APPLAUSE FOR
SIMON BRETT AND
HIS CHARLES PARIS MYSTERIES

"[An] irresistible, roguish actor-sleuth. . . . Wicked, biting satire on the show-biz world."
—*Washington Post Book World*

"Charles Paris is a refreshment and a delight."
—*San Francisco Examiner*

"Paris is probably current crime fiction's most complex and developed series character."
—*Chicago Sun-Times*

"Brett is both a clever writer and a funny one."
—*Philadelphia Daily News*

"No one delivers more pure entertainment. His plots are fresh, his characters are enjoyable, and his wickedly witty view of backstage life is by itself worth the price of admission." —*San Diego Union*

Simon Brett

FOUR COMPLETE MYSTERIES

Simon Brett

FOUR COMPLETE MYSTERIES

An Amateur Corpse

Star Trap

So Much Blood

Cast, In Order of Disappearance

WINGS BOOKS
New York•Avenel, New Jersey

This omnibus was originally published in separate volumes under the titles:

An Amateur Corpse, copyright © 1978 by Simon Brett.
Star Trap, copyright © 1977 by Simon Brett.
So Much Blood, copyright © 1976 by Simon Brett.
Cast, In Order of Disappearance, copyright © 1975 by Simon Brett.

This 1993 edition is published by Wings Books, distributed by Outlet Book Company, Inc., a Random House Company, 40 Engelhard Avenue, Avenel, New Jersey 07001, by arrangement with Charles Scribner's Sons, an imprint of Macmillan Publishing Company.

Random House
New York · Toronto · London · Sydney · Auckland

Printed and bound in the United States of America

Library of Congress Cataloging-in-Publication Data

Brett, Simon.
　　[Novels. Selections]
　　Four complete mysteries / Simon Brett.
　　　　p.　　cm.
　　Contents: An amateur corpse — Star trap — So much blood — Cast, in order of disappearance.
　　ISBN 0-517-09330-8
　　1. Paris, Charles (Fictitious character)—Fiction.　2. Detective and mystery stories, English.　3. Actors—England—Fiction.　I. Title.
PR6052.R4296A6　1993
823′.914—dc20　　　　　　　　　　　　　　　　　　　　93-17193
　　　　　　　　　　　　　　　　　　　　　　　　　　　　　　CIP

8　7　6　5　4　3　2　1

CONTENTS

An Amateur Corpse

Dedicated to
SOPHIE

CHAPTER 1

THE CAST PARTY for the Breckton Backstagers' production of *The Seagull* was held, like all their cast parties, in the rehearsal room. Drinks were served in the bar (known to the members as the Back Room) and were paid for by a collection made during the run by the Assistant Stage Manager. The choice, displayed on the bar, was cheap Spanish red in two-litre bottles or cheap Spanish white in two-litre bottles.

Charles Paris was the first to arrive in the Back Room after the curtain fell on the Saturday night. His friend Hugo Mecken had stopped off in the Gents on the way from the theatre. The cast were still creaming off their make-up and slipping out of costumes and most of their hangers-on were hanging on in the dressing rooms, spraying out wild congratulations and faint praise. Hugo, Charles noticed without surprise, had not gone backstage to congratulate his wife Charlotte on her performance as Nina.

Charles was conscious of his interloper status. So, judging from his sour expression, was the thin man in a cravat who stood behind the bar. Charles tried, "A glass of red, please."

"Are you a member?"

It was a perfect example of what Charles remembered being taught about in Latin school—a question expecting the answer no. It got it.

"Then I'm afraid I can't give you a drink."

"My name is Charles Paris. I was invited down here this evening to see the show because I'm leading the Critics' Circle discussion on Tuesday."

"Ah. Well, in that case, a member will be able to get you a drink."

"But I can't get one for myself?"

"Not unless you are a member."

Charles was beginning to get angry. "And how much would it cost me to become a bloody member?"

"Two pounds a year Social Membership or five pounds Acting Membership. Though for that, of course, you have to pass an audition."

With difficulty Charles didn't say what he thought of the idea of himself, as a professional actor, having to audition for a tin-pot suburban amateur dramatic society. He channeled his annoyance into slamming two pounds down on the counter. "Right, there you are. I'm a Social Member. Now give me a drink."

"I'm afraid your application has to be endorsed by a member."

Hugo appeared slap on cue from the Gents. "Right, here's my endorsing member—Hugo Mecken. I'm Charles Paris, there's my two pounds, now give me a drink."

"What's the trouble, Charles?" asked Hugo.

"I'm joining the bloody society, so that I have a license to breathe in this place."

"Oh, you don't need to—"

"I've joined. Red wine, please."

"And for me too, Reggie."

Sour Reggie paused for a second, searching for another rule that was being contravened. Failing to find one, he ungraciously half-filled two wine-glasses.

They drank. Charles contemplated Hugo. Olive-colored skin, his head a bald dome fringed with black hair, dark eyes darting about uneasily. The lips, heavy with indulgence in the good things of life, turned down, registering that the Backstagers' Spanish plonk wasn't among them.

Charles was conscious of the silence. He often had difficulty in thinking of what to say to Hugo. It had always been the same, even when they first met at Oxford back in 1947. They had been friends, but conversation had never flowed easily.

And when they had remet a couple of months previously it had been exactly the same. A great warmth, affection for each other, but not a lot to say. A good working-relationship, socially no overt strain. Just a slight tension within Charles from a sense of Hugo's dependence on him. Hugo was almost too hospitable, inviting Charles down to Breckton all the time, pressing a spare house key on him, telling him to use the place as his own.

But the re-established contact had been a godsend at least from the financial point of view. Hugo seemed likely to put a lot of work his way after what had been a very lean year, even by the modest standards of Charles Paris's theatrical career.

Hugo Mecken was the Creative Director of Mills Brown Mazzini, a small but thriving advertising agency in Paddington, and he had introduced Charles to the lucrative world of commercial voice-over work. It was a strange world to Charles, one that he was still trying to come to terms with, to fit into his picture of what being an actor meant.

The pause had gone on too long for comfort. "Charlotte's very good." Charles volunteered.

"Should be. Professionally trained." The shortness of Hugo's response confirmed his suspicion that all was not well with the marriage.

"I feel like getting obscenely pissed," Hugo continued suddenly, and drained his glass.

It was a familiar cry. The word "pissed" was of the seventies but the intention was one which Charles had often heard from Hugo thirty years before at Oxford. Sometimes it had been a danger signal. A sudden lurch of mood, a lot to drink and then bizarre midnight exploits, wild destruction of college windows or other fierce extravagances until the passion subsided into somnolence and, later, self-abasing recrimination.

While Hugo outstared sour Reggie into refilling their glasses Charles reviewed his friend's marital history. First wife, Alice, married straight out of Oxford. Rather swish do in Worcester College Chapel at which Charles had been present. Two children soon after, all set on conventional course.

Then, over twenty years later, news from a mutual friend, Gerald Venables, that Hugo had contacted him in his professional capacity as a solicitor and wanted a divorce. He had upped and left Alice with two teenagers, and moved in with some twenty-two-year-old actress with whom he'd done a commercial.

A couple of years later, a scribbled note on Snoopy paper (strong contrast to the heavy die-stamped invitation to Worcester Chapel) asked Charles to a post-registry office piss-up in an expensive Soho trattoria.

Through hazes of alcohol, Charles could recall that riotous meal. Hugo and Charlotte dressed in identical oyster-grey velvet suits, a lot of advertising people, a lot of showbiz. A truly glittering occasion. Charlotte so young, so unbelievably beautiful, her complexion glowing and red hair sparkling in the colored lights of the restaurant. And Hugo boisterous as a schoolboy, his bald dome gleaming, his face alive with the knowledge that every man in the room envied him.

Then it had all seemed possible. That one could start again. It even convinced Charles how right he had been to leave his own wife Frances. Somewhere, round some corner, there was a perfect young girl waiting for him, someone who could make it all happen again.

Mostly it had been the drink thinking for him. But there had been more than that. Hugo, in a good mood, was a fierce romantic and he could infect others with his enthusiasm. He could make everyone believe that the world was perfectible, that it was only a matter of time before paradise was re-established on earth.

Charles remembered acting in a play which Hugo had written at Oxford, a play full of soaring, impossible romanticism. But that had been a long time ago, when Hugo had been going to be the world's greatest playwright, when he had been in love with Alice, when he'd been on a permanent high.

As he returned with the drinks, Hugo was patently not on a high. He looked ill at ease, vulnerable, potentially petulant.

The rehearsal room was beginning to fill up now, as the stars of the Backstagers emerged in their party finery. Charles was relieved to see they all got the same vinegary reception from Reggie at the bar. (Maybe he had made the mistake of trying the wine.)

Hugo seemed to know many of the people who came in. Though not involved in the acting side, he was a regular of the Back Room, using it as his local, often dropping in for a drink on his way home from work. He dished out some abrupt nods and deterrent smiles to acquaintances, but seemed anxious to stay with Charles. It was reminiscent of parties in their first terms at Oxford, staying together shy against the wall until they had had enough to drink to risk a social foray.

A young man in jeans and a denim shirt came over to them. His face still glowed with the scrubbing it had taken to remove the make-up and there were streaks of grease-paint behind his ears. Charles recognized him from the stage, where less than half an hour before he had gone out to shoot himself in the character of Konstantin. In his own character, he didn't look suicidal. Cocky would be a better word. A handsome young face, pulled out of true by lines of arrogance around the mouth.

"Hugo! How'd you like it?" He must have been nearly thirty years younger, but the tone was patronizing.

"Fine." Hugo was unexpansive.

"Little lady did well."

Hugo flicked a one-frame smile across his face.

Konstantin looked speculatively at Charles. Then, deciding that Hugo was not going to introduce them, he reached out a man-of-the-world hand. "I'm Clive Steele."

"Charles Paris."

"Thought you must be. Charlie said the old man was bringing you." Charles felt Hugo stiffen. Difficult to tell whether it was at his wife's nickname or his own designation. The boy continued with a self-deprecating smile. "Well, how did it seem to you, Charles? How did the stumbling efforts of the amateurs seem to you as a professional theatre man?"

The boy was not really asking his opinion; he was fishing for compliments. Charles didn't know whether to give a vague reassurance as he would to any professional actor after a performance or to do exactly as he had been asked and give professional criticism.

It was something he was going to have to sort out before the Critics' Circle on the Tuesday.

He made some trimming remark about the show with an ambiguous comment on Clive's performance. It was a waste of ambiguity; Clive took it as a straight compliment.

The conversation eddied. Clive, unprompted, but assuming its unfailing interest, provided his life story. He was becoming an accountant. The next week he had to go to Melton Mowbray on an audit. All bloody week. He had done a lot of productions with the Breckton Backstagers, mostly leads.

Charles couldn't resist it. "Yes, amateur dramatic societies are always hard-up for young men."

But Clive was well armored with self-opinion. "Certainly for ones who can act and are anything like decent-looking."

Charles didn't bother any more. The conversation was nearly dead, now he had withdrawn. But the boy kept talking. Like Hugo, Clive didn't seem to want to leave this particular corner. They both seemed to be waiting for something. Charles wondered if it was Charlotte.

A new couple came over and gave the conversation the kiss of life. This time Hugo remembered his social graces. "This is Charles Paris. Charles, Denis and Mary Hobbs."

"Oh dear," Mary giggled, "you're the one who's going to pass judgement on our performance. Now I do hope you'll treat us just like professionals."

It took him a minute or two to place her. She looked so different in the turquoise trouser suit, orange silk blouse and rainbow lamé slippers. And the blonded hair and too-young make-up. But when he added a rust-colored pre-Revolutionary Russian dress and a high-piled black wig. . . . "Of course. Madame Arkadina. I'm so sorry. I just didn't recognize you."

Yes, he was full of admiration for her make-up. On her performance he hoped he wouldn't be drawn. That kind of criticism could well wait till the Tuesday. In spite of himself, he found he was forming phrases of his real critical opinion. Such a pity that amateurs are always tempted by classic plays. Just because they're classics, it doesn't mean they're easy to do. In fact, often just the reverse. Arkadina is one of the great roles of the theatre and not to be handed out at random to anyone who happened to have recited nicely at the Women's Institute Concert. Amateurs should stick to what's within their range—Agatha Christies, frothy West End comedies, nothing that involves too much subtlety of characterization. Leave Chekhov to the professionals.

Good God, there were only two people in that cast tonight who got within a mile of what it was about—Charlotte as Nina and the guy who played Trigorin. The rest should take up something else to fill their evenings—like stamp-collecting.

Even as he framed the thoughts, he knew he was overreacting. It was the irrational but instinctive response of anyone who made his living by acting. The very existence of amateur dramatic societies seemed to cast doubt on the seriousness of his profession.

Mary Hobbs was in full theatrical spate. "Oh God, there was a terrible moment in the first act, when we were meant to be watching Konstantin's play and I had this line about there being a smell of sulphur, and I think one of the stage managers had brought some fish and chips into the wings, because suddenly we all got this amazing whiff of vinegar across the stage, and I caught Geoff's eye and I'm afraid I just went. Total, absolute corpse. I turned upstage. I don't know if anyone noticed in the audience . . ."

Charles had noticed. Any experienced actor would have been aware of the tell-tale snort and sudden movement. And how typical of the Backstagers that they should have all the theatrical slang. A "corpse" was a breakdown into laughter on stage.

Mary Hobbs appealed to her husband. "Did you notice it, Den?"

"Blimey, no. Couldn't take my eyes off your missus, Hugo, I didn't see much else, eh?"

He erupted with laughter. Not particularly amused laughter, just the sort that some hearty people use around their speech like quotation marks.

The reactions to his remark were interesting. Hugo grimaced in an irritated way, as if he didn't want to be reminded of Charlotte's existence. Mary Hobbs flashed a look of reproof which quelled her husband. He looked like a schoolboy who had spoken out of turn, gauche as if he shouldn't have said anything in his rough voice while his wife was present to elocute for the two of them.

Mary's admonition was over in a second and she resumed her theatrical reminiscence. "Of course, Geoffrey didn't break up. He is marvellous. Didn't you think he was marvellous, Charles? Geoffrey Winter, our Trigorin. He's so clever. We really all think he ought to go on the stage professionally. He's so much better than most professional actors you see on the telly-box."

Charles didn't know whether this was meant to be deliberately rude, but let it pass. Mary Hobbs didn't seem to need reaction to impel her dialogue. She sighed dramatically, "Oh, it's all over. *Quelle tristesse.*"

"Till the next one." Denis supplied her cue promptly, as if to make up for his earlier faux pas.

"Till the next one. *Winter's Tale.* Dear old Shakespeare. Start rehearsing next week."

There was a moment of silence and Hugo seemed to wake up to some sort of social duty. But his question showed he had not been listening to the conversation. "Now the show's over, Denis, will you be able to get some weekends down at the cottage?"

Denis gave his punctuation of laughter. "Yes, not before time. I must say we've been living Chekhov this last couple of months. And what with all the Sunday afternoon rehearsals, we only got away one weekend since August."

"Still we are going away this weekend." Again the edge of reproof in his wife's voice.

Denis compensated quickly. "Oh yes. It's just one of the penalties of marrying talent, eh?" Another unmotivated eruption. Mary smiled and he reckoned he could risk a little joke. "She's spent so much time here recently I kept saying why didn't she move in? After all, we're only next door." This too was apparently very funny.

Mary graciously allowed him this little indulgence and then felt it was time to draw attention to her magnanimity. "Still, this weekend I'm going to make it all up to you, aren't I?" She took her husband's hand and patted it with a coquettishness which Charles found unattractive in a woman in her fifties. "First thing in the morning, when all the rest of the naughty Backstagers are sleeping off their hangovers, we'll be in the new Rover sweeping off down to the cottage for a little delayed weekend. All tomorrow, and all Monday—well, till nine or so when we'll drive back. Just the two of us. A second honeymoon—or is it a third?"

"Three hundredth," said Denis, which was the cue for another explosion of merriment.

Charles escaped to get more drinks. Soon the wine would cease to taste of anything and his bad temper would begin to dissipate.

While he queued at sour Reggie's bar, he looked around at the kindling party. There was music now, music rather younger than the average age of those present. But the pounding beat was infectious.

As the room filled, he was increasingly aware of the common complaint of amateur dramatic societies—that there are always more women than men. And some of them were rather nice. He felt a little glow of excitement. No one knew him down in Breckton. It was like being given a whole new copybook to blot.

Some couples were dancing already. Charlotte Mecken was out there, with her arms around Clive Steele. They were moving together sensuously to the slow pounding of the music. But what they were doing was paradoxically not sexy. It had the air of a performance, as if they were still on stage, as if their closeness was for the benefit of the audience, not because it expressed any real mutual attraction.

The same could be said of the Trigorin, Geoffrey Winter. He was dancing with a pretty young girl, whose paint-spattered jeans suggested she was one of the stage staff. They were not dancing close, but in a jerky slow motion pantomime. Geoffrey moved well, his body flicking in time to the music, like a puppet out of control. But again it was a performance of a body out of control, not genuine abandon. Each movement was carefully timed; it was well-done, but calculated.

Charles had noticed the same quality in the man's stage performance. It had been enormously skillful and shown more technique than the rest of the cast put together, but it had been mannered and ultimately artificial, a performance from the head rather than the heart.

The man was good-looking in an angular way. Very thin, with grey hair and pale eyes. He wore a black shirt, black cord jeans and desert boots. There was something commanding about him, attractive in not just the physical sense of the word.

As Charles watched he saw the man change partners and start a new dance with another little totty. "Enjoying himself, isn't he?"

He turned to the owner of the voice which had spoken beside him. A young woman of about thirty. Short mousy hair, wide green eyes. Attractive. She was following Charles's gaze towards the dancing Trigorin. "My husband."

She said it wryly. Not bitterly or critically, but just as if it were a fact that ought to be established.

"Ah. I'm Charles Paris."

"Thought you must be." Charles felt the inevitable actor's excitement that she was going to say she recognized him from the television. But no. "You're the only person down here I didn't recognize. And I knew you'd be in tonight because you're doing the crit on Tuesday, so, by a process of elimination. . . ."

"I'm Vee Winter, by the way. Though I act here under my maiden name, Vee le Carpentier. I always think if people see in programs that the leads are played by people with the same surname, they get to think the Backstagers are awfully cliquey." Before Charles had time to take in this statement, she went on, "Have you met Geoffrey?"

"No, just seen him on stage. He's very talented." Charles didn't volunteer whether he thought the talent was being appropriately used.

"Yes, he's talented." She changed the subject abruptly. "Since you're coming down to do this thing on Tuesday, why not have a meal with us beforehand?"

"That's very kind," said Charles, wondering if he ought to check whether Hugo and Charlotte were expecting him.

Vee took it as assent. "About half-past seven. The Critics' Circle isn't till eight-thirty. I'll give you our phone number in case you have problems."

"Fine." Charles made a note of the number. Then he added,

because he was beginning to understand suburban timetables, "Seven-thirty then. After the children are asleep."

"We don't have any children," said Vee Winter.

Sour Reggie dispensed Charles's order for drinks as if the country were threatened by imminent drought. Vee helped carry the glasses back to the group.

She seemed to know them all. She made some insincere compliment to Mary Hobbs about her Arkadina.

"Oh, that's sweet of you to say so, darling. Actually . . ." The voice dropped with the subtlety of a double declutch on a worn gear-box. ". . . I still think you would have made a better Nina, but, you know, Shad gets these ideas. . . ."

The circle had enlarged in Charles's absence to include an elderly man with a white goatee beard. And Hugo's mood had shifted into something more expansive. "Charles, I don't think you've met Robert Chubb. Bob, this is Charles Paris. Bob's the founder of the whole set-up. Started the Backstagers back in . . . ooh. . . ."

"Nineteen hundred and mind-your-own-business," supplied Robert Chubb jovially. "First productions in the Church Hall, mind you. Come some way since then. Started the fund for this complex in 1960 . . . and ten years later it was all finished." He gestured to the rehearsal room and theatre.

It was an impressive achievement. Charles bit back his cynical views on the subject of amateur theatre and said so.

Robert Chubb seemed to have been waiting for this cue to launch into the next installment of his monologue. "Well, I thought, I and a few like-minded cronies, that there should be some decent theatre in Breckton. I mean, it's so easy for people in the suburbs to completely lose sight of culture.

"So we damned well worked to set up something good—not just your average amateur dramatic society, performing your Agatha Christies and your frothy West End comedies, but a society with high professional standards, which kept in touch with what was happening in the theatre at large. And that's how the Backstagers started."

Charles felt he was being addressed like a television interviewer who had actually asked for this potted history. And his interviewee continued. "And now it's grown like this. Enormous membership, great waiting list of people from all over South London keen to join in the fun. Lots of Press coverage—particularly for our World Premières Festival.

"It just keeps getting bigger. Now we run our own fortnightly newsletter to keep people informed of what we're up to—called *Backchat,* don't know if you've seen it?"

"No."

"Then of course this bar's called the Back Room."

"I see, everything's Back-something-or-other?"

"Yes. Rather nice, isn't it?"

Charles's mind began seething with new permutations of Back-, most of them obscene. It was perhaps as well that Hugo spoke before he launched into any of them. "We must get Charles down here to do a production, eh, Bob?"

It was Charles's turn to be self-deprecating. "Oh, come on, Hugo, I'm a professional actor. Much as I'd like to do it, I'm likely to be off touring or something at a moment's notice."

"Nonsense. This voice-over campaign's really going to take off. You'll be stuck in London with more work than you can cope with."

"When that happens—" Charles joked, "and I won't believe it until it does—I'll be prepared to do a production for the Backstagers." That seemed to get him safely off the hook.

But a new voice joined the circle and qualified his remark. "If, of course, you do a successful One-Act Productions Audition and your choice of play is approved by the Directorial Selection Sub-Committee." Charles was not surprised to find that the voice came from sour Reggie, the walking rule-book.

"Oh, Charles has had rather a lot of experience as a director." It was Hugo coming to his rescue. Charles didn't want rescuing. He thought doing a production for the Breckton Backstagers was a consummation devoutly to be avoided. The atmosphere was getting claustrophobic.

But Hugo's defense was quite impassioned. Again Charles was conscious of the other man's need for him. He was being paraded for the benefit of Hugo's local crowd. In a strange way, it seemed to tie in with Charlotte's behavior, as if Hugo's ignoring his wife was justified by the fact that he had a genuine professional actor to show off.

Charles was being used and he didn't like it, but Hugo continued with his sales campaign. "Charles is a bit of a playwright too. You should get him to write something for the World Premières Festival."

Charles made some suitably modest response, but Robert Chubb seized on the cue. "Oh really, if you've got something that hasn't been performed tucked away in a cupboard, do let us see it. We're getting the next Festival sorted out at the moment and one of our expected scripts has just fallen through, so we'd be very interested."

Charles was tempted. There was in fact an unperformed play sitting in a drawer in his room in Hereford Road. He'd written it after his one successful play, *The Ratepayer*. A light comedy, called *How's Your Father?* It would be quite gratifying to have it done under any circumstances.

But the patronizing tone in which Robert Chubb continued changed his mind. "It could do you a lot of good, Charles. Lots of plays we've premiered here have gone on to do awfully well. It's a real chance for an unknown playwright. I don't know if you know George Walsh's *Doomwomb?*"

Charles shook his head. Robert Chubb smiled indulgently at his ignorance. "That started here."

"Really?" Suddenly he wanted to scream, wanted to do something appalling, be very rude to someone, break something, get the hell away from all these pretentious idiots.

Rescue came from an unexpected source. He felt an arm round his waist and a female body pressed close to his. "Dance with me."

It was Vee Winter.

CHAPTER 2

SHE WAS A strange woman. She clung to him tightly and he could feel the nervous excitement coursing through her body. In other circumstances, he would have interpreted this as a sexual message and responded in kind, but that somehow didn't seem appropriate. The excitement had nothing to do with him.

He was being used for some purpose of her own. Certainly she was working to give the appearance of a sexual encounter, but it was for the benefit of the rest of the room, not for her partner.

Charles wondered at first if it was a ploy to make her husband jealous. Geoffrey was across the room, dancing with circumscribed abandon in front of yet another little dolly and Vee was very aware of his presence. But her behavior did not seem designed to antagonise him; instead Charles received an inexplicable impression of complicity between husband and wife, as if their performances were co-ordinated parts of an overall plan and would later be laughed over when they were alone together.

This annoyed him. Again he was being used as a counter in a game he didn't understand. The heavy beat of a rock number changed to a soupy ballad and Vee snuggled closer, pressing the contours of her body tightly against his. He realized with surprise that he didn't find this arousing. Vee Winter was an attractive woman, but he didn't fancy her. This gave him a perverse sense of righteousness, as if confirming that his randiness was not absolutely indiscriminate.

He commented rather coldly on her forwardness. "Is this to give food for scandal to the gossip columnist of *Backbite?*"

"Backbite?"

"Your fortnightly magazine."

"That's called *Backchat.*" She corrected him without humor. "Anyway, it doesn't have a gossip columnist."

Charles unwisely chose to continue in facetious vein. "So there's no one to chronicle the backslidings of the Backstagers bopping to Burt Bacharach and their bacchanalian orgies?"

"No." Vee's reply was absolutely straight. Charles wouldn't have minded if she had said it as a put-down (his attempt at humor had been pretty feeble), but for her not to notice even that the attempt had been made, that he found galling.

"Do you act much here?"

She laughed with incredulity at his question, rather as if someone had asked the Queen if she had any jewelry. "Oh I have done a few things, yes."

"But not *The Seagull?*"

"No." She stiffened slightly. "I really felt I needed a rest. Also I've played so many leads in the past year, I didn't want it to look as if Geoff and I were monopolizing the entire society. Ought to give some of the newer members a chance. And then Shad, who directed, had this strange notion that Nina ought to have red hair. He's a rather quirky director, if you know what I mean."

Through the excuses, Charles knew exactly what she meant.

He took the end of a record as an opportunity to end their clinch. He looked over at the group round Hugo and couldn't face it yet. He needed just to get out of the place for a moment. The sweet wine was making him feel sick. Pausing only to pick up someone's full glass off a table, he left the rehearsal room.

The change was as welcome as he had anticipated. In spite of the summery days of that fall, October was nearing its end and the evenings were chilly. The slap of cold air was refreshing. He leaned against the inside of the porch and breathed deeply.

Then he heard the voices. Charlotte Mecken and Clive Steele. Arguing in fierce whispers. First Charlotte's voice, the veneer of drama school thinned by emotion to reveal its Northern Irish origin. ". . . I'm sorry, Clive, you've got it completely wrong. I never knew you were thinking that."

"What was I meant to think, after all those rehearsals, when you suddenly got all emotional and confided in me when I drove you home?"

"I'm sorry. I shouldn't have broken down. I just . . . it was all too much. . . ."

"Well, I made the perfectly natural assumption that—"

"It may have seemed perfectly natural to you, but—"

"It bloody well did. Look, if it's your husband you're worried about, forget it. It's bloody obscene you being married to him anyway. Reminds me of all those jokes about young girls on their wedding nights feeling old age creeping all over them—"

"Clive, stop it. You've got the wrong end of the stick. So completely the wrong end. It's all much more complicated than you can begin to imagine. Look, I'm sorry if you've been hurt, but I can assure you—"

"Oh, stuff that! All right, you've made your point. I see what's been happening now. There is a word for women who lead men on you know."

"Clive, if I'd had any idea of what was going through your mind—"

"Oh shut up. I'm going."

"Be careful."

"Don't worry, I will. I'm not like Konstantin—I'm not going to go off and shoot myself because some tart's let me down. If I were to do anything, I can assure you it would be something a lot more practical. Goodbye!"

Charles heard a few brisk footsteps across the gravel, a car door open and slam, then a powerful sports car engine starting and tires screeching off down the road.

He assumed Charlotte was still there. He gave her two minutes, then, not being an actor for nothing, did his impression of someone coming noisily out of the rehearsal room.

He was aware of her perfume before he saw her. It was very expensive, very distinctive. Whatever Hugo's relationship with his wife, he didn't stint her expenses. Her clothes were also of the best.

She was a trendy fashion plate amidst the pervading dowdiness of the Backstagers.

She was leaning against the bonnet of a Volvo in the car park and didn't look as if she had moved for some time. Her face was infinitely miserable.

"Hello, Charlotte. What's up?"

"I don't know. Last night blues," she lied. "You should understand about that."

"Yes. What I usually do is get wildly pissed. Then I don't notice. And the next morning I feel so bad physically that I forget about any emotional upset."

"Hmm. I'm rather off alcohol at the moment."

Silence. She looked sensational in the bluish light shed from the rehearsal room. The pain of her expression increased rather than diminished her beauty. The face framed in red hair looked pale and peaky in the thin light. Very young, very vulnerable, a child being brave.

Charles found being with her a relief. She seemed more like a real person than the lot in the rehearsal room. He felt protective towards her. And that made him feel better. He didn't like the boorish bloody-mindedness which the massed Backstagers kindled in him.

"You know, your Nina was very good."

"Thank you. What are you going to say—I ought to take it up professionally?"

"That's what you were trained for."

"Yes. A bit pathetic, isn't it really—fully trained actress mucking about with amateur dramatics."

"Oh, I don't know. I'm sure, if you pass your Juvenile Lead Audition and are approved by the Big Parts Selection Sub-Committee, you'll get some very juicy roles here."

Charlotte laughed. "You seem to have caught on to the atmosphere of the place very quickly. God, what a load of creeps they all seem when you think of them objectively. All with their oversize egos and silly stage names—all those abbreviations and hyphens and extra middle names—it makes me sick when I think about it. I make a point of using their proper names just to annoy them."

"Do you think you'll do more here?"

"Maybe. I don't know. What's the alternative? I can't see Hugo being keen on my having a real acting career. Anyway, I've lost all the few contacts I ever had in the theatre. Just a housewife with dreams, I suppose."

"I'm sure you could make it in the real theatre."

" 'You should go on the stage,' says Arkadina. 'Yes, that is my one dream,' replies Nina. 'But it'll never come true.' "

"Could do."

But Charlotte's temporary serenity was broken by some memory. "No, it'll never—oh, everything's such a mess. God knows what's in store for me anyway."

"Anything you can talk about?"

She hesitated for a moment, on the verge of sharing her burden. But decided against it. "No. Thanks for the offer, but I'm rather against shoulders to cry on at the moment. It's my own mess and I must sort it out somehow." She moved resolutely away from the Volvo.

"Are you coming back in, Charlotte?"

"No, I can't face that lot right now. I'm just going to . . . I don't know . . . have a bit of a walk, try to clear my head or . . . I don't know, Charles. Tell Hugo I'll be back later. You're staying with us tonight, aren't you?"

"If that's okay."

"Sure. I'll see you in the morning." She walked off into the night, pulling her long Aran cardigan round her against the cold.

Hugo had been hard at the Spanish red when Charles got back into the rehearsal room. But the mood that was settling in was one of catatonic gloom rather than manic violence.

They both continued to drink, resolutely and more or less silently. The party was livening up, with more and more couples clinched on the dance-floor. There were still plenty of spare women, but Charles had lost interest. The intensity of Vee Winter and Charlotte's troubled words had changed his mood. He and Hugo drank as they might have done thirty years earlier at an Oxford party where all the women had been bagged before they arrived.

It was about three when they left. Charles murmured something about Charlotte making her own way home, but Hugo didn't react. He drove them back to his house with the punctilious concentration of the very drunk.

As the Alfa-Romeo saloon crunched to a halt on the gravel in front of the house, he said determinedly. "Come in and have a nightcap."

Charles didn't want to. He was tired and drunk and he had a potentially difficult day ahead of him. Also he had a premonition that Hugo wanted to confide in him. Ignobly, he didn't feel up to it.

But Hugo took his silence for assent and they went into the sitting room. Charles stood with his back to the empty fireplace, trying to think of a good line to get him quickly up to bed, while Hugo went over to the drinks cupboard. "What's it to be?"

He opened the door to reveal a neat parade of whisky bottles. There were up to a dozen brands. Hugo always rationalised the size of the display on the grounds that everyone has a favorite Scotch, but it was really just the potential alcoholic's insurance policy.

Charles missed the opportunity to refuse and weakly chose a Glenmorangie malt. Hugo poured a generous two inches into a tumbler and helped himself to a Johnnie Walker Black Label.

Then they just stood facing each other and drank. Hugo kept the Johnnie Walker bottle dangling in his free hand. The silence became oppressive. Charles downed his drink in a few long swallows and opened his mouth for thank you and goodnight.

Hugo spoke first. "Charles," he said in a voice of uneven pitch, "I think I'm cracking up."

"What do you mean?"

"Cracking up, going round the bend, *losing control*." The last two words came out in a fascinated whisper.

"Oh come on, you're pissed."

"That's part of it. I drink too much and I just don't notice it. It doesn't make me drunk, it doesn't calm me down, I just feel the same thing—that I'm . . . losing control."

"Control of what? What do you think you are going to do?"

"I don't know. Something terrible. I'm going to say something awful, hit somebody or. . . . All the constraints I've built up over the years, they're just breaking down . . . I. . . ." He mouthed incoherently.

"Oh come on. You've just had too much to drink. It's nothing."

"Don't tell me it's nothing!" Hugo suddenly screamed. As he did so, he hurled the whisky bottle at the stone mantelpiece to the right of Charles. It shattered. Glass fell into the fireplace and spirit dripped down on to it.

Charles thought the outburst contained more than a dash of histrionics. If his friend wasn't going to believe him, then Hugo was damned well going to give a demonstration of his lack of control. "Like that, you mean?" asked Charles. "Out of control like that?"

Hugo looked at him defiantly, then sheepishly, then with a hint of a smile, seeing that his bluff had been called. He sank exhausted into a chair. "No, not like that. That was just for effect. I mean worse than that. I get to a flashpoint and I feel I'm going to lash out —I don't know, to kill someone."

Charles looked straight at him and Hugo looked away, again slightly sheepish, admitting that the homicidal threat was also for effect.

"Who are you going to kill?" Charles teased. "Charlotte?"

Hugo was instantly serious. "No, not Charlotte. I wouldn't touch Charlotte. Whatever she did, I wouldn't touch her."

"Then who?"

Hugo looked at Charles vaguely, distantly, as if piecing together something that had only just occurred to him. Then he said slowly, as if he didn't believe it, "Friends of Charlotte."

Charles took a risk and laughed. Hugo looked at him suspiciously for a moment and then laughed too. Soon after they went to bed.

Charles didn't think too much about what Hugo had said. Obviously his friend was under pressure and all wasn't well with his marriage, but most of the trouble was the drink.

Anyway, Charles had domestic problems of his own to worry about. His last thought, before he dropped into the alcohol-anesthetized sleep which was becoming too much of a habit, was the next day he had to see his wife for the first time in five months. At the christening of their twin grandsons. Grandsons, for God's sake.

CHAPTER 3

THE CHRISTENING WENT okay, he supposed. Difficult to say, really. It was a long time since he had been to one with which to compare it. The twins were healthy five-month-old boys and they were successfully received into the Church of England in Pangbourne in Berkshire, which was where Charles's daughter Juliet and her husband Miles (who was apparently carving a successful career for himself in insurance) lived. The boys were named Damian and Julian, which would not have been their grandfather's choice.

So everything went as it should have done. But it was not an easy day for Charles. Being with Frances and behaving as if they were still conventional man and wife had been strange. In some ways seductively appealing. His mind was still full of the bourgeois morality of Breckton and he found himself wondering whether it could have worked, he and Frances as a couple, growing old together, building a family, having Juliet and the kids over for Sunday lunch and so on.

But deep down he knew that he'd followed the only course open to him when he'd left Frances in 1961. He still loved her, still often would rather spend time with her than anyone else, but he never wanted to get back into the claustrophobia of always being there, always being answerable.

In a way, his leaving her had been as romantic as Hugo's leaving of Alice. But, unlike Hugo, Charles hadn't thought it was all possible, that a new woman could make it all all right again. He had left so as to keep some illusions. He didn't want just to sink into a middle age of disappointed bickering. Nor did he want to feel guilty if he had affairs with other women.

Of course, it hadn't worked. Guilt had remained in some form in all his affairs and much of the time he had been just lonely. But his single state gave him a kind of perverse integrity.

The situation had been complicated when it transpired that Frances had developed some sort of boyfriend. Charles never knew how serious the relationship was. The only thing he did know was that, illogically, it made him jealous.

And so, even more illogically, did seeing Frances so wrapped up in the twins. He felt excluded, as he had when she had been pregnant with Juliet.

That was the trouble. Whenever he saw Frances, unwelcome emotional confusion crowded into his mind. When he didn't see her, he could exist quite happily from moment to moment, without thinking all the time that feelings had to be defined and formalized.

At the christening he hardly saw her. It was a public occasion, there were other people there, he had no real chance to ask her the sort of questions he wanted to. Or felt he ought to.

He went through it all in the train on the way back to London. He must ring Frances—soon. They must meet and talk, really talk.

The day had increased the unease which the atmosphere between Hugo and Charlotte had fomented in him.

He tried to think if there was anything comforting that had emerged. Only the fact that his son-in-law Miles, Mr. Prudent, king of the insurance world, with a policy for every hazard, had not insured against twins.

The Monday recording session was for a series of radio commercials, which was much less hairy than the voice-to-picture session which had preceded it. All Charles had to do was to read some copy in the same voice that he had used in the television commercials.

Not very hard work. And well spread out. Even this simple job was to be done in two sessions: half of the commercials were to be recorded the following Tuesday morning.

The whole voice-over business still puzzled him. Giving a couple of dozen readings of a banal endorsement for some product which no self-respecting housewife should be without didn't fit into his definition of acting.

Still, the money was good, potentially very good. And it was different. And so long as one didn't take it too seriously, it was better than sitting at home waiting for the telephone to ring.

It had started out of the blue some two months before with a bewildered call from his agent, Maurice Skellern. Someone from Mills Brown Mazzini had been enquiring about Charles Paris's availability for voice-over work. That had led to a series of in-house voice tests in a tatty studio at the advertising agency.

Presumably (though no one ever actually told him so) these had been successful, because within a week he had been summoned to a session of voice-to-picture tests. These had been more elaborate, in a swish professional dubbing theatre, and attended by an enormous gallery of advertising people, all of whom, it seemed, had the right to give him notes on his performance.

Again (though nobody actually said so) he must have been successful, because soon after he was summoned to put his voice to three television commercials, which were apparently on test transmission in the Tyne-Tees area.

It was Hugo Mecken he had to thank for this new development in his acting career. It seemed that Hugo had secured the account for a new bedtime drink which was being launched by a huge Dutch-owned drugs company. The drink was to be called Bland and the campaign had been agreed on some months before. It was to be led by a cartoon character called Mr. Bland who wore a top-hat and tails. In the launching series of animated television commercials he was to visit a tribe of little fuzzy red creatures called the Wideawakes. When presented with cups of Bland on a silver salver by Mr. Bland, they gradually turned pale blue and fell asleep. Over their snoring, Mr. Bland intoned the words, "Bland soothes away the day."

The voice of Mr. Bland, which, if the campaign took off as it was hoped, would be a very lucrative assignment, had gone to Christopher Milton, a well-known stage and television actor (who, apart from his current success in the musical *Lumpkin!* at the King's The-

atre, was said by Hugo recently to have signed a contract for
£25,000 to do an in-vision commercial for instant coffee).

All this had been agreed with the Brand Manager for Bland, the
animation voice-track was recorded and the animation work was
started. From which point all should have gone well until the
launching of the product.

But during the interval between the agreement of the campaign
and the completion of the three test commercials the Brand Manager for Bland had been appointed European Marketing Manager
for the huge Dutch-owned drugs company. His successor on
Bland, a Mr. Farrow, saw the commercials and, as a matter of
principle, didn't like them. Because of the proximity of the launch
date and because of the enormous cost of the animation, he
couldn't afford to make radical changes in the campaign. So he
homed in on the voice.

It was totally wrong, he cried. Far too patronizing, too light, it
didn't treat the product seriously enough, suggested that the whole
sales campaign was a bit of a joke. Hugo and his associates held
back their view that little fuzzy red figures called Wideawakes were
not going to look very serious however funereal the voice that
addressed them and said yes, of course he was right and they had
rather suspected this might be a problem from the start and they'd
go straight off and find another voice.

By coincidence, on the very evening of the meeting at which this
decision had been made, Charles Paris was appearing in a television play. It was one of the few jobs he had had in a very lean year
and he was playing an avuncular Victorian solicitor. His voice was
somewhat deeper than usual because he had had a cold at the time
of the recording.

Whether it was this odd voice quality or the fact that he had
worn tailcoat and top-hat that made him seem to Hugo to be the
ideal Mr. Bland, Charles never knew. Secretly he thought it was
partly that Hugo knew that he would be easy to work with and that
the Creative Director desperately needed to come up with something new. It was evident that Hugo, in a business that thrives on
ideas, was beginning to run out of them.

He could feel the pressure from the inventive minds of younger
copywriters and the task of finding the new voice for Mr. Bland was

a competitive issue in the agency. There were other members of the staff with other candidates and the results of the voice-to-picture tests could well cause some realignment in the creative hierarchy of Mills Brown Mazzini.

So when the new Bland Brand Manager, Mr. Farrow, chose Charles Paris from the test, Hugo was over the moon. It was then that he had started the showing off and parading of his new discovery which had so annoyed Charles at the Backstagers' party.

(For Charles the success was not without irony, because it involved getting one up on Christopher Milton, whose path he had crossed during the accident-haunted rehearsals for the musical *Lumpkin!.*)

Charles was now familiar with the small commercial recording studio where he was to work. Through the glossy foyer with its low glass desks and low oatmeal couches, downstairs to the tiny Studio Two.

God knows what the building had been before conversion. A private house maybe, with the studio as a larder. The conversion had consisted mainly of sticking cork tiles on every available surface. In spite of the expensive recording hardware, the whole operation looked unfinished and temporary, as if all the cork could be stripped off and the studio equipment dismantled in half an hour so that the real owner would never know what his premises had been used for during his absence.

Hugo and Farrow were already sitting in the control cubicle. Hugo looked tired and nervous.

They started recording. The copy was so similar to the television version that any notes on performance given in those sessions were still applicable, but Farrow was determined to give them all again. Like all Brand Managers (indeed it is an essential qualification for the job), he was without artistic judgement.

Charles had now done enough of these sessions to know how to behave. Just take it, do as you're told even if it's wrong, don't comment, don't suggest, above all don't try to put any of yourself into it. The agency and, indirectly, the client had hired his voice as a piece of machinery, and it was their right to use it as they thought fit, even if the owner of the machinery knew it wasn't being used in the best way. At worst, there was the comfort that the session was only booked for an hour and he was being paid for it. Thirty-five quid basic, with possible repeats.

So, with his voice lowered an octave to recapture the coldy quality of his Victorian solicitor, Charles gave every possible reading of the lines. He hit each word in turn to satisfy Farrow. BLAND soothes away the day. Bland SOOTHES away the day. Bland soothes AWAY the day. Bland. . . . It did seem a rather pointless exercise for a grown man.

Within half an hour all possible inflections of the lines had been recorded and Charles went from the studio into the control cubicle. Farrow was still not happy. After some deliberation, he pronounced, "I think it may not be the actor's fault this time." Charles found that charming. "No, I think it's the copy that's wrong."

Hugo's voice was extremely reasonable as he replied. "But you have already passed the copy as suitable for the television commercials, and I thought the idea was to keep the two the same."

"If so, the idea was wrong," said Farrow accusingly.

"Well, it was your bloody idea," Hugo suddenly snapped.

Farrow looked at him in amazement, as if he must have misheard. In times when there was so much competition for big accounts, no member of an agency would dare to disagree with a client. After a pause, he continued as though Hugo had not spoken. "I'm afraid you advised us wrongly on that. The radio campaign must be entirely rethought. I can see it's easy for you to use the same copy but I'm not the sort of man to take short cuts. I care about this product and I'm looking for a campaign that's going to be both effective from the sales point of view and also artistically satisfying."

This was too much for Hugo. "Christ, now I've heard it all. Artistically satisfying—what the hell do you know what's artistically satisfying? I've listened to enough crap from you and all the other jumped-up little commercial travelers who try to tell me how to do my job. Stick to what you're good at—peddling pap to the masses—and leave me to get on with what I'm good at—making advertising."

There was a long pause. Mr. Farrow collected together his papers and put them in his briefcase. Had he left the room in silence, it could have been a dignified exit. But he let it down by trying an exit line. "More powerful men than you, Mr. Mecken, have tried to beat me and failed."

This delivered in his nasal London whine was suddenly unaccountably funny, and Charles and Hugo both erupted with laughter almost before the door had closed behind the aggrieved Brand Manager.

Hugo's laughter was a short, nervous burst and when it had passed, he looked ghastly, drained of color. "Oh shit I shouldn't have done it. I'll have to go after him and apologize. I wasn't thinking—or I was thinking about other things. I just snapped."

He rose to leave. Suddenly Charles was worried about him. He couldn't forget their drunken conversation on the Saturday night. The outburst against Farrow had sounded like an overdue expression of home truths, but now he wondered if it had been a more fundamental breakdown of control.

Hugo stood dazed for a moment and then started for the door. "I've booked a table at the Trattoria for twelve-thirty. See you there. I'll get along as soon as I can."

CHAPTER 4

CHARLES WALKED ROUND Soho until it was time to go to the restaurant for another expense account meal. He gave Hugo's name and was shown to a table where there were already two young men.

One he recognized as Ian Compton, a bright copy-writer of about twenty-four who was under Hugo at Mills Brown Mazzini. He was wearing a double-breasted gangster-striped suit over a pale blue T-shirt. Around his neck hung a selection of leather thongs, one for a biro, one for a packet of Gauloise, one for a Cricket lighter and others whose function was not immediately apparent. His lapels bristled with badges, gollies, teddy bears, a spilling to-mato ketchup bottle and similar trendy kitsch.

The other was more soberly dressed in a dark jacket and open-necked brown shirt. "Diccon, this is Charles Paris. I told you about him." Ian's tone implied that what he had told hadn't been wholly enthusiastic. "This is Diccon Hudson."

"Hello." The name rang a bell. Charles had heard Diccon spo-ken of as one of the few who made a very good living exclusively from voice-over work.

Diccon looked at him appraisingly. Not rudely, just with great interest, sizing him up professionally. "So you're the guy who got the Mr. Bland campaign."

" 'Fraid so," said Charles inanely.

"Oh, don't apologize. You win some, you lose some."

So Diccon had been one of his rivals for the job. Intuition told him that he was facing Ian Compton's candidate.

"Who's your agent?" asked Diccon suddenly.

"Maurice Skellern."

"Never heard of him." Was there a hint of relief in the voice? "You want a specialist voice-over agent if you're going to get anywhere in this business."

"Where's the old man?" asked Ian, as Charles ordered a Scotch.

"Hugo? Oh, he's . . . he'll be along shortly." Charles felt it prudent to keep quiet about the scene with Farrow.

It was Diccon's turn for a sudden question. "Do you know Charlotte?"

"Hugo's wife? Yes."

"How is she?" The inquiry was poised midway between solicitude and insolence.

"Fine." Not the moment to share her anxieties of the Saturday night. "You know her well?"

"Used to. Before she got married. Drama school together. Used to go around with her." There was a shading of sexual bravado in his tone. "Quite cut up when she went into the geriatric ward, I was."

Charles ignored the implied rudeness. "But now you've managed to forgive Hugo?"

Diccon looked at him very straight. "Well, he's work, isn't he, love?"

At that moment the subject of their conversation arrived. He was deathly pale. It was impossible to guess at the outcome of his interview with Mr. Farrow. He was in need of a drink. "Got a lot of catching up to do. Marcello, vodka and Campari for me, please. And the same again for the others."

Hugo started drinking as if he were trying to catch up on a whole lifetime. He became very jovial, swopping flip dialogue, scandal and crude anecdotes with the two young men in a way that was jarringly out of character. Charles didn't like the sight of Hugo being one of the boys. And he didn't like the way the two young men were responding to it either. Hugo didn't seem to notice the covert smiles that passed between Ian and Diccon, or the hint of mockery in their tones as they spoke to him. It was not just at home that Hugo had problems.

As the drink got through, he became increasingly like a salesman in a dirty joke. At one point he leaned nudgingly across to Diccon. "What do you say to that bit over there? Chick by the wine rack, eh? Lovely pair of tits."

"Not bad." Diccon gave a superior smile. He knew Hugo was making a fool of himself and was enjoying every minute of it.

"That's what women should be like," Hugo went on in drunken man-of-the-world style. "Nice firm little tits. Don't let 'em have children. Never have children. Not worth the effort. Little buggers don't give a damn about you and look what they do to their mothers—make 'em bloody sag, ruin their figures, stop 'em being sexy. That's what women should be about—they're meant just to give you a bloody good time in bed, that's all."

They had reached the coffee stage. Charles looked round desperately for a waiter to come and bring a bill. He couldn't bear to see Hugo destroying himself much longer.

Diccon Hudson leaned across the table and said to Hugo in a very sincere voice, "So I take it you and Charlotte won't be starting a family?"

"No chance. I've been through all that and it doesn't work."

"So you've managed to persuade her to go on the Pill. Funny, she always used to be against the idea."

Diccon's ambiguous indiscretion had been quite deliberate, but Hugo didn't rise to it. "Huh," he snorted, "there are other ways, you know. We didn't have any Pills in our young days, but we managed, didn't we Charles? Eh, we managed."

Charles had had enough of this barrack-room talk. He rose, "I've got to be going now actually, Hugo."

"No, don't go." The appeal was naked, almost terrified. Charles sat down.

They left the Trattoria an interminable half-hour later, just after three. Diccon Hudson (who had drunk Perrier water through the meal) said he had to go off to his next recording session.

"They keep you busy," Charles observed and was rewarded by a complacent smile.

"Got an evening session tonight, have you, Diccon?" asked Ian in his usual insolent style.

Diccon colored. "No," he said and left without another word.

After Ian Compton had also gone, Charles turned to his friend. "Well, Hugo, thanks for the lunch. Look, I'll no doubt see you tomorrow down in Breckton for this Critics'—"

"Don't go, Charles. Let's have another drink. 'S a little club in Dean Street where I'm a member. C'mon, little quick one."

The club was a strip joint with gold chairs and a lot of hanging red velvet. A party of Japanese executives and a few morose single men watched a couple of girls playing with each other.

Hugo didn't seem to notice them. He ordered a bottle of Scotch. The boisterous, vulgar stage of drunkenness was now behind him; he settled down to silent, cold-blooded consumption.

Charles drank sparingly. He had the feeling that Hugo was going to need help before the day was out.

He tried asking what was the matter; he offered help.

"I don't want help, Charles, I don't want talk. I just want you to sit and bloody drink with me, that's all."

So they sat and bloody drank. Clients came and went. The girls were replaced by others who went through the same motions.

Eventually, Hugo seemed to relax. His eyelids flickered and his head started to nod. Charles looked at his watch and put his hand on his friend's arm. "Come on, it's nearly six. Let's go."

Hugo was surprisingly docile. He paid the bill (an amount which took Charles's breath away) without noticing. Out in the street he looked around blearily. "'S find a cab, Charles. Get the six-forty-two from Waterloo."

They were lucky to find one and got to the station in good time. Charles went off to buy a ticket and returned to find Hugo on the platform with a copy of the *Evening Standard* tucked under his arm. Charles made to move a little further down the platform. "No, Charles, here. Right opposite the barrier at Breckton."

Sure enough, twenty minutes later they got out of the train opposite the ticket collector. Hugo showed his season ticket with an unconscious reflex movement, turned right out of the station and started to walk along a footpath by the railway line. After a few steps he stopped.

"Come on, Hugo, let's get back to your place. See Charlotte."

"Charlotte." There was a deep misery in his echo.

"Yes, Come on."

"No," Hugo dithered like a recalcitrant two-year-old. "No, let's go up to the Backstagers and have a drink."

"Haven't we had enough drinks?" Charles spoke very gently.

"No, we bloody haven't! Don't you try to tell me when I've had enough!" Hugo bunched his fist and took a wild swing. Charles was able to block it harmlessly, but he felt the enormous strength of frustration in the blow.

Hugo went limp. "I'm sorry, Charles. I'm sorry. Silly. Come on, come to the Backstagers—just for a quick one. Often go there for a quick one on the way home."

"All right. A very quick one."

In the Back Room bar (manned that evening by Robert Chubb) Hugo recommenced his silent, systematic drinking. Charles, himself no mean performer with a bottle, was amazed at his friend's capacity. What made it unnerving was the fact that after the outburst by the station, it no longer seemed to have any effect. Hugo spoke with great care, but without slurring. And still the alcohol poured in, as if fueling some inner fire, which must soon burst out into a terrible conflagration.

There were a good few Backstagers about. Apparently, this was one of their rare lulls between productions. The Critics' Circle for *The Seagull* the next day and then, on Wednesday, rehearsals for *The Winter's Tale* would start. Charles visualized Shakespeare getting the same perfunctory treatment as Chekhov.

Hugo introduced him liberally to everyone in sight and then left him to fend for himself. Geoffrey Winter was lounging against the bar with a middle-aged balding man dressed in a navy and white striped T-shirt, white trousers, plimsolls and a silly little blue cap with a gold anchor on it.

This refugee from *H.M.S. Pinafore* turned out to be Shad Scott-Smith, director of *The Seagull*. "Now, Charles," he emoted when they were introduced, "promise me one thing—that when you do the Critics' Circle you will really criticize. Treat us just as you would a professional company. Be cruel if you like, but please, please, do be constructive. There's an awful tendency for these meetings to end up just as a sort of mutual admiration society, which really doesn't help anyone."

"I'll do my best to avoid that."

"Oh, super. I'm just here actually buying the odd drink of thanks for members of my hardworking cast—libations to my little gods, you could say. Oh, the whole gang did work so hard. I tell you, I'm still a washed-out rag at the end of it all. Still, I at least get a bit of a break now. Do you know, Geoff's going straight on to play Leontes in *The Winter's Tale*. Honestly, I don't know where he gets the energy. How do you do it, Geoff?"

Geoffrey Winter shrugged. Charles thought that was a pretty good answer to a totally fatuous question. He warmed to the man.

Shad went on. "Oh, something happens, I know. The old adrenalin flows. Leave it to Doctor Footlights, he'll sort you out."

He breathed between gushes and changed the subject. "By the way, Geoff, do you know if Charlotte's going to be in this evening? I do want to buy my darling Nina a drink."

"I've no idea what she's up to. Ask Hugo."

Charlotte's husband was hunched over a large Scotch at the bar. Shad swanned over. "Any idea what the little woman's up to this evening?"

"Little woman?" Charles heard a dangerous undertone in Hugo's echo.

"Darling Charlotte," Shad explained.

"Darling Charlotte . . ." Hugo began, unnecessarily loud. "Darling Charlotte may be in hell for all I know. Don't ask me about Charlotte the harlot. She's a bloody whore!"

After the shocked silence which followed this pronouncement, Shad decided that he'd ring Charlotte from home. As he minced away, other Backstagers joined the exodus with desultory farewells. Charles felt guilty, responsible. "Geoffrey, has Hugo driven them away? He's drunk out of his mind."

"No, it's not that. This place is used to dramatic outbursts. The mass evacuation is due to the telly. *I, Claudius* tonight. Nine o'clock. Becoming a great cult show. I haven't seen any, been rehearsing. But I'm told it's just the thing for bourgeois commuters' wish-fulfillment. Lots of rapes and murders."

"Living vicariously."

"Yes, well, we don't get all that at home. At least, not many of us."

Charles laughed. "Actually, I'd better get Hugo home. I hate to think how much alcohol he's got inside him." He moved over to the bar. "Hugo, time to go, don't you think?"

Once again this suggestion touched some trigger of violence.

Hugo shouted, "Just keep your bloody mouth shut!" and dashed his glass of Scotch in Charles' face.

Charles was furious. Unaware of the shocked gaze of the remaining Backstagers, he turned on Hugo. "You're drunk and disgusting!"

"Get lost!"

"You ought to go home. You've had enough."

"I'll go home when I bloody choose to. And that won't be before closing time." Hugo banged his glass down on the bar and then, as if to deny the force of his outburst, asked politely, "May I have another Scotch, please?"

As Robert Chubb obliged with the drink, Charles stormed out. In the lobby he found Geoffrey Winter had followed him. Geoffrey offered a blue and white handkerchief to mop up his jacket. "Thanks. Is there a phone?"

"There. Just behind the door."

Charles got through to Charlotte. "Look, I've just left Hugo. He's in the Backstagers' bar. Says he won't be leaving till it closes. He's extremely drunk."

"Won't be the first time," she said dryly. "Thanks for the warning."

Geoffrey Winter was still waiting outside. "I'd offer you a lift, but we don't run a car. Still, I can show you a quick way down to the station. There's a footpath."

"Thank you."

They walked past a large house next door to the Backstagers. It was neo-Tudor with diamond window panes. No light on. Outside the porch, horrible out of period, a pair of grotesque stone lions stood on guard.

Charles drew in his breath sharply with distaste. Geoffrey followed his glance and chuckled. "The Hobbses. Mr. and Mrs. Arkadina. Advertising their money. Ostentatious buggers. But, nonetheless, a good source of free drinks."

Charles laughed, though inwardly he was still seething from the encounter with Hugo.

"By the way," said Geoffrey, "I gather we see you tomorrow."

"Yes, Vee invited me down for a meal. If that's still okay."

"Fine. Love to see you. I'll show you the way when we get to the main road."

They walked across a common where a huge pile of wood and rubbish announced the approach of Bonfire Night.

"Good God, November already," observed Geoffrey. "Guy Fawkes to be burnt again on Friday. How time flies as you get older."

"You think you've got problems," Charles mourned. "It's my fiftieth birthday this week."

They talked a little on the way to the main road, but most of the time there was silence except for the soft pad of their rubber soles on the pathway. Charles didn't notice the lack of conversation. His mind was still full of hurt after the clash with Hugo.

He didn't really notice saying goodbye to Geoffrey. Or the train journey back to Waterloo. He was still seething, almost sick with rage.

CHAPTER 5

CHARLES SPENT AN unsatisfactory Tuesday mooching round his bed-sitter in Hereford Road, Bayswater. It was a depressing room and the fact that he stayed there to do anything but sleep meant he was depressed.

He was still fuming over the scene with Hugo. No longer fuming at the fact that Hugo had hit him, but now angry with himself for having flared up. Hugo was in a really bad state, possibly on the verge of a major breakdown, and, as a friend, Charles should have stood by him, tried to help, not rushed off in a huff after a drunken squabble.

As usual, his dissatisfaction with himself spilled over into other area of his life. Frances. He must sort out what his relationship with Frances was. They must meet. He must ring her.

Early in the afternoon he went down to the pay-phone on the landing, but before he dialed her number, he realized she wouldn't be there. She was a teacher. Tuesday in term-time she'd be at school. He'd ring her about six, before he went down to Breckton.

To shift his mood, he started looking through his old scripts. *How's Your Father?* He read the first few pages. It really wasn't bad. Light, but fun. A performance by the Backstagers would be better than nothing. Rather sheepishly, he decided to take it with him.

He left without ringing Frances.

* * *

Vee Winter opened the door. She had on a P.V.C. apron with a design of an old London omnibus. She looked at him challengingly again, part provocative, part exhibitionist.

"Sorry I'm a bit early, Vee. The train didn't take as long as I expected."

"No, they put on some fast ones during the rush-hour. But don't worry, supper's nearly ready. Geoff's just got in. He's up in the study. Go and join him. He's got some booze up there."

The house was a small Edwardian semi, but it had been re-arranged and decorated with taste and skill. Or rather, someone had started rearranging and decorating it with taste and skill. As he climbed the stairs, Charles noticed that the wall had been stripped and rendered, but not yet repapered. In the same way, someone had begun to sand the paint off the banister. Most of the wood was bare, but obstinate streaks of white paint clung in crevices. The house gave the impression that someone had started to renovate it with enormous vigor and then run out of enthusiasm. Or money.

The soprano wailing of the *Liebestod* from Wagner's *Tristan und Isolde* drew him to Geoffrey Winter's study. Here the conversion had very definitely been completed. Presumably the room had been intended originally as a bedroom, but it was now lined with long pine shelves which extended at opposite ends of the room to make a desk and a surface for an impressive selection of hi-fi. The shelves were covered with a cunning disarray of books, models, old bottles and earthenware pots. The predominant color was a pale, pale mustard, which toned in well with the pine. On the wall facing the garden French windows gave out on to a small balcony.

Geoffrey Winter was fiddling with his hi-fi. The Wagner disc was being played on an expensive-looking grey metal turntable. Leads ran from the tuner to a small Japanese cassette radio.

"Sorry, Charles, just getting this on to cassette. So much handier. It's nearly finished."

"This room's really good, Geoffrey."

"I like it. One of the advantages of not having children—you have space."

"And more money."

Geoffrey grimaced. "Hmm. Depends on the size of your mortgage. And your other bills. And how work's going."

"What do you do?"

"I'm an architect." Which explained the skill of the decor.

"Work for yourself?"

"Yes. Well, that is to say, I work for whoever will pay for my services. So at the moment, yes, I seem to work just for myself. No one's building anything. Can I get you a drink?"

"Thank you."

"It's sherry or sherry, I'm afraid." And, Charles noticed, not a particularly good sherry. Cypress domestic. Tut, tut, getting spoiled by the ostentatious array of Hugo's drinks cupboard. It would take a distressingly short time to pick up all the little snobberies of materialism.

While Geoffrey poured the drinks, Charles moved over to the shelves to inspect a theatrical model he had noticed when he came in. It was a stage set of uneven levels and effectively placed columns. Plastic figures were grouped on the rostra.

Geoffrey answered the unspoken question as he handed Charles his sherry. "Set for *The Caucasian Chalk Circle*. I'm directing it for the Backstagers in the new year."

"You're a meticulous planner."

"I think as a director you have to be. In anything to do with the theatre, in fact. You have to have planned every detail."

"Yes, I could tell that from your Trigorin."

"I'm not sure whether that's meant to be a compliment or not, Charles."

"Nor am I."

Geoffrey laughed.

"No, Geoffrey, what I mean is, you had more stagecraft than the rest of the company put together, but occasionally . . . one or two tricks—like that very slow delivery on key lines, separating the words, giving each equal emphasis—well, I was conscious of the artifice."

Geoffrey smiled, perhaps with slight restraint. "Don't waste it, Charles. Keep it for the Critics' Circle. Professional criticism."

The record had ended. The stylus worried against the center groove. Geoffrey seemed suddenly aware of it and, with a look at Charles, he switched off the cassette player. He replaced the disk in its sleeve and marshalled it into a rack.

The conversation dipped. Charles found himself asking about the previous night's television. Dear, oh dear. Slipping into commuter habits. "Did you get back in time for your ration of rape and murder in *I, Claudius* last night?"

"No. I was back in time but I left Vee to watch it on her own. I did some work on Leontes. Trying to learn the bloody lines."

"Shakespearean verse at its most tortured. How do you learn them? Have you any magic method?"

" 'Fraid not. It's just read through, read through. Time and again."

"It's the only way."

At that moment Vee called from downstairs to say the meal was ready.

There was quite a crowd in the Back Room before the Critics' Circle. And for once they had a topic of conversation other than the theatrical doings of the Breckton Backstagers.

Denis and Mary Hobbs had been burgled. They had come home from their weekend cottage at about midnight the previous night and found the house full of police. A burglar had smashed one of the diamond panes in a downstairs front window, reached through and opened it, gone upstairs and emptied the contents of Mary's jewel box.

". . . That's what's so horrible about it," she was saying into her fourth consolatory double gin, "—the idea of someone in your house, going through your things. It's ghastly."

"Were they vandals too? Did they dirty your bedclothes and scrawl obscenities on your walls?" asked sour Reggie hopefully.

"No, at least we were spared that. Remarkable tidy burglars, closed all the cupboards and doors after them. No fingerprints either, so the C.I.D. boys tell us. But . . ." After her proprietary reference to the police force, she warmed to her role as tragic queen. ". . . that only seems to make it worse. It was so coldblooded. And the idea of other people invading our privacy—ooh, it makes me feel cold all over."

"Did they get much?" asked Reggie, with morbid interest.

"Oh yes, there was quite a lot of good stuff in my jewelry box.

Not everyday things—I dare say a lot of them I don't wear more than twice a year. But I'd got them out of the bank for this Masonic do of Denis's last Monday and it didn't seem worth putting them back, because next week there's this dinner-dance thing at the Hilton—did I tell you about that?"

The snide expressions on the faces of the surrounding Backstagers suggested that Mary missed no opportunity to give them details of her posh social life. Anyway, the question seemed to be rhetorical. The role was shifting from tragic queen to wonderful person.

"Oh, I don't care about the stuff as jewelry. I'm not materialistic. But they're presents Den's given me over the years, birthday, Christmases and so on. That's the trouble—the insurance will cover the value in money terms, but it can never replace what those things mean to me."

"It serves us bloody right," said her husband. "We've talked enough times about having a burglar alarm put in. But you put it off. You think it'll never happen to you."

"Do the police reckon there's a chance of getting the culprits?"

"I don't know. Never commit themselves, the buggers, do they? But I think it's unlikely. They seem to reckon the best chance was missed when Bob first saw the light."

"What light?"

"Oh, didn't you hear? You tell them, Bob."

Robert Chubb took his cue and graciously moved to center stage. "I was the one who discovered the ghastly crime. Proper little Sherlock Holmes. Perhaps I should take it up professionally.

"I'd been sorting through some stuff in the office last night after I handed the bar over to Reggie and I was walking home past Denis and Mary's at about ten-fifteen, when I saw this light."

Years of amateur dramatics would not allow him to miss the pregnant pause. "The light was just by the broken window. It shone on the jagged glass. I thought immediately of burglars and went back to the office to phone the police. Incidentally—" he added in self-justification, in case Denis's last remark might be construed by anyone as a criticism, "the boys in blue told me I was absolutely right not to try to tackle the criminal. Said they get as much trouble from members of the public who fancy themselves as heroes as they do from the actual crooks.

"Anyway, my intervention does not seem to have been completely useless. They reckon the burglar must have seen me and that's what frightened him off. He appears to have scampered away in some disarray."

"Yes," Mary Hobbs chipped in, temperamentally unsuited to listening to anyone for that length of time. "He left his torch behind in the window sill. The police are hoping to be able to trace him through that."

Robert Chubb, piqued at losing his punch-line, changed the subject. Like a child who dictates the rules of the game because it's his ball, he brought them back to his dramatic society. "Oh, Charles, about the World Premières Festival, did you bring along that play of yours? The committee would really like to have a look at it. Need a good new play, you know."

Embarrassed at the fact that he actually had got it with him, Charles handed over the script with some apology about it being very light.

"Oh, the lighter the better. I'm sure it has the professional touch. And, talking of that, I do hope that in your criticism this evening you will apply professional standards to *The Seagull*. We always do and hope others will. So please don't pull your punches."

"All right. I won't."

As soon as Charles started speaking to the rows of earnest Backstagers in the rehearsal room, it was clear that they did not like being judged by professional standards.

He began with a few general observations on Chekhov and the difficulties that his plays presented. He referred to the years of work which had gone into the Moscow Arts Theatre's productions. He then went into detail on Chekhovian humor and stressed the inadvisability of playing Russian servants as mugging Mummerset yokels.

He moved on from this to the rest of the cast. He gave a general commendation and then made detailed criticism. He praised Charlotte's controlled innocence as Nina and the technical skill of Geoffrey's Trigorian. He faulted Clive Steele's Konstantin for lack of discipline and regretted that the part of Madame Arkadina was beyond the range of all but a handful of the world's actresses. But, rather against his better judgement and to sugar the pill, he congratulated Mary Hobbs on a brave attempt.

He thought he had been fair. Out of deference to their amateur status and because he had no desire to cause unpleasantness, he had toned down the criticism he would have given a professional cast. He thought his remarks might have been overindulgent, but otherwise unexceptionable.

The shocked silence which followed his conclusion indicated that the Backstagers did not share his opinion. Reggie, who seemed to get lumbered with (or perhaps sought after) all official functions, was chairing the meeting. He rose to his feet. "Well, some fairly controversial views there from Mr. Parrish. I don't think everyone's going to agree with all that." A murmur of agreement came back from the audience. "Still, thank you. Any questions?"

There was an "after you" silence and then Shad Scott-Smith rose to his feet. He spoke with a heavy irony which obviously appealed to the mood of the gathering. "Well, first of all, I'd like to thank Mr. Parrish for his comments and what I'd like to offer is not so much a question as a humble defense.

"As perpetrator of the terrible crime of *The Seagull* . . ." This sally drew an appreciative titter. "I feel I should apologize, both to the cast, whom I misled so disastrously, and to the good folk of Breckton, who so unwisely bought all the tickets for all four performances and who made the terrible mistake of enjoying the production very much."

This got an outright laugh of self-congratulation. "And I would also like to apologize to the local newspaper critics who, out of sheer malice and stupidity, gave such good reviews to my production of *The Cherry Orchard* last year, since they didn't know they were dealing with someone who had no appreciation of Chekhov. And while I'm at it, I'd better tick off the adjudicators of the Inter-Regional Drama Festival who were foolish enough to award my production of *The Bear* a Special Commendation."

He sat down to a riot of applause. Charles saw he was going to have an uphill fight. "All right, I'm sorry. I had no intention of offending anyone. I am here as a professional actor and director and I'm giving you my opinions as I would to the members of a professional company. Everyone keeps saying that these Critics' Circles are not just meant to be a mutual admiration society."

"No, they're certainly not," said Robert Chubb with unctuous charm. "I set them up as a forum for informed discussion, for the give-and-take of intelligent ideas. I'm sure we can all take criticism and that's what we are all here for."

Charles thought maybe at last he had got a supporter. But Robert Chubb soon dispelled the idea as he went on. "The only comment I would have is that it does seem to me rather a pity that the only member of the cast for whom you managed unstinting praise was one of our newest members and that you were somewhat dismissive of some of our most experienced actors and actresses. Particularly of a lady to whom we all owe many splendid performances, not least her Lady Macbeth last year."

This spirited defense of Mary Hobbs produced another warm burst of applause. Charles was tempted to ask what relevance a performance in a production of *Macbeth* he couldn't possible have seen should have to a production of *The Seagull* he had seen, but there didn't seem any point.

He had misjudged the nature of the meeting entirely. All that had been required of him had been a pat on the back for all concerned, not forgetting the charming young man who tore his ticket and the good ladies who made the coffee for the interval. All he could do now was to insure that that meeting ended as soon as possible and get the hell out of the place. And never come back.

Mentally he cursed Hugo for ever letting him in for it, or at least for not briefing him as to what to expect.

He then realized with a slight shock that Hugo wasn't there. Nor was Charlotte. Nor Clive Steele. It seemed strange.

As he thought about it, he started again to feel guilty about the way he had left Hugo the night before. He hated to let things like that fester. Stupid misunderstandings should be cleared up as soon as possible. He was too old to lose friends over trivialities. Once he'd stopped the Backstagers baying for his blood, he'd go round and see Hugo and apologize.

But there was still more Critics' Circling to be weathered. It was hard work. There was no common ground for discussion. The Backstagers were only capable of talking about the Backstagers. When Charles made a comparison with a West End production of *The Three Sisters*, someone would say, "Well, of course, when Walter directed it down here . . ." When he praised the comic timing of Michael Hordern, someone would say, "Oh, but Philip's a wonderful actor too. If you'd seen him in *The Rivals* . . ." It was like talking to a roomful of politicians. Every question was greeted, not by an answer, but by an aggrieved assertion of something totally different.

It did end. Eventually. Reggie gave an insipid vote of thanks with some vague remarks about "having been given lots of food for thought . . . interesting, and even surprising, to hear the views of someone from the outside."

Charles prepared his getaway. He thanked Geoffrey and Vee for the meal and made for the exit, hoping that he was seeing the last of the Breckton Backstagers.

As he reached the door, he overheard a lacquered voice commenting, "Don't know who he thinks he is anyway. I've never seen him on the television or anything."

Charles Paris knew who they were talking about.

Hugo opened the front door. His eyes were dull and registered no surprise at the visit. He was still wearing the clothes he had had on the day before and their scruffy appearance suggested he hadn't been to bed in the interim. The smell of whisky which blasted from him suggested that he hadn't stopped drinking either.

"I came round to apologize for going off like that last night."

"Apologize," Hugo echoed stupidly. He didn't seem to know what Charles was talking about.

"Yes. Can I come in?"

"Sure. Have a drink." Hugo led the way, stumbling, into the sitting room. It was a mess. Empty whisky bottles of various brands bore witness to a long session. He must have been working through the collection. Incongruously, the scene was cosily lit by an open fire, heaped with glowing smokeless fuel.

"Was cold," Hugo mumbled by way of explanation. He swayed towards the fire and removed the still burning gas poker. "Shouldn't have left that in." He unscrewed the lead with excessive concentration. "Whisky?"

"Thank you."

Hugo slopped out half a tumbler of Glenlivet and handed it over. "Cheers." He slumped into an armchair with his own glass.

Charles took a long sip. It was welcome after the idiocies of the Critics' Circle. "Where's Charlotte?"

"Huh. Charlotte." Hugo spoke without violence but with great bitterness. "Charlotte's finished."

"What do you mean?"

"Charlotte—finished. The great love affair, Charlotte and Hugo —over."

"You mean she's left you?"

"Not here." Hugo was almost incoherent.

"She wasn't here when you got back last night?"

"Not here."

"Where do you think she's gone?"

"I don't know. To see lover boy."

"Is there a lover boy?"

"I suppose so. That's the usual story. Pretty young girl. Middle-aged husband. Don't you read the Sunday papers?" Hugo spoke in a low, hopeless mumble.

"Have you been in to work today?" Hugo shook his head. "Just drinking?" A small nod.

They sat and drank. Charles tried to think of anything he could say that might be helpful. There was nothing. He could only stay, be there.

After a long, long silence, he started to feel cold. The fire was nearly dead. Charles got up briskly. "Where's the coal, Hugo? I'll go and get some more."

"You'll never find it. Let me. Come on, I'll show you."

Hugo led the way unsteadily into the kitchen. He picked up a torch and fumbled it on.

They went out of the back door. There was a shed just opposite. "In there," said Hugo.

Charles opened the door. Hugo shone the torch.

In its beam they saw Charlotte. She was splayed unceremoniously over the coal. A scarf was knotted unnaturally round her neck. She was very dead.

CHAPTER 6

CHARLES RANG THE police and stayed beside Hugo in the sitting room until they arrived. Hugo was catatonic with shock. Only once did he speak, murmuring softly to himself, "What did I do to her? She was young. What did I do to her?"

When the police arrived, Charles steeled himself to go out once again to the coal shed. The beams of their torches were stronger and made the color of Charlotte's cheeks even less natural, like a detail from an over-exposed photograph.

The richness of her perfume, which still hung in the air, was sickly and inappropriate. The staring eyes and untidy spread of limbs were not horrifying; the feeling they gave Charles was more one of embarrassment, as if a young girl had been sick at a party. And his impression of callowness was reinforced by the Indian print scarf over the bruised neck, like a teenager's attempt to hide love-bites.

The bruises were chocolate brown. On one of them the skin had been broken and a bootlace of dried blood traced its way crazily up towards Charlotte's mouth.

Hugo remained dull and silent and Charles himself was dazed as they were driven to the police station. They were separated when they arrived and parted without a word. Each was taken into a separate interview room to make a statement.

Charles had to wait for about half an hour before his questioning began. A uniformed constable brought him a cup of tea and apologized for the delay. Everyone was very pleasant, but pleasant with that slight restraint that staff have in hospitals, as if something unpleasant is happening nearby but no one is going to mention it.

Eventually two policemen came in. One was in uniform and carried a sheaf of paper. The other was fair-haired, early thirties, dressed in a brown blazer and blue trousers. He spoke with the vestiges of a South London twang. "So sorry to have kept you waiting. Detective-Sergeant Harvey. Mr. Paris, isn't it?"

Charles nodded.

"Fine. I must just get a few personal details and then, if I may, I'll ask a few questions about . . . what happened. Then Constable Renton will write it down as a statement, which you sign—if you're happy with it. Okay?"

Charles nodded again.

"It's late, and I'm afraid this could take some time. Say if you'd like more tea. Or a sandwich or something."

"No, I'm fine, thanks."

So it started. First, simple information, name, address and so on. Then details of how he came to know Mr. and Mrs. Mecken. And then a resume of the last two days.

As he spoke, Charles could feel it going wrong. He told the truth, he told it without bias, and yet he could feel the false picture that his words were building up. Everything he said seemed to incriminate Hugo. The more he tried to defend him, the worse it sounded.

Detective-Sergeant Harvey was a good poker-faced questioner. He didn't force the pace, he didn't put words into Charles's mouth, he just asked for information slowly and unemotionally. And to damning effect.

"After your lunch on Monday you say that you and Mr. Mecken went on to a drinking club?"

"Yes, a sort of strip joint in Dean Street."

"And what did you drink there?"

"Hugo ordered a bottle of whisky."

"So, by the time you left there, you had both had a considerable amount to drink?"

"I didn't drink a great deal in the club." Immediately Charles kicked himself for prompting the next question.

"But Mr. Mecken did?"

"I suppose he had quite a bit by some people's standards, but you know how it is with advertising people—they can just drink and drink." The attempt at humor didn't help. It made it sound more and more of a whitewash.

"Yes. But you then both returned to Breckton and continued drinking at the theatre club. Surely that made it rather a lot of alcohol, even for an advertising man."

"Well, yes, I agree, we wouldn't normally have drunk that much, but you see Hugo was a bit upset and . . ." Realizing that once again he had said exactly the wrong thing, Charles left the words hanging in the air.

"Upset," Detective-Sergeant Harvey repeated without excitement. "Have you any idea why he should have been upset?"

Charles hedged. "Oh, I dare say it was something at work. He was involved in a big campaign to launch a new bedtime drink—that's what I was working on with him—and I think there may have been some disagreements over that. You know, these advertising people do take it all so seriously."

"Yes. Of course." The slow response seemed only to highlight the hollowness of Charles's words. "You have no reason to believe that Mr. Mecken was having any domestic troubles?"

"Domestic troubles?" Charles repeated idiotically.

"Worries about his marriage."

"Oh. Oh, I shouldn't think so. I mean, I don't know. I don't think anyone can begin to understand anything about another person's marriage. But I mean Charlotte is a—I mean, was a beautiful girl and . . ." He trailed off guiltily.

"Hmm. Mr. Paris, would you describe Mr. Mecken as a violent man?"

"No, certainly not. And if you're trying to suggest that—"

"I am not trying to suggest anything, Mr. Paris. I am just trying to get as full a background to the death of Mrs. Mecken as I can," Detective-Sergeant Harvey replied evenly.

"Yes, of course, I'm sorry." Blustering wasn't going to help Hugo's cause. As his interrogation continued, Charles kept thinking of his friend, in another interview room, being asked other questions. Where were Hugo's answers leading?

"You say Mr. Mecken is not a habitually violent man. Is he perhaps the sort who might become violent when he's had a few drinks? I mean, for instance, did he show any violence towards you during your long drinking session on Monday?"

Charles hesitated. Certainly he wasn't going to go back to Hugo's bizarre outburst while an undergraduate and his instinct was to deny that anything had happened on the Monday. But Hugo's second swing at him had been witnessed by a bar full of Backstagers. He couldn't somehow see that self-dramatizing lot keeping quiet about it. He'd do better to edit the truth than to tell a lie. "Well, he did take a sort of playful swing at me at one point when I suggested he ought to be getting home, but that's all."

"A playful swing." Detective-Sergeant Harvey gave the three words equal emphasis.

The questioning ended soon after and the information was turned into a written statement. Detective-Sergeant Harvey courteously went through a selection of the questions again and Constable Renton laboriously wrote down the answers in longhand on ruled paper.

Inevitably it was a slow process and Charles found his mind wandering. He didn't like the way it was heading.

Previously he had been numb with shock, but now the fact of Charlotte's death was getting through to him. The feeling of guilt which his initially casual reaction had prompted gave way to a cold sensation of nausea.

With it came a realization of the implications for Hugo. As Charles went through the details for his statement, he saw with horror which way the circumstantial evidence pointed.

There were so many witnesses too. So many people who had heard Hugo's denunciation of his wife and his violent burst of aggression towards Charles. Unless Hugo could prove a very solid alibi for the time at which his wife had been murdered, things didn't look too good for him.

At this point it struck Charles that he was assuming Hugo was innocent and he paused to question the logic of this. On reflection, it didn't stand up very well. In fact the only arguments he could come up with against Hugo's guilt were Hugo's own denial that he would ever hurt Charlotte and Charles's own conviction that someone he knew so well would be incapable of a crime of such savagery.

And those weren't arguments. They were sheer emotion, romantic indulgence.

The thought of romanticism only made it worse. It suggested a very plausible motive for Hugo to kill his wife. Hugo was a romantic, unwilling to accept the unpleasant facts of life. He had built up his own life into a romantic ideal, with his writing talent supporting the professional side and his love-affair with Charlotte the domestic.

When it became clear to such a man that the twin pillars of his life were both illusions, anything could happen.

He finished the statement and was asked to read it through, signing each page. At one point he hesitated.

"Anything wrong?" asked Detective-Sergeant Harvey.

"Well, I . . . it seems so bald, so . . ." He couldn't think of anything that didn't sound like protesting too much. "No." He signed on.

He was amazed to discover it was nearly five o'clock. Dully he accepted the offer of the lift home in a squad car. He gave his Hereford Road address.

He didn't notice the drabness of the bedsitter as he entered. He homed in on the bottle of Bells straight away and sank half a tumblerful. Then he lay down on the bed and lost consciousness.

When he woke, it was still dark. Or rather, he realized after looking at his watch, dark again. Quarter past six. He'd slept round the clock.

He was still dressed. He left the house and walked along Hereford Road to Westbourne Grove. There was a newspaper seller on the corner. He bought an *Evening Standard*.

It didn't take long to find the news. Hugo Mecken had been arrested, charged with the murder of his wife, Charlotte.

And Charles Paris felt it was his fault.

CHAPTER 7

IN SPITE OF logic, the feeling of treachery remained. Charles Paris had deserted his friend in a crisis. Charles Paris had incriminated his friend by his statement.

He had to do something. At least find out all the circumstances, at least check that no mistakes had been made.

He hurried back to the house in Hereford Road, went to the pay-phone on the landing and dialed Gerald Venables's office number.

Gerald was a successful show business solicitor whom Charles had known since Oxford. Armed with a boyish enthusiasm for the whole business of detection, he had collaborated with Charles on one or two investigations, starting with the strange death of Marius Steen. In the current circumstances, it was an immediate instinct to ring Gerald.

An efficient, husky voice answered the phone.

"Is that Polly?"

"Yes."

"It's Charles Paris. Could I speak to Gerald, please?"

"I'm sorry, he's not here."

"Oh, sod it. Is he on his way home?"

"No, he's out with a client, I'm afraid. He was called down to Breckton mid-morning and he's been there all day."

"Oh my God, of course. He's Hugo Mecken's solicitor, isn't he?"

"Yes. That's who he's with. I gather you've heard the news."

"Yes." It wasn't worth going into details of how he had been the first to hear it. "Stupid of me. I'd forgotten. Gerald sorted out Hugo's divorce, didn't he?"

"Yes. And he was a bit shocked when he discovered what it was about this time."

"That I can believe. Look, Polly, have you any idea when he'll be back? I mean, is he reckoning to go back to the office?"

"No. He rang about half an hour ago to say he'd go straight to Dulwich from Breckton. And asked me to ring Mrs. Venables and say he'd be late."

"Why didn't he ring her himself?" Charles asked irrelevantly.

"I think it sounds more businesslike if I do." Polly replied with a hint of humor.

Yes, that was Gerald all over. "Polly, when he says 'very late,' what do you reckon that means?"

"I honestly don't know. He said I was to say ten-thirty at the earliest to Mrs. Venables."

"Okay. Thanks, Polly. He didn't say anything else about . . . you know, the case . . . or Hugo . . . or anything."

"No. Well, there isn't really much to say, is there?"

"I suppose not."

Charles spent an unsatisfactory evening and drank too much. He thought of ringing Frances, but put it off again. Round eight he realized he hadn't eaten for over twenty-four hours. He didn't feel hungry, but he thought he ought to have something.

Going out to a restaurant was too much effort. He was too jumpy to sit down and relax over a proper meal. He looked round the room. There was an opened packet of cornflakes on the table. No milk. He tried a handful. They were soft, cardboard.

He rooted through the grey-painted cupboard, shoving aside scripts, half-finished plays, empty bottles, socks and crisp packets. All he came up with was a tin of sardines without a key and a tin of curried beans.

The menu was dictated by his antiquated tin-opener, which wouldn't grip on the sardine tin. He slopped the beans into a saucepan still furred with boiled milk from the previous week and put it on the gas-ring which was hidden discreetly behind a plastic curtain.

The curried beans didn't improve anything. He took a long swill from the Bell's bottle as a mouthwash. Except he didn't spit it out.

Then he addressed his mind to thought. Serious thought. He had been in criminal situations before and he had even, by a mixture of luck and serendipity, solved crimes before. But this one mattered. He had to concentrate, sort it out. He was motivated by his affection for Hugo and his abiding sense of guilt.

His first assumption remained Hugo's innocence. No logic for this, just a conviction.

If only he could see Hugo face to face, talk to him, ask him. Then he would know, he felt sure.

But how do you get to see a man who has just been arrested for murder? Gerald would know. All action seemed to hinge on speaking to Gerald.

Half past nine. The evening was passing, but slowly. Perhaps another generous Bell's would speed up the process.

He looked at the floor through the slopping spirit in his glass. The image was refracted and distorted. Like his thought processes.

The obvious solution was that Hugo had killed his wife. In a wild reaction to the collapse of his dreams he had taken the terrible kamikaze course of the disillusioned romantic. "Yet each man kills the thing he loves . . . ," as Oscar Wilde wrote in his despair.

The only way to escape the obvious solution was to provide a feasible alternative. Either to prove Hugo was doing something else at the time that Charlotte was killed. Or to prove that someone else did it.

Charles's brief experience of the Backstagers told him that emotions ran high in the group. Charlotte had antagonised the established stars by her success as Nina. Vee Winter, for one, felt herself usurped by the newcomer.

But that kind of jealousy wasn't sufficient motive for murder. A sexual impulse was more likely. A woman as beautiful as Charlotte was bound to cause reverberations wherever she went and no doubt her appearance among the Backstagers had led to the snapping-off of a few middle-aged husbands' heads by middle-aged wives who saw eyes lingering with too much interest. Indeed, Charles had seen evidence of this with the Hobbses.

But that was still not something for which a sane person would kill.

It must be a closer attachment. Clive Steele. Charles thought back over the conversation he had heard in the car park. The young man's passions had been demonstrably immature, but they had been strong. He was supposed to be away working in Melton Mowbray for the whole week, but it might be worth investigating his movements.

Or then again, why should the murderer have anything to do with the Backstagers? Charlotte did have other contacts. Not many but a few. Diccon Hudson, for instance. He had made some sour reference to having gone around with her before her marriage. Probably nothing there, but anything was worth looking into to save Hugo.

After all, Diccon could have been the mysterious lover of whom Hugo had spoken. Charles didn't know whether to believe in this personage or not. It could just be a creation of Hugo's fevered imagination. But if such a person did exist, the possible permutations of violent emotions were considerably increased.

Equally, if he did exist, Hugo's motive for killing his wife was that much stronger. But Charles put the thought from his mind. He had to start by assuming Hugo's innocence.

He was full of nervous excitement. He wanted to do something, get started, begin his task of atonement.

He looked at his watch. Twenty-five to eleven. Thank God, he could try Gerald again. The need to do something was now almost unbearable.

Kate, Gerald's wife, sounded disgruntled. No, he wasn't home yet. Yes, Charles could try again in half an hour if it was important, but not much later because she was going to bed.

Charles stood by the phone, seething with energy. There must be something else he could do. He could start piecing together Hugo's movements from the time he left the Back Room on Monday night. Someone must have seen him leave, someone might even have walked him home. Details like that could be vital.

The only Backstager's number he had was Geoffrey and Vee's. Geoffrey answered.

"Have you heard about Hugo?"

"Yes, Charles. Horrible, isn't it?"

"Horrible. Look, I'm trying to find out what he did when he left the bar on Monday night."

"Amateur sleuth work."

"I don't know. Maybe. Thing is, you'd know—who are the real barflies up at that place? Who was guaranteed to have been there at closing time and seen him go?"

"Well, Bob Chubb's the obvious one. He was on the bar, wasn't he?"

"Do you have his number?"

"Yes, sure. I'll get it. I—what's that love?" Vee's voice was asking something in the background. "Just twiddle the aerial round to the right. Sorry, Charles, our television's on the blink. Extremely unwilling to get a decent picture on BBC2. Comes of buying cheap junk. Ah, here it is." He gave Charles Robert Chubb's number. "I only hope it bears fruit. It seems incredible, doesn't it? The idea that Hugo . . . I keep thinking that it'll all turn out to be a mistake and all be cleared up somehow."

"It depends what you mean by cleared up. Charlotte will still be dead."

"Yes."

Robert Chubb answered the phone. His voice was bland and elocuted. When he heard who was calling, it took on a colder note. And when he heard what Charles wanted to know, it became positively snappish.

"As I have already told the police, Mr. Mecken left the bar at about ten-thirty. On his own. I don't really know why I should waste my time repeating this to you. I know everyone likes to see themselves as a private eye, but I really do suggest, Mr. Parrish, that you should leave criminal investigation to the professionals."

"And I really do suggest, Mr. Chubb, that you should do the same with the theatre." Charles slammed the phone down.

He was beginning to run out of small change. He rested his penultimate 10p on the slot and dialed Gerald's number again.

The solicitor answered, sounding formal, even pettish. "Oh, hello, Charles, Kate said you'd rung. Look, could you ring me later on tomorrow? I'm dog-tired. I've just got in and I'm sure whatever you've got to say will keep."

"Gerald, it's about Hugo."

"Oh. Oh yes, of course, you were with him when he found the body—or claimed to find it."

"Yes. How's it going?"

"What do you mean—how's it going?"

"With Hugo."

"Charles, I'm sorry." Gerald sounded exasperated and professional. "I know you are a friend and we are talking about a mutual friend, but I'm afraid, as a solicitor, I can't discuss my clients' affairs."

"You can tell me where he is, can't you? Is he in prison—or where?"

"He'll be spending tonight in the cells at Breckton Police Station."

"And then what?"

Gerald sighed with annoyance. "Tomorrow morning he'll appear at Breckton Magistrates' Court where he'll be remanded in custody. Which means Brixton. Then he'll be remanded again every week until the trial."

"Hmm. When can I get to see him?"

"See him—what do you mean?"

"You know, see him. I want to ask him some questions."

"Well, I don't know. I suppose it may be possible for him to have visitors when he's in Brixton. I'm not sure how soon—"

"No, I want to see him tomorrow."

"That's impossible."

"Will you be seeing him?"

"Yes, of course. As his solicitor, I'll be in court and see him before he's taken off to Brixton."

"Well, can't I come along with you and be passed off as one of your outfit?"

"One of my *outfit?*" Gerald italicized the last word with distaste.

"Yes, surely you have colleagues in your office, articled clerks and what have you. Pretend I'm one of them."

"Charles, do you realize what you're saying? You are asking me to indulge in serious professional misconduct. Have you been drinking?"

"Yes, of course I have. But that's not the point. I am completely serious."

"Charles, I am also serious. This is an extremely serious matter. We are talking about a case of murder."

"What about the death of Willy Mariello? Wasn't that a case of murder? You were keen enough to help me on that. Indeed, whenever I meet you, you get all schoolboyish and ask me when I'm going to get involved in another case and beg that I'll let you know and work together with you on it."

"Yes, but that's different."

"No, it isn't. The only difference is that this case happens to be one in which you are already involved professionally. So far as I'm concerned, this is a case of murder which might well need investigation and, according to your frequently expressed desire, I am asking you if you will help me on it."

Gerald was silent for a moment. When he spoke again, it was with less certitude. "But, Charles, this is a fairly open-and-shut case. I mean, I know I shouldn't say this about a client, but it seems to me that there's little doubt Hugo did it. It all fits in too neatly. And anyway the police wouldn't have arrested and charged him so quickly if it hadn't been pretty definite."

"Okay, I agree. It is most likely that Hugo murdered Charlotte. But I feel that so long as there's even the vaguest alternative possibility, we should investigate it. Well, I should, anyway. Just for my peace of mind."

"What do you mean by an alternative possibility?"

"Say an alibi. Suppose Hugo saw someone, talked to someone during that missing twenty-four hours. . . ."

"But if he did, surely he would have told the police."

"Yes, probably. Look, I haven't worked it all out yet, but I feel guilty about it and—"

Gerald was continuing his own train of thought. "Anyway, we are only talking of a fairly short period for which he'd need an alibi. The preliminary medical report came in while I was down at the Breckton Police Station. They'll get the full post mortem results in a couple of days. It seems that when you discovered Charlotte's body she'd already been dead for twenty-four hours."

"Good God. So she was killed on the Monday night."

"Yes. The police theory is that Hugo arrived back from the theatre club smashed out of his mind, had an argument with his wife—possibly over sexual matters—and then . . . well, strangled her and hid the body. It fits. He'd had a hell of a lot to drink."

"I see. And I suppose the theory is that he continued drinking through the Tuesday to get over the shock."

"Something like that, yes."

"Hmm. This makes it even more imperative that I see Hugo."

"Charles, I have a professional reputation to—"

"Oh, stuff that, Gerald. For God's sake. You're always complaining to me how bloody boring your work is, how sick you get of fiddling about with theatrical contracts all day, how you wish you could get involved in something really exciting like a murder. Well, here's one right in your in-tray. . . ."

"Yes, and it's just because it's there that I have to treat it with professional propriety."

"Gerald, stop being so bloody pompous. I've got to see Hugo. Look, there's hardly any risk involved. Okay, so you've got a new Mr. Paris on your staff. No one knows you down in Breckton. No one's going to check."

"Well . . ." wavering.

Press home advantage. "Come on, Gerald. Live a little. Take a risk. Being a solicitor is the business of seeing how far laws can bend—why not test this one out?"

"I'm not sure."

"Look, you're nearly fifty, Gerald. I don't believe you've ever taken a risk in you life. Even the shows you put money into are all box office certainties. Just try this. Come on, I'll be the one who gets clobbered if anything goes wrong. But nothing will, anyway. Go on, what do you say?"

"Well . . . Look, if I do agree, and if you do find out there's anything to be investigated, you will keep me in the picture, won't you?"

"Of course."

There was a long pause. The pay-tone on the phone beeped insistently. Charles crammed in his last 10p. By the time the line was clear, Gerald had reached his decision.

"Okay, buster. We give it a whirl, huh?"

It was going to be all right. When Gerald started talking like a fifties thriller, he was getting interested in a case.

"But one thing, Charles. . . ."

"Yes."

"People who work in my office tend to look extremely smart and well-groomed. So will you see to it that you are wearing a suit, that you've shaved and that you've brushed your hair? I don't want you rolling up in your usual guise of an out-of-work gamekeeper who's just spent a long night with Lady Chatterley."

"Don't worry, Gerald. I'll look as smooth as you do."

CHAPTER 8

GERALD WAS GRUDGING. "Well, I suppose it'll do."

"What do you mean—do?" Charles was aggrieved. He had spent the journey down to Breckton in vivid fantasies of Charles Paris, the legal whiz-kid. As an actor, he could never escape being dictated to by his costumes.

"Never mind. I suppose there are scruffy solicitors," Gerald conceded.

"Scruffy? I'll have you know, in 1965, this suit was considered daringly trendy."

"Yes, maybe, but one or two things have changed since 1965. In fact, most things have."

"Except the British legal system, which hasn't changed since 1865."

Gerald ignored the gibe. He looked preoccupied. "Charles, I've been thinking about this business. As a solicitor, I will be taking a risk which is really unjustifiable. In the sense—"

"It's decided. I've got to see Hugo."

"You'll have to give your name when we enter the court. If there ever is any follow-up—"

"Let's assume there isn't. Come on, Gerald, where's your spirit of adventure?"

"Currently hiding behind my fear of being struck off for professional misconduct."

They entered the Magistrates' Court building. Mr. Venables and his colleague from the office, Mr. Paris, checked in and were directed to the relevant court. They sidled on to a solicitors' bench on which the profession was represented by every level of sartorial elegance.

"That suit on the end's a darned sight older than mine," Charles hissed. "Looks like it escaped from a Chicago gangster movie."

Gerald switched him off with a look. Charles scanned the courtroom. It all seemed a bit lethargic, like a rehearsal where some of the principal actors were missing and their lines were being read in. The court was as empty as a summer matinée. And as in a theatre, where the audience is scattered in little groups, he was more conscious of the comings and goings in his immediate vicinity than of the main action taking place between the magistrates' dais and the dock. Solicitors shuffled in and out, reading long sheets of paper to themselves in states of bored abstraction.

One disturbing feature of the proceedings, for which his ignorance of the British legal system had not prepared him, was the large number of policemen around. That in itself was not worrying, but it soon became apparent that for each case the arresting officer had to be present. He wasn't sure who the arresting officer would be in Hugo's case, but if it were one of the policemen he had met on the Tuesday night, Charles's imposture could have serious consequences. He decided not to mention this new anxiety to Gerald. It would only upset him.

It was after twelve, and after some dreary cases of drunkeness, thefts and a taking and driving away, that Hugo was called. He came up into the dock accompanied by a policeman whom, thank God, Charles had never seen before. The prisoner was not handcuffed; in spite of the seriousness of the charge, he was not regarded as a public danger.

Charles turned round with some trepidation and discovered to his relief that there were no familiar faces among the policemen who had just entered the court.

He transferred his attention to his friend. Hugo looked lifeless. There was a greyish sheen to his face and bald dome; his eyes were dead like pumice-stone. Charles recognized that extinguished expression. He'd seen it in Oxford tutorials, in recording studios, at the various ports of call during their Monday drinking session. Hugo had retreated into his mind, closing the door behind him. Nobody could share what he found there, no friend, no wife.

This time the deadness seemed total, as if Hugo had withdrawn completely from the body. His movements when brought to the dock had been those of an automaton. Presumably he must still be suffering from a brain-crushing hangover—it would take a week or so to get over the sort of bender he had been on—but that wasn't sufficient to explain the absolute impassivity of his expression. It was as if he had opted out of life completely.

The proceedings were short. The charge was read by the magistrate, the police said that they were not yet ready to proceed and the accused was remanded in custody for a week.

Suddenly Hugo was being led off down to the cells again. Gerald shook Charles by the shoulder. "Come on. We go down now."

The jailer was in a lenient mood and gave the two solicitors permission to go into the accused's cell rather than leaving them to conduct their interview through the covered slot in the metal door.

The door was unlocked with caution, but as it swung open, it was apparent that no one need fear violence from the inmate.

Hugo sat on the bed, looking straight at the wall ahead of him. He did not stir as the genuine and false solicitors were ushered in or as the door clanged shut and was locked behind them.

"How are you feeling?" asked Gerald with professional joviality.

"All right," came the toneless reply.

"Headache better?"

"Yes, thank you."

Charles took the moment for his revelation. Perhaps it would be the necessary shock to shake Hugo out of his lethargy. "Look, it's me—Charles."

"Hello." The response was again without animation. Without even surprise.

Unwilling to lose his coup, Charles continued, "I came in under cover of Gerald's outfit."

The solicitor winced predictably at the final word. To gain another predictable wince and maybe to shift Hugo's mood by humor, Charles added, "There's no substitute for knowing a bent lawyer."

Gerald's reaction was as expected; Hugo still gave none. Charles changed tack. "Look, Hugo, I know this is one hell of a situation and I feel partly responsible for it, because I'm sure if I hadn't said certain things in my statement, you wouldn't be here and—"

Hugo cut him off, which at least demonstrated that he was taking in what was being said. But the voice in which he spoke remained lifeless. "Charles, if it hadn't been you it would have been someone else. You only told them the truth and that was all they needed."

"Yes, but—"

"So there's no need for you to feel guilty about me or feel you have to make quixotic gestures and come down here to save me from a terrible miscarriage of justice. I don't blame you. I'm the only person to blame, if blame is the right word."

"What, you mean you think you killed her?"

"That's what I told the police."

"You've confessed?"

"Yes."

Charles looked at the solicitor. Gerald shrugged. "I didn't tell you because you didn't ask. You swept me along with some wild scheme of your own and—"

"But, Hugo, is it true?"

"Oh, Charles." The voice was infinitely weary. "I've spent some days going through this, both on my own and with the police. And . . . yes, I think I did it."

"But you can't remember?"

"Not the exact details. I know I staggered back from the Backstagers when the bar closed and I was full of hatred for Charlotte and drunk out of my mind. The next thing I remember with any clarity is waking up on the sitting room floor on Tuesday morning with the feeling that I'd done something terrible."

"But everyone feels like that when they've had a skinful."

Hugo ignored him. "It's no secret that Charlotte and I hadn't been getting on too well, that . . . the magic had gone out of our marriage. . . ." For the first time, there was slight intonation, a hint of bitterness as he spoke the cliché. "And it's no secret that I'd started drinking too much and that when I drank, we fought. So I imagine it's quite possible that, if I met her, smashed out of my mind, on Monday night, I laid hands on her and . . ." In spite of the detachment with which he was speaking, he was unable to finish the sentence.

"But you can't remember doing it?"

"I can't remember anything when I'm that smashed."

"Then why did you confess to killing her?"

"Why not? It fits the facts remarkably well. The motivation was there, the opportunity. I think my guilt is a reasonable deduction."

"Did the police put pressure on you to—"

"No, Charles. For Christ's sake—" He mastered this momentary lapse of control. "I reached the conclusion on my own, Charles. I was under no pressure." Realizing the irony of his last remark, he laughed a little laugh that was almost a sob.

"So you are prepared to confess to a murder you can't even remember just because the facts fit?"

Gerald came in at this juncture with the legal viewpoint.

"I think this may be one of the most fruitful areas for the defense, actually. If you really can't remember, of course we won't be able to get you off the murder charge and that's mandatory life, but the judge might well make some recommendation and you could be out in eight years."

"You're talking as though his guilt were proven, Gerald."

"Yes, Charles. To my mind—"

"For Christ's sake, both of you shut up! What does it matter? What's the difference?"

Charles came in, hard. "The difference is, that if you are found guilty of murder, you'll be put away for life. And if you are not found guilty. . . ." He petered out.

"Exactly," It was only then that Charles realized the depths of Hugo's despair. His friend was bankrupt of any kind of hope. It made little difference whether he spent the rest of his life in prison or at large. Except if he were free, drink might help him shorten his sentence.

Gerald got to his feet in an official sort of way. "You see, Charles, I didn't really think there was much point in your coming down here. I'm afraid it's an open-and-shut case. All we can do is to ensure that it's as well presented as possible. Actually Hugo, I wanted to discuss the matter of instructing counsel. I felt—"

"Stop, Gerald, stop!" Charles also stood up. "We can't just leave it like this. I mean, as long as there's even a doubt. . . ."

"I'm afraid a signed confession doesn't leave much room for doubt. Now come on, Charles, I've taken a foolish risk in bringing you down here; I think we should move as soon as possible and—"

"No, just a minute. Hugo, please, just look at me and tell me that you did it, tell me that you strangled Charlotte, and I'll believe you."

Hugo looked at Charles. The eyes were still dull, but somewhere deep down there was a tiny spark of interest. "Charles, I can't say that definitely, because I can't remember. But I think there's a strong chance that I killed Charlotte."

"And you're prepared to leave it like that?"

Hugo shrugged. "What's the alternative? I don't see that it's going to be possible to prove that I didn't."

"Then we'll just have to prove that someone else did." The remark came out with more crusading fervor than Charles had intended.

It affected Hugo. A new shrewdness came into his eyes. "Hmm. Well, if you think that's possible, then you have my blessing to investigate until you're blue in the face."

The new animation showed how little Hugo had even considered the possibility of his innocence. Whether from his own remorse or because of the prompting of C.I.D. men anxious to sew up the case, he had not begun to think of any alternative solution.

But the shift of mood did not last. Hugo dropped back into dull despair. "Yes, if it'll amuse you, Charles, investigate everything. I'd like to feel I could be of use to someone, if only as something to investigate. And if you can't clear *my besmirched name*"—the italics were heavy with sarcasm—"then take up another hobby. Amateur dramatics, maybe?"

Gerald got purposeful again. "Charles, I think Hugo and I—"

"Just a minute. Hugo, I've got to ask you a couple of things."

"Okay." The voice had reverted to tonelessness.

"You said the other evening that Charlotte was having an affair. Do you know who her lover was?"

"Oh God, here we go again. I've been through all this with the police and—"

"Look, Charles, I don't think—" Gerald butted in instinctively to defend his client.

"No, it's all right, Gerald. I can go through it once again. No, Charles, I don't know who Charlotte's lover was. No, I'm not even certain that she was having an affair. It just seemed a reasonable assumption—like so much else."

"What led you to that assumption?"

"She was a young, attractive woman. She was trapped in a marriage that was getting nowhere. She was bored, lonely. I spent more and more time out getting pissed. If she didn't start something up, then she had less initiative than I gave her credit for."

"But you had no proof?"

"What sort of proof do you want? No. I never caught her in *flagrante delicto,* no, I never saw her with a man, but if coming in at all hours, if going out on unexplained errands during the day, if saying she didn't have to stay with me, she could go elsewhere . . . if that kind of thing's proof, then I had it."

"But you never asked her directly?"

"No. Towards the end we didn't talk too much. Only to make domestic arrangements or to shout at each other. Oh, I'm sure she had a man somewhere."

"When did you start to think this?"

"I don't know. Two, three months back."

"Round the time she started rehearsing *The Seagull.*"

"Possible. And, in answer to your next question, no, I have no idea whether she was having an affair with any of the Backstagers. I just felt she was having an affair with someone." Hugo's voice was slurred with fatigue. Charles could feel Gerald's protective restlessness and knew he hadn't got much longer for his questioning.

"Hugo, I'll leave you now. Just one last thing. I want to find out more about Charlotte. Did she have any friends I could talk to, to ask about her?"

Hugo replied flatly, "No, no friends in Breckton. No close

friends. That's what she always complained about. That's why she joined the Backstagers, to meet people. No, no friends, except lover boy."

"Didn't she keep in touch with people she'd known before you married?"

"One or two. Not many. Diccon Hudson she used to see sometimes. And there was a girl she'd been at drama school with, used to come round sometimes. Not recently. I didn't like her much. Too actressy, hippy . . . young maybe is what I mean."

"What's her name?"

"Sally Radford."

"Thank you. I will go now, Hugo. I'm sorry to have to put you through it all again. But if there's a chance of finding something out, it'll be worth it."

Hugo spoke with his eyes closed. His voice was infinitely tired. "I wouldn't bother Charles. I killed her."

CHAPTER 9

CHARLES SAT OVER a pint in the bay-window of a coach lamp and horse brasses pub and looked out at the main shopping street of Breckton.

It was dominated by a long parade of shops with flats overhead, built in the thirties by some neat planning mind which had decreed that this would be enough, that there was room here for a baker, a butcher, a grocer, a greengrocer, a fishmonger, an ironmonger and one of everything else that the area might need. It would all be neat, all contained, all readily accessible.

Maybe it had had five years of this neat, ordered appearance. But soon shops had changed hands or identities and the uniformity of the original white-lettered names had been broken down by new signs and fascias. Now the line above the shop-windows was an uneven chain of oblongs in neon and garish lettering. And the frontages of the flats had been variously painted or pitted with the acne of pebbledash.

The original parade had quickly proved inadequate to the demands of the growing dormitory suburb. New rows of shops had sprung up to flank it, each date-stamped by design, and each with its uniformity broken in the same way.

As the final insult to symmetry, opposite the old parade an enormous supermarket had been built in giant Lego bricks.

The street was crowded with shoppers. Almost all women with children. Outside the pub Charles saw two young mothers, each with a child swinging on the end of one arm and another swaddled in a baby buggy, stop and chat. And he began to feel the isolation of Charlotte in this great suburban incubator.

The whole place was designed for young couples with growing families and all the daytime social life revolved around children.

What could a girl like Charlotte have done all day in a place like this? Little more than a girl when she married, she had presumably come from some sort of lively flat life in London. The shock of her lonely incarceration in the suburbs must have been profound.

What had she done all day? At first there had been thoughts of her continuing her acting career, but, as time went on, the terrible slump of unemployment which all young actors go through while they are building up their contacts must have extended hopelessly to the point where she lost those few contacts she had. Hugo, while probably not actively discouraging her career, had come from nearly twenty years of marriage to a woman who had done nothing but minister to him and, however vehement his protests that his second marriage was going to be totally different from his first, was too selfish to give real encouragement to something that could take his new wife away from home. So Charlotte's horizons were limited before the marriage had gone sour.

What had gone wrong with the marriage? Charles felt he knew. Something comparable had happened to him. With a mental blush he remembered himself equally dewy-eyed two years before, equally certain that a young girl called Anna could put the clock back for him, that he could fall in love like an adolescent in a romantic novel. In his case, the disillusionment had been rapid and total, but he could still feel the pain of it.

With Hugo the realization must have been slower, but even more devastating. As the relationship progressed, he must have understood gradually that he had not married a goddess, only a girl. She wasn't a symbol of anything, just a real person, with all the attendant inadequacies and insecurities. Even her beauty was transient. In the short years of their marriage, he must have seen her begin to age, seen the crinkles spread beneath her eyes and know that nothing had changed, that he was the same person, growing older yoked to a different woman. And a woman in many ways less suitable than the wife he had left for her.

No doubt the sexual side of the marriage had also palled. Charles knew too well the anxieties men of his age were prey to. Perhaps Hugo had left Alice when their sex-life had started to fail, making the common male mistake of blaming the woman. He had married Charlotte as the new cure-all and then, slowly, slowly found that all the old anxieties had crept back and left him no better off than before.

Once the marriage had started to go wrong, deterioration would have been rapid. Hugo had always had the ability to shrink back into himself. No doubt when love's young dream began to crack, he didn't talk to Charlotte about it. He probably ceased to talk to her at all, morbidly digging himself into his own disappointment. He took to drinking more, arriving home later, leaving her longer and longer on her own. Again the question—what did she find to do all day?

Charles decided that was the first thing for him to find out. And he knew where to start. Still in his pocket was the spare key which Hugo had pressed on him so hospitably. He set off towards the Meckens' house.

The road of executive residences was almost deserted. Distantly an old lady walked a dog. The houses looked asleep, their net curtains closed like eyelids.

Charles felt chilly as he crunched across the small arc of gravel in front of Hugo's house. There was a strong temptation to look round, to see if he was observed, but he resisted it. There was no need to be surreptitious; he was not doing anything wrong.

Inside everything was tidy. Very different from the Tuesday night. The police had been through every room, checking, searching. And they had replaced everything neatly. Too neatly. The house looked like a museum.

He didn't know what he was looking for, but it was something to do with Charlotte. Something that would explain her, maybe even answer the nagging question of how she spent her time. He had thought he understood her in the Backstagers' car park on Saturday night, but it was only since her death that he was beginning to feel the complexity of her character and circumstances.

Like the Winters, Hugo and Charlotte had had the luxury of space in a house designed for a family. Their double bed was in the large front bedroom which had a bathroom en suite. But when Charles had come to stay with them for the first time, some three months before, Hugo had slept in one of the small back bedrooms and used the main bathroom. Husband and wife lived in a state of domestic apartheid.

The bed in the mistitled master bedroom was strangely pathetic. It was large with a white fur cover, a defiant sexual status symbol. It had been bought for a new, hopeful marriage, a marriage that was going to work. But now the pillows were only piled on one side and one of the bedside tables was empty.

He looked through the books on the other side. Nothing unexpected in Charlotte's literary taste. A few thrillers, a Gerald Durrell, a copy of *The Seagull*. All predictable enough.

On the shelf below was something more interesting. A copy of a Family Health Encyclopedia. It was not a new book, printed in the fifties, probably something Hugo had brought from his previous married home. Not a great work of medical literature, but useful for spot diagnosis of childish ailments.

But why was Charlotte reading it? Was she ill? And why was she reading it in a slightly surreptitious way, half-hiding the book. Surely, if she thought she were really ill, she'd have gone to a doctor. Or at least consulted some more detailed medical work. Unless it had been the only work of reference to hand. Unless she had a panic about something she didn't dare to discuss. . . .

Good Lord, had Charlotte been worried that she was pregnant? Suddenly the thought seemed attractively plausible. A lot of what she had said in the Backstagers' car park would be explained if that were the case. That business about being off alcohol. It could be checked through the police post mortem. Mental note to ask Gerald.

If she were pregnant, a whole new volume of possible motives for killing her was opened. He felt a catch of excitement.

He tried the drawer next. That didn't seem to offer anything unexpected. A couple of rings, a broken string of beads, no doubt awaiting mending, a polythene bag of cotton wool balls, a nail-file, an empty key-ring, a jar of nail polish and . . . what was that at the back? He pulled it out. A small book covered in red leather.

It was a Roman Catholic missal. Inside the cover was written, "To Charlotte. On the occasion of her first communion, with love from Uncle Declan and Auntie Wyn."

Yes of course, the Northern Irish background. Good little Catholic girl. Which might raise problems if she had got herself pregnant. And moral issues over contraception. Difficult to know how strong the Catholic influence would have remained. She had married Hugo in spite of his divorce. But Charles had gathered from his friend's unworthy ramblings in the Trattoria that she had let Hugo take the responsibility for birth control in the relationship. Which might mean that Charlotte would be in danger of getting pregnant if she started sleeping with someone else. Which would make sense.

He opened the fitted wardrobe on Charlotte's side of the room. The sight of her fashionable clothes gave him a sharp pang. She had worn them so well, been so beautiful. And now they hung lifeless, misshapen by the bony shoulders of the clotheshangers.

Charles ruffled through the dresses and looked with care among the litter of shoes in the bottom of the wardrobe. He still didn't know what he was looking for, but he didn't feel the time was wasted. Somehow, among her things, he felt closer to Charlotte, closer to understanding what had been going through her mind in the days before her death.

Her clothes smelt strongly of her scent, as if she were still alive. He wouldn't have been surprised to see her walk in through the door.

The wardrobe revealed nothing unexpected. Nor did the rows of drawers which flanked it. He was about to start looking round the bathroom when he stopped. There had been nothing unexpected among her clothes, but equally there had not been something that might have been expected there either.

Charlotte Mecken had been strangled with a scarf. Hugo had identified it as her own scarf and yet there were no others among her clothes. There were any number of dresses, skirts and shirts for her to choose from, any number of pullovers and pairs of shoes. But only one scarf.

When he came to think of it, Charles realized he had never seen Charlotte wearing a scarf. And what was more, even his sketchy knowledge of current fashion told him that scarves were not "in." Certainly not those crude Indian prints like the one he had seen knotted around Charlotte's neck. No, those had had a vogue in the late sixties, they now looked rather dated. Charlotte, with her sharp fashion sense, would not have been. . . . He smiled wryly as his mind formed the phrase "been seen dead in one."

What it meant was that Charlotte was most unlikely to have been wearing the scarf with which she was killed. Which made the accepted picture of the murder, of Hugo reaching out to her in a drunken fury and throttling her, unlikely. Whoever killed Charlotte must have gone to get the scarf with which to do it.

The bathroom did not offer much space for secrets. The pale green bath, basin, bidet and lavatory were modern and functional. Fluffy yellow towels hung from the heated rail. Only the mirror-fronted cabinet gave any opportunity for concealment.

The contents were predictable. Make-up, various creams, nail scissors, a tin of throat sweets, shampoo, an unopened box of Tampax, cough medicine, a roll of sticking plaster.

The decor of the bathroom was recent. The walls were olive green and the floor was covered with the same mustardy carpet as the bedroom. It was all very neat, very attractive, like a picture out of *Homes and Gardens*.

The only blemishes were two small screw-holes above the cabinet. It must have been set too high initially and been moved down to the right level for Charlotte. Maybe it had been moved when Hugo exiled himself to the other bedroom and bathroom.

Now it had been moved down, the cabinet's bottom edges rested on the top row of white tiles which surrounded the wash-basin. As a result it was tilted slightly and there was a narrow triangle of space between it and the wall.

Charles knew there would be something in there. He didn't know why. It was part of the understanding he was beginning to feel for Charlotte. She had been so young, so young, almost child-like in some respects. It was in character for her to have a hiding place for her secret things, like a girl at boarding school making one little corner of total privacy that the teachers would never know about. It was a way of maintaining her identity in a challeng-ing situation.

Charles pressed his face to the wall and squinted along the gap. Then, very calmly, he fished in with a pen and slid out a brown envelope. It was not sealed. As he raised it to shake out the con-tents, the front door-bell rang.

He shoved the envelope in his pocket and swallowed his first im-pulse to run and hide. After all, he wasn't doing anything wrong. Hugo had given him the key without prompting. He wasn't even trespassing on his friend's property.

He tried to calm himself with such thoughts as he walked se-dately downstairs, but he still felt as guilty as a schoolboy caught with an apple in his hand in an orchard.

This mood was intensified when the opened front door revealed a uniformed policeman.

"Good afternoon, sir," said the policeman in a tone that indi-cated that he was prepared to start quite reasonably, but was ready to get tough when the need arose.

"Good afternoon," Charles echoed foolishly.

"Might I ask what you're doing here, sir?"

"Yes, certainly," Charles affected man-of-the-world affability, to which the policeman seemed immune. "My name's Charles Paris. I'm a friend of Hugo Mecken. I've stayed here a few times. He gave me a key, actually." Charles reached into his pocket as if to demon-strate until he realized the fatuity of the gesture. "Said I could drop in any time."

"I see, sir." The policeman's tone remained reasonable, but it had a strong undercurrent of disbelief. "Rather an unusual time to drop in, sir. Or haven't you heard what's been happening here?"

"Oh yes, I know all about it." Charles replied eagerly and, as he said it, recognized his stupidity. If he'd claimed ignorance of the whole affair, he could just have walked away.

"I see, sir. In fact, we had a call from someone in the road who had seen you go into the house and who thought, under the circumstances, it was rather odd."

Good God, you couldn't blow your nose in Breckton without someone seeing. There must be watchers behind every curtain. Time for a tactical lie. "In fact, officer, the reason I am here is that, as I say, I stayed with the Meckens a few times and on the last occasion Mrs. Mecken was good enough to wash out a couple of shirts for me. Now all this terrible business has happened, I thought I'd better pick them up without delay."

The policeman seemed to accept this. "And have you found them?"

"Found what? Oh, the shirts—no, I haven't yet. I've been looking around, but I'm not sure where Mrs. Mecken would have put them."

"Ah. Well. Would you like me to accompany you round the house while you find them?" It was phrased as a question, but it wasn't one.

Like Siamese twins they went through the house. They looked in the airing cupboard, they looked in the wardrobes. Eventually Charles produced the solution he had been desperately working out for the last few minutes. "Do you know, I think Mrs. Mecken must have mixed them up with her husband's clothes and put them away in his drawer."

"Well, sir, I dare say you'll want to be off now."

Charles didn't argue.

"And, sir, I think, if you don't mind, you'd better give me that key. I'll see that it gets put with the rest of Mr. Mecken's belongings. I think, under the circumstances, with the possibility of further police investigations, the less people we have walking around this property, the better. I quite understand why you came in, sir, but if a key like this got into the wrong hands . . . well, who knows, it might be awkward."

"Of course." Charles had no alternative but to hand it over.

"Thank you, sir." The policeman ushered him out of the front door and closed it behind them. Then he stood in the middle of the doorstep. "Goodbye, sir."

Charles walked across the gravel and along the road in the direction of the station, conscious of the policeman's eyes following him. He wasn't going to get another chance to get inside that house without breaking and entering.

Still, the search had not been fruitless. In his pocket there was an envelope.

CHAPTER 10

"YOU REALIZE IT's probably illegal," said Gerald grumpily. "It's withholding evidence . . . or stealing evidence or . . . I'm sure there's something they could get you for."

Gerald was being unhelpful over the whole thing. He didn't want to hear how Charles had spent the rest of the morning and manifested the minimum of interest in his findings. Also it was clear that he didn't like having his friend round the Grosvenor Street office. Charles Paris was a reminder of the Mecken case and Gerald didn't want to be reminded. He wanted to reimmerse himself in his regular work, wrangling over small clauses in film and television contracts, or even sorting out the odd divorce. Having clients charged with murder upset him; he thought it was irresponsible and didn't want to dwell on it.

"I don't care," said Charles, "I think it's important. I had a look at the book on the train, but couldn't make much of it, so I thought two heads might be better than one. You always said you wanted to be included in any of my cases."

"Charles, there is a difference between what one does professionally and what one does as a hobby." Gerald could be insufferably stuffy.

"Murder's a funny sort of thing to have as a hobby. Anyway, just give me five minutes of your time to look at this stuff and then I'll leave you alone." Gerald looked dubious. "Good God, do I have to pay for your time?"

This at least brought a smile to Gerald's lips. "You'd never be able to afford my rates, Charles."

He took advantage of the shift of mood to redirect attention to the envelope on the desk. He shook it and out came a thin, blue-covered book and a beige plastic envelope. "Let's concentrate on the diary first."

He flicked through the pages. Gerald, in spite of himself, craned over to look. "Not much in it, Charles."

"No, that's what makes it interesting. Why make such a palaver about hiding a book that contains so little information?"

"Presumably because the little information it does contain is extremely secret."

"Yes. In other words, it had to be kept secret from Hugo. I mean, there was no one else in the house to hide things from, was there?"

"No."

"The interesting thing is that there's nothing at all until May. Then we have this entry—Saturday May 23rd, Backstagers' Party. Now I know that Charlotte hadn't been a member of the society long, so I reckon that could well have been her first contact."

"Seems reasonable, but it doesn't get us far."

"No. Then we get these four dates in early June—*Seagull* auditions. That's self-explanatory. And isn't it typical of that Backstagers lot to make a big production out of it and have four whole evenings of auditions.

"As we know, Charlotte was successful in the audition, because then in July we start getting rehearsals marked. Okay, that makes sense. She started the diary when she started getting involved in amateur dramatics."

"Not really something you'd treat as a big secret, is it, Charles?"

"No, the secret bit comes later. But there's something odd about this diary even from what we've seen so far. I mean, I can understand why she enters all the rehearsals—they're quite complicated and she'd need to make a note of them—but why are there no engagements before the Backstagers' party? I'm not going to believe that was the first time she went out in the year."

"No." Gerald sounded as if he was losing interest again.

Charles picked up the pace. "I think I know what it was. Not the first time she had gone out, but the first time she had arranged to go out herself. So far as I can tell, it was round that time that she and Hugo ceased to communicate. I think starting this diary was an identity thing for her. All right, if Hugo and I are not having a life together, I'll damned well make a life of my own. And this little diary was a symbol of that determination, of her separateness. And if that's why she started the diary, it explains the later entries. The Affair." He pronounced it portentously to whet Gerald's appetite. "Look."

Starting late August, in the midst of all the *Seagull* rehearsals, there was a new series of notes. Lunchtimes. 1:00—Waterloo. 1:00 —Charing Cross. 1:00—Charing Cross again, then back to Waterloo. A whole sequence of them.

The last was different. It was for the Tuesday of that week. 1:00 —Victoria. But that was one railway station rendezvous Charlotte Mecken did not make. Because by then she was dead.

"You reckon it was a lover?"

"It would fit rather cosily, wouldn't it, Gerald?"

"But I thought you were working on the idea that she was having an affair with someone in the Backstagers. Surely that'd be strictly local."

"Not if they wanted any degree of privacy. To have an affair in a place like Breckton would be like having it off in the middle of Wembley Stadium on Cup Final day."

"Hmm. So you reckon it was someone who worked in Town."

"Which would apply to every man in Breckton."

"Yes. It still seems odd to me that she should write all these things down. Surely it was courting disaster. I mean, if Hugo had found this book. . . ."

"I think that danger was part of the excitement. Anyway, it would have been just as damning if Hugo had found these." Charles indicated the small beige plastic envelope.

Gerald picked it up and slid out a rectangle of foil round the edge of which was a line of transparent blister, some of which contained small white pills. The solicitor looked up blankly. "What is it?"

Charles laughed "Oh Gerald, what touching naïveté. Have you never seen these before? Of course, they're not really of our generation. We and our wives and girl friends did not have such modern conveniences at our disposal."

Gerald colored. "You mean these are contraceptive pills?"

"Exactly." Charles couldn't resist a little further tease. "I think that's a very heart-warming comment on your marriage, Gerald. That you shouldn't even recognize these new-fangled inventions. Fidelity is not dead. If you'd spent as much time as I have hopping in and out of unsuitable young women's bedrooms, you'd know sure enough what—"

Gerald was not amused. "I think you'd better put them away, Charles. Polly might come in."

"You're beautifully old-fashioned, Gerald. I rather think Polly would recognize them."

Gerald took refuge in a look at his watch. "Look, I've got rather a lot to get on with."

"Okay. I'll stop sending you up and be quick. These pills are the final proof that Charlotte was having an affair. Not only because of the way in which they were hidden, but because I happen to know that Hugo was in favor of more primitive methods of contraception."

Gerald's eyes opened wide. "How on earth do you know that? It's hardly the sort of thing you'd talk about."

Charles laughed again at his friend's sedateness. "He did mention it actually. But look, that's not the only thing these pills tell us. There's something else strange about them. Look."

Gerald cast an embarrassed eye over the foil and shrugged. "Don't see anything."

"The last pill was taken on a Wednesday."

"So?" Gerald was looking distinctly uncomfortable. The conversation was straying beyond the boundaries of what he considered suitable masculine subject matter.

"Charlotte was killed on Monday night and yet the last pill was taken on a Wednesday. It wasn't the end of her cycle because there are still pills left. So it means that she stopped taking the pills at least five days before she died."

"Maybe she just forgot them." Gerald's interest was beginning to overcome his embarrassment.

"Unlikely. Though I suppose she was very tied up with the play and it's possible. But you would have thought a married woman in the middle of an affair would be extra careful."

"Unless the affair had broken up and she no longer had any use for the pills . . ."

"That's a thought. That *is* a thought." The existence of a jilted lover opened new vistas of motivation. But there was a snag. "On the other hand, if we look back at the diary, there's that Victoria assignation for the Tuesday, not to mention a Charing Cross one for the Monday. Which rather suggests that the affair was still swinging along. So that can't be why she stopped taking the pills."

The flow of logic had stopped. Charles sighed. He was buzzing round something important, but he hadn't found it yet. He had got the right pieces, but he wasn't putting them in the right order. "Oh well, I suppose the first thing is to find out who the lover was."

"I should think, if he exists, the police would know by now."

"Do you reckon?"

"Of course. They're not stupid. Maybe you can keep that sort of thing secret from the nosey parkers of Breckton, but the police can go around and question everyone who knew Charlotte, they can talk to the railway staff who saw her traveling up on her assignations, all that sort of thing."

"Yes. Well, if the police happen to tell you who the lover was—or any other useful snippets of information, you will pass them on, won't you?"

"If they are the sort of things I think I should pass on, yes."

Charles had an urge to punch Gerald right in the middle of his formal solicitor's face, but he decided it wasn't worth losing friends that way. "Maybe I'd better go."

"Yes. I am meant to be getting on with my work. I do have clients depending on me, you know."

"Yes, I'm sure we can depend that one of them is paying for your time at the moment."

Gerald didn't rise to the running joke.

There was a copy of *Spotlight* in the outer office where Gerald's secretary Polly sat. Charles picked up *Actresses L-Z*.

Sally Radford was under *Juvenile and Juvenile Character*. The photograph showed a strong face dominated by a largish nose. Straight dark hair parted in the middle and looped back like curtains behind the ears. It was one of those faces which in the flesh would either look very attractive or not quite make it. Depend to some extent on the coloring. Beneath the black and white photograph it said "5ft. 6in" and "Blue Eyes." The blue eyes were unexpected and promising.

There was no name and number for an agent. Just "C/O *Spotlight*" as a contact. That was revealing to Charles as an actor. Probably meant she had not yet got very far in her career and either couldn't find an agent willing to represent her until she had more experience or had decided that for the moment she was going to do as well finding work for herself. It also probably meant that she was based in London rather than doing a season out at some provincial rep. If she were out of town she'd want an agent as a point of contact for inquiries.

Polly graciously granted him the use of her phone and he got through. The girl on the *Spotlight* switchboard said that Sally Radford was likely to be ringing in and could he leave a number where he could be contacted? He explained that that was rather difficult as he wasn't sure of his movements.

"Is it important?" asked the girl, meaning "Is it work?"

"Yes, it is," Charles replied, glad that she'd phrased it in a way that enabled him to reply without lying.

"Okay then, I can give you a number to contact her."

"Thank you very much."

Sally Radford answered straight away. Her voice was husky and well-articulated without being actressy. It confirmed the strength of character implicit in the photograph.

"Hello, my name's Charles Paris. I got your name through *Spotlight*."

"Yes."

He heard the catch of excitement in her voice and realized that that was a rotten way to introduce himself to an out-of-work actress. He had better disillusion her quickly. "Sorry, it's not about work."

"Oh." The disappointment could not be disguised.

"No, I'm sorry, it's a rather awkward thing I'm ringing about. I believe you were a friend of Charlotte Mecken."

"Yes." The voice went serious. Charles began to think that she was probably a talented actress; her inflections on small words were telling. She continued, not playing it tragic queen, just sad, "I thought somebody might be in touch. I suppose I was her closest friend—though with Charlotte that did not necessarily mean very close. Are you police?"

"No, I'm not actually. I'm a . . ." He resisted the temptation to say "private investigator," which was a bit grandiose for what he was doing and probably an offence under the Trades Descriptions Act. ". . . friend of Hugo's."

"Ah." Again the intonation was informative and reminded him that Hugo and Sally had not got on well.

"As you probably know, Hugo's been arrested for murder. . . ."

"Yes."

"Well, I'm by no means certain that he's guilty. That's why I'd like to meet you and talk if I may."

"Sure. Anything I can do to help."

"Can we meet soon?"

"Soon as you like, I don't have a lot happening at the moment." The understatement spoke of some weeks of sitting by the telephone.

Charles arranged to go round to her flat in Maida Vale at six and put the phone down with the small satisfaction of having made a date.

CHAPTER 11

SALLY RADFORD DID look better in color than in monochrome. The strength of the face and its potential hardness were made less daunting by the piercing blue of her eyes. She was dressed in a collarless man's shirt with a brown stripe, well-cut jeans and cowboy boots. Almost flat-chested, but very feminine. A hint of some musky scent.

Her flat showed the same kind of style. Obviously rented furnished, but with sufficient touches of her own to take the curse off the Identikit furniture. A Japanese paper kite in the shape of a bird dangled over the fireplace. Tall grasses in the old green bottle balanced the slumped display of books on a low shelf. The decor was minimal, but assured.

The girl emanated the same confidence. Not the go-getting brashness that Charles had encountered in so many young actresses, but an inner patience, an impression that everything she did was logical and right.

Charles found her relaxing. Partly because of her directness, but also because she was an actress, a real actress to whom he could talk about the theatre without fearing the stupid or exaggerated responses he had come to expect from the Backstagers. It was only as he talked to her that he realized how long it was since he had been with real actors.

She sat him down and offered him tea or coffee. He chose tea, which came in a blue and grey earthenware mug. China with lemon. Good.

"Okay, what do you want me to tell you?" Down to business as soon as the social formalities had been observed.

"Let me fill you in a bit on what I'm doing first. I was with Hugo when he found Charlotte's body. . . ." He then filled her in on the background of Hugo's confession and his own reasons for believing that it was not necessarily conclusive.

Sally was silent for a moment, then made up her mind. "Okay, let's accept your hypothesis for the time being. What can I do for you?"

"Just a few questions about Charlotte. I'm sorry, I know you didn't like Hugo, but I would like to clear up—"

"I didn't dislike him. I don't think he even disliked me. I think he just resented my friendship with Charlotte. Partly because he was jealous of what he imagined to be our closeness—he was terribly aware of their age difference and was afraid of Charlotte seeing too much of her contemporaries in case they took her away from him—which is ironic, seeing how the marriage turned out. Also I'm an actress and I tended to talk about the theatre. I don't think Hugo really wanted Charlotte's career to develop, in case that took her away from him."

"That's rather what I thought."

"So he got very uptight if I started talking about contacts or auditions coming up or prospects for jobs or. . . . Though," she added on a personal note of bitterness, "I don't think he need have worried if Charlotte's success had been anything like mine over the last couple of years."

"Work not coming?"

She shook her head wryly. "You're a master of understatement. No, I'm not exactly fighting the offers away from my door. I've had a few radios, one or two close calls on West End auditions, but. . . ." She straightened up. "But you know all that. It's familiar country."

"Right." There was a pause of great togetherness, of shared experience. "I don't know Charlotte well, Sally. I only really met her through Hugo and, you know, you view your friend's wives and girl friends through a kind of refracting glass of the friends themselves. What I've been trying to do since Charlotte was killed is to see her on her own, to know what her own personality was like, apart from Hugo. What I really want you to do is tell me if I'm on the right lines in understanding her, or if I'm hopelessly wrong."

"How do you see her?"

"It's funny, I keep coming back to the image of her as terribly young. I don't mean just in age. I mean young for her years. Immature even."

Sally nodded slowly. "That's quite shrewd. Yes, she was. I knew her right through drama school and she was always very naïve, sort of wide-eyed about things. She never looked it. So beautiful, for a start, and she had such superb dress sense that everyone thought she was the ultimate sophisticated woman, but it was only a front— no, not even a front, because she didn't put it up consciously. It was when I realised this that I first started to like her. Suddenly I saw that she wasn't a daunting, challenging woman, but just a rather earnest child. I think we're always drawn to people by knowledge of their weaknesses. It's so comforting, that moment when you realize that you don't have to be afraid and competitive any more.

"I think Charlotte had had a very sheltered upbringing. Northern Ireland. Straight-laced, inward-looking family so far as I can gather. Convent education."

"It seems odd Sally, considering that, that she was allowed to go to drama school. You'd think there would have been family opposition."

"Yes, it was strange. But she was strong-minded about certain things. And she knew she could act and that that was what she wanted to do. I don't think anyone could cross her once she'd really made up her mind about something."

"Hmm. She was a good actress. I only saw her in one thing, tatty amateur production of *The Seagull*, but by God it was all there."

"Oh yes, she was good. That's what made her marrying Hugo so sad. He didn't want her to be a successful actress. He was miserly about her, wanted to keep her to himself."

"Do you think he even objected to her joining the amateur society?"

"I don't think he was keen. That was something she decided to do very much on her own. Anyway, he could hardly object—I gather he had been a member to take advantage of the bar for some time. But I doubt if they discussed it. By then they were hardly speaking."

Charles nodded. It was satisfying to have his diagnosis of the marriage and Charlotte's motivation confirmed. "So she joined as a deliberate attempt to assert her own individuality?"

"Yes. I think she also saw it as a step of getting herself back on the road to the professional theatre. You know how it is in the business—if you don't work for a bit, you lose confidence. I think she had to do something to prove to herself that she could still act."

"It's surprising that she started at such a local level, that she didn't just up and leave Hugo and go back to the real theatre world."

"I don't think she really wanted to leave him. She had been very much in love when they married. It was only when he withdrew completely into himself that the marriage foundered. I think she still hoped that one day he would come out of his sulk and everything would be all right again. Deep down she had a great belief in the sanctity of marriage. The Catholic background again. She wouldn't have left her husband lightly."

"Hmm. But she would have an affair with another man lightly?"

Sally Radford appraised him coolly. "You know about that then. In fact, I don't think that was entered into lightly either. Charlotte was a very serious girl—as I said, an earnest child. No, I think the affair was because she just had to do something to get out of her spiral of loneliness. And also because she was very attracted to the man in question."

"You don't, by any chance . . . ?" Charles hazarded hopefully.

Sally shook her head. " 'Fraid not. I have this sneaking feeling that she did once mention a man's name to me, but I'm sorry, I can't for the life of me remember what it was."

"But she did tell you she was having an affair?"

"Not directly. But she came to me for practical advice, and I put two and two together."

"Practical advice?"

"Yes. It's back to the naïveté we were talking about. Charlotte had always been a bit backward in sexual matters. I mean, at drama school, where all the rest of us were screwing away like rabbits, she kept herself to herself."

"You don't mean she managed to come through drama school a virgin? I thought that was a technical impossibility."

Sally smiled. "I don't know if she was actually a virgin, but I do know that she was pretty inhibited about such things. Needless to say, all the men were panting round her like puppies, but I don't know if any of them got anywhere."

"Not even Diccon Hudson?"

"Ah, you know Mr. Golden Voice. Yes, he certainly tried as hard as any of them, but I just don't know. He made a point of trying to have everything in sight, really put it about. What do they reckon that kind of manic screwing's a sign of? Latent homosexuality? Not in his case, I think."

"But did he make it with Charlotte?"

"I think probably not. And I'm sure if he didn't it made him furious. Great blow to the great pride. No, for Charlotte, Hugo was the first big thing in her life. I think perhaps she found the slower approach of the older man less frightening than the ravenous groping of her contemporaries."

"Yes, of course, we old men do slow down quite a bit," Charles agreed with mock-seriousness.

Sally Radford realized what she had said and giggled. She looked at him and a new awareness came into their conversation. "Anyway, Charles, to come up to date. . . . Some time in July, Charlotte rang and asked if we could meet for lunch. We did and, after some small talk and embarrassment on her part, she asked me how she should set about getting on the Pill. Since she had got that far into her married life without it and because she was so surreptitious about the inquiry, I reckon that that meant she had started sleeping with someone other than her husband."

"Yes, that would fit." Charles quickly summarized his discovery of the pills in their hiding place in Charlotte's bathroom.

"Anyway," Sally continued, "for some reason she didn't want to go to her local G.P. So I recommended the Brook Clinic in Totty Court Road. I'd been there myself, they're very helpful."

"So we can assume that they fitted her out and the affair continued."

"I imagine so. I found it a bit sad that she came to me actually. I mean, not that she was so ignorant, that was just part of her character, but the fact that I was the only person she could talk to. I didn't know her that well, and yet she was in a strange way dependent on me."

"Hmm. When did you last see her or hear from her?"

"We had lunch again quite soon after the time I mentioned. Since then, just the odd phone call."

"Did she talk again about the contraception business?"

"Only once. Otherwise it was as if it had never happened."

"And the once?"

"That was quite recently. I think the last time I heard from her. She must have read some scare article about the Pill in a magazine or something. She asked all kinds of things about the dangers of it. Not straight away, but she maneuvered the conversation round to it."

"What sort of things did she ask?"

"Practically everything—about the dangers of embolism, could the Pill cause obesity, was it liable to raise the blood pressure, could it harm the fetus if a pregnant woman took it, could it lead to sterility, did it upset the cycle irrevocably—just about every Pill scare that has ever been put out, and a few old wives' tales thrown in for good measure."

"Did she sound worried?"

"She didn't actually *sound* worried, but she was a good actress and the fact that she raised the subject suggested to me that she must be."

"You didn't get any impression which of the particular dangers she was worried about?"

" 'Fraid not. If there was one in particular she was asking about, she managed to put up an effective smoke-screen with all the other. I assumed that the Pill had just affected her cycle. It often does at first. If her periods had always been regular before, it would probably worry her if things suddenly got out of phase."

Charles was silent, his passivity hiding the speed with which his mind was working. There were other things that could cause an upset in a woman's cycle.

Sally Radford suddenly spoke again, with more emotion than

hitherto. "God knows why she asked me. That's what I meant by being sad, that there was no one else she could ask, no family, no friendly doctor. As if I were an international expert on contraception."

The bitterness in the last sentence made Charles look up and he was surprised to see the glint of a tear in her eye.

She dashed it away. "I'm sorry. It's just that it seems so inhuman —Charlotte dead and presumably dissected on some police mortuary slab while we meticulously pick through her gynecological history."

"Yes, but there's something else worrying you, isn't there?"

She looked up at him, giving the full benefit of those blue eyes. "You're shrewd, Charles Paris. Yes, it was ironical her coming to me with her contraceptive problems. I learned the hard way."

"An abortion?"

"Yes. Sixth form at school."

"I'm sorry." He offered the useless comfort of someone who knew nothing of the circumstances.

"Oh yes." She tossed her head back to signify her return to a controlled mood. "Yes, it's not really the emotional shock in my case. It's just the fear that, you know, something might have gone wrong, that I might not be able to conceive again as a result. I mean, not that there's anyone around at the moment whose baby I want to have, but . . . I don't know, you just have this fear that if you couldn't have children, it'd warp you in some way. Oh, it's all irrational. Forget it."

Charles changed the subject, but he didn't forget it. "Sorry to have dragged you through all this, but I'm very grateful to you for giving me your time and for being so frank. Can I take you out for a drink to say thank you?"

"Why not?" She consulted her watch. "Twenty to eight. Yes, I think we can safely assume that all the major impresarios of London have packed their briefcases for the night and that I can leave the telephone unattended without jeopardizing my chances of becoming a STAR."

They went to a rather camp Victorian pub in Little Venice and drank large amounts of red wine. Then Charles took Sally to a little Italian restaurant where they drank more red wine. When he saw her back to her flat, there didn't seem to be any question of his leaving.

"Why are we going to sleep together?" asked Charles with the deep philosophy of the drunk as he hopped round the bedroom trying to get his trousers off.

"In my case," Sally replied, pulling her shirt over her head, "because I like you and on the whole I do sleep with people I like. Also . . ." She paused profoundly, "I'm after experience."

"Experience that will one day be seen in a stage performance before the paying public?"

"Maybe."

"Well, it may surprise you to know that even at my advanced age I'm still after experience." He mused. "Do you know, I'm fifty this week. Fifty."

"There, there." She took him in her arms. "Rejuvenate yourself with the body of a young woman. Like Dracula."

"You're nothing like Dracula. If you were you'd have run screaming from the garlic in the *pollo sopreso*."

"There, there. Let's hope your body's not as decrepit as your wit. Otherwise I'm left out in the cold."

"There, there. And there." She drew in her breath sharply as he touched her. "I think you'll find all's in working order."

"Remember," she whispered as they rolled together, "no strings. Experience."

"No strings," he echoed as their bodies' heats fused.

"And no babies," she said, nimbly detaching herself and reaching into her bedside drawer. "Good God, considering our conversation, it's amazing I forgot it." She flicked the small white pill into her mouth and swallowed it down jerkily.

"Tell me . . ." Charles's mind fumbled through the fogs of alcohol. ". . . if you were having an affair with someone, what would stop you from taking your pill? Apart from just forgetting it?"

"I suppose if the bloke walked out, I might—except that I wouldn't because I always live in the hope that something else is going to come along. Or if I wanted to get pregnant—except then I'd be more likely to do it at the end of the cycle."

"Or . . ."

"Or, I suppose, if I thought I was pregnant, I'd stop as soon as I realized . . . for fear of hurting the baby."

Charles smiled in a satisfied way as he took Sally back into his arms and crushed her flat but oh so feminine chest to his.

It was unhurried and good. As they snuggled together to sleep, Charles murmured, "It simplifies everything, doesn't it? Sex therapy. Frees the mind."

"Yes," Sally agreed lazily, "it's freed my memory."

"What do you mean?"

"I've just remembered the name that Charlotte mentioned, the guy who I think must have been her lover."

Charles was instantly alert. "Yes?"

"Does the name Geoff make any sense?"

"Yes," said Charles. "Yes, it does."

CHAPTER 12

Charles got back to Hereford Road at half-past nine the next morning, feeling pretty good. So it wasn't all over; it could still happen. His mind started to generalize, filling with images of other nubile young girls through whose beds he would flit.

An envelope on the doormat quickly dislocated his mood. A birthday card. Right on cue. Friday, November 5th. The card was a well-chosen reproduction of an El Greco grandee and continued the message "Congratulations on half a century. Love, Frances." It served as a brutal reminder not only of his age but also of his neglected responsibilities. Images of future girls gave way to wistful recollection.

To stop himself getting maudlin, he brought his concentration to bear on Charlotte's murder. Now he knew the identity of her lover, the case seethed with new possibilities. The first thing he must do was to talk to Geoffrey Winter.

The sound of the phone ringing broke into his train of thought. Expecting it would be a boyfriend of one of the beefy Swedish girls who lived in the other bedsitters, he answered. It was his agent, Maurice Skellern.

That was unusual. Maurice was terribly inefficient and never rang his clients. Since he had never got any work for them, there was no point; they could ring him to find that out.

"Charles, I've had an inquiry from an advertising agency about your availability for a voice-over."

"What, Mills Brown Mazzini?"

"No, another one."

"That's good. Hugo said that once somebody uses you in this field, you start getting lots more inquiries. Perhaps I've become Flavor of the Month."

"Well, they want you to do a voice test."

"When?"

"This morning. At eleven."

"Shee. I'd better get straight along. What's the address and who do I ask for?"

Maurice gave the details. "Incidentally, Charles, about this voice-over business. I don't know much about it . . ."

"Well, there's an admission."

"What I was going to say was, I'm glad about all the work, but we don't seem to have had too many checks through yet."

"No, we'll have just the basic studio session fees so far. A few thirty-five quids. It's when the commercials go out and get repeated that the money really starts to flow. I mean, if this Bland campaign takes off . . . well . . . Exclusive contract has even been mentioned. And, you see, it's already leading to other inquiries."

"So you reckon there's a lot of work there?"

"Could be. Some people do dozens of voice-overs a week. Mix it in with film dubbing, reading books for the blind, other voice work. Make vast sums. Mostly people with specialist agents, of course," he added maliciously.

Maurice was too used to Charles's snide lines about their relationship even to acknowledge this one. "Well, good, good. Obviously the right step for you career-wise. Haven't I always been telling you you should be extending your range, finding a wider artistic fulfillment?"

"No, you've always been telling me I should make more money. By the way, anything else about?"

"There's a new permanent company being set up in Cardiff. Might be worth trying for that."

"Hardly me, is it—Cardiff? Anyway, if this voice-over business gets under way, I'm going to have to be based in London for a bit. Till I've made enough to keep the taxman quiet. No nice convenient little tellies coming up, are there?"

"Haven't heard of anything. London Weekend are supposed to be setting up a new series about Queen Victoria's cooks, but I haven't heard when."

"Then let's live in hope of the voice-overs. I'd better get along to this place for the test. By the way, did they say what the product was?"

"Yes. Something for . . . depopulation, was it?"

"For depopulation? You mean, like napalm?"

"No, no. For removing unsightly hair."

"Depilation, Maurice."

The new depilatory about to be launched on the armpits of the world was called No Fuzz and the selling line was "There's no fuss with No Fuzz."

Charles used his heavy cold voice again, because that was what they wanted. (If he had to keep grinding it down like that, he was going to ruin his vocal cords.) He dropped into the routine of giving every possible intonation to the new line, waiting for the fatuous notes from the account executive in charge ("Give it a bit more *brio*, love" and "Try it with just a smidgeonette of sex in the voice") and let his mind wander. He couldn't lose the suspicion that a properly programmed computer could sew up the entire voice-over business.

He was kept for an hour, told he was super and that they'd give him a tinkle. And he had earned another thirty-five pounds.

In the reception of the agency he met Diccon Hudson. Charles saw the other man's eyes narrow at the sight of a potential rival. Diccon worked hard to maintain all his agency contacts and wouldn't take kindly to being aced out by a non-specialist. "You up for the No Fuzz campaign?" he asked directly.

"Yes."

"Becoming rivals, aren't we. First Mr. Bland, now . . ."

"I haven't necessarily got this one."

"No." Diccon Hudson seemed to gain comfort from the fact. His ferrety face could not conceal what was going through his mind.

Charles recalled suddenly that Diccon was on his list of people to check out in his investigation. "You heard about Charlotte?"

The name sent a spasm across Diccon's over-expressive face. "I heard. I was pretty cut up about it."

Charles nodded. "Terrible, yes. I suppose you hadn't seen her for a long time."

"I saw her quite recently actually."

"Not on Monday night, I suppose," Charles joked, to draw Diccon out.

"No, not on Monday night. I—" Diccon suddenly stopped short, as if he'd thought better of what he was going to say.

"What were you doing on Monday night then, buddy?" Charles dropped into a New York cop accent to take the curse off his interrogation.

"Nothing." Diccon hurried on. "I last saw Charlotte about a fortnight ago. We used to meet for the odd lunch."

"Regularly?" Charles was beginning to wonder if, in spite of Sally Radford's recollection of the name "Geoff," there was any connection between Diccon and the dates in Charlotte's diary.

But the theory was shattered before it was formed. "I was away in Crete for all of August, but I saw her a few times before and after. A few times." The repeat was accompanied by a smug smile, enigmatic, but probably meant to be taken as a form of sexual bragging.

"Did Hugo know?"

Diccon gave a contemptuous shrug; the question wasn't worth answering.

Now for Geoffrey Winter. Charles was glad that Sally had come up with the name, because it confirmed a conclusion towards which his mind had been moving.

He had decided that, if Charlotte had chosen her lover from the ranks of the Backstagers, then Geoffrey was the only candidate. Perhaps it was *The Seagull* which had led him to the conclusion. Trigorin, after all, was the older man who seduced Nina. Or maybe it was just that Geoffrey seemed the only one of the Backstagers sufficiently attractive and interesting to be worthy of Charlotte.

He had first got an inkling of something between the two of them at the cast party. Not that they had been together; they had been apart. They had both danced so ostentatiously, both putting on such a show with other people. There had been something studied about the way they had avoided each other. All of the rest of the cast had been constantly reforming and forming in little knots to remember some near disaster or ill-disguised corpse, but Geoffrey and Charlotte had always ended up in different groups.

So Charles liked to think that he would have looked up Geoffrey's office address in the phone book even if Sally hadn't mentioned the name.

When he did, the address gave him further confirmation. Listed under Geoffrey Winter Associates, Architects. And an office in Villiers Street, adjacent to Charing Cross Station and just over Hungerford Bridge from Waterloo.

The office was on the top floor. A door with a frosted glass window bore the name on a stainless steel plaque. He tapped on the window, but, getting no response, tried the handle.

The door opened. He found himself in a small outer office. It was very tidy, box files upright in rows along the shelves, cardboard tubes of plans stacked on brackets on the walls. The color scheme and the choice of the sparse furniture showed the same discrimination as Geoffrey's study.

But the outer office gave no feeling of work. It was like the Meckens' house after it had been tidied by the police—too neat to be functional.

The typewriter on the desk was shrouded in its plastic cover, as if its typist had long gone. There were no coats on the row of aluminum pegs.

But there was someone in the next room. Or presumably more than one person, because Charles could hear a voice. Talking loudly, in a rather stilted way.

He drew close to the connecting door, but couldn't make out the words. He couldn't even be sure that they were in English. He tapped on the door, but there was no break in the speech. He turned the handle and pushed the door open.

There was only one person in the room. The first thing Charles saw was the soles of a new pair of shoes resting on the desk. Behind them, a pair of hands holding an Arden edition of *The Winter's Tale*. And behind that the surprised face of Geoffrey Winter.

"Good God. Charles Paris."

"Yes."

"Have you come to commission me to build a second National Theatre?"

"No such luck, I'm afraid. It's not work."

"It never is."

"Bad at the moment?"

"Not a good time for the architect on his own. No one's building anything."

"The economic situation."

"Yes."

"Like everything else. Like why theatres are cutting down on resident companies, why managements are putting on less shows . . ."

This banter was conducted at a pleasant enough level, but they both knew that it was only a formal observance preceding something more important. Charles decided there was little to be gained by further prevarication. "I've come to talk about Charlotte Mecken."

"Ah." Geoffrey Winter tensed fractionally at the name, but he didn't give anything away. Charles got the same message that he had got from the performance as Trigorin, that here was a man of considerable emotional depth, but with great control over his reactions. He did not let anything emerge until he had fully considered how he wanted to present it.

Charles had hoped for more reaction and was thrown when he didn't get it. So he blundered on and, after a brief explanation of his belief in Hugo's innocence, asked point blank if Geoffrey had been Charlotte's lover.

The response was an "Oh," delivered absolutely flat; it gave nothing. But Geoffrey Winter was only playing the pause for maximum dramatic effect. Charles recognized the acting technique and let the silence ride. At last Geoffrey spoke.

"Well, congratulations. You've done your homework well.

There's no point in my denying it, you're right. Since the police know, no doubt it'll all come out at Hugo's trial, so why should I pretend? Yes, I was Charlotte's lover until she . . . died."

He changed pace suddenly on the last word, straightened up in his chair and turned to look out over the irregular roofs of London. As if in the grip of strong emotion. Charles always found it difficult to judge with actors. Since their lives were devoted to simulation, it was often hard to distinguish when their feelings were genuine.

He didn't offer any comment; he let Geoffrey play the scene at his own pace. Sure enough, when the pause had extended far enough to make even a Pinter audience feel uncomfortable, Geoffrey turned back from the window and looked piercingly at him. "I suppose your next question is going to be—did I kill Charlotte?"

In fact, that was not where Charles's suspicions were leading, but he decided to play along with the scene. "I was going to be a bit more subtle than that."

"Well, Charles, the answer is no. I didn't kill her. It would have been perverse for me to . . . I had no cause to break up what was happening . . . about the best . . . thing that . . ." Again he was overcome by real or simulated emotion (or, most likely, an amalgam of the two). He turned back to the window.

"I'm sorry to put you through this, Geoffrey. I realize it must be painful. But Hugo is a friend and I have to investigate every avenue."

Geoffrey was once again master of himself (if indeed he had ever relinquished control). "I quite understand. I've been through all this with the police."

"How did they find out?"

"Not difficult. They checked Charlotte's comings and goings with the staff at Breckton Station, realized the convenient position of my office for such an affair, then came and asked me, more or less as you have done. It seemed pointless to try and hide the facts. It would only have made things worse."

"Did they ask you if you'd killed her?"

"They, as you intended to be, were a bit more subtle than that. But they did ask a few pertinent questions about my movements on Monday. I think they were just checking; I didn't get the impression they had much doubt about Hugo's guilt. In fact, they came to see me after he had been arrested, so I suppose they were just building up the background to the case."

Charles must have been looking at Geoffrey quizzically, because the architect seemed to read his thoughts. He gave a dry laugh. "Yes, I'll tell you what I told the police. I'll establish my alibi for you —as I believe the saying goes.

"Part of it you know, because you were with me in the Back Room. As you recall, we left there together and walked down to the main road. Now, in case you're thinking that I might have immediately doubled back and taken the insane step of strangling someone I loved, it seems that there is proof that Charlotte was still alive and well at nine o'clock. Shad Scott-Smith, you may remember, in the Back Room buying drinks for *The Seagull* cast. Because Charlotte wasn't there, he rang her from his home at about ten to nine. He rang off at nine. The reason he could be so specific is that he heard the opening of *I, Claudius* on the telly and he wanted to watch it."

"It seems to have cut a swathe through the lives of an entire generation, that programme."

"It did. Big success. Pity you weren't in it."

"Yes, there'd be some pretty useful repeats on something like that. I'm afraid I've never been in what's been hailed as a television success."

The change of subject relaxed the tension between the two men and Geoffrey continued in almost a bantering tone. "Right, on with my alibi. I arrived home just before nine to find that Vee, as another member of the generation decimated by *I, Claudius*, was all geared up to watch. I left her to it and went upstairs to do some work on my lines for *The Winter's Tale*.

"For the next bit, I have cause to be thankful that I have a bloody-minded neighbor. Apparently, old Mrs. Withers next door, who goes to bed at about nine, could hear me ranting away through the wall—her bedroom's right next door to my study. Apparently she's not a great fan of Shakespeare and later on, when I got a bit carried away with the character, she took it upon herself to ring up the police and complain. A very apologetic constable was round at our place for some time saying that old ladies could be very difficult. Apparently, according to the police in the murder case, this means that I'm covered for the time of the death."

He paused, not with satisfaction or triumph, but as if he had reached a natural conclusion. Then he added, "Fortunate, really. Most evenings spent at home, it would be very difficult to account for one's movements."

"Thank you very much for going through it all again. And for bearing with my wild accusations."

"That's quite okay. I sympathize with your motives. I'm as keen as you are to find the person who killed Charlotte. I just thought he had already been found."

"You may well be right. Certainly the fact that she was having an affair would give Hugo even more of a motive. Do you know if he knew about it?"

"No idea. Charlotte and I didn't discuss him."

"From my conversations with him, I got the impression that he thought she was having an affair, but didn't know who with."

Geoffrey smiled painfully. "Ironic though it may seem, Charlotte and I did try to be discreet about it. I mean, never let on what we felt for each other round Breckton. We didn't want to be gossip-fodder for the Backstagers."

"Very wise. So she always came up here?"

Geoffrey nodded sadly. "Yes. It started in the summer. You remember the long, hot summer?"

This new note of wistfulness, like everything else, sounded contrived. Charles didn't respond to it. "Tell me, why did Charlotte come sometimes to Charing Cross and sometimes to Waterloo?"

Geoffrey raised his eyebrows and nodded in appreciation. "Ten out of ten for homework. To answer that question, I think you have to understand what Charlotte was like. It was her first affair, she treated it with great excitement, and I think much of the excitement came from the secrecy. Coming to different stations was her idea of discretion, of covering her tracks. She was very young. As you see," he continued with irony, "the smoke-screen was not very effective. It didn't take the police—or you—long to see through it."

Charles felt a glow of satisfaction for his understanding of Charlotte's character. "And was it for the same reason that she planned to go to Victoria on the day after she died?"

"Victoria?"

"I'd better explain. I found Charlotte's engagement diary down at the house. She'd listed all your meetings by a time and the name of the terminus she was coming to. The last two entries were one o'clock at Charing Cross on the Monday, the day she died, and then one o'clock on the Tuesday at Victoria."

"Ah, I didn't know she'd done that."

"What—put the places down in the book?"

"Yes. Yes, that must have been it." For the first time in their interview he seemed to be in the grip of some emotion that was more powerful than his control. "I'm sorry, it's just so typical of her, to think that that kind of subterfuge would fool anyone. Going to Victoria instead . . . I mean, to go out of her way like that to be inconspicuous and then write all the details down in a diary. I think a lot of the affair was just a game for her, like a schoolgirl having a midnight feast."

"But it was serious on your side?"

Geoffrey looked pained. "Serious on both sides—in our different ways. It was very good."

"And it was still going well when she died? I mean, you hadn't had a row or . . . ?"

Geoffrey looked at Charles with some distaste, pitying his lack of subtlety. "I know what you mean. No, we hadn't had a lover's tiff which would inspire me with hatred to go and kill her. It was all going very well." He was becoming wistful again.

"And was it going to change?"

"Change?"

"I mean, were you likely to get divorced and marry?"

Geoffrey shook his head and slowly. "No, it was an affair. I wanted to go on as long as possible, but I suppose some time it would have ended. I've had other affairs. They all end sooner or later. I wouldn't have left Vee. People can never understand how close Vee and I are. I'm just one of those men who's capable of loving more than one woman at a time. Do you understand?"

"I think I do. Did Vee know about Charlotte?"

"I assume so. I never told her, but she's not stupid."

"Didn't she get jealous?"

"Vee would only get jealous if she thought someone was likely to take me away from her. She knew that no one would. According to my own rules of morality, I'm very loyal."

Charles nodded. Geoffrey had a male chauvinist vanity which was quite strong enough to blind him to his wife's real feelings. No woman, however liberated, actually welcomes the knowledge that her husband is sleeping around. And Charles knew from the way that Vee had watched her husband at the cast party, she had a strong possessive instinct.

There wasn't a lot more Charles could find out. "I must go. I mustn't keep you from your work any longer."

Geoffrey laughed cynically and flapped his copy of *The Winter's Tale*. "Ah, my work. Geoffrey Winter Associates haven't had a decent size job now for four months."

"Where are the Associates?"

"Disassociated—or should it be dissociated? I never know. All gone their separate ways, anyway. Even the secretary's gone."

"So you just come up here and do nothing all day?"

"Sometimes things come up. Odd little jobs, through friends in various government departments. That's the answer these days— work in the public sector. No room for men on their own. I keep applying for jobs in local government and things, but as yet no luck. So I stay on here and wait. May as well, until the lease is up."

"When's that?"

"A couple of months."

"And then what?"

Geoffrey Winter's shrug started expansive as if it encompassed every possibility in the known world, but shrank down to nothing.

"So what do you live on?"

"Credit." He laughed unconcernedly. "And the confidence that something will turn up."

Charles went back to Hereford Road feeling excited. He had been glad to hear Geoffrey's watertight alibi because that removed him from the running. And enabled Charles to follow the suspicions which were hardening in his mind. It wasn't Geoffrey he suspected; it was his wife. He could not forget the tensed-up energy he had felt in Vee's body as they had danced together. She was a woman capable of anything.

The chain of motivation was simple. Vee's jealousy of Charlotte had started when she was beaten for the role of Nina which she had regarded as hers by right. It had been compounded by the discovery of her husband's affair with the upstart. That, however, she could have borne; what drove her to murder was the discovery that Charlotte was giving Geoffrey the one thing that their marriage could not—a child.

The opportunity for committing the crime was equally easily explained. Geoffrey had been at such pains to establish his own alibi that he hadn't thought about his wife's. While he was upstairs ranting through Leontes, she was assumed to be downstairs watching *I, Claudius*. So far as Geoffrey was concerned, that was what she was doing. He could presumably hear the television from upstairs.

But a television set conducts a one-way conversation, regardless of whether or not there is anyone watching. Vee, knowing that Geoffrey would get carried away by his performance, had every opportunity to leave the house after the show had started. There was plenty of time for her to have gone up to the Meckens'. Charlotte would have recognized her and let her in. A brief exchange, then Vee had taken Charlotte by surprise and strangled her. Put the body in the coal shed to delay its discovery and a brisk walk home to be back in time for the end of *I, Claudius*.

It was all conjecture, but it fitted. And, what was more, Charles thought he could prove it.

The proof lay on the table of his bedsitter. For reasons mainly of masochism (to see how much work other actors were getting), Charles always had the *Radio Times* delivered. Since he had no television and rarely listened to the radio, it was frequently thrown away unread. But on this occasion he felt sure it was going to be useful.

It was the Wednesday that interested him. He thought back to the Wednesday night when he had rung the Winters to get Robert Chubb's number. He remembered the time. Twenty-five to eleven, because he had looked at his watch after speaking to Kate Venables. And when he had spoken to Geoffrey Winter, there had been a break in their conversation while Vee was given advice on how to adjust the television for a good picture on BBC2.

Charles almost shouted out loud when the *Radio Times* confirmed his suspicions. At ten o'clock until ten-fifty on BBC2 on Wednesday night there had been a repeat of the Monday's episode of *I, Claudius*. Geoffrey Winter would not have been watching it, because he had missed so many of the earlier episodes.

So why should his wife watch the same program for a second time in three days? Unless of course she hadn't been there to see it the first time.

CHAPTER 13

CHARLES HAD CAUSE to be grateful to sour Reggie for forcing him into joining the Breckton Backstagers. As a Social Member, it was quite legitimate for him to be propping up the Back Room bar at a quarter past seven that evening.

There were not many faces he recognized. Robert Chubb gave him the sort of glance most people reserve for windows and a few others offered insincere half-smiles. The only person who greeted him with anything like conviviality was Denis Hobbs, who bought him a large Bell's. "You going to do some show or something down here then, Charles?"

Denis without Mary Hobbs was a refreshing change. He remained hearty, but didn't seem to have the same obligation to be raucously jovial which he had demonstrated on their previous meeting.

Charles denied that he was likely to break into amateur dramatics. "Just a handy bar." he explained, hoping that Denis wouldn't ask why it was handy for someone who lived fifteen miles away.

But Denis was a man without suspicion. He leaned forward to Charles and confided, "Exactly the reason I joined. I mean, you can't turn up the chance of a bar on your doorstep, can you?"

"So you don't act?"

Denis erupted with laughter. "Me? Bloody hell, I could no sooner act than have a baby. Blimey, me an actor—no, I'm a builder, that's what I am. Although Mary keeps trying to get me to say I work in the *construction industry.*"

The mimicry which he put into the last two words suggested that he was not as devoid of acting talent as he had implied. "No, the acting bit's all Mary's. Very keen she is on all this arty-farty stuff. I tell you," he confided like a schoolboy with a dirty story. "I've been more bored in that theatre next door than a poof in a brothel. Still, Mary enjoys it. Keeps her out of my hair and keeps her off the streets, eh?" He laughed again robustly. "I'm only here for the beer—and I like to look at the scenery. The young female scenery, that is." He winked.

They were silent for a few moments. It wasn't an uncomfortable silence, just a pause of drinking companionship. Then, idly, to make conversation, Charles asked whether there had been any further developments on the burglary.

"No, not a thing. The police seem to think their best hope is to catch the villains when they try to get rid of the stuff. Apart from that, apparently there's not much chance. I mean, they've been all through the house and they haven't got any fingerprints or anything to go on."

"They left it very tidy?"

"Oh yes, everything put back, all the doors closed—very neat job."

"Nasty thing to happen, though."

"Yes. Still, we were insured, so it could have been worse. Mary was a bit cut up about what was taken, sentimental value, all that, but I went out and bought her a load more gear and that seems to have calmed her down a bit."

At that moment the Winters came in. Perhaps it was what Geoffrey had said in the morning, but they did look very together to Charles. As if they did share the complete relationship which he had described.

Denis Hobbs seemed to be slightly uneasy at their appearance, as if he suddenly had to be on his best behavior. Mary continually told him what a privilege it was to know such artistic luminaries as the Winters.

Geoffrey did a light take, but greeted Charles cordially. As if by mutual agreement, they did not mention their earlier encounter.

Charles offered them drinks heartily. "What's it to be? I'm just taking advantage of my new membership."

Geoffrey wasn't fooled by that, but he made no comment. Charles wondered if the architect knew that he wanted to talk to Vee.

It was possible. Certainly Geoffrey seemed to be keeping his wife at his side to inhibit private conversations. A new thought struck Charles. Maybe Geoffrey had discovered his wife's crime and was set to defend her against investigation. That could make things difficult. Geoffrey's was a formidable mind to have in opposition.

But the architect's protection couldn't last long. The *Winter's Tale* rehearsal started at seven-thirty "and he gets furious if you're late, so I'd better go. Will you be going straight back home, Vee?"

The question was delivered with studied casualness, but Charles could sense the tension beneath it. Vee, either deliberately or not, didn't take the hint. "No, not straight away. I'll just buy Charles a drink. See you later. Hope it goes well."

"Fine." Geoffrey went through to the rehearsal room with a cheery wave. Or was it his impression of a cheery wave? Charles was getting paranoid about Geoffrey Winter's sincerity or lack of it.

He asked for a Bell's and Vee bought him a large one. Denis and a lot of the others round the bar had left and so, whether Geoffrey wanted it or not, Charles and Vee were alone together.

She commented on her husband's departure. "You know, he almost sounded as if he was jealous."

"What, of us?"

Vee shrugged. Charles laughed loudly, as if it was the best joke he had heard for a long time.

Interesting—straight away she put their meeting into a sexual context, just as she had done at the cast party. Once again he wasn't interested. And once again he felt she wasn't really interested either.

He decided that he would have to be a bit more subtle in questioning Vee than he had been with her husband. Better start at an uncontroversial level. "What are they rehearsing tonight?"

"Blocking the first two acts. So I'm not wanted."

"Oh, I didn't even realize you were in the production. What are you playing?"

"Perdita. Since yesterday." She pronounced it with triumph.

"You mean it was going to be . . . ?"

"Charlotte, yes. Of course, it's a terrible way to get a part, but it's an ill wind . . ." Her regret was merely formal.

At least she wasn't disguising her satisfaction at Charlotte's removal from the scene. She was now back in her position as undisputed queen of the juve leads in the Breckton Backstagers. Charles would have thought she was a bit long in the tooth to be "the prettiest low-born lass that ever ran on the greensward" and a symbol of youthful beauty and regeneration, but now she was the best that Breckton had to offer. If she had killed Charlotte, then the returns were immediate.

Charles knew he had to play her gently. She was highly-strung and information would have to be wheedled out of her. He hoped Geoffrey had been discreet and not mentioned their meeting earlier in the day. He did not want her to be on her guard.

Starting with flattery seemed the best approach with someone as self-absorbed as she was. He asked her about her acting career at Breckton, regretting that he had never had the pleasure of seeing her in a production.

She needed no second invitation. He had in his time met a good few professional actors and actresses who assumed that everyone shared their own consuming interest in their theatrical doings, but never one as voluble as Vee Winter. Perhaps living with another king-size ego who also liked to talk about his acting, she didn't often get the chance to let rip in this way.

He got it all—the early aptitude for mimicry noted by loving parents, the success in elocution exams, the outstanding ability remarked upon by an English teacher, commendations at local festivals, the agonizing decision of the late teens as to whether to try for drama school and take it up professionally, then parental pressure and the final regrettable resolution to deprive the greater public of her talents.

At this point a pause was left for Charles to murmur some suitable insincerity about tragic waste.

"And then of course I married and decided that it would be

wrong for me to do something that would take me away from
Geoffrey for long periods of time. He is a complex character and
can be a full-time job. I often think it's as well that we don't have
children, because he needs so much of my attention that they
might not get a look-in."

In this speech Charles could hear two threads of oft-repeated
self-justification. First, the very common suburban housewife's explanation of why she never did anything more with her life, how
the cares of marriage cut off in its bloom a career of unbelievable
promise. In some cases—like, he reflected, that of Charlotte
Mecken—it's true, but in most, where only moderate talent is involved, it's no more than a comforting fiction.

There was also the second well-rehearsed self-justification, for
her childlessness. It was sad that this was felt necessary, but there
was a defensive quality to her remarks about Geoffrey's demands
on her time. Ironic to Charles, with his knowledge of the other
women among whom Geoffrey spread those needs.

But she gave him a cue to find some purely practical information. "You talk about Geoffrey being a full-time job. Do you actually
have a real one?"

"Job? Yes. I teach Speech and Drama at a local private school."
"Oh."

This again seemed to need justification. "It's very close and convenient. I get home for lunch. And of course I think one can give a
lot to young minds. If you've got an enthusiasm for the theatre, it
does communicate and stimulate their interest."

"Oh, certainly."

"Also the little extra money comes in handy."

Knowing what he did about Geoffrey's business affairs, Charles
felt sure it did. He would imagine they must have been living more
or less exclusively on Vee's income for some time. Perhaps Geoffrey
even conducted his affair with Charlotte on a grant from his wife.

But this digression on Vee's work did not divert her long from
the main subject of her dramatic triumphs. She started to list the
shows she had been in through a few more drinks, and Charles's
attention was wavering when he suddenly heard himself being
asked back to the house to see some of her scrapbooks.

Instinctively he said yes, not certain whether scrapbooks were the latest form of etchings as a seduction bait. The more time he could spend with Vee, the more relaxed she became, the easier it was going to be to ask the questions he wanted to.

It might also be useful to get inside the Winters' house again. If Vee Winter did kill Charlotte, he was going to need some tangible proof of it to convince the police.

Vee made their exit from the Back Room pointed, with loud goodbyes to everyone and messages that she'd see Geoffrey later. Again Charles felt the overtones of sexual intrigue. Vee wanted to be seen leaving with him, possibly to stimulate gossip among the Backbiters. But that was all; she seemed to want the aura of an illicit liaison rather than any illicit action. Or at least that was the impression he got.

He would presumably find out if he was right when they got back to the house.

As they walked back along the path to the main road, Charles looked covertly at his companion. If she had murdered Charlotte as he suspected, then this was the route she must have taken on the Monday night. But her face betrayed nothing.

The air was full of explosions and the sudden screams of rockets. Of course, fireworks. November the Fifth. His birthday. He recalled the old family joke that his mother had been frightened into delivery by a wayward jumping cracker.

On the common the celebrations were under way round the huge bonfire. Presumably there had been an effigy of Guy Fawkes hoisted on top of the pile, but now all was consumed in the tall rippling flags of flame.

To one side of the bonfire, in a roped-off area, some responsible fathers were donating Roman candles and Catherine wheels. Charles knew that this was the new approved policy; for greater safety, families were encouraged to pool their fireworks into this kind of communal party. To him it seemed to take away the excitement and make the exercise rather pointless. Like drinking non-alcoholic beer in motorway service cafés.

And in this case it didn't even seem to be particularly safe. The leaping flames spat up lumps of burning debris, some of which had landed in a nearby tree and kindled the branches. The conflagration was in danger of getting out of hand.

Still, there were lots of responsible fathers to deal with the problem. Lots of over-insured men in their early forties who no doubt drove Volvos with the side-lights on in the daytime. As Charles and Vee passed, there seemed to be an argument among them as to whether they should call the fire brigade or not.

To his amusement, Charles saw that the organizing spirit in the pro-fire brigade lobby was sour Reggie from the Backstagers. Taking his role as professional wet blanket literally this time. He scurried about issuing orders, followed by two small children of one sex or the other whose faces were as sour as their father's. It was strange to see the niggling committee man in another context.

Vee waved at Reggie, but he didn't see her. Once again she seemed to be drawing attention to her being with Charles, to set tongues wagging.

A group of overexcited children rushed towards them, involved in some inexplicable, but evidently very funny, game. Vee moved aside to let them pass. As she did so, the flames suddenly threw a spotlight on her face. The expression was one of infinite pain and bitterness.

They walked in silence down the paved path to the main road. There Vee stopped outside an off-license. "No drink in the house, I'm afraid."

She selected a cheapish bottle of Italian red wine. Charles insisted on paying for it and she didn't argue. His new knowledge of the Winters' financial plight made sense of such details.

As Vee put her key in the front door, they heard the distant siren of a fire engine. Sour Reggie had triumphed. For the firework party-goers the evening's entertainment was ending.

But, as Vee Winter laid her arm on his shoulder and ushered him into the house, Charles Paris felt that perhaps his evening's entertainment was only beginning.

CHAPTER 14

CHARLES SIPPED HIS wine and tried not to look too downcast when Vee came in loaded with her theatrical memorabilia. Scrapbooks, programs, a box of photographs and—most daunting of all—the cassette recorder that he had seen Geoffrey using. Oh dear, it looked as if he was going to get an Action Replay of her entire dramatic career.

He settled down to be bored out of his mind. Vee, he knew, was inflicting this on him because he was a professional actor. She wanted his commendation, she wanted him to say how impoverished the British theatre had been by her decision to turn her back on it. Maybe she even wanted to gain his praise so that she would compare favorably with those whom he had condemned at the Critics' Circle.

He found her exhibitionism sad. The fact that she needed this bolstering. It showed that Geoffrey had too simple an interpretation of his wife's character. Her insecurity spoke in every nervous action. To think that she would not be jealous of another woman was totally wrong.

The overtones of sexuality which she gave to the proceedings also revealed her insecurity. She needed attention, she needed Charles to be aware that the two of them together was a potentially sexual scenario, but he felt that was all she needed. If he had made a pass at her, he would have got a considerate rebuff. She wouldn't have minded—in fact, she would rather have welcomed it as a boost to her ego and as something else to feel martyred about. She liked to think of herself as a tragic queen, resisting all blandishments from other men, because of her devotion to one man who was not really worthy of her.

Charles had not realized this vein of contempt which ran through Vee's feelings for her husband until the subject of children came up again. It was prompted by a photograph of Vee with another girl in Elizabethan dress who, apparently, had been a terribly good actress, but had given it all up when she started to have children. "Four I believe she's got now. Four. I suppose that could have been me, if things had turned out differently." She responded to Charles's quizzical look. "I mean, if I had married someone else."

"Oh." He sounded slightly embarrassed, as if he ought not to inquire further, knowing that this was the sure way to make her continue.

"Yes, with another man, no doubt I would be surrounded with the little brats, spending all my days at coffee parties and tea parties, talking about nappies and nursery schools." The edge she put into the words showed how much she was an outsider in the great incubator of Breckton. All the thoughts he'd had about Charlotte being ostracized by her childlessness applied even more strongly to Vee.

He continued his embarrassed act. "Well, er . . . I understood that nowadays there were things that could be done about infertility and . . . er . . . clinics and so on."

Vee smiled a martyred smile. "Maybe, but I don't think you'd ever get Geoffrey along to one of those. He couldn't admit to himself that . . . male pride in virility or . . . I'm sure you know all about that."

Again the remark was sexually loaded. Not quite a come-on, but a reminder that they were a man and woman alone together.

Charles thought quickly as he worked through the file of meaningless photographs. Vee's conviction that Geoffrey was to blame for their lack of family was obviously one of the supports of their marriage. She believed it, because it gave her superiority over him.

She could watch with indulgence his philandering with other women, knowing his secret. And she was not afraid to divulge it.

Charlotte's pregnancy must have threatened the entire fabric of that illusion and Charlotte had had to be removed so that Vee could remain protected in her cocoon of fiction.

He knew he was right. All he needed was proof. It was time he got down to the details of his investigation.

In broaching the subject he was helped by the photographs. There was a picture of Vee surrounded by adolescent youths in togas with laundry marks.

"Portia in *Julius Caesar* at school," she supplied.

"Ah, real *I, Claudius* stuff," he commented, grateful for the cue. She laughed.

"Have you been watching it, Vee?" he asked casually.

"Oh yes. Seen every one. That was the big advantage of not doing *The Seagull*. Meant I could make it a regular date."

"Every Wednesday."

"No, I watch it on Mondays."

Charles took a risk. What he had to say next was going to sound more like interrogation than casual conversation. He hoped she wouldn't notice. "That's strange. I rang Geoffrey on Wednesday and I could have sworn he said you were watching it then."

He played it very light, but still threw her. She looked at him, flustered and bewildered. "Oh . . . oh yes, I did watch it on Wednesday this week."

He didn't volunteer any comment. Just left her to explain.

She did a good performance as someone sorting through her memory. "Oh, of course. My mother rang on Monday just after it had started. She always natters on so, the show was practically over by the time I got off the phone."

Charles joked, as if the information meant nothing to him, "I think everyone's mother's like that." But he felt sure she was lying.

"Yes, mine always rings at inconvenient times. Still, I suppose I shouldn't grumble, if the odd phone call keeps her happy. Better than continually traipsing up to Lytham St. Anne's to see her."

That was very helpful. He knew Vee's maiden name was le Carpentier. There shouldn't be too many old ladies of that name in Lytham St. Anne's with whom to check her alibi.

Eventually (and it seemed to take for ever) they came to the end of the photographs. "Fascinating," Charles lied.

Vee looked disappointed, as if she had expected more. What did she want him to do, for God's sake, say that she was the greatest actress to tread the boards on the evidence of a load of amateur snapshots?

But it seemed there was more evidence about to be offered. Vee was now turning her attention to the cassette player and the black plastic-covered box of cassettes. "Actually," she said with elaborate casualness, "I've got recordings here for some of the stuff I've done."

"Oh, really?" Charles gave the last dreg of his supply of simulated interest. "What, recorded off stage?"

"Some of them. Some I've just done at home—really just for my own benefit, so that I can get a kind of objective view of what I'm doing."

"I see."

"I thought you might like to hear one or two little bits. It'd give you some idea of how I do act."

Charles quarried a smile from his petrifying features. "Great." She fiddled with the machine. "Geoffrey lets you borrow his recorder then?"

"It's not his, it's mine. He occasionally borrows it when he's learning lines."

"And to dub off his music."

"What? Good God, no. He's far too much of a purist for that. Only happy when music is being perfectly reproduced on all that hi-fi stuff he's got upstairs. He always says I'm a bit of a Philistine about it. I mean, I've got some music cassettes—popular stuff—which I play round the house, but he gets very sniffy about them. This recorder's only mono for a start and he says you're missing ninety per cent of the enjoyment if you don't hear music in stereo."

"So he would never use it for music?"

"Not a chance. Look, there's a bit here that's an extract from a production of *The Country Wife* that we did. I played Mrs. Pinchwife. Got very good press. I think this speech is quite amusing. Would you like to hear it?"

The affirmative smile was another triumph of engineering.

Just before she switched it on, they both heard a strange wail from outside. A sound like a child in pain. Vee rose and Charles looked at her with some alarm.

"I must go to the kitchen to let him in," said Vee.

"Who is he?"

"Vanya."

"Vanya?"

"The cat."

As soon as she was out of the door, he leapt to the cassette box. Her recorded voice wound on, but he didn't listen. His mind was too full.

When he had first gone up to the study, Geoffrey Winter had been copying Wagner's *Liebestod* from his expensive stereo on to this cheap mono cassette machine. Geoffrey had given some specious line about it being handier, which had seemed reasonable at the time, but which now seemed extremely suspicious.

If you don't want a cassette copy of a piece of music, then why copy it? Only one answer sprang to mind—in order to cover something already on the cassette.

He felt a prickle of excitement. Now at last he was on to something. Geoffrey's recording of the Wagner had taken place on the Tuesday, the day after Charlotte's murder. The architect must somehow have found out about his wife's crime and known that there was incriminating evidence on a cassette, which had to be removed. But Charles was due for supper just after he made the discovery, so he had to destroy the evidence while their guest was there without raising his suspicions. What was easier than to record over it?

Charles found the distinctive yellow and green container which held the cassette Geoffrey had used. There was a chance, a very long chance, that some part of its previous recording remained unerased. He slipped the thin rectangle into his pocket.

Meanwhile Vee Winter's interpretation of Wycherley ground on.

Suddenly the door opened and Geoffrey walked in. "Hello, Vee, I—"

The surprise was so great that even his well-controlled emotions were caught off their guard. In the flash of time before he recovered himself, Geoffrey's face bared his thoughts. He found another man alone in his house with his wife. And he was extremely suspicious.

CHAPTER 15

GERALD VENABLES WAS much more friendly when Charles rang him the next morning. Maybe he was less tired and the arrival of the weekend had cheered him. Or maybe the fact that it was the weekend meant he could relax his professional guard. Outside the office he could see Hugo's predicament as a case to be investigated rather than as an inconvenient and time-consuming legal challenge.

Whatever the cause, he agreed that they should meet and invited Charles down to Dulwich for lunch. As he signed off on the phone, he said, "So long, buster. See you at my joint round twelve. Okay, coochie-coo?" An encouraging sign.

As Charles walked from West Dulwich Station, he found that he was casting a Breckton eye over everything he saw, assessing the suburb from a suburban point of view. He hadn't quite got to the stage of pricing the houses he passed, but he could feel it wasn't far off.

Dulwich had the same air as Breckton of quiet desperation. Paranoid car-cleaning, wives pulled in every direction by children, buggies and shopping, determinedly jovial husbands taking the kids for a walk, track-suited executives sweating off some of the week's lunches in unconvinced jogging, others bearing their loads of wood and ceiling tiles from the brochured neatness of the Do-It-Yourself shop to the bad-tempered messes of a constructive weekend.

Gerald's house was predictably well-appointed. Part of a newish development, with that fraction more room between it and the next house which is the mark of success in the suburbs. The front door had a brass lion knocker and was white, with small square Georgian panels. The up-and-over garage door was panelled in the same way. In fact the whole scheme of the house was Georgian, with thin-framed white windows set in neat red brick. It was exactly the sort of house that anyone in Georgian England who happened to own two cars, a central heating oil tank, a television and a burglar alarm would have had.

Gerald was manifesting the schizophrenia of a Monday to Friday worker. He was dressed in a pale blue toweling shirt and evenly faded jeans (the summery image made possible by the blast of central heating which greeted Charles as he entered). His feet were encased in navy blue sailing shoes and a Snoopy medallion hung around his neck. This last was worn a bit self-consciously. Perhaps it was a fixture, always round the solicitorial neck beneath the beautifully-laundered cotton shirts and silk ties, but somehow Charles doubted it.

The shock of Gerald without a suit made him realize that it must have been nearly twenty years since he had seen his friend in informal gear. For a moment he wondered if he had come to the right house.

"Kate's taken the kids to some exhibition in Town, so we've got the place to ourselves. She sent love and so on. There's some kind of basic pâté lunch in the fridge for later. Have a beer?"

Predictably Löwenbräu. Charles descended into the depths of a light brown leather sofa and took a long swallow. "Well, are you beginning to think I might have a point?"

"Hardly, Charles, but I am willing to go through the evidence with you and see if there's anything. What do you reckon might have happened?"

Charles outlined his current view of Charlotte's death, moving swiftly from point to point. As he spoke, his conjectures took a more substantial form and he could feel an inexorable pull of logic.

Gerald was impressed, but skeptical. "I can see that that makes a kind of sense, but in a case like this you've got to have evidence. If you're ever going to convince the police that their nice neatly-sewn-up little case is not in fact nice and neatly-sewn-up at all, you're going to have to produce something pretty solid. All we've got so far is the slight oddness of a woman watching her favorite television program twice in three days. And that could well be explained if it turns out that her story about her mother's phone call is true."

"I'd care to bet it isn't. Anyway, that's not all we have. We've also got this." With an actor's flourish Charles produced the yellow and green cassette box from his pocket.

"Oh yes." Gerald was not as overwhelmed by the gesture as he should have been. "You mentioned that. I'm afraid I don't quite see where you reckon that fits into the scheme of things."

"What, you don't want me to repeat all that business about my coming in and finding Geoffrey copying the Wagner?"

"No, I've got that. What I don't understand is what you are expecting to find on it. Except for Wagner. I mean, he could just have been copying it for a friend or something."

Charles wasn't going to shift from his proudly-achieved deduction. "No, I'm sure he was trying to hide something, to erase something."

"But what? What could possibly be put on tape that was incriminating? The average murderer doesn't record a confession just to make it easy for amateur detectives."

"Ha bloody ha. All right, I don't know what it is. I just know it's important. And the only way we're going to find out what's on it is by listening to the thing. Do you have a cassette player?"

"Of course," Gerald murmured, pained that the question should be thought necessary.

In fact he had a cassette deck incorporated into the small city of matt grey Band and Olufsen hi-fi equipment that spread over the dark wooden wall unit. The speakers stood on the floor like space age mushrooms.

"Now I reckon," said Charles as Gerald fiddled with the console, "our best hope is that there's something right at the beginning, that he started recording too far in and didn't wipe all the . . ."

The opening of the *Prelude* from Wagner's *Tristan and Isolde* gave him the lie.

"Well, if that was our best hope . . ." Gerald observed infuriatingly, as he bent to fiddle with more knobs.

When he was happy with the sound, he sat down with a smug smile on his face, waiting to be proved right. The *Prelude* wound moodily on. Charles remembered how cheap he had always found the emotionalism of Wagner's outpourings. He began to get very bored.

After about five minutes it became clear that Gerald was going through the same process of mental asphyxiation. "Charles, can't we switch it off? Kate's taken me to this stuff, but I've never cared for it much."

"No. Some American once said Wagner's music is better than it sounds."

"It needs to be. I think it's going to go on like this for some time and we're not going to get any dramatic murder confessions."

"I agree. Let's spool through. There might be something where he changed sides. That's a C90 cassette, forty-five minutes each way. The LP could only have had about twenty minutes each side, so he must have flipped the disc. Might be something there."

There wasn't. They could hear the blip of the pick-up being lifted off, then the slight hiss of erased tape until the bump of the stylus back on the other side, the tick of the homing grooves and the return of the music.

"No." Gerald's smugness was increasing.

"Let's try the end. Yes, if there's only forty minutes on the disc and it's a forty five minute tape . . ." Charles felt a new surge of excitement at the thought.

He tensed as Gerald spooled through till nearly the end of the tape and uttered a silent prayer as the replay button was pressed.

God was apparently deaf. Tape hiss. Again, nothing but tape hiss. "I think he just left the Record button down and let the tape run through until it was all erased."

"Yes, I suppose so," Charles agreed gloomily. Then, with sudden memory—"No, but he didn't. I was there. I remember quite distinctly. Perhaps he had intended to do that, but because I was there he switched it off when the music stopped. He must have erased the last bit after that. Which would suggest to me that he did have something important to hide." Suddenly he got excited. "Look, suppose he missed a bit just at the end of the music . . ."

"Why should he?"

"Well, with some of these cheap cassette players it's difficult to press the Play button and Record at exactly the same time. He might have put down the Play a moment earlier and left something unerased."

"But surely he would have heard anything and gone back over it."

"Not necessarily. Most of these machines have another button with which you switch off the sound to prevent microphone howlround. So he wouldn't have heard it. And, given his great respect for music, even in this situation I don't think he'd want to risk going back and wiping the final reverberation of his Wagner."

"It sounds pretty unlikely to me."

"It is. But it's possible. Spool back to the end of the music."

With the expression of someone humoring the mentally infirm, the solicitor returned the controls. It was the end of the *Liebestod*. The soprano warbled to death and the orchestra rose to its sullen climax. The regular hiss of the stylus on the center groove seemed interminable. Then abruptly it was lifted off. This sound was followed by the woolly click of the recorder being switched off. Then another click as it had been restarted and, seconds later, a third as the Record button had been engaged.

Between the last two clicks there was speech.

Charles and Gerald looked at each other as if to confirm that they had both heard it. They were silent; the evidence was so fragile, it could suddenly be blown away.

Charles found his voice first. "Spool back. Play it again," he murmured huskily.

Again Wagner mourned in. Again the pick-up worried against the center of the record. Then the clicks. And, sandwiched between them, Geoffrey Winter's voice. Saying two words—no, not so much —two halves of two words.

"-ed coal-" Charles repeated reverentially. "Play it again."

Gerald did so. "It's cut in the middle of some word ending in *ed,* and it sounds as though the *coal* is only the beginning of a word too."

"What words begin with *coal?*"

Charles looked straight at Gerald. "*Coal shed,* for one."

"Good God." For the first time the lines of skepticism left the solicitor's face. "And what about words ending in *ed?* There must be thousands."

"Thousands that are spelled that way, not so many that are pronounced like that."

"No. I suppose there's *coal shed* again. If the two parts came the other way around . . . ?"

"Or there's *dead,* Gerald."

"Yes," the solicitor replied slowly. "Yes, there is."

"May I use your phone, Gerald?"

"What for?"

"I'm going to crack Vee Winter's alibi."

"Oh."

"Don't sound so grumpy about it. Cheapest time to phone your friends—after six and at weekends. I'll pay for the call, if you like."

"No, it's not that. The firm sees to the phone bill anyway."

"Of course. I'd forgotten. You never use your own money for anything, do you?"

"Not if I can help it." Gerald smiled complacently.

Given Lytham St. Anne's and the unusual name of le Carpentier, Directory Inquiries had no difficulty in producing Vee's mother's phone number. Charles put his finger down on the bar of Gerald's Trimphone and prepared to dial.

"Are you just going to ask her direct, Charles? Won't she think it's a bit odd?"

"I'm not going to ask her direct. I have a little plan worked out, which involves using another voice. Don't worry."

"But that's illegal," wailed Gerald as Charles dialed. "You can't make illegal calls on a solicitor's telephone."

Mrs. le Carpentier answered the phone with the promptness of a lonely old lady.

"Hello. Telephone Engineer." Charles was pleased with the voice. He had first used it in a stillborn experimental play called *Next Boat In* ("Captured all the bleakness and, I'm afraid, all the tedium of dockland" —*Lancashire Evening News*). He thought it was a nice touch to be Liverpudlian for Lytham St. Anne's.

"Oh, what can I do for you? I hope there's nothing wrong with the phone. I'm an old lady living on my own and—"

The Telephone Engineer cut in reassuringly over Mrs. le Carpentier's genteel tones. "No, nothing to worry about. Just checking something. We had a complaint—somebody reported that your phone was continually engaged when they tried to ring, so I just have to check that the apparatus was in fact in a state of usage during the relevant period."

"Ah, I wonder who it could have been. Do you know who reported the fault?"

"No, Madam."

"It could have been Winnie actually. She lives in Blundellsands. We play bridge quite often and it's possible she was trying to set up a four for—"

The Telephone Engineer decided he didn't want to hear all of Mrs. le Carpentier's social life. "Yes, Madam. I wonder if we could just check the relevant period. The fault was reported last Monday. Apparently someone tried to call three times between nine and half past in the evening. Was the apparatus being used at this time?"

So confident was he of a negative response that the reply threw him for a moment. "I beg your pardon, Madam?"

"Yes, it was in use."

"Oh. Oh." Still, it wasn't necessarily Vee to whom she was speaking. "Local calls, were they, Madam?"

"Oh no, it was just one call. Long distance."

"Where to? We have to check, Madam, when it's been reported."

"It was a call to Breckton. That's in Surrey. Near London."

Charles felt the concoction of logic he had compounded trickling away from him. "Are you absolutely confident that that was the time, Madam?"

"Absolutely. It was the time that that *I, Claudius* was on the television."

"Oh."

"Yes, you see, I saw it for the first time last week and I thought it was a shocking program. So much violence and immorality. My daughter had mentioned that she watched it, but after I'd seen what it was all about, I thought it was my duty as a mother to ring her up while it was on, so that she couldn't watch it. Do you see?"

"I see," Charles replied dully. Yes, he saw. He saw all his ideas suddenly discredited, he saw that he must flush every thought he'd ever had about the case out of his mind and start again with nothing.

Mrs. le Carpentier was still in righteous spate. "I think too many parents nowadays neglect their duties as their children's moral guardians. I mean, Victoria's over thirty, but she still needs looking after. She mixes with all kinds of theatrical people and—"

"Victoria?"

"My daughter."

"Good God."

"That's another thing I don't like in young people today—taking the name of the Lord in vain. It's—"

"Mrs. le Carpentier, thank you very much. You've been most helpful. I can confirm that there is nothing wrong with your apparatus."

"Oh good. And do you think maybe I should ring Winnie?"

"Yes, I would."

He slumped on to the sofa, not hearing Gerald's remonstrances about the illegality of impersonating people over the telephone and the number of laws under which this action could be charged and how the fact that the owner did not stop the crime might well make him an accessory.

It all flowed past Charles. The void which had been left in his mind by the confirmation of Vee's alibi had only been there for a few seconds before new thoughts started to flood in. He pieced them together into a rough outline and then spoke, shutting Gerald up with a gesture.

"Vee's real name is Victoria."

"So what? What about her alibi? Was she telling the truth?"

"Oh yes." Charles dismissed the subject.

"Well then, that seems to put the kybosh on the whole—"

"But don't you see—her real name is Victoria."

"Yes, but—"

"I should have guessed. The way all these amateur actors fiddle about with their names, it should have been obvious."

"I don't see that her name is important when—"

"It is important, Gerald, because it means that it was Vee whom Charlotte was going to see at one o'clock the day after she was murdered. During the school lunch hour. Charlotte couldn't stand all those affected stage names, so she would have called her Victoria as a matter of principle. And I bet that the reason she was going to see Vee was to tell her she was pregnant."

"So Vee didn't already know?"

"No."

"But surely that throws out all your motivation for her to have done the murder and—"

"She didn't do the murder. Forget Vee. She doesn't have anything to do with it."

"Then who did kill Charlotte?"

"Geoffrey Winter."

"But Geoffrey didn't have any motivation to kill her. He had a very good affair going, everything was okay."

"Except that Charlotte was pregnant."

"We don't even know that."

"I'll bet the police post mortem showed that she was. Go on, you can ask them when you're next speaking."

"All right, let's put that on one side for the moment and proceed with your wild theorizing." The lines of skepticism were once again playing around Gerald's mouth.

"Geoffrey and Vee Winter are a very close couple. In spite of his philandering, he is, as he told me, very loyal to her. Now all marriages are built up on certain myths and the myth which sustains Vee is that her childlessness is Geoffrey's fault. His infertility gives her power. She can tolerate his affairs, secure in the knowledge that he will come back to her every time. But if it were suddenly proved that in fact he could father a child, everything on which she had based their years together would be taken away from her. I think, under those circumstances, someone as highly-strung as she is could just crack up completely.

"Geoffrey knew how much it would mean to her, so when Charlotte told him she was pregnant, he had to keep that knowledge from his wife. No doubt his first reaction was to try to get her to have an abortion, but Charlotte, nice little Catholic girl that she was, would never have consented to that. Equally, being a conventional girl, she would want to have the whole thing open, she'd want to talk to his wife, even maybe see if Vee would be prepared to give Geoffrey up.

"So she rang Vee up and fixed to meet her on the Tuesday during her lunch hour. On the Monday she went up to Villiers Street for her assignation with Geoffrey and told him what she intended to do. He could not allow the confrontation of the two women to take place. He decided that Charlotte must never go and see Vee. So he killed her."

Charles leaned back with some satisfaction. The new theory felt much more solid than the old one. It left ~~less~~ details unaccounted for.
    FEWER

Gerald said exactly what Charles knew he would. "I'm impressed by the psychological reasoning, Charles, but there is one small snag. Geoffrey Winter had an alibi for the only time he could have murdered Charlotte. He was at home rehearsing his lines so loudly that his next door neighbor complained to the police. How do you get around that one?"

Gerald couldn't have set it up more perfectly for him if he had tried. "This is how he did it." Charles picked the cassette box up off the table.

"So easy. He even told me he used the cassette recorder for learning his lines. All he had to do was to record a full forty-five minutes of *The Winter's Tale* on to this cassette, put it on, slip out of the French windows of his study, go and commit the murder, come back, change from recording to his own voice and insure that he started ranting loudly enough to annoy his neighbor with whom his relationship was already dodgy. After previous disagreements about noise, he felt fairly confident that she would call the police, thus putting the final seal on his watertight alibi."

Gerald was drawn to this solution, but he was not wholly won over. "Hmm. It seems that one has to take some enormous imaginative leaps to work that out. I'd rather have a bit more evidence."

"We've got the cassette. And I've suddenly realized what it means. The words—it's Leontes."

"It's what?"

"Leontes in *The Winter's Tale*. One of the most famous lines in the play. When he speaks of Hermione's eyes, he says; 'Stars, stars! And all eyes else *dead coals*.' That's the bit we've got on the tape."

Gerald was silent. Then slowly, unwillingly, he admitted, "Do you know, you could be right."

"Of course I'm right," said Charles. "Now where's that lunch you were talking about?"

CHAPTER 16

CHARLES DIDN'T WANT to hurry things. He was now confident that he knew how Charlotte had been killed, and he could afford to take time to check it. There was no point in confronting Geoffrey Winter or going to the police with an incompletely researched solution.

He left Gerald late on the Saturday afternoon. (Gerald wanted to watch *Doctor Who* and Charles didn't really much.) They agreed that Charles should make various further investigations and then report back. Gerald was now more or less convinced by the new solution, but his legal caution remained.

Since there was nothing useful he could do that day, Charles went for the evening to one of his old haunts, the Montrose, a little drinking club round the back of the Haymarket. As he expected, it was full of out-of-work actors (and even, after the theatres finished, some in-work ones). A great deal of alcohol was consumed.

He woke feeling pretty ropey on the Sunday morning and did the tube and train journey to Breckton on automatic pilot. It was only when he emerged into the stark November sunlight outside the suburban station that consciousness began to return.

Blearily he reminded himself of the plan he had vaguely formed the day before. He had come down to Breckton to check the timing of the crime, to retrace the steps that Geoffrey Winter had taken on the Monday night and see if it was feasible for him to have killed Charlotte in the forty-five minutes the tape allowed.

Charles was early. Since he didn't want to run the risk of meeting any of the principals in the crime, he had decided to conduct his exploration after two-thirty when they would all be emoting over *The Winter's Tale* up at the Backstagers.

He arrived just after twelve, which was a remarkably convenient time for him to go into a pub and kill time and his hangover at one blow.

There was a dingy little Railway Tavern adjacent to the station which was ideal for his purposes. The railway line was at some distance from the posher residential side of Breckton and he was in no danger of meeting any of the Backstagers down there.

When he entered the pub, it was clear that the clientele came from "the other side of the railway," an expression of subtle snobbery that he had heard more than once from the theatrical circle. On the "other side of the railway" there was a council estate, yet another socio-geological stratum in the complex structure of Breckton. At the bottom was the bedrock of "the other side of the railway line," then the unstable mixture of rising lower middle and impoverished upper middle class "the other side of the main road" (where Geoffrey and Vee lived), then the rich clay of the newer detached executive houses like the Meckens' and finally the lush topsoil of extreme affluence which manifested itself in mock-Tudor piles like the Hobbses'. Across the strata ran the faults and fissures of class and educational snobbery as well, so that a full understanding of the society would be a lifetime's study.

Charles ordered a pint which made his brain blossom out of its dessication like a Japanese flower dropped in water.

Being a Sunday, there was nothing to eat in the pub except for a few cheese biscuits and cocktail onions on the bar, but Charles was quite happy to resign himself to a liquid lunch.

As he sat and drank, his mind returned to Charlotte's murder. Not in a depressed or panicky way, but with a kind of intellectual calm. He felt as he had sometimes done when writing a play, the comforting assurance that he'd sorted out a satisfactory plot outline and only needed to fill in the details.

And little details were slotting into his scenario of the death of

Charlotte Mecken. One was disturbing. He was beginning to think that Geoffrey might be on to his suspicions.

First, the interrogation in his office must have put him on his guard, if Charles's phone call on the evening of Hugo's arrest hadn't already done so. But there was something else. On the Friday night, when Geoffrey had discovered Charles in his sitting room, he had looked extremely suspicious. At the time, Charles had assumed that the suspicion had a sexual basis.

But, as he thought back over the circumstances, he found another interpretation. When Geoffrey arrived, the cassette player was running, reproducing Vee's performance of Wycherley's Mrs. Pinchwife. Geoffrey had entered speaking to Vee, as if he expected her to be in the room. Maybe the suspicion arose when he saw that he had been fooled by the sound of the cassette player, that in fact he had been caught by his own deception. If that were the case, then he might have thought that Charles was further advanced in his investigation than he was and that playing the tape of Vee had been a deliberate set-up to see how the supposed murderer would react.

It was quite a thought. Geoffrey was a cold-blooded killer and if he could dispose of his mistress without a qualm, he would have little hesitation in getting rid of anyone else who stood in his way. Charles would have to tread warily.

Because if Geoffrey Winter did try to kill him, he would do the job well. He was a meticulous planner. Charles thought of the set model for *The Caucasian Chalk Circle* in Geoffrey's study. Every move carefully considered. Little plastic people being manipulated, disposed (and disposed of) according to the director's will.

The thought of danger cast a chill over the conviviality of the pub and the glow of the fourth pint. Well, the solution was to get to the source of the danger as soon as possible, to prove Geoffrey's guilt and have him put away before he could make a hostile move.

The pub was closing. Charles went to the Gents with the uncomfortable feeling that the amount he had consumed and the cold weather were going to make him want to go again before too long.

* * *

It was after two-thirty when he reached the Winters' road. He walked along it at an even pace, apparently giving their house no deeper scrutiny than the others. Somehow he felt that the watchers of Breckton were still alert behind their net curtains on Sunday afternoons.

The Winters themselves had resisted the suburban uniform of net curtains, so from a casual glance he could feel pretty confident that they were out. But he did not start his timed walk from then. He felt sure there must be a route from the back of the house.

When he got to the end of the road, his hunch was proved right. The gardens of the row of identical semis (identical to everyone except their proud owners) backed on to the gardens of the parallel row in the next road. Between them ran a narrow passage flanked with back gates into minute gardens.

The alley was concreted over, its surface cracked and brown, marked with moss and weeds. Suburban secrecy insured that the end fencing of all the gardens was too high for anyone walking along the alley to see in (or, incidentally, to be seen).

As Charles walked along, he could hear sounds from the gardens. The scrape of a trowel, a snatch of conversation, the sudden wail of a child, very close the snuffling bark of a dog. But except for the occasional flash of movement through the slats of fencing, he saw no one.

And this was in the middle of Sunday afternoon. After dark one could feel absolutely secure in passing unseen along the alley. And Geoffrey Winter must have known that.

When he reached the Winters' garden gate, he pressed close to the fence and squinted through a chink. He could see the distinctive wall-coloring of Geoffrey's study and, outside it, the little balcony and staircase, so convenient for anyone who wanted to leave the room unnoticed after dark.

As anticipated, the pressure on his bladder was becoming uncomfortable and he stopped to relieve himself where he stood. He was again struck by the secluded nature of the alley, which enabled him to behave impolitely in such a polite setting.

* * *

Then he started his timed walk. He reckoned Geoffrey must have allowed a maximum of forty minutes. *I, Claudius* lasted fifty, but he could only get forty-five minutes of *The Winter's Tale* on one side of the tape. Five minutes would be a buffer to allow for the unexpected.

Charles set off at a brisk walk. If Geoffrey had run, the timing would have been different, but Charles thought that was unlikely. A man running after dark attracts attention, while a man walking passes unnoticed.

The alley behind the houses came out on to the main road exactly opposite the footpath up to the common. There was a "No Cycling" notice at the entrance. The path was paved until it opened out onto the common.

It was the first time Charles had seen this open expanse in daylight. In the center were a couple of football pitches, which were reasonably well maintained, but the fringes of the common were ill-tended and untidy and had been used as a dumping ground by the nice people of Breckton. Superannuated fridges and rusty buckets looked almost dignified beside the more modern detritus of garish plastic and shredded polythene. It was an eyesore, the sort of mess about which aggrieved ratepayers no doubt wrote righteous letters to the local paper. To Charles it seemed a necessary part of the suburban scene, the secret vice which made the outward rectitude supportable.

The half-burnt crater of the bonfire doused by the fire brigade at sour Reggie's behest gave the dumping ground an even untidier and more melancholy appearance.

The bonfire had been built where the footpath divided into two. The right-hand fork went up towards the Backstagers' club-rooms and the Hobbses' house. Charles took the other path which led towards the Meckens'.

He was feeling the need for another pee, but resolutely hung on, because any unscheduled stop would ruin his timing. He wished he had got a stopwatch, so that he could suspend time long enough to make himself comfortable. But he hadn't.

Even on a Sunday afternoon there were not many people up on the common. A few bored fathers trying to feign interest in their toddlers, one or two pensioners pretending they had somewhere to go. Breckton boasted other, more attractive parklands, equipped with such delights as swings and duck-ponds, and most of the inhabitants were there for their exercise.

It had rained during the week, but the path had dried out and was firm underfoot as Charles continued his brisk stroll. When he got to the other side of the common, the footpath once again had a proper surface of dark tarmac. His desert boot soles sounded dully as he trod.

To maintain his excitement he made a point of not looking at his watch until the journey was complete. He didn't stop when he got to Hugo's house. His memories of the new curtain snooper made him unwilling to draw attention to himself.

When he had gone one house-length beyond (which he reckoned would allow for going over the gravel drive to the front door), he looked at his watch.

Sixteen minutes. Geoffrey, with his longer stride, might have done it in fifteen. Say the same time each way. That gave eight to ten minutes in the house. Charlotte would have recognized him and let him in immediately, so there would have been no delay.

And eight or ten minutes was plenty of time for a determined man to strangle a woman.

If, of course, the murder weapon was to hand. On that kind of schedule, Geoffrey couldn't afford time to look for a scarf. He must have known where it was or . . . no, there was something missing there.

Charles tried to focus his mind on the problem. He summoned up the image of Charlotte in the coal shed, surprised untidily by the torch beam. He remembered her face. The red hair that framed it had looked unnatural, as if it were dyed, against the horrible greyness of her flesh. And that thin knotted Indian print scarf which couldn't hide the trickle of dried blood and the purply-brown bruises on her neck. Bruises almost like love-bites. He remembered what he had thought at the time, how she had looked so young, embarrassingly unsophisticated, like a teenager with a scarf inadequately hiding the evidence of a heavy petting session.

Good God—maybe that's what it had been. After all, she had seen Geoffrey at lunchtime. By then he must have planned the murder. It would be typical of the man's mind if he had deliberately marked her neck, knowing that, respectable married woman that she was, she would be bound to put on a scarf to cover the bruising.

Then Geoffrey could go round in the evening, confident that the murder weapon would be to hand. Under the circumstances, he did not have to leave long for the strangling.

Charles shivered as he thought of the cold-bloodedness with which the crime had been planned.

He felt like an athlete in training for a major event. Everything was moving towards a confrontation with Geoffrey Winter. It was going to be risky to confront the villain with what he had deduced, but he couldn't see any way round it. The evidence he had was minimal and certainly not enough to persuade the police to change their tack. So his only hope was to elicit some admission of guilt from Geoffrey.

The fear of the man was building inside Charles. He felt increasingly certain that Geoffrey had read his suspicions and he wanted to keep the advantage by going to see his adversary rather than waiting for his adversary to search him out.

Within the next twenty-four hours, Charles knew, something conclusive was going to happen.

He went back to Hereford Road on the Sunday evening and rang Sally Radford. He had the sensation of a condemned man deserving a final treat.

But he didn't get his treat. Sally was glad to hear from him, but, sorry, she'd got a friend coming round that evening. Yes, maybe another time.

It shouldn't have hurt him. They'd agreed no strings, but it did cause a pang. The idea of a completely casual encounter with no obligations had always appealed to him, but now it had happened he was full of the need to establish continuity, to keep it going, to make something of it.

When he'd rung off from Sally, he contemplated ringing Frances, but procrastinated once again. He wrote off the idea of female company for the evening and went back to the Montrose. If he could keep on topping up his alcohol level, he might retain his mood of confidence and face the ordeal ahead without too much introspection.

CHAPTER 17

IN SPITE OF the knowledge of inevitable confrontation, Charles still had a career to pursue. Whatever the outcome of his meeting with Geoffrey Winter, he was still meant to be recording the second batch of Bland radio commercials on the Tuesday morning. The events of the week had pushed that from his mind.

It was only when he thought about it on the Monday morning that he realized he had better check the details. After all, it was Hugo Mecken's campaign and Hugo would not be able to conduct it from the remand wing of Brixton Prison.

He rang through to Mills Brown Mazzini and asked for Ian Compton. It turned out to be the right choice. Ian told him with no little complacency that he had taken over the Bland account. Charles wondered how much more of Hugo's authority the young wheeler-dealer had managed to annex since the Creative Director had been off the scene.

"I was just ringing to check that tomorrow's still on as per arrangement. Eleven o'clock at the same studio for the rest of the radios."

"Yes, I should think that'll stand, though there's a slight question mark over it. May need some time for reworking of the copy. I'm having a meeting with Farrow this afternoon. Won't really know for sure till after that. Can I ring you in the morning?"

"Not quite sure of my movements."

"You should be. Got to always be on call in the voice-over business."

Charles ignored the young man's patronizing tone. "I'll ring you. Either at the office in the morning or—have you a home number where I can get you this evening?"

"Won't be in. Got a film dubbing session at Spectrum Studios."

"For the Bland campaign?" Charles pricked up his ears. Was Ian Compton getting some other voice-over work done on Bland behind his back?

"No, no. It's a private film production I'm working on. Doing a session with Diccon, just dubbing the voice."

"Oh, I see." It was hard to know whether to believe it or not. Ian Compton wouldn't hesitate to lie if it served his ends. On the other hand, he did work on a lot of other projects apart from Bland. "How is Diccon?"

"Oh, he's in a pretty lousy mood at the moment."

"What, not getting work?"

"You must be joking. That cookie is one of the busiest voices in the business. Clears twenty grand a year easy. No, he seems very cut up about Hugo's wife. I think he had quite a thing for her."

"She was a very nice lady."

"So I hear. It seems everyone thought so except Hugo." Ian did not attempt to disguise the note of triumph in his voice. He was giving a reminder that Hugo Mecken was no longer a challenge to the bright young whiz-kid of Mills Brown Mazzini.

Charles decided that the confrontation should take place in Geoffrey's office. It would be quiet, no danger of interruptions. He told Gerald what he was going to do. Gerald disapproved, but Charles wanted someone to know in case he didn't return from the interview.

It was about a quarter to eleven on the Monday morning when he entered the building in Villiers Street. He mounted the stairs with one part of his mind immobilized by fright and the other irreverently providing sound track music and offering Sydney Carton's dramatic lines for use when mounting scaffolds to the sneers of unruly mobs.

All of which build-up was somewhat wasted when he found the door of Geoffrey Winter Associates firmly locked.

There was no light on inside. His mind, still running on romantic rails, summoned up the image of Geoffrey Winter sprawled over his desk, the smoking revolver clutched in his hand, his brains spattered on the wall behind. The villain who knew he had been found out and who had done the decent thing.

Wisely recognizing that this image was a little fanciful, he started knocking on the door to attract attention. A light tap produced nothing from inside, so he tried a more robust blow and then heavy hammering.

The last did raise a reaction, but it came from the floor below. An aggrieved young man with elastic bands holding up his shirt sleeves came and complained. So far as he knew, Mr. Winter wasn't in. He hadn't heard him coming up the stairs that morning. And surely the fact that there had been no reply to "that bloody awful din you're making" indicated that there was nobody in the office.

Charles apologized and left the building. But he was too keyed up to drop it there. He had steeled himself to a meeting with Geoffrey Winter that day and somehow he had to arrange it.

He went into Charing Cross Station and rang the Winters' number from a call-box.

Vee answered. That in itself was strange. If she was a teacher, she should surely be in class at that time. Also she sounded even tenser and more emotional than usual. She had snatched up the phone on the first ring.

"Could I speak to Geoffrey, please? It's Charles Paris."

"No, I'm sorry, he's not here." She sounded near to tears.

"Do you know when he's likely to be back? I've been to his office and I couldn't find him there."

"No, I've no idea. He's . . ." She stopped, leaving the word dramatically in the air. Charles was conscious of her acting instincts vying with genuine emotion.

"Is he likely to be in this evening? Do you know?"

"No. I don't. I—" Again she cut short, uncertain whether to confide more. Charles felt a new panic. Had Geoffrey done a bunk?

But Vee could not keep her secrets to herself. In the same way that she had confided Geoffrey's supposed infertility to Charles, she couldn't resist the dramatic and martyring implications of her latest piece of news. "Oh, what the hell. I might as well tell you. The whole country will no doubt know soon enough. Geoffrey's been arrested."

"Arrested?"

"Yes, the police came round this morning before he left for work."

Charles murmured some suitable words about how sorry he was and how sure he was that it would soon all be cleared up and how it must all be a ghastly mistake, but he had stopped thinking what he was saying. He concluded the conversation and then walked slowly, numbly, down to the Embankment.

He looked into the murky, swirling Thames. He tried to tell himself all kinds of other things, but ultimately he couldn't deny that he felt profoundly disappointed.

So that was it. The police must have been following his investigations in exact parallel. They must have worked out in just the same way how Geoffrey had contrived his alibi and managed to leave his room for the vital forty minutes.

Or no, perhaps he was flattering himself. The police had probably far outstripped his feeble investigations. They must have done. They wouldn't make an arrest without convincing evidence. He felt diminished and unnecessary.

He tried to argue himself out of this selfish mood. After all, what did it matter who had found the truth, so long as it had been revealed? Hugo could now go free, that was the main thing.

It didn't help. Depressingly he thought how little Hugo cared whether he was free or not. The release might well be a license for him to commit suicide or, more slowly, drink himself to death.

Still, right had triumphed. He tried to feel glad about it.

With an effort he drew himself away from the river and started back to the station. Better ring Gerald and bring him up to date. Though if charges against his client were about to be dropped, he'd probably know already.

He didn't. He reacted strongly when Charles told him. But the reaction was not that of Gerald Venables the amateur sleuth; it was all solicitor. This new development changed circumstances for his client. He would get on to the Breckton police immediately.

"Okay," said Charles dismally. "Well, I'm going back to Hereford Road. So if there's any interesting development, just let me know."

But he didn't really think any new development would concern him. He felt excluded, the one boy in the class without a party invitation.

He bought a new bottle of Bell's on the way back to Hereford Road. He was going to drink himself into a stupor. After the tension of the last week, this sudden anti-climax had let him down like a punctured air-bed.

The phone was ringing when he entered the house. He ran up to the landing and picked it up.

It was Gerald. Very cross. "Are you trying to make me look like a complete fool? I've just spoken to the Superintendent at Breckton. He must think I'm a bloody lunatic. And you're not the most popular person down at the station either.

"Geoffrey Winter has been arrested, yes. But it has nothing to do with the Mecken murder at all. He's been arrested for stealing some jewelry from a couple called Hobbs."

"Oh my God." Charles saw the bottom card being withdrawn from the great edifice he had built up.

"So you were right, Charles. Geoffrey Winter did have something to hide about what he was doing last Monday night. But it wasn't what your fertile imagination gave him to do."

"But—"

"And what's more—just for your information—I've heard about the post mortem. Charlotte Mecken was not pregnant."

CHAPTER 18

LIKE THE CAT in a Tom and Jerry cartoon, Charles Paris continued running after the ground had crumbled away beneath his feet, before the inevitable realization and the windmill-armed plummeting descent to the depths.

Geoffrey Winter must be guilty of Charlotte's murder. All the motivation fitted; Charles couldn't start again the laborious reconstruction of emotion and opportunity with another subject. He refused to accept it.

But like the cat, he became increasingly aware that he was running on air. Whichever way he worked it, Geoffrey could not have committed both crimes on the Monday evening.

Unwilling to relinquish his theory, Charles went down to Breckton to time it all out again. He felt none of the elation of the previous day; as time passed he saw his logic falling apart.

He tried the trip from the Winters' house to the Meckens' via the Hobbses', he tried it the other way round, going to the Meckens' first, but there was just not enough time for anyone to have committed the two crimes.

Visiting the two houses added another five minutes to the round trip. Which left five or less for murder. Which was cutting it fine by the standards of the most experienced assassin. He tried adding the extra five minutes which he had reckoned Geoffrey would have left as a safety margin, but the sums still seemed pretty unlikely.

They seemed even unlikelier when he remembered that he had

not allowed any time for the actual theft from the Hobbses' house. He had only timed the round trip of going past the house. If that were all that had been involved, the murder might have been possible. But even if Geoffrey knew the house well and knew exactly where Mary Hobbs kept her jewelry, it was still going to take him some time to break in, get through the house in the dark armed only with a torch and grab the loot. The absolute minimum was four minutes. In fact, considering the care with which Geoffrey had covered his tracks, it must have been six or eight.

Which left very little time to murder Charlotte Mecken.

Charles sat down on a bench on the common as it started to get dark. He was furious. There was no way it would work.

It wasn't just the timing. If Charlotte hadn't been pregnant, then none of his complex sequence of motivation worked either.

Depression took over. So everything was as obvious as it seemed. Hugo Mecken had killed his wife and Geoffrey Winter, in desperate financial straits because of his failing architect's business, had stolen some jewelry from the richest people he knew. The fact that the two incidents had taken place on the same evening had been mere coincidence.

The new turn of events changed his opinion of Geoffrey. While he had thought of the architect as Charlotte's murderer, he had had a kind of respect for him, for the cold-blooded intellect that could plan such a crime. But now he knew that all that planning had been for a petty theft, a mean robbery from some supposed friends.

And Geoffrey's was not a great intellect. He had shown remarkable ineptitude in the execution of his crime, however clever the original conception of the cassette alibi. For a start, there had been his confused exit from the Hobbses' house when he saw Robert Chubb pass. Leaving his torch behind on the window sill was the real mark of the amateur.

The way he had been caught had been equally incompetent. Charles had heard it all from Gerald. The thief had gone along the jewelers' stands in the Portobello Road on the Saturday morning trying to sell his loot. One of the dealers had bought some and then, becoming suspicious, alerted the police. From a description and from some remarks Geoffrey had carelessly let slip to the stall-holder, they had had little difficulty in tracking the culprit down.

So Geoffrey was relegated to the status of a shabby sneak-thief and Charles had either to concede that Hugo had killed Charlotte or start investigating somebody else.

The only two people left who seemed to have had any emotional relationship with Charlotte were Clive Steele and Diccon Hudson. Clive was supposed to have been in Melton Mowbray auditing at the time of the murder and no doubt Diccon would have some equally solid alibi. Still, wearily Charles supposed he must try to get interested again and check their movements. But the spark had gone. Any further investigation was going to be just a chore.

Since he was down in Breckton, he might as well start with Clive Steele at the Backstagers. The Back Room opened at six. Just sit a little longer on the common to kill time.

"Evening, sir. A bit dark to be out here, wouldn't you think?"

He looked up to see the outline of the same policeman who had found him inside the Meckens' house the previous week.

"Yes, I suppose it is dark." While he had been wrapped up in his thoughts, it had changed from dusk to blackness.

"You intending to sit there all night?"

"No, I wasn't. I was just going."

The policeman held his ground and watched Charles out of sight along the footpath towards the Backstagers. He obviously thought he was watching a potential rapist or, at the very least, a flasher.

Charles decided that, considering how low his stock stood with the Breckton police, any alternative murder solution he took to them was going to have to be backed up by absolutely incontrovertible evidence.

There was no sign of Clive Steele in the Back Room, nor of anyone else Charles knew until Denis Hobbs came in at about half-past six.

He was his usual boisterous self, though there was a slight strain beneath the bonhomie.

He had come in for a quick one on his way home from work. Charles wondered if he needed his regular drink to fortify him to face the redoubtable Mary.

They got talking naturally and Charles bought drinks. Denis had a pint, Charles a large Bell's. After some social chit-chat, Charles said, "So you've got your man."

Denis recoiled. "What do you mean?"

"Your burglar."

The builder's eyes narrowed. "What do you know about it?"

"I know who's been arrested."

Denis Hobbs looked at him steadily for a moment and then downed the remaining half of his beer. "We can't talk here. Come round to my place for a drink."

Inside, the Hobbses' house was, decoratively, exactly what the mock-Tudor exterior with its brash stone lions would lead one to expect. The tone was set before you entered. A china plaque by the doorbell showed a little girl in a crinoline and a boy in a tasselled cap leaning forward to kiss over the legend "Denis and Mary live here."

It must have been Mary's taste. The same eyes which had chosen her turquoise trouser suit and rainbow-colored lamé slippers had certainly picked the jungle wallpaper. And the Raspberry Ripple carpet. And the green leather three-piece suite. And the miniature cluster of swords and axes tastefully set behind a red shield on the wall. And the three-foot-high china pony pulling a barrel. And the wrought iron drinks trolley with the frosted glass top and gold wheels. Denis was content to let her make decisions about such things. After all, she was the artistic one.

It was to the drinks trolley Denis went first. He poured a pink gin for his wife, a Scotch for Charles and got out a can of beer for himself. When he had poured it into his glass, he crushed the can in his huge paw. The metal flattened like tinfoil.

Mary's greeting to Charles was distinctly frosty. She had not forgotten his reservations about her Madame Arkadina.

But Denis cut through the atmosphere by saying, "He knows."

"What?"

"About the burglary."

"Oh." Mary looked downcast, as if rehearsing for a tragedy.

"How did you find out?" asked Denis.

"I spoke to Vee on the phone this morning. She told me."

"Damn. I hope she's not telling everyone."

"Why? What does it matter? Presumably everyone'll know when it comes up in court."

"If it does come up in court. I'm trying to see that it doesn't."

"I wouldn't have thought you stood much chance. I mean, if the police picked him up, they're going to bring charges."

"I don't know. I'm going to ask them not to proceed. I'm going to stand bail for him and try to keep it as quiet as possible."

"But why? I mean, there's no question as to whether he did it or not."

"No, he's admitted it."

"Then why shouldn't he pay the price of his actions?"

"Well, he's . . ." Denis was having difficulty in framing his thoughts (or his wife's thoughts) into words. "He's a friend."

Mary took over. "It's terribly embarrassing. I mean, he's been in and out of our house so often. This place becomes a sort of Backstagers' annex when the Back Room closes—particularly when we've got a show on. Geoffrey's a very close friend."

"I can see it's embarrassing, but the fact remains that he has stolen your property."

"Yes, but people are so materialistic, Mr. Parrish. What's a bit of jewelry?" Mary sat surrounded by the fruits of middle class affluence as she posed this ingenuous query.

"The thing is," Denis contributed, "we didn't realize the financial state he was in. We could have helped, lent him some money or something, not driven him to this."

"Hardly driven. He did it of his own free will, presumably to get himself out of a spot." Charles was bewildered by their reactions. Instead of being affronted and disgusted by Geoffrey's betrayal of their friendship, they were trying to justify his actions.

Mary gave Charles the patronizing smile of sainthood. "It may be difficult for you to understand, but we feel an enormous loyalty to Geoffrey. He is a wonderfully talented person and we just didn't understand the terrible time he had been going through. To steal from us was a terrible lapse, which I'm sure he's regretted bitterly, but it's only an expression of the dark side of his impulsive artistic temperament."

Now Charles had heard it all. That old fallacy about artists being answerable to a different code of morality from the rest of society. It was a view he had never subscribed to in the cases of the extremely talented writers and actors of his acquaintance who had tried it on, but for it to be used in the context of a moderately talented amateur was ridiculous.

Denis Hobbs nodded as his wife continued to expound her views. Charles was saddened by the sight of a man so emasculated by marriage. He wanted to get Denis on his own again and find out what the man really thought, not just hear him echoing Mary's opinions.

"You see, Mr. Parrish," she continued, "it's often difficult to explain to people that we don't just believe in materialistic values, that we have an appreciation of art—the theatre, poetry, painting." She gestured vaguely in the direction of a Hawaiian sunset scene luminously painted on black velvet.

"We've been lucky, we've made a lot of money . . ." Charles thought it was magnanimous of her to include Denis in this statement. She spoke of money as if it were an unfortunate skin condition. He was surprised Denis didn't get up and knock her block off. But her husband's brainwashing had been completed too long ago for him even to notice the slight.

"So what we feel is, Mr. Parrish, that it's our duty—being of limited artistic talent ourselves—" She simpered in expectation of some complimentary remonstrance, but then remembered Charles's expressed view of her acting abilities and moved hurriedly on. "—to share some of our good fortune with more artistic people. That's why we make this room a second Back Room and provide lots of drinks and things . . ." (She couldn't resist quantifying their altruistic generosity.) ". . . so that we can do our bit for the spread of cultural ideas, stimulate lively conversation, discussion of the arts and so forth."

Charles began to understand her cock-eyed reasoning. Mary Hobbs saw herself as the leader of an artistic salon, the Madame de Staël of Breckton. Geoffrey Winter's crime was just the errant behavior of one of the young geniuses she was nurturing. In fact, it was a challenge to her values, an opportunity for her to show how far above material considerations she was.

He wondered to what extent Geoffrey had anticipated this reaction. If he had known that the theft, if it ever came out, rather than ruining him socially, might increase his stock among the Backstagers and build up his mildly roué image as a man above conventional morality, then it was not such a risk as it might have appeared.

"Oh dear." Mary Hobbs gave a tragedienne's sigh. "I wonder if the police will be persuaded to drop the charges against him."

This abstraction seemed to be directed at Denis. "I don't know, dear. I doubt it. But perhaps Willy will be able to get him off lightly. Our solicitor's looking after Geoffrey," he explained for Charles's benefit.

Good God. The man broke into their house and stole their property and there they were leaning over backwards to defend him. "What'll happen, Denis? Will he be up before Breckton magistrates in the morning?"

"Yes. My solicitor's going to ask for bail. We'll be going down to give moral support. We've got to get him free as soon as possible."

Mary agreed. "Otherwise it's going to interfere dreadfully with *Winter's Tale* rehearsals."

Charles kept having to remind himself that these people were real when they came up with remarks like that. "And then straight on as before . . . Geoffrey rehearsing, no mention of the theft, coming back here for drinks after the Back Room closes . . ."

"And why not? Geoffrey's a friend." Mary's constant repetition of this was like a child's assertion that someone is "my best friend." In children it is always symptomatic of insecurity and only heard from those who have difficulty in making real friends. And in adults too.

Charles found something infinitely pathetic about the Hobbs trying to buy friendship with a constant supply of free drinks and afraid to lose a friend even when he abused their trust so disgracefully.

Denis seemed to think Mary's view of Geoffrey needed endorsement. "Oh, he's a very lively bloke, Geoffrey. I don't suppose you've ever seen him in full flood. Life and soul of the party. Always full of ideas for games and what-have-you. What was that thing he started here after the first night of *The Seagull*, love?"

Mary Hobbs giggled with the memory. "Oh yes, it was a great game. One of you goes out of the room and dresses up and then when they come back in, you all have to ask questions to find out who they're meant to be. You know, you can be politicians or show biz people—or members of the Backstagers, if you like." She laughed again, a comfortable "in" laugh. Her Backstagers' identity was a vital support to her life. "Do you remember, I pretended to be Reggie, the secretary?"

Denis guffawed at the recollection.

"Actually he wasn't very pleased, was he, Den?"

"No, can't take a joke, our Reggie."

"Did Geoffrey himself have to go?" asked Charles.

"Oh yes. He was a riot. He did Margaret Thatcher. He found a wig of mine and a smart overcoat and . . . oh, it was hysterical. He'd got the voice just right, hadn't he, Den?"

Denis agreed on cue. "He was great. Oh, it was a great party, that. Charlotte—she looked really lovely that evening—wore this long check sort of smock thing."

"Yes, well, she's dead," snapped Mary with unnecessary brutality. Denis recoiled as if struck. Mary hastened to paper over the rift. "Oh, it was a marvellous night. We had so much fun. Of course, Charlotte spent most of the evening with young Clive Steele."

This seemed to be put in as another rebuff to her husband. His attraction to Charlotte must have been the subject of some marital tiff. She went on. "Such a clever boy, Clive. And so good-looking. You know, I think he had rather fallen for Charlotte. He certainly seems very cut up about her death."

"I suppose he's only just heard," said Charles.

"What do you mean?"

"Well, he was away working all last week in Melton Mowbray, wasn't he?"

"Oh, no, apparently that was called off. No, Clive was here all last week."

CHAPTER 19

THIS TIME CLIVE Steele was at the Back Room bar when Charles went in. The young man greeted him patronizingly and graciously accepted the offer of a drink. "Don't know why I bothered to turn up this evening. I get here to find the rehearsal's off."

"Oh."

"Yes, we were meant to be doing all the Florizel/Perdita scenes tonight. But Vee Winter's cried off. Apparently not well."

Or too upset over her husband's arrest to face anyone, Charles reflected. "You're playing Florizel?"

"Yes. Terribly drippy part. But I suppose I really am too young for Leontes," he conceded as if youth were the only possible bar to his being given the lead. "Still, it's parts like Florizel that need real acting. It takes a bit of talent to make something of that kind of weed, so I suppose it's quite a challenge."

Charles saw a chance to move the conversation his way. "So, but for recent events, it would have been another Clive Steele/Charlotte Mecken partnership. Florizel and Perdita."

"Yes." Clive looked shaken, childishly near to tears. "Oh my God, it was terrible. For her to die—Charlotte who had so much to give—for her just to be strangled by that drunken brute."

"Hugo?"

"Of course Hugo. You know why it was . . . ?" Clive leaned across to Charles confidingly. "Hugo was jealous."

"Oh yes. Of whom?"

"Of me."

"You?"

"Yes. It's no secret that Charlotte and I got pretty close over *The Seagull*. There was a very strong mutual attraction. I think Hugo must have realized and killed her in a fit of jealousy."

Charles was almost amused by the young man's arrogant assurance. "Are you saying you were having an affair with Charlotte?"

"Ssh," Clive hissed loudly and waved his hand in a rubbing-out movement. "Don't say a word about it here." His dramatic behavior must have drawn the attention of everyone in the bar. Fortunately, for a moment there was no one there.

"Well, were you?"

"Not exactly. I mean, nothing had actually happened. You know, she had a few scruples and I didn't want to rush things, but it was inevitable the way it would go. Only a matter of time."

This seemed very much at odds with the state of the relationship which Charles had gathered from the conversation he overheard in the car park. He had surmised from that that Clive had misinterpreted Charlotte's natural niceness as a come-on and that she was disillusioning him in no uncertain terms. But Clive seemed to have forgotten that encounter and retained his belief in his irresistible magnetism for her. Maybe, now she was dead, he found that a reassuring fiction to cling to. It flattered his ego and gave him an opportunity to feel tragic.

He was certainly putting on a performance of feeling tragic. "And now she's dead—it's awful. She was so young, so ripe for loving. I think love is for the young and beautiful." This was clearly a category in which he would include himself. "I mean, it was disgusting, the idea of Charlotte being groped by an old man. Someone like Hugo."

Charles didn't rise to the implied insult. He was a great believer in letting people ramble on when they were in spate. It was a much easier method than interrogation and often quite as informative.

"Or Denis Hobbs," Clive continued.

"Denis? Did he grope Charlotte?"

"Well, he was always putting his arm around her, you know, casually, like it didn't mean anything, but I got the feeling he was enjoying handling the goods."

"There was one night I remember—Wednesday before last it was, first night of *The Seagull*—we all went round to the Hobbses' place. I think Denis must have been a bit pissed, but he certainly seemed to be after Charlotte."

"Oh."

"We'd all decided we wanted to play silly games and Denis kept saying we ought to play Postman's Knock (which I should think is about his level), because that meant kissing people—and he made a sort of grab at Charlotte to demonstrate."

"But you didn't play Postman's Knock?" Charles fed gently.

"No, we played a much better game that Geoff Winter knew. Dressing up sort of thing. But Denis didn't give up. I went upstairs with Geoff to sort out some dressing-up clothes and then I came down while he was changing—actually he got himself up as Margaret Thatcher, he was bloody marvellous—anyway, when I got down, there was Denis with his arm round Charlotte. He was pretending it was all casual again and she was sort of joking, but I don't think she really liked it. And I'm damned sure Mary Hobbs didn't like it. She came out into the hall at that moment and you should have seen the look she gave Denis."

"When did you last see Charlotte?"

"After the cast party."

"That was the last time? You didn't talk to her again or anything?"

"Well, actually I did. I rang her on the Monday afternoon."

"The day she died."

"Yes." Clive seemed poised to launch into another self-dramatizing lament, but fortunately didn't. "I was trying to fix to meet her that evening. The fact is, we hadn't parted on the best of terms after the cast party . . ."

Ah, now the truth, thought Charles.

"Silly thing, really," Clive continued. "She was talking about leaving Hugo for me and I was saying no, it was too soon, we should let things ride for a bit . . . you know, the sort of disagreement you get between two people in love."

Charles couldn't believe it. Clive's self-esteem was so great that he actually seemed to have convinced himself that he was talking the truth. Charles was glad that he had heard the real encounter between the two; otherwise he might have found himself taking Clive seriously.

The young man rambled on mournfully. "So I wanted to meet for a drink, you know, to chat, sort it all out. But she said she couldn't, so I got a bit pissed off and went to the flicks with an old girlfriend."

"Did Charlotte say why she couldn't meet you?"

"She said someone was coming round."

"She didn't say who?"

"Some friend from drama school."

Charles took a taxi from Waterloo to Spectrum Studios in Wardour Street. He told the uninterested commissionaire that he wanted to see Diccon Hudson and was directed to the dubbing theatre.

The red light outside was off to indicate that they weren't recording at that moment, so he went on through the double door. It was a large room, walls covered with newish upholstered sound-proofing. At one end was a screen above a television which displayed a film footage count. On a dais at the other end was the dubbing mixer's control panel. On a low chair in front of this Ian Compton lolled.

He looked quizzically as Charles entered. Some explanation of his presence was called for.

Charles hadn't really thought of one and busked. "I was in the area and I thought I'd just drop in to find out about tomorrow's session. Save the phone call."

Ian Compton looked skeptical and Charles realized it did sound pretty daft. But no comment was made. "No, in fact tomorrow's off, Charles. Farrow's not happy with the radio copy and I'm afraid it's all got to be rewritten. Take a few days. I should think we'd be in touch by the end of the week."

"Fine."

"And don't worry, you were booked for the session, so you'll get paid."

"Oh thanks." Charles's instinct was to say, "Don't bother about that," but he bit it back. He must develop more commercial sense.

Ian Compton looked at him with an expression that signified the conversation was over.

"Actually, I wanted to have a word with Diccon too."

A raised eyebrow. "Really?"

"Yes."

"Well, we're just about to start doing a few more loops. Then we'll break in about half an hour when we've got to set up a new machine."

"May I wait?"

Ian Compton shrugged permission.

The film that was being dubbed appeared to be about a young bronzed man fishing for octopus on a Greek island. Charles need not have worried about Bland work being done behind his back.

Diccon Hudson was working at a table in a box of screens. He wore headphones. The film was cut down into loops of about thirty or forty-five second durations. On each loop a chinagraph pencil line had been scored diagonally, so that it moved across the screen when the film was run. When it reached the right hand side, it was Diccon's cue to speak, adding his voice to the Music and Effects track.

He worked smoothly and quickly. He needed only one run of each loop and timed the words perfectly each time. A master of all forms of voice work.

When they had to break, Ian Compton went out to the control room, where the new machine was being set up. Charles went into the box of screens. Diccon Hudson looked up nervously. "To what do I owe this pleasure? Coming to get some tips on voice technique?"

"No."

"On dubbing? The great con-trick. Wonderful the things you can perpetrate in dubbing. That bloke on the screen, the diver who does all the talking, is Greek. Talks English like a broken-winded turkey. But by the wonders of dubbing, he can speak with my golden cadences. It's magic. He does his talking at one time, I add my voice at another and in the cinema, so far as the audience is concerned, it all happened at the same time." He had taken this flight of fancy as far as it would go and paused anxiously. "But you didn't come here to talk to me about dubbing."

Charles shook his head slowly. "No, I've come to talk about Charlotte Mecken."

Diccon colored at the name. "Oh yes, what about her?"

"When we last met, you said you used to see her from time to time. The odd lunch."

"So?"

"I've come along to ask if you saw her a week ago today. Last Monday."

It was a shock. Diccon gaped for a moment before replying. "No, of course I didn't. Why should I? What are you insinuating?"

"I'm not insinuating anything. I'm just asking you what you were doing last Monday."

"I was out."

"Out where?"

Diccon hesitated. "Out with friends."

"Friends who I could check with?"

"No, I . . ." He tailed off in confusion.

"Did you speak to Charlotte that day?"

"On the phone, yes. When I got back to my flat after an afternoon session, there was a message on the Ansafone for me to ring her."

"Someone else she spoke to that afternoon was told that she had a friend from drama school coming down in the evening."

"She wanted me to go down and see her, but I couldn't."

"You went out with friends instead."

"Yes. What are you suggesting—that I strangled her?"

Charles shrugged. "Well, I don't think Hugo did."

"I didn't. I swear I didn't go down there. I went out."

"But you won't tell me where."

Diccon hesitated and seemed on the verge of saying something. But then, "No."

"But you did speak to her?"

"I've told you, yes. She wanted my advice."

"On what?"

"She wanted to know if I knew the name of an abortionist."

This time it was Charles who was put off his stroke for a moment. "But she wasn't pregnant. The police post mortem showed that."

"Well, she thought she was. And she said she'd decided she couldn't keep the baby."

"Why not?"

"I don't know. Presumably because Hugo didn't want children."

"You think it was Hugo's?"

"Why not?"

"Not yours?"

"What?" His surprise seemed genuine. "Good God, no, I never scored with Charlotte, I'm afraid. Though I tried a few times."

"Then why did she ask you about the abortionist?"

"I don't know. I suppose I was the only person she knew who might have that sort of information. I have been around with quite a few women, you know," he added with a touch of self-assertive bravado.

It had the ring of truth. If Charlotte had wanted to get rid of a baby, in her naîveté, she wouldn't have known where to begin. She could only ask a friend. Why not Sally Radford? Perhaps Charlotte knew of the girl's emotional reaction to her own abortion and didn't want to upset her by asking.

As to the pregnancy, that must have been a phantom, some freak of Charlotte's cycle, probably a side-effect of going on the Pill.

But if what Diccon had said was true, why was he being so evasive about the night of the murder? "I'd like to believe you, Diccon, but I'd feel happier with an alibi I could check. Where were you at the time Charlotte was strangled?"

"I . . . I won't tell you."

"You tell him." A new voice came into the room, harsh and electronic. It was Ian Compton on the talkback from the control room. He must have had Diccon's microphone up and been listening to their conversation for some time.

Diccon turned towards his friend behind the glass screen and shouted, "No!"

"All right then, I'll tell him."

"*NO!*" Diccon Hudson rose and ran out of the screens towards the glass as if he could somehow smother Ian's speech.

But the talkback talked on inexorably. "Diccon was with me. We went together to a club called The Cottage, which you may know is a resort of homosexuals or gays as we prefer to call them. We went there because we are both gay."

"No," muttered Diccon, tears pouring down his face.

"For some reason, Charles, as you see, Diccon does not like to admit this fact in public. God knows why. He's only discovered his real nature recently and still tries to put up a straight front. That's why he lunches all these pretty little actresses, like Charlotte Mecken—to maintain the image of the great stud. Which is in fact far from the truth."

Diccon Hudson found his voice again. "Shut up," he said feebly.

Charles decided it was time for him to go. He didn't want to get into a marital squabble and he didn't think much more useful information was likely to be forthcoming. "I'm sorry to have caused a scene. Thank you for telling me all you have. It's going to help me clear Hugo."

"Clear Hugo?" Diccon repeated in amazement. "You can't still think that I—"

"No, not you."

But something that Diccon had said had released a block in Charles's mind and he was now certain who had killed Charlotte and how.

The next day he was going to confront that person.

CHAPTER 20

CHARLES FELT CERTAIN that the person he wanted to see would be at Breckton Magistrates' Court the next morning.

It was nearly twelve o'clock when the little group came out of the main entrance. Geoffrey was in the middle with Vee, and they were flanked by Denis and Mary Hobbs. A man in a pin-striped suit, presumably the Hobbses' solicitor, followed slightly behind. The atmosphere was more celebration of the return of a conquering hero than the release on bail of a man accused of petty theft from a friend.

Charles went forward to meet them. "I'm terribly sorry, Geoff. Vee inadvertently told me what had happened."

"That's all right. Thanks for coming." Geoffrey wore a mask of relaxed affability. "I suppose everyone will know soon."

"Yes, but it'll blow over pretty quickly," asserted Denis Hobbs. "Don't you reckon, Willy?"

"We live in hope," the solicitor replied smugly. Charles wondered whether smugness was something that all solicitors have to take on when they're articled in a sort of primitive ceremony like a circumcision rite.

"Anyway, don't let's talk about it," said Denis. "Charles, we're all going out to lunch—how'd you like to join us? We're going to put all this behind us and think of the future. I hadn't realized how badly things were going with poor Geoff. But I think over lunch we might have a bit of a discussion about one or two openings there might be for architects in my business."

He looked to Mary for approval. She smiled and he glowed visibly. So that was it. Not only was Geoffrey going to be forgiven for his crime; he was also going to get a new job to sort out his financial problems. Mary Hobbs loved being in the Lady Bountiful position, using her husband's money and influence to share a little of the reflection of Geoffrey's talent. And to gain power over him.

Charles declined the lunch invitation with thanks, but said he'd walk along with them a little way.

He fell into step beside his quarry. "I wonder if we could have a chat at some point. Something I'd like to discuss."

"Certainly. How about this afternoon? I'll be at home when we get back from this lunch."

"Okay, fine."

"About three."

Charles nodded. It had all been very casual, but they both knew it was a confrontation.

The house was empty but for the two of them.

"Well, Charles, what can I do for you?"

No point in beating around the bush with social pleasantries. It had to be direct. "I know how you did it."

"Did what?"

"Killed Charlotte."

"Ah." Charles had to admire the other's control. Even total innocence should have given more reaction. "So that's what it is, is it? All right, intrigue me, tell me how I did it."

"It was a very carefully worked out plan. A work of genius, one might say."

"I'm touched by the compliment, but I think it may be misapplied. Incidentally, before you tell me how I committed this crime, would you be so good as to tell me why I did it?"

"You did it, Geoffrey, because Charlotte told you she was pregnant and as a good Catholic she said she wouldn't have an abortion. So you had to get rid of her out of loyalty to Vee. She was coming to see Vee the day after she died. She'd fixed it by phone. You couldn't risk Vee finding out about the pregnancy. It would have destroyed your marriage."

Geoffrey left a pause before he responded. Maybe it was in reaction to what he had heard, but when he came back, his voice was as firm as ever. "I see. So that's why I did it. Now perhaps you will continue with telling me how I did it."

"Right. Last Monday night, after we parted at the main road, you went home. Vee wanted to watch *I, Claudius,* as you knew she would. As soon as it had started, you put on a previously prepared cassette of yourself doing the lines for *The Winter's Tale,* then left this room by the balcony. You walked briskly along the path at the back, over the main road and—"

"Look, I hate to break in on this magnificent piece of deduction, but I would just like to congratulate you and say you're absolutely right. Except in one detail. I did all this, but the crime which I committed in the time thus gained was not Charlotte's murder, but the theft from Denis and Mary for which I appeared in court this morning."

"If you will wait a moment, Geoffrey, I was coming to that. This is where your plan was so clever, because it involved a double alibi. If anyone worked out the cassette dodge, then you had a second line of defense that during the relevant time you were doing the robbery. On Friday you thought I was on to the cassette—in fact, you flattered me, I hadn't quite got there by then—but that was sufficient to frighten you into implementing your second plan, getting rid of the stolen jewelry in such an amateur manner that you knew it was only a matter of time before the police arrested you."

"I see." Geoffrey's voice was heavy with irony. "So, according to the Charles Paris theory, in the time I had at my disposal, I stole the jewelry and strangled Charlotte in two different houses half a mile apart. Hmm. You obviously have a very high opinion of the speed at which I work."

"No, I haven't finished the Charles Paris theory. What I am saying is that you didn't do the robbery."

"Oh, I see. Magic, was it? The jewelry suddenly appeared in my pocket. Or maybe I had a leprechaun as a henchman and he spirited the stuff away. Was that it?"

"No. You did the robbery, but you didn't do it on the Monday evening."

"But that's when it was done. That's when Bob Chubb saw the light in the Hobbses' house, that's when the police came and found it had been done."

Charles shook his head slowly. "All you did on the Monday night was to break the window, open the catch and leave the switched-on torch on the window sill, so that Bob Chubb or whoever else happened to pass couldn't fail to see it. You'd actually taken the valuables on the previous Wednesday evening when you'd been round at the house. You'd put a lot of planning into the thing. You'd suggested the game of charades at the Hobbses' and while you were upstairs dressing up as Margaret Thatcher in Mary Hobbses' clothes, you helped yourself to the jewelry.

"So, on the Monday, you only had to stop at their house for thirty seconds rather than five minutes. That was why everyone was so surprised at the tidiness of the burglary. Everything left as if it hadn't been touched. It hadn't been. No one went inside the house that evening.

"The crime was done like a dubbed film—one part of the action at one time and the other later on. The theft was committed before the break-in. And everyone thought they had been done at the same time."

Geoffrey's face remained impassive. Impossible to judge what was going on behind that mask.

Charles pressed on. "Then you went to Meckens's house. It was easy. Hugo played into your hands. Apart from the convenience of his constant outspoken attacks on Charlotte, you knew he wasn't going to leave the Back Room until it closed. And that then he'd be in a state where his reactions and memory could play him false.

"Charlotte was all set up. You'd seen her at lunchtime. In the excess of your passion you'd marked her neck with a lovebite, so you knew she'd have a scarf round her neck. Maybe you'd even said you'd drop in, so that she'd open the door quickly and you wouldn't be seen.

"Strangling her must have been quick. She was totally unsuspicious, off her guard. Then you put her body in the coal shed to delay its discovery and you were off home. Back before the end of

I, Claudius. Just in time to pick up from the cassette and start bellowing your lines with such vigor that your next-door neighbor was bound to complain, thus even getting the police to corroborate your first alibi."

There was a long pause. Geoffrey kept the usual tight rein on his emotions. "Well, Charles, you give me credit for a lot of ingenuity."

"I do."

"And I can see that, if all your assumptions are correct, it would have been possible for me to kill Charlotte. But you need a ripe imagination to follow the twists of what you've just told me. I think you might have difficulty persuading the police of it all—particularly as at the moment they have two crimes and for each one they have a self-confessed criminal."

"But Hugo only confessed because he couldn't remember and because he didn't care."

"If he didn't care, then why should we?"

"I don't know. I just want the truth to come out."

"Admirable sentiments. Well, I'm sure as soon as you can produce evidence to back up your preposterous allegations, the truth will come out."

Yes, there was the rub. Charles knew he had nothing except his own convictions to support his theory. It was right, but, as Geoffrey observed, it was going to be almost impossible to persuade the police to take it seriously. Particularly if the persuader was someone who stood as low in the estimation of Breckton Police Station as Charles Paris.

He felt his confidence begin to ebb and, with an effort, tried to regain momentum. Maybe he could shock a confession out of Geoffrey. "What makes the whole crime so ironic, even tragic, is the fact that Charlotte wasn't even pregnant."

"What!" This time Geoffrey reacted. This time, for a moment, the mask crumbled. And from that instant Charles knew for certain that he was right. He might have got some of the details of the plan's execution wrong, but Geoffrey Winter definitely killed Charlotte Mecken.

"No," he continued coolly. "The police post mortem revealed that she wasn't pregnant."

"But—"

"Oh, she thought she was, but it was just some freak effect of her going on the Pill. If she'd had the nerve to go to her doctor about it, he could have quickly disillusioned her. But no, she told you she was pregnant; she said, as a Catholic, she was going to keep the baby and, what was more, if you wouldn't tell your wife about it, then she would. When she made that decision, she signed her death warrant."

Geoffrey's eyes were closed and he was breathing deeply. Charles turned the knife in the wound. "And, if you're looking for further ironies, between the time that she saw you on the Monday lunchtime and the time that you killed her, Charlotte had decided that she would have an abortion. She rang up a friend for advice on how to end the pregnancy that never was. So her death was doubly unnecessary."

Geoffrey was badly shaken, but he rallied. There was only slight tension in his voice when at last he spoke. "This has been very interesting. May I ask what you are going to do now, Charles?"

"Nothing. I'm going to go away. I'm going to leave you with the knowledge that I know exactly what happened and see how you react. Maybe you'll come round to the conclusion that you ought to devise another equally ingenious method of disposing of me. My knowledge makes me just as much of a threat to your way of life as Charlotte was."

"You sound almost as if you are issuing a challenge."

"Yes, Geoffrey. I am."

CHAPTER 21

THE NEXT FEW days were an agony of vigilance for Charles. He hadn't really meant to challenge Geoffrey to kill him, but without evidence he saw no other way of drawing the man out into the open. All he had to do was to keep on his guard and see Geoffrey before Geoffrey saw him.

In case the worst happened, he wrote down a detailed reconstruction of what had taken place on the night of Charlotte's murder and lodged it with Gerald. Then if Charles Paris were found murdered, it could be delivered to the police, who would know where to start looking for their murderer.

But Charles didn't intend to be murdered; he intended to catch Geoffrey Winter attempting to murder him. That attempt would be tantamount to a confession to Charlotte's murder.

Charles tried to live as normally as possible. He stayed round Hereford Road a lot, so that Geoffrey should have no difficulty finding him. He drank less, so as to remain alert. He rigged up an elaborate alarm over the door of his bedsitter so that he should not be surprised in the night. And he waited.

Meanwhile he tried to continue his career, as funds were getting low. In this he encountered an unexpected setback.

He rang through to Mills Brown Mazzini on that Friday to find out when the next Bland recording session would be. Ian Compton told him with ill-disguised glee that the housewives of the Tyne-Tees area had given the thumbs-down to the Mr. Bland television commercials. They had found the animation too frivolous for something as important as a bedtime drink and they didn't like the name.

As a result, Ian had worked out a completely different approach for the product, and it had been approved by Mr. Farrow. The new campaign for the drink (now renamed Velvet-Sleep) was to feature a young couple who had just finished a hard day's decorating. The voice-over was going to be done by Diccon Hudson.

So that was it. Charles was paid off for the Tuesday's cancelled recording session and suddenly the heady vistas of infinitely re-peated commercials bringing in infinite repeat fees shrank down to a few solitary session payments. Needless to say, there had been no long-term contract signed. The dazzling prospects had existed only in conversations between Charles and Hugo. With his sponsor still remanded in custody, Charles was suddenly out of the voice-over world. He never heard the result of the No Fuzz test.

He rang Maurice Skellern and said he would audition for the Cardiff company. He had to live on something.

He also kept thinking he should ring Frances, but didn't get round to it.

On the Saturday morning he received a letter.

Dear Mr. Parrish,
    Thank you so much for letting us see your play, *How's Your Fa-ther?*, which we read with some amusement.
    We regret that we do not feel it to be suitable for our World Premières Festival, as we feel it is too slight and commercial a piece for production in what has increasingly become one of the main outlets for modern experimental theatre in this country.
    We have also been fortunate to receive a new play by George Walsh. It is called *Amniotic Amnesia* and concerns the thoughts of a group of fetuses awaiting a fertility drug-induced multiple birth. It

raises many interesting questions of philosophy and ecology and is much more the sort of work we feel the Backstagers should be doing.

We will hope to see you down here for our next production, *The Winter's Tale* by William Shakespeare.

> Yours sincerely,
> Robert Chubb
> World Premières Festival
> Sub-Committee

PS Your script is being returned under separate cover.

It was over a week before the truth sank in. That Geoffrey was not going to be drawn, that so long as he didn't rise to Charles's challenge, he was safe. He knew that there was no evidence and he did not intend to supply any.

Charles felt ridiculous when this dawned on him. He had nothing; he should have realized. Geoffrey Winter had killed Charlotte Mecken, but it could never be proved.

Charles was furious. Having got so near, to be thwarted at the end . . . Hugo would be sentenced to life imprisonment and maybe come out after eight years to drink himself to death. Geoffrey would get a fine or a short sentence or maybe—if Willy, the Hobbses' solicitor, were really good—a suspended sentence for the crime he'd had to commit as a cover-up. Then he'd take up a job with Denis Hobbs in the "construction industry" and continue to play all the leads at the Breckton Backstagers. And Mary Hobbs would have the satisfaction of feeling that she had done something direct and positive for the artistic life of the community. And memories would heal over and the case would trickle away.

He couldn't stand the thought. He resolved to get back to Breckton for one last try. There must be something he had missed.

It was Monday. Exactly two weeks from the night that Charlotte had died. Monday, November 15th. It had been a bright autumn day, but was dark by the time Charles arrived once again at Breckton Station.

Nearly seven o'clock. Instinctively he walked towards the Winters' house. As he rounded the corner of their road, he stopped.

Geoffrey and Vee were walking ahead of him towards the main road.

Of course. Rehearsal. Up to the Back Room for a quick one, and then ready to give artistically at seven-thirty. Leontes and Perdita, played by Geoffrey Winter and Vee le Carpentier. The stars of the Breckton Backstagers. Oh yes, he knocks around a bit with other women, but they're really very close. No children, no. But they're very close.

He tailed them at about fifty yards distance, but they didn't look round. It was uncannily silent. Geoffrey, like Charles, must be wearing his favorite desert boots and Vee's shoes also must have had soft soles, for there was no sound of footfalls on the pavement of the footpath. Just the occasional chuckle from up ahead. Geoffrey sounded more relaxed alone with his wife than Charles had ever heard him in company. Oh yes, he needed Vee. When Charlotte threatened that relationship, she had to go.

Charles followed them all the way, keeping the same distance behind. It was sickening. He knew what had happened, the criminal was right in front of him and yet he could do nothing about it. Nothing without proof.

By the time Charles got to the Hobbses' house, Geoffrey and Vee had disappeared inside the Backstagers. Everything went on just the same—drink, rehearsal, home, work, drink, rehearsal . . . Why should he try to break it up? Hugo was long past hope—what did it matter whether he despaired in prison or at large? He had nothing to live for. Geoffrey Winter at least had his love for his wife, his acting, his little affairs. What was the point of trying to break that pattern?

Charles decided he would go back to the station, get the train back up to Town and forget the case had ever happened.

A feeling almost of nostalgia for the time he had spent retracing Geoffrey's movements made him take the long way round past the Meckens' house.

It stood dark and unfriendly. Presumably, after Hugo's trial it would go on the market, someone would buy it. There would be stories of what had happened there. If the buyer were imaginative, Charlotte's ghost might even be seen. If not, it would all be forgotten. Sooner or later, all would be forgotten.

As he stood there, he was seized by an impulse to do it once again. One more retracing and that was it.

This time just as Geoffrey must have done it two weeks before. He slipped across the gravel drive to the side gate. He no longer cared about the net curtain snoopers. Let them report him if they wanted to. He was about to leave Breckton for the last time.

The side gate was not locked. He lifted the latch and let himself into the back garden. He had a small pencil torch in his pocket and he shone it on the ground before his feet as he walked towards the coal shed.

It was a shock not to find Charlotte's body still there. That embarrassingly sprawled figure had so etched itself on his subconscious that he felt cheated when there was only coal in his torchbeam.

He stood there for a moment looking round. Nothing. Not the perfect crime, but a crime that was by now undetectable. Maybe at the time, maybe if Geoffrey had been the first suspect, there might have been something which would have given him away. Maybe the blood from the abrasion on Charlotte's neck had been on his hands as he walked home. But if so, that blood had been long washed away, long dispersed and unidentifiable. Now there was nothing. Not a chance of anything.

Charles's footsteps crunched in the coal-dust as he sighed and left the coal shed. Back across the drive, along the road and down the tarmac footpath to the common.

There was no one about, of course. No one to see him, just as there had been no one to see Geoffrey Winter a fortnight before.

He walked doggedly along the hard mud path skirting the football fields towards the path to the main road. He passed the untidy bit, the dumping ground, still dominated by the washed-out crater of the Guy Fawkes bonfire.

He reached the paved path and walked a couple of paces. Then he stopped.

He felt a little tremor of excitement. Twisting one foot round on the paving, he heard the crunch of coal-dust.

Good God, it stayed on. He'd have thought it would have been wiped off by the walk across the common, but no. The little grains of coal embedded themselves into the rubber sole of the desert boot and took a lot of shifting.

And if he had noticed the difference in sound when he came on to the paving, so would someone else have done two weeks before. Could Geoffrey have taken the risk of carrying that incriminating dust into his own house?

No, surely he would have tried to remove the evidence. Charles looked at his own sole with the pencil torch. Little chips of coal glinted in the beam. He tried to scrape them off. Some came, some stayed. He could have got them all out, but it would have taken time. And time was the one commodity which Geoffrey hadn't had. His tape gave him a maximum of forty-five minutes.

And on the morning Charles had visited him in his office, Geoffrey had been wearing new shoes.

Charles looked round. There was only one obvious place to dispose of a pair of shoes. You could throw them into the bushes, but there they'd be retrieved by the first nosey dog who came along. But in the bonfire . . .

After all, so long as suspicions were held off for four days, the evidence would be burnt publicly and no one any the wiser. And as soon as Geoffrey heard about Hugo's arrest, he could relax. He had only to wait till November 5th to be absolutely secure.

But sour Reggie had reckoned the fire was out of control and it had been doused by the fire brigade. There was still that soggy mess of ash. If Geoffrey had shoved the shoes into the middle at the bottom to be inconspicuous, there was a long chance that they might still be there.

Charles scrabbled through the damp debris of ash, half-burnt sticks and charred rubbish by the light of his torch. He spread it all flat on the ground. There was nothing big enough to be a shoe. One half of a heel might have come from a lady's sandal, but otherwise nothing.

He sat down deflated, mindless of the debris. Oh well, it had been a good idea. Too easy though, really. Geoffrey wasn't stupid.

He'd have found a way round the shoes, scrapped them or changed them, destroyed them at home. Or just put them high enough in the bonfire to ensure that they would burn quickly.

No, the case was over. Charles put one hand down on the ground to lever himself up.

And felt close round a soft flesh-like lump.

He had the object up in his torch-beam. At first it seemed to be a plastic-covered ball, which had survived by rolling to the bottom of the fire before it was doused. It was shapeless and blackened with ash.

But then he saw that it had once been a pair of plastic gloves, rolled together. Now deformed and fused by the heat, but recognizably a pair of gloves.

But that wasn't what brought a catch of excitement to his throat. It was the fact that the gloves had been wrapped round something. Something soft.

The melted plastic had made a little envelope which gave easily to his fingernail. Inside, preserved like a packet on the supermarket shelf, was a handkerchief.

A blue and white handkerchief he had last seen when Geoffrey Winter had lent it to him in the Back Room. On the night of Charlotte's murder.

The brown smudge across it showed why it had been thrown away to be burned in the fire.

It was blood.

Blood that could be identified by a police laboratory.

Blood from the scratch on Charlotte Mecken's neck.

And was it fanciful for Charles to catch a hint of a familiar expensive scent?

As expected, the police took a lot of convincing. When he first started to expound his reconstruction of events, Charles could feel how unlikely it sounded.

But when he showed them the handkerchief, they got more interested. After about an hour they agreed to go up to the common with him to look at the bonfire. A plain-clothes man and a uniformed constable.

They didn't talk much. They inspected the scene and started assessing times and distances. Charles didn't push his luck by saying anything.

Eventually the plain-clothes man spoke. "Well, it's just possible. Of course, we won't really know until we get this handkerchief looked at by forensic. But I think we'll go and talk to Mr. Winter, get his version of events. Where did you say he lived?"

"He won't be there at the moment. He's rehearsing a show for the Breckton Backstagers."

The rehearsal was in full swing when they arrived. The cast were doing the awakening of the statue of Hermione.

The queen stood frozen center stage, with Geoffrey as Leontes on one side of her and Mary Hobbs as Paulina on the other. Vee, as Perdita, knelt behind her husband. By her side stood Clive Steele as Florizel.

As Charles and the policemen entered at the back of the rehearsal room, Geoffrey was declaiming. They stood in silence while he continued.

> "O! thus she stood,
> Even with such life of majesty,—warm life,
> As now it coldly stands,—when first I woo'd her.
> I am asham'd: does the stone rebuke me
> For being more stone than it? Oh—"

As he acted, Geoffrey took them in. Charles could see the pale grey eyes flicker from him to the uniformed policeman, then to the plain-clothes man and finally come to rest on the soiled handkerchief which the detective was still holding gingerly in front of him.

When Geoffrey saw the handkerchief, his voice wavered. There was a little gasp like the beginning of a giggle.

The supposed statue of Hermione let out the snort of a suppressed laugh. Then Mary Hobbs went off into uncontrollable giggles. Vee and Clive started laughing too.

None of them knew what the joke was, but soon all the Backstagers in the room were roaring their heads off. It was one of those moments that often happen at rehearsal, when suddenly a tense scene breaks down into the ridiculous. A mass "corpse."

Gradually, one by one, the actors stopped, slowing down to gasping breaths, and wiping tears from their eyes. Then they turned to look, with growing concern, at Geoffrey Winter.

But he just kept on laughing.

Star Trap

*To my Parents, with thanks
for all that education*

*And with special thanks to
Bill and Chris, who know
all about it*

PART 1

London

CHAPTER 1

"ACTUALLY," SAID GERALD Venables, after a sip from his wine glass, "there's a bit more to it than that."

"Ah," said Charles Paris. "I thought there might be."

Gerald took a long pause and twiddled the stem of his wine glass. Charles wondered what the catch would be. Gerald was a good friend but was unlikely to be offering him a job from purely altruistic motives. And if it were just a gesture of goodwill, he wouldn't have made it over lunch at Martinez.

"In fact," the solicitor picked out his words like a philatelist handling stamps, "there may be something rather odd going on in this show."

"Odd?"

"Well, as you know, a West End musical is a very large financial undertaking and with any large financial undertaking there are probably as many people who wish it to fail as succeed. And the . . . people whom I represent are very anxious that this particular show should succeed."

"You mean you've got money in it?" Charles knew this would make Gerald bridle. Though well known in theatrical circles as a speculator, the solicitor would never admit to his involvement.

"One of the people whom I represent," came the frosty professional reply, "has a considerable financial stake in the venture. It is on his behalf that I am approaching you."

Charles winked. Gerald deflated, smiled and moved the

conversation away from money. "Listen, Charles, the reason that we want you in the show is that we need an investigator on the spot to keep an eye open for anything untoward."

"I see."

"And, of course" (remembering that even as cynical an actor as Charles Paris had his professional pride) "because you would be absolutely ideal for the part."

Charles inclined his head graciously and looked up for more information.

"You see, Charles, the reason I thought of you was because of that business in Edinburgh that you sorted out . . . the murder of that boy—what was his name—Marinello?"

"Something like that. I'm flattered, Gerald, but I think to say I sorted it out is a slight exaggeration. I was there. . . ."

"It comes to the same thing. And then there was the Marius Steen business."

"Again I would hardly say that I—"

"Don't worry what *you* think. I think you can do the job required and I'm asking you. I mean, it may be that there's nothing to investigate. In that case think of it just as an acting job. After the tour, you'd have a contract for nine months in the West End, you'd be pretty well paid—it's not a bad offer, is it?"

"No."

"And you haven't got anything else major coming up at the moment, have you?"

As an actor, Charles replied instinctively. "Well, there are one or two things I'm considering, which may possibly. . . ." Then he decided there was no point in trying to impress Gerald. "No, nothing major." Or why not be completely honest? "Nothing minor either, as it happens. And I had a somewhat uncharitable letter from the Inland Revenue this morning."

"So you'll take the job?"

"I suppose so."

"That's terrific." Gerald punctuated the agreement by refilling their wine glasses. He seemed relieved, which amazed Charles. Surely he never thought the offer might be refused. Or perhaps, from his position of extreme opulence, Gerald was unaware of the general scarcity of acting work at a time when theatres were paring down the size of their permanent companies, when big cast plays were no longer being written or produced and when even the BBC was making cutbacks in its programme hours. Nor was he probably aware of the precarious system of final demands and delaying letters by which Charles conducted his financial affairs.

"What about a sweet?" Gerald airily summoned the waiter with a well-tailored gesture and, as often before, Charles was impressed and amused by his friend's smoothness. He did not envy it, he had long ago decided that certain sorts of success did not interest him, but it was still entertaining to see a successful man at work. Everything about Gerald was right—the beautifully cut charcoal grey pin-striped suit, the residual tan from an August spent with his family in their villa in Corsica, the silver hair cut just long enough to be trendy, the chunky gold ring and identity bracelet, the almost imperceptible aura of expensive after-shave. Charles was always amazed by people who could live like figures in glossy magazines and by people who wanted to. For him the basic challenge of getting from day to day more than occupied his time.

The sweets were sorted out and they both tucked into monster slices of strawberry gâteau. Charles wiped a stray blob of cream from the side of his mouth and asked, "What's been happening, Gerald?"

"In the show, you mean?"

"Yes. There must be something strange for you to go to these lengths to get me involved."

"Yes. Two things have happened. They may both have been accidents, and they may be completely unconnected, but it's just possible that someone's trying to sabotage the whole venture."

"What were the 'accidents'?"

"The first came on the second day of rehearsal. There was a guy called Frederick Wooland who was rehearsal pianist for the show. As he was on the way to the Welsh Dragon Club where they're rehearsing, he was shot at."

"Shot at? You mean someone tried to kill him?"

"No, not really. It was only an air rifle. He just got a pellet in his hand. Not very serious except that he won't be able to play for a couple of weeks and they've had to find a new rehearsal pianist."

"Usually if you hear of someone being shot at with an air rifle, it's just kids fooling about."

"Yes, I agree. That may well be what it was in this case. It's a fairly rough area down there."

"Where is the Welsh Dragon Club?"

"Elephant and Castle."

"Hmm. Presumably the pianist didn't see who shot at him?"

"No. First thing he knew was a stinging pain in his hand."

"Were the police told?"

"Oh yes. It was all official. They seemed to think it was kids. No great surprise. It's not the first time that it's happened round there."

"In that case, I can't see why you think there's anything odd about it. It doesn't sound as if it had anything to do with the show at all. Perhaps the only lesson is that managements should be prepared to pay a bit more money to get rehearsal rooms in slightly nicer areas." He pronounced the last two words in his best Kensington Lady accent.

"Okay. Yes, I admit, on its own, that doesn't sound much. But exactly a week later there was another accident. The day before yesterday."

"What happened this time?"

"One of the actors fell down some stairs and broke his leg."

"Where? At the rehearsal rooms?"

"No. At his digs."

"So why should that have anything to do with the show?"

"It's just the coincidence of the two of them, exactly a week apart, at exactly the same time of day, both people in the show."

"What time of day was it?"

"Early in the morning both times. Frederick Wooland was shot on his way to rehearsal, say at quarter to ten, and Everard Austick was found in his digs at about half past nine this Tuesday."

"Did you say Everard Austick?"

"Yes."

Charles burst out laughing. "You can't be serious."

"What do you mean?"

"Well, Everard Austick is the greatest piss-artist in the business. He's a bottle-a-day man. Always drunk out of his mind. If you think that him having a fall in his digs is a sign of foul play, you're way off beam. I'd be much more suspicious if a day went by when he *didn't* fall down something."

Gerald looked discomfited. "Oh, I thought the coincidence was too great. I mean, both on the same day."

"Well . . . it doesn't sound much to me. Listen, Gerald, I'm very grateful to you for getting me this job and certainly once I get inside the company I will investigate anything that needs investigating, but from what you've said, I'm not going to have much to do. Is that really all you've got?"

"Well, I suppose that's all the actual facts. But it means that the show has got off to an unlucky start and we—they don't want anything to go wrong. There's a lot of money at stake."

"Whose money?"

Gerald didn't rise to the bait. "Amulet Productions are putting up most of it and they're working in association with Arthur Balcombe, who is one of my clients. Hence my involvement."

"I see. All the big boys."

"Yes. And then of course Christopher Milton has a stake because he's got the rights of the show."

"Christopher Milton?"

"Yes, he bought it as a vehicle for himself."

"Really?"

"Didn't you know?"

"Gerald, you didn't tell me anything. You just asked if I would be prepared to take a part in a West End musical for nine months and keep my eyes open for any possible sabotage attempts. You've told me nothing about the show. But I see now, it's this musical based on *She Stoops to Conquer,* isn't it?"

"That's right."

"I've seen stuff about it in the Press. Now let me think. . . ." he mused facetiously. "If it's a musical based on *She Stoops to Conquer* for a West End audience, then what would it be called? Um. How about *Conkers?* With an exclamation mark."

"No, it was going to be," said Gerald with complete seriousness, "but then it was decided that that didn't really give the right impression of the sort of show it is."

"So what's it called now?"

"Lumpkin!"

"With an exclamation mark?"

"Of course."

"With Christopher Milton as Tony Lumpkin?"

"Of course. That was another reason for the title. It means a neat billing—'Christopher Milton as *Lumpkin!'* See what I mean?"

"Yes, I do. Tony Lumpkin. Of course. One of the all-time great upstaging parts. Hmm. What's the script like?"

Gerald was reticent. "It's okay."

"Anything to do with Goldsmith?"

"No. He hasn't any money in it."

"I didn't mean Goldsmith the impresario. I meant Oliver Goldsmith who wrote the thing."

"Oh, I'm sorry. I think the show makes the occasional nod in his direction."

"But presumably it's not designed for fans of Oliver Goldsmith?"

"No, it's designed for fans of Christopher Milton. He's riding very high at the moment, with the telly show at the top of the ratings."

"What telly show?"

"Oh, come on, Charles, don't be affected. You must have seen *Straight Up, Guv.*"

"I don't think I have. I'm not a great telly viewer." He did not possess a television in his Bayswater bed-sitter. He was not enthusiastic about the medium. It was a necessary evil for his career as an actor, because it was well paid, but he had never enjoyed the work (or the product).

"Well, let me enlighten your ignorance. The show gets massive audience figures and it has made Christopher Milton just about the hottest property around. He's very big box office."

"So it doesn't really matter what show you put him in."

"Ah, but it does, and *Lumpkin!* is just right. Could make a lot of money. That's why I—the people I represent—are so anxious that nothing should go wrong. Either to the show—or to the star."

"I see. Who's written it?"

"Well, it's basically a show which the Ipswich Warehouse Company put on last year to celebrate the bicentenary of Goldsmith's death."

"Oh yes, I remember reading a notice of that in *The Stage*. What was it called then?"

"*Liberty Hall.*"

"That's right."

"Book by a chap called Kevin McMahon, with music by some bloke whose name I forget. Anyway, Christopher Milton's agent, Dickie Peck—do you know him, by the way?"

"By reputation."

"Well, he went down and saw the show and reckoned it had potential for his boy, got Christopher Milton himself down to see it, and they bought up the rights. I think they got them pretty cheap. Could be a good investment. I mean, the stage show should run at least a couple of years on Christopher Milton's name, and then there might be a chance of a film. . . ."

"And the script is more or less as at Ipswich?"

"Hardly. No, there's been quite a lot of surgery. They've scrapped the original music and lyrics—or most of them anyway. And got in Carl Anthony and Micky Gorton to write new ones."

"You look at me as if I should have heard of them."

"You certainly should, Charles. They've written a whole string of Top Ten hits. *Heart Doctor* . . . *Gimme No More Lies* . . . *Disposable Man*—all that lot!"

"Ah."

"Really, Charles, you are square." Gerald prided himself on his sudden knowledge of the pop scene.

"Some of us age quicker than others, man."

Gerald ignored the dig. "The new music is excellent. It fits the style of the period, but it's also very . . . funky." He tried too hard to deliver the last word naturally.

Charles laughed. "It sounds a riot. I hope I don't have to sing anything funky. I wouldn't know where to begin. Incidentally, I should have asked before—what part am I playing?"

"You're playing Sir Charles Marlow. Do you know the play?"

"Yes, I did a production of it once in Cardiff—with Bernard Walton of all people, when he was very new in the business. He played Young Marlow—his first starring rôle. And I'm the father . . . hmm. Only comes in at the end."

"That's right."

"Good."

"Why good?"

"Last act parts are good. You can spend the whole evening in the pub."

"It was Everard Austick's part," said Gerald reprovingly.

"Ah, yes, that was probably his downfall. A lifetime of last act parts is the short route to alcoholism."

"Hmm." Gerald pondered for a moment. "I sometimes think I drink too much. Difficult to avoid in my line of work. Occupational hazard."

"That's what I feel about my line of work too," Charles agreed. "Though I must admit at times I worry about the amount I put away."

"Yes." There was a reflective pause. Then Gerald said, "How about a brandy?"

"Love one."

When it arrived, Charles raised his glass. "Many thanks, Gerald. This is the most painless audition I've ever undergone."

"My pleasure."

"Incidentally, I don't know anything about the time-scale on this show yet. What's this—the second week of rehearsal?"

"That's right. Second of five. Then the show does one week in Leeds. . . ."

"Ah, Leeds. . . ."

"Friends up there?"

"You could say that."

"Then a week at Bristol, a week at Brighton, a week of final rehearsal and previews in town and then it should open at the King's Theatre on November 27th."

"Isn't that a bit near Christmas? I mean, it's a dodgy time for audiences."

Gerald smiled smugly. "No problem. Christopher Milton's name will carry us over Christmas. And then . . . we'll be all right. Ideal family entertainment. Nothing to offend anyone."

"I see. And when do I start rehearsal?"

"Tomorrow morning, if all goes well."

"If all goes well? You mean, if I'm not poisoned overnight by the mysterious saboteur."

"You may laugh, but I've a feeling there's something up."

"I will keep my eyes skinned, word of honor." Charles made a Boy Scout salute.

"And if you do find out anything . . . untoward or criminal, let me know first."

"Before the police?"

"If possible. We have to watch the publicity angle on this."

"I see."

"We don't want the fuzz queering our pitch."

Charles smiled. It was reassuring to hear Gerald dropping into his thriller slang. The solicitor had always had the sneaking suspicion that crime held more exciting dimensions than the minor infringements of contracts which occupied his working life. His thirst for criminal glamour had to be satisfied by thrillers and, in moments of excitement, his language showed it. Gerald was excited now. He thought they were on to a case.

Charles didn't. He felt certain that the whole idea of saboteurs had been dreamt up by nervy managements suddenly counting up the amount of money that they had invested in one stage show and one star. They were scared and they had to give what frightened them a tangible form. Sabotage was as good an all-purpose threat as any other.

Still, he wasn't complaining. Nine months' work, however boring it might be, was nine months' work. It could sort out the taxman and one or two other pressing problems.

"I'll be very discreet, Gerald, and tell you everything."

"Good."

"Now let me buy you a brandy."

"I wouldn't worry. It's all on Arthur Balcombe. You didn't really think I was taking you out on my own money?"

"No, Gerald, I know you never do anything on your own money. Still, let's have another brandy on Arthur Balcombe and imagine that I've bought it to thank you for the job."

"Okay. There is one thing, though."

"Yes."

"I've offered you the job, you've accepted it, but in a way it isn't mine to offer."

"Now he tells me."

"I mean, I don't think there'll be any problem, but it's just that you'll have to go and see Dickie Peck before it's all definite."

"Oh."

"Just to check details of your contract."

"*Just* to check details of my contract."

"Well, it's also . . . sort of . . . to get to know you, to see if you are the kind of person who's likely to get on with Christopher Milton, if you see what I—"

"What you mean by that formula of words is that Christopher Milton has an Approval of Cast clause in his contract and I've got to go and see Dickie Peck to be vetted."

Gerald tried to find another formula of words, but eventually was forced to admit that that was exactly what he meant.

"I get it. When do I see Peck?"

"You've got an appointment at four o'clock."

CHAPTER 2

DICKIE PECK WORKED for Creative Artists Ltd, one of the biggest film and theatre agencies in the country, and he was big. His clients were said to be managed by "Dickie Peck at Creative Artists" rather than just by "Creative Artists." In the agency world this designation often preceded a split from the parent company when an individual member of the staff would set up on his own (usually taking his best clients with him). But Dickie Peck had had this individual billing ever since anyone could remember and showed no signs of leaving the Creative Artists umbrella. There was no point in his making the break; he was a director of the company and worked within it in his own way at his own pace.

It was the pace which was annoying Charles as he sat waiting in the Creative Artists Reception in Bond Street. He had been informed by the over-made-up girl on the switchboard that Mr. Peck was not yet back from lunch and as the clock ticked round to half past four, Charles felt all the resentment of someone who has finished lunch at half past three.

He was not alone in Reception. A young actress with carefully highlighted cheek-bones was reading *The Stage* and sighing dramatically from time to time; an actor whose old, hollow eyes betrayed his startlingly golden hair gave a performance of nonchalance by staring at his buckled patent leather shoes. The girl on the switchboard kept up a low monologue of "A call for you . . .," "I'm sorry, he's tied up at the moment . . ." and

"Would you mind hanging on?" She deftly snapped plugs in and out like a weaver at her loom.

It was nearly a quarter to five when Dickie Peck came through Reception. The girl on the switchboard stage-whispered, "Mr. Peck, there've been a couple of calls and there's a gentleman waiting to see you."

He half-turned and Charles got an impression of a cigar with a long column of ash defying gravity at its end. Ignoring his visitor, the agent disappeared into his office. Five minutes later a summons came through on the receptionist's intercom.

The office was high over Bond Street and Dickie Peck's chair backed on to a bow-window. Cupboards and dusty glass-fronted book-cases lined the walls. The paint-work must once have been cream, but had yellowed with age. The dark red carpet smelt of dust. Nothing much on the desk. A current *Spotlight,* Actors LZ (to check what Charles Paris looked like) and a circular ashtray in the center of which was a decorative half golfball. The channel around this was full of lengths of cigar ash, long and obscene, like turds.

The ash was long on the cigar that still drooped from the agent's lips. It was an expensive one, but the end was so chewed and worried that it looked like the cheap brown-wrapping-paper sort.

The face which the cigar dwarfed was grey and lined, crowned by a long tongue of hair brushed inadequately over baldness. The head was disproportionately small and accentuated the stocky bulk of body below it. Dickie Peck was dressed in a dark grey suit with thin lapels. A plain blue tie askew across a grubby white shirt. Tie and jacket dusted with cigar ash. It was not the traditional image of the big show business agent; more like a Town Hall clerk.

"Charles Paris, isn't it? Take a chair." He gestured expansively, but the ash at the end of his cigar miraculously stayed intact.

Charles sat on a low gilt chair whose red plush upholstery was as hard as wood.

"Now, Mr. Paris, I gather you've seen a representative of Amulet Productions about this part."

"Yes." So Gerald wasn't just acting as solicitor for Arthur Balcombe.

"And he explained what it was about?"

"Yes."

"Good. As you gather, the part became vacant due to an accident to one of the cast."

"I know." Charles didn't volunteer any comment. Gerald had been uncertain whether Dickie Peck shared his suspicions of sabotage or not and had asked Charles to play it carefully. The fewer people knew that there was an investigator in the company, the better.

Dickie Peck gave no sign of suspicion. He took a long draw at his cigar, extending the column of ash to an even more precarious length. He leant back and blew a slow jet of smoke to the ceiling. "This show, Mr. Paris, is a very big one."

"So I gather." Charles was getting tired of being told about the size of the operation.

"It's likely to be a very big success."

"Good," said Charles, feeling that some sort of comment was required.

"And so it's important that everything about it should be right."

Again Charles helped out the pause with a "Yes."

"Because what we have here is a show with a very big star. Christopher Milton, no less."

Here a longer pause was left for some comment of amazed approbation. Charles produced a grunt which he hoped was appropriate.

"Yes, Christopher Milton. Let me tell you, Mr. Paris, I have been in this business a very long time and I have never before seen someone who had so much star quality written all over him."

"Ah." Charles found it difficult to get interested in the idea of stardom. It was not the end of show business in which he was involved.

But Dickie Peck's litany had started and couldn't be stopped. "Oh yes, I've seen them all sitting in that chair. They've all come to me for advice. Because they know, if they want to get ahead in this business, then they should come and see old Dickie Peck. Oh yes." For the first time in the interview he looked at the crumbling end of his cigar, but decided it didn't need attention yet. "I remember once back in 1960, I had four young men from Liverpool in this office. Four ordinary lads, got their own group—would I be interested in representing them? And you know who they were? Only the Beatles.

"They asked my advice and I gave it. I said, Lads, you've got a lot of talent, but the act isn't right. What you've got to do is split up, go your own ways, separate careers, that's what you need if you're really going to make it." He paused for dramatic emphasis, then delivered his triumph. "And look at them now—separate careers."

He leant back with satisfaction, then, instinctively sensing the imminent collapse of his cigar ash, deposited another neat cylinder into the ash-tray.

"There have been others too—Frank Sinatra once when he was over here, wanted a bit of advice on which way I thought his career should go. Glenda Jackson, Tom Jones, oh yes, they've all sat in that chair and asked for a bit of help from old Dickie Peck."

Charles looked at the chair on which he was sitting with what he hoped was due reverence and didn't believe a word of it.

"But let me tell you, Mr. Paris, of all the big stars I've ever seen, Christopher Milton is the biggest. That boy has so much talent, he can do anything. I mean, when you think that he is now only thirty-four, a mere baby, at the beginning of his career, I tell you in the future there's going to be no stopping him. And *Lumpkin!* is the show that's really going to put him in the big time." Realizing that this could be constructed as diminishing his protégé, he covered himself. "Not of course that he isn't in the big time already. With the television show, a few films, oh yes, he's right at the top. And it's not that we haven't had offers—oh, there have been plenty of scripts come along, plenty of managements with ideas, chance of a big musical on Broadway, Hollywood positively begging, but we said no. We preferred to bide our time, wait for the right show, the one that was absolutely right. Christopher Milton had got the telly, he was doing okay, he could afford to wait. That's an important thing in this business, choosing the right work. Oh yes, you've got to be selective."

Which is nice if you can afford to be selective, thought Charles. Most actors have to do what comes along or starve.

Dickie Peck's monologue was evidently self-propelled, so Charles gave up providing nods and yesses and grunts of agreement to stimulate it. "Now, of course, when you're talking about an artist of Christopher Milton's caliber, you want to be sure that all the work he does is done in the right atmosphere, that he works with people who he gets on with, people who are sympathetic to what he's doing." Charles pricked up his ears. They were finally getting round to the vetting part of the interview. "Because what happens when you get someone with more talent than most people is that you do tend to get jealousy developing. And that doesn't make for a healthy working atmosphere in a company. Now Christopher Milton is a charming boy, very easy to get along with, but he is a person of considerable genius and he does have strong ideas. Now because of his great sense of theatre his ideas are very often right. And obviously in the context of a show being rehearsed under pressure, too many arguments over the way things are done can only be counter-productive. Do you see what I mean?"

He leant back, nursing another two inches of cigar ash. This time a response was definitely needed.

And it was not an easy one to give. Oh yes, Charles knew what Dickie Peck meant. Through all the verbiage, the message was quite clear—if you want this job, you will have to undertake to do as Christopher Milton says. He's not the director of the show, but his word is law, and if you don't like the sound of that, remember he has an Approval of Casting clause and the world is full of unemployed actors.

Under normal circumstances Charles liked to think he'd tell the agent to stuff his job and walk out. But these weren't normal circumstances. He tried to conciliate his conscience. Gerald had offered him the job, and Gerald was a friend. It wouldn't do to let him down. Anyway, it wasn't really an acting job. He was being infiltrated into the company as an investigator of sabotage. Yes, it was quite legitimate for him to accept the conditions; it would only raise suspicion if he didn't. But as he replied, he knew that his real motive was the tax bill lying on the table in his room in Hereford Road. "Yes, I fully understand, Mr. Peck. I know that Christopher Milton owns the rights of the show and so obviously he will be deeply concerned in all aspects of the production, and I'm sure I will respect his ideas."

Dickie Peck looked at him suspiciously, but evidently decided to take the reply at face value. "Good, fine. Well, we have Mr. Venables' word as to your suitability for the part. . . ." Then, just as Gerald had done, he gave a token nod to actor's pride. "And of course I know your work. I have a script of the show here. Did Mr. Venables tell you about the tour and the length of contract?"

"Yes."

"Fine. Well, good luck."

"Thank you. There is just one thing. . . ."

"Oh, yes, of course, money."

"Yes. Look, I'll give you my agent's number. He deals with all that."

"Fine. Will I catch him there now? I'd like to get this sorted out today. And it's after half past five now."

"Maurice'll be there. He works from home anyway."

"Fine. I'll give him a buzz."

"Well, thank you very much, Mr. Peck. I hope that show's going to be a great success."

"With Christopher Milton in it it's bound to be. That boy is what stardom's all about. Oh yes, it'll be a big success. And if anyone tries to stop it being a success, there'll be hell to pay. Christopher Milton is going right to the top and no one is going to get in his way."

He said the last words with a fierce, almost religious, intensity.

Charles pressed twopence into the coin-box when he heard the voice say, "Maurice Skellern Artistes."

"Maurice."

"Who's calling him?"

"Oh, for God's sake, Maurice, don't you ever recognize my voice? It's me—Charles."

"Ah well, can't be too careful in this business. Don't want to give anything away."

"You don't give much away by answering to your name. Anyway, never mind that. Did Dickie Peck get through to you?"

"Yes, Charles. Sounds very good, this musical. I think it's about time you got into that sort of show. I mean, haven't I been saying for years that you ought to be doing shows that are more . . . more important?"

"No. You've been saying for years that I ought to be doing shows that are better paid."

"Ah, now that's not fair, Charles. Okay, I've always said you should keep out of these fringe capers, this experimental stuff, but I've always been thinking primarily of your career, of your artistic development."

"That's very generous of you."

"I do my best."

"So what am I getting for the current artistic development?"

"Well, Charles, Dickie Peck was offering, on behalf of the management, twenty-five for rehearsal, forty on tour and sixty for the run and I said you wouldn't consider it for under forty for rehearsal, eighty on tour and a hundred for the run and I wouldn't budge from that and that was my final word on the subject."

"So?"

"You're getting thirty for rehearsal, fifty on tour and eighty for the run."

"Oh well, could be worse. Christopher Milton's in this show. Got any form on him?" While Maurice Skellern was pretty useless as an agent, he was an invaluable source of theatrical gossip.

"Nothing much, no. He doesn't do a lot of work, really."

"It's just that everything he does is massively successful."

"Yes, if you look back on his career it's all award-winning shows. Not a lot, but it's all been chosen just right."

"That's what having a good agent is about."

Maurice didn't seem to notice the edge in the remark. "He's a talented boy, Charles."

"Where did he start?"

"I'm fairly sure he came out of one of the stage schools, but I don't know which one. Think he may have been a child star in films. Not sure, though."

"Know anything of his working reputation?"

"A bit temperamental, I've heard. But that's third hand. I mean stories like that go around about every big name in the business."

"Yes. Is he gay or anything?"

"No, I don't think so. Sure not, actually. He married that girl who was in that film . . . you know."

"I'm afraid I don't."

"Oh, the one who played opposite Nigel Thingummy in that. . . . Oh, you know. Name like Elsa or Virginia or—Charlotte Fable, that's it!"

"I've heard of her. Still together?"

"No, I think they split up eighteen months or so ago."

"Divorce?"

"Haven't seen anything about it. No, I shouldn't think he'd like the publicity. Rather lets down the image of lovability, and that's what the public expects of him."

"Hmm. Oh well, thanks."

"If you really want form, ask Johnny Wilson. He worked with him on the telly show."

"Oh yes. What's that called?"

"*Straight Up, Guv.* Surely you must have seen it."

"No, I haven't."

"Oh, it's a very funny show, Charles. I never miss it. It's on tonight at seven-thirty. These are repeats, actually, second time round, or is it third? Think of the money on a show like that. Probably sells round the world. That's what you need, Charles, a big, long-running television series."

"As part of my artistic development?"

"Of course."

That evening Charles watched television. He went round to see Jim Waldeman, a fellow actor who lived in Queen's Gardens with his wife Susie and a fairly new baby. He took a bottle of Bell's to ensure his welcome, but it was unnecessary. As he entered the door, both Jim and Susie's eyes lit up and, with a cry of "Babysitter!", they installed him in an armchair in front of the television and went off to the pictures. "Imagine," said Susie, "actually going to see a film. The excitement. We used to go about twice a week, but since *that* came along, we just haven't. At all. Bless you, Charles."

"What happens if it—"

"Oh, he won't. He's terribly good. But if he does, there's some Phenergan on the dresser. Cheerio." And the door slammed.

"What's Phenergan?" asked Charles weakly, but he realized they couldn't hear. He also realized that the slam of the door had woken the baby.

He switched on the television, determined that the child would soon be asleep again. It was a color set (Jim's career was obviously flourishing), but Charles caught the end of an old black and white movie. It was British, some story about a small boy bringing together his estranged parents. The father was an airman and there was a lot of stiff upper lip stuff about one last mission. The boy was a beautiful child, with a perfectly proportioned baby face and blond curls. Charles wondered idly if it was Christopher Milton in his child star days.

It was becoming clear that the baby was not going back to sleep. The keening cry sawed through the noise of the television. Charles looked at his watch. Twenty-five past seven. The crying showed no signs of abating and he didn't want to miss the beginning of the show. He went into the night-lit nursery and mumbled soothingly over the cot. The screams redoubled in volume. In the sitting-room music built to an heroic conclusion. He picked up the baby in its blanket and returned to the television.

The film credits flashed past. The child star was not Christopher Milton. Gareth Somebody, another who had no doubt vanished without trace to become an accountant or an estate agent or a double glazing salesman. After the film came a trailer for a program on Northern Ireland to be shown the following night.

The baby was not taking kindly to its move. The little mouth strained open like a goldfish and the pebble eyes almost vanished in folds of skin as it screamed. It was a long time since Charles had held a baby and he had forgotten the little tricks he had used when his own daughter Juliet was small. He tried rocking the little bundle and murmuring the Skye Boat Song. It didn't work.

On the television screen the credits rolled. Inevitably, "CHRISTOPHER MILTON" came first. Then "in STRAIGHT UP, GUV— by WALLY WILSON." Then "with" the names of a couple of those comedy supports who are never out of work and the inevitable wild studio applause faded into the show proper. (Why do studio audiences always applaud signature tunes and credits? The fact that they clap when nothing has happened casts serious doubts on the credibility of their subsequent reactions.) The episode started; Charles couldn't hear a word above the baby's howls.

In desperation he dipped a finger in his Scotch and proffered it to the bellowing mouth. The tiny lips closed round it as if determined to remove the skin. But there was silence.

It didn't last. After a few moments the suction was released and the bellowing recommenced. Charles hastily dipped his finger back in the glass and the mouth clamped on again. By repeating the process every two minutes he found he could watch *Straight Up, Guv* in comparative comfort.

It was not bad. The show was built around the adventures of a second-rate con-man Lionel Wilkins (played of course by Christopher Milton), whose attempts to pull off the big coup were always crowned with disaster. Wally Wilson's script was workmanlike, but uninspired; it was Christopher Milton's performance which raised it above the ordinary. Lionel Wilkins was a genuine comic creation, whose doomed cockiness was strangely engaging. He was the original Wobbly Man; every time you pushed him over, he bounced back up again. As catastrophe followed catastrophe and his face crumpled into crestfallen embarrassment, the audience roared. Each time he picked himself up with some new incongruous scheme and the audience roared again. Even Charles found himself laughing out loud at times. Christopher Milton's face in repose was unremarkable, but in the character it seemed capable of infinite comic variation. It was easy to see why the show had become a cult.

And, like many cult shows, it had a catch-phrase. As the worst reversal hit him, Lionel Wilkins paused in horror, the audience laughed in anticipation, and then, with perfect timing, he said, "I beg yours?" As Charles heard it, he recognized it, recognized it from shouting schoolboys in the street, giggling secretaries in the tube and half-heard impressionists on the radio. "I beg yours?" was Christopher Milton; he said it and the entire nation followed him.

When Jim and Susie returned, Charles and the baby were still watching television, and between them they'd got through half the bottle of Bell's.

CHAPTER 3

The Welsh Dragon Club near the Elephant and Castle had been built in more elegant times as a meeting-place for expatriate Welshmen of the upper and middle classes. It then boasted four tennis courts (grass), fielded six rugby teams and held very proper dances on Saturdays. The members tended to wear blazers or tweed, they had strong religious principles and, when drunk, broke into mournful song.

The club was now lost in a forest of concrete blocks. Two of the tennis courts had been sold for development and the others were now pink shale stained with moss. The only rugby discussed in the bar was what was seen on the television and the Saturday dances had been replaced by intermittent bookings for disco-parties (which were rarely profitable because of the number of broken windows). The members had gone down in class and numbers. They tended to lounge around in jeans and patterned pullovers, propped against the moth-eaten baize of the old notice-boards, occasionally throwing a desultory dart or pulling without hope at the arm of the one fruit machine. When they got drunk, they still broke into mournful song.

The club had one paid employee, who doubled the rôles of caretaker and barman. His name was Griff and he spent whole days propped over the bar reading an apparently inexhaustible copy of the *Sun*.

The club activities could not possibly make any profit, but the

Welsh Dragon stayed open. All its revenue came from hiring out rehearsal rooms. There were two—one where old cue-racks and brass score-boards against treacle-colored panels accentuated the absence of the long-sold billiard tables, and the other, grandly called the "Ballroom," a long expanse of bare boards with a tiny stage at one end and a wall of French windows which in the old days were left open for dances after summer tournaments. Many of the window panes had been broken and covered with asymmetrical offcuts of hardboard.

Charles was directed to the Ballroom, where a flotsam of chairs and upturned benches represented the expensive set of *Lumpkin!* (The designs, by Derbyshire Wilkes, were elaborate and featured considerable use of revolves and flown pieces.) The scene was like any morning in any rehearsal room. Actors and actresses sat on chairs round the edges of the room like the sad wallflowers who had once moped there after missing vital backhand returns in the mixed doubles. Little clusters formed round crosswords or gossip. Bleary bodies shuffled slowly out of the cocoons of their coats. A member of the stage management moved purposefully around the room, following some logic of her own. Hangovers and television were discussed, knitting was unwound.

The director, David Meldrum, was poring over the script at a small table isolated in the middle of the room. He was balding, with rimless glasses and somehow managed the pinched look of a clerk from a Dickens serial. Charles knew him by sight and introduced himself.

"Ah, Charles, hello. I gathered your name was being mentioned for the part. Nice to see you." He did not seem particularly interested in the addition to his cast. "Gwyneth will give you a rehearsal schedule."

At the mention of her name, the stage management girl homed in and handed Charles a cyclostyled sheet of times and scenes. Instinctively he assessed her. Old habits die hard and one of the first moves on joining any company is to examine the available crumpet. He decided that Gwyneth looked too dauntingly efficient for his taste. Not a high cuddlability rating.

As he sat down to study the schedule, Charles reflected that it was rather pathetic for him still to be studying the crumpet. He was nearly forty-nine years old and his emotional track record was not spectacular. There was a nice wife, Frances, in Muswell Hill, with whom he hadn't lived for fourteen years (in spite of occasional reconciliations) and who was now reputed to have a boy friend. Apart from her, it was a history of intense casual affairs, which were either too intense or too casual. Thinking about it depressed him, so he channeled his thoughts in another direction.

It was strange that David Meldrum had accepted his appearance so casually. Indeed, it was strange that the director had had no part in his selection for the rôle. "I gathered your name was being mentioned for the part." As if it had nothing to do with him. Charles racked his brains for any stray comments he had heard about the director and from some source he couldn't identify he remembered the words, "A good technician, love, but about as much imagination as a bread-board. Ought really to be in local government. Approaches a production like planning a car park." That made sense. David Meldrum was a director who would see that the show got on the stage. He might not have many ideas of his own, but at least he wouldn't argue with anyone else's. Charles felt certain that Christopher Milton's contract also included an Approval of Director clause.

He looked round for the star, but there was no sign of him. Five to ten. Perhaps he was one of those actors who makes a point of arriving just at the moment of the call.

As the room filled up, there were one or two familiar faces from a long time ago. He saw Michael Peyton, with whom he'd worked on his own production of *She Stoops to Conquer* in Cardiff. They grinned at each other across the room. A couple of other actors smiled vaguely, as unable to remember Charles' name as he was to remember theirs.

There were few actresses. Thinking of the original play, Charles could only remember three female characters—Mrs. Hardcastle, Kate Hardcastle and Miss Neville. He identified them easily. The middle-aged lady in a tweed trouser-suit and a scallop of blue-grey hair he recognized as Winifred Tuke. Good workmanlike actress. He remembered once overhearing her saying, "Been a feature player all my life and very happy at it—I've never wanted to be a star." She must be playing Mrs. Hardcastle. The thin girl with aquiline nose and straight blonde hair must be Miss Neville and the shorter one whose mouth and teeth were attractively too large looked absolutely right for Kate Hardcastle.

Michael Peyton came over to chat and confirmed the identification. The girl playing Kate was called Lizzie Dark, apparently only a year out of Sussex University and generally believed to have a glowing future.

"Nice looking kid, isn't she?" Charles observed.

"Yes. Fairly regular boy friend. Often comes and picks her up after rehearsals."

"Oh, I wasn't thinking. . . ."

"Of course you were."

"Well. . . ."

"There's always the tour."

"Hmm."

"And the dancers."

"When do they join us?"

"Next week. They're rehearsing separately."

"How the hell do dancers fit into *She Stoops to Conquer?*"

"If you think this show bears any relation to the play as we did it in Cardiff, you can't have read the script."

"True. I've only read my scenes."

"There's an actor for you. I hope you didn't count your lines."

"No," he lied.

David Meldrum stood up and moved to the center of the set in a rather apologetic way. "Um, perhaps we ought to start. . . ."

He was interrupted by the entry of a man in a donkey-jacket, who whispered something to him and sat down on a chair adjacent to the table. He had brown curly hair and a boyish face with a snub nose, but his skin belied the impression of youth. It had that *papier-mâchée* quality which is the legacy of bad acne.

"Who's he?" Charles hissed.

"Spike. He's the stage manager. Nice bloke. He must be down to see if we're actually going to be able to negotiate Derbyshire Wilkes' amazing set. Of course, there's always the stage staff," he added irrelevantly.

"What do you mean?"

"Potential crumpet."

"I'm too old."

"Come off it. Nothing like a warm little props girl to comfort a chap in his old age."

"Um, I think we should make a start," said David Meldrum.

"Where's the star, Michael?"

"Oh, he's never called till ten-thirty. It's in his contract."

In 1773 Oliver Goldsmith decided that Sir Charles Marlow should not appear in his play until the fifth act, so Charles Paris' rehearsal schedule was not too onerous. That much had survived the translation of *She Stoops to Conquer* into *Liberty Hall* and even the transmogrification of *Liberty Hall* into *Lumpkin!* The result was that, although there was ground to be made up and Charles would have to go through his scenes with the assistant director and be taxied off to Soho for a costume fitting that afternoon, he was not actually called for the morning. And because Griff the barman interpreted such concepts as club membership and licensing hours with a commendable degree of independence, by ten-thirty Charles and Michael Peyton were sitting in the bar over a couple of pints of bitter.

Griff was hunched over the *Sun,* reading between the lines of a photograph. In the corner a gloomy figure in denim battledress confronted the fruit machine, willing it to swallow his money and confirm his failure. Charles decided it might be a good moment to find if Gerald's suspicions about the two accidents were shared by an ordinary member of the company like Michael Peyton. "Funny way of coming into a show for me, you know, Mike. After an accident. Sort of dead men's shoes situation."

"Ah well, it's an ill wind."

"Yes. Poor old Everard."

"No one can expect to drink that much and stay perpendicular. Against the laws of physics."

"Yes. I suppose he just fell. . . ."

"Suppose so," said Michael without interest and certainly without suspicion.

"Hm." No harm in probing a bit further. "Funny, though, that accident coming straight after the other one."

"Other one?"

"The rehearsal pianist."

"Who? Alec?"

"No, the one before him."

Michael jutted forward his lower lip in an expression of ignorance. "Didn't know there was one."

"Oh, I heard some rumor. Must have got it wrong." Obviously to the ordinary member of the company there was nothing bizarre going on. There was no general feeling of doom, of a "bad luck" show. Gerald's imagination had been overstimulated by thoughts of the size of his financial investment. For Charles, it was just an acting job. He raised his glass to his lips and reflected on the differences between unemployed drinking and drinking with a nine-month contract. A warm glow filled him.

"Griff love, can you do me a port." The new voice belonged to a good-looking young man in a smart blazer and check trousers. "I've got the most frightful throat coming on and David's just sent me to go through my songs with Alec up in the billiard room."

"Port, 'eh?"

"It's the only thing for a throat, Griff."

"Huh."

"Mark, have you met Charles Paris?"

"No, Mike, I haven't. Hello, I'm Mark Spelthorne." He left an infinitesimal pause for Charles to say, "Yes, of course, I recognize your face from the television," but Charles didn't, so he continued. "You're taking over from poor old Everard?"

"That's right."

"Well, don't drink too much of that, or you'll go the same way."

"I'll be careful." It wasn't worth objecting to the young man's patronizing tone.

"Do you know, Mike," said Mark Spelthorne, though he was addressing the world in general rather than anyone in particular, "my agent is a bloody fool. He had a call yesterday from Yorath Knightley—do you know him?"

"No."

"BBC. Telly. Drama. Wanted me for a play, super part. Rehearsals the week after this opens. Lovely, just what I need. But my damn fool agent says, oh no, out of the question, they may have some rerehearsal and what have you on *Lumpkin!* Honestly, I said, well, surely, love, we can get a few days off, sort round the contract, organize the filming round the schedule for this show. Oh no, he says, you're under contract. No bloody imagination. I think I must get another agent."

"Sorry it took so long. Had to open a bottle. Don't get much call for port here. One or two of the ladies has it with lemon, but most of the gents drink beer or spirits."

"Never mind, Griff. Bless you," said Mark Spelthorne bountifully. He took a sip of the drink and gargled it gently, then swallowed. "Better." He repeated the process. Charles and Mike watched in silence as the glass slowly emptied. "Ah, well, better test out the old singing voice."

"If you want to hear real singing," said Griff morosely, "you want to listen to a Welsh male voice choir."

"Ah." Mark was nonplussed, not certain what his reaction should be.

"We used to have a choir here at the Welsh Dragon. Lovely singing. Better than anything I've heard since you lot've been here."

"That's a matter of opinion." Mark hesitated, uncertain whether or not that was a good enough exit line. Failing to come up with a better one, he exited to the billiard room.

"Should I know him, Mike? He behaved as if I should."

"Not unless you're a fan of *The Fighter Pilots*, Charles."

"What's that?"

"You're obviously not. It's an ITV series. Another cashing in on the nostalgia boom. Mark Spelthorne plays Flying Officer Falconer, whose daring missions and dreary love life fill up most of each episode."

"Oh. I've never heard of him in the theatre."

"I don't think he's done much. Presumably he did his forty weeks round the provinces to get the Equity card, but I think that's it. He's one of the media mushrooms who has sprung up overnight as a fully developed television star."

"Then why is he in this?"

"Publicity, Charles. So that he can be billed on the poster as Mark Spelthorne of *The Fighter Pilots*. That's to mop up the one per cent of the population who haven't come to see Christopher Milton of *Straight Up, Guv.*"

"The television takeover is complete."

"Yes."

"He seemed to have a fairly inflated opinion of himself."

"Ah, he would like to be a big star, Charles."

"And will he make it?"

"I don't know. Somehow I don't think so. Don't think he's got what it takes."

"What's he playing?"

"Your son, Young Marlow."

"That's the best part in the play."

"Was, Charles, was. Maybe that's what Goldsmith intended, but that was before Christopher Milton got his hands on the script."

"Yes," the gloomy man at the fruit machine chipped in suddenly and savagely. "Before Christopher Milton got his bloody hands on the script."

There was a moment's pause before Michael Peyton recovered himself sufficiently to make the introduction. "Charles Paris—Kevin McMahon."

"Ah yes. You wrote *Liberty Hall.*"

"In a previous existence, I think." His voice had the rough blur of a hangover and there was a large Scotch on a table beside the fruit machine. Having registered his protest, he seemed to lose interest in the two actors and, with an air of self-mortification, pressed another ten pence into the slot. Or maybe he turned away as a deliberate snub to the man entering the bar. "Morning, everyone. Hello, Griff. Charles Paris, isn't it?"

"That's right."

"Delighted you're with us on the show."

Charles took the offered firm handshake and looked into the clear, honest face. "My name's Christopher Milton."

CHAPTER 4

THE NEXT FEW weeks were an education for Charles. The sort of theatre he had always concentrated on had not depended on stars. Christopher Milton was a star.

At their initial meeting he was charming. There was only a short break in rehearsal, but he devoted it all to the new member of the company. And he had done his homework. He referred to incidents in Charles' career which he could not have guessed at, but which showed genuine interest or research. He spoke flatteringly about the one successful play Charles had written, *The Ratepayer*. In fact all the right things were said and Charles was impressed. He saw once again the distorting mirror of show-biz rumor at work. Reputations get inflated and diminished by gossip and scandal. One bitchy remark by a jealous actor can give the permanent stigma of being "difficult" to another. Time and again Charles had encountered supposedly "lovely" people who were absolute monsters and been charmed by supposed monsters. And he found Christopher Milton charming.

As rehearsals developed and he began to feel part of the company, it was increasingly difficult to take Gerald's fears of sabotage seriously. There was an air of tension about the production, but no more than one would expect from any show at that stage of development. Charles' rôle was not an onerous one, and Griff's ever-open bar was an ideal place to toast Gerald's excessive anxiety which had got him the job.

He had a slight twinge of misgiving as the Tuesday approached. Gerald had made such an issue of the fact that the two accidents had taken place exactly a week apart. If there were a psychopathic wrecker about, determined to ruin the show, then he would strike again on the Tuesday.

Charles went to rehearsal that morning with some trepidation but the day passed and there wasn't so much as a cold among the cast. He decided that he had just landed on his feet in an acting job. Eighty pounds a week and sucks to the taxman.

He had not seen much of the show except for the scenes which involved him, but on the Wednesday he decided to stay on after he'd finished. They were rehearsing the Chase Scene at the end.

Now Goldsmith did not write a Chase Scene. In his play Tony Lumpkin meets Hastings and describes how he has just led Mrs. Hardcastle and Miss Neville on a circular wild goose chase until, "with a circumbendibus, I fairly lodged them in the horse-pond at the bottom of the garden." But description is not the stuff of West End musicals. Kevin McMahon had written a small chase into *Liberty Hall* and had been persuaded to expand it for *Lumpkin!* The result was a massive production number with song and dance, as Tony Lumpkin actually led the two ladies in their coach through mire and thicket. The dancers, playing a series of misdirecting yokels, buxom country wenches and a full-scale fox hunt which would have amazed Goldsmith, were rehearsing elsewhere on their own, and the special effects of fog, rain and snow were not yet available. Nor was it possible to simulate the moving trees and revolving cottages which were to add visual excitement to the scene. But it was already a complicated sequence and an interesting one to watch.

It also gave Charles his first opportunity to see Christopher Milton in action, building a part. The result was impressive. Tony Lumpkin was emerging as a complete comic character, totally different from Lionel Wilkins. The London whine of the television con-man had been replaced by a rich West Country accent and instead of sentimental incompetence, there was a roguishly knowing confidence. Charles began to feel that Dickie Peck's claims for his client's talent were not so ridiculous.

David Meldrum had by now been nicknamed David Humdrum and it fitted. He ordered people round the acting space like a suburban gardener laying a patio. Everything had to be exactly in place, every move exactly matching the neat plans in his script. But it was not the perfectionism of genius; it was the predictability of a man who had worked out his blocking with pins on a stage model long before rehearsals had started.

Still, it was professional and efficient. The production advanced. And for a complex commercial show it's probably better to have a good journeyman than a genius.

Anyway, David Meldrum was only providing the skeleton; the flesh was the performances. And Christopher Milton was fleshing up nicely. He had a song called *Lead 'em Astray*, for which Micky Gorton had written some most ungoldsmithian lyrics.

> *"Get them going*
> *The wrong way*
> *There's no knowing*
> *What they'll say.*
> *Hey, hey, hey,*
> *Lead 'em astray."*

If Gorton's lyrics did have a fault it was a tendency to the nonspecific. They had been written not to advance the plot, but to be taken out of the show and recorded by pop stars. However, Carl Anthony's tunes were good and *Lead 'em Astray*, in spite of its anachronism, captured the excitement and mischief of Tony Lumpkin. In Christopher Milton's performance, even with just the rehearsal piano, it was a potential show-stopper.

It was also very funny. His movements were beautiful. They showed the clodhopping clumsiness of the character and yet they were very precise. He darted round the two chairs which represented Mrs. Hardcastle's coach and wove his way through the other chairs which were trees. On the chorus of the song he froze for a moment, then jerked forward like a car left in gear, then stopped and flashed a look of sheer devilment at the audience. The timing made the gesture hilarious; even the cast who had seen it many times before laughed spontaneously. He seemed encouraged by the reaction and in the next verse his movements became more grotesque and jerky. He bounced up to the coach and pecked forward like a chicken with a head that suddenly seemed disconnected from his body. There was a splutter from Miss Neville, the unmistakable sound of someone "<u>corpsing</u>." Christopher Milton rose to it and varied the steps of his dance into a strange little jig. This struck Miss Neville as even funnier and soon she was gasping, incapable with laughter, while tears flowed down her cheeks.

The laughter spread. Mrs. Hardcastle started, then one by one, the watching actors caught it. Charles found himself giggling uncontrollably. It was one of those moments of communal hysteria which cannot be explained, but where everything suddenly gets funnier and funnier.

Only Christopher Milton stayed in control. The pianist was laughing too much to continue playing, but the star sang and danced on to the end of the number. His movements got faster and stranger and funnier until suddenly at the end he dropped flat on his back.

The timing was immaculate. It was the perfect end to the sequence. And it was impossible not to applaud. Charles, who was almost in pain from laughing, joined the others clapping.

As the noise subsided into scattered gasps and deep breaths, a strange stillness came over the room. Christopher Milton was still the focus of attention, but the mood had changed. Everyone watched him as he sat up, but he did not seem to be aware of them. He rose pensively to his feet, and moved slowly forward. "I think we can do more with that," he said.

The remark did not seem to be addressed to anyone in particular, but David Meldrum, as director, felt that he should pick it up. "What do you mean, Christopher?"

"I mean there's not enough happening on stage in that number."

"Well, of course, we haven't got the dancers yet, and the—"

"Shut up. I'm thinking." He said it dismissively, as if he were swatting a fly. Then slowly: "We need more movement from me, bobbing up all over the place. . . . Yes, we need doubles."

"Doubles?"

"Yes, doubles for me. People my height, dressed in the same costume. So that I can disappear behind one tree and appear behind another, come out of trap doors. Really make it into a silent film sequence."

"But it works very well like this and—"

"I told you to shut up. That's how we're going to do it. The whole thing will have to be replotted."

"But we haven't got time."

"We'll make time."

"Look, it's a tight rehearsal schedule—"

"Sod the rehearsal schedule. We can reblock this tomorrow afternoon."

"We're meant to be doing the Young Marlow/Kate scenes tomorrow."

"You can do those on Friday."

"No," Mark Spelthorne's voice drawled out. "I can't do Friday. I'm released for the day. Doing a pilot of a radio series."

"You're contracted here."

"Agent cleared the release, Christopher old boy."

"I don't care what your sodding agent's done. You're contracted here."

"Listen, it's a pilot of my own show."

"Your own show. Huh." The laugh was loaded with scorn. "A pilot for your own show. I wouldn't bother. Don't do it. It'll save you disappointment when they turn the idea down."

"What do you mean?"

"I mean that you'll never have a show of your own. You haven't got it in you. Adequate, you are. The word adequate was invented to describe people like you."

"What the hell do you mean?" Mark had risen sharply, as if he were about to strike his antagonist. Christopher Milton looked at him with contempt.

There was a long pause. Then Mark Spelthorne backed away. He muttered, "Bloody prima donna" in an unsuccessful tone of defiance, and walked out of the room.

A long silence followed. Everyone except Christopher Milton looked horribly embarrassed. But they all waited for him to speak first.

When he did, it was as if the argument had never happened, as if he had just been thinking. "We'll reblock this Chase Scene tomorrow afternoon."

"Yes," agreed David Meldrum. "Fine."

Charles was glad when the rehearsals were over that day. The atmosphere was uncomfortable, although Christopher Milton seemed oblivious of it.

By chance, Charles found himself leaving at the same time as the star. They walked out of the Welsh Dragon Club in silence. Charles felt ill at ease, as though he were about to be asked to take sides, to say what he thought of Mark Spelthorne.

But that was not at all what happened. As they emerged from the Club, Christopher Milton was suddenly surrounded by small boys from the tower blocks opposite. One of them must have seen the star go in earlier in the day and spread the word. They were a rough lot, of various colors and degrees of scruffiness. They all clamored up to Christopher Milton with scraps of paper for autographs.

As the kids moved in, a stocky figure in a dark suit detached himself from a parked Rolls Corniche and moved forward as if anticipating trouble. A gesture from Christopher Milton stopped him and he moved back to lean against the metallic brown flank of the car.

"All right, all right. Who's first?" The voice was instantly that of Lionel Wilkins.

It was exactly what the audience wanted. They all howled with laughter and clamored even louder for autographs. "All right, all right. Give me a pen," whined Lionel Wilkins. A biro was thrust into his hands. He dropped it with a distinctive Wilkins gesture. The audience howled again.

"All right. You first. What's your name?"

"Mahendra Patel."

The timing was immaculate. An eyebrow shot up, the mouth dropped open and Lionel Wilkins said, "I beg yours?"

The catch-phrase produced screams of delight and the little crowd jostled and shouted as their hero signed all the grubby comics, pages torn out of school books, and cigarette packets they thrust at him. He was punctilious about getting every name right and signed nearly thirty, by the time he had supplied sisters and cousins (and a few imaginary sisters and cousins to be sold at school for profit).

Eventually, they were all done. With a few more Lionel Wilkins lines and a demonstration of the Lionel Wilkins walk, Christopher Milton edged towards the back door of the Corniche. The driver opened it smartly and the star was inside. The electric window came down and the cabaret continued. The car started, the kids shouted louder, Christopher Milton waved, called out, "Cheerio, Charles, see you tomorrow," and the car drew away.

Charles had felt awkward during the autograph session. He didn't want to sneak off quietly, nor to come too much into the center of things in case it looked as if he wanted to be asked for his signature too. But now Christopher Milton had drawn attention to him by mentioning his name, he felt the focus of a dozen pairs of questioning eyes.

He made a vague wave in their direction and started to turn hoping something wouldn't happen.

It did. Two little Indian boys, Mahendra Patel and a younger brother, came towards him. "May I have your autograph?" asked the elder in perfect Cockney.

"Oh, you don't want it." He tried to laugh it off, but the lolly wrapper which had been thrust forward was not withdrawn. Blushing furiously, he signed. The other boys stood and stared. With an ineffectual cheery wave, he gave the paper to Mahendra. Then he turned and hurried away. But not fast enough to avoid hearing the little Cockney voice say, "No, it isn't him."

He drank rather more than he should have done that evening at his depressing local in Westbourne Grove. He felt emotionally raw, on the edge of depression for the first time since the rehearsals had started. And, as he knew from experience, when he felt in that mood, things got out of proportion.

The afternoon's flare-up had left a nasty taste. It cast doubt on the whole atmosphere of the show. Charles realized the fragility of what he had taken to be such a good company spirit. Maybe he had condemned himself to nine months of unnecessary unpleasantness.

But after the third large Bell's he felt more able to analyse what had happened at the rehearsal. All Christopher Milton had done was to be rude to David Meldrum and Mark Spelthorne. In a good cause—he had only been thinking of improving the show. And David Meldrum's passivity positively invited rudeness. So did the affectations of that little tit Mark Spelthorne. In fact, all Christopher Milton had done was to express the opinions held by most of the cast. In fact, he had shown pretty good judgment in his choice of butts.

Having rationalised that, Charles felt better. He went and got another large Bell's.

The next day Christopher Milton was all over the *Sun* newspaper. "It's Nightshirt Week in the Sun!" said the front page and the centerspread was a large photograph of the star in a long Dickensian nightshirt and drooping nightcap, holding a candle. He wore the familiar Lionel Wilkins expression of appalled surprise.

When it comes to nightwear, Christopher Milton, better known as Lionel Wilkins, says a nightshirt's the answer—so long as it's a long one. "Otherwise you get very cold round the . . . round the . . . um, er . . . round the middle of the night. It's no fun waking up in December with your nightie round your neck." 34-year-old Christopher is currently rehearsing a big new musical, *Lumpkin!*, which opens in the West End late November. "The part I'm playing's a bit different from Lionel Wilkins. Tony Lumpkin's a chap who likes making trouble for everyone—oh yes, he's always getting the girls into trouble—Ooh, that's not what I meant. I beg yours!" With lovable Christopher Milton around, *Lumpkin!* should be a show worth seeing.

Lovable Christopher Milton's behavior at rehearsals became more erratic. There were more breaks in the flow, more orders to David Meldrum to shut up, more long pauses while he worked out how a comic effect should be achieved. It was intolerable behavior on the part of a professional actor, and yet Charles could forgive it, because he was gaining an increasing respect for the man's theatrical instinct. Christopher Milton was always right, he knew what would work for an audience. And, given David Humdrum's total lack of this quality, *Lumpkin!* needed some inspiration.

But it wasn't popular with the rest of the cast, because Christopher Milton's comic instinct was only applied to his own part. The rest of the action was hurried through and substantial cuts were suggested. Only occasionally would there be a long discussion about one of the straight scenes, and that was only if the opportunity was seen for another entrance by Tony Lumpkin.

"Um, Christopher. . . ."

"Shut up, David. I'm thinking."

"Look, we want to get on with this first meeting between Young Marlow and Kate."

"Yes, I was thinking it might be better if Tony Lumpkin overheard this scene. I could be behind the screen and. . . ."

"Oh, for God's sake," snapped Mark Spelthorne. "This is one of the most famous scenes in English drama. It would make nonsense of the plot if Lumpkin overheard it. It wouldn't add anything."

Christopher Milton did not seem to hear the objection; he was still working the scene out in his own mind. "I mean, it's not a very interesting scene, no jokes or anything. I think it could be improved with Lumpkin there."

Mark Spelthorne grew apopleptic. "That's a load of absolute balls!"

"Um, Christopher," said David Meldrum tentatively, "I think we probably will be better off doing the scene as it is."

"Hmm." Again he was distant, still mentally planning. There was a long pause. "I'll have a look at it." He moved from the center of the stage, picked up his script and sat quietly in a corner looking at it. The rehearsals continued.

Such confrontations were not conducive to good feeling. Griff's bar became a center of disaffection and at any time of day there would be a little knot of actors there discussing their latest grievance against the star. Mark Spelthorne was always one of the most vociferous. "I mean, let's face it, when Goldsmith wrote the play, he intended Young Marlow to be the hero. There's no question about that. Which was why I took the part. Of course, my bloody agent didn't check the script, just assumed that I would be playing the lead. At least one has the comfort that all this mucking about with the show is making a complete nonsense of it. It'll never run. Doubt if we'll actually come in, die quietly on the tour, I shouldn't wonder. And that won't do a great deal for the career of Mr. Christopher Milton. Maybe teach him the dangers of overexposure."

"I don't know, Mark. He doesn't actually do that much work. He's very selective in what he does. Anyway, you can't talk. You're doing plenty yourself."

"Oh yes, that's always a danger if one's popular. Have to watch it. I mean, no doubt there'll be another series of *The Fighter Pilots*. And then if this radio takes off. . . ."

"Oh yes, that was the pilot show. How did it go?"

"Bloody marvellous. Really went a bomb. The planners'll be fools to themselves if they turn that one down. So I suppose I'll be stuck with doing a series of that early next year. Not that I mind. I mean, radio doesn't take long and in fact I have quite an affection for it. The main thing is it's comedy, and really comedy's my best thing. The radio might persuade the telly boys how good I am at it. That's the trouble in telly, they do so like to pigeon-hole people. After this *Fighter Pilots* thing, they seem to think I'm only good for the handsome young hero type, whereas of course. . . ."

There were plenty of others in the company with complaints about Christopher Milton, but Charles put it down to the ordinary ineffectual bitching of actors. No one seemed sufficiently motivated to want to sabotage the show. As time went on, Gerald's fears seemed more and more insubstantial.

* * *

It was on the Tuesday of the fourth week of rehearsals that Charles began to wonder. By then the scale of the production had got larger. The dancers had joined the company, though they kept somewhat aloof in their self-contained, camp little world. None of them had identifiable parts, except for the prettiest girl who had been given the wordless rôle of Bet Bouncer. There had also been a music rehearsal with the full orchestra ("We can't afford more than one with the band, because of the expense"), and the musicians added another element of an alien culture. The rehearsals became more concerned with details. There were constant discussions with Derbyshire Wilkes, the designer, and Spike, the stage manager, about exact sizes of parts of the set. The pieces of tape which marked their outlines were constantly rearranged. Actors were continually being rushed off in taxis for final costume fittings. The whole production was building up to its first appearance in a theatre on the Saturday week. On that day, their last in London before the tour, *Lumpkin!* was going to have a run on an improvised set in the King's Theatre.

The presence of the augmented company did not stop Christopher Milton's continual interruption of rehearsals while he worked out new entrances and business for Tony Lumpkin. His fits of temperament did not worry the dancers or musicians. Both were well used to hanging around at the whim of whoever happened to be in charge. Whether the break was for a broken microphone or a tantrum did not make a lot of difference to them. They just waited impassively until it was time to continue. And the male dancers had a stage-struck camp affection for stardom. They would have felt cheated if Christopher Milton hadn't behaved like a star.

On the Tuesday they were rehearsing the closer (that is, the last new song of the show, not the acres of reprises which followed it). It was called *Never Gonna Marry You* ("gonna" was a favorite word in Micky Gordon's lyrics) and it sewed up the Lumpkin side of the plot by getting him out of marriage to his cousin and into marriage with Bet Bouncer (while, incidentally, leaving the rest of the plot totally unresolved). It was the only moment in the show when

Charles had to sing, which was a great relief to him. Just one couplet and he was quite pleased with it. The lines rose above the general level of Micky Gorton's wit.

> *"Marriage is like a hot bath, I confess—*
> *The longer you're in it, the colder it gets."*

It probably wasn't an original line and it didn't rhyme properly, but it was a line that would get a laugh, and that was quite a bonus to an actor in a supporting rôle. Charles cherished it; it was the only laugh he stood to get in the show.

After he had sung the couplet in rehearsal that Tuesday, there was a long pause. Christopher Milton had the next line, but he let the music continue and was silent. He looked at Charles with the preoccupied expression he always wore when he was working something out. As the accompaniment died down to untidy silence, he spoke. "You know, that line will probably get a laugh."

"I hope so," said Charles cheerily. "Unless I cock it up."

"Hmm. I think I ought to sing it."

"I beg your pardon."

"I think I ought to have the line rather than you."

"What?" Charles was stunned by the directness of the approach. He was a fairly easy-going actor and didn't make scenes over minor details as a rule, but the brazenness of this took him off his guard. "Oh, come on, Christopher, you can't have all the laughs in the show."

"I think I should have that line." Christopher Milton's voice had the familiar distant quality of previous encounters with other actors whose parts he had raided.

"But it strikes me, Christopher, that that line would come much more naturally from Old Marlow, the man of the world, than from Tony Lumpkin, who, let's face it, is meant to be fairly uneducated and—"

"I think I should sing it."

"Look, I'm not claiming that I'd deliver it better than you or anything. It's just that—"

"Huh." The laugh came out with great savagery. "I should think not. You'd hardly expect great delivery of lines from a tired old piss-artist. I'm sure there are lots of actors who get through their careers with your level of *competence*, but don't you start comparing yourself with me."

The suddenness of the attack hurt like a blow in the face. Charles tried some acid line about people who felt they should have all the lines and about acting being a team effort, but it misfired. He appealed to David Meldrum for a decision and—surprise, surprise —David thought Christopher Milton probably had got a point.

Charles spent the rest of the day's rehearsal in a state of silent fury. He knew that his face was white and he was hardly capable of speech. He felt sick with anger.

As soon as he was released, he got a taxi back to Bayswater. Too churned up even for the distant conviviality of the pub, he stopped at an off licence on the way and went back to his room with a bottle of Scotch.

The room in Hereford Road was an untidy and depressing mess, with grey painted cupboards and yellow candlewick on the unmade bed. Its atmosphere usually reduced him to a state of instant depression, but on this occasion it had too much anger to compete with and he hardly noticed his surroundings. He just sat and drank solidly until there was a slight shift in his mood and he could think of something other than his fury.

It was only a line, after all. Not even a particularly good line at that. And the show was hardly one that was very important to him or one that was going to make any difference to what was laughingly called his career. It wasn't like him to get so upset over a detail.

And then he began to realize the power of Christopher Milton's personality. From his own over-reactions Charles understood the intensity of resentment that the man could inspire. Which made him think that perhaps there were people who felt sufficiently strongly to sabotage any show Christopher Milton was in.

Charles decided that he would make a belated start to the business of investigation for which Gerald Venables had engaged him. Since he had no rehearsals the following morning, he would go and see Everard Austick.

CHAPTER 5

EVERARD AUSTICK'S ADDRESS was a block of flats in Eton College Road, near Chalk Farm Underground Station. Charles found it in the phone book and went along on the off-chance that its owner would be out of hospital. He could have rung to check, but felt disinclined to explain his inquiries on the telephone. Also there was a chance that the dry agony of his hangover might have receded by the time he got there.

In fact the tube journey didn't help much and, as he stood in the old lift gazing ahead at its lattice-work metal door, he felt in need of a red-hot poker to burn out the rotten bits of his brain. The only coherent thought he could piece together was the eternal, "Must drink less."

The block of flats was old, with long gloomy corridors interrupted by the stranded doormats of unwelcoming doorways. Number 108 was indistinguishable from the others, the same blue gloss paint, the same glass peephole to warn the inmate of approaching burglars, rapists, etc.

Charles' pressure on the doorbell produced no reaction. Perhaps it wasn't working. He pressed again, his ear to the door, and caught the distant rustle of its ring. Oh well, maybe Everard was still in hospital, or away convalescing. One more try.

This time there was a distant sound of a door opening, a muttered curse and the heavy approach of a plaster-cased foot. The door opened and Everard Austick peered blearily out into the shadows of the corridor. He looked a mess. His grey hair stuck out in a series of Brylcreemed sheaves as he had slept on it. He had only shaved sketchily for a few days and the areas he had missed sprouted long bristles. A dilapidated camel dressing-gown was bunched around his large frame. His right leg was grotesquely inflated by its plaster. He was probably only in his fifties, but he looked an old man.

"Can I help you?" he asked in a public school voice furred with alcohol.

"Yes. I'm sorry to trouble you. My name's Charles Paris."

Fuddled incomprehension.

"We worked together once for a season in Glasgow."

"Ah. Ah yes, of course." But he didn't remember.

"Look, I've taken over the part you were playing in *Lumpkin!*"

"Oh. Do you want to come in?"

"Thank you." Everard Austick backed away and Charles moved past him into the dim hall. A door gave off on to a large sitting-room and he made towards it. "Er, not in there if you don't mind."

Charles had seen the smart decor of the room and looked back quizzically at Everard. "Fact is, old boy, I don't use all the flat. No point in using it all when I'm away so much . . . I . . . er, there's a young couple who also live here. Just on a temporary basis. Helps out with the old rent, what?" The jovial tone could not hide the facts. Everard Austick was so hard up that he had to rent out almost all his flat to keep his head above water.

This impression was confirmed when Charles was led into Everard's bedroom, obviously the smallest in the flat. The air tasted as if it hadn't been changed for a fortnight. A pile of dusty magazines against them showed that the windows hadn't been opened for months, and the bed was rumpled not just by one night's occupation, but by long days and nights of simply lying and staring at the ceiling rose.

A half-empty bottle of vodka on the dressing-table was evidence of the only activity the room had seen for some time. "Sorry it's a bit of a tip," said Everard, attempting to play the line with light comedy insouciance. "Can I offer you a drink? There's only the vodka, I'm afraid. Well, I suppose I could make some coffee, but. . . ." His mind was unable to cope with the incongruity of the idea.

"A little vodka would be fine." A hair of the dog might possibly loosen the nutcrackers on Charles' head.

He received a clouded toothmug half-full of vodka . . . Everard Austick's hand shook as he passed it over and topped up his own tumbler. "Down the hatch, old boy." The long swallow he took was not an action of relish, but of dependence. He grimaced, shuddered and looked at Charles. "Now, what can I do for you, old man? Want a bit of help in your interpretation of the part, eh?" Again the cheerfulness sounded forced.

"No, actually I just wanted to pick your brains about something." Charles paused. It was difficult. He did not want to reveal his rôle as an investigator into the show. He realized that he had not done enough preparation for the encounter; he should have worked out some specious story to explain his interest, or even made the approach in some other identity. Still, too late now. Better to try the direct question and hope that Everard's bemused condition would prevent him from being suspicious. "You know when you broke your leg—what happened?"

"I fell down the stairs."

"Just an accident?"

"Oh, God knows. I'd had quite a skinful the night before, met a few chums, celebrating actually being in work, it had been a long time. And I had a few more in the morning, you know, to pull me round, and I managed to leave late, so I was hurrying, so I suppose I could have just fallen."

"Or?"

"Well, there was this chap on the stairs, ran down from behind me, I thought he sort of jostled me. I don't know though."

"And that's what caused you to fall?"

"Could have been. I don't know."

"Did he stop to help you when you fell?"

"No, he seemed to be in a hurry."

"Hmm. Did you see what he looked like?"

"No."

"Not even an impression?"

"Nothing."

"Did you tell the police?"

"No. Who's going to believe me? I'm not even sure it happened myself. Could just have fallen."

"Yes." The interrogation did not seem to be getting anywhere. Everard Austick was so fogged with alcohol that he didn't even trust his own memory. No one was going to get anything else out of him. Charles drained his glass and rose to leave.

"You're off?" Everard seemed to accept the departure with as little surprise as he had the arrival. Nothing seemed strange in his half-real world. "Actually, there is one thing, old boy."

"Yes?"

"This damned leg, I find it so difficult to get about, you know, get to the bank and so on, a bit short of cash, for the . . . er . . . you know, basic necessities of life."

The expansive gesture which accompanied the last four words was meant to signify a whole range of food and domestic essentials, but it ended up pointing at the nearly-empty vodka bottle.

Out of guilt or something, Charles gave him a fiver. Then a thought struck him. "Everard, why didn't you use the lift that morning?"

"Wasn't working."

"Sure?"

"I pushed the button for it and it didn't come for a long time. I told you I was in a hurry."

"Yes. Thank you."

Charles walked slowly along the dim corridor until he came to the lifts. He looked at them closely. Both were the old sort with sliding doors. A notice requested users to close both doors firmly. Otherwise the lifts would not function. So it would be possible to immobilize both by calling them to another floor and leaving them with their doors ajar. It would then be possible to linger in the gloomy corridor until Everard Austick staggered out of his flat, watch him call unsuccessfully for the lift and then help him on his way when he started downstairs. Unlikely, but possible.

* * *

"Hello, Gerald, it's Charles. I got your message at the rehearsal rooms and I'm afraid this is the first chance I've had to call."

"Okay. How's it going?"

"Nothing to report really. Nothing else has happened."

"No tension in the company?"

"No more than in any show with Christopher Milton in it which starts its pre-London tour in a week."

"Hmm. Maybe I was being alarmist."

"Maybe. Anyway, thanks for the job."

"Any time. Keep your eyes skinned."

"Okay. Though I don't know what for. There's nothing to see."

"Unless something else happens."

"Hello, is that Ruth?"

"Yes. Who's speaking?"

"Charles Paris."

"Good God. I thought the earth had swallowed you up long ago."

"No. Still large as life and twice as seedy."

"Well, to what do I owe this pleasure? Tidying out your room and just found a seven-year-old diary?"

"No."

"Joined Divorcees Anonymous have you, they gave you my number?"

"Actually I'm still not divorced."

"Separated though?"

"Oh yes."

"And you just phoned for the Recipe-of-the-Day, did you? It's stew."

"No, the fact is, I'm in a show that's about to start a pre-London tour and our first week's in Leeds and, with true actor's instinct, I thought, well, before I fix up any digs, I'll see if I've got any old friends in Leeds. . . ."

"You've got a nerve."

"Sorry, I shouldn't have asked. I'll—"

"No. It might be quite entertaining to see you after all these years. At least a change from the sort of men who hang around divorcees in Leeds. When do you arrive?"

"Sunday."

As Charles put the phone down, Ruth's voice still rang, ominously familiar, in his ears and he had the feeling that he had done something stupid.

If all went well on the tour, *Lumpkin!* was to take over the King's Theatre from a show called *Sex of One and Half a Dozen of the Other*, which had long outstayed its welcome. It had been put on in 1971 by Marius Steen and had celebrated a thousand performances just before the impresario's mysterious death in which Charles Paris had become involved. As the Steen empire was slowly dismantled, the show had continued under different managements with increasingly diluted casts until even the coach party trade began to dwindle. It limped through the summer of 1975 on tourists, but had no chance of surviving the pre-Christmas slump. The theatre-going public had been too depressed by rising ticket prices and the fear that the terrorist bombs might return with the dark evenings to make the effort to see a tired old show. *Sex of One . . .* had made its London killing and was now off to pick up the residuals of national tours, the depredations of provincial theatre companies and finally the indignities perpetrated by amateur dramatic societies.

On Saturday, October 25th, the last day of London rehearsals, the *Lumpkin!* cast assembled for a pre-tour run-through in the King's. The idea was to gain familiarity with the place before the ceremonial entry on November 27th.

The call was for nine o'clock, so that everything should be ready when Christopher Milton arrived at his contractual ten-thirty. Time was tight. *Sex of One . . .* had a three o'clock matinée and their set (most of which had been dismantled and piled up against the naked brick walls at the back of the stage) had to be reassembled by two-thirty. This meant that an eleven o'clock start would just allow a full run, with only half an hour allowed for cock-ups.

The run was not to be with costume or props. Everything had been packed up into skips and was already on its way to Leeds. The set was in lorries on the M1, scheduled to arrive for the get-in at ten-thirty that night when the current show at the Palace Theatre (a second-rate touring revival of *When We Are Married*) finished its run. Spike, the stage manager, was going to see the run-through, then leap on to the five to four train to Leeds and maybe grab a little sleep in anticipation of the all-night and all-day job of getting the set erected and dressed. The actors' schedule was more leisurely. After the run, their next call was at seven o'clock on the Sunday evening for a technical rehearsal. At eleven the next morning there was a press conference in the bar of the Palace Theatre, a dress rehearsal at one, and at seven-thirty on Monday, October 27th, *Lumpkin!* was to meet a paying audience for the first time.

The audience in the King's Theatre on the Saturday morning had not paid. They were all in the circle. David Meldrum, with a rare display of personality, had taken over all of the stalls and set up a little table in the middle. A Camping Gaz lamp was ready to illuminate his interleaved script and notes when the lights went down. Two chairs were set there, one for him and one for Gwyneth, ever efficient, never passing comment.

Up in the circle were some of the backers, who joked nervously like race-horse owners, frightened of coughs, lameness and nobbling. Dickie Peck was there, salivating over his cigar until it looked like a rope-end. There was a representative of Amulet Productions, who looked as if he had gone to a fancy-dress ball as a merchant banker. Gerald Venables was too cool to turn up himself and reveal his anxiety, but a junior member of the office was there representing the interests of Arthur Balcombe. Some other seats were occupied by Press representatives and a few girl and boy friends who had been smuggled in.

The stage manager had imposed dress rehearsal discipline and the cast were not allowed out front. Nor were they encouraged to make themselves at home in the dressing-rooms, so there was a lot of hanging around in the green room and the wings. Charles decided that once the run started he would adjourn to the nearest pub. Even with a totally trouble-free run, Sir Charles Marlow could not possibly be required onstage until one o'clock. He knew he should really hang about the green room listening to the gossip and trying to cadge a lift up to Leeds. But he hated cadging and would rather actually spend the travel allowance he had received on a train ticket than try it.

He listened to the beginning of the run-through on the Tannoy. It sounded pretty pedestrian. He left a message as to his where abouts with one of the stage management and started towards the pub.

But just as he was leaving the green room, he met Mark Spelthorne. "Good God, Charles, it's pitch dark out there on the stage. There's just some basic preset and no working lights on in the wings. I just tripped over something and went headlong."

"What did you trip over?" he asked, suddenly alert.

"Don't know. Something just by the back exit from the stage."

Charles moved quietly in the dark behind the black tabs which represented the limits of the *Lumpkin!* set. He had a chilly feeling that he was about to discover something unpleasant.

His foot touched a soft shape. Soft cloth. He knelt down in the dark and put his hands forward reluctantly to feel what it was.

Just at that moment someone became aware of the lack of light backstage and switched on working lights. Charles screwed up his eyes against the sudden brightness, then opened them and looked down.

It was a cushion. A large scatter cushion, part of the set dressing for *Sex of One* . . . , which had been dropped when the set was cleared. Charles felt sheepish and looked round, embarrassed. He was alone. He shut off the flow of melodramatic thoughts which had been building in his head.

Still, he was there in a watchdog capacity. Better safe than sorry, he argued in self-justification. To reinforce this illusion of purpose he went across to the pile of tall, heavy flats leant haphazardly against the brick wall. They did not look very safe, some nearly vertical, some almost overhanging. He inspected more closely. Oh, it was all right, there was a pair of thick ropes crossed over the flats, restraining them. They were fixed to rings at the top and the loose ends were wound firmly round a large wooden cleat on the wall. No danger there. Charles tried not to feel a fool and went off to the pub.

That morning's run-through had all the animation of a bus queue. Nothing went wrong, but, God, it was dull. Everyone seemed to feel this and there was a great sag as they came to the end of the final reprise. "Excellent," said David Meldrum's voice from somewhere near the Camping Gaz glow. "Two hours, fifty-seven minutes," as if the stopwatch were the only criterion of theatrical excellence. "Right, well done, everybody. Now we must clear the theatre as soon as possible. I've got one or two notes on that run, but I'll give them to you before the Tech. run on Sunday. Okay. See you all in Leeds. That run was really super, loves."

The cast, who didn't agree and didn't think saying "loves" suited him, dispersed grumbling. There was a communal feeling of apathetic gloom. The *Sex of One . . .* stage crew came onstage to start rebuilding their set for a few coachloads of sweet-paper-rustling pensioners. Dickie Peck arrived and started to talk in an undertone to Christopher Milton. The star's driver, who had also appeared from somewhere, stood at a respectful distance. The cast hurried off to tie up the loose ends of their shopping, or sex lives, which had to be done before they left London. Charles made for the exit.

It was at that moment that all the working lights went out again. This was greeted by the usual curses and cheap jokes. Then suddenly there was another sound, an ominous heavy scrape of wood. It merged into a thud and a scream of pain. Voices, suddenly serious, shouted, "Lights!"

The working lights revealed a silent tableau. The pile of flats had toppled forward from the wall and lay almost flat on the ground. Protruding from under them was the torso of Mark Spelthorne. Christopher Milton, his driver and Dickie Peck were frozen where the flats had just missed them. Other members of the cast and stage crew stood aghast.

Suddenly everyone rushed forward and started heaving at the wood and canvas to lift it off Mark's body.

"It's all right," came the familiar drawl. "Don't fret."

The helpers stood back as Mark extricated himself. He stood up and rubbed his shoulder.

"Are you all right?"

"I think I'll have a bit of a bruise tomorrow, but otherwise, fine."

"God, you were lucky," said Spike, who was looking at where the top edges of the flats had come to rest. "Look."

The wall had been Mark's salvation. Because the flats had been a little longer than the floor on which they fell, they had been stopped short when they met the wall, which had taken their weight. Scraping and chipping on the brick showed the force with which they had fallen.

"No one else under there, is there?"

Spike crouched and looked into the triangle of darkness under the flats. After what seemed a long time he straightened up. "No. Look, could some of you lads help me to get these back?"

"Certainly. Let me give a hand." Mark Spelthorne, having inadvertently been cast in the rôle of hero, continued to play it.

"That could have been a very nasty accident," said Christopher Milton.

"All in a day's work for Flying Officer Falconer of *The Fighter Pilots*," said Mark Spelthorne smugly.

"Whoever tied up those flats should get his cards," Spike grunted with professional disgust.

"Don't know who did it," mumbled one of the *Sex of One* . . . crew.

"Oh well. It happened, not much we can do about it now," said one of the dancers brightly. "Don't want to cry over spilt milk, do we? Just mop it up and squeeze the rag back into the bottle, eh?"

This seemed to break the atmosphere. They all helped to push the flats against the wall again and went off laughing and chatting.

Except for Charles Paris. He had seen how firmly the restraining ropes had been fixed to the cleat. He knew what had happened had not been an accident.

PART 2

Leeds

CHAPTER 6

ON THE TRAIN up to Leeds that Sunday afternoon Charles cursed his lack of detective instinct. He had been present at what was probably a crime and just when his mind should be flashing up an instant recall of every detail of the scene it was providing only vague memories and woolly impressions. Perhaps it was Oliver Goldsmith's fault. By delaying Sir Charles Marlow's entry until the fifth act, he had ensured that Charles Paris had had at least two pints too many at the Saturday lunchtime, so that the ideal computer print-out of facts and details was replaced by a child's picture in Fuzzy Felt.

He couldn't even remember exactly who had been there. Christopher Milton, certainly, and Dickie Peck and the driver. And David Meldrum and Gwyneth were somewhere around, though he couldn't remember whether they were on stage or in the auditorium at the time of the accident. Mark Spelthorne had been there, of course, and Spike and some of the King's Theatre stage staff. . . . And then who else? Two or three male dancers—Charles didn't know their names, but he'd recognize them again—and the two girl dancers. Then one or two of the supporting actors and actresses. Charles screwed up his eyes and tried to see the scene again. Lizzie Dark certainly, she'd been there, and Michael Peyton, and some others. The edges of the picture were cloudy.

"Damn!" he snapped, and opened his eyes to find that the word had attracted the gaze of a large Bradford-bound Pakistani family.

Embarrassed, he closed his eyes and tried to concentrate again. A little chill of anxiety about seeing Ruth kept getting in the way.

Well, the identity parade of suspects wasn't very impressive, because it was incomplete. But, assuming a crime had been committed, it must have a motive and that might give a clue to the criminal.

The first question—was Mark Spelthorne the intended victim or was it just chance that caught him? Christopher Milton was not far behind and it was possible that the criminal was after him, but misjudged his timing in the dark. Or it could have been meant for any one of the people on stage. Or just a random blow for whoever happened to be there. The last would tie in with Gerald's original view that someone was trying to wreck the show and didn't mind how. If it was a personal vendetta against Christopher Milton, then why had the perpetrator bothered to make his first attacks on the pianist and Everard Austick? Why not go straight to his quarry? And why not use a more selective method than a tumbling pile of flats? If, on the other hand, Mark Spelthorne was the intended victim. . . .

Oh dear. He knew it wasn't getting him anywhere. Any of the people on stage at the time of the accident could have unwound the rope from the cleat. Equally, any of them could have been the intended victim. And since he couldn't remember exactly who had been there, the possibilities were infinite. Add the difficulty of tying the motivation for that crime in with the other two and the problem was insoluble, or at least insoluble to a forty-eight-year-old actor who had spent too long in the bar at King's Cross and who was having serious misgivings about going to stay with a woman with whom he had had a brief and not wholly glorious affair seven years previously.

He looked out of the window at the matt flatness of the Midlands. He closed his eyes, but sleep and even relaxation kept their distance. A new question formed in his mind—Did the 15:10 train from King's Cross to Leeds have a bar? He set out to investigate.

* * *

Ruth was disagreeable. As soon as he saw her again he remembered. Not disagreeable in the sense of being unattractive; her trim body with its sharp little breasts and well-defined calf muscles remained as good as ever; she was disagreeable in the sense that she disagreed with everything one said. Charles never had known whether it was a genuine defense from a reasoned feminist standpoint or sheer bloody-mindedness. But it came back to him as soon as she spoke. Her voice was marinated in cynicism. Charles felt a great swoop of despair, as if all his worst opinions of himself were suddenly ratified, as if the thoughts that infected him in his lowest moods had suddenly been classified as gospel. He saw himself as an Everard Austick, an alcoholic whose failure in his chosen profession was only matched by his failure as a human being.

It wasn't that cynicism struck no chord. He himself tended to attribute the worst motives to everyone and was distrustful of optimists. But like all practitioners of an art, he liked to feel that his version of it was a definitive one. His cynicism could still be unexpectedly erased by the sight of a child or the shock of a sudden kindness or a moment of desire, while Ruth's blanket coverage seemed to debase the currency of cynicism.

It wasn't that she'd had a particularly bad life. True, its emotional path had been a bit rocky. In her twenties she had had a series of affairs which never stood a chance of going the distance (Charles would have put himself in that category) and eventually at the age of thirty married a central heating systems salesman five years her senior. The marriage lasted three years until he went off with a croupier and they got a divorce. The fatalism with which Ruth accepted this reverse suggested that she had never had much faith in the marriage and had been undermining it for some time.

"So you came." She spoke with that exactness of enunciation which is more revealing than an accent.

"Yes, I said I would."

"Oh yes." The disbelief in her tone instantly put the clock back seven years. "And how are you, Mr. Charles Paris?"

"Fine, fine."

"Good, And your lady wife?"

"I don't know. Well, when I last saw her. It's a few months back now. I believe she has a boy friend, someone from the school where she teaches."

"Good for her. Not going to wait forever on your filing system, is she? Can I get you a cup of tea or a drink or something? Or should I show you up to your room in true landlady fashion?" She leant against the kitchen table in a way that could have been meant to be provocative. It was always difficult to know with Ruth. But seeing her, Charles remembered how much he had fancied her. That was really all there ever had been to the relationship. If there were nothing to life except bed, they'd still have been together. He felt a warm trickle of desire in spite of all the gloom which she had generated inside him.

He overcompensated by the heartiness of his reply. "A cup of tea would be really . . . grand." Her flash of suspicion made him wish he had chosen another word. He'd forgotten how sensitive she was to anything that could be construed as criticism of her Yorkshireness.

She made the tea and Charles kept up a relentless flow of banter to stop himself from making a pass at her. "How are things in Headingley then?"

"They don't change. I've lived here thirty-four years and lost hope that they ever will."

"Still in the same job?"

"Oh yes. I think Perkis and Levy, Solicitors and Commissioners for Oaths, would cease to function without my secretarial assistance."

"Enjoy it?"

She spread open her hands in a gesture which showed up the pointlessness of the question.

"And socially?"

"Socially life here is okay if you're a teenybopper going down the discos or an elegant blue-rinse who likes bridge and golf. I'm neither."

"No." The little gusts of interest which had been propelling the conversation along died down to silence. Charles was morbidly aware of the outline of Ruth's nipples through the cotton of her patterned blouse.

She broke the silence. "This show you're doing, is it the one at the Palace?"

"Yes."

"With Christopher Milton in it?"

"Yes."

"He's good," she said with more enthusiasm than usual. "What's he like?"

The classic question, as asked by every member of the public about every star. And virtually unanswerable. No reply can possibly satisfy the questioner, who usually has only thought as far as the question.

Charles tried. "Well, he's . . ." And then realized he could not even answer to his own satisfaction. "I don't know."

He was glad of the seven o'clock call at the Palace Theatre, as it temporarily took off the pressure of Ruth's presence.

After David Meldrum's tentative notes on the Saturday run-through (interrupted by less tentative ones from Christopher Milton), Charles sorted out a later call with the stage management and set off to investigate the adjacent pub.

It was small and dingy, one of the few old buildings which had survived the extensive modernization of Leeds city center. A few regulars sat around in despairing huddles while a younger group played silent, grim darts. Charles ordered a large Bell's, which they didn't have, and got a large Haig. As he turned to find a space on one of the railway waiting-room benches, he recognized a figure in a blue donkey jacket hunched against the bar. "Hello, Kevin."

The bleary eyes showed that the writer had been there since opening time. Charles received an indifferent drunken greeting.

"Not a bad theatre, is it?"

"Not a bad theatre? Huh. Are you telling me about the Palace Theatre? That's good. I've been seeing shows at the Palace since I was six. Pantomimes, all sorts. I was brought up here. Meanwood. Went to the grammar school. We were always brought on outings to the Palace, when there was anything cultural on, touring companies, all that. Always came to the Palace. It was my ambition, when I was in my teens, to have something of mine done, performed at the Palace. That and losing my virginity."

"And now I assume you've managed both."

"One happened, near as dammit, in the back row of the Cottage Road Cinema." He let out an abrupt, dirty laugh. Then his face darkened. "But the other. . . ."

"The other you achieve tomorrow. First night."

Kevin looked him straight in the eyes for a moment before he spoke. "Oh yes. Tomorrow. First night. But first night of what? Do you think I'll feel any pride in *that*?"

"Don't worry. It's going to be a good show. It's inevitable that everyone's a bit jumpy just before it starts." Charles had not decided yet what he really thought of the show, but he thought reassurance was required.

As it turned out, he was wrong. "That's not what I mean. I mean that what'll go on at that theatre tomorrow will have nothing to do with me."

"Oh, I know it's changed a bit from the original production, but that's inevitable when—"

"Changed a bit—huh! There's almost nothing in that show that I put there."

"I'm sure a lot of it's still quite close to the original."

"Balls. I should never have agreed. If I'd known what a total cock-up they were going to make of it . . . okay, they wanted to get in somebody else to do the music . . . all right, maybe Joe Coatley's music wasn't that commercial, but I thought at least they'd leave my text alone. I felt bad about dropping Joe at the time, but now I bloody envy him. I'd give anything to be out of it."

Deliberately crude, Charles mentioned the money.

"Oh yes, there'll be plenty of money. Run forever, a show like this, or at least until his Lordship gets bored with it. You know, I used to think I'd do anything for money—that was when I hadn't got any—thought I'd write anything, pornography, all sorts. I did, I wrote a real hard-core porn book—filth, all about whips and Alsatians, real muck. I got a hundred pounds for that, but I tell you, I'm more proud of that than I will be when this load of shit's running in the West End and bringing me in my so many per cent a week." He was in full flow, spurred on by the drink. "Look, I'm a

writer, a writer. If I didn't want to be a writer, I'd be some other
bloody thing, an accountant, a clerk in the Town Hall, I don't care
what. But that's not what I wanted to be. I wanted to be a writer.
And why does someone want to be a writer?"

Charles had his own views on the subject, but didn't volunteer
them. Anyway, Kevin's question turned out to be rhetorical. "I'll
tell you why someone wants to be a writer. Because what he writes
is his own. It may be rubbish, but it's his own rubbish. No one can
take that away from him. He wrote it." He seemed to realize he was
becoming almost incoherently repetitive and paused to collect his
thoughts before continuing. He swayed slightly.

"And that is why I don't like my work being destroyed by some
jumped-up idiot of an actor, who couldn't even write his own
name."

Charles found himself (not for the first time) taking up a position
of boring middle-aged reasonableness. "Kevin, one has to face it
that there are some things which work on the page that don't work
in performance."

"I accept that. Good God, I've worked on plays before. I'm used
to doing rewrites and changing things and cutting things down,
but in the past it's always been a matter of discussing it, not just
some prima donna ballsing up whole scenes so that he gets all the
lines."

Charles smarted at the remembrance of his own suffering from
Christopher Milton on a line-hunt, but continued his defence.
"Look, I know he's got an unfortunate manner, but he does have a
real genius for the theatre. He knows what's going to work and
what—"

"He knows what's going to work for him, yes, but he doesn't give
a bugger about the rest of the show. He's already made nonsense of
the plot by cutting down the Young Marlow scenes to nothing. The
show'll be a great shapeless mess."

"The audience will love it."

"Audience, huh. What the hell do they know? The audience that
comes to this show will be so force-fed with television they won't
notice what it's about. They'll spend all their time waiting for the
commercials. They'd come and see him if he was peeling potatoes
onstage. They'd come and see anything that they saw on their

screen. A jug of water, *as featured on the Nine O'Clock News,* that's what they'd come to see."

He paused for breath. Charles took the opportunity to buy more drinks, hoping to break the monologue. But when he'd handed Kevin a large whisky, raised his own and said "Cheers," it was instantly resumed. "There's a lot of good stuff in that show which has just been dumped. Dumped and replaced by corny rubbish. I know. I'm not saying I'm the greatest writer there ever was, but I know when I've written a good line, and I don't write them so that some idiot can just come along and. . . ." He lost his thread and when he came back his voice was cold with concentration. "If he takes anything else out of this show, I'll kill the bastard. I've warned him, I've warned him that I can get nasty, and I will. Do you know, last Friday he was even saying he didn't know whether *Liberty Hall* was a good number or not. *Liberty Hall,* I mean that's the best number in the show. It's the only one they kept from the original. They had to, they'd never get a better number than that, would they? Go on, you say what you think of it. Of that song."

Charles, who hated being button-holed for opinions, murmured something about it being a very good number.

"Too right it is. A bloody good number. I tell you, if he tries to get rid of that song, I will kill him."

Kevin became more violent and unintelligible as the drink seeped in and Charles was relieved when it was time for him to return to the theatre. As he traveled back to Headingley in the 33 bus, he thought about Kevin. Most of it he put down to the drink, but it was another example of the violent reactions Christopher Milton inspired. Kevin had plenty of motive for wishing ill to the show, if he was really as disgusted with it as he claimed. And he had said something about having warned Christopher Milton, which could be a reference to the previous crimes. And, Charles suddenly remembered, the writer had been onstage at the King's Theatre when the flats fell. A new thought came into his mind. Suppose the first two accidents were genuine and the campaign of persecution only began with the falling flats. And suppose the object of the persecution was not the show, but just Christopher Milton. Someone hated the star so much that he wanted to kill him.

* * *

Back at the semi in Headingley Ruth had gone to bed, but her door was ajar and the light on. Charles knocked softly and went in.

She looked up without surprise. "So you've finished." Her voice could imbue the simplest sentence with criticism.

"Yes." He sat heavily on the bed.

"Drunk, I suppose."

"Moderately."

"You're a wreck, Charles." She said it hard, without affection. Then she reached forward and touched his hand. The scent of talcum powder rose to his nostrils. He looked at her. And then he kissed her.

She responded, as he knew she would. As he had known when he had first heard he was going to Leeds. From that moment a guilty fascination had led him to this. His unwillingness, his positive knowledge that it was idiotic to restart the affair, was swamped by animal urgency. His right hand scrabbled roughly at her nightdress, pulling it up.

"I know what you want." Even as her hands reached down hungrily to fight with the clasp of his trousers, she made it sound like an accusation.

CHAPTER 7

IN THE AUDIENCE at *Lumpkin!*'s first public performance on Monday, October 27th, 1975, were some people with a special interest in the show. There were the Friends of the Palace Theatre who spent the performance preparing witty things to say at the discussion with the cast which their secretary, Miss Thompson, had arranged to take place on stage after the final curtain. There were Kevin McMahon's parents whom he hadn't been able to dissuade from coming. There was Dickie Peck, just arrived from London to see that everyone was doing exactly what his protégé wanted. And there was Gerald Venables, up in theory in his legal capacity to extort money from a wealthy mill-owner, and in fact to keep an eye on his investment and get a progress report from Charles Paris.

The performance they watched was unusual, in that it started with one central character and ended with another. Charles saw it all from the fly gallery. It was strictly against theatre discipline for him to be up there, but he had asked Spike, who didn't seem to mind. Spike was easy-going about most things. He had that equable technician's temperament that never failed to amaze Charles. The ability to continue hard physical work up to seventy-two hours without ever losing his resource and surly good humor. And all without any sort of public recognition. The extrovert actor part of Charles could not understand that. What made people like Spike tick? Where did they come from?

He looked across at the intent acne-ridden face as the stage manager pulled on a thick rope and delicately eased a huge piece of scenery up between two metal bars with their heavy load of lights. Charles instantly remembered stories of flying disasters, of cumbersome pieces plummeting down on actors below, of faulty counterweighting snatching technicians up from the stage to dash them against the chipping machine of the grid in the roof. But the sight of Spike's strength and control put away such thoughts. The eternal stage manager. As the name implied, he could always manage. There was no point in thinking what Spike might have done before; it was impossible to imagine him in any other world.

As the show progressed, Charles' attention soon moved from speculations about the stage staff to the strange transformation which was taking place onstage, the transformation of the character of Tony Lumpkin. Christopher Milton's performance started as it had been in rehearsal. The knowing yokel dominated the stage, his voice deeply rustic and his movements capturing the clumsy grace of the farm-boy. Charles settled down to enjoy it.

The change, when it came, was quite abrupt. Audience reaction was a bit slow, but no slower than one would expect from a Monday night house of stuffed shirts from the clothing industry and a few stray television fans, awestruck by the unaccustomed space of a theatre. Charles had been in many shows which had got worse reaction at this tender stage of their lives.

But Christopher Milton was worried. His anxiety was not apparent to the audience, but to Charles, who knew the performance well, the fear showed. There was a hesitancy in delivery, a certain stiffness in dancing that betrayed the inward unrest. It came to a head in the *Liberty Hall* number. This involved a parodic country dance for Tony Lumpkin and the dancers. It was a well-choreographed routine, which started with heavy deliberation and speeded up until Christopher Milton was spinning giddily on a rostrum center stage, from which he did a final jump to a kneeling position, an inevitable cue for applause.

He'd done it perfectly in rehearsal, but on the first night he mistimed it. He came out of the spin into the jump and landed untidily on one leg. It was not a serious error and certainly did not hurt him, but it was messy. The audience realized it had gone wrong, lost their own natural timing and did not come in with instantaneous applause.

The pause was tiny, the audience goodwill to clap was there, but the mistake had thrown them. Christopher Milton felt the hiatus and came in quickly with the line, "Ooh, I done it all wrong."

This time the reaction was enormous. An instant laugh, the loudest of the evening, which melted naturally into vigorous clapping, as if the audience wanted to make up for missing their first cue.

As a professional Charles could recognize Christopher Milton's immaculate timing of the line, but it was not that which struck him most about it. It was the voice in which it had been delivered. The star had not used his own voice, nor that of Tony Lumpkin. The line had been spoken by Lionel Wilkins of the television series *Straight Up, Guv.*

And from that point on, Lionel Wilkins took over. For the next ten minutes or so, Tony Lumpkin fought a desultory rearguard action, but he was defeated before he started. The rustic burr was replaced by a London whine. The brown frock coat was thrown into the wings and the part was played in timeless shirtsleeves. Oliver Goldsmith, who had probably done a few gyrations in his grave over the previous weeks, must by now have been turning fast enough to power the National Grid. One of the central themes of his play, the contrast between Town and Country, had just vanished. The plot lost yet another of its tenuous links with sense.

And the audience loved it. Familiarity gave them the confidence they needed to express their enthusiasm. It may have been a bit difficult to follow the twists and exposition of an old-fashioned story, but to be presented with an instantly recognizable character from their television screens, that made it all simple. Charles watched from the fly gallery in amazement. "What the hell is he doing?" he murmured to Spike, who was leaning on the rail beside him.

"His own thing," Spike grunted. "Never does anything else."

"What will David Humdrum say?"

Charles knew the answer to his question, but Spike supplied it. "He'll say, 'Fine'."

* * *

And he did. Charles saw the encounter between star and director in the green room at the interval. "Christ, this needs a lot more work," said the star.

"It's going fine, Christopher, just fine," soothed the director.

"That *Liberty Hall* number will have to come out for a start. I always thought it was a load of crap."

"I'm sure, with a bit more rehearsal—"

"Shut up! It's coming out." Christopher Milton went up to his dressing-room.

Charles decided that it was in his interests as the show's secret watchdog to keep his eyes on the movements of Kevin McMahon. If the writer lived up to half of his drunken threats, there was going to be trouble.

The trouble started as soon as the curtain had come down on the final call. Kevin McMahon was in the green room to greet the cast as they came offstage. He went straight up to Christopher Milton and shouted, "What the hell do you mean by performing my stuff like that? This isn't one of your tatty TV comedies!"

The star seemed to look through him and greeted a man with greasy swept-back hair and a cheap suede zip-up jacket. "Hello, Wally. What did you think?"

"Good bits, bad bits," said Wally Wilson in broad Cockney.

"Never mind. Nothing that can't be changed."

"Too right. Soon be up to the *Straight Up, Guv* standard!"

"Now you bloody listen to me, Mr. Christopher Bloody Milton . . ." Kevin began belligerently.

The response came back like a whip-lash. "Shut up, I'm talking to a writer."

The implication was too much for Kevin McMahon. With a cry of fury, he drew his fist back for a blow.

Christopher Milton moved fast. He sidestepped with a dancer's ease. Kevin swung himself off balance and at that moment Dickie Peck, who had moved from the doorway at amazing speed when the fracas started, flicked up Kevin's head with his left forearm and smashed a hard right knuckle into the writer's mouth. The knees gave, the body crumpled and blood welled from a cut lip. "Don't you ever dare lay a finger on him." Dickie Peck hissed.

The action had all been so quick that it left behind a shocked silence. The unexpectedness of the fight paled into insignificance compared to the transformation of Dickie Peck, suddenly converted from a middle-aged joke figure to a bruiser. Charles recollected a distant rumor that the agent had started his career as a boxer.

Christopher Milton broke the silence. He continued in an even tone, as if nothing had happened. "Wally, come up to my dressing-room and have a chat."

"Love to." Wally's casualness was more studied.

"Um, er, Mr. Milton." A young man who had been hovering uneasily round the edges of the green room, stepped forward, blushing furiously.

"What?"

"I'm, er, um . . . my name is Bates and, er, I'm representing Mr. Katzmann, who, as you know, is, er, the general manager of the theatre and—"

"What the hell are you burbling about?"

"Well, er, as you know, the, er . . . the, er. . . ." He ran out of syntax. "The Friends."

"Are you coming, Wally?"

"Mr. Milton." Panic made the young man articulate again, and he blurted out his message. "The Friends of the Palace Theatre are about to hold their discussion of the show on stage and, as Mr. Katzmann arranged, you and the other members of the cast will be joining in the discussion."

"I bloody won't. It's the first I've heard of it. If you think I'm going to piss around talking crap to old ladies, you can forget it."

"But—"

Dickie Peck cut the young man short with a gesture and again took control. "Has this been advertised?"

"Yes. Mr. Katzmann arranged it months ago."

"Not through me, he didn't. You'd better do it, Chris."

"Look, I've just done a bloody performance, I've just been assaulted by a lunatic hack-writer, I'm not going to—"

Dickie Peck raised his hand and the voice petered out. "You've got to do it, Chris. It's a bloody lumber and—" with a glance at Mr. Bates, who trembled visibly—"there'll be hell to pay for someone in the morning when I find out who made the cock-up. But if it's been advertised . . . you can't afford to get the reputation of someone who jacks out of that sort of thing."

Christopher Milton swore obscenely and loud, but accepted the logic of the argument. He went upstairs to take off his make-up and, as often happened when he left the room, the atmosphere relaxed. People started to drift away. Charles went across to Kevin McMahon, who had dragged himself quietly to a sofa and was dabbing at his lip with a handkerchief. "I think it's time to take the money and run, Kevin. Put this down to bad experience. Reckon that it's just a grant of money to buy you time to go off and write what you really want to."

"I really wanted to write *Liberty Hall*."

"Yes, but there must be other things, more original, more your own that you want to get on with."

"Oh yes, things where I express the real me, things that the world has been waiting to have written by some genius who only needs time to get on with it."

Charles ignored the heaviness of the irony. "Yes, that sort of thing."

"Don't you patronise me!" Kevin stood up. "I'm going to kill the bastard," he said and walked out of the theatre.

"But," said Mrs. Crichton-Smith, whose husband owned a sock factory and played off an eight handicap, "I remember doing *She Stoops to Conquer* at school and I must say a lot of the original plot seems to have been obscured in this production."

Christopher Milton flashed her a frank, confiding smile. "I agree, Mrs. Crichton-Smith, but Goldsmith was writing for his time. This is 1975, we can't just do a production as if nothing has changed since the play was written. And, anyway, this is not *She Stoops to Conquer*, this is a new musical. What we're trying to do, and I think our writer, Kevin McMahon, would agree with me here," he added, as if to impress the image of a big-happy-family, all-working-towards-the-same-end company, "is to create an original show. I mean, entertainment is variety. Your husband wouldn't think much of you if you produced the same meal for him every night—however good it was."

His middle-class half-joke produced the right middle-class half-laugh and Charles was once again impressed with Christopher Milton's ability to adapt to any audience and say the right things. It was not an intellectual gift; he probably did not have the intelligence or knowledge to argue the merits of the piece on a literary level; it was just an instinct that never failed.

Miss Thompson, the secretary, next introduced a question from: "Mr. Henry Oxenford, one of our keenest members, who's interested in all things theatrical." Mr. Oxenford, one of the bow-tied types who hang about amateur dramatic societies, content to be precious rather than queer, stood up and put his well-rehearsed inquiry, "I would like to know whether you, as a performer, be it as Tony Lumpkin or Lionel Wilkins, find the danger that a part tends to take over your private life and you become like that person?"

Christopher Milton laughed boyishly. "You mean when I'm working on the television series, do I go around trying to con money off everyone I meet?"

"Well, not exactly."

"Oh, I beg yours." The Lionel Wilkins line was, as ever, perfectly delivered and got its laugh. Charles watched Christopher Milton's eyes and saw him decide to continue in the Wilkins voice and prolong the misunderstanding. "Oh, I see what you mean—do I go up to people in the street and say, Look'ere, I've got this great project. Wouldn't you like to buy shares in the first motel on the moon? Not only do you get the normal dividends, but you also get a free weekend every year once the motel is completed. Now the shares aren't yet officially on the market, but I can let you have some at a price which. . . ." And he was away, recreating the plot of a recent episode of *Straight Up, Guv*. The Friends of the Palace Theatre loved it.

As he drew to the end of his routine, before Miss Thompson could introduce Mrs. Horton who had been waving her arm like a schoolgirl know-all between each question, he glanced at his watch. "Oh, look at the time. I'm afraid we've gone on much longer than we intended. We've still got a lot of work to do on this show—oh, you may have liked it, but there are a good few things to be altered yet—so we must draw it to a close there."

The Friends of the Palace Theatre started to leave through the stalls. An autograph cluster gathered round the star. The other members of the cast, who hadn't got much of a look-in on the discussion, trickled back through the curtains. Mark Spelthorne dawdled, seeing if there were any fans of *The Fighter Pilots* on the autograph trail. When it became apparent there weren't, he vanished smartly.

Christopher Milton finished the signings and waved cheerily from the stage until the last Friend had gone out of the doors at the back of the stalls. When he turned his face was instantly twisted with rage. "Cows! Stupid, bloody cows!" He pushed through the curtains, shouting imperiously, "Wally! Dickie! Come on, we've got to get this script altered, even if we have to work all bloody night."

As Charles waited to hear the inevitable news that there would be a rehearsal call at ten the following morning, he began to understand the personality-splitting pressure of a public image.

Gerald Venables was sitting waiting in his car, a Mercedes 280 SL, with the lights doused, by the stage door. He had the collar of his raincoat turned up and was slumped against the window in an attitude cribbed from some B-movie. He was trying so hard to be inconspicuous that Charles saw him instantly. "Hello."

"Ssh. Get in." The passenger door was slipped open. Charles climbed in clumsily. "So, what gives?" Gerald hissed, his eyes scanning the empty road ahead.

"Just been a bit of a dust-up, boss," Charles hissed back.

Gerald didn't realise he was being sent up, but ran out of slang. "What? You mean a fight?"

"Too right, boss."

"Irons?"

"I beg your pardon."

"Irons—you know, guns. God, don't you watch any television?"

"Not much."

"Well, give us the dirt. Who swung a bunch of fives at whom?"

The grammatical resolution of the question rather weakened its underworld flavor.

Charles gave a quick account of the scene in the green room and the solicitor nodded knowingly. "So you reckon this McMahon could be our cookie?"

"Our saboteur, the man devoted to the destruction of the show . . . ?"

"Yes."

"I don't know. Certainly he hates Christopher Milton. If anything were to happen to the star tonight, I would have no doubt about who to look for. But I don't think Kevin can have been responsible for the other accidents, not the first two, anyway."

"Why not?"

"Because why should he? When the pianist was shot at, Kevin didn't know what was going to happen to his script, rehearsals had hardly started. I reckon at that stage he must have been full of excitement, you know, his first West End show and all that."

"But it can't have taken long for him to realize the way things were going."

"Yes, I suppose he could have built up a sufficient head of resentment by the time Everard Austick met with his accident."

"Yes, surely, and—"

"There's another snag, Gerald. Kevin's resentment is completely against Christopher Milton. Sniping at these minor figures may be bad for the show, but it doesn't hurt the star much. Christopher Milton doesn't care who his supporting cast are, so long as they don't argue with him or do anything better than he does. If Kevin McMahon did want to get at anyone he'd go straight for the one who was bugging him—and, with the star out of the way, there might be a chance that his musical could survive in another production."

"Yes. So we've got to look for someone else as the mastermind behind the whole sequence of crimes."

"If there is a sequence, Gerald, if there are any crimes. So far the only evidence I have of misdoing is what happened at the King's Theatre. I know someone tampered with the rope holding those flats up. All the others could be genuine accidents. In fact, the thing at the King's may have a perfectly legitimate explanation."

"I don't know, Charles. I still have the feeling that they're all linked and that something funny's going on."

There was a silence. "Hmm. Yes, I can feel a sort of foreboding too, but I don't know why."

As he spoke, light spilled across the road from the stage door. Christopher Milton, Dickie Peck, Wally Wilson and the show's musical director, Pete Masters, came out, escorted by Milton's driver, who smartly moved forward to the parked Corniche and opened the doors. They all got in. "Let's follow them," whispered Charles, more to satisfy Gerald's love of the dramatic than anything else.

They let the Rolls disappear at the junction on to the main road, confident that Leeds' central one-way system would make it difficult to lose their quarry, and started up in pursuit.

Gerald's "Follow that car" routine was as exaggerated as his "I am waiting unobtrusively" one, involving many sudden swivels of the head and bursts of squealing acceleration alternating with dawdling so slowly that it drew hoots of annoyance from other road-users. But the inhabitants of the Rolls did not appear to notice them. There were none of the sudden right-angled swerves up side-roads beloved of gangsters in movies. They drove sedately round the one-way system and into Neville Street, where they swung off the main road and came to rest at the entrance of the Dragonara Hotel. Gerald, who hadn't been expecting the stop, overshot, screeched to a halt and reversed to a spying position, flashed at by the righteous headlights of other drivers in the one-way street.

The party disembarking from the Corniche still did not take any notice of their pursuers. The four of them walked straight into the foyer and the driver slid the car away to the hotel car park.

"Well . . ." said Gerald.

"Well, I guess we've found out where he's staying."

"Yes. Yes, we have."

"I could have asked him and saved us the trouble."

"Yes, but at least this way we can tell if he's lying."

"What on earth do you mean? Why should he lie about staying in the newest, poshest hotel in Leeds?"

"I don't know." They both felt very foolish.

"By the way, Gerald, why aren't you staying at the Dragonara? I thought that was your usual style."

"I didn't know it existed. Polly, my secretary, booked me into the Queen's. More traditional, I think . . . I'm only here for the one night. I suppose I could try and get transferred, see if there's a room here."

"What good would that do?"

"Well, then I'd be in the hotel, I could spy, I. . . ."

"What are we spying on? What do we want to find out?"

"I don't know."

"All we want to do is see that Kevin McMahon doesn't get a chance to have a go at Christopher Milton."

"Yes."

"And since he's got Dickie Peck and his driver in the hotel there with him, I think we're superfluous."

"So what should we do?"

"Go to our several beds," said Charles, with mingled desire and depression at the thought of his.

"All right. I suppose we'd better. Mind you, we're going to feel pretty silly in the morning if we hear that Christopher Milton's been murdered."

They needn't have worried. Christopher Milton survived the night unharmed. But Kevin McMahon was found beaten up in the car park by the bus station.

CHAPTER 8

CHARLES DIDN'T HEAR about the new accident until he reached the theatre for rehearsal. A silent breakfast with Ruth had been followed by a silent lift in her Renault 5L to the city center. She started work at nine, so he had time to kill. They parted in silence and he wandered off in the direction of the Dragonara for no apparent reason.

To occupy his mind with trivialities, he pretended he was trailing the man in front of him. The head he followed was completely bald with enormous ears like the handles of a loving cup. Charles varied his pace, playing a game with himself, committing details to memory, checking the time. At five to nine the man went in the front entrance of the Dragonara and the game was over.

Charles looked round for someone else to use as a dummy and then felt a wave of hopelessness. What was the point of playing at detectives when his performance was so abysmal on the occasions that required real detective abilities?

The "what was the point?" gloom deepened to embrace his emotional life too. Another night of angry sex with Ruth had depressed him. What was the point of it? He had left Frances to get away from the ties and twists of a "relationship," hoping to find some kind of freedom. And he had accepted the limitations which the emotional free-lance shares with all other free-lances—delays between engagements and sudden terminations of contracts. But it wasn't just that. Casual sex didn't give him enough and anything deeper soon got claustrophobic. If he was going to go through all the hard work of making something work, he might just as well try again with Frances. At least he had got a start there.

But Frances had got a boy friend. So the rumor went, and he had no cause to disbelieve it. And that seemed to change it all. It twisted his emotional outlook. He would not admit to himself that he was prey to so simple an emotion as jealousy, but the fact that Frances was not floating unattached in the background made any other relationship more threatening, as if now he was really looking for something lasting. Which he wasn't. . . . Oh, hell, why couldn't he just think of Ruth as a nice time in Leeds, all to be over and forgotten in a week? But guilt crept in, and though he was conscious of his depression over-dramatising everything, he was unable to get out of the pointless spiral of his thoughts.

He quickly got news of Kevin's accident when he arrived at the theatre. The police were there. They had taken over one of the dressing-rooms, where they were questioning members of the cast. There were constant assurances that no one in the company was suspected, but certain facts had to be established—who Kevin was, where he was staying and so on.

The details of the beating spread quickly. Kevin was in the Infirmary though he was not seriously hurt. Apparently he had spent the evening drinking, moving on to a small club when the pubs closed. He had been kicked out of there at about two, and wandered round for some time—he couldn't remember how long —and then been jumped by someone who punched him in the face, kicked him about the rest of his body, left him unconscious and stole his wallet. The police regarded it as a simple mugging and were looking for someone local.

They did hear about the altercation between Kevin and Dickie Peck and when the agent arrived with his protégé at ten-thirty, he was questioned. But it transpired that the two of them, along with Wally Wilson and Pete Masters, the young musical director, had been up most of the night working on a new number to replace *Liberty Hall*. They had mutually dependent alibis.

That was a blow to Charles' simple reading of the situation. He had leapt to the conclusion that Dickie Peck must have got at Kevin, continuing the scene that had started in the green room. And if there had only been Christopher Milton and Wally Wilson to corroborate Dickie's alibi, he would still have believed it. But if Pete, the M.D., also vouched for him, that changed things. He was not one on the star's immediate entourage and the most unlikely person to submit to intimidation. So maybe it was just an attack by a mugger unknown. But it did seem too much of a coincidence.

And if it was a coincidence, it was a very happy one for Christopher Milton. There was no dissenting voice when he announced that *Liberty Hall* was to be dropped and that the whole day until the evening performance would be spent rehearsing the new number which had been written overnight.

He was very ebullient and cheerful. He made no pretence now that David Meldrum was directing the show and leapt around the stage telling everyone what to do and demonstrating. He showed no fatigue after the long night and was supremely creative. His enthusiasm for the new song was infectious and they all worked hard to give it life.

Pete Masters, the M.D., had written a simple but catchy tune and was very pleased with himself. Wally Wilson had written the lyric and when Christopher Milton first sang it through with the piano, Charles could feel the gyrations of Oliver Goldsmith in his grave accelerate yet again.

> *When you're out of the fiddle*
> *And you're trying to pull a con*
> *And the cops come in the middle*
> *Of the trick you're trying on,*
> *Then all you've gotta do*
> *Is just give a little pause,*
> *Give a little smile*
> *And come back with "I Beg Yours?"*
>
> *Not "I beg to differ" or "I beg to remain . . ."*
> *Not "I beg your pardon," but an easier refrain,*
> *Not "I've lost my bottle" and not "I've lost my*
> *drawers"—*

The answer's very simple—
All you say is "I Beg Yours?"

When you're selling some jew'l'ry
And the jew'l'ry don't exist
And the victim of your fool'ry.
(Who you thought was very . . . drunk)
Turns out to be a cop
And says he'll bring down the laws,
Don't lose your cool,
But come back with "I Beg Yours?"

Not "I beg to differ" or . . . and so on through four more verses of variable scansion and anachronism. Christopher Milton ended the song with a flourish and Charles couldn't help joining in the applause that followed it. He was once again struck by how good Christopher Milton was. The applause was not sycophancy; it was the genuine praise of professionals.

But in spite of the performance, the song was hopelessly wrong for the show. Charles knew it and felt he had to say something. He was just assembling a tactful objection when Mark Spelthorne came in with his own drawling complaint. Typically, it was completely selfish. "But we can't really have that number there, Christopher. I mean, that would make it three solos for you in a row. Surely, it would be better for the balance of the show if we had an ensemble number at this point." (What he really meant was, "I had a lot to do in *Liberty Hall*. Now I've lost a number.")

Christopher Milton did not snap back at Mark. He didn't bother when Dickie Peck was present to do it for him. "That's nonsense," barked the agent. "The audience will have come here to see Christopher Milton and the more of him they see, the happier they'll be."

"There is such a thing as overexposure," Mark Spelthorne observed in a voice that wouldn't remain as cool as he wanted it.

"Something you're never going to have to worry about, sonny," Dickie flashed back. "No, it's a great number. Really good. Just done overnight, you know—" (appealing for admiration from the company. Charles' admiration conformed with Dr. Johnson's comment about a dog walking on its hinder legs—"It is not well done, but you are surprised to find it done at all.") "—No, I think this is going to be the number of the show. Make a great single too. I don't see actually why it shouldn't be the title of the show. *I Beg Yours?*, I mean it's catchy and it's—"

"All the publicity's already gone out," David Meldrum interposed, thus at least killing that ridiculous idea. But Charles still thought someone ought to question the suitability of the number for a show which, in spite of major surgery and transplants, was still set in the eighteenth century and was about Tony Lumpkin rather than Lionel Wilkins. It would stick out like go-go dancers in the middle of the Ring Cycle.

He cleared his throat to remonstrate, but fortunately Winifred Tuke anticipated him. "We can't have this song."

"Why not?" asked Dickie Peck aggressively, pausing with match held up to a new cigar.

"Well, honestly, darling, I mean, I know we're not doing *She Stoops* . . . straight, but this does make nonsense of it." It was daring and impressive and she should have left it at that. Instead she went on, getting more actressy and vague. "I mean, the whole thing about this play is that it's Town life versus Country and we're already losing that by playing Tony London, but if we start putting in bits from other shows then—"

"It isn't a bit from another show," said Christopher Milton softly.

"Not exactly, darling, but this song is absolutely based on that divine character you play in the telly, and I mean it just isn't Tony Lumpkin . . . is it?"

Her ginny voice faltered as he gazed at her coldly. The tableau was held in silence for a full minute. Then Christopher Milton turned to David Meldrum and said, unfairly, "Come on, we should be rehearsing if we're to get this number in by tonight."

"And are we?"

"Yes, we bloody are. For Christ's sake assert your authority." Which was rich, coming from the person who had done most to undermine it.

* * *

I Beg Yours? was in the show on the Tuesday night. It was under-rehearsed and a little untidy, but the audience loved it. Once again, Christopher Milton's instinct seemed to have been vindicated. The reaction to the rest of the show was mixed, but they latched on to that number.

Ruth was out front. Charles had given her a ticket, though after their silent parting in the morning he wasn't certain that she'd come. However, there she was at the stage door after the show. When he saw her, he felt an awful sense of shame. It was not exactly that he was ashamed of her, but he felt wrong with her. He tried to hurry her away, but Michael Peyton called out to him just as they were leaving, "Hey, everyone's going out for a curry. You want to come?"

Charles started to refuse, but Ruth chipped in and said she hadn't eaten and would love to go.

He hated the meal, because he hated being thought of in conjunction with Ruth. He knew how cruel it was to resent someone's company in that way and the knowledge only made him feel guiltier. Ruth, on the other hand, enjoyed herself. Surprisingly, Christopher Milton and Dickie Peck had joined the party, the star having decided to be one of the boys for a night, and he chatted up Ruth shamelessly. She luxuriated in this and Charles, embarrassed by her naïve questions and provincial tastes, was annoyed to find that he felt jealous too. To be jealous about a woman whom he was embarrassed to be with, it all got far too complicated to cope with. He drank heavily and wished Frances were there.

Ruth was drunk too and drove back unsteadily, chattering about Christopher Milton, to the grim inevitability of bed.

There was a small paragraph in the *Yorkshire Post* on the Wednesday morning, which mentioned the mugging of Kevin McMahon. From the management's point of view, it could have been worse. It didn't make a big issue of the incident and, on the bonus side, it was a free advertisement for the show.

The morning's rehearsal schedule was more work on *I Beg*

Yours?, which didn't involve Charles, so, hoping to shrug off the depression engendered by the scene with Ruth, he set off for the home of Kevin McMahon's parents. Remembering a mention of Meanwood in their conversation in the pub, he easily found the right McMahons in the phone book and rang them to check that Kevin was out of the Infirmary.

He traveled by bus. The pebble-dash semi had a two-tone doorbell.

Mrs. McMahon was small and sixtyish, with fuzzy white hair. She went on about how nice it was for one of Kevin's friends from the play to come along and treated Charles like one of her son's school friends. She also muttered regretfully about this terrible thing happening to Kevin on the night of his great triumph.

"You enjoyed the show on Monday?"

"Oh, we thought it was grand. That Christopher Milton, he's lovely, isn't he? I bet he's one of those who's just the same offstage as he is on. No *side,* if you know what I mean, isn't that right?"

Charles replied appropriately, making a mental note that Kevin was beyond the age for confiding in his parents.

The writer was in his childhood bedroom and seemed to have grown younger to match his surroundings. There was a poster of the Leeds United team of 1961. Uneven piles of magazines and carefully dusted Airfix airplane models suggested that his mother had kept his room "just as he liked it" for whenever he decided he needed the comfort of home. But this could hardly have been the return she had hoped for.

Kevin's eyes were nearly closed by puffy blue lids. Face criss-crossed with strips of plaster and open scratches. His right hand was bandaged in gauze and one finger stiffened with the square outline of a splint. No doubt the covers hid comparable injuries on the rest of his body.

"How're you doing?"

"Not too bad, Charles. It's good of you to come." He was subdued and formally polite, as if his surroundings brought back years of being taught good manners.

"No problem. I wasn't called for rehearsal this morning. They're doing the new—something that doesn't involve me."

Kevin showed no interest in what was happening to the show. There was a silence.

"Was it very bad?"

"I don't know. I think I was more or less anesthetized by alcohol at the time it happened." Charles chuckled encouragingly. "And when I came round, the hangover was so bad I hardly noticed my injuries. It's only today I'm really beginning to feel it."

"Sorry."

"Not too bad. Just very stiff all over. As if every bone in my body has been pulled out of its socket and reassembled by an enthusiastic amateur."

"Hmm. Do you mind talking about it?"

"No, but there's nothing to say."

"Why not?"

"I was so honked I can't remember anything. There was one bloke, that's all I know. And no, I didn't get a look at him. The police have asked me all this."

"You couldn't even say whether he was old or young?"

"No. Why do you ask that?"

Charles decided honesty might elicit the best response. "I was wondering if it was Dickie Peck who got at you."

"Dickie Peck? Why?" The question was dully asked; there was no animation.

"Well, you had that fight earlier in the evening. . . ."

"Yes." He sounded very tired. "Look, Charles, I was mugged. It's not nice, but it happens. I have no reason to believe it was anyone I know who did it. My only comfort is that it was hardly worth his while. I'd drunk away practically all the money I had, so all he got was a couple of credit cards."

"Did he say anything to you, or just hit?"

"Just hit." Kevin winced at the recollection.

"Surely the average mugger starts by asking for the goods and then comes in with the heavy stuff when you refuse."

"I don't know." The intonation was meant to end the conversation, but Charles had to continue. "Kevin, Dickie Peck protects Christopher Milton like a eunuch in a harem. If anyone argues with his blue-eyed boy, he stops them. And I don't think he's too fussy about his methods. He used to be a boxer and, as we saw the other night, he's still pretty tough."

"I was mugged," said Kevin doggedly.

"You're not holding out on me? There is nothing to make you think it could have been Dickie?"

"I am not holding out on you. There is nothing to make me think it could have been Dickie," came the repetition in a monotone.

Charles sighed. "Okay. Thanks. Well, I expect you'll soon feel better. What'll you do—come down and join us in Bristol?"

"No, I don't think I'll bother."

"What?"

"I think I'll follow your earlier advice—take the money and run. What was it you said—that I must think of it as a grant to buy time to go off and write what I really want to? That's what I'll do. There's no point in going on banging my head against a brick wall."

"Or having your head banged against a brick wall." But Kevin did not rise to the bait. Whoever it was had got at him had achieved the objective of the Christopher Milton/Dickie Peck camp. There would be no more interference in *Lumpkin!* by the writer of *Liberty Hall*.

He managed to get a word with Pete Masters, the musical director, during a break in the morning rehearsal. "Good number, that *I Beg Yours?*" he offered. Compliment is always conducive to confidence.

Pete, however, showed discrimination. "It's all right. Rather cobbled together. I don't really think it's that great. Lyric could do with a bit of polishing. The basic tune's okay, but it needs a proper arrangement. I'll do it as soon as I get time."

"Still, the product of one night. A whole song. Did you find it hard?"

"What, doing it in the time? Not really. Did lots of revue at— university and got used to knocking up stuff quickly."

"People who hesitate before they say "university" either went to somewhere so unmentionably awful that they're afraid of shocking people or went to Oxbridge and are afraid of being thought toffee-nosed."

Pete's boyish face broke into a smile. Charles' guess had been right. "Cambridge, actually."

"Ah, the Footlights."

"Exactly. By the way, you're right, people do get a bit shirty if you talk about it. Especially in the music business."

"Did you read music?"

"Yes."

"So this is slumming for you."

Again the tone had been right. Pete laughed. "You could say that." As he relaxed, his nondescript working-with-musicians voice gave way to his natural public school accent.

"Tell me, when you wrote that new song, did you actually stay up all night?"

"Oh yes."

"In the Dragonara?"

"In Christopher Milton's suite, yes."

"And you all worked on it, him and you and Wally and Dickie Peck?"

"Yes. Well, we talked it through first and then Wally and I went down to the ballroom, which was the only place where there was a piano. I think Christopher Milton and Dickie may have got some sleep while we did that."

"Or I suppose they could have gone out. . . ."

Pete treated the idea as a joke rather than as grounds for suspicion, which was just as well. "What, in Leeds? There's nothing to do here during the daytime, leave alone at night."

Charles chuckled. "So how long did it take you and Wally actually to write the number?"

"I don't know exactly. I suppose we went down to the piano about two-thirty and maybe finished about five."

So it was possible that Dickie Peck could have left the hotel to get Kevin McMahon. If, of course, he knew where to find him. Which was unlikely. But possible. The case seemed full of things that were possible, but not likely.

* * *

Charles wandered aimlessly around Leeds, trying to work it out, just to get one line of logic through all the strange events of the past few weeks. But it seemed as impossible to impose a pattern as it was to work out the geography of Leeds town center. After half an hour of circling round identical pedestrian shopping precincts, he went into a little restaurant called "The Kitchen" in Albion Street.

Over the Dish of the Day and a glass of red wine, he got out a notebook and pencil bought for the purpose in a W. H. Smith's he'd passed three times in the last half hour. James Milne, whom he'd met in Edinburgh over the Mariello murder the previous summer, had taught him the advantages of writing things down to clarify thoughts.

Three headings—"Incident," "Suspect" and "Motive." In the first column—"Pianist shot at," "Everard Austick pushed downstairs," "Flats allowed to fall" and "Kevin McMahon beaten up." He filled in a question mark after the first two, thought for a moment, and put one after the third. He started on "Suspects." Dickie Peck and Christopher Milton's driver for the second two "Incidents" and question marks for the first two. "Motive" offered "Protection of C.M., seeing that he gets his own way," again only for the second two. More question marks.

If only he could get some line which linked the first two victims with the later ones. He'd asked Michael Peyton about any altercations between the star and the pianist or Everard and received the information that, in the first case, the two didn't even meet at rehearsal, and in the second, an atmosphere of great cordiality had been maintained. So, unless there were some unknown link in the past, the motive for the first two attacks couldn't be the same as for the subsequent ones. Oh dear. He had another glass of wine.

In one respect at least the attack on Kevin McMahon had changed the situation. It had been publicly recognised as a crime by the cast, the police, the Press. That meant that any subsequent incidents might be related by people other than Charles and

Gerald Venables. The criminal, if criminal there were, would have to be more careful in future.

Having come to this conclusion, Charles looked at his watch. Five to two. God. There was a two-thirty matinée on Wednesday and if he hadn't signed in at the theatre by the "half," there'd be trouble.

In fact, there was trouble, but not the sort he feared. It was gastric trouble, and it only affected one member of the cast, Winifred Tuke.

Very interesting. If the pattern of accidents Charles suspected did exist, and if the motivation he had assumed were correct, then it was natural that Winifred Tuke should be the next victim. Since her clash with Christopher Milton over *I Beg Yours?*, she had made no secret of her feelings and, being a theatrical lady, she made no attempt to make her umbrage subtle. Gastric trouble also fitted. After the dramatic fate of Kevin, the criminal was bound to keep a low profile. Winifred Tuke had to be punished for opposing the will of Christopher Milton, but it couldn't be anything too serious, just an embarrassing indisposition which would put her out of action while the new number was rehearsed and became an established part of the show.

She had started to feel queasy at the end of the matinée, and only just managed to get through the last number. She did not appear for the curtain call. The company manager questioned her in her dressing-room and gathered, not so much from her genteel explanations as from her constant departures to the Ladies, that she was suffering from acute diarrhea. She was sent back to her digs in a taxi, moaning imprecations against the previous night's curry, and her under-rehearsed understudy took over for the evening performance.

Charles was not convinced about the curry. For a start, he would have expected food poisoning to manifest itself more quickly, and also it seemed strange that Winifred Tuke should be the only one affected by it. The meal had been one of those occasions when everyone ordered something different and had a bit of everything.

But nobody else seemed worried and certainly no one talked of links between the incident and Kevin's mugging. It seemed strange to Charles that in a large company of actors, who are the most superstitious of people, no one had spoken of bad luck or a jinx on the show. Perhaps he was too close to it. If it hadn't been for his unconventional recruitment, he probably wouldn't have found anything odd himself.

But at least this could be investigated. If Winifred Tuke had been slipped something, the chances were it had happened in the theatre. So, in the dead time between the matinée and evening performance, Charles took a look around.

The silence of empty dressing-rooms is almost tangible. He could feel the great pull of sentimentality which has led song-writers to maunder on about the smell of grease-paint, the limpness of unoccupied costumes, the wilting flowers, the yellowing telegrams of congratulation and all that yucky show business rubbish. Distant sounds from the stage, where the indefatigable Spike and his crew were going through yet another flying rehearsal, served only to intensify the silence.

Fortunately, Winifred's hasty exit had left her dressing-room unlocked. Inside it was almost depressingly tidy. A neat plastic sandwich-box of make-up, a box of tissues and a Jean Plaidy paperback were the only signs of occupation. Someone with Winifred's experience of touring didn't bother to settle in for just a week.

What Charles was looking for was not in sight, but it didn't take him long to find it. His clue came from the smell on Winifred Tuke's breath during rehearsals and, more particularly, performances. It was in the bottom of the wardrobe, hidden, in a pathetic attempt at gentility, behind a pair of boots. The middle-aged actress's little helper, a bottle of Gordon's gin.

The investigation was an amateur detective's dream. It was so easy Charles almost felt guilty for the glow of satisfaction it gave him. He opened the bottle and sniffed. Gin all right. He took a cautious sip and immediately felt suspicious. It wasn't the taste, but the consistency, the slight greasiness the drink left on his lips.

He poured a little into a glass and his suspicions were confirmed. Though it didn't show through the dark green of the Gordon's bottle, in the plain glass it was clear that the liquid had separated into two layers. Both were transparent, but the one that floated on top was viscous and left a slight slime round the glass. He dabbed at it and put his finger to his tongue. Yes, he wouldn't forget that almost tasteless taste in a hurry. It was his prep school matron's infallible cure for constipated boys—liquid paraffin. *way???*

He was excited by the discovery, but controlled his emotions while he washed up the glass. The slime clung on stubbornly and he had to wipe at it with a tissue.

A doubt struck him. If he had discovered the doctoring of the drink so easily, why hadn't Winifred noticed it? But the concealment of the gin bottle in the wardrobe answered that. If she kept her drinking a secret (or at least thought she did), then probably she would only whip the bottle out for a hasty gulp and pop it straight back to its hiding place. And if she'd been drinking during the show, she would probably put the greasy taste down to make-up on her lips.

Charles felt breathlessly excited. Here at last was evidence. Though every other apparent crime could have been an accident or the work of a vindictive outsider, the bottle was evidence of deliberate misdoing, committed within the company.

He had to keep it. In a case where facts were so thin on the ground he couldn't afford not to. Winifred Tuke was far too genteel to report its disappearance and, considering the bottle's contents, he was doing her a favor by removing it.

His holdall was in the green room, so he set off there, gin bottle in hand. Stealth was unnecessary; nobody would be in for the evening performance for at least an hour. He trod heavily on the stairs, awaking the echoes of the old building. He pushed open the green room door with a flourish and realized that he had forgotten the stage staff.

Spike and some others were slumped on sofas, reading newspapers. Charles made an involuntary movement to hide the bottle.

He needn't have worried. Spike was the only one who stirred. He looked up mildly and said, "Didn't think that was your usual tipple, Charles."

Charles made some half-joke about ringing the changes, put the bottle in his holdall and went out to the pub. He gave himself a mental rap over the knuckles for bad security. It didn't really matter, because only Spike had seen him. But it could have been someone else and it was his job as investigator to keep a low profile.

Still, he'd got the bottle. Perhaps a diarrhea weapon lacked the glamour of a murder weapon, but it certainly warranted a large whisky.

Now all he had to do was find a link between the bottle and his chief suspect. Difficult. Dickie Peck had returned to London that afternoon. Never mind, the investigation would keep until he rejoined the company.

Significantly, with the agent away, in spite of occasional flashes of temper from Christopher Milton, there were no more incidents while *Lumpkin!* was in Leeds.

PART 3

Bristol

CHAPTER 9

CHARLES WAS GLAD to get to Bristol. He hadn't enjoyed the previous few days. Investigations apart, Leeds had ended in scenes of cynical recrimination with Ruth. After a final fierce coupling on the Sunday morning and a silent drive to the station, he had had a long slow journey to King's Cross for her unspoken accusation to fester in his mind. He couldn't just laugh it off. As many times before, he cried out for the ability to say, that was good while it lasted, or that didn't work, oh well, time to move on. But he was bad at the sort of insouciance that should have accompanied his style of sex life. Feelings kept snagging, he kept feeling sorry for people, kept feeling he was using them. And, as always, lacking the self-righteousness necessary for anger, he ended up feeling self-disgust.

A half-day in London hadn't helped his mood. The bed-sitter in Hereford Road had not got less depressing in his absence. With the change in the weather it was as cold as a morgue when he opened the door. Nor did Sunday papers he'd bought offer any cheer. Bombs in London restaurants and the continuing apparent hopelessness of the Herrema siege led to fears of the imminent collapse of society, that terrible plunging feeling that tomorrow everything will stop and animal chaos will reign.

He rang his wife Frances in an attempt to shift the mood. But her phone just rang and rang and he stood, his finger dented by the twopence in the coin-box and his mind drifting, trying to remember what she had said in their last conversation about this new man she was seeing, forming silly fantasies of her with the new man, even of her upstairs in their bed with him, hearing the phone and saying, "Shall we answer it?" and him saying, "No." It was stupid, childish; it was as if he were again a sixteen-year-old, his stomach churning as he asked his first girl out to the pictures. And this was Frances, for God's sake, Frances whom he knew so well, who was so ordinary he had left her. But his feelings swirled around, unanchored. He put the phone down.

Back in his room (the telephone was outside on the landing) he had turned immediately to the obvious solace, a half-full (or, in his current mood, half-empty) bottle of Bell's. He drank with the kamikaze spirit of self-pity, sadly identifying with Everard Austick.

So Bristol, by comparison, was pleasant. He got a lift down on the Monday morning with a couple of the dancers who lived in Notting Hill and, apart from the fact of being in company, the staged sparkle of their camp chatter put him in a good mood. Then there was where he was staying. Julian Paddon, an actor friend from way back, was a member of the resident company at the Old Vic and had issued an immediate invitation when he heard *Lumpkin!* was coming to Bristol. His wife Helen was charming and had the enormous advantage after Ruth that Charles didn't fancy her at all (and even if he had, she was eight months pregnant and thus satisfactorily *hors de combat*).

Julian, whose nesting instinct, always strong, had been intensified by regular employment and the prospect of an addition to his family, had rented a flat in a Victorian house in Clifton and Charles was made to feel genuinely welcome.

Lumpkin! too responded to the new town. The day's break after the heavy rehearsal schedule in Leeds meant that everyone came to it with renewed vigor. The makeshift musical arrangement for *I Beg Yours?* had been improved and expanded by Leon Schultz, an American arranger flown over at enormous expense by an edgy management. The song was greatly enhanced and on the first night in Bristol it stopped the show. Once again Christopher Milton's theatrical instinct had been vindicated. The management was so pleased with the song that they asked Schultz to do new arrangements for all other numbers in the show. It would mean a lot more rehearsal, but in the new mood of confidence no one complained.

Away from the gloom of Leeds, Charles found it difficult to believe in thoughts of sabotage. The long sequence of crimes he had rationalised became unreal, another part of the general confusion over the show and Ruth which Leeds had meant for him. When he unpacked at Julian's flat, he had to look closely at the Gordon's gin bottle to convince himself that anything criminal had ever happened.

Part of his relaxation was due to Dickie Peck's absence. His suspicions had now homed in firmly and until the agent rejoined the company, he did not fear further incidents. What he should do when another occurred was something he tried not to think about.

Anyway, rehearsals kept him busy. Desmond Porton from Amulet Productions was to come and see the show on the Thursday and give the final all-clear for the scheduled first night at the King's Theatre on Thursday, November 27th. That gave a sense of urgency and a healthy edge of determination to everyone in the show.

The first two nights made Charles begin to think he was, for possibly the first time in his life, about to be connected with a success. Apart from reflections on the irony of a fate which withheld major triumph from shows he had cared about in favor of the commercial banality of *Lumpkin!*, it was a pleasant feeling.

He was sitting in the pub during the Tuesday performance (having dutifully checked in for the "half" and let the stage manager know where he'd be) when the girl approached him. Her pale blue eyes had the unfocused stare of contact lenses, but there was nothing vague about her manner. "Are you in *Lumpkin!?*" she asked, the directness of the question emphasised by an American accent.

"Fame at last," he replied with irony. "Yes, I am."

"Good, I thought I recognized you. I saw the show last night."

"Ah." Charles left the pause for comment on his performance which no actor can resist.

But the girl didn't pick up the cue. "My name's Suzanne Horst," she said. "I'm a free-lance journalist."

He emitted another "Ah," again succumbing to an actor's instinctive reaction that the girl wanted to write something about him.

She soon put him right on that. "I'm trying to make contact with Christopher Milton."

Of course. He blushed for having suspected anything else, and let out another multi-purpose "Ah."

"Would you introduce me to him?"

"Well. . . ." This was rather difficult. The past month with Christopher Milton had revealed to Charles how carefully the star's contact with the press and media was regulated by his agent. To introduce an unexpected journalist could be a serious breach of professional etiquette. "I think probably the best thing you could do would be to make contact with his agent. It's Dickie Peck of Creative Artists."

"I don't want to mess with agents. Anyway, I'm here in Bristol. What's the point of contacting a guy in London about someone who's only a hundred yards away at this moment?"

There wasn't a great deal of logic about it, but that was the way stars worked, Charles explained.

She was not put down. "Yes, I know that's the correct way to go about things, but I don't want to go the correct way. I want to go the way that'll get me the interviews I'm after."

"Well, I don't know what to suggest." Charles felt churlish, but thought he was probably doing the right thing. "What are these interviews you are after?"

"One's for radio. Only got Radio Brighton interested at the moment, but I'm sure I'll be able to get it on one of the networks. That's only secondary, anyway. The main thing I want him for is an article I'm doing on the nature of stardom. Want to know what makes him tick, you know."

"Who's that for?"

"Don't know who I'll offer it to yet. *Cosmopolitan,* maybe."

"It hasn't been commissioned?"

"No, but I'll sell it all right." Whatever Miss Horst lacked, it was not confidence.

In fact she didn't lack much. Certainly not looks. Her shoulder-length hair was that streaky yellow which might be the natural result of sun on brown hair or the unnatural result of hairdressers on any color. Her belted Burberry formalised but did not disguise her lithe figure, and though her overpowering confidence might be a slight deterrent, the general effect was distinctly tangible. "Can I get you a drink?"

"Thank you. A vodka and tonic, please." The barman eyed Charles knowingly as he supplied the drink. Suzanne didn't seem to notice. "Are you sure you can't introduce me?"

"Honestly, it is difficult. You know, people like Christopher Milton have to guard their privacy very carefully. I'm afraid they tend to be a bit resistant to journalists."

"But, look, I'm not going to do a big exposé or anything. It'll be an appreciative piece. I mean, I'm a fan."

"I don't think that's really the point. It's rather difficult to get near him."

"But you see him at rehearsal, don't you?"

"Well, yes, but—"

"Then you could ask him if he'd be prepared to do an interview with me."

Her persistence didn't make it easy. Charles cringed with embarrassment at the thought of putting the girl's request to Christopher Milton. It was difficult to explain to someone outside the closely defined relationship that exists between actors in a working context. "Look, I'm sorry, I really don't think I can."

"Why not? You do know him, don't you?"

"Yes, I do, but—"

"Well then," she said, as if that concluded the syllogism.

"Yes." Under normal circumstances he would have given a categorical "No," but under normal circumstances the people who made this kind of request didn't look like Suzanne Horst. He said something about seeing if he had a chance to raise the matter at rehearsal (which he had no intention of doing) and asked the girl how much journalism she had done.

"Oh, quite a lot in the States. I got a degree in it, but the scene over there isn't very interesting, so I decided to check it out over here."

"What, you've given yourself a sort of time limit to see if you can make it?"

"Oh, I'll make it."

Charles was beginning to find this self-conviction a little wearying, so he brought in a damper. "Yes, unfortunately it's a bad time to get started in that sort of area at the moment. Journalism's getting more and more of a closed shop. It's like acting, getting increasingly difficult to make the initial break into the business."

"Don't worry," said Suzanne, as though explaining to a child, "People with talent always get through."

He couldn't think of anything to say after that.

But Suzanne suddenly got an idea. "Hey, you could actually be quite useful on this stardom article."

"In what way?"

"Well, you could give me a bit of background on Christopher Milton. After all, you're working with him."

Charles was hesitant, but overruled. She had whipped out a new shorthand notebook and a freshly-sharpened pencil and was poised in the attitude of someone who had taken a degree in journalism. The question came out formal and rehearsed. "Tell me, as an actor, what do you think it is that makes some people stars?"

"And some dreary old hacks like me? Hmmm. Well now—" dropping into an American accent—"what is a star? What is it that picks out one from the myriad throng of the moderately talented and gives him that magic name? What is it that sets one talent glowing in the limelight, that scatters the moondust of stardom on that one chosen head? Is it of the earth or is it made in heaven? Perhaps in that Great Casting Agency in the Sky, there sits the one Eternal Agent who—"

"Look, are you taking the rise out of me?" *FROM AN AMERICAN GIRL ???*

He lapsed back into his normal voice. "No, sorry. I was just getting my bearings. Stardom? I don't know really. In the sort of theatre I normally do it's rarely an issue.

"But I suppose, if I had to give an opinion. . . . Well, talent certainly, that must be there. Not necessarily a great deal of it, nor anything very versatile. In fact, there should be no versatility. The star must always be recognizable—if he puts on voices, he must put them on almost badly, so that everyone knows it's him. That's talent. Okay. What else? Dedication certainly, the conviction that what he does is more important than anything else in the world."

"Isn't that likely to lead to selfishness?" Suzanne interposed with studied professionalism.

"Inevitably. Bound to. Hence, presumably, all the stories that one hears of stars hating competition and being temperamental and slamming dressing-room doors and that sort of thing."

He realized that it could get a little awkward if Suzanne asked him to relate his last observation to the star of *Lumpkin!*, and hurried on before she had the chance. "I think there's also something about the way the entertainment industry works, certainly for actors. Being an actor is, potentially, the most passive function on earth. Most actors are completely dependent on directors, because it's directors who control the jobs. Some manage to assert themselves by deep commitment to their work, or by directing or writing and devising shows. Some do it by political affiliations—starting street theatres, workshop communes, even— in cases of extreme lunacy—joining the Workers' Revolutionary Party. Some do it by forming their own companies, that kind of thing. But what I'm getting at is that, given this lack of autonomy, when an actor becomes very much in demand, as a star might be, he wants to dictate his own terms. It's years of frustration at living on someone else's terms. It's also a self-preservation thing—once someone's got to the top, he tries to do everything to ensure that he stays there, and that may involve being careful about the people he works with, seeing that none of them are too good. I mean, often when you see a show with one big star name above the title and the rest of the cast nonentities, it's not just because the star's fee has exhausted the budget, it's also that he shows up in such mediocre company. The Whale among Sprats syndrome.

"Then there's management, which is very important. Choosing work, not doing anything that's beneath the star's dignity, or anything in which he's not going to shine. Can't take a risk, everything that is done has to be right, even at the expense of turning work down. For that reason you often find that a real star won't do anyone a favor, won't step in if someone's ill. It's not just bloody-mindedness, it's self-preservation. When someone's at the top, there are any number of people sniping, ready to read the signs of a decline, so it never does to be too available."

"Do you think a star has *magic?*" asked Suzanne, with awestruck italics.

"I don't know. I—"

"Oh, Mr. Paris, there you are." Gwyneth of the stage management stood before him, her customary calm ruffled by anxiety. "You should have been back in the theatre half an hour ago."

On the Wednesday morning they were rehearsing the first act finale, *Ooh, What a Turn-up,* which had been rearranged by Leon Schultz. Pete Masters, the M.D., was not in the best of moods. Having seen his own arrangements thrown out of the window, he found it galling to have to teach the new ones to the impassive band. The musicians had long since lost any spark of interest that they may have had for the show and sat mentally sorting out their VAT returns, eyes occasionally straying to their watches to see if the rehearsal would spread over into another session at M.U. rates. Christopher Milton was onstage directing, while David Meldrum sat at the back of the stalls reading *The Stage.*

The rehearsal had reached an impasse. Leon Schultz's new arrangement introduced a short violin figure which bridged from the verse into the chorus and there was no dancing to cover it. The cast tried freezing for the relevant three seconds, but that lost the pace of the number. A couple of the dancers improvised a little jig, which looked alien and messy. There was a long pause while Christopher Milton stood center stage, the ominous faraway expression in his eyes.

Suddenly he was galvanized into action. "Where's the sodding choreographer?"

"She wasn't called for this rehearsal," said the musical director smugly, "following assurances that the new arrangements would not involve any major changes in the choreography."

Christopher Milton seemed not to hear the dig. It was as if his mind could only focus slowly. "Then what can we do?" He enunciated the words very clearly and without emotion.

"No idea." Pete Masters shrugged. "Unless we cut the meaningless little bit of schmaltz altogether." His tone was calculated to provoke, but produced no reaction. Emboldened, he pressed on: "Or go back to the original arrangements, which were quite as good and a darned sight less fussy."

"What, your arrangements?" Christopher Milton asked slowly.

"Yes."

"Your sodding arrangements." The build to anger was slow, but now it had started it built to a frightening intensity. "Your little tuppenny-ha'penny amateur teashop quartet arrangements. This is the bloody professional theatre, sonny, not some half-baked student revue. Your arrangements! This isn't Penge Amateur Operatic Society, you know."

Pete Masters' face had gone very red, but he fought to keep his voice calm and give a dignified reply. "There's no need for you to speak to me like that. You may prefer the new arrangements to mine, but there's no need to be offensive about it."

"Oh, I'm sorry, was I being offensive?" The last word was pronounced with savage mimicry that exactly echoed Pete's public school tone. "How foolish of me. I had forgotten that I was speaking to someone who has a degree in music and therefore knows everything about the subject. What a silly-billy I am."

The impersonation was funny and, though Charles cringed in the wings and the musicians continued to stare impassively, it did produce an unidentified laugh from somewhere up in the flies where the stage crew were invisibly watching the proceedings. It gave Christopher Milton a stimulus and he continued to vent his lacerating irony on Pete.

Eventually the M.D. struck back. Still he tried to sound in control, but his wavering voice let him down. "Listen, if you're going to speak to me like that, I'm going."

"Go. See if anyone cares. Just don't think you can treat me like that. You've got to get it straight, boy, what matters in this show. You don't. You go, there are a hundred second-rate musicians can take over tomorrow. I go, there just isn't a show. Get your priorities right, boy."

Pete Masters mouthed, but couldn't produce any words. He did the only possible thing in the circumstances and walked off stage.

The musicians looked at their watches with satisfaction. A row like this made it almost certain that they'd go into another session. The atmosphere in the theatre was heavy with embarrassment.

It blew over. Of course it blew over. That sort of row can't go on for long. The pressures of keeping the show going don't allow it. Pete and Christopher Milton were working together again within a quarter of an hour, with neither apologizing or commenting on the scene. All the same, Charles Paris was relieved that Dickie Peck had not been present to witness the latest challenge to his protégé.

It wasn't just the clash at rehearsals that morning, but something changed the company mood on the Wednesday afternoon. Perhaps it was a small and silent house at the matinée. Perhaps it was Desmond Porton's impending visit and the fear of having the show assessed. Or perhaps it was The Cold.

Actors, whose working tools are their voices, are naturally terrified of colds, sort throats, flus and other infections which threaten their precious vocal cords. They all have their own favorite remedies and preventative methods when germs are in the air, or, in some cases, even when they aren't. Large doses of Vitamin C are swallowed, dissolved or crunched. (So are most other vitamins of the alphabet, with a kind of pagan awe.) Strange elixirs of lemon and honey (with bizarre variations involving onions) are poured down tender throats. Aspirin, codeine, paracetamol, Anadin, Veganin and others are swilled down, discussed and compared as connoisseurs speak of malt whiskies. Names of doctors who can "do wonders for throats" (as well as others who deal with backs and nervous twinges) are exchanged like rare stamps. It is all taken very seriously.

When a show involves singing, the panic and precautions are doubled. Vocal sprays are brought into play. Little tins and envelopes of pills are ostentatiously produced and their various merits extolled. Some favor Nigroids, small pills which "blow your head off, dear, but really do wonders for my cords"; others will not stir without "The Fisherman's Friend"—"quite strong, darling, but they really relax the throat"; there are Friar's Balsam, Vocalzones,

Sanderson's Throat Specific and a whole gallery of other patent medicines available, all of which have their staunch adherents.

The Cold started with one of the dancers, who had difficulty in preventing his sneeze during the matinée. Then Mark Spelthorne, quick to seize any opportunity for self-dramatization, thought he might have one of his throats coming on. During the evening performance many of the cast were walking round backstage massaging their throats, talking in whispers ("conserving the voice, dear—may have a touch of "flu coming on") and generally putting on expressions of private suffering which they had learnt when rehearsing Chekhov. It helped to make the atmosphere around *Lumpkin!* suddenly spiky.

Charles just made it to the pub as time was being called after a sedate Bristol house had given its qualified support to the evening performance. He was the only one of the company who went. Most went straight home to nurse themselves in anticipation of The Cold.

He managed to get in an order for a pint of bitter (performing always made him thirsty) and was letting the first mouthful wash down when the girl came up to him. The American voice twanged. "Did you ask him?"

"Who? What?" He pretended innocence, but knew full well what she meant.

"Christopher Milton. You were going to ask him about the interview."

"Oh yes, of course. I hadn't forgotten. Trouble is, today was very busy, what with the two shows. And we were rehearsing some new arrangements this morning." It sounded pretty feeble.

But she didn't seem to notice. "Never mind. You'll do it sometime." Surprisingly benign. He'd expected her to tear him apart for his omission. "Some time," she repeated and he realized that she was drunk.

"Can I get you a drink?"

"Haven't they closed?"

"Nooo. Never. Barman. What is it, Suzanne?"

"Vodka tonic."

"One of those, please."

She took the drink and gulped it down like water. She stood close to him and swayed so that they almost touched. "How'd the show go?"

"Not world-shattering."

"Smy birthday today."

"Ah."

"Had a few drinks to celebrate. Alone in a foreign country."

"Ah."

She leant against him. "Give me a birthday kiss. Back in the States I never go without a birthday kiss."

He kissed her dryly on the lips as if she were a child, but he felt uncomfortably aware of how unchildlike she was. Her breasts exercised a magnetic attraction as she swayed towards him. He drained his beer. "Well, better be off. They'll be turfing us out shortly."

"You going to see me home?" she asked kookily. Miss Suzanne Horst with a few drinks inside her was a very different proposition from the hyper-efficient lady who was about to set British journalism afire.

"Is it far?"

"Not far. Staying at a hotel."

"Ah." Charles found he said a lot of "Ahs" in conversation with Suzanne. Because he couldn't think of anything else to say.

They hadn't got far from the pub when she stopped and rolled round into his arms. "Kiss me properly," she mumbled. Light filtered across the road from the lamp over the stage door.

He held her warm and cozy in his arms. He didn't kiss her. Thoughts moved slowly but with great clarity through his mind. The girl was drunk. He was nearly fifty. He should keep away from women; it always hurt one way or the other. The silent resentment of Ruth was too recent a memory. And before that there had been Anna in Edinburgh. And others. A wave of tiredness swept over him at the eternal predictability of lust.

He felt a shock of depression, as if the pavement in front of him had suddenly fallen away. What was the point of anything? Women could alleviate the awareness of the approach of death, but they could not delay it. He was cold, cold as though someone was walking over his grave. The intensity and speed of the emotion frightened him. Age, it must be age, time trickling away. He thought of Frances and wanted her comforting touch.

The girl in his arms was still, half dozing. He took her elbow and detached her from him. "Come on. I'll get you back to your hotel." Gently.

At that moment he heard the clunk of the stage door closing and looked across to see Pete Masters emerge with a briefcase under his arm. The M.D. didn't see him, but started to cross the road, going away from him.

The Mini must have been parked near by, but Charles wasn't aware of it until it flashed past. He turned sharply, seemed dumb for a moment, then found his voice, too late, to shout, "Look out!"

Pete Masters half-turned as the wing of the Mini caught him. He was spun round on his feet and flung sprawling against a parked car. From there he slid down to lie still in the road. The Mini turned right at the end of the street and disappeared.

CHAPTER 10

AND DICKIE PECK had not been in Bristol at the time of the accident. Charles tried to reason round it, but the fact was incontrovertible. According to Christopher Milton, the agent was not expected to come and see *Lumpkin!* again until Brighton. In case that information wasn't reliable, Charles went to the extreme of phoning Creative Artists to check it. He used a disguised voice and pretended to be a policeman investigating the accident to Pete Masters. It was a risky expedient, one that had turned sour on him before, but he couldn't think of another. As soon as he put the phone down, he realized that if Dickie Peck had anything to hide, he was now going to be a hundred times more careful. And he could well have been lying about his movements anyway.

All the same, Charles had already started to remove the agent from the front rank of his suspicions. Though he might be involved, might be directing operations, Dickie Peck wasn't the one to do the heavy stuff. The more Charles thought about it, the more incongruous it became—a successful agent, with a lot of artists on his books, going round running people over and slipping them liquid paraffin? No. What was needed was a logical reappraisal of the situation.

He sat in Julian Paddon's sitting room on a bright autumn day and once again wrote down James Milne's headings, "Incident," "Suspect" and "Motive." He only filled in the middle column.

Three names—Dickie Peck, Christopher Milton and Christopher Milton's driver.

Then, as if imposing logic by committing conjecture to paper, he wrote another heading, "Reasons for Innocence." Against Dickie Peck's name he filled in, "Not on scene of last incident (i.e. in London)—position to keep up—discovery would ruin career." Against Christopher Milton—"Last point above to nth degree—v. concerned with public image—could not afford the risk of personal action." Against the driver he put a neat dash, then changed his mind and wrote, "The only question is who he's taking orders from —D.P. or C.M.—or is he acting off his own bat?"

Written down it looked convincing, Charles felt a satisfaction akin to completing *The Times* crossword. He couldn't imagine why he hadn't thought of the driver before. Very distinctly he remembered the first time he had seen the man, advancing threateningly towards the crowd of boys who mobbed Christopher Milton outside the Welsh Dragon Club. He remembered how the driver had been halted by a gesture and how he had hovered protectively until the star wanted to leave. Like a bodyguard. It was quite logical that Christopher Milton should have a bodyguard. People in the public eye are instant targets for freaks and lunatics. And in a way everything untoward that had happened on the show could be put down to an exaggerated interpretation of a bodyguard's role. Whether the man interpreted it that way for himself or at someone else's suggestion was a detail which could wait until there was some actual evidence of guilt.

In Charles' new mood of logical confidence he felt sure that proof would not be difficult to find now that he had a definite quarry. He took his sheet of paper with the winning formula on it and burnt it carefully in the grate of the fireplace, pulverizing the black ash until it could yield nothing to forensic science. Even as he did so, a sneaking suspicion that he concentrated too much on the irrelevancies of detection started to bore a tiny hole in his shell of confidence.

"Charles, what the hell's going on?"

"What do you mean, Gerald?"

"Well, there's a little piece in the *Evening Standard* about this M.D. being run over."

"Ah."

"It also mentions Kevin being mugged in Leeds. No comment, just a juxtaposition of the two facts. It's worse than if they actually said it's a bad luck show."

"Oh, come on. If someone's run over, it doesn't necessarily mean there's anything odd. Accidents do happen."

"But don't you think this is another in the series?"

"As a matter of fact I do, but nobody else does. There's no talk about it in the company, beyond the sort of relish actors always have for dramatic situations."

"Have the Press made much of it down there?"

"Not a lot. Small report, just the facts. M.D. of *Lumpkin!*—hit and run driver in stolen car—details of injuries, that's all."

"What were his injuries?"

"Mainly bruising. I think he may also have broken his patella."

"His what?"

"Kneecap to you."

"And he's out of the show?"

"Certainly for a bit. Leon Schultz has taken over as M.D."

"Has he?" Gerald sounded gratified. "Ah, well, it's an ill wind. Good. I always said they should have got a big name from the start rather than that boy. It'll bump the budget up a bit."

The welfare of the show seemed to be Gerald's only concern. So long as his investment was protected, nothing else mattered. Charles felt bitter, particularly as his friend continued. "But look, do keep a watchful eye on Christopher Milton. If he gets clobbered, the show really is a non-starter."

"And if anyone else gets clobbered, it doesn't matter?"

"Well, yes, it does, of course, because it's very bad publicity for the show, but it's Christopher Milton who's the important one. And they must be aiming for him eventually, otherwise there's no point in all this, is there?"

"That's not the way I see it. I don't think I should worry about Christopher Milton; I should be protecting everyone else in the show."

"What do you mean?"

"Nothing. I can't explain it now. Suffice to say that my view of the case has changed since we last spoke."

"Oh. But do you know who's doing it all?"

"Yes. I think I do."

"Well, get him arrested and stop him."

"I haven't got any evidence yet."

"Then get some."

"I will."

Charles felt furiously angry when he put the phone down. The whole thing was getting out of proportion. The protection of Christopher Milton must continue, whoever got hurt on the way. It was hearing such blinkered lack of consideration from Gerald that made him so cross. The world, even his friends, would forgive anything done in the name of Christopher Milton. Gerald had asked for evidence and an arrest and he'd get them, though they might not be what he expected. Charles felt a wave of anger against the whole star set-up, the charming public persona that needed the support of thuggery to survive. Whether or not Christopher Milton was directly involved in the crimes, the rottenness and meanness of what had been going on should be exposed to the public. From now on Charles wasn't working for Gerald Venables representing Arthur Balcombe. He was working for himself.

After the Thursday show, he dressed carefully for his midnight jaunt. As an actor, he knew how much the right costume could help in a difficult rôle, and the rôle in which he had cast himself was a very difficult one.

He wore a pair of his own black trousers and a black sweater borrowed from Julian (in what he hoped was a casual manner). He had bought a pair of plimsolls in Woolworth's and, since Woolworth's doesn't sell ready-dirtied plimsolls for housebreakers, he had shabbied them up with earth from Julian's garden. Other investments were a balaclava helmet and a pencil torch. He knew the preparations were overelaborate, but they took his mind off what he had to do.

With the balaclava on, he looked like a very young photograph of himself as Second Sentry in *Coriolanus* ("Leaden production"—

Richmond and Twickenham Times). Without it, he looked a cross between himself as Lightborn in a modern dress *Edward II* ("Flamboyantly sinister"—*Birmingham Evening Mail*) and as Jimmy Porter in *Look Back in Anger* ("Ill-considered"—*Luton Evening Post*). He crept down the stairs to the front door and realized he was using the walk he'd perfected for *Rookery Nook* ("Uneven"—*Jewish Telegraph*).

Unfortunately he met Julian coming in. "Where are you going dressed like that, Charles? You look as if you're about to commit a burglary."

That didn't help.

Residents of the Holiday Inn in Bristol park their cars in the adjacent multi-story car park. It was a simple matter to walk in. He found Christopher Milton's distinctive Rolls on the first level without any problem.

And his luck held. The Corniche was unlocked. He slipped in by the passenger door and closed it quickly to douse the interior light. He reached to get the torch out of his pocket, but his hand was shaking too much. He closed his eyes and practiced rib-reserve breathing, trying to keep the thought of what he was doing at bay. But a schoolboy fear of being found out remained. He wished he could remember some of the relaxation exercises various experimental directors had tried to put him through. None came.

Still, the deep breathing helped. He opened his eyes and, very slowly, like a man under water, he got out the torch and switched it on.

The glove pocket opened easily. A tin of boiled sweets came first into the light. He prised it open and found nothing but the sugary debris that should have been there. Next a large stiff envelope. He felt inside. The shiny surface of photographs. He pulled one out and shone the torch on it. Christopher Milton grinned cheerily at him. Fan photographs. The sight of the familiar face brought on another pang of guilt. At the same moment he noticed that his thumb had left a perfect print on the photograph. The light caught it on the shiny surface. That was one that the police wouldn't need powder to spot. He wiped at it roughly, but seemed only to add more prints. He shoved the photograph back into the envelope and replaced it.

Sweat prickled on his hands and he thought he'd done enough. His grandiose schemes for following the raid on the car with a search of the driver's hotel bedroom were evaporating fast.

Finish the glove pocket and go. He ran his fingers along the angle at the back and felt some small beadlike objects under his fingernails. He picked one out, held it between thumb and forefinger and turned the light on it.

And at that moment his whole attitude to what he was doing changed. What he held was a small-waisted piece of lead. The shape was unmistakable. It was an airgun pellet. Just the sort of airgun pellet which had hit *Lumpkin!*'s first rehearsal pianist in the hand on the second day of rehearsal. It was evidence.

He grabbed three or four more of the slugs and put them in his pocket. His panic had changed to surging confidence. He reached forward for one more sweep into the glove pocket and his hand closed round the firm outline of a small bottle. Hardly daring to hope, he drew it out and flashed the torch on it. LIQUID PARAFFIN (Liquid Paraffin BP). The bottle was half-empty. He could not believe his good fortune.

There was a noise of a door banging. He turned. Someone was coming from the direction of the hotel. A guest going to another car. He'd wait for them to drive off and then beat a hasty retreat. He shrank down into the leather seat and slipped the balaclava helmet over his head. He pulled it round to cover his face.

The silence was unnaturally long. No slam of a car door, no choking of an engine. He began to think that the visitor must have gone out down the ramp and slowly eased himself up to look.

At that moment there was a click of the door opening and he felt light through the latticed wool of the balaclava. He was face to face with Christopher Milton's driver, who was leaning forward to get into the car.

The man's eyes bulged as he saw the intruder and in shock he jerked his head back sharply. There was a loud crack which shook the car and he slid gracefully from view.

Charles, his mind full of ugly pugilistic visions, edged slowly across to the driver's seat and looked down over the edge.

The driver lay neatly on the ground with his eyes closed. He was out cold. Charles got out of the car, shut the door to put the light out and turned his torch on the body on the ground.

There was no blood. Regular breathing. Strong heartbeat. Strong pulse. Probably just concussion. He loosened the man's tie and put a cushion from the back of the car under his head.

Then, with the precious pellets and bottle in his pocket, Charles crept down the stairs out of the garage. As he emerged into the street, he removed the balaclava.

There was a phonebox opposite. It seemed a natural conclusion to the dreamlike flow of luck which had characterized the previous half-hour. Charles dialed 999 and asked for the ambulance service in his own voice before thinking to disguise it. When he was connected, he had a moment's agonizing decision choosing a voice. Northern Irish seemed the most natural for this sort of thing, but it might be unduly alarmist in a bomb-conscious Britain. The voice that came to hand was American-Italian. Sounding like something out of *The Godfather,* he said, "Could you send an ambulance to the big car park beside the Holiday Inn." He was tempted to say, "There's a stiff there," but made do with, "There's somebody injured."

"What's happened to them?" asked the voice and it was only by putting the phone down that Charles could prevent himself from saying, "Someone made him an offer he couldn't refuse."

He hung about until he saw the ambulance safely arrived, and then went briskly back to Julian's place, using the walk he'd developed when playing a gangster in *Guys and Dolls* ("This guy didn't like it and nor did the doll he was with"—*Bolton Evening News*).

CHAPTER 11

CHARLES WOKE IN an excellent mood. The events of the previous night were very clear to him. It was as if he had found the instant cure-all he had always dreamed must exist somewhere. All his problems had been resolved at once. He now had evidence of the wrong-doing of the driver and just to make his job easier, the driver himself was temporarily removed from the scene. There was still the minor question of what he should do about it—confront the villain and threaten police proceedings, go direct to the police or send them an anonymous deposition advising investigation—but that would keep. The warm completed-*Times*-crossword sensation had developed into an even better feeling, as if his solution to the puzzle had won a prize.

Helen Paddon cooked him an enormous breakfast, which he consumed with that relish which only a fulfilled mind can give. She was pleased to have something to do. The last heavy weeks of pregnancy were dragging interminably.

He finished breakfast about nine and took the unusual expedient of ringing Gerald at home. After pleasantries and must-see-you-soons from Kate Venables, the solicitor came on the line. "What gives?" he asked in his B-film gangster style.

"It's sorted out."

"Really?"

"Uhuh." Charles found himself slipping into the same idiom.

"You know who's been doing it all?"

"I know and I've got evidence."

"Who?" The curiosity was immediate and childlike.

"Never mind." Charles was deliberately circumspect and infuriating. "Suffice to say that I'll see nothing else happens to threaten the show, at least from the point of view of crime or sabotage. If it fails on artistic grounds, I'm afraid I can't be held responsible."

"Is that all you're going to tell me?"

"Yes."

"Damn your eyes." Charles chuckled. "But you're sure that Christopher Milton is in no danger?"

"I don't think he ever has been in any danger from anyone but himself." On that cryptic note he put the phone down, knowing exactly the expression he had left on Gerald's face.

There was a ten-thirty call for the entire company to hear what Desmond Porton of Amulet Productions had thought of *Lumpkin!* and what changes he had ordered before the show could come into London. Charles ambled through the streets of Bristol towards the theatre, his mood matched by the bright November sun. The people of the city bustled about their business and he felt a universal benevolence towards them. His route went past the Holiday Inn and he could hardly repress a smile at the memory of what had happened the night before. It was strange. He felt no guilt, no fear that the driver might have been seriously hurt. That would have spoiled the rounded perfection of the crime's solution.

The people of Bristol looked much healthier than those of Leeds. His mind propounded some vague theory about the freedom of living near the sea as against the claustrophobia of a land-locked city, but it was let down when the sun went in. Anyway, the people didn't look that different. In fact, there was a man on the opposite side of the street who looked exactly like the bald man with big ears whom he'd idly followed in Leeds. He kicked himself for once again trying to impose theories on everything. Why could he never just accept the continuous variety of life without trying to force events into generalizations?

There was a lot of tension at the theatre. The entire company sat in the stalls, exchanging irrelevant chatter or coughing with self-pity to show that they'd got The Cold. There were three chairs on the stage and, as Charles slumped into a stalls seat, they were filled by the company manager, David Meldrum and Christopher Milton.

David Meldrum stood up first as if he were the director and clapped his hands to draw attention. The chatter and coughing faded untidily. "Well, as you all know, we had a distinguished visitor in our audience last night, Desmond Porton of Amulet, who, you don't need reminding, are putting up a lot of the money for this show. So for that reason, if no other, we should listen with interest to his comments and maybe make certain changes accordingly."

"Otherwise the show will never make it to London," added the company manager cynically.

"Yes." David Meldrum paused, having lost his thread. "Um, well, first let me give you the good news. He liked a lot of the show a lot and he said there is no question of the London opening being delayed. So it's all systems go for November 27th, folks!" The slang bonhomie of the last sentence did not suit the prissy voice in which it was said.

"And now the bad news. . . ." For this line he dropped into a cold German accent which suited him even less. "We were up quite a lot of the night with Desmond Porton going through the script and there are quite a lot of changes that we're going to have to make. Now you probably all realize that over the past few weeks the show has been getting longer and longer. Our actual playing time is now three hours and eight minutes. Add two intervals at fifteen minutes each and that's well over three and a half."

A derisive clap greeted this earnestly presented calculation. David Meldrum appeared not to hear it and went on. "So that means cuts, quite a lot of cuts. We can reduce the intervals to one, which would give us a bit of time, and the King's Theatre management won't mind that because it saves on bar staff. But we've still got half an hour to come out of the show. Now some of it we can lose by just shortening a few of the numbers, cutting a verse and chorus here and there. We can probably pick up ten minutes that way. But otherwise we're going to have to lose whole numbers and take considerable cuts in some of the dialogue scenes.

"Now I'm sorry. I know you've all put a lot of work into this show and I know whatever cuts we make are going to mean big disappointments for individuals among you. But Amulet Productions are footing most of the wage bill and so, as I say, we have to listen carefully to their views. And after all, we have a common aim. All of us here, and Amulet, we all just want the show to be a success, don't we?"

The conclusion of the speech was delivered like Henry V's "Cry God for Harry, England and St. George!" but was not greeted with the shouts of enthusiasm which follow Shakespeare's line in every production. There was an apathetic silence punctuated by small coughs until one of the dancers drawled, "All right, tell us what's left, dear."

David Meldrum reached round for his script, opened it and was about to speak when Christopher Milton rose and said, "There was another point that Desmond made, and that was that a lot of the show lacked animation. Not enough action, not enough laughs. So as well as these cuts, there will be a certain amount of rewriting of the script, which Wally Wilson will be doing. It's all too sedate at the moment, like some bloody eighteenth-century play."

"But it is a bloody eighteenth-century play." Charles kept the thought to himself and nobody else murmured. They were all resigned—indeed, when they thought about it, amazed that the major reshaping of the show hadn't come earlier. They sat in silence and waited to hear the worst.

David Meldrum went through the cuts slowly and deliberately. They were predictable. Oliver Goldsmith, whose revolutions in his grave must by this time have been violent enough to put him into orbit, was left with almost nothing of his original play. The trouble with most musicals based on other works is that the songs are not used to advance the action. A musical number is merely a break in the continuity and, when it's over, you're four minutes further into the show and only two lines further into the plot. Carl Anthony and Micky Gorton's songs, written with an eye to the Top Ten and continuing profitable appearances on LPs, were particularly susceptible to this criticism. But because the songs were the set-pieces and the items on which most rehearsal time and money had been spent, they had to survive at the expense of the text. Charles, who remembered Goldsmith's play well from his own Cardiff production, saw the plot vanishing twist by twist, as one of the most beautiful and simple comic mechanisms in English literature was dismantled and reassembled without many of its working parts.

But the cuts were selective. It was clear that Christopher Milton had been up through the night with David Meldrum and Desmond Porton, watching each projected excision with a careful eye. Tony Lumpkin's part came through the massacre almost unscathed. One rather dull number was cut completely and a verse and chorus came out of another. And that was it. While all the other characters had their parts decimated.

The one who suffered most was the one who Goldsmith, in his innocence, had intended to be the hero, Young Marlow. Cut after cut shredded Mark Spelthorne's part, until he had about half the lines he had started the day with.

For some time he took it pretty well, but when the proposal to cut his second act love duet with Lizzie Dark was put forward, his reserve broke. "But that's nonsense," he croaked. (He was suffering from The Cold and was determined that no one should miss the fact.)

"Sorry?" asked David Meldrum mildly, but the word was swamped by a sharp "What?" from Christopher Milton.

"Well, putting on one side for a moment the fact that the play no longer has a plot, if you cut the love duet, there is absolutely no romantic content from beginning to end."

"Yes, there is. There's my song to Betty Bouncer."

"But that song has nothing to do with the plot. Betty Bouncer doesn't even appear in the original play."

"Sod the original play! We aren't doing the original play."

"You can say that again. We're doing a shapeless hotch-potch whose only *raison d'être* is as a massive trip for your overinflated ego."

"Oh, I see. You think I'm doing all this work just to give myself cheap thrills."

"I can't see any other reason for you to bugger up a plot that's survived intact for two hundred years. Let's face it, it doesn't matter to you what the show is. We might as well be performing a musical of the telephone directory for all you care. Just so long as you've got all the lines and all the jokes and all the songs. Good God, you just don't know what theatre's about."

"I don't?" Christopher Milton's voice was ominously quiet. "Then please tell me, since I am so ill-informed on the matter, what the theatre is about."

"It's about teamwork, ensemble acting, people working together to produce a good show—"

"Bullshit! It's about getting audiences and keeping in work. You go off and do your shows, your 'ensemble theatre' and you'll get nobody coming to see them. People want to see stars, not bloody ensembles. I'm the reason that they'll come and see this show and don't you kid yourself otherwise. Let me tell you, none of you would be in line for a long run in the West End if this show hadn't got my name above the title. So don't you start whining about your precious lines, Mark Spelthorne. Just think yourself lucky you've got a job. You're not going to find them so easy to come by now they've dropped that bloody awful *Fighter Pilots*."

That got Mark on the raw. "How the hell did you know that?"

"I have contacts, sonny. As a matter of fact, the Head of London Weekend Television was down this week trying to get me to do a series for them. He told me."

"It's not definite yet," said Mark defensively. "They're still considering it. The producer told me."

"It's definite. The producer just hasn't got the guts to tell you the truth. No, your brief taste of telly stardom is over and let me tell you, no one's too anxious to pick up the failed star of a failed series that didn't make the ratings. So if I were you, I'd keep very quiet in this show, take what you're given and start writing round the reps."

The public savagery of the attack gave Mark no alternative but to leave the theatre, which he did. What made the denunciation so cruel was that it was true. Mark Spelthorne had risen to public notice in advance of his talents on the strength of one series and without it he wasn't much of a prospect.

As usual the star continued addressing his audience as if nothing had happened. "Now the next scene we come to is the Chase, the *Lead 'em Astray* sequence. I don't think we need cuts in this one. In fact I don't think we've begun to develop that scene yet. I discussed this with Desmond Porton and he agrees that we can add a whole lot more business and make it a really funny slapstick sequence. We're going to do it in a sort of silent film style, with a lot more special effects. And I think we can pep up the choreography a bit in that scene. Really get the girls jumping about."

"You try jumping about in eighteenth-century costume," complained an anonymous female dancer's voice.

Christopher Milton did not object to the interruption; he continued as if it were part of his own train of thought. "Yes, we've got to change the girls' costumes there. Get more of an up-to-date feel. Like go-go dancers. Really get the audience going."

"Why not have them topless?" drawled one of the dancing queens.

"Yes, we could—no." His objection was, needless to say, not on grounds of anachronism. "We've got to think of the family audience. I think this Chase Scene can be terrific. Wally Wilson's working on it now and we can make it into something really exciting. Going to mean a lot more work, but it will be worth while. Oh, that reminds me, we're going to need flying equipment for it. . . ."

"What?" asked David Meldrum weakly.

"Flying equipment for the Chase Scene. I'm going to be flown in on a Kirby wire. Have we got the stuff?"

"No, I don't think so. We'd have to get it from London."

"Well, get it. Who organizes that?"

"I suppose the stage manager."

"Is he about?"

"Yes, I think he's backstage somewhere."

"Then get him to organize that straight away. I want to start rehearsing with it as soon as possible." As if under hypnosis, the man whose title was "director" wandered offstage to find Spike. "Now, in that sequence, we're also going to be making a lot more use of the trapdoors and doubles for me. . . . Okay. It's going to make that bit longer, but I think it'll give the show a great lift towards the end. . . ."

* * *

Charles' part was so small that, short of cutting it completely (and in the current climate, that did not seem impossible), the management could not do it much harm. As it was he lost four lines and left the theatre for the pub feeling that it could have been a lot worse. Just as he went through the stage door, he met Spike coming in. "Oh, they were looking for you. Something about a Kirby wire."

Spike's *papier mâché* face crumpled into a sardonic grin. "They found me. Yes, so now his Lordship wants to fly as well as everything else. It'll be walking on the water next."

Charles chuckled. "I wonder if he's always been like this."

"What do you mean?"

"Always ordering everyone about. I mean, he couldn't have done it when he started in the business, could he?"

"With him anything's possible."

"Where did he start? Any idea?"

"Came out of stage school, didn't he? Suppose he went straight into rep."

"You've met lots of people in the business, Spike. Ever come across anyone who knew him before he became the big star?"

There was a pause. "I don't know. I'm trying to think." Spike wrinkled his face; when the acne scars were in shadow, he looked almost babylike. "There was an actor I once met who I think had been with him a long time back. Now what was his name . . . ? Seddon . . . Madden, something like that. Paddon, that's right."

"Not Julian Paddon?"

"Yes, I think that was the name. Why, do you know him?"

"I'm only staying with him here in Bristol."

Mark Spelthorne was sitting in the corner of the pub. It was only eleven-thirty and there weren't many people about. Charles felt he couldn't ignore him. "Can I get you a drink?"

"Brandy, please. Medicinal. For the cold." He looked frail. His nose was comically red, the lines of his face were deeply etched and for the first time Charles realized that the hair was dyed. Mark

Spelthorne was older than the parts he played. As Christopher Milton had said, overcoming the current setback in his career wouldn't be easy.

Charles ordered the brandy and a pint of bitter for himself. That meant he was in a good mood. He drank Scotch when he was drinking to change his mood or delay a bad one and beer when he wanted to enjoy the one he was in.

"Cheers." They drank. Charles felt he could not ignore what had happened. "Sorry about all that this morning. Must've been pretty nasty for you."

"Not the most pleasant few minutes of my life."

"That I believe. Still, he says things like that in the heat of the moment. He doesn't mean them."

"Oh, he means them."

Though he agreed, Charles didn't think he should say so. He made do with a grunt.

"Yes, he means them, Charles, and what's more, he's right."

"What do you mean?"

"They aren't going to do any more *Fighter Pilots*."

"Well, so what? Something else will come up."

"You reckon? No, he's right about that too. They launched that series to see if it caught on. If it had, I'd have been made, got star billing from now on. But now it's failed, nobody'll touch me."

"Oh, come on. You'll keep in work."

"Work, yes. Supports, but not star billing. My career's ruined."

Charles tried to remember if he'd ever thought like that. So far as he could recollect, his aim in the theatre had always been for variety rather than stardom. Still, it obviously mattered to Mark. He tried another optimistic tack. "But there'll be other chances. I mean, you made this pilot for your own radio show . . . ?"

"Yes. They don't want it. It's been heard and they don't want to make a series."

"Ah, ah well." Charles searched through his store of comforts for such situations and could only come up with cliché. "Never mind, one door closes, another one opens." It was patently untrue. In his own experience life's doors worked like linked traffic lights —one closed and all the others closed just before you got to them.

Mark treated the platitude to the contemptuous grunt it deserved. "My God, he's such a sod. I feel so angry, just so angry."

"Yes," Charles said, inadequately soothing.

"And the world loves him. *Lovable* Christopher Milton. Every time he's mentioned in the Press, there it is, lovable Christopher Milton. Doesn't it make you puke? If only his precious public could see him as he was this morning, could see all the meanness that goes to make up his lovability. My God, do people have to be that unpleasant to appear lovable?"

"He works hard at his public image. It's all very calculated."

"Yes, calculated and untrue. He has no integrity, his whole life is a masquerade." Mark Spelthorne spoke from a position of extreme righteousness, as if his own life had never been sullied by a shadow of affectation. "You know, I think I'd give anything to expose him, show him to the public for what he really is—a mean-minded, egotistical, insensitive bastard."

"But talented."

"Oh yes. Talented." Even in the violence of his anger Mark could not deny the facts.

Charles thought a lot about what Mark had said. Because possibly he held in his hands the power to expose the star. If the series of accidents which had happened to *Lumpkin!* and been perpetrated by his driver could ever be traced back to Christopher Milton, that would be exactly the sort of scandal to bring the star down in the public estimation.

And yet Charles did not believe that Christopher Milton was directly involved. True, all the crimes turned out to the star's advantage, but Charles was convinced that the driver had either been acting off his own bat or on the orders of Dickie Peck. Either way, the motive had been a protective instinct, to keep the star from the harsh realities of life (like people disagreeing with him). Somehow Christopher Milton himself, in spite of all his verbal viciousness, retained a certain naïveté. He assumed that everything should go his way and was not surprised to find obstacles removed from his path, but his was more the confidence of a divine mission than the gangster's confidence in his ability to rub out anyone who threatened him. The star might have his suspicions as to how he was being protected, but he was too sensible to ask any questions about such matters. And far too sensible to take direct action. For a person so fiercely conscious of his public image it would be insane and, when it came to his career, Christopher Milton seemed to have his head very firmly screwed on.

The Friday performance was scrappy. The cuts had been only partly assimilated and the show was full of sudden pauses, glazed expressions and untidy musical passages where some of the band remembered the cut and some didn't. With that perversity which makes it impossible for actors ever to know what will or won't work onstage, the audience loved it. . . .

Charles was taking his makeup off at speed—even with the cuts, it was still a close call to the pub—when there was a discreet knock on his door. Assuming that someone must have got the wrong dressing-room, he opened it and was amazed to be confronted by his daughter Juliet and her husband Miles. What amazed him more was that Juliet, who had a trim figure and was not in the ordinary way prone to smocks, was obviously pregnant.

"Good heavens. Come in. . . . Sit down," he added hastily, overconscious of Juliet's condition. It confused him. He knew that everything about having children is a continual process of growing apart and could remember, when Frances first brought the tiny baby home, the shock of its separateness, but seeing his daughter pregnant seemed to double the already considerable gulf between them.

"Enjoyed the show very much," Juliet volunteered.

"Oh good," Charles replied, feeling that he should have kissed her on her arrival, but that he'd been too surprised and now he had missed the opportunity (and that the whole history of his relationship with his daughter had been missed opportunities to show affection and draw close to her). "I didn't know you were coming. You should have let me know. I could have organized tickets," he concluded feebly, as if free seats could compensate for a lifetime of non-communication.

"I didn't know I was coming till today. Miles had to come to a dinner in Bristol and then I was talking to Mummy yesterday and she said you were in this show and I thought I'd come and see it."

That gave him a frisson too. He had not told Frances about *Lumpkin!* How had she found out? At least that meant she was still interested in his activities. He couldn't work out whether the thought elated or depressed him.

"I didn't see the show, of course," Miles stated in the plonking consciously-mature manner he had. "I had to attend this dinner of my professional body."

Charles nodded. He could never begin to relate to his son-in-law. Miles Taylerson did very well in insurance, which was a conversation-stopper for Charles before they started. Miles was only about twenty-five, but had obviously sprung middle-aged from his mother's womb (though, when Charles reflected on Miles' mother, it was unlikely that she had a womb—she must have devised some other more hygienic and socially acceptable method of producing children). Miles and Juliet lived in a neat circumscribed executive estate in Pangbourne and did everything right. They bought every possession (including the right opinions) that the young executive should have and their lives were organized with a degree of foresight that made the average Soviet Five-Year-Plan look impetuous.

When Miles spoke, Charles took him in properly for the first time. He was dressed exactly as a young executive should be for a dinner of his professional body. Dinner jacket, but not the old double-breasted or now-dated rolled-lapel style. It was cut like an ordinary suit, in very dark blue rather than black, with a discreet braiding of silk ribbon. Conventional enough not to offend any senior members of the professional body, but sufficiently modern to imply that here was a potential pacesetter for that professional body. The bow tie was velvet, large enough to maintain the image of restrained panache, but not so large as to invite disturbing comparisons with anything flamboyant or artistic. The shirt was discreetly frilled, like the paper decoration on a leg of lamb. In fact, as he thought of the image, Charles realized that that was exactly what Miles looked like—a well-dressed joint of meat.

Recalling a conversation that Miles and he had had two years previously on the subject of breeding intentions, he could not resist a dig. "When's the baby due?" he asked ingenuously.

"Mid-April." Juliet supplied the information.

"You've changed your plans, Miles. I thought you were going to wait a couple more years until you were more established financially."

"Well, yes. . . ." Miles launched into his prepared arguments. "When we discussed it, I was thinking that we would need Juliet's income to keep going comfortably, but of course, I've had one or two rises since then and a recent promotion, so the mortgage isn't taking such a big bite as it was, and I think the general recession picture may be clearing a little with the Government's anti-inflation package really beginning to work and so we decided that we could advance our plans a little."

He paused for breath and Juliet said, "Actually it was a mistake." Charles could have hugged her. He spoke quickly to stop himself laughing. "I'm sorry I can't offer you anything to drink . . . I don't keep anything here." With a last act entrance and an adjacent pub, there didn't seem any need.

"Don't worry, I'm not drinking much, because of the baby."

"And I had up to my limit at the dinner. Don't want to get nabbed on the M4." The image came of Miles sitting at the dinner of his professional body, measuring out his drinks drop by drop (and no doubt working out their alcoholic content with his pocket calculator).

"You say you heard from your mother yesterday," said Charles, with what attempted (and failed) to be the insouciance of a practitioner of modern marriage, unmoved by considerations of fidelity and jealousy.

"Yes."

"How was she?"

"Fine."

"How's the new boy friend?" He brought in the question with the subtlety of a sledge-hammer.

"Oh, what do you . . . ?" Juliet was flustered. "Oh, Alec. Well, I don't know that you'd quite call him a boy friend. I mean, he just teaches at the same school as Mummy and, you know, they see each other. But Alec's very busy, doesn't have much time. He's a scoutmaster and tends to be off camping or climbing or doing arduous training most weekends."

Good God. A scoutmaster. Frances must have changed if she'd

found a scoutmaster to console her. Perhaps she'd deliberately looked for someone as different as possible from her husband.

Juliet tactfully redirected the conversation, a skill no doubt refined by many Pangbourne coffee mornings. "It must be marvellous working in a show with Christopher Milton."

"In what way marvellous?"

"Well, he must be such fun. I mean, he comes across as so . . . nice. Is he just the same off stage?"

"Not exactly." Charles could also be tactful.

But apparently Christopher Milton united the Taylersons in admiration. Miles thought the television show was "damn funny" and he was also glad "that you're getting into this sort of theatre, Pop. I mean, it must be quite a fillip, career-wise."

"What do you mean?"

"Well, being in proper commercial theatre, you know, West End, chance of a good long run, that sort of thing. I mean, it's almost like having a regular job."

"Miles, I have done quite a few shows in the West End before, and if I have spent a lot of my life going round the reps, it's at least partly because I have found more variety of work there, more interest."

"But the West End must be the top."

"Not necessarily. If you want to be a star, I suppose it might be, but if you want to be an actor, it certainly isn't."

"Oh, come on, surely everyone in acting wants to be a star."

"No, actors are different. Some want to open supermarkets, some just want to act."

"But they must want to be stars. I mean, it's the only way up. Just as everyone in a company wants to be managing director."

"That principle is certainly not true in acting, and I doubt if it's true in the average company."

"Of course it is. Oh, people cover up and pretend they haven't got ambitions just because they see them dashed or realize they haven't got a chance, but that's what everyone wants. And it must be the same in the theatre, except that the West End stars are the managing directors."

"If that's the case, where do I come on the promotion scale?"

"I suppose you'd be at a sort of . . . lower clerical grade." And then, realizing that that might be construed as criticism, Miles added, "I mean, doing the job frightfully well and all that, but sort of not recognized as executive material."

They were fortunate in meeting the managing director on the stairs. Christopher Milton was leaving alone and, suddenly in one of his charming moods, he greeted Charles profusely. Miles and Juliet were introduced and the star made a great fuss of them, asking about the baby, even pretending to be interested when Miles talked about insurance. They left, delighted with him, and Charles reflected wryly that if he'd wanted to organize a treat, he couldn't have come up with anything better.

Christopher Milton's mood of affability remained after they'd gone. "Fancy a drink?"

"Too late. The pubs have closed."

"No, I meant back at the hotel."

"Yes. Thank you very much." Charles accepted slowly, but his mind was racing. The offer was so unexpected. If Christopher Milton were behind the accidents which had been happening over the past weeks and if he knew that Charles had been inspecting his car the night before, then it could be a trap. Or it could be an innocent whim. Acceptance was the only way of finding out which. And Charles certainly felt like a drink.

"Good. I've got a cab waiting at the stage door."

"I thought you usually had your car."

"Yes. Unfortunately my driver had an accident last night."

The intonation did not sound pointed and Charles tried to speak equally casually. "Anything serious?"

"Got a bang on the head. Don't know how it happened. He'll be in hospital under observation the next couple of days, but then he should be okay."

"Do you drive yourself?"

"I do, but I don't like to have that to think about when I'm on my way to the theatre. I do quite a big mental buildup for the show." Again the reply did not appear to have hidden layers of meaning. No suspicion that Charles was mildly investigating the accident to Pete Masters.

In his suite at the hotel Christopher Milton found out Charles' predilections and rang for a bottle of Bell's. It arrived on a tray with a bowl of cocktail biscuits. The star himself drank Perrier water. ". . . but you just tuck into that."

Charles did as he was told and after a long welcome swallow he offered the biscuits to his host.

"I don't know. Are they cheese?"

Charles tried one. "Yes."

"Then I won't, thanks."

There was a long pause. Charles, who had the feeling he was there for a purpose, did not like to initiate a topic of conversation. Christopher Milton broke the silence. "Well, how do you think it's going?"

"The show? Oh, not too bad. A lot of work still to be done." Clichés seemed safer than detailed opinions.

"Yes. This is the ugliest part." Christopher Milton paced the room to use up some of his nervous energy. "This is where the real work has to happen." He stopped suddenly. "What do you think of the cuts?"

"Cuts were needed."

"That tells me nothing. We both know cuts were needed. I'm asking what you thought of the cuts that were made."

"Well, it depends. If you're thinking of how much sense we're now making of Goldsmith's play—"

"We're not. We're thinking of the audience. That's what theatre's about—the people who watch the stuff, not the people who write it."

"I agree with you up to a point, but—"

"What you're trying to say is that the cuts could have been spread more evenly, that I myself got off pretty lightly. Is that it?"

"To an extent, yes." Asked a direct question, Charles felt bound to give his real opinion.

"I thought you'd think that. I bet they all think that, that it's me just indulging my oversized ego." Charles didn't confirm or deny. "Go on. That's what they think. That's what you think, isn't it?"

The sudden realization came that all the star wanted that evening was someone to whom he could justify himself. The fact that it was Charles Paris was irrelevant. Christopher Milton was aware of the bad feeling in the cast and he wanted to explain his actions to someone, to make him feel better. Obviously he had more sensitivity to atmosphere than Charles had given him credit for. "All right," Charles owned up, "I did think other cuts would have been fairer."

Christopher Milton seemed relieved that he'd now got a point of view against which to deliver his prepared arguments. "Yes, and I bet every member of the cast is sitting in his digs tonight saying what a bastard I am. Well, let me tell you, all I think is whether or not this show is going to be a success, and I'm going to do my damndest to see that it is. That's my responsibility.

"You see, *Lumpkin!* just wouldn't be on if I weren't in it. *She Stoops to Conquer*'s been around for years. No commercial management's likely to revive it unless they suddenly get an all-star cast lined up. I suppose the National or the RSC might do a definitive version for the A-level trade, but basically there's no particular reason to do it now. But I said I was interested in the project and the whole bandwagon started.

"Now we come to the point that I know you're thinking—that we're buggering up a fine old English play. No, don't deny it, you're a kind of intellectual, you're the sort who likes literature for its own sake. What I'm trying to tell you, to tell everyone, is to forget what the play was. We're doing a show for an audience in 1975. And that, in your terms, is probably a debased audience, an audience force-fed on television. Their ideal night out at the theatre would probably be to see "live" some soap opera which they see twice a week in the privacy of their sitting-rooms. Okay, that's the situation. I'm not saying it's a good situation, it's just the way things are, and that's the audience I'm aiming for.

"Because of television, I'm one of the people they want to see. And they want to see a lot of me. They don't give a bugger about the twists and turns of Goldsmith's quaint old plot. They want to see Lionel Wilkins of *Straight Up, Guv,* simply because he's something familiar. I've only realized this since we started playing the show in front of audiences. That's why I stopped playing Lumpkin rustic—oh, yes, I saw the expression of disapproval on your face when I did that. But I am right. Give the audience what they want."

"All right, I agree they want to see you, but surely they'd be even more impressed if they saw your range of abilities, if they saw that you could play a very funny rustic as well as Lionel Wilkins."

"No, there you're wrong. They want what they recognise. Popular entertainment has got to be familiar. This is a mistake that a lot of young comedians make. They think the audience wants to hear new jokes. Not true, the average audience wants to hear jokes it recognizes. No, in this show they see sufficient variety in me, they see me sing and dance—most of them probably didn't know I could do that—but they never lose sight of Lionel Wilkins, and it's him they came for. And it's my business to give them Lionel Wilkins.

"So, when I said to Mark Spelthorne this morning that I felt responsible for the entire company, I meant it. It's up to me to hold this company together and if that looks like just ego-tripping, well, I'm sorry."

Charles couldn't think of anything to say. He had been surprised to hear such a cogently reasoned justification and, although he could not agree with all the arguments, he could respect it as a point of view. Christopher Milton himself obviously believed passionately in what he said. He broke from the unnatural stillness he had maintained throughout his exposition and started his restless pacing again. He stopped by a sofa and began rearranging the cushions. "And it's the same reason, my duty to the audience, which makes me so concerned about my public image. I just can't afford to do anything that lowers me in their estimation.

"Oh, don't look so innocent, as if you don't know why I've moved on to this subject. People think I'm blind, but I see all the little looks, the raised eyebrows, the remarks about me putting on the charm. Listen, my talent, wherever it came from, is all I've got. It's a commodity and, like any other commodity, it has to be attractively packaged. I have to be what the public wants me to be."

"Even if at times that means not being yourself?"

"Even if that means most of the time not being myself. That's the way of life I've chosen."

"It must put you under incredible strain."

"It does, but it's what I've elected to do and so I must do it."

This messianic conviction seemed almost laughable when related to the triviality of *Lumpkin!*, but it was clear that this was what made Christopher Milton tick. And though the strength of his conviction might easily overrule conventional morality, he was never going to commit any crime whose discovery might alienate the precious audience whom he saw, almost obsessively, as the arbiters of his every action.

Charles left the Holiday Inn, slightly unsteady from the whisky, but with the beginnings of an understanding of Christopher Milton.

CHAPTER 12

THE LIGHTS WERE still on in Julian's flat when Charles got back there, though it was two o'clock in the morning. Julian himself was in the front room, marooned wretchedly on an island of bottles, glasses and ashtrays. "Oh, Charles, thank God you've come back. I need someone to talk to. It's started."

"Started?"

"The baby."

"Oh yes." He nearly added "I'd completely forgotten," but decided that might show an unwelcome sense of priorities.

"Waters broke, or whatever it is they do, about nine. I took her down to the hospital, they said nothing'd happen overnight, suggested I come back to get some sleep. Sleep, huh!"

"She'll be okay."

"Yes, I'm sure she will, but that doesn't make the time till I know she is any easier. It's like quoting the statistics of normal childbirths, it doesn't make you any more convinced that yours is going to be one."

"No. Well, you have a drink and keep your mind off it."

"Drink, huh, I've had plenty of drinks." Julian was playing the scene for all it was worth. Charles had the feeling that he often got with actor friends in real emotional situations, that they rose to the inherent drama and, though their feelings at such moments were absolutely genuine, their acting training was not wasted. "Oh

God," Julian went on, "the waiting. It's much worse than a first night."

"For a small Paddon it is a first night."

"Yes. Oh God!"

"Talk about something else. Take your mind off it."

"All right. What shall we talk about?"

"The Irish situation? Whether *Beowulf* is the work of one or more writers? The Football League? Spinoza's *Ethics*? Is pay restraint compatible with democracy? Is democracy compatible with individual freedom? Is individual freedom compatible with fashion? Is fashion compatible with the Irish situation? Do stop me if you hear anything that sounds interesting."

"Nothing yet. Keep talking."

"You sod."

"All right. Let you off. Tell me what you've been doing all day. I'm sure the wacky world of a pre-London tour must be more interesting than a day of rehearsal in a resident company."

"Yes, I suppose today has been quite eventful. Desmond Porton of Amulet came down last night to pass sentence."

"And are you still going in?"

"Oh yes, but today has been spent disemboweling the show."

"Ah, that's familiar. A different show every night. Oh, the thrills of the open road."

"You sound very bourgeois as you say that."

"Well, I am. Respectable. Look at me—regular company, in the same job for at least six months. Married. . . ."

"Prospective father. . . ."

"Oh God!"

"I'm sorry. I'm meant to be taking your mind off that. I wonder what that makes you in the hierarchy."

"What?"

"Being in a resident company. I suppose it's not quite a managing director but it's better than a lower clerical grade. A sort of rising young executive. Middle management, that's probably the level."

"What are you talking about?"

"Nothing. I'm sorry. I'm a bit pissed."

"Well, get stuck into that whisky bottle and get very pissed."

"Okay."

"Who have you been drinking with until this time of night?"

"With no less than Christopher Milton. The Star. Tonight I was given the honor of being the repository of his guilty secrets."

"Not all of them, I bet."

"Why, what do you—oh, of course, you knew him." Spike's words of earlier in the day suddenly came back. "You knew him before he was big."

"Yes, I had the dubious pleasure of being with him in the first company he went to as an adult actor. He'd done quite a lot as a child, but this was his first job as a member of a company. Cheltenham, it was."

"How long ago was this?"

"I don't know. Fifteen years—no, twenty. I remember, I celebrated my twenty-first birthday there."

"Christopher Milton must have been pretty young."

"Eighteen, I suppose."

"No, fourteen. He's only thirty-four now."

"My dear Charles, you must never allow yourself to be a victim of the publicity men."

"What do you mean?"

"Christopher Milton is thirty-eight, at least."

"But it says in the program—"

"Charles, Charles, you've been in the business too long to be so naïve. As you know, in this game everyone gets to play parts at the wrong age. People who play juveniles in the West End have almost always spent ten years grafting round the provinces and are about forty. But it doesn't have quite the right ring, does it? So when Christopher Milton suddenly became very big, he suddenly shed four years."

"I see. It figures. Do you remember him from that time?"

"Difficult to forget."

"What—the star bit?"

"Oh yes, give him his due, he never made any secret of what he wanted to be. He spent a good few years rehearsing for the big time."

"Was he good?"

"Very good. But no better than any number of other young actors. Indeed there was another in the company at the time who was at least as good. He'd come from the same drama school, also done the child star bit—what was his name? Garry Warden, that was it. And who's heard of that name now? I don't know what happens to the products of the stage schools. They almost always vanish without trace. . . ."

"Perhaps most of them haven't got Christopher Milton's single-mindedness."

"Single-mindedness is a charitable word for it. God, he was terrible. Put everyone's backs up. Used to do charming things like ringing up other actors in the middle of the night to give them notes. And as you know it's very difficult to have that sort of person in a small company."

"Did he drive everyone mad?"

"Funny you should say that." Julian held his glass up to the light and looked through it pensively. "No, he drove himself mad."

"What do you mean?"

"He had a breakdown, complete crackup. Couldn't live with an ego that size, maybe."

"What form did the breakdown take?"

"Oh, the full bit. None of this quiet sobbing in corners or sudden keeling over in the pub. It was the shouting and screaming that everyone was trying to murder him sort. He barricaded himself in the dressing-room with a carving knife. I tell you, it was the most exciting thing to happen in Cheltenham since the Ladies' College Open Night."

"Did he go for anyone with the knife?" Charles was beginning to feel a little uncomfortable.

"Went for everyone. One of the stage staff got a nasty gash on the forearm. It took three policemen to calm him down. Well no, not calm him down, hold him down. He was screaming blue murder, accusing us all of the most amazing things. Yes, it was a pretty ugly scene."

"And did he come back to the company when he'd recovered?"

"No, he was taken off in a traditional little white van and that's the last time I saw him. Then suddenly four or five years ago I started reading all this publicity about the great new British star and there he was."

"And you've no idea what happened to him after Cheltenham?"

"Not a clue. I suppose he went to some loony bin and got cured or whatever they do to people with homicidal tendencies."

"Yes. Strange, I've never heard about that incident before."

"Well, he's not going to go around advertising it. Lovable Lionel Wilkins, the well-known loony."

"No, but it's the sort of story that gets around in the business."

"Probably he's deliberately tried to keep it quiet. I suppose there aren't many people who would know about it. The Cheltenham company was pretty small—what was it the director used to call us? 'A small integrated band.' A cheap integrated band, anyway. God, when I think of the money they used to give us, it's a wonder we didn't all die of malnutrition."

"You don't still see any of them?"

"No, not for years. I should think a lot of them have died from natural causes—and one or two drunk themselves to death."

"Can you remember who was in that company?"

"Yes. Let me think—" At that moment the telephone rang. Julian leapt on it as if it were trying to escape. "Hello. Yes, I am. What? When? But you said nothing would happen till the morning. Well, I know, but—what is it? Good Lord. Well, I . . . um . . . I mean. . . . Good Lord. But I wanted to be there. Can I come down? Look, it's only five minutes. No, I'll be there straight away. Good God, having effectively stopped me being there, you can bloody well keep them up for five minutes for me to see them!" He slammed the receiver down and did a jaunty little walk over to the fireplace. He turned dramatically to Charles and threw away the line, "A boy. Just a little boy. Damian Walter Alexander Robertson Paddon."

"Congratulations. That's marvellous."

"Yes, it is rather good, isn't it? I must dash. The cow on the phone wanted me to wait till the morning. God, I should take her something." He started frantically scanning the room. "I don't know what—grapes or . . . where would I get grapes at three in the morning? Oh, I'd better just—"

"Julian, I'm sorry, but who was in that company?"

"What?"

"In Cheltenham."

"Oh look, Charles, I've got to rush. I—"

"Please."

"Well, I can't remember all of them." He spoke as he was leaving the room. Charles followed him through the hall and out of the front door to the car. "There was Miriam Packer, and Freddie Wort . . . and Terry Hatton and . . . oh, what's the name of that terrible piss-artist?"

Charles knew the answer as he spoke. "Everard Austick?"

"Yes."

"And was there a pianist called Frederick Wooland?"

"Good Lord, yes. I'd never have remembered his name. How did you know? Look, I've got to dash."

Julian's car roared off, leaving the road empty. And Charles feeling emptier.

It was with a feeling of nausea, but not surprise, that he heard next day that Mark Spelthorne had been found hanged in his digs.

PART 4

Brighton

CHAPTER 13

IT SEEMED STRANGE to continue working with Christopher Milton after that. Or perhaps the strangeness lay in how easy it was, how much of the time it was possible to forget the grotesque suspicions which had now hardened in Charles' mind. And they were busy. *Lumpkin!* was scheduled to open at the King's Theatre on November 27th and the problems of rerehearsing great chunks of the show were now exacerbated by extra rehearsals for Mark Spelthorne's understudy. (The management were dithering in London as to whether they should leave the part in the understudy's hands or bring someone else with a bit more name value. The boy who'd taken over wasn't bad . . . and he was cheaper than his predecessor . . . but was his name big enough . . . ? Or with Christopher Milton above the title, did one perhaps not need any name value in the supports . . . ? And after the cuts Young Marlow wasn't much of a part anyway. . . . The usual impersonal management decisions continued to be made a long way from the people they concerned.)

There was not much fuss over the death. Police were round asking about Mark's state of mind before the incident and there were rumors that some representatives of the company might have to attend the inquest, but the assumption of suicide was general. The coincidence of the failure of the radio pilot, the demise of the *Fighter Pilots* and troubles over *Lumpkin!* were thought to be sufficient motive. To a character like Mark Spelthorne, whose life was driven by ambitions of stardom, this sequence of blows, with the implication that he was never going to make it in the way he visualized, could be enough to push him over the edge.

Even Charles found the explanation fairly convincing and tried to make himself find it very convincing. But other thoughts gate-crashed his mind.

An unwelcome logical sequence was forming there. What he had heard from Julian provided the thread which pulled all the wayward strands of the case together into a neat little bundle. Christopher Milton's history of mental illness was just the sort of thing that he would fight to keep from his adoring public. The mass audiences for popular entertainment are not the most liberal and broad-minded section of the population and they would not sympathize with anything "odd."

Everard Austick and the pianist Frederick Wooland had passed unnoticed through Dickie Peck's Approval of Cast net and Christopher Milton must have recoiled in shock when he saw them at rehearsals. They were links with the one episode in his past he was determined to keep quiet and so far as he was concerned, they had to be removed. Not killed or even badly injured but kept out of *Lumpkin!* Hence the airgun pellet and the shove which sent poor, pissed Everard downstairs. Charles kicked himself for being so blinkered about the evidence he had found in the Corniche. He had been looking for something to incriminate the driver and had found what he wanted, without considering that its location could be equally damning to the car's owner.

Because now he had no doubt of Christopher Milton's personal involvement. Apart from anything else, at the time of Mark's death, Dickie Peck was in London and the driver was in hospital. And everything became quite logical if the star was considered as potentially unbalanced. In his morbid self-obsession he saw everyone who challenged him as a serious threat to his personality and as such someone who should be removed or punished. It wasn't a case of Dickie Peck or the driver being overprotective; it was a paranoid man protecting himself. And it meant that Charles was dealing with a madman.

Only a madman would believe that he could continue to behave like that without ultimate discovery and disgrace. Only someone totally locked in his own world, someone who had lost touch with everyday reality. Christopher Milton's unshakable belief in his talent was matched by a belief in his immunity from discovery.

And he had been skilful. All of the crimes had the appearance of accidents or unrelated acts of violence. Charles felt certain that no one else in the company saw any pattern in them. And because *Lumpkin!* was on the move, it was unlikely that the different police forces involved would be aware of a sequence of crimes.

But now, with the death of Mark Spelthorne, the whole situation became more serious. Beating up people who get in your way is one thing; killing them puts you in a different league.

And Charles was still left with the dilemma of what he should do about it. Gerald's original instructions to him to protect the show and its star from sabotage now seemed grotesquely irrelevant. The situation had got beyond that. But he still did not have enough evidence to go to the police with a tale which must strain their credulity. The airgun pellets and the liquid paraffin were unsubstantiated evidence; he could have planted them, and anyway his own behavior in snooping around the Holiday Inn car park could be liable to misinterpretation. He didn't have any proof that Christopher Milton was at the scene of most of the incidents.

He considered the possibility of talking directly to his suspect, but he couldn't imagine what he would say. A quiet word in the ear may stop a schoolboy from smoking behind the cycle sheds, but in a case of murder it's seriously inadequate. And if he was dealing with a potentially homicidal maniac, it was asking for trouble to draw attention to such suspicions. But the alternative was sitting and waiting for someone else to get hurt or even killed.

He wanted to discuss it with someone, but Gerald Venables, who was the only suitable confidant, was too involved in the situation and might panic.

So he would have to work it out on his own. He thought through the known facts and wished there were more of them. He made vague resolutions to find out as much as he could about Christopher Milton's past and current activities. One useful idea did come into his head. He recollected that the first two crimes had been committed between nine and ten in the morning and suddenly tied this up with the unusual "no calls before ten-thirty" clause in the star's contract. It would be interesting to find out what he did in the mornings. Was it just that he liked a lie-in? That did not tally with the voracious appetite for work he demonstrated the rest of the day. He was prepared to stay up all night getting a new number together and yet the day never began until half past ten. That was worth investigating.

But it was one stray positive thought in a scrambled mind. Everything else circled round uselessly, tangling with emotions and producing nothing.

The Queen's Theatre, Brighton, was one of the great old touring theatres of Britain. It had been built for more spacious times, in the 1870s, before the cinema had cheapened illusion by comparisons with the real thing. When the Queen's was put up, people went to the theatre for spectacle and they got it. Entertainments were built round special effects—shipwrecks, fires and falling buildings, magic, ghosts and live animals. And the theatres were designed to cope.

The original stage machinery had been built for the Rise and Sink method of set changing, whereby the stage was made up of separate narrow sections, which could be raised and lowered with different sets on them by an elaborate system of pulleys and counterweights. There was a cellar below the stage as deep as the proscenium was high and above the audience's sight lines there was equivalent space in the flying gallery. The complex of girders and hawsers in the cellar was a feat of engineering comparable to one of the great Victorian railway bridges.

When the stage was designed, it had been equipped with the full complement of trap doors which were written into many plays of the period. Downstage were the corner traps, small openings used for the appearance or disappearance of one actor. Often these would be used as Star Traps, so called because the aperture was covered with a circle made up of triangular wooden segments like cake slices, hinged with leather on the outside, which would open like a star to deliver the actor on to the stage and then fall back into place.

Then there was the Grave Trap center stage, which was always

used for the Gravediggers' scene in *Hamlet*. And originally the
theatre had had the most elaborate trap of all, the Corsican Trap,
or Ghost Glide. This had been developed for the 1852 play *The
Corsican Brothers* and enabled a ghost to rise from the grave as he
moved across the stage.

Charles found it fascinating. He had always been intrigued by
the mechanics of theatre and just being in the old building gave
him that pleasantly painful feeling of hopeless nostalgia which
always comes from the knowledge that, however much one
exercises the imagination, however much one researches, it is
never possible to know what earlier times were really like. He
picked the brains of Len, the stage doorman, about the theatre's
history and tried to spend as much time as he could alone there,
sensing the building's past, hearing echoes of old triumphs,
tantrums and love affairs.

But it was not easy to indulge this sentimentality. For one thing,
the theatre had undergone many changes. The divided stage had
been replaced in the forties and now most of the old equipment
was boarded over. Only the Star Trap on the forestage was still kept
working for the annual pantomime appearances of the Demon
King (complete no doubt with miscued puff of smoke).

Then again the frantic rerehearsal schedule for *Lumpkin!* was not
conducive to luxuriating in nostalgia. But, most of all, the looming
problem of what should be done about his knowledge of
Christopher Milton's criminal activities kept Charles' mind
naggingly full.

As in the other towns of the tour, the local Press greeted the arrival
of *Lumpkin!* in Brighton with a big spread about the show's star.
There was a photograph of Christopher Milton in one of his
lovable poses and the column was headed "BACK TO SCHOOLDAYS FOR
LIONEL WILKINS." Intrigued, Charles read on.

> Lovers of television's *Straight Up, Guv* are in for a surprise this week
> at the Queen's Theatre when they see the show's lovable star
> Christopher Milton in a different rôle as an eighteenth-century
> rogue by the name of Tony Lumpkin.

"Actually, he's not that different from Lionel," confides boyish 34-year-old Christopher. "They're both conmen. I think, if anything, Tony Lumpkin is slightly more successful than Lionel. Well, let's face it—that wouldn't be difficult."

Offstage, Christopher Milton is nothing like his bungling television counterpart. He is a hard-working performer with a great belief in the live theatre. "Television is strange," he muses. "It's in one way the most intimate of the media, because everything you do on it is very small, you know, just for the camera, and because the viewers are just sitting in their living rooms to watch. And yet in a strange way, for the performer, it's a distant feeling playing to a camera, even when there's a studio audience. It doesn't bear comparison with the contact you can get with a live theatre audience. That's electrifying, intoxicating, magic."

For Christopher, being in Brighton is almost like coming home. "I spent seven years of my life here at Ellen da Costa's Stage School. I came when I was a very young ten-year-old and left when I went into full-time professional theatre. In many ways, Ellen taught me all I know. I think she's retired now, but I certainly hope to see her while I'm in Brighton. I hope she'll come and see the show—and no doubt rap me over the knuckles for sloppy enunciation! She used to be very hot on enunciation. I can't think that she'd approve of Lionel Wilkins' style of speech. . . ."

The article went on to complete the plug for *Lumpkin!* with information about Carl Anthony and Micky Gorton. It made no mention of Mark Spelthorne's death. But then the whole thing read like an Identikit PR interview which had been prepared long in advance.

Still, the information about the stage school was interesting. If the key to Christopher Milton's behavior lay deep in his past, then it might be worth paying a visit to Miss Ellen da Costa.

The rehearsals were hard. They started with a ten-thirty call on the Monday morning and it was like working on a new show. Wally Wilson's typewriter had been busy and few scenes had escaped "improvement." The charming cadences of Goldsmith's lines had now completely vanished and were replaced by the staccato banality of television comedy. There was more work for everyone. At enormous cost, the band had special rehearsals with Leon Schultz. The choreographer kept snaffling dancers away to learn new routines in the theatre bar. Actors were rarely seen without scripts in their hands as they tried to flush the old lines out with the new. Wherever there was a piano it was surrounded by a knot of actors struggling to pick up altered songs. The atmosphere was one of intense pressure.

But surprisingly it was cheerful. The company seemed more united than ever. And this was almost solely due to Christopher Milton. His enthusiasm was infectious and he inspired everyone to greater and greater efforts. He made them think that they were working on the greatest show that had ever happened and that every change was only going to make it that much greater. Charles could not help admiring the Pied Piper strength of the man's personality. The company was carried along on the wave of his vitality. Even the previous doubters, like Winifred Tuke, made no more comments on the evisceration of Oliver Goldsmith. The triumph of Christopher Milton was total.

He was everywhere. David Meldrum no longer even made a pretence of directing. He acted as a glorified messenger boy for the star, organizing rehearsal schedules as instructed and fixing the details of the increasingly elaborate technical side of the show.

Christopher Milton shared Charles' fascination for the mechanics of theatre and seemed to feel the magic of the old building. But he didn't just want to stand and dream while a sense of history seeped into him; he wanted to recapture that history and recreate the splendors of Victorian illusion. The Star Trap was quickly enlisted into the Chase sequence to fire Tony Lumpkin on to the stage from the bowels of the earth. (It was hoped to accompany this entrance with a flash from an electrically-fired maroon, but with the IRA bombers again in action, managements were nervous of sudden bangs in their theatres.) Moments later, Tony Lumpkin descended from the flies on a Kirby wire, then shot behind a tree only to reappear within seconds (thanks to the judicious use of a double) rising from the Grave Trap flanked by two eighteenth-century go-go dancers. The sequence was a far cry from *She Stoops to Conquer,* but it was moving towards the

Chaplinesque quality the star wanted. Of course as the business got more and more detailed, so it expanded and yet more of the original plot had to be cut to accommodate it. At the current rate of progress, by the time the show got to London it would have no more substance than a half-hour episode of *Straight Up, Guv*. "This week lovable conman Lionel Wilkins fools some supporting actors into believing that a private house is a pub—with hilarious consequences."

But *Lumpkin!* was beginning to work. Taking Christopher Milton's advice and forgetting Goldsmith, Charles began to see what was emerging, and it was something with enormous potential. In his own strange way, Christopher Milton was a considerable artist. His instinct for the theatrical and particularly the comic was unerring. Charles began to see the situation as a Faustian one in which the star was achieving earthly success at the cost of his immortal soul. The dark side of madness and crime was a necessary complement to the genius of the public image.

After a very hard day's rehearsal on the Tuesday Charles was leaving the theatre to grab a quick bite before the evening performance when he met Suzanne Horst. "Ah," she said accusingly, "there you are. Have you asked him yet?"

"What?" His mind was completely blank. He could only remember Suzanne drunk in his arms at the time of Pete Masters' accident.

"About the interview. You said you'd ask him."

"Oh, did I?" He tried to sound ingenuous and squirm out of it.

"Yes, and you didn't do it in Bristol, which means I've lost some time. So look, I want to do the radio interview this week. It's for Radio Brighton and I've promised them I'll do it while he's down here." The last sentence was not an appeal for help from a position of weakness; it was a reproof to Charles for failing to discharge a duty. Suzanne was a sharply efficient young lady once again; the warmth of their last encounter was only a product of the drink. Either she had forgotten it or was determined that it should be forgotten. "So look, when am I going to be able to do it?"

"Well, I don't know," he prevaricated. "We're rehearsing very hard at the moment and—"

"Have you asked him yet?"

Faced with the point-blank question, Charles could only admit he hadn't.

Suzanne Horst gave a contemptuous grunt. "Do you realize, you've wasted a lot of my time. I thought you were asking him."

"I'm sorry," he mumbled inadequately, trying to remember how he'd got into the position of agreeing to help her. "Does that write off the magazine article as well?"

"No, it only slows that down too." Her mind did not accommodate the idea of failure. "But I've been doing quite a lot of background research on it."

"Oh."

"Yes, I went to see the old lady who ran his stage school, that sort of thing." A firm reminder to Charles that that was his next priority. He started to make leaving noises, but did not escape without the final rap over the knuckles. "I'm very disappointed in you, Charles. I was relying on you. Now I'll have to try my own more direct methods."

Maybe it was the meeting with Suzanne that decided Charles to present himself at the Ellen da Costa Stage School in the guise of a journalist, or maybe it was just the obvious rôle to take when seeking information. Some inner warning mechanism told him not to go as Charles Paris.

There were some good old clothes shops near the station in Brighton and he had kitted himself out well. The suit was cheaply cut, but looked newish, and the tie was a touch of psychedelic bravado, too young for its wearer and too old to be fashionable. His hair was greyed and Brylcreemed back like raked grass. A pair of pebble glasses changed the shape of his face and made seeing almost impossible. He stained two fingers of his right hand yellow and bought a packet of cigarettes. He didn't shave and rubbed a little Leichner No. 16 on to darken his jowl. Then an unfamiliar aftershave to cover the greasepaint smell.

He studied the effect in the mirror and thought he looked sufficiently anonymous. The face that looked back at him was like a child's Potato Man, random features stuck on to a vegetable. He adopted a slightly hunched stance, as if shrinking from the cold. It looked all right.

Now just a name and a voice. He fabricated Frederick Austick from the names of the first two victims of the accidents, then decided it was too obvious and amended it to Alfred Bostock. Despite temptations to go fancy or double-barreled, he stuck at that. He tried a few words in his *Moby Dick* voice ("Allegorically inconsistent"—*Coventry Evening Telegraph*), but was more satisfied with the one he'd used as Bernard in *Everything in the Garden* ("Authentic suburban twang"—*Surrey Comet*).

He didn't really know who he was disguising himself from—the rest of the *Lumpkin!* company were rehearsing on the Wednesday morning—but as usual he felt more able to cope with a difficult task in character.

The Ellen da Costa Stage School had closed some years before, but its principal still lived in the building (and still kept her hand in by giving elocution lessons to the young people of Brighton who had impediments or social aspirations). The school was a tall Victorian private house off one of the seafront squares. Its owner's reduced circumstances were indicated by the cluster of tenants' doorbells attached with varying degrees of permanency to the old front door frame. Charles pressed the one whose plastic window showed a copperplate "Ellen da Costa" cut from a visiting card.

She answered promptly, a long gaunt lady in black, whose flowing dress and shawl combined with a tangle of hanging beads to make her look like a bentwood hatstand. Her hair was swept back in flamenco dancer style, as if to justify her Spanish surname, but the white line at the roots gave the lie to its sleek blackness. The skin of her face was drawn tight over her cheekbones, as if, like the hair, its tension was maintained by the system of asymmetrical combs at the back of the head. She was made up with skill, but a skill which belonged to an earlier age and survives now only in opera.

But she had style and must once have been a beautiful woman. Though probably seventy, she behaved with the assurance of a woman who has no doubt of her sexual magnetism. There was no coquetry, but a grace and dignity, heightened by her theatrical manner.

"Good morning," she enunciated with the attention to each vowel and consonant which she had instilled into generations of young hopefuls.

"Hello, I'm Alfred Bostock." He slipped easily into his *Everything in the Garden* twang. "I'm a journalist. I'm researching an article on Christopher Milton and I'm here because I've heard that you had so much to do with shaping his early career."

She laughed a clear, tinkling laugh, only shown to be staged by the overdramatic intake of breath which followed it. "Ah, dear Christopher. Everyone wants to know about him."

"Other members of the Press, you mean?"

"Yes, dear boy. There was the cub from the local rag, then a charming American girl, and now you."

"Yes, I hope you don't mind going over the ground again."

"Mind? But, *mon cher,* I am always delighted to speak about my little ones. And when it is *the* one, the one of all others who had the *je ne sais quoi,* the unknowable something that is stardom, why should I refuse? We who serve genius must do our duty. Do come in."

Charles, who was beginning to find her language a bit excessive, followed her up a couple of staircases to a dark sitting-room. It needn't have been as dark as it was, but much of the window was obscured by an Art Deco glass firescreen with a colorful design of a butterfly. The splashes of pale green, blue and red which the sun cast over the floor and furniture gave an ecclesiastical flavor to the room and this was intensified by the rows of photographs in ornate metal frames on the walls. They looked like images of saints and youthful miracle workers, with their slicked hair and unearthly smiles. They were presumably the "little ones," the pupils who had taken their theatrical orders under Miss da Costa's guidance and gone on to work in the field.

Two untimely candles added to the stuffy atmosphere of Italian Catholicism which the room generated. Every surface was crowded with souvenirs, more tiny framed photographs, dolls, masks, gloves, programs, massed untidily like offerings before a shrine.

The votaress sank dramatically into a small velvet chair and lay back so that the candlelight played gently over her fine profile. It reminded Charles of *Spotlight* photographs of ten years before, when every actor and actress was captured in a fuzzy light which picked out their bones in a murk of deepening shadows. (Nowadays actors tend to be photographed as if they've just come off a building site or are about to start life sentences for rape.) "Well," she said, "you want to ask me about Christopher."

She didn't ask for any credentials, which was a relief, because Charles hadn't thought through the details of what Alfred Bostock was meant to be researching.

"Yes, I'm after a bit of background, you know, what was he like as a child?" Charles mentally practiced his Alfred Bostock voice by repeating "Ford Cortina," "double glazing" and "ceiling tiles" to himself.

"Christopher came to me when he was ten." Ellen da Costa settled down to her recitation from *Lives of the Saints*. "Just a scrap of a boy, but with that same appealing charm and, of course, the talent. Even then, when he was unformed, the talent was there. Quite exceptional. His parents had died, in a car crash, I think, and it was an aunt who brought him to me. Very self-possessed he was."

"When was this that he first came to you?"

Ellen da Costa gave him a look for talking in prayers, but she answered his question, revealing that she had not been in on the shedding of four years considered necessary to the star's career.

She then continued at some length describing the evolution of the embryo talent under the ideal laboratory conditions of her school. Charles was beginning to feel sated with superlatives when she offered to illustrate her lecture with a collection of Press cuttings pasted into large blue ledgers.

They weren't very revealing. One or two good notices for the young Christopher Milton, but nothing which suggested a performer set to take the world by storm. Charles mentioned this to Ellen da Costa in suitably reverential tones.

"Ah well, the Press has never been notorious for its recognition of true quality, particularly in the theatre. I once knew an actor, ..." the pause was deliberately left long to summon up images of years of wild passion. ". . . a very great actor, who was nearly crucified by the critics. It was a martyrdom, a true martyrdom, very *triste*. Pardon my speaking so of your chosen occupation—" for a moment Charles couldn't think what she was talking about—"but in my experience the Press has never, in this country anyway, had the *delicatesse* to understand the workings of genius."

Charles did not attempt to defend his assumed calling, but murmured something suitable. "Also," she continued, her finely modulated voice drawing out the final "o" almost to breaking point, "perhaps Christopher was not fully realized at first. The potential was there, massive potential. Of course, with my experience I could see that, I was *sympathique* to it, but it was slow to blossom. At first there were others who appeared more talented than he, certainly who attracted more public notice, more Press reaction, more work."

"They worked while they were here?"

She at once became guarded, as if this were a patch of coals over which she had been hauled before. "Most stage schools also act as agencies for child performers and a lot of our pupils do a great deal of work, subject of course to the legal restrictions of only working forty days in the year and with adequate breaks. All the children are chaperoned and—"

But Charles was not writing a muck-raking article on the exploitation of child actors, so he tactfully cut her short, and asked if she would show him some of the early photographs of Christopher Milton.

She obliged readily. "Here are some from 1952." They looked very dated. Styles of period stage costume change quite as much as current fashion and the starched ruffs and heavy Elizabethan garments the children wore had the same distant unreal quality as Victorian pornography. "This is from a production of *Much Ado* my students did. Christopher was playing Claudio."

Charles took the photograph she proffered. Christopher Milton's face was instantly recognizable, even under a jeweled and feathered hat. All twenty-three years had done was to cut the creases deeper into his skin.

But it was the other two children who intrigued Charles. They were beautiful. Their grace in the heavy costumes made them look like figures from an Elizabethan painting and showed up Christopher Milton as very twentieth century, almost gauche in doublet and hose. The girl had a perfect heart-shaped face and long-lashed eyes whose grave stare, even from the old photograph, was strongly sensual. She appeared to be looking at the boy, who returned her gaze with the same kind of intensity. He had the epicene grace which some adolescent boys capture before they coarsen into adults. The face was almost babylike in its frame of long blond curls. The eyes were deep-set and powerful.

"Claudio," Charles repeated after a long pause. "That's not the best part in the play. Presumably this young man played Benedict?"

"Yes."

"Was he good?"

"Yes, he was very good. He did a lot of film work in his teens. Gareth Warden, do you remember the name?"

"It rings a bell." Yes, Julian Paddon had mentioned it and, now he saw the photograph, Charles realized that Gareth Warden had been in the film he'd caught the tail-end of on Jim Waldeman's television. That seemed so long ago it was like a memory from a previous incarnation. "And the girl?"

"Prudence Carr. She was a clever little actress, so clever."

"And she played Beatrice?"

"Yes."

"Any idea what happened to her? Or to Gareth Warden, come to that?"

"I don't know, Mr. Bostock. The theatre brings its share of heartbreaks to everyone who is involved in it." She gave a long sigh, which was a good demonstration of the breath control so vital for elocution and which was also meant to imply a lifetime of theatrical heartbreaks. "Neither of them did much so far as I know. Dear Garry had the misfortune of early success. It's so difficult for them to make the transition from playing child parts to adult ones. As you see, he was a beautiful boy. Perhaps he decided the theatre was not the career he wanted. *Je ne sais pas.* He hasn't kept in touch at all."

"And the girl?"

"The same story. I haven't seen her since she left my care. Maybe she didn't go into the theatre."

"She should have done. With looks like that. And if she could act as well as you say."

"Ah, she was magic. But things change. Fate takes a hand. Maybe she settled down and got married. How many promising careers have been cut short by matrimony. And how many only started by the failure of matrimony," she added mysteriously with a suffering gaze out of the window to some distant memory. "But *c'est la vie*. Some rise and some fall. Of those three, all the same age, all so talented, one was chosen, one who was more talented, one who had the real magic of stardom, and that was dear Christopher. He triumphed and left his rivals standing."

With recent knowledge of Christopher Milton's methods of leaving his rivals standing, Charles wondered if there was some story from the past which might show a parallel. "Presumably, Miss da Costa, with three students who were so talented in the same area, there must have been moments of jealousy between them?" he probed.

"Ah, the young are always jealous. They are so afraid, they feel that if they are not the absolute best in the world, then they are the absolute worst. Only with time can they understand that most are destined to be fairly good or fairly bad, that the world is made up of mediocrity and that only a chosen few, like dear Christopher, will be the best."

Charles tried to move her from generalizations to the specific. "You mean they were jealous of each other?"

"But of course. They would not be normal if they weren't."

"And was that jealousy ever expressed in violence?"

"Violence?" Her eyes widened and again she stiffened as if he were trying to find scandal. "Of course not. I kept a respectable school, Mr. Bostock. Nowadays, if one can believe the newspapers, violence in the classroom is commonplace. I did not allow it in my school."

"No, of course not. That's not what I meant." Charles covered his retreat clumsily, realizing that he wasn't going to get any answers to that question. But then it struck him that a bit of well-placed journalistic boorishness might be productive. "Of course,

Miss da Costa, another thing we keep reading about in the newspapers is sex in the classroom."

"Sex." She gave the word Lady Bracknell delivery.

"Yes, I mean, a group of young adolescents together, it's inevitable that they're going to form relationships. I was wondering, I mean, say these three youngsters, was there also some kind of emotional attachment between them?" He was glad he had come in disguise. Charles Paris could never have managed this crudeness of approach.

The question touched a nerve which had apparently been exposed before. "Mr. Bostock, I don't think there is any need to go over this ground again. The investigation by the local education authority in 1963 revealed that I was quite blameless in that matter."

Intriguing though it was, Miss da Costa's dark secret had no relevance to his current enquiries, so Charles tried to retrieve some of the ground he had lost. "I'm sorry, I think you misunderstand me. I'm not talking about 1963. As you know, I'm interested only in Christopher Milton. What I meant by my question was, was there maybe some early schoolboy romance we could mention? You know, the women readers go for all that stuff. 'My first romance.' It was a perfectly innocent enquiry."

It worked. "Oh, I see." She sat back. "I'm sorry, but I have had cause in my life to be somewhat wary of the Press. When one has figured in the private life of the great . . ." Again she left the hint of her wildly romantic past dangling to be snapped up by anyone interested. Charles wasn't, so she continued after a pause. "Well, of course, when you are speaking of young people, of beautiful young people, yes, *l'amour* cannot be far away. Oh, I'm sure at one time or another, all three of them were in love with each other. All such sensitive creatures. Yes, I have seen the two boys wildly, madly in love. I have seen them both look at Prudence in a way . . . in a way one can recognize if one has seen it directed at oneself. Then one understands. Ah, I sometimes wonder if one has loved at all if one has not heard a lover's voice reciting Swinburne soft in one's ear. Don't you?"

He thought that Charles Paris' and Alfred Bostock's answers to that question might well be identical, so he tried to get the conversation back on the subject and avoid the Ellen da Costa Anthology of Love Poetry. "Hmmm," he offered, in a way that he hoped dismissed Swinburne. "I was wondering, do you know if either of the affairs with Prudence continued after they left the school?"

"Mr. Bostock, I do not like your word 'affair'; it implies impropriety at my school."

"I'm sorry. You're misunderstanding me again. I just meant, you know, the . . . friendships."

"That, Mr. Bostock, I'm afraid I don't know. For the first year after they left, I heard a little of them—well, that was inevitable. I act as agent for all my pupils for their first year out of school."

"You mean you put them under exclusive contract?"

"I prefer to think that I protect them from some of the sharks and exploiters in the agency business. But after the year, I heard nothing of Garry or Prudence. Of course, I heard a great deal about Christopher. Everywhere these days, one hears about Christopher. Did you see this in the local paper?" She opened one of the blue ledgers and pointed to the cutting from the previous day's paper. It was already neatly glued in. Charles found the promptness of its filing sad. It opened a little window on to the great emptiness of the old lady's life. He told her that he had seen the article and rose to leave.

Now she seemed anxious to detain him. "Did you notice, he said in the interview that he'd try to come and see me while the show's down here?"

"Yes. Well, I believe that the company are doing a great deal of rehearsal at the moment."

"Oh yes, I fully understand." She reclined elegantly in her chair, the High Priestess of the Cult, prepared to wait forever for her Mystic Experience.

CHAPTER 14

CHARLES RANG JULIAN Paddon from a phone-booth on the front. "Hello, how's the family?"

"Sensationally well. Damian has inherited my own innate sense of the theatre. I went to see them yesterday and he shat all over the nurse who was changing him. What timing. I think he'll grow up to be a critic."

"And Helen?"

"Fine. Uncomfortable, which is I believe a feature of the condition, but extremely cheerful. Normal cervix, I understand, will be resumed as soon as possible. No hint of purple depression or whatever it is. Can't wait to get home."

"When will that be?"

"Monday, I hope."

"Listen, Julian, I wanted to pick your brains again. You remember we were talking last week about the old Cheltenham company you were in with Christopher Milton."

"Oh yes."

"You did say that an actor called Gareth Warden was also in the company?"

"Yes."

"Seen anything of him since?"

"No. Why do you ask?"

"Oh, it's just something I'm trying to work out. You've no idea what happened to him?"

"Vanished off the face of the earth so far as I know."

Julian's words gave substance to a thought which had been forming in Charles' mind. Christopher Milton tended to make people who challenged him "vanish off the face of the earth." Was the key to the current set of crimes in a crime which had been committed long before?

"Hmmm. I see. Another thing—you don't remember by any chance what Christopher Milton's sex life was like at the time?"

"Good God. What do you want—times, dates, with whom, number of orgasms achieved? It was twenty years ago, Charles. It's hard enough to remember what my own sex life was like."

"I mean just in general terms."

"Blimey. Well, let me think—I don't remember him being gay, though I could be wrong. I don't remember him taking up with anyone in the company—mind you, there wasn't much spare there, they tended to get snapped up pretty quickly. I don't even recall a sort of regular popsie coming down for weekends. Oh, it's a long time ago. I honestly don't know, Charles. I mean, keeping track of actors' love-lives is like doing a National Census of rabbits. Sorry, I just can't remember."

"Oh well, never mind. And you can't ever recall hearing him speak of a girl called Prudence Carr?"

"Nope."

"Does the name mean anything to you?"

"Nope."

"Oh. Well, I—ooh, one last thing—when he had his breakdown, was it caused by anything personal, you know, a girl who'd chucked him or. . . ."

"I don't think so, Charles. I think it was solely due to the fact that the world did not at that time share his inflated opinion of himself. As I remember him, sex was a long way down his list of priorities. In fact everything was a long way down his list of priorities—except for his career and becoming a star."

The strain of the extra rehearsals and the difficulties of remembering a continuously changing text began to show on the Wednesday evening performance. Perhaps the matinée was the last straw which made the cast suddenly realize how tired they were. Whatever the reason, the mood of united endeavor was replaced in a moment by an atmosphere of bad temper and imminent disintegration.

It was small things that went wrong. Lines were missed and lighting cues were slow. As the show progressed, the contagion spread and by the end everyone felt they were doing everything wrong. There weren't any major errors of the sort that an audience is likely to notice, but they worried the cast and undermined the communal confidence.

The Chase Scene was all over the place. Entrances were missed and special effects failed to function. The Star Trap didn't work. Because of other stage management crises, the crew forgot about it completely and Christopher Milton rushed down to the cellar to find the locking bar which held the wooden platform firmly in position and no sign of the four members of the crew who were meant to man the ropes and eject him on to the stage. As a result he had to rush back up on stage mouthing obscenities at everyone and make a very tame entrance from the wings. The comic timing of the scene's slapstick was ruined.

Even Charles didn't escape the epidemic of cack-handedness. He actually fell over in his first scene. To give him his due, it wasn't his fault. Because of the general panic of the stage management, including some local help who'd only been brought in that day, the rostrum on to which he had to move at a given point had not been anchored to the ground and was freemoving on its wheels. So, as soon as he put his foot on it, it sped away, forcing an ungainly splits movement which deposited him flat on his face. It got a good laugh from the audience, but, since it took place in the course of Tony Lumpkin's romantic song to Bet Bouncer, it was perhaps not the sort of laugh the show wanted.

The only person who came through the performance unscathed was Lizzie Dark. In fact, she was at her very best. She had an advantage. She was only eighteen months out of Sussex University and still had a lot of friends there who had come *en masse* to see her. They were wildly partisan and applauded her every action. The general mediocrity of the performance made her seem even better and the reaction grew increasingly fulsome. It was only a small group in the audience, but they were noisy. At the curtain call, they screamed and shouted "Bravos!" and "Encores!" at her. It was an elaborate private joke, recapturing no doubt the heady atmosphere of a campus first night, and it was out of place in a professional theatre. But Lizzie seemed to be carried along by it, to be instantly transported back to amateur night. She played to her gallery shamelessly.

Christopher Milton exploded as soon as the curtain was down. Surprisingly he didn't turn on Lizzie or any other of the cast who had miscued him or let him down. He let the stage management have it. Of all the errors of the show, it was his ignominious return to the stage from the Star Trap which really rankled. He bawled them all out. Four-letter words flew around as he lambasted their incompetence, called them amateurs, provided a few choice images of things he wouldn't trust them with and some equally vivid ones of fates that would be too good for them. This display of temper was the most violent Charles had witnessed from the star and it made him uncomfortable. The great hiss of anger came like steam from a pressure cooker and before long the pressure cooker was going to explode and scald everyone in sight. Charles couldn't keep his knowledge to himself and do nothing much longer.

The inefficiency which had characterized the performance continued. While the star was unleashing his diatribe onstage, a group of schoolkids had somehow eluded Len the stage doorman's vigilance and invaded the dressing-rooms. They had only been driven by enthusiasm and were in fact fans of Christopher Milton, but he was in no mood for one of his sudden switches to charm. He added a few lacerating sentences against Len and said he'd remain on stage until the fans had been cleared. The rest of the cast shuffled sheepishly off to get changed.

Charles started to follow them. He was in a bad mood; the limping performance and the ensuing row had ruled out any possibility of getting to the pub before closing time. But just as he was at the pass door he noticed Christopher Milton going off into the wings and down the stairs to the cellar. Presumably just to have another look at the offending Star Trap. What made it interesting was that Lizzie Dark followed him.

There was another way down to the cellar backstage. Charles

moved silently, though there was no one about. The cellar was lit by a couple of isolated working lights, but the vertical and horizontal girders of the old stage machinery made forests of shadow through which he could creep to a good spying position. Somewhere over the other side Spike or one of the stage crew was hammering nails into a broken flat, but he paid no attention to the intruders.

As Charles anticipated, Christopher Milton was looking balefully at the Star Trap mechanism. Four wooden beams boxed in the small platform on which the person to be ejected stood. The platform was in the up position, almost flush with the stage underneath the hinged Star top. The locking bar, a solid piece of two by four, was firmly in position, blocking any movement. The star slapped it petulantly. He seemed aware of Lizzie Dark's presence, but, though he spoke out loud, he did not speak to her. "Sodding thing. Why we're stuck with this sort of old-fashioned crap I don't know. Four people to operate it. You'd think with a system of counterweights, you could make it self-operating. Get this bloody locking bar out and leave it preset, so that it's ready when I am and not when the bloody stage crew are."

"But," Lizzie hazarded tentatively, "if you took out the locking bar and had it down for too long someone onstage might step on and fall through."

"Yes, so we're back relying on incompetents." His anger had drained away, leaving him tired and listless.

"Christopher. . . ."

"Yes."

"I wanted to apologize for tonight."

"Eh?"

"That load of lunatics in the audience. My so-called friends. I'm afraid they did rather misbehave. It can't have made it any easier for you to concentrate."

"Oh, never mind. There are good nights and bad nights." His voice was philosophical and very tired. The violent outburst Charles had expected didn't come. That was what made being with Christopher Milton so exhausting. There was never any indication of which way he was going to jump.

"Well, I'm sorry. I shouldn't have played up to them. It was a bit unprofessional."

"Never mind." He put his arm round the girl's waist affectionately. "We all have to learn."

This avuncular, kindly Christopher Milton was a new one on Charles and he found it unaccountably sinister. The arm stayed round her waist as Lizzie asked, "How do you think it's going, Christopher?"

"It's going all right. It'll be very good—if we all survive to see the first night."

"Am I doing all right?"

"Yes, you're good. Could be better in bits."

No actress could have resisted asking which bits.

"That song in the second half, the romantic one. There's a lot more to be got out of that."

"Yes, I'm sure there is, but the trouble is, David never actually gives any direction and I'm not experienced enough to know what to do myself. . . . It's difficult."

"I'll take you through it when I've got a moment."

"Would you?"

"Sure. When? What's the rehearsal schedule tomorrow?"

"The afternoon's free. We're all meant to be in need of a rest."

"And how." The deep weariness in the two words reminded Charles of the intense physical pressure that the star had been under for the past months. "But okay. Let's go through it tomorrow afternoon."

"No, I don't want to take up your time. I—"

"Here. At three o'clock."

"Well, if you really. . . ."

"I really."

"Thank you. I'm sorry, I just feel so amateur in this company. I mean, it's jolly nice getting good jobs, but I've only done a year round the reps and I've got so much ground to make up."

"Don't worry. You'll make it. You've got talent."

"Do you really mean it?"

"I do. You'll be a big star. Probably bigger than me."

"Come off it."

"I'm serious. It's a long time since I've seen an actress who had your kind of potential. There was a girl I was with at drama school, but no one since then."

"What was her name?"

"Prudence."

"And what happened to her?"

"Ah." There was a long pause, during which Charles felt that water, defying the laws of gravity, was being poured up his back. "What does happen to talented girls who work with me?"

Christopher Milton moved suddenly. The hand on Lizzie Dark's waist was brought up sharply to her neck where his other hand joined it. Charles started forward from his hide to save her.

They didn't see him, which was just as well. Because far from being strangled, as he feared, Lizzie Dark was being passionately kissed. Charles melted back into the shadows. The hammering in the distance continued, but otherwise the cellar was silent as he crept out, feeling like a schoolboy surprised with a dirty book.

The next morning Alfred Bostock took over the case again. For the next part of the investigation it would not do to be recognised and, after the previous night's unsatisfactory spying, Charles wanted the comfort of disguise.

He'd hung around the stage door until Christopher Milton and Lizzie Dark left the building. They had come out separately and set off in opposite directions. Charles trailed Christopher Milton to the Villiers, his sea-front hotel. (It was so near the theatre that there was no point in having a car, even for a star.) That made him think that Lizzie at least was safe for the night. What had gone on in the cellar after he'd left fed his imagination. It was a good half-hour before they emerged, so most things were possible.

But the urgency of the case was inescapable. The star's violent outburst, the strangeness of his behavior with Lizzie, and a vague but unpleasant idea of what had happened to Gareth Warden and Prudence Carr made Charles realize that he could dither no longer. And the most obvious thing to do was to find out what Christopher Milton did during that missing hour in the morning.

Charles was very organised. He got up at five o'clock after a disbelieving look at the alarm clock and started making up as Alfred Bostock.

At six-thirty he rang the Villiers. A night porter answered. Charles said he was ringing on behalf of Dickie Peck, Mr. Milton's agent, and was Mr. Milton up, he knew he sometimes got up very early. No, Mr. Milton was not up. Yes, he was in the hotel, but he was sleeping. Yes, he was certain that Mr. Milton had not gone out, because he'd been on all night. Yes, he thought it would be advisable if the representative of Mr. Peck rang back later. Mr. Milton normally ordered breakfast in his suite at eight o'clock. And, incidentally, the Villiers Hotel looked forward to Mr. Peck's arrival later in the day.

At eight o'clock the representative of Mr. Peck—who incidentally used the accent Charles Paris had used as Voltore in *Volpone* ("Lamentably under rehearsed"—*Plays and Players*)—rang again and asked to be put through to Mr. Milton. He was connected, but as soon as Christopher Milton spoke, there occurred one of those unfortunate cutoffs which are a feature of the British telecommunications system. Charles Paris, in a phone-booth on the sea-front opposite the Villiers Hotel, knew that his quarry was inside and was determined to follow him wherever he went. He had checked the entrances and exits and, unless Christopher Milton left through the kitchens (which would be more conspicuous than the main door in terms of witnesses), he would have to come out on to the front. Now it was just a question of waiting.

Charles sat in a shelter with a miserable-looking couple of old men who were realizing their lifetime's ambition of retiring to the south coast. They depressed him. It was cold. He saw himself with the deadly X-ray eye of a third person. A middle-aged actor play-acting on the front at Brighton. Someone who'd never managed to create a real relationship with anyone, a man whose wife was forced to take solace with a scoutmaster, a man whose daughter spoke the language of another planet, a man who would sink into death without even disturbing the surface of life, unnoticed, unmourned. How would he be remembered? As an actor, not for long. Maybe the occasional unfortunate accident might stick in people's minds: "There was an actor I knew—what was his name?—Charles Paris, that's right, and he. . . ." Or would he just live on as a sort of Everard Austick, an archetypal heavy drinker in the mythology of the theatre? "There was an incredible piss-artist in a company I was once in, bloke called Charles Paris, and he used to drink. . . ." No, he wasn't even an exceptional drinker, not the sort of wild alcoholic around whom Rabelaisian stories gathered. He drank too much, but not interestingly too much.

Perhaps it was the sea-front in winter that made him so introspective, but he found big questions looming in his mind, big unanswerable cliché questions, all the *whys?* and *why bothers?* and *what does it matters?* Life was very empty.

There was a man walking along the street towards the Villiers Hotel. Charles stiffened. Here at last was something, something real and tangible.

The man he saw was bald, with big ears. When he had seen them in Leeds, Charles had thought the ears looked like handles of a loving cup. The man had hardly registered in Bristol, Charles had just thought he looked like the one in Leeds, but now seeing him for the third time there was no question. It was the same man.

And each time the man had appeared near Christopher Milton's hotel early in the morning. Charles felt he was near to solving the mystery of who did the star's dirty work.

He crossed the road and followed the bald man into the Villiers Hotel. He hadn't really planned his next move, but it was made easy for him. There was temporarily no one in Reception. The bald man rang for a lift. Charles stood by his side, assessing him. A bit old for a heavy, but he was well-built and had the bear-like shape of a wrestler. His mouth was a tight line and the eyes looked mean.

The lift came. The bald man got in and asked for the fourth floor. Charles, who hadn't acted in fifties detective films for nothing, also got in and asked for the fifth. There wasn't one. "Oh, so sorry," he said, feeling that this wasn't a very auspicious start. "I mean the fourth—third."

The bald man did not seem to notice his companion's gaucheness and Charles was decanted on the third floor. It was a matter of moments to find the stairs and scurry up to the fourth. He hid behind the firedoor and watched the bald man walk along the corridor to room 41, knock and enter.

Charles followed, treading noiselessly in the soft pile of the expensive carpet. He stopped by room 41 and put his ear to the door. He could hear two voices, one of them recognizably Christopher Milton's, but they were too far away for him to distinguish the words.

Anyway, he was in a rather exposed position for listening. A Hoover stood unattended in the corridor and muffled singing also indicated the presence of cleaners. He'd have to move quickly.

The cleaners had left a key with its heavy metal label in the door of room 42. He opened the door and sidled in.

He had expected an immediate confrontation with a suspicious cleaner but miraculously the suite was empty. He moved to the wall which was shared with room 41 and put his ear to it. They were still talking, but, though the speech was clearer, it was again impossible to hear individual words. The effect was of badly tuned radio.

Remembering another movie, Charles fetched a tooth-glass from the bathroom. Pressed against the wall it improved the sound quality, but still not enough to make it intelligible. People who paid for their privacy at the Villiers Hotel did not waste their money.

He was almost despairing when he thought of the balcony. A sea view was another of the perks for those who were prepared to pay the astronomical rates charged for a fourth-floor suite at the Villiers.

He slid the galvanized steel door back. The cold slap of air made him realize how grotesquely overheated the hotel was.

The balcony of room 42 adjoined that of 41. Only a bar separated them. By sliding along the wall of the building, Charles could get very close to Christopher Milton's window and still remain out of sight from the room. The window was slightly open in reaction to the central heating. Charles could hear what was being said inside quite clearly.

He stood high above the seashore on a cold November morning in Brighton and listened.

Christopher Milton's voice came first, strangled with passion. ". . . And I can't stand the way they are always looking at me, always assessing me. I hate them all."

"What do you mean, you hate them?" The other voice was toneless, without any emotion.

"I mean I want something to happen to them."

"What?"

"I want them out of my way. The others went out of my way."

"Yes." The dry voice gave nothing. "What do you want to happen to them?"

"I want them to die. I want them all to die." He could hardly get the words out.

"Who are you talking about?"

"All of them."

"Not all. We can't just kill them all, can we? Who do you really want dead?"

"Charles Paris." The name was hissed out. "I want Charles Paris dead."

CHAPTER 15

AT THAT MOMENT someone came into the room behind Charles and let out an incomprehensible shriek. It was one of the cleaners, a slender Filipino girl in a blue nylon overall. She looked at him with widening black eyes. He had to think quickly. "Room 32?" he offered. And then, to cover himself in case she knew the occupant of Room 32, "Toilet? Toilet?" Unaccountably the words came out in a comedy sketch Spanish accent.

"Toilet," the girl echoed, as if it were a word she had heard before, but did not understand.

"Si, si," Charles continued insanely, "dondo este el toilet?"

"Toilet," the girl repeated, now uncertain whether she had actually heard the word before.

"Si, toiletto." He thought adding the final "o" might help, but it didn't appear to. The girl looked blank. Charles pointed to his fly as a visual aid to the word "toilet."

This time the girl understood. Or rather she misunderstood. Throwing her hands in the air, she cried "Rape!" and rushed out into the corridor.

Charles followed at equal speed. He too wanted to get away in a hurry. Unfortunately the Filipino girl took his movement for pursuit and redoubled her screams. They rushed along the corridor in convoy, because she had chosen to run in the direction of the lifts. Doors opened behind them and bewildered faces stared. Charles decided he couldn't wait for the lift and took to the stairs. He managed to get out of the building without being stopped.

He sat in the shelter opposite the Villiers Hotel and tried to control the breath which was rasping in his throat. It wasn't only the physical effects of the chase that made him feel so shaky. It was also the unpleasant feeling which comes to people who have just heard a contract being taken out on their lives. He gasped and trembled and, although a diluted sun was now washing the sea-front, the morning seemed colder.

The two old men were still sitting in the shelter, overtly ignoring him, but with sly side glances. They didn't depress him now. They were part of a humanity he did not want to leave. Dr. Johnson's adage about the proximity of death concentrating the mind wonderfully was proving true. The depression he had felt so recently seemed a wicked affront to life, to all the things he still wanted to do. And yet within fifty yards of him a lunatic was giving a paid killer instructions to murder him.

It was ridiculous. He had that feeling he could recall from prep school of getting into a fight and suddenly realizing that it was becoming more vicious than he'd expected and suddenly wanting to be out of it. Like a recurrent nightmare in which, after a long chase, he always capitulated and apologized and pretended it had all been a joke. But this was not a joke.

The question of what to do about the whole case had now taken on more than a dilettante interest. It had become an issue of red-hot urgency. But the answer didn't come any more readily.

Though the sequence of Christopher Milton's (or his hit-man's) crimes and their motives were now clear as daylight, Charles still had no real evidence. Just the gin bottle, the airgun pellets and the liquid paraffin, but none of those could be pinned on the criminals and none related to the most serious crimes.

He still needed positive proof of wrongdoing. Or, since he was apparently the next person to be done wrong to, positive proof of the intention to do wrong might be preferable. He decided to follow the bald man in the hope of catching him red-handed. (The details of how he would himself catch red-handed someone whose criminal mission was to eliminate him he left for the time being. They would supply themselves when the occasion arose.)

He counted his advantages and there weren't many. First, he knew they were after him, so he was on his guard. Secondly, he was in disguise and so could spy on them without automatic discovery. Not much, but better than nothing.

At about five past ten the bald man came out of the hotel. He walked without suspicion, no furtive glances to left and right. Charles had the advantage of hunting the hunter.

The bald man was an ideal candidate for tailing. He walked straight ahead at a brisk pace, not stopping to look in shop windows or dawdling aimlessly. All Charles had to do was to adjust his own pace to match and follow along about fifty yards behind. Brighton was full of shoppers and the pursuit was not conspicuous.

It soon became clear that the man was going to the railway station. He walked briskly and easily up the hill, fitter than his appearance suggested. Charles thought uncomfortably of the strength he had seen in middle-aged wrestlers on the television. If it came to direct physical confrontation, he didn't reckon much for his chances.

The man didn't stop to buy a ticket. He must have a return, because he showed something at the barrier. He went on to Platform 4, for trains to London. At first Charles was going to buy a single, but that showed a depressing lack of faith in the outcome of his mission, so he got a return.

He also bought a *Times* for burying his face in. Tabloid newspapers, he decided, must be unpopular with the criminal fraternity; they hide less.

The train came soon, which implied that the bald man knew the times and was hurrying for this specific one. Charles began an irrelevant conjecture about the idea of the commuting assassin, always catching the same train. "Had a good day at work, dear?" "Oh, not too bad. Had a bit of trouble with one chap. Had to use two bullets. Still, always the same on a Friday, isn't it?" But the situation was too tense for that sort of fantasy.

The assassin got into an open-plan carriage, which was ideal. Charles went into the same one by another door and positioned himself in a seat from which he could see the man's leg and so would not miss any movement. He opened *The Times,* but his eyes slipped over the words without engaging or taking them in. He turned to the crossword on the principle that mental games might take his mind off the icy trickling in his stomach.

"I know that death has ten—several doors/For men to take their exits—Webster (8)." The fact that he recognized the quotation from *The Duchess of Malfi* and could fill in the word "thousand" gave him small comfort.

He felt ill, on the verge of violent diarrhea. He could still see the man's leg round the edges of the seats. It didn't move, but it mesmerized him. He tried to imagine the mind that owned the leg and the thoughts that were going through it. Was the man coolly comparing methods of killing, trying to come up with another crime that could look like an accident? Had his paymaster given him a deadline by which to get Charles Paris? The word "deadline" was not a happy choice.

Come to that, if his quarry was supposed to be in Brighton, why was he going to London anyway? Charles' fevered mind provided all kinds of unpleasant reasons. There was some particularly vicious piece of killing equipment that had to be bought in London. Or the job was going to be subcontracted and the bald man was on his way to brief another hitman with the details. Even less attractive solutions also presented themselves.

The pressure on his bowels was becoming unbearable. He'd have to go along to the toilet at the end of the carriage.

That meant going past the bald man. Still, it might be useful to get a closer look. Charles walked past. The man did not look up.

His reading matter was unlikely for a hired killer. The *Listener* was open on his lap and a *New Scientist* lay on the seat beside him. Obviously a new class of person was turning to crime. Presumably in times of rising unemployment, with a glut of graduates and a large number of middle-aged redundancies, the criminal social pattern was changing.

Charles felt a bit better after he had used the lavatory, but the face that stared at him from the stained mirror as he washed his hands was not a happy one.

The Alfred Bostock disguise made him look seedier than ever. The pebble glasses perched incongruously on the end of his nose (the only position in which they enabled him to see anything). The makeup on his jowl looked streaked and dirty. The bright tie mocked him. What was he doing? He was forty-eight, too old for this sort of masquerade. What was he going to do when he got to London? He couldn't spend the rest of his life following the bald-headed man. The confidence that he would know what to do when the occasion arose was beginning to dissipate.

The journey to Victoria took just over an hour and during that time the assassin sat quietly reading the *Listener*. Charles supposed that one would have to relax and behave normally in that line of work or go mad. His own *Times* lay unread on his knee and no subsequent crossword clues were filled in.

At Victoria the man got out and gave in his ticket at the barrier. Charles tried a little detective logic. If the man had a return ticket and yet was carrying no luggage except his newspapers, it was possible that he had started from London that morning, gone down to Brighton just to get his instructions and was now returning to base. This deduction was immediately followed by the question, "So what?"

The bald man walked purposefully to the Underground with Charles in tow. He bought a 15p ticket from the machine and Charles did likewise. The man went on to the platform for the Victoria Line northbound. Charles followed.

They travelled in the same compartment to Oxford Circus. The bald man was now deep into his *New Scientist*, apparently unsuspicious.

He climbed out of the Underground station and walked along Upper Regent Street into Portland Place. He walked on the left, the British Council side rather than the Broadcasting House one. His pace was still even. Nothing in his behavior betrayed any suspicion. And equally nothing in his behavior would make any passerby think of him as anything but a professional businessman on his way to work.

He turned left at New Cavendish Street, then right up Wimpole Street and left on to Devonshire Street. After two hours of tailing, Charles was becoming mesmerized and he almost overshot the man when he stopped.

Though they were only feet apart, the bald man still did not notice his pursuer. He walked in through the yellow painted front door of a white Georgian house.

Charles, in a panic over nearly bumping into his quarry, walked on a little so as not to make his behavior too obvious, then turned back and walked slowly past the house. It was expensive. Net curtains prevented snooping inside. A worn brass plate on the door —"D. M. Martin." No initials after the name, no indication of professional qualifications.

Charles paused, undecided. It was an expensive area of London. Contract killing must be a lucrative business, if the man lived there. All around were expensive private doctors and architects. He looked up and down the road. A policeman about fifty yards away was watching him curiously.

That decided him. The Law was there to back him up if need be, and the thing had to be done. He couldn't stand the strain of being under sentence of death any longer. It was time to take the bull by the horns.

The door gave easily when he turned the handle and he found himself in a carpeted hall. The smartly suited girl behind the desk looked up at him, surprised. "Can I help you?"

It was all too ridiculous. He had seen films about organized crime where the whole operation was run like big business with secretaries and receptionists, but he never expected to see it with his own eyes.

He was no longer afraid. Somehow here in the center of London he felt safe. There was a policeman just outside. He could manage. "Did a bald man just come in here?" he asked brusquely.

"Mr. Martin just arrived, but—"

"Where is he?"

"He's in his room, but do you have an appointment?"

"No. I just want to see him."

The girl treated him warily, as if he might be important.

"Look, if you like to take a seat in the waiting room, I'll speak to Mr. Martin and see what we can do. He's got someone coming to see him at twelve, but I'll—"

"Waiting room!" It was farcical. Charles started to laugh in a tight, hysterical way. "No, I'm not going to sit in any waiting room.

I haven't come along with a list of names of people I want killed. I—"

The noise he was making must have been audible from the next room, because the door opened and Charles found himself face to face with the assassin. "What's going on, Miss Pelham?"

"I'm not sure. This gentleman—"

"I've come to tell you I know all about what you've been doing, Mr. Martin. There's a policeman outside and I have proof of what's been going on, so I think you'd better come clean." Somehow the denunciation lacked the punch it should have had. The bald-headed man looked at him gravely. "I'm sorry. I've no idea what you're talking about."

"Oh really. Well, I'm talking about Christopher Milton and the instructions he gave you."

The name had an instantaneous effect. Mr. Martin's face clouded and he said coldly, "You'd better come in. Ask the twelve o'clock appointment to wait if necessary, Miss Pelham."

When they were inside, he closed the door, but Charles had now gone too far to feel fear. He was going to expose the whole shabby business, whatever it cost him.

"Now what is all this?"

"I know all about what you and Christopher Milton have been doing."

"I see." The bald man looked very displeased. "And I suppose you intend to make it all public?"

"I certainly do."

"And I suppose you have come here to name a price for keeping your mouth shut?"

"Huh?" That was typical, the feeling that money can solve anything. "No, I intend to let everyone know what's been going on. You won't buy me off."

"I see. You realize what this could do to Christopher Milton?"

"Nothing that he doesn't fully deserve. He may think he's a god, but he's not above the law. He is a public danger and should be put away."

"It's that sort of small-minded thinking that delays progress. If you—"

"Small-minded thinking! I don't regard disapproving of murder as small-minded. What, do you subscribe to the theory that the artist is above the law, the artist must be cosseted, the artist—?"

"What the hell are you talking about? Who are you?"

"Charles Paris." This was no time for pretence.

The name certainly registered with Mr. Martin.

"Yes, I'm Charles Paris. I'm in the company with Christopher Milton. You know all about me."

"Oh yes. I know about you. So it was you all the time. And now, blackmail."

It was Charles' turn to be flabbergasted. "What are you talking about?"

"Christopher Milton mentioned that a lot of sabotage had been going on in the show, that someone was trying to get him. It was you. And now you want to expose what he does with me."

The voice was sad, almost pitying. It checked the impetus of Charles' attack. "What do you mean? It's Christopher Milton who's been responsible for the sabotage and you're the one who's done the dirty work for him. And this morning he gave you orders to kill me. Don't try to pretend otherwise, Mr. Martin."

The bald man gazed at him in blank amazement. "What?"

"I know. I saw you in Leeds, and in Bristol, and in Brighton. I know you did it. All those early morning meetings when he gave you instructions. You are Christopher Milton's hitman."

"Mr. Paris," the words came out tonelessly, as if through heavy sedation, "I am not Christopher Milton's hitman. I am his psychotherapist."

Charles felt the ground slowly crumbling away beneath his feet. "What?"

"As you may or may not know, Christopher Milton has been prone in the past to a form of mental illness. He has had three or four major breakdowns, and has been undergoing treatment by me for about seven years. His is a particularly stressful career and at the moment the only way he can support the pressures it places on him is by having an hour of psychotherapy every day of his life."

"And that's why he always has his call at ten-thirty?"

"Exactly. The hour between nine and ten is our session."

"I see. And so you travel round wherever he goes?"

"He doesn't leave London much. Under normal circumstances he comes to me. This tour is exceptional."

"And what happens to your other patients or subjects or whatever they're called?"

"It was only the week in Leeds when I had to be away. I commuted to Bristol and Brighton. Mr. Milton is a wealthy man."

"I see." Money could buy anything. Even a portable psychiatrist.

"Needless to say, the fact that Mr. Milton is undergoing treatment is a closely-guarded secret. He believes that if it got out it would ruin his career. I've argued with him on this point, because I feel this need for secrecy doubles the pressure on him. But at the moment he doesn't see it that way and is desperately afraid of anyone knowing. I only tell you because of the outrageousness of your accusations, which suggest that you have completely—and I may say—dangerously misinterpreted the situation."

"I see." Charles let the information sink in. It made sense. It explained many things. Not only the late morning calls, but also the obsessive privacy which surrounded the star. Even little things like Christopher Milton's nondrinking and unwillingness to eat cheese would be explained if he were on some form of tranquilizers as part of his treatment.

"I take it, Mr. Paris, from what you said, that you overheard part of our session this morning and leapt to a grotesquely wrong conclusion?"

"Yes. I may as well put my cards on the table. I was brought into the show by the management to investigate this sabotage business."

"If that's the case then I apologize for suggesting that you were responsible for the trouble. It seems that both of us have been victims of delusions. But, Mr. Paris, why did your investigations lead you to eavesdrop on our session this morning?"

"The fact is, Mr. Martin, that my investigations so far have led me to the unfortunate conclusion that Christopher Milton is himself responsible, either directly or indirectly, for all of these incidents."

The psychotherapist did not reject the suggestion out of hand. "I can understand what you mean—that all of the . . . accidents have in fact benefited him, that they disposed of people he wanted out of the way."

"Exactly."

"Yes. The same thought had crossed my mind." He spoke the words sadly.

"You know his mental condition better than anyone. What do you think?"

"I don't know." He sighed. "I don't think so."

"Having heard the violence of what he said about me this morning. . . ."

"Yes, but that is a feature of the analysis situation. You mustn't take it literally. The idea of analysis is—in part—that he should purge his emotions. He says the most extreme things, but I don't think they should be taken as expressions of actual intent."

"You don't sound sure."

"No."

"I mean, at the time of his first breakdown he attacked people with a knife."

"I see you've done your homework, Mr. Paris. Yes, there is violence in him. He's obsessed by his career and he is slightly paranoid about it. He does turn against anyone who seems to threaten him in even the tiniest way. I mean, I gather that the crime which provoked this morning's outburst was your falling over and getting a laugh during one of his songs."

"An accident."

"Oh yes, I'm sure, but he's not very logical about that sort of thing."

"But he has expressed antagonism to most of the other people who've been hurt."

"Yes, I'm afraid so. And a strange bewildered relief after they've disappeared from the scene. I suppose it is just possible that he could have done the crimes. You say you have evidence?"

"Some. Nothing absolutely conclusive, but it seems to point towards him."

"Hmmm. I hope you're wrong. It would be tragic if it were true."

"Tragic because it would ruin his career?"

"No, tragic because it would mean the ruin of a human being."

"But you do think it's possible?"

"Mr. Paris, I think it's extremely unlikely. Behavior of that sort would be totally inconsistent with what I know of him from the past and with all that I have ever encountered in other cases. But I suppose, if you force me to say yea or nay, it is just possible."

Charles Paris looked at his watch. It was a quarter to one. In two and a quarter hours Christopher Milton had a meeting arranged on the stage of Queen's Theatre, Brighton, with the girl who had stolen the show from him the night before.

CHAPTER 16

THERE IS NO stillness like the stillness of an empty theatre. As Charles stepped on to the stage, he could almost touch the silence. And the fact that the building wasn't completely empty seemed to intensify the loneliness. Somewhere behind the circle people were busy in the general manager's office. In a distant workshop someone was using an electric drill. Traffic noise was filtered and reduced by the ventilation system. But onstage there was a deep pool of silence.

Len the stage doorman had not been in his little room, though he had left his radio on and was presumably somewhere around in the silent building. But he didn't see Charles enter.

It was ten to three. The stage had been preset for the evening performance after the morning's rehearsal. One light in the prompt corner alleviated the gloom. Charles stood behind a flat down right in a position from which he could see the entire stage. He looked up to the fly gallery. If sabotage were planned, the easiest way would be to drop a piece of scenery or a bar loaded with lights from above. But the shadows closed over and it was impossible to distinguish anything in the gloom.

The old theatre had an almost human identity. The darkness was heavy with history, strange scenes both on- and offstage that those walls had witnessed. Charles would not have been surprised to see a ghost walk, a flamboyant Victorian actor stride across the stage and boom out lines of mannered blank verse. He had in his bedsitter a souvenir photograph of Sir Herbert Tree as Macbeth from a 1911 *Playgoer and Society Illustrated,* which showed the great actor posed in dramatic chain mail, long wig and moustache beneath a winged helmet, fierce wide eyes burning. If that apparition had walked onstage at that moment, it would have seemed completely natural and right.

There was a footfall from the far corner near the pass door. Charles peered into the shadows, trying to prise them apart and see who was approaching. Agonizingly slowly the gloom revealed Lizzie Dark. She came to the center of the stage, looked around and then sat on a rostrum, one leg over the other swinging nervously. She looked flushed and expectant, but a little frightened.

She hummed one of the tunes from the show, in fact the song with which Christopher Milton had promised to help her. It was five past three, but there was no sign of her mentor.

As Charles watched, she stiffened and looked off into the shadows of the opposite wings. She must have heard something. He strained his ears and heard a slight creak. Wood or rope taking strain maybe.

Lizzie apparently dismissed it as one of the unexplained sounds of the old building and looked round front again. Then she rose from her seat and started to move gently round the stage in the steps of the dance which accompanied the song she was humming. It was not a flamboyant performance, just a slow reminder of the steps, the physical counterpart to repeating lines in one's head.

Charles heard another creak and slight knocking of two pieces of wood from the far wings, but Lizzie was too absorbed in her memorizing to notice. The creaks continued, almost in rhythm, as if something were being unwound. Lizzie Dark danced on.

Charles looked anxiously across into the wings, but he could see nothing. His eye was caught by a slight movement of a curtain up above, but it was not repeated. Just a breeze.

The noise, if noise there was, had come from the wings. He peered across at the large flat opposite him and wished for X-ray eyes to see behind it. There was another, more definite movement from above.

He took in what was happening very slowly. He saw the massive scaffolding bar with its load of lights clear the curtains and come into view. It hung suspended for a moment as if taking aim at the oblivious dancing girl and then started its descent.

With realization, Charles shouted, "Lizzie!"

She froze and turned towards him, exactly beneath the descending bar.

"Lizzie! The lights!"

Like a slow motion film she looked up at the massive threatening shape. Charles leapt forward to grab her. But as he ran across the stage, his feet were suddenly jerked away from him. His last thought was of the inadvisability of taking laughs from Christopher Milton, as the Star Trap gave way and plummeted him down to the cellar.

CHAPTER 17

THE FIRST THING he was conscious of was pain, pain as if his body had been put in a bag of stones and shaken up with them. And, rising above all the others, a high, screaming pain of red-hot needles in his right ankle.

He lay like an abandoned sack at the bottom of the Star Trap shaft. It was even darker in the cellar. He didn't know whether or not he had passed out, but time, like everything else, seemed disjointed. He remembered crying out to Lizzie, then crying out as he fell and then he remembered being there swimming in pain. There was an interval between, but whether of seconds or hours he didn't know.

He was aware of some sort of commotion, but he couldn't say exactly where. Onstage maybe, or in the auditorium. A door to the cellar opened and light flooded in.

Len was the first to arrive. The old doorman came towards him nervously, as if afraid of what he would see. "It's all right. I'm alive," Charles said helpfully, hoping he was speaking the truth.

"Who is it? Mr. Paris?"

"That's right. Is Lizzie all right?"

"Lizzie?"

"Lizzie Dark. Onstage. There was a bar of lights that—"

"It missed her. She's all right."

"Thank God."

"Can you move?"

"I wouldn't like to make the experiment."

Other people came down to the cellar. Lizzie. She looked pale and on the verge of hysterics. Some of the staff from the general manager's office who had heard the commotion arrived. So did Dickie Peck. Spike and a couple of his stage crew came from the workshop. Charles lay there in a daze of pain. He knew that he had been the victim of another of Christopher Milton's insane jealousies, but there seemed nothing to say and talking was too much effort.

They carried him upstairs. Spike and another of his men took an arm each. As the shock of the various pains subsided, it was the ankle that hurt most. It was agony when it dragged on the ground, so they lifted him up to sit on their joined hands. It still hurt like hell.

Since the dressing-rooms were up more stairs they took him into Len's little room by the stage door. There was a dilapidated sofa on which he was laid. The general manager's staff went back to phone for an ambulance. Len went off to take some tea, which was his remedy for most conditions. Dickie Peck and Lizzie Dark vanished somewhere along the way. Spike stayed and felt Charles' bones expertly. "Used to do a bit of first aid." His diagnosis was hopeful for everything except the ankle. Charles wouldn't let him get near enough to manipulate it, but Spike insisted on removing his shoe. Charles nearly passed out with pain.

"Spike," he said, when he was sufficiently recovered to speak again. "That Star Trap, it must have been tampered with."

"Yes."

"The locking bar was right out of position."

"Yes, and someone had scored through the leather hinges with a razor blade. It was a booby-trap, meant for anyone who stepped on it."

"I think it was meant specifically for one person."

"What do you mean?"

"Never mind. You'll all know soon enough."

"Hm?"

"Well, this sabotage to the show can't go on, can it?"

"You think it's a connected sequence of sabotage?"

"Sure of it. And after today I think a police investigation can be started. It's sad."

"Sad?"

"Sad because we're dealing with a madman."

"Ah."

There was no point in hiding the facts now. It would all come out soon. "Christopher Milton. A good example of the penalties of *stardom!*"

"So it was him all along. I wondered." There was suppressed excitement in Spike's voice as if at the confirmation of a long-held suspicion.

"Yes."

A pause ensued and in the silence they both became aware of Len's radio, which was still on. ". . . so all I can say in answer to that question is—I beg yours?"

It was Christopher Milton's voice. An American female voice came back, "Well, on that note, thank you very much, Christopher Milton."

A hearty male voice took it up. "Well, there it was—an exclusive for us here in the studio on Radio Brighton—for the past half hour you've been listening to Christopher Milton live. And just a reminder that *Lumpkin!* is at the Queen's Theatre until tomorrow and it opens in the West End at the King's Theatre on November 27th. And incidentally the interviewer with Christopher Milton was Suzanne Horse."

"Horst," said Suzanne's voice insistently.

Spike went to turn off the radio. Too quickly. He turned back defensively to Charles. The light caught him from behind and only the shape of his face showed. The blurring marks of acne were erased and the outline of his features appeared as they must have done when he was a boy.

Charles recognized him instantly and like the tumblers of a combination lock all the details of the case fell into place and the door swung open. "Gareth Warden," he said softly.

"What?"

"Gareth, if Christopher Milton has just been in the studio at Radio Brighton, he couldn't have been here tampering with the Star Trap."

"He could have done it earlier and left it as a booby-trap."

"And released the bar of lights to fall on Lizzie Dark?"

There was a silence. Spike, or Gareth Warden, seemed to be summoning up arguments to answer this irrefutable logic. The ambulance arrived before he had mustered any.

Len fussed around as Charles was loaded on to a stretcher and taken to the ambulance. The doors were about to close when Charles heard Spike's voice say, "I think I'll come with him."

The realization of the true identity of the criminal he had been seeking seeped slowly into Charles' mind. Strangely he didn't feel afraid to have the man beside him in the ambulance.

They traveled in silence for some minutes. Then Charles asked softly, "Why did you do it all?"

Spike's voice had lost its hard professional edge and now showed more signs of Ellen da Costa's painstaking elocution lessons. "To show him up. To let people see what he was really like."

"What do you mean?"

"I mean I just realized his ambitions. All he ever wanted to do was to get his own way and destroy anyone who challenged him. He was always totally selfish. And yet the public loved him. Look at the Press, everywhere—it always says *"lovable"* Christopher Milton. I just wanted to show the public what a shit their idol really was. All I did was to put into action what he was thinking. It was wish-fulfillment for him. Everyone who got in his way just vanished. That's what he wanted."

"But he never actually hurt anyone."

"But he wanted to, don't you see? He was never lovable, just evil."

"And you hoped to bring public disgrace on him?"

"Yes."

"But how? You must have realized that sooner or later you were going to make a mistake, commit some crime at a time when he had an alibi. Like this afternoon, for instance. He'd never have been convicted."

"He didn't need to be convicted. The disgrace of the allegation would have been enough. Reports of the investigation would have brought up all the rows at rehearsals and showed the kind of person he really was."

"But what made you think that there would be an investigation? The management have done everything to keep the whole affair quiet."

"Ah, but they put you in the cast."

"You knew I was there to investigate?"

"I was suspicious early on and when I saw you with Winifred Tuke's gin bottle, I was certain. That's why I fed you so much information, why I planted the clues for you in his car, why I told you to ask Julian Paddon about him."

"I see." Charles' detective achievements were suddenly less remarkable. "Why did you hate him so much?"

"I've known him a long time. He's always been like this."

"No, there's more to it than that. Has it anything to do with Prudence Carr?"

Spike/Gareth flinched at the name. "What do you know about her?"

"Just that you were all three at stage school together, that she was very beautiful and talented, that nothing has been heard of her for some time, that you and he were both maybe in love with her."

"I was in love with her. He was never in love with anyone but himself. His marriage broke up, didn't it?"

"But he wasn't married to Prudence," Charles probed gently.

"No, he wasn't. He didn't marry her."

"What do you mean?"

"He just took up with her, he unsettled her. He . . . I don't know . . . he changed her."

"In what way?"

"He destroyed her confidence. He crushed her with his ego. She could have been . . . so good, such a big star, and he just undermined her. She never stood a chance of making it after she met him."

"A lot of people don't make it in the theatre for a lot of reasons."

"No, it was him. He destroyed her. Because he knew she was better and more talented than he was. She stood in his way." His words were repeated in the monotone of obsession.

"And where is she now?"

"I've no idea. But wherever she is, she's nothing—nothing to what she could have been."

"And you loved her?"

"Yes."

"Did she love you?"

"Yes, at first. Then he came along . . . I wanted to marry her. She refused. Said she loved him. That's impossible. There is nothing about him to love."

"And what happened to you? Why did you give up acting? I know you started at Cheltenham."

"My, you have done your homework. Why did I give up acting? I gave it up because nobody wanted to employ me. I'd had a good run as a child star, but it's difficult to make the break from child to juvenile. And I lost my looks, which didn't help. I developed this acne, my hair turned darker. Nobody thought I was pretty any more. I had three years of nothing. And then I thought, stuff it, I'll go into the stage management side."

"But didn't Christopher Milton recognize you when you started on this show?"

"I don't know. I doubt it. He's totally unaware of other people."

There was another pause. The ambulance moved slowly through the Friday afternoon traffic.

Charles began again. "But, Spike, why? I can see that you hated him, I can see that you wanted revenge, but why do it this way?"

"I had to show him up in public for what he was," Spike repeated doggedly.

"But the things you had to do to achieve that . . . I mean, beating up Kevin McMahon, running Pete Masters over. . . . It's all so cruel, so mean."

"Exactly," said Spike as if this proved his point. "Christopher Milton is cruel and mean. That's what I had to show the public. I have seen inside his mind. That's what he would have wanted to happen to people."

"But he didn't do it, Spike. You did it."

"He wanted to." The line came back insistently.

"But, Spike, people got hurt. Mark Spelthorne got killed. That's murder, Spike."

"It was suicide. I had nothing to do with that."

"Do you mean it?"

"Christopher Milton drove him to suicide."

"And you didn't help him on his way?"

"No." The answer came back so casually that Charles believed it.

"But, Spike, I still can't understand why you did it."

"Perhaps you can't, but then you didn't grow up with him, you didn't see him use people, destroy people, always. You didn't see the smile of satisfaction on his face when someone was removed from his path. You didn't feel him all the time undermining your confidence. You didn't see him grinning with triumph every time he came out on top. He is a monster and the public should know it. Someone like that shouldn't be allowed to win all the time."

"What do you think made him like that?"

"Ambition for stardom. He wants to be the best. Oh, I know what it's like. I was big in my teens. I was hailed as the great white hope of English theatre. I was going to get to the top. I understand the kind of pressure that puts you under. And I know that you've got to get out of it and love people, not treat them like dirt."

"Hmm." Charles was about to comment on how Spike had treated people but he went on on another tack. "Do you think he's happy?"

"Happy? So long as he's on top, yes."

So Charles told him what he had discovered that morning, how Christopher Milton could not face life without an hour of psycho-analysis a day, how he lived in fear of discovery of his weakness, how his life was split between public acclamation and private misery. "How can he be happy when he doesn't even know who he is? His changes of mood are so violent because he has no real identity. That's why he clings to his fictional self. Lionel Wilkins is more real to him than Christopher Milton and it is only when he is in that character, hearing the adulation of an audience, that he feels alive. You hate him, you can despise his behavior, but don't ever think he's happy. His desperate concern for his career is only because he lives through it. Take it away and you kill him."

There was another long silence. Then Spike grunted, "He's a bastard." His mind couldn't cope with an idea that challenged his long-held obsession.

The ambulance swung round into the gates of the hospital.

Charles felt weak. The pain in his ankle was burning fiercely again. "The question now is," he said with effort, "what are we going to do about it."

"I suppose you report me to the police." Spike's voice was dull. "That's presumably what the management put you into the company to do—find the wrong-doer and see him brought to justice."

"On the contrary, they brought me in to the company to find the wrong-doer and to hush up the whole affair."

"Ah."

"And I don't see why I shouldn't do just that. That is, if you've been persuaded of the pointlessness of your vendetta. You cannot do worse to him than he does to himself. You cannot destroy the real Christopher Milton, because it doesn't exist."

"So in fact you're letting me off?"

"Yes, but, by God, if anything else happens in this show, you'll have the entire police force descending on you from a great height."

"And if I actually strike at the *star* himself?"

"I don't think you will."

"Well, thanks." The ambulance came to a stop and the men got out to open the back door. "So you reckon he's a real wreck?"

"Yes. If that gives you any cause for satisfaction."

"Oh, it does, it does."

"What will you do—leave the show?"

"I'll have to, won't I?"

Charles was pulled out and placed on a trolley. Spike still didn't seem able to leave. He wanted to taste the last drop of news of his rival's degradation. "So it's driven him mad. That happens. There's a danger of that with anyone who's ever been even vaguely in contact with stardom. They lose all touch with reality."

"Yes," said Charles, but, locked in his own world, Gareth Warden seemed unaware of the irony.

PART 5

First Night

CHAPTER 18

THE FIRST NIGHT of *Lumpkin!* at the King's Theatre on Thursday, November 27th, 1975, was a major social and theatrical event. Everyone was there.

Included in everyone, though less famous and glamorous than many of the rest of everyone, were Charles Paris and his wife Frances. She had somehow heard about his accident and come down to visit him in the Brighton hospital. His injuries were not too bad. Apart from extensive bruising, the only real damage was a broken ankle. In fact, the rather gloomy young doctor who dealt with him described it as a Pott's fracture and said that with a fall like that, he was lucky not to have crushed a few vertebrae, fractured his calcaneum and broken his sternum. He was out within a week, complete with a cartoon plaster on his foot and a pair of authentic-looking tubular crutches. There was no chance of his appearing in the show and there was talk of compensation from the company. The wheel had come full circle; his identification with Everard Austick was now complete.

It was difficult to say where he stood with Frances. She had accepted his invitation to the first night and there had been no mention of Alec, the scout-master. And yet she seemed distant. Perhaps just making her point that she was no longer around whenever he needed picking up out of depression. It wasn't a tangible change, but it made him feel that if really he did want her back, he'd have to work for her.

It was like going out with someone for the first time, not knowing which way the evening would turn out.

In the crowded foyer they met William Bartlemas and Kevin O'Rourke, a pair of indefatigable first-nighters resplendent in the Victorian evening dress they always affected for such occasions. "Why, Charles . . ." exclaimed Bartlemas.

"Charles Paris . . ." echoed O'Rourke.

"What *have* you been doing to yourself . . . ?"

"You have been in the wars. . . ."

"What was it—some tart stamp on your foot . . . ?"

"I don't think you've met my wife, Frances."

"Wife? Dear, oh dear. Never knew you were married. . . ."

"Lovely to meet you though, Frances. . . ."

"Lovely, Frances darling. Such a pretty name. . . ."

"But Charles, I thought you were *in* this show. . . ."

"But obviously the leg put you out. You know what it was, O'Rourke, someone wished him luck. You know, the old theatrical saying—break a leg. . . ."

"Break a leg! Oh, that's too divine. . . ."

"Going to be a marvellous show tonight, isn't it, Charles . . . ?"

"Well, of course you'd *know*, wouldn't you? I mean, you've been working with him. Such a clever boy, isn't he, Christopher . . . ?"

"Clever? More than clever. That boy is an A1, thumping great star. If the national Press don't all agree about that in the morning, I'm a Swedish *au pair* girl. . . ."

"Oh, but they will. He is such a big star. I think he's really brought stardom back into the business. We've had all those dreary little actors with Northern accents who spend all their time saying how they're just like ordinary people. . . ."

"But stars shouldn't be like ordinary people. Stars should be larger than life. . . ."

"And Christopher Milton is . . . so big. We were reading an interview with him in one of the Sundays. . . ."

"By some American girl, Suzanne somebody . . . very good it was. . . ."

"Oh, super. And you've been working with him, Charles. That must have been wonderful. . . ."

"Yes, but wonderful. . . ."

* * *

It was very strange seeing a show he had been with for so long from out front, but perhaps less strange with *Lumpkin!* than it would have been with anything else. It had changed so much since he last saw it that it was like seeing a new show. The cast must have been working every hour there was since Brighton. And they did well. The first-night sparkle was there and they were all giving of their best.

The show had gained in consistency of style. Wally Wilson had also been working away like mad and, for all the part he played in the final product, Oliver Goldsmith might as well have taken his name off the credits. Charles reflected that in the whole case there had only been one murder—that of *She Stoops to Conquer*.

The changes had involved more cuts and now Tony Lumpkin's part totally overshadowed all the others. In less skilled hands than those of Christopher Milton it would have overbalanced the show, but the star was at his brilliant best. He leapt about the stage, singing and dancing whole new numbers with amazing precision and that perfect timing which had so struck Charles at the early rehearsals in the Welsh Dragon Club. The show would be a personal triumph. It was bound to be if it succeeded at all, because no other member of the cast got a look in.

At the interval there was a buzz of satisfaction in the audience. Charles, who was feeling tired and achey after his bruises, couldn't face the rush for the bar and sat quietly with Frances. Greatly daring, like a schoolboy on his first date, he put his hand on hers and squeezed it. She returned the pressure, which made him feel ridiculously cheerful. Their hands interlocked and he felt the familiar kitchen-knife scar on her thumb.

He looked at the busy stalls. He could see Kevin McMahon in the middle of a congratulatory throng, smiling with satisfaction. Gwyneth, David Meldrum's assistant, was coming up the aisle towards him. They were like creatures from a previous existence.

Gwyneth stopped by his seat to ask how he was. He told her, but she hung around, for the first time in their acquaintance seeming to want a conversation. He asked a few idle questions about the company and production details. Running out of things to say, he asked, "Who's the new stage manager?"

"New one? Why, it's still Spike."

"Still Spike?"

"Yes, of course. He's in charge in the fly gallery tonight."

A familiar cold trickle of anticipation crept into Charles as the lights dimmed for the second act.

It continued to go well. The audience, enlivened by their gins and tonics, seemed more relaxed and receptive. The show was building up to the climax of the Chase Scene. The profusion of comic business meant that no one was aware of the butchery that the plot had undergone. The audience exploded with laughter time and again. Only Charles Paris was silent.

The Chase Scene arrived and the audience roared. Charles held his breath when it came to the Star Trap moment, but the machinery of the King's Theatre delivered its burden safely on stage at the correct time and gained an enormous laugh.

But the respite for Charles was only temporary. He knew what was happening behind the scenes. While doubles onstage continued their interweaving and dancing, the real Tony Lumpkin climbed to the gallery where he would have the Kirby wire attached to the corset he was already wearing. The audience laughed away at the action onstage while Charles fought with the nausea of horror.

Bang on cue, Christopher Milton appeared. He descended slowly from the heavens and his appearance gathered the round of applause that always attends spectacular stage effects.

The pace of his descent suddenly accelerated. The applause died as if it had been switched off. No longer was the star coming down at a controlled speed; he was free-falling. The real panic in his eyes and the jerking of his arms and legs communicated his fear to the audience. For about twenty feet he fell and then sharply the wire was taken up again and he came to rest bobbing about five feet above the stage.

There was a long pause while Charles could feel the agony of the corset cutting under the star's arms. Then Christopher Milton pulled a Lionel Wilkins face and said, "I beg yours?" The house erupted into laughter and applause.

And that was how the rest of the show went. Everything that should have got laughs did, every song was applauded to the echo and Christopher Milton could do no wrong. At the end there were twelve curtain calls and the audience was still shouting for more when the curtain came down for the last time.

Afterwards Charles, who was the least showbiz-conscious person in his profession, felt he had to go round backstage. There was an enormous melée of people outside the stage door.

He met one of the stage management struggling out against the crowd (no doubt sent by thirsty actors to stock up with drinks before the pubs closed). She recognized him. "How are you? Wasn't it marvellous tonight?"

"Great. Barbara, where's Spike?"

"Well, that's strange. I don't know. He was in the gallery and then there was that cock-up in the Chase Scene. Did you notice it?"

"I think the whole audience noticed it."

"Oh no. Apparently most of them thought it was deliberate. Anyway, Spike went off straight after that. It was very strange, he said something about some things you can't beat and that he was leaving and wouldn't be coming back. And he went. Amazing, isn't it? He always was a funny bloke."

"Yes," said Charles. "He was."

At that moment the stage door crowd surged forward and Charles and Frances found themselves swept into the theatre. Standing in the green room (he had been mobbed before he could even get to his dressing-room) was Christopher Milton. He was smiling, radiant, happy, as the world milled around him and everyone said how marvellous he was.

He saw Charles and reached out a hand to wave across the throng. "Hello. Are you better? What did you think of it?"

"Bloody fantastic," said Charles. And he meant it.

So Much Blood

Dedicated to
The City of Edinburgh

Chapter headings by Thomas Hood
(1799–1845)

CHAPTER 1

My brain is dull my sight is foul,
I cannot write a verse, or read—
Then, Pallas, take away thine Owl,
And let us have a Lark instead.

TO MINERVA—FROM THE GREEK

"MAURICE SKELLERN ARTISTES," said the voice that answered the telephone.

"Maurice—"

"Who wants him?"

"Maurice, for God's sake. I know it's you. Why you always have to go through this rigmarole of pretending you've got a staff of thousands, I don't know. It's me—Charles."

"Ah, hello. Pity about the telly series."

"Yes, it would have been nice."

"And good money, Charles."

"Yes. Still, in theory it's only been postponed. Till this P.A.s' strike is over."

"When will that be, though?"

"Don't know."

"What is a P.A. anyway? I can never understand all that B.B.C. hierarchy. Do you know what a P.A. is?"

"Vaguely." Charles Paris had a feeling that a P.A. was either a Production Assistant or a Producer's Assistant, but his knowledge of the breed was limited to an erotic night in Fulham with a girl called Angela after recording an episode of *Dr. Who.* And they had not discussed the anomalies of the P.A.s' conditions of service that led to the strike which in August 1974 was crippling B.B.C. Television's Drama and Light Entertainment Departments. "Anything else on the horizon, Maurice?"

"Had an inquiry from the Haymarket, Leicester. Might want you to direct a production of . . ." he paused, ". . . the Head Gabbler?"

"Hedda Gabler?"

"That's it."

"Could be fun. When?"

"Not till the spring."

"Great." Heavy sarcasm.

"Might be a small part in a film. Playing a German football manager."

"Oh yes?"

"But that's very vague."

"Terrific. Listen, Maurice, I've got something."

"Getting your own work, eh?"

"Somebody's got to."

"Ooh, that hurt, Charles. I try, you know, I try."

"Yes. My heart bleeds, an agent's lot is not a happy one, mournful violin plays *Hearts and Flowers.* No, it's for *So Much Comic, So Much Blood.*"

"What?"

"You know, my one-man show on Thomas Hood. Thing I did for the York Festival and the British Council recitals."

"Oh yes." The tone of Maurice's voice recalled the tiny fees of which he had got ten per cent.

"A friend of mine, guy I knew in Oxford who now lectures in the Drama Department at Derby University, has offered me a week at the Edinburgh Festival. Some show's fallen through, one the students were doing, and they're desperate for something cheap to fill the lunchtime slot. Just for a week."

"Charles, how many times do I have to tell you, you mustn't ever take something cheap? It's not official Festival, is it?"

"No, on the Fringe. I get fifty per cent of box office."

"Fifty per cent of box office on a lunchtime show on the Fringe of the Edinburgh Festival won't buy you a pair of socks. There's no point in doing it, Charles. You're better off down here. A voice-over for a commercial might come up, or a radio. Edinburgh'll cost you, anyway. Fares, accommodation."

"I get accommodation."

"But, Charles, you've got to ask yourself, is it the right thing for you to be doing, artistically?" Maurice made this moving appeal every time Charles suggested something unprofitable.

"I don't know. It's a long time since I've been to Edinburgh."

"Charles, take my advice. Don't do it."

As he emerged from Waverly Station, Charles Paris sniffed the caramel hint of breweries in the air and felt the elation which Edinburgh always inspired in him. It is, he thought, a theatrical city. The great giant's castle looms stark against the cyclorama, and from it the roofs of the Royal Mile tumble down a long diagonal. There are so many levels, like a brilliant designer's stage set. Plenty of opportunities for the inventive director. The valley of Princes Street, with a railway instead of a river and the Victorian kitsch of the Scott Memorial instead of an imposing centerpiece, is ideal for ceremonial entrances. From there, according to the play, the director can turn to the New Town or the Old. The New Town is designed for comedy of manners. Sedate, right-angled, formal, George Street and Queen Street, regularly intersected and supported by the tasteful bookends of Charlotte and Saint Andrew Squares, stand as Augustan witnesses to the Age of Reason.

The director should use the Old Town for earthier drama, scenes of low life. It is a tangle of interweaving streets, wynds and steps, ideal settings for murder and mystery, with a thousand dark corners to hide stage thugs. This is the city of Burke and Hare, of crime and passion.

The Old Town made Charles think of Melissa, an actress who had been in a show with him at the Lyceum fifteen years before. After a disastrous three months he had returned to London and his wife Frances, but Melissa had made Edinburgh seem sexy, like a prim nanny shedding her gray uniform behind the bushes in the park.

On Sunday August 11, 1974 the city still felt sexy. And this time Charles Paris was free. He had left Frances in 1962.

Everything smelt fresh after recent rain. Charles felt vigorous, younger than his forty-seven years. He decided to walk. Frances would have caught a bus; she had an uncanny ability for comprehending any bus system within seconds of arrival in town. Charles would walk. He set off, swinging his holdall like a schoolboy. The only shadow on his sunny mood was the fact that Scottish pubs are closed on Sundays.

He couldn't miss the house in Coates Gardens. Among the self-effacing homes and hotels of the Edinbourgeois there was one whose pillars and front door were plastered with posters.

D.U.D.S. ON THE FRINGE!
Derby University Dramatic Society presents
*FOUR WORLD PREMIÉRES!
ONE GREAT CLASSIC!
*A Midsummer Night's Dream—Shakespeare's Immortal Comedy REVISUALIZED BY Stella Galpin-Lord.
*Mary, Queen of Sots—A Mixed-Media Satire of Disintegration by Sam Wasserman.
*Isadora's Lovers—Lesley Petter's Examination of a Myth in Dance and Song.
*Who Now?—a Disturbing New Play by Martin Warburton.
*Brown Derby—Simply the Funniest Late-Night Revue on the Fringe.

There followed lists of dates, times and prices for this complicated repertoire, from which Charles deduced that the show he was replacing was *Isadora's Lovers*. For some reason Lesley Petter was unable to Examine the Myth in Dance and Song. He felt annoyed that the poster had not been amended to advertise *So Much Comic, So Much Blood*. They had known he was coming for more than a week. And publicity is enormously important when you're competing with about two hundred and fifty other shows.

The doorbell immediately produced a plain, roly-poly girl in irrevocably paint-spattered jeans.

"Hello, I'm Charles Paris."

"Oh Lord, how exciting, yes. I'm Pam Northcliffe, Props. Just zooming down to the hall to make the axe for *Mary*. Going to build it around this." She waved a squeezy washing-up liquid bottle. "So the blood spurts properly."

"Ah."

"Brian's in the office. Through there." She scurried off down the road, bouncing like a beach-ball.

The shining paint on the partitions of the hall was evidence that the house had only recently been converted into flats. The door marked "Office" in efficient Letraset was ajar. Inside it was tiny, the stub-end of a room unaccounted for in the conversion plans. A young man in a check shirt and elaborate tie was busy on the telephone. He airily indicated a seat.

"Look, I know it's the weekend, I know you're working every hour there is. So are we. It's just got to be ready. Well, what time tomorrow? No, earlier than that. Midday . . ."

The wrangle continued. Charles looked at a large baize-covered board with the optimistic Letraset heading, "What the Press says about D.U.D.S." So far the Press had not said much, which was hardly surprising, because the Festival did not begin for another week. In the middle of the board was one cutting. A photograph of a girl, and underneath it:

UNDERSTUDY STEPS IN

It's an ill wind, they say, and it's certainly blown some good the way of Derby University Dramatic Society's Anna Duncan. When one of the group's actresses, Lesley Petter, broke her leg in an accident last week, suddenly 20-year-old Anna found she was playing two leading rôles—in a play and a revue, both to be seen at the Masonic Hall in Lauriston Street when the Festival starts. Says Anna, "I'm really upset for poor Lesley's sake, but it's a wonderful chance for me. I'm very excited." And with lovely Anna onstage, Fringe-goers may get pretty excited too!

The reporter, whatever his shortcomings in style, was right about one thing. Even in the blurred photograph the girl really was lovely. She was pictured against the decorative railings of Coates Gardens. Slender body, long legs in well-cut jeans, a firm chin and expertly cropped blond hair.

The telephone conversation finished and Charles received a busy professional handshake. "I'm Brian Cassells, Company Manager."

"Charles Paris."

"I recognized you. So glad you could step in at such short notice. Nice spread, that." He indicated the cutting. "Helps having a pretty girl in the group. Important, publicity."

"Yes," said Charles.

The edge in his voice was not lost on Brian Cassells. "Sorry about yours. That's what I was on to the printer about. Posters and handouts ready tomorrow."

"Good. Did you get the stuff I sent up? The cuttings and so on."

"Yes. Incorporated some in the poster. They were very good."

Yes, thought Charles, they were good. He particularly cherished the one from the *Yorkshire Post*. "There are many pleasures to be had at the York Festival, and the greatest of these is Charles Paris' *So Much Comic, So Much Blood*."

The Company Manager moved hastily on, as if any pause or small talk might threaten his image of efficiency. "Look, I'll show you the sleeping arrangements and so on."

"Thanks. When will I be able to get into the hall to do some rehearsal?"

"It's pretty tied up tomorrow. Stella's having a D.R. of the *Dream*. Then Mike's in with *Mary*. That's Tuesday morning. Tuesday afternoon should be O.K. Just a photocall for *Mary*. A few dramatic shots of Rizzio's murder, that sort of thing, good publicity. Shouldn't take long."

The sleeping arrangements were spartan. The ground-floor rooms were filled with rows of ex-army camp-beds for the men, with the same upstairs for the girls. No prospects of fraternization. "It's not on moral grounds," said Brian, "just logistical. Kitchen and dining-room in the basement if you want a cup of coffee or something. I'd better get back. Got to do some Letrasetting."

Charles dumped his case on a vacant camp-bed which wobbled ominously. The room had the stuffy smell of male bodies. It brought back National Service, the first dreary barracks he'd been sent to in 1945, to train for a war that was over before he was trained. He opened a window and enjoyed the relief of damp-scented air.

He felt much more than forty-seven as he sat over the skinny coffee in the basement, surrounded by blue denim. An epicene couple were wrapped round each other on the sofa. A plump girl was relaxing dramatically on the floor. Three young men with ringlets were hunched over the table discussing The Theatre.

"What it's got to do is reflect society, and if you've got a violent society, then it's got to reflect that."

The reply came back in a slightly foreign accent. German? Dutch? "Bullshit, Martin. It's more complex than that. The Theatre interprets events. Like when I'm directing something, I don't just want to reflect reality. Not ordinary reality. I try to produce a new reality."

Charles winced as the other took up the argument. "What is reality, though? I reckon if people are getting their legs blown off in Northern Ireland, if they're starving in Ethiopia, you've got to show that. Even if it means physically assaulting the audience to get them to react."

"So where is the violence, Martin? Onstage? In the audience?"

"It's everywhere. It's part of twentieth-century living. And we've got to be aware of that. Even, if necessary, be prepared to be violent ourselves, in a violent society. That's what my play's about."

"That, Martin, is so much crap."

The youth called Martin flushed, stood up and looked as if he was about to strike his opponent. Then the spasm passed and, sulkily, he left the room. Charles deduced he must be Martin Warburton, author of *Who Now?* a Disturbing New Play.

The other ringletted youth looked around for someone else to argue with. "You're Charles Paris, aren't you?"

"Yes."

"What do you think about violence in the theatre?"

"There's a place for it. It can make a point." Charles knew he sounded irretrievably middle-aged.

The youth snorted. "Yes, hinted at and glossed over in West End comedies."

Charles was riled. He did not like being identified exclusively with the safe commercial theatre. His irritant continued. "I'm directing *Mary, Queen of Sots.* That's got violence in perspective. Lots of blood." He turned on Charles suddenly. "You ever directed anything?"

"Yes." With some warmth. "In the West End and most of the major reps in the country."

"Oh." *Mary, Queen of Sots'* director was unimpressed. "What, long time ago?"

"No, quite recently." Charles' anger pushed him on. "In fact I'm currently considering a production of *Hedda Gabler* at the new Haymarket Theatre in Leicester."

"Big deal." The ringletted head drooped forward over a Sunday newspaper.

Without making too much of a gesture of it, Charles left the room. In the hall he checked with a D.U.D.S. program for details of his antagonist.

MICHAEL VANDERZEE—After work in experimental theatre in Amsterdam and in Munich under Kostbach, he made his directorial debut in this country with *Abusage* by Dokke at the Dark Brown Theatre. He has been responsible for introducing into this country the works of Schmiss and Turzinski, and recently directed the latter's *Ideas Towards a Revolution of the Audience* at the Theatre Upstairs. Drawing inspiration from the physical disciplines and philosophies of East and West, he creates a theatre indissolubly integrated with working life.

"Huh," said Charles to himself. As he started towards his dormitory, a key turned in the front door lock and a middle-aged man in a sandy tweed suit appeared. He smiled and extended his hand. "Hello, you must be Charles Paris."

"Yes."

"I'm James Milne, known to the students as the Laird. I live in the flat on the top floor. Would you like to come up for a drink?"

It was the most welcome sentence Charles had heard since he arrived. Edinburgh regained its charm.

"Yes, I agree. I am an unlikely person to be involved with Derby University Dramatic Society. It's a coincidence. I've only moved into this house recently and I sold my previous one in Meadow Lane to a lad called Willy Mariello. Have you met him yet?"

"No."

"No doubt you will. He's with this lot. Well, the conversion here was more or less finished, but the summer's not a good time to get permanent tenants—holidays, the Festival and so on. So when Willy said this crowd was looking for somewhere, I offered it for six weeks."

"Brave."

"I don't know. They pay rent. There's no furniture, not much they can break. And they've sworn they'll clean everything up before they go. I just hurry in and out and don't dare look at the mess."

"What about noise?"

"This flat's pretty well insulated."

"Largely by books, I should imagine. And this has only just been converted too? I can't believe it."

The Laird glowed. Obviously Charles had said the right thing. But the flat did seem as if it had been there for centuries. Brown velvet upholstery and the leather spines of books gave the quality of an old sepia photograph. A library, an eyrie at the top of the building, it reminded Charles of his tutorials at Oxford. Dry sherry and dry donnish jokes. True, the sherry was malt whisky, but there was something of the don about James Milne.

"You like books?" He half-rose from his chair, eager, waiting for the slightest encouragement.

Charles gave it. "Yes."

"They're not first editions or anything like that. Well, not many of them. Just good editions. I do hate this paperback business. Some of the Dickens are quite good. And that *Vanity Fair* is valuable . . ."

Charles wondered if he was about to receive a lecture on antiquarian books, but the danger passed. ". . . and this edition of Scott might be worth something. Though not to the modern reader. Nobody reads him nowadays. I wonder why. Could it be because he's a dreary old bore? I think it must be. Even we Scots find him a bit of a penance." He laughed. A cozy-looking man; probably mid-fifties, with a fuzz of white hair and bushy black eyebrows.

Charles laughed, too. "I've read half of *Ivanhoe*. About seven times. Like *Ulysses* and the first volume of Proust. Never get any further." He relaxed into his chair. "It's very comforting, all those books."

"Yes. 'No furniture is so charming as books, even if you never open them or read a single word.' The Reverend Sydney Smith. Not a Scot himself, but for some time a significant luminary of Edinburgh society. Yes, my books are my life."

Charles smiled. "Wasn't it another Edinburgh luminary, Robert Louis Stevenson, who said, 'Books are all very well in their way, but they're a mighty bloodless substitute for real life?' "

James Milne chuckled with relish, which was a relief to Charles, who was not sure that he had got the quotation right. "Excellent, Charles, excellent, though the point is arguable. Let me give you a refill."

It turned out that the Laird had been a schoolmaster at Kilbruce, a large public school just outside Edinburgh. "I retired from there some five years ago. No, no, I'm not as old as all that. But when my mother died I came into some money and property—this house, an estate called Glenloan on the West coast, a terrace of cottages. For the first time in my life I didn't have to work. And I thought, why should I put up with the adolescent vagaries of inky boys when I much prefer books."

"And inky boys presumably don't appreciate books?"

"No. Some seemed to—appeared to be interested, but . . ." He rose abruptly. "A bite to eat, perhaps?"

Half a Stilton and Bath Olivers were produced. The evening passed pleasantly. They munched and drank, swapped quotations and examined the books. Their crossword minds clicked, and allusion and anecdote circled round each other. It was the sort of mild intellectual exercise that Charles had not indulged in since his undergraduate days. Very pleasant, floating on a cloud of malt whisky above everyday life. The book-lined room promised to be a welcome sanctuary from the earnest denim below.

Eventually Charles looked at his watch. Nearly one o'clock. "I must go down to the bear-pit."

"Don't bother. I'll make up the sofa for you here."

"No, no. Downstairs is the bed I have chosen, and I must lie on it."

The bed he had chosen had been left vacant for good reason. At half-past three he woke to discover it had come adrift in the middle and was trying to fold him up like a book. He wrestled with it in the sweaty breathing dorm and then tottered along to the lavatory.

It was locked and a strange sound came from inside. As Charles took advantage of the washbasin in the adjacent bathroom, he identified the noise through a haze of malt. It was a man crying.

CHAPTER 2

The very sky turns pale above;
  The earth grows dark beneath;
The human Terror thrills with cold,
    And draws a shorter breath—
An universal panic owns
  The dread approach of DEATH!

THE ELM TREE

THE EDINBURGH FREEMASONS' revenue must shoot up during the Festival, because they seem to own practically every strange little hall in the city. Each year the gilded columns of these painted rooms witness the latest excesses of Fringe drama, and the gold-leaf names of Grand Masters gaze unmoved at satire, light-shows, nudity or God-rock, according to theatrical fashion.

On the Monday morning the Temple of the Masonic Hall, Lauriston Place, was undergoing *A Midsummer Night's Dream*, Shakespeare's Immortal Comedy Revisualized by Stella Galpin-Lord. As Charles Paris slipped in, it was clear that the process of revisualization had hit a snag. The snag was that Stella Galpin-Lord was having a directorial tantrum.

"Where are those bloody fairies? Didn't you hear your bloody cue? For Christ's sake, concentrate! Bottom, get up off your backside . . ."

As she fulminated, it was clear to Charles that Stella Galpin-Lord was not a student. Far from it. The over-dramatic name fitted the over-dramatic figure. She was wearing rehearsal black, a polo-

necked pullover tight over her presentable bosom, and clinging
flared trousers less kind to her less presentable bottom. Honey-
blonded hair was scraped back into a broad knotted scarf. The efforts of make-up—skillful pancake, elaborate eyes and a hard
line of lipstick—drew attention to what they aimed to disguise.
The slack skin of her face gave the impression of a badly erected
tent, here and there pulled tight by misplaced guyropes. The
tantrum and her twitchy manner with a cigarette spelled trouble to
Charles. Neurotic middle-aged actresses are a hazard of the profession.

"Well, don't just amble on. You're meant to be fairies, not nav-
vies. For God's sake! Amateurs! This show opens in less than a week
and we don't get in the hall again till Thursday. Good God, if you
don't know the lines now . . . Where is the prompter? Where is
the bloody prompter!"

Charles, who had only come down to check the details of staging
in the hall, decided it could wait and sidled out.

Back in Coates Gardens he looked for somewhere to work. In
the men's dormitory a youth was strumming a guitar with all the
versatility of a metronome. Sounds from upstairs indicated a revue
rehearsal in the girls' room. Charles felt tempted to seek sanctuary
with James Milne again, but decided it might be an imposition. He
went down to the dining room. Mercifully it was empty.

With a tattered script of *So Much Comic, So Much Blood* open on
the table, he started thumbing through an ancient copy of Jerrold's
edition of Hood, looking for *The Dundee Guide,* an early poem
which might add a little local interest for an Edinburgh audience.
It was not there. He was perplexed for a moment, until he remembered that only a fragment of the work survived and was
in the *Memorials of Thomas Hood.* He started thumbing through
that.

So Much Comic, So Much Blood had begun life as a half-hour radio
program. Then Charles had added to the compilation and done
the show for a British Council audience. Over the years he had
inserted different poems, played up the comic element and drama-
tized some of the letters. The result was a good hour's show and he
was proud of it.

He was also proud that its evolution predated the success of Roy

Dotrice in John Aubrey's *Brief Lives,* which had set every actor in the country ransacking literary history for one-man shows.

"I'm going to make some coffee. Would you like some?" Charles looked up at the girl in the photograph, Anna Duncan.

"Please." She disappeared into the kitchen. He stared with less interest at the extant fragments of *The Dundee Guide.*

"Here's the coffee. Do carry on."

"Don't worry. I like being disturbed. I'm Charles Paris."

"I know. Recognize you from the box. It's very good of you to step into the breach."

"I gather you did more or less the same thing."

"Yes. Poor Lesley." A brief pause. "What is your show about?"

"Thomas Hood."

She did not recognize the name. "Why's it called what it is?"

"Because he once wrote 'No gentleman alive has written so much Comic and spitten so much blood within six consecutive years.' In a letter to *The Athenaeum* actually."

"Oh. I don't think I've even heard of Thomas Hood."

"I'm sure you know his poems."

"Do I?"

"Yes. 'I remember, I remember . . .' "

" '. . . the house where I was born?' That one? I didn't know that was Hood."

"It was. And *No-vember. Faithless Sally Brown.* Lots of stuff."

"Oh."

Her eyes were unusual. Very dark, almost navy blue. Her bare arm on the table was sunburned, its haze of tiny hairs bleached golden.

"What are you reading at Derby?"

"French and Drama in theory. Drama in practice."

"Last year?"

"One more. If I bother." The navy eyes stared at him evenly. It was pleasantly disconcerting.

"I've just been down to the hall. Saw the lovely Stella Galpin-Lord. A mature student, I thought."

Anna laughed. "She lectures in Drama."

"Ah. She seemed rather to have lost her temper this morning."

"That's unusual. She's always uptight, but doesn't often actually explode."

"She was exploding this morning."

"Everyone's getting on each other's nerves. Living like sardines in this place. I'm glad I'm in a flat up here." (On reflection, Charles was glad she was too.) "And people keep arguing about who's rehearsing what when, and who's in the hall. It's purgatory."

"You're rehearsing the revue at the moment?"

"Yes, but I've got a break. They're doing a new number—about Nixon's resignation and Ford coming in. Trying to be topical."

"Is the revue going to be good?"

"Bits."

"Bits?" Charles smiled. Anna smiled back.

At that moment Pan Northcliffe bounded into the room, her arms clutching two carrier bags which she spilled out on the table. "Hello. Oh Lord, I must write my expenses. I'm spending so much on props."

"What have you been buying?" asked Charles.

"Oh Lord, lots of stuff for *Mary*."

"Did you get the cardboard for my ruff?"

"No, Anna, will do, promise. No, I was getting black crepe for the execution. And all these knives that I've got to make retractable. And some make-up and stuff."

"Good old Leichner's," said Charles, picking up a bottle which had rolled out of one of the carriers. It was labeled "Arterial Blood."

"What other sort is there?"

"There's a brighter one, for surface cuts. It's called . . ." Pam paused for a moment. ". . . oh, I forget." And she bustled on. "Look, I'm not going to be in your way, am I? I've got to do these knives. I was going to do them on the table, if you . . ."

"No, it's O.K. I've finished." Charles resigned himself to the inevitable. Anna returned to her rehearsal and he went to see if the men's dormitory was still being serenaded.

Passing the office, he heard sounds of argument, Michael Vanderzee's voice, more Dutch in anger, struggling against Brian Cassells' diplomatic tones. ". . . and the whole rehearsal was ruined yesterday because that bloody fool Willy wasn't there. Look, I need more time in the hall."

"So does everyone."

"But I've lost a day."

"That's not my fault, Mike. Look, I've worked out a schedule that's fair to everyone."

"Bugger your schedule."

"It's there on the wall-chart—"

"Oh, bugger your wall-chart!" Michael Vanderzee flung himself out of the office, past Charles, to the front door. The windows shook as it slammed behind him.

Brian Cassells appeared in the hall looking flushed. When he saw Charles, he smoothed down his pin-striped suit as if nothing had happened. "Ah, morning." The efficient young executive was reborn. "I've . . . er . . . I've got your posters. Just picked them up."

"Oh, great."

"In the office."

On the desk were two rectangular paper parcels. "A thousand in each," said Brian smugly. "Did the Letrasetting myself. Do have a look."

Charles tore the paper and slid one of the printed sheets out. As he looked at it, Brian Cassells grinned. "O.K.?"

Charles passed the paper over. It was headed:

D.U.D.S. ON THE FRINGE
. . . and the greatest of these is Charles Paris' *So Much Comic, So Much Blood*.

"Oh," said Brian, "I am sorry."

Undisturbed rehearsal in the Coates Gardens house was clearly impossible. Charles decided a jaunt to one of his Edinburgh favorites, the Museum of Childhood in the Royal Mile, might not come amiss. It was only Monday and there was a whole week till he had to face an audience. And with Brian Cassells in charge of publicity, the chances were against there being an audience anyway.

Back at the house late afternoon, he found Martin Warburton hovering in the hall, as if waiting for him. "You're Charles Paris, aren't you?"

"Yes."

"I've written this play. *Who Now?* We're doing it. I want you to read it." A fifth carbon copy was thrust forward.

"Oh, thank you. I'd like to."

"You don't know. You might like to; you might think it was a waste of time."

"I'm sure you wouldn't have written it if you thought it was a waste of time."

The boy looked at Charles fiercely for a moment, then burst into loud laughter. "Yes, I might. That's exactly what I might have done."

"Everything we do is just random. I happened to write this. It's just chance. I might have written anything else. It's nothing."

"I know sometimes it seems like that, but very few things are random—"

"Don't patronise me!" Martin's shout was suddenly loud, as if the volume control on his voice had broken. He reached out to snatch the play back, then changed his mind, rushed out of the house and slammed the door.

In spite of Brian Cassell's assurances, the Masonic Hall was not free for Charles to rehearse in on the Tuesday afternoon. When he arrived at two o'clock Michael Vanderzee had just started a work-shop session with the *Mary* cast and most of the *Dream* lot too. Brian was not there to appeal to (he'd apparently gone down to London for a Civil Service interview), so Charles sat at the back of the hall and waited.

Everyone except Michael was lying stretched out on the floor. ". . . and relax. Feel each part of your body go. From the extremi-ties. Right, your fingers and toes, now your hands and feet. Now the forearms and your calves—feel them go . . ."

Charles' attitude to this sort of theatre was ambivalent. He had no objection to movement classes and workshop techniques. They were useful exercises for actors, and kept them from getting over-analytical about their "art." All good stuff. Until there was a show to put on. At that point they became irrelevant and the expediency of getting everything ready for the opening left no time for self-indulgence.

Michael Vanderzee (who drew inspiration from the physical disciplines of East and West and created a theatre indissolubly integrated with working life) obviously did not share these views. "Right. O.K. Now I want you to sit in pairs, and when I clap, you start to tell each other fairy stories. And you've got to concentrate so hard, you tell your story and you don't listen to the other guy. Really concentrate. O.K. I clap my hands."

While the assembly shouted out a cacophony of Red Riding Hood and Goldilocks, Charles looked down at Anna. Squatting on the floor, mouthing nonsense, she still appeared supremely self-possessed. Her T-shirt did nothing to hide her contours and the interest she had started in him was strengthened.

The door of the hall opened noisily. An enormously tall young man in blue denim with a Jesus Christ hairstyle strolled purposefully up the aisle. "Willy!" roared Michael. "Where the hell have you been? Why weren't you at rehearsal this morning?"

"I had things to do." The voice was sharp and the accent Scottish.

"You've got things to do here as well. I had to drag you in yesterday."

"Piss off." Willy collapsed into a chair in the front row, ungainly as a stick insect.

"Look, do you want to be in this show or not? You've got to rehearse."

"I don't mind rehearsing. But I don't see why I should waste time poncing about with relaxation and pretending I'm a pineapple and all that. I'm only meant to be doing the music."

"You're playing Rizzio in the show, and you're meant to be part of an ensemble."

Willy gave a peculiarly Scottish dismissive snort. "All right, all right. What do you want me to do?"

"I want you to shout, all of you. Scream your heads off. Really uninhibited screams. Let everything go. Right. When I clap."

The noise was appalling. Charles sunk into his chair with hands over his ears. It was going to be a long time before he got the stage to himself.

When the baying mouths onstage had finally closed, he uncovered his ears and heard another sound close behind him. A sniff. He turned to see the ship-wrecked face of Stella Galpin-Lord, who had just slipped into the hall. She saw him and blew her nose.

At that moment Pam Northcliffe bustled in, her arms as ever full of parcels and packages. "Hello, Charles," she hissed loudly. He grinned at her.

"Just brought down the props for the *Mary* photocall."

"All O.K.?" he whispered.

"Oh Lord, I suppose so. Just about. I was up till two last night doing the daggers."

"Work all right?"

"Yes." She showed him her artifacts proudly. Charles picked up one of the knives. Its metal blade had been replaced by silver-painted plastic which slid neatly back into the handle. He pressed it into his hand. "Very good."

"Oh. I'm afraid the paint's not quite dry."

Charles looked down at the silver smudge on his palm. "Never mind."

"What's Mike up to now?"

"God knows."

"All right. Now we're relaxed, all uninhibited. Now an ensemble is people who know each other. Love each other, hate each other. We try hate. Right, as we've done it before. Somebody stands in the middle and the others shout hatred at him. Doesn't matter what you say, any lies, anything. Hate, hate. We purge the emotions.

"O.K., Willy, you first. Stand in the middle. We form a circle round. And we shout. Ah, hello, Stella, you join our workshop?"

"Might learn something," she said patronizingly.

"You might, you might. Hey, Charles Paris. You want to learn something too?"

Charles choked back his first instinctive rejoinder and meekly said, "Yes, O.K." Enter into the spirit of the thing. Don't be a middle-aged fuddy-duddy.

The large circle round Willy Mariello waited for the signal. Michael clapped his hands and they shouted. Abuse poured out.

Young faces swelled with obscenities. Stella Galpin-Lord screamed, "Bastard! Bastard!" her mouth twisting and pulling a whole map of new lines on her face. Anna's expression was cold and white. Martin Warburton almost gibbered with excitement. And Charles himself found it distressingly easy to succumb, to scream with them. It was frightening.

Another clap. They subsided, panting. "Good. Catharsis. Good. O.K. Now someone else. Charles."

It was not pleasant. As the mob howled, he concentrated on Sydney Carton, borne on his tumbril to the scaffold. "It is a far, far better thing that I do now . . ." It still was not pleasant.

But a clap ended it and another victim was chosen. Then another and another. The repetition took the edge off the discomfort of being abused. Just an exercise. They finished, breathless.

"O.K. Another concentration exercise. Truth Game. You sit on the ground in pairs and ask each other questions. You have to answer with the truth instantly. If you hesitate, you start asking the questions. And don't cheat. It's more difficult than you think."

They started forming pairs. Charles saw Willy Mariello speak to Anna. She turned away and sat down opposite a colorless girl in faded denim. Willy and Charles were the only ones left standing. They squatted opposite each other.

The Scotsman sat awkwardly, his long legs bent under him like pipe-cleaners. Stuck to his denim shirt was a purple badge with white lettering: *It's Scotland's Oil.* The long messianic hair was full of white powder and the hands were flecked with white paint. His expression was aggressive and he had the hard mouth of a spoilt child. But the brown eyes were troubled.

Charles tried to think of something to ask. "What do you make of all these exercises?"

"I think they're a bloody waste of time." The answer was instant, no question about the truth there. Voices started up around and made concentration difficult.

"Um. Are you happy?"

"No."

"Why not?"

"A lot of hassles."

"Anything specific?"

"Yes."

The concentration of talking and listening over the other voices was intense. Everything seemed focused in this one conversation. Charles pressed further. "What's worrying you?"

Willy hesitated. Then, "I've found out something I'd rather not know, something that might be dangerous."

"Something about a person?"

"Yes."

"Someone connected with this group?"

A slight pause. "Yes." There was fear in the brown eyes.

Charles pushed on, mesmerized by the direction of the conversation. "Who?"

Willy opened his mouth, but paused for a moment. Stella Galpin-Lord's piercing voice was suddenly isolated. ". . . and lost my virginity when I was fourteen . . ." The spell was broken. "No, I didn't come in quick enough," said Willy. "I ask. How old are you?"

The exercise continued, but Charles felt a vague unease.

The Truth Game was followed by a Contact Game. "O.K.? We close our eyes and move around. When you touch somebody, you make contact. Feel, explore, encounter. Get to know them with your hands. This will increase your perceptions. O.K.?"

Perhaps it was by chance that the first person Charles touched was Anna. In accord with his director's instructions, he made contact, felt, explored, encountered and got to know her with his hands. Her eyes opened to a slit of navy blue. He smiled. She smiled.

"Are you rehearsing tonight?"

"No."

"Fancy dinner?"

"O.K."

Charles moved away to feel, explore and encounter someone else. His probing hand felt the arm of a tweed jacket, then up, over a chest criss-crossed with leather straps to the bristly wool of a beard.

"What the hell do you think you're doin?" The voice had the broken-bottle edge of Glasgow in it. "I'm the photographer. Who's Michael Vanderzee?"

Getting people into costume took some time. The photographer fretted and cursed. Then Michael announced he did not want posed shots; he wanted natural action shots. That involved rehearsing whole chunks of the play. The photographer cursed more.

"Right, come on. Let's do the scene of Rizzio's murder. O.K.? You'll get some good shots from this. Action stuff. Violence."

"How long's the bloody scene?"

"We'll only do the end. Three, four minutes."

"Why you can't just pose them . . . I've got some fashion pictures to do later this afternoon."

"I don't want them to look like amateur theatricals."

"Why not? That's what they bloody are."

The scene started and Charles sat under a light at the back of the hall to watch. *Mary, Queen of Sots* was written in a blank verse that was meant to sound archaic but only sounded twee. Since Willy needed a prompt every other line, it was heavy going.

"Willy, for God's sake!"

"Shut up, Michael!" The tall figure looked incongruous in doublet and hose.

"Look, for Christ's sake, can't we get these bloody photos taken? My time's expensive and these models are waiting."

"I say, we haven't got the daggers," said Martin Warburton suddenly from the recesses of a dramatic conspirator's cloak.

"Oh, Pam, where the hell are they? Here, quick. Look, the blades retract on the spring like this. O.K.? Now come on, let's get it right first time." Charles started to scan his *So Much Comic* . . . script.

Suddenly his eyes were jerked off the page by a scream. Not a theatrical workshop scream, but an authentic spinetingling cry of horror from Stella Galpin-Lord.

Onstage the scene was frozen. Anna stood white-faced in her black Tudor costume, looking down at Willy Mariello, whose great length had shrunk into a little heap on the stage. Around him were a circle of cloaked conspirators clutching daggers with retracted blades. In the center Martin Warburton gazed fascinated at the weapon in his hand. Its blade was metal and the Arterial Blood which dripped from it was not made by Leichner's.

CHAPTER 3

The BLOODY HAND significant of crime,
That glaring on the old heraldic banner,
Had kept its crimson unimpaired by time,
In such a wondrous manner.

THE HAUNTED HOUSE

THE POLICE ARRIVED promptly and were very efficient. An ambulance took Willy to hospital, but he was dead on arrival. Everyone gave statements and was told to expect further inquiries. Pam North-cliffe and Martin Warburton were taken away for questioning. A distraught Pam was returned to Coates Gardens in the early hours of the Wednesday morning and treated in the girls' dormitory with sleeping pills and inquisitive sympathy.

The atmosphere in the house throughout the Wednesday was charged with tension. The accumulated pressures of living to-gether and building up to the shows' openings were aggravated by the shock of Willy's death. Rehearsal schedules were thrown out and the continual reappearance of policemen at the house and hall got on everyone's nerves. All day Coates Gardens was full of uneasy jokes, sudden flares of temper and bursts of weeping.

Charles escaped the worst of it. Fortunately James Milne had suggested that he might be glad of a little seclusion from the com-munity hysterics and offered the sanctuary of his flat. It was a great relief to be with someone who did not want to discuss the death. Milne dismissed the subject. "I didn't know the boy well and I wasn't there at the time, so I don't feel too involved. It's an unpleasant business. And the best thing to do about unpleasant things is to put them out of your mind."

But Charles did not find it so easy. He felt he was involved and, as much as he tried to concentrate on revising *So Much Comic . . .* , his mind kept returning to the scene in the Masonic Hall. He suffered from the communal shock. And another uncomfortable feeling which he did not want to investigate.

By the Thursday morning the atmosphere among the D.U.D.S. was more settled. The Procurator-Fiscal's inquiry (which is held instead of a public inquest in Scotland) was no doubt following its private course, but the students were unaffected by it. Only Martin Warburton remained hysterical, which was hardly surprising after his long ordeal of questioning.

The police were not making any charges against him and, though the investigation was far from complete, the general impression was that they considered the death to have been a ghastly accident. The real knife had been put in one of Pam's carrier bags with the treated ones by mistake and foul play was apparently not suspected.

On the Thursday afternoon rehearsals restarted in earnest. More than in earnest, in panic. Everyone realized at the same time that a day and a half had been lost and there were still three shows opening on the following Monday. Brian Cassells' rehearsal schedule was ignored. (Since its originator was still in London he could not argue.) Stella Galpin-Lord commandeered the Masonic Hall for the rest of the day as her right and Michael Vanderzee demanded it for the Friday. Charles began to think he would be lucky to get onstage there for his actual performances. Rehearsal in the house was equally impossible. In the basement Pam and a couple of A.S.M.s were building a wall for Pyramus and Thisbe. Three smelly technicians lay over a greasy lighting plot in the men's dormitory. The Laird's flat was locked and silent. In fact Charles was relieved; his mind was too full for serious rehearsal.

Still, as a gesture of good faith, he tucked his script and Hood's *Collected Poems* under his arm before he set off into the city. It was a warm afternoon and only five o'clock. There were lots of places to sit and study in Edinburgh—Princes Street Gardens, the Castle, or it might even be worth a stroll down to Arthur's Seat. He weighed the possibilities, but was not surprised when he went straight into the nearest pub and ordered a large whisky.

He sat hunched at the bar and realized that he could not put off thinking any longer. And the one thought which he had been holding back for nearly two days resolved itself clearly in his mind.

Whatever the police thought, Willy Mariello had been murdered.

Charles could not forget the expression in those brown eyes during the Truth Game, when Willy had spoken of finding out something about someone that he would rather not know. There had been pain in that look, but also there had been fear, even horror. Whatever it was that he had found out it was nasty. Nasty enough for someone to commit murder to keep it quiet.

Charles had tried to express this suspicion to the detective who took his statement, but he knew the man did not take it seriously. Somehow the words had not come out right. "It was a moment of such concentration . . . I could see such fear in his eyes . . . It made me feel a sense of danger . . ." The further he got into it, the more tenuous the idea seemed and the more Charles knew he sounded like an effete actor emoting. In spite of polite assurances about complete investigations, that was obviously what the detective took him for. By the time he got to Charles, he had probably had a bellyful of the "vague feelings" and "premonitions" of self-dramatizing students.

And, objectively, it did sound pretty nonsensical. Charles, whose normal thought processes involved reducing everything he did to the absurd and seeing if there was anything left, was surprised that the conviction remained so strong. But it did. It was an instinct he could not deny.

Facing the fact that Willy had been murdered led automatically to the question of what should be done about it. Charles had done his duty as a citizen by voicing his suspicions, and it was quite possible that the police were already way ahead of him, working on investigations of their own. He was no longer involved.

But involvement does not cease like that. It was easy enough for James Milne to say he wanted to forget about it; he had not sat opposite Willy in the Truth Game, he had not been present at the killing.

Charles knew he had to get to the bottom of it. He recalled an earlier occasion when he had come up against crime, in the case of Marius Steen. Then he had been forced into involvement by circumstance; this time he was making a positive decision. He was not driven by any crusading fervor for the cause of justice, but he knew he would not feel at peace until he had found out all the facts.

And the only facts he had were that Willy Mariello had found out something unpleasant about one of the people involved with the Derby University Dramatic Society in Edinburgh. And that he had subsequently been killed by a dagger in the hand of Martin Warburton.

No more facts. Now on to feelings. Charles had a strong feeling that the one person who did not kill Willy was Martin Warburton. Unless he were a lunatic or playing some incredibly devious game of his own, no one would commit a premeditated murder in front of thirty people, under stage lights, with a photographer on hand. And unless Charles' suspicions about the motive were wrong, the murder was premeditated.

The elimination of Martin still left about forty suspects. Any of the students themselves or of the hangers-on who surrounded the D.U.D.S. could have switched one of the treated knives for a real one, and so stood a reasonable, though not infallible, chance of killing Willy Mariello.

Charles ordered another large whisky. A little mild investigation was called for.

Things could not have worked out better when he returned to Coates Gardens. Pam Northcliffe was in the dining room alone mixing porridge to roughcast Pyramus and Thisbe's wall. The cooks of the day were clattering about in the kitchen preparing a dinner whose main ingredient smelled like cabbage.

Pam looked up, red-eyed and guilty when he entered. "Hello."

"Hi. Feeling better?"

"Yes." Spoken with determination.

"I was going down to the pub for a drink and looking for someone to join me. Do you fancy it?"

"What? Me?"

"Yes."

"Well, I . . ." She wiped a porridgy hand on the back of her jeans, adding another streak to the existing collage. "All right."

A half of lager for Pam and, since he was now thirsty, a pint of "heavy" for Charles. "How are the props? Coming together?"

"I think so. I'm spending over my budget on them."

"D.U.D.S. will find the money."

"I hope so." She spoke with great care, as if the accumulated tension inside her might break out at the slightest provocation.

Charles knew that discussion of Willy's death might be exactly that sort of provocation. But it was what he had to investigate. He approached obliquely. "Everyone settling down a bit now."

"Yes, I suppose so. All too busy to think about it."

"That's a blessing."

"Yes." Silence. Charles tried to think how he could get her back on to the subject without causing too much pain. But fortunately he did not have to. She seemed anxious to talk it out of her system without prompting. "I don't think I'll ever get over it. It's the first time I've ever seen someone dead."

"It is nasty. But you do forget."

"I mean, you see it on films, and on the box and it all . . . well, it doesn't seem important. But when you actually see . . ." Her lower lip started to quiver.

"Don't talk about it."

As Charles hoped, she ignored his advice. "And the trouble is . . . apart from just the shock and things, I feel responsible. I mean, I was in charge of the props, so I must have got the knives mixed up."

"Do you really think you did?"

"Oh Lord, I just don't know now. I would have said definitely not. I remember counting them before I put them in my carrier bag. The police asked me all this and, you know, at the end I couldn't remember what I'd done. You think so much about something, after a time you just don't know what's true any more . . ."

"I know what you mean."

"And it's so stupid, because I shouldn't have done the knives like that anyway. Michael Vanderzee told me what he wanted, and I thought the best thing would be to get real knives with hollow handles and unscrew them and take the blades out. And Michael said that was daft and expensive and I should have improvised and . . ." Her voice wavered with the remembered rebuke. "It's the first time I've done props. And I got it all wrong. If I hadn't done the knives that way, Willy would still be alive."

Charles did not feel so certain of that. He felt sure that if the knives had not been to hand, the murderer would have found some other method. But it was not the moment to voice such suspicions. "Pam, you really mustn't blame yourself. Even if you did mix the knives up. And it's quite possible that you didn't. Somebody else may have been playing about with them and made the mistake. I mean, presumably they were just lying round the house, so anyone could get at them?" He left the question hanging disingenuously in the air.

"Yes. I suppose so."

"Toy knives have a fascination for people. Anyone might have started fooling around with them. How long were they there?"

"I was up late finishing them on Monday night. And I left them out on the table till the next morning."

"Why? So that the paint could dry?"

"Yes, but it didn't actually. I got some awful oily lacquer that stayed sticky for ages."

"Was the real knife with the others?"

"Yes, it was. You see, it was daft, but I was sort of rather proud of the ones I'd made because they did look so realistic. So I left them all out on the table."

"So that people would see them when they came down to breakfast?"

"Yes." She looked sheepish. "I haven't made lots of things and I thought they looked good."

"They did. Look very good." He almost added "Unfortunately" but realized that might be tactless. "So then they were put away while people had breakfast?"

"Yes, I put them in a carrier bag, and I thought I left the real one in a box with my scissors and sellotape and glue and all that rubbish."

"And they stayed in your carrier bag in the sitting room till you brought them down to the hall at about three o'clock?"

"Yes."

"So there was lots of time for anyone in the house to play around with them during the day and mix them up?"

"I suppose so."

"You weren't there during the morning?"

"No, I had to go out to buy some cardboard and stuff."

"Well, I should think that's what happened. Someone was fooling about with them on the Tuesday morning and mixed them up." It was not what he really meant, but Pam looked reassured. What he did mean was that the knives had been on show for every member of the company, that the murderer had realized their potential and arranged the switch when the sitting room was empty at some point during the Tuesday morning. Then he had had to wait and see what happened. Which might well have been nothing. The chances were that someone would notice the real knife before the stabbing could take place, and the murderer would have to find another method. But the impatience of the photographer at the photo-call had given no one time to inspect their weapons closely.

Though the murder method was now clear, the identity of its deviser remained obscure. From Pam's account, virtually anyone who was in the house on the Tuesday morning could have switched the knives. And that meant virtually every member of the D.U.D.S. company. Which in turn meant checking everyone's movements. Which sounded a long, boring process.

"Did you know Willy Mariello well?" Charles tried another tack. Pam blushed. "No, hardly at all."

"But you must have seen him round the University."

"What do you mean?"

"During term-time. If he was involved in the Dramatic Society."

"Oh, but he wasn't. He was nothing to do with the University."

"Then where did he come from?"

"He used to play with Puce."

"What?"

"The rock band. He was lead guitar. Until they broke up earlier this year. Oh, come on, you've heard of Puce?"

Charles had to confess he hadn't.

* * *

They walked back to Coates Gardens together. Pam seemed calmer; she had almost recaptured her customary bounce. A nice girl. No beauty, but good-natured. Needed a man who appreciated her.

She was telling him about her parents' home in Somerset as they entered the hall. At that moment Anna Duncan came out of the Office. "Hello," said Charles. She grinned.

Pam paused in mid-sentence: He realized his rudeness. "I'm so sorry. I . . . what were you saying?"

"Oh, it wasn't important. I'd better get on with my wall." And she disappeared gracelessly downstairs.

"Taking other women out when you've already stood me up," said Anna with mock reproach.

"I hardly think we'd have had a very relaxed dinner with policemen taking statements between courses."

"No, I didn't mean it."

"Rehearsing tonight?"

"Finishing at half past eight."

"Shall we pretend the last two days haven't happened, and pick up where we left off?"

"That sounds a nice idea."

"Shall I see you here?"

"No. If Mike gives us another of his rolling about on the floor workshops, I'll need to go back to the flat and have a quick bath."

"Well, let's meet at the restaurant. Do you know L'Etoile?"

"In Grindlay Street?"

"That's the one. I'll book a table for half past nine. O.K.?"

"Fine. I must get back upstairs and pretend to be a banana."

"Another of Michael Vanderzee's wonderful ideas?"

"Yes. The perception through inanimate transference of pure emotion."

"Wow."

Anna grinned again and left. Charles knocked on the office door. If Brian was back, perhaps it would be possible to arrange some rehearsal time at the Masonic Hall.

The Company Manager was wearing another executive suit, this time a beige three-piece. Charles explained his requirements and was not wholly reassured by Brian's assurance that he'd sort it out and the movement of some colored strips on the wall chart. There are certain sorts of efficiency which do not inspire confidence.

The efficiency had obviously been at work on the "What the Press says about D.U.D.S." board. It was smothered with cuttings about the death of Willy Mariello. The one person to have made a definite profit from the killing was the disgruntled Glaswegian photographer. He seemed to have sold the pictures to every newspaper in the country. Charles felt a frisson of shock at seeing the scene again. "You're not actually going to use those as publicity?"

"No," said Brian regretfully, "wouldn't be quite the thing. Not to display them. Mind you, it is an amazing spread. It's really fixed the name of D.U.D.S. in people's minds. Better than any publicity stunt you could devise. I remember last year Cambridge staged something about pretending Elizabeth Taylor was in Edinburgh. They got a girl to dress up as her and so on. Quite a lot of coverage. But nothing like this."

The note of unashamed satisfaction in Brian's voice made Charles look at him curiously. Insensitivity of that order would be wasted in the Civil Service; he should try for advertising or television. "I'm sure Willy would be glad to think that his life was lost in the cause of full houses for the D.U.D.S."

"Yes, it's an ill wind." Brian was impervious to irony.

"One thing . . . I was interested to hear that Willy Mariello wasn't a member of the University."

"No."

"How did he come to be involved in this then?"

"I don't know. I suppose he was a friend of someone."

"Who? Do you know?"

"No. I don't know any of them very well. I wasn't in D.U.D.S. I was Chairman of Ducker."

"Ducker?"

"D.U.C.A. Derby University Conservative Association."

"Oh."

"They only brought me into this because of my administrative ability."

* * *

The men's dormitory was mercifully empty and Charles managed an undisturbed run of *So Much Comic, So Much Blood*. He was encouraged to find how much he remembered. The intonation of the poems came back naturally and he began to feel the rhythm of the whole show. A bit more work and it could be quite good.

So he felt confident as he sat opposite Anna in the French restaurant in Grindlay Street. Her appearance contributed to his mood. The "quick bath" back at her flat had included a flattering amount of preparation. Just-pressed pale yellow shirt with a silly design of foxtrotting dancers on it, beautifully cut black velvet trousers. Eyelashes touched with mascara, lip-colored lipstick, cropped hair flopping with controlled abandon. All very casual, but carefully done.

"I'm looking forward to seeing the show. I'm sorry, as I said, I don't know anything about Hood."

"Not many people do."

"Was he Scottish?"

"No. His father came from Dundee, but Thomas himself only went there a couple of times. Wasn't very struck with it either. Particularly the cooking. I sicken with disgust at sight of a singed sheep's head. I cannot bring myself to endure oatmeal, which I think harsh, dry and insipid. The only time I ever took it with any kind of relish was one day on a trouting party, when I was hungry enough to eat anything. Sorry, I've just been working on it, hence the long trailer."

"What do you do in the show—dress up as Hood?"

"No, it wouldn't work. I don't like all that emotive bit—this is what the bloke was *really like*. It seems to remove the subject from reality rather than making him more real. Like historical novels about Famous People. I'm just an interpreter of Hood's work; I don't pretend to be him. Let the poems and lyrics speak for themselves. Certainly in the case of poems, it would falsify them to read them in character. They were written as public entertainments to be recited and that's how I treat them."

"So it's more a sort of recital than an acting thing?"

"I suppose so. It's mid-way between. And it has the great advantage that I don't have to learn it all and can actually refer to the book when I want to."

"Handy. So you just wear ordinary clothes for it?"

"A suit, maybe. I'd look daft dressed as Thomas Hood anyway. I haven't the figure of a stunted Victorian consumptive."

"He was another one, was he?"

"Yes. Hence the *So Much Blood* of the title. Actually there is some question as to whether it was consumption—T.B. or not T.B. It may have been rheumatic heart disease. But he spat blood, that's the main thing. It was very difficult to be a literary figure in Victorian times without spitting blood. Healthy writers started at an enormous disadvantage."

Anna laughed. "If he was ill, I think you're showing great restraint in not acting it out. Most actors leap at the chance of doing hacking coughs and their dramatic dying bit."

"So do I. But unfortunately it wouldn't be right for this show. Oh, I've died with the best of them. You should have heard my death rattle as Richard II after Sir Pierce of Exton stabbed me."

There was a moment's pause. They were both thinking the same, both seeing Willy Mariello lying on the stage at the Masonic Hall. Anna went pale.

"Sorry. Shouldn't have said that. I wasn't thinking."

"It's all right. It's just . . . so recent."

"Yes." Charles hesitated. He had decided to investigate Willy's death, but dinner with Anna was not intended to be part of that investigation; her attraction for him was not primarily as a source of information. On the other hand, here was someone who knew all the people involved, and the conversation had come round to the subject. The detective instinct overcame his baser once. "Did you know Willy well?"

"No, I wouldn't say well. I knew him."

"I was amazed to discover that he wasn't at the University. How on earth did he get involved with your lot?"

"Oh, he . . . You know he used to play with a band?"

"Yes. Puce."

"That's right. They came and did a gig at our Student's Union. I think Willy stayed around a bit. It was just round the period the band broke up. He must have met the drama lot then."

"And somebody asked him to do this show?"

"I suppose so, yes. Because he lived in Edinburgh and was kind of at a loose end. He wrote all the music, you see. I think he wanted to do something different, after the band."

"*Mary, Queen of Sots* sounds pretty different. You don't know if he made any particular friends at Derby?"

"No." She seemed to remember something. "Oh, yes. Sam. Sam Wasserman. He's the guy who wrote *Mary*. I think Willy was friendly with him. Probably it was Sam who asked him to do the music."

"I don't think I've met Sam."

"No. He's not up here. On holiday in Europe somewhere. He's American so it has to be Europe rather than any specific country. They seem to think Europe is just one country."

"So Sam's not likely to be up here at all?"

"I think he's coming up for the opening of *Mary*."

"When's that?"

"Third week. Opens on the 2nd September."

"Ah." A week after Charles' engagement finished. No chance of picking Sam Wasserman's brains. The investigation did not seem to be proceeding very fast. He decided that he would forget it for the rest of the evening. "How's your show going?"

"*Mary*'s still all over the place. We spend so much time improvising and so on, we hardly ever get near the actual script."

"And the revue?"

"Still bits. Bits are O.K. One or two of the songs are quite exciting, but . . . I don't know. See what the audience thinks on the first night."

"Monday. I'll be there. Hmm. I wonder what I should call my opening. A first lunch?"

"Why not? I'll come and see it, rehearsals permitting."

"Good." Charles refilled her glass from the cold bottle of Vouvray. "Do you want to make the theatre your career?"

"Yes." No hesitation. "Always have. Totally stage-struck."

"Hmm."

"There was a world of cynicism in that grunt. You, I take it, are not stage-struck?"

"More stage-battered at my age."

"Don't you still find it exciting?"

"Not very often, no. I can't really imagine doing anything else, but as a profession it leaves a lot to be desired. Like money, security . . ."

"I know."

"There's a lot more to it than talent. You need lots of help. You have to be tough and calculating."

"I know."

"I'm sorry. I sound awfully middle-aged. I think the prime reason for that is that I am awfully middle-aged. No, it's just that I'd hate to think of anyone going into the business who didn't know what it was about."

"I do know."

"Yes. So you're prepared for all that unemployment they talk about, sitting by the telephone, sleeping with fat old directors."

"I only sleep with who I want to sleep with." She gave him the benefit of a stare from the navy blue eyes. It was difficult to interpret whether it was a come-on or a rebuff.

He laughed the conversation on to another tack and they cheerfully talked their way through coq au vin, lemon sorbet, a second bottle of Vouvray, coffee and brandy.

The Castle loomed darkly to their left as they climbed up Johnston Terrace, but it seemed benign rather than menacing. Charles' arm fitted naturally round the curve of Anna's waist and he could feel the sheen of her skin through the cotton shirt. Edinburgh had regained its magic.

She stopped by a door at the side of a souvenir shop on the Lawnmarket. The city was empty, primly correct, braced for the late-night crowds that the Festival was soon to bring.

"Good Lord, do you live here? A flat full of kilts and whisky shortbread and bagpipe salt-cellars?"

"On the top floor."

"That's a long way up."

"A friend's flat. Student at the University here. Away for the summer."

"Ah. All yours."

"Yes. Do you want to come in?"

"What for?" Charles asked fatuously.

She was not at all disconcerted and turned the amused navy blue stare on him. "Coffee?"

"Had coffee."

"Drink?"

"Had brandy."

"Well, we'll have to think of something else."

They did.

CHAPTER 4

And the faulty scent is picked out by the hound;
And the fact turns up like a worm from the ground;
And the matter gets wind to waft it about;
And a hint goes abroad and the murder is out.

A TALE OF A TRUMPET

HE WAS ALONE in the bed when he awoke. There was a note on the pillow. GONE TO REHEARSAL. IF I DON'T SEE YOU DURING THE DAY, SEE YOU TONIGHT? He smiled and rolled out of bed to make some leisurely coffee.

He drank it at the window, looking down on shoppers and tourists, foreshortened by the distance, scurrying like crabs across the dark cobbles of the Lawnmarket. He thought of Anna's brown body with its bikini streaks of white, and felt good. The cynicism which normally attended his sex life was not there. An exceptional girl. Willy Mariello's death became less important.

Rehearsal for an opening in four days' time, on the other hand, was important. He finished the coffee and set out for Coates Gardens.

Martin Warburton was sprawled over a camp-bed in the men's dormitory, reading. Reading *So Much Comic . . .* , Charles noticed with annoyance. The boy looked up as he entered. His expression was calmer than usual and he was even polite. "Sorry. I shouldn't be reading this. But it was on your bed. I started it and got interested."

Given such a compliment, however unintentional, Charles could not really complain. "There's more to Hood than many people think."

"I don't know. Is there? I mean he's clever, there's a lot of apparent feeling, but when you get down to it, there's not much there. No certainty. All those puns. It's because he doesn't want to define things exactly. Doesn't want anything to define him. There's nothing you can identify with."

It was a surprisingly perceptive judgment. "You think that's important, identifying?"

"It must be. You can only respond to art if you identify with the artist. That's how I worked. I'd read into everything someone had written, until I felt the person there at the center. And then I'd identify. I'd become that person and know how to react to their work."

"You're reading English, I assume."

"No, History."

"Ah."

"Just taken my degree."

"OK?"

"Yes, got a First."

"Congratulations."

"Not that it means anything." Martin's mood suddenly gave way to gloom. "Nothing much does mean anything. I criticize Hood for not believing in things and there's me . . ." He looked up sharply. "Have you read my play?"

"No, I'm sorry. I will get around to it, but—"

"Wouldn't bother. It's rubbish. Nothing in the middle."

"I'm sure it's going to be very interesting." Charles tried not to sound patronizing, but was still greeted by a despairing snort. Martin rose suddenly. "I must go. I'm late. Got to rehearse *Mary*. The composer's body not yet decomposed and we rehearse."

"You're punning yourself, like Hood," said Charlie, trying to lighten the conversation.

"Oh yes. I'm a punster. A jolly funny punster." Martin let out one of his abrupt laughs. "A jolly punster and a murderer. I killed him, you know."

"No. You were the instrument that killed him."

This struck Martin as uproariously funny. "An instrument. Do you want to get into a great discussion about Free Will? Am I guilty? Or is the knife guilty perhaps? Where did the will come from? The knife has no will. I have no will?"

"Martin, calm down. You mustn't think you killed him."

"Why not? The police think I did."

"They don't."

"They asked so many questions."

"It's the police's job to ask questions."

"Oh yes, I know."

"Why? Have you been in trouble with them before?"

"Only a motoring offence, sah!" Martin dropped suddenly into an Irish accent.

"What was it?"

"Planting a car bomb, sah!" He burst into laughter. Charles, feeling foolish for setting up the feed-line so perfectly, joined him. Martin's laughter went on too long.

But Charles took advantage of the slight relaxation of tension. "Listen, the police can't think you did it. No one in their right mind would commit murder in front of a large audience."

"No," said Martin slyly, "no one in their right mind would." This again sent him into a paroxysm of laughter. Which stopped as suddenly as it had begun. He looked at Charles in a puzzled way, as if he did not recognize him. Then, in a gentle voice, "What's the time?"

"Twenty-five to eleven."

"I should be at rehearsal." He rose calmly. "Do try to read my play if you can."

"I will."

"See you." He slouched out of the room.

Charles lay for a moment thinking. Martin seemed to be on the edge of a nervous breakdown. The end of finals is a stressful time for most students. Charles suddenly recalled the state he had been in after Schools in 1949. Three years gone and then the apocalyptic strain of assessment. How good am I? What will I do in the real world? Or, most simply, who am I?

He tried to imagine the effect of a shock like Willy's death on someone in that state. A harsh cruel fact smashing into a mind that could hardly distinguish reality from fantasy. Inside his sick brain Martin might think he was a murderer, but Charles felt sure he was not. Martin Warburton needed help. Medical help possibly, but certainly he needed the help of knowing that he was only an unwitting agent for the person who planned the murder of Willy Mariello. The facts had to come out.

And the show had to go on. He turned to the script. On sober reflection, though the day before's run-through had been promising, there was a lot that needed improvement. Particularly the Pathetic Ballads. They should have been the easiest part of the program with their well-spaced jokes and obvious humor. But it was hard to find the balance between poetry and facetiousness. He concentrated and began to recite *Tim Turpin*.

> *Tim Turpin he was gravel blind,*
> *And ne'er had seen the skies:*
> *For Nature, when his head was made,*
> *Forgot to dot his eyes.*
> *So like a Christmas pedagogue—*

"Um. I'm so sorry." Brian Cassells was peering apologetically around the door.

"Yes."

"Look, I'm sorry to break into your rehearsal, but I wonder if you could give me a hand to carry something." And *So Much Comic* . . . was shelved again.

Outside the Office stood Willy Mariello's forlorn guitar in its black case, leaning against a large amplifier. It had been brought up from the Masonic Hall after Tuesday's drama. By the door was a thin girl with long brown hair and those peculiarly Scottish cheeks that really do look like apples. Tension showed in the tightness of her mouth and the hollows under her eyes. "Charles, this is Jean Mariello. Mrs. Mariello, Charles Paris."

She nodded functionally. "I've come to collect Willy's things."

"Yes. Charles, I wonder if you could give me a hand with this amplifier. If we just get it out on to the street, I've phoned for a taxi."

"O.K." Brian was patently embarrassed and wanted to get rid of Jean Mariello. His administrative ability did not run to dealing with recent widows.

They placed the heavy amplifier on the pavement. Willy's wife followed with the guitar. Brian straightened up. "I'd better go. I've go some Letrasetting to get on with."

"What am I going to do the other end?"

Brian paused, disconcerted by her question. Charles stepped in. "It's all right. I'll go with you. I wanted to go over that way. Off Lauriston Place, isn't it?"

"Yes."

"Oh . . . Oh well, that's fine. I'll go and get on with the . . . er . . . Letrasetting." Brian scuttled indoors.

Charles felt he should say something fitting. "I'm sorry."

Jean Mariello shrugged. "Thank you."

The taxi arrived and they traveled for a while in silence. Charles felt the need for some other inadequate condolence. "It must be terrible for you. We were all very shaken."

"Yes, it's been a shock. But please don't feel you have to say anything. Will and I weren't love's young dream, you know." The accent was Scots and she spoke quietly, but there was a hard note in her voice.

"Did you live together?"

"Up to a point. Though one or other of us always seemed to be touring or something."

"You're a musician too?"

"Yes. I sing in folk clubs. Not Willy's sort of music. We grew apart musically as well as everything else." She leant forward and tapped the glass partition. "If you drop us just here . . ."

Meadow Lane was lined with gray houses, considerably smaller than those of Coates Gardens. They had the dusty shabbiness of the Old Town. Most of the windows were shrouded with gray net. But on the house they stopped by the windows were clean and unveiled.

Charles let Jean pay the driver. She turned to him. "Can you manage that on your own? It's heavy."

It certainly was. Also an awkward size. His hands could not quite clasp around it. But he was determined to manage.

As she opened the front door, he noticed a worn stone slab over it which dated the house: 1797. Inside, however, the place had been extensively modernized. There was no sign of a fireplace in the front room, but there were new-looking central heating radiators. Everything gleamed with fresh white paint. There was even a smell of it. The room was empty of furniture, but a ladder and a pile of rubble in the corner indicated decorating in progress.

He lowered the amplifier gratefully on to the uncarpeted floor. "Would you mind putting it against the wall there where people can't see it? The catch has gone on the window and I don't want to encourage burglars."

Another effort moved the amplifier to the required position. He stood up. Jean Mariello had left the front door open and stood with her arms folded. He was expected to go.

And he was never likely to get such a good opportunity for finding out more about Willy. No point in beating about the bush. "Mrs. Mariello, do you think your husband was murdered?"

She was not shocked or angry, she seemed to expect the question. "No, I don't."

"Why not?"

"No one wanted to kill him. Listen, Willy wasn't a particularly nice person. He was mean and lazy. But those aren't reasons for anyone to murder someone."

"No. But you can't think of anything he might have done to antagonise anyone in that Derby lot?"

"I've hardly met any of that Derby lot, so I wouldn't know. Listen, Mr. Paris, I can understand your curiosity, but the police have asked me all these questions and so has everyone I've met for the past two days. I'm getting rather bored with it, and I'd be grateful if you would stop."

"I'm sorry, Mrs. Mariello, but I do have a reason for asking." And he told her of his encounter with Willy in the Truth Game. At the end he paused dramatically.

She did not seem over-impressed. "You say he seemed troubled?"

"Yes."

"Probably some horse he'd backed had been beaten."

"No, it was more than that. I'm sure it was. Something that really went deep."

"Nothing went very deep with Willy. That Truth Game could have meant anything. What makes you so sure it was something serious?"

He could only supply a lame "Instinct."

To give her her due, Jean Mariello did not actually laugh out loud. "Well, instinct tells me, from knowing him pretty well, that the only thing that upset Willy was not getting his own way. He was spoilt. He'd had a lot of success and it went to his head. Used to be just a builder's laborer, playing guitar in his spare time. Then the group took off and suddenly he was famous. Everyone gave him everything he wanted and he started getting bad-tempered if anything didn't fall into his lap. If he was upset, it must have been that some girl had slapped his face."

"There were a lot of girls?"

"Yes."

"Do you know if he'd been particularly involved with anyone recently?"

"We didn't discuss it. We went our own ways. Listen, Willy was a slob. All right, I'm sorry he died, but he was no great loss."

Charles was shocked by her honesty and his face must have betrayed it. Jean laughed. "Yes, you're wondering why I married him. Well, I was only seventeen, I wanted to be a musician and I wanted to get away from my parents. And Willy was different then —it was before he became successful. He was less sure of himself and, as a result, less selfish. We both changed. He became a bastard and I got a lot tougher. In self-defense."

There was a slight tremor on the last words, the first sign of human feeling that she had shown. The callous attitude to her husband's death was a protective shell, distancing her from reality. It was true that she had not loved him, but the killing had affected her. Charles changed his approach slightly. "When did you last see him?"

"Last Friday. I went down to Carlisle to start a tour of folk clubs. Then this happened. I'll be joining the tour again as soon as I've got things sorted out."

"And Willy didn't seem upset when you left?"

"He was exactly as usual."

"And you've no idea what he was doing over the weekend?"

"Screwing some bird probably. Decorating here maybe. Rehearsing his bloody show. I don't know."

The edge was creeping back into her voice. She wanted Charles to leave. She wanted to be on her own. Maybe so that she could break down and cry her heart out. There was not time for many more questions. "Why did he get involved in the show in the first place?"

"Puce split up. Willy had delusions of grandeur—wanted to get it together as an all-round entertainer. Another Tommy Steele. No big impresario offered him a contract, but Derby University offered him a part in their tatty show. I supposed he saw it as a rung on the ladder to *stardom*." She put an infinity of scorn into that word.

"Sounds unlikely."

"Maybe there was some other reason. Look, Mr. Paris—"

"I'm sorry. I'll go. Can I just ask you again—was there anyone you can think of, however unlikely, who might have profited by your husband's death?"

"First let me ask you—why are you so interested in all this? It's nothing to do with you."

"No, you're right, it's just . . . I was there . . . I saw it . . ." He petered out. Tried again. "There are people who will feel happier when the facts are known. I mean, there's so much gossip and speculation and accusation down at Coates Gardens . . ." As he spoke, he knew it was not true. In fact there had been surprisingly little discussion among the students. Once they had exhausted the inherent drama of the situation, they all seemed quite happy to accept that it was an accident and get back to the more important drama of the shows they were putting on. "No, I'm sorry, I can't really answer your question."

"Hmm. I'll answer yours. The only person who stood to benefit from Willy's death was his widow, who would thus get out of an unsatisfactory marriage without the fuss of divorce. In other words, the only person with a motive was me." She laughed sharply. "Goodbye, Mr. Paris."

* * *

He wandered disconsolately along Meadow Lane and looked back at the house. It was in a better state of repair than the others, walls and chimney repainted, missing slates replaced. And inside, was Jean Mariello as tidy and controlled? Or was she crying? He'd never know. All he did know was that she did not kill her husband. Her talk of motives had just been a contemptuous challenge to him. She had not been in Edinburgh at the time of the murder, and in the Truth Game Willy had specified that the person whose secret he had discovered was connected with the Derby group. No progress.

He felt in need of company. As a long shot, he tried the bell of Anna's flat as he passed. Just after twelve, no reason why she should be there.

She wasn't. He went into the Highland chic of the Ensign Ewart pub opposite and started drinking whisky. As he drank, the whole business of playing at detectives seemed increasingly pointless. If only there were someone around he could discuss the case with. Maybe some great detectives manage on their own, he thought as he downed the second large Bell's, but right now I'd give anything for Dr. Watson to walk through that door.

But the Doctor did not come and Charles drank too much on his own. The whisky did not make him think any more clearly. He looked round the pub. The office workers of Edinburgh were in huddles with their backs to him. A loud group of American tourists was being ignored at one table. The Festival influx was not welcomed by the residents. Charles tried to get another drink, but could not attract anyone's attention. Being invisible at a bar is one of the loneliest experiences in life and he felt depressed for the first time since his arrival.

It was the interview with Jean Mariello that had done it. Up until then he had been cheerful, even buoyant after the night with Anna. But Anna was not there and it did not take long for her image to get distorted. He needed her presence to restore reality. But she was as elusive as Dr. Watson.

His eyes gave up trying to catch the barman's attention and wandered over to a noticeboard on which the grudging management had stuck a few of the dozens of handbills which earnest theatrical groups had thrust on them. They were on a metal clip. Oxford Theatre Group on top. That was inevitable. Their head-quarters was opposite the pub and so they had a head-start on that pitch in the popular Fringe game of sticking your poster over everyone else's.

Beside the Oxford bill was another that looked familiar. Good God, it was one of the greatest D.U.D.S. on the Fringe, Charles Paris' *So Much Comic, So Much Blood,* opening Monday, August 19th, at one fifteen p.m. He felt a sense of urgency that amounted almost to panic.

"Yes, sir, what can I get you?"

"Nothing. I've got to rehearse." The barman's bewildered stare followed him out of the pub.

Outside in the street he realized that he had had an excessive lunch for a working actor and trod with care down the steep steps of Lady Stair's Close to the Mound. The light seemed very bright. He thought he saw the familiar figure of Martin Warburton ahead. He hurried to catch up. "Martin!"

But the figure did not stop. It turned right at the bottom of the steps and Charles saw the beard and glasses. It was not Martin.

He awoke on his camp-bed at about five with the worst sort of afternoon hangover. The urgent rehearsal schedule he had promised himself had petered out rather quickly. He hoped that he had not been seen lying there by too many of the group. A middle-aged man asleep in the afternoon. No doubt snoring. The monotone of the piano upstairs indicated a revue rehearsal. He hoped Anna had not seen him.

A cup of coffee might help. He eased himself downstairs to the kitchen. The day's cook, a large girl with corkscrew curls, was chopping up more of the inevitable cabbage.

"Where's the coffee?"

"Over there, behind the cornflakes."

"Oh yes."

"I'll make you some . . ."

"Thanks." He made to sit on a chair by the table.

". . . if you don't mind doing something for me."

"What?"

"Just empty that, would you?"

"That" was a large cardboard box full of rubbish—papers, sweepings, cigarette ends, kitchen refuse. The bottom felt unwholesomely soggy on his hands. Charles Paris, haulage contractors. Amplifiers, refuse—distance no object. He negotiated the load through the kitchen door and made his way to the dustbins.

There was a little room at the top of one of them. He balanced the box on the edge and tried to let the contents slip gently in.

They all came with a rush, covering his hands with tea-leaves and a yellow slime that had been food. Little scraps of paper scattered all around the bin.

He pushed down the smelly pile and bent to pick up some of the litter. A lot of the paper appeared to have been torn from a big poster photograph. He picked up a piece which had printing on it.

WI
PU

He scrabbled among the other bits until he found the adjacent one which spelled out the title.

WILLY MARIELLO
PUCE

It was a publicity poster of Willy that someone had shredded into a thousand pieces.

CHAPTER 5

How bless'd the heart that has a friend
A sympathizing ear to lend
  To troubles too great to smother!
For as ale and porter, when flat, are restored
Till a sparkling bubbling head they afford,
So sorrow is cheer'd by being poured
  From one vessel to another.

MISS KILMANSEGG AND HER PRECIOUS LEG

FROM BIBLICAL TIMES the restorative properties of a young woman's body have been acknowledged, and Charles felt better after another night with Anna. He was amazed how much she affected him. She was beautiful, and she was knowledgeable in bed, but it was not just that. There was something about the honesty of her responses. No extravagant protestations of love, no questions about the future, just an acceptance that what was happening was good. Most people reveal their weaknesses in a close relationship and endear themselves by failure. But the nearer Charles got to Anna the more complete and integrated she seemed. And she made him feel complete too. Not two lost souls leaning against each other for support, but two independent people who complemented each other.

The alarm woke them at nine. Charles reached his hand round to the small of her back and kissed the elastic skin of her breasts. Anna smiled. "Got to get up."

"Saturday."

"No weekend for us. The revue opens on Monday. We've got a tech. run at ten."

"Yes, the show must go on." She got up. Charles squatted ruefully on the bed with his elbows on his knees. Anna paused in the bathroom doorway and grinned. "You look like a dog that's had its bone taken away."

"Yes, I fancied a nice bit of marrow-bone jelly. Isn't that what Prolongs Active Life?"

"You needn't worry." She closed the bathroom door. Charles smiled, gratified. He spoke up over the sound of running water. "Hey, look, I've got a lot of rehearsal to do, too. Can I use the flat? It's so difficult to find anywhere quiet at Coates Gardens."

A gurgle from the bathroom gave him permission. "What are the technical lot like, Anna? All the sound and lighting people?" Another gurgle said they were fine, there was a good course in the Department of Drama. "I hope so. I'm only getting a few hours' rehearsal in the hall—Sunday and Monday mornings is all I'm allowed."

The bathroom door slid open and Anna appeared, naked, her hair spiked with damp. "Not fair, is it, you poor old thing?" she said as she crossed to her clothes on the chair.

He grabbed at her ankle as she passed and she flopped on to the bed. "Got to go and rehearse, Charles."

"Rehearse and become a big star."

"Yes."

"Even stars have five minutes."

The rehearsal went well too. Given somewhere to work on his own. Charles concentrated and put more subtlety into his readings. He was very organized. Once straight through, then a laborious line-by-line analysis of what had gone wrong. Another run—improvements in individual items but too uniform a pace overall. More detailed work, and finally a run that he would not have been ashamed to show to an audience. "There are many pleasures to be had at the Edinburgh Festival, and the greatest of these is Charles Paris' *So Much Comic, So Much Blood.*" Silly, however old and cynical he got, there were times when his mind raced and fantasies of success made him deliciously nervy and excited.

After rehearsal he found the pubs were shut and that made him feel virtuous. A brisk walk was called for. He popped into a little café aptly called the Poppin and bought a couple of floury ham rolls. Then started a leisurely stroll up to the Castle.

The Esplanade was flanked with tiers of seats ready for the Military Tattoo. The head of a statue and the point of an obelisk came through the disciplined rows to be capped incongruously by green tarpaulin covers. But the Castle itself still looked impressive as Charles mounted the gentle incline to its heraldic gateway. "Nemo me impune lacessit." The motto's translation came to his mind in the accent of a Glasgow thug—"No one provokes me and gets away with it."

It was like a pilgrimage. Every time he came up to Edinburgh, he had to look around the Castle. Climb up to Mons Megs, maybe look inside St. Margaret's Chapel. Then on the level below he would lean against the ramparts and gaze down over the city, whose grays merged to distant greens, which were lost in the gleam of the Firth of Forth.

It was a clear, sparkling day. He had a beautiful girl and he felt confident about his show. And yet . . .

And yet there was a nagging unease in his mind. Willy Mariello's murder. Each time he tried to dismiss it, he saw the fear in those brown eyes. And he knew that the pleasures of Edinburgh could only allay his unrest temporarily. Peace would not come until he knew the full facts.

The facts he had found out did not take him far. There were still some forty suspects who had had equal opportunity to switch the knives. Of those two had had greater opportunities than the others to stage-manage the murder—Martin Warburton and Pam Northcliffe. Martin had struck the fatal blow and he was an unstable character with strange obsessions about violence. But it seemed too obvious, and Charles felt an understanding, even an affinity with the boy's tormented mind. He could not think of him as a murderer.

The same applied to Pam. However, it was she who had actually issued the murder weapon and there were other strange features of her behavior. He had a strong suspicion that she was responsible for the torn poster. The pieces that he had found had burst out of a paper bag full of crêpe paper scraps which Pam had been using to make props. He had not challenged her with it, but he was fairly certain. So she had something to hide.

But not murder. Why not? Because I, Charles Paris, like the girl. The same goes for Martin. It is a hopelessly subjective, emotional judgment. I have an old-fashioned, middle-class view that murderers are, by definition, nasty people. Whereas, in fact, they are just nice, ordinary people who get into situations they can't cope with and take what seems to them the only way out.

Again he desperately wanted someone to talk to about his suspicions. Someone detached and objective. Not Anna. She was involved with the other students and he did not want the murder to intrude on their growing relationship. But there was always Gerald.

Gerald Venables was a show business solicitor with a child-like relish for the cloak and dagger aspect of detection. Charles had enlisted his help earlier in the year to sort out the Marius Steen affair and, when that mystery was solved, Gerald had insisted that he should be included in any future venture of criminal investigation. This looked like his opportunity.

"Hello, Gerald."

"Who's that? Charles?"

"Yes. I think I may be on to another case."

"Really." Excitement sprang into Gerald's voice. "Where?"

"Edinburgh, I'm afraid. It'd cost you a lot in fares."

"Don't worry. I've got lots of Scottish clients. I can put it on one of their bills. What's the crime?"

"Murder."

"Fantastic. Will it keep?"

"What do you mean?"

"Keep for a few days. I'm going to Cannes for a long weekend to stay with a client."

"Work?"

"Well, it'll be on his bill, but I don't intend to do anything."

"When are you back?"

"Probably Wednesday."

"Some weekend."

"Pity to rush it."

"Hmm." Wednesday seemed a long way off. Charles wanted someone there to talk to at that moment.

Gerald continued. "And then at the end of next week—Saturday —I'm taking the family out to our villa in Corsica for a month."

"Just the month?"

"Yes. I have to get back to work then," said Gerald piously, not catching Charles' sarcasm.

"So you might be free for a couple of days next week?"

"Might. The case won't be solved by then, will it?"

"No, I shouldn't think so." Depression swooped and Charles feared he was speaking the truth. "I'll give you a buzz when you get back if there's anything left to investigate. O.K. Fine. Have a good weekend." It was not worth saying how pointless it would be for Gerald to come up for two days. Oh, well, another good idea gone west.

"Oh, it's you, Charles." James Milne was standing at the foot of the stairs in the hall. "I wondered who was using the phone. That one's just an extension to mine upstairs. It's meant to be disconnected soon and I'd put it in the cupboard so that it shouldn't be used."

"I'm sorry. It was just here on the floor when I came in."

"Don't worry. One of the Derby lot found it, no doubt. How's Thomas Hood?"

"Fine. Positively going well."

"Good, good." The Laird stood with one foot on the stair, posed like an old-fashioned print. His stocky figure was dressed in a biscuit-colored tweed suit with a Norfolk jacket. "Can I offer you a cup of tea?"

A slow grin spread over Charles face. "Dr. Watson," he said.

"I beg your pardon."

* * *

Over a cup of Earl Grey tea and chocolate-covered <u>Bath Olivers</u>, Charles explained. He told of his suspicions about the murder and the small progress of his investigations.

James Milne looked at him in silence for a moment. "What an amazing idea. And what do you want me to do? Crawl around the rooftops with firearms and beard villains in their dens? I don't know whether that's quite my style. I used sometimes to try to catch poachers on my mother's estate at Glenloan, but I'm not exactly a private eye."

"Look, all I want you to do is address your mind to the problem. I want to hear what you think. You've met most of the people involved. You know, two heads are better than one and all that. And I'm really getting nowhere on my own. My suspicions just go round and round in circles . . . I want you to be a kind of sounding board for my ideas."

"Hmm. I think a ouija board for contacting Willy Mariello might be more useful."

"You're probably right. What do you say?"

"Well, Charles, I'm certainly prepared to help you in any way you think might be useful. But I must say right from the start that I don't share your certainty that a murder has been committed. From what I heard it sounded like a very unfortunate accident. What makes you so sure it's murder?"

Again Charles had to fall back on his feeble cry of "Instinct."

"Instinct is a great matter, I was a coward on instinct. Hmm. Dear old Falstaff. Instinct. Do the Police share your instinct?"

"Not so far as I know."

"They don't think it was murder?"

"I don't think so, though that won't really be clear until they've finished their inquiries."

"No. Hmm. Good."

"Why good?"

"Well, when our investigations reach their dramatic dénouement, we can feel confident that Inspector Flatfoot of the Yard won't pip us at the post."

"You mean you agree?"

"Yes, I'll be your sounding board. It could be fun."

"Good. Thank you."

The Laird immediately regressed to his school-mastering days. "Right. Now have you made any notes on the case?"

"No."

"Well, I'm sure you should." Charles watched amazed as his Dr. Watson began to organize him. "Right, paper, fountain pen, sharp HB pencil. And a column, so. Headed 'Suspects.' And another— 'Reason for Suspicion.' Now who have we got?"

"We've just been through all that."

"No harm in doing it again. There is nothing so effective for stimulating the memory and provoking thought as writing things down."

Charles felt he was right back in the First Form. (On his present investigative form, in the corner with a big "D" on his hat.) But he humored his new partner and they made out their list.

It did not take long. The "Reason for Suspicion" column looked particularly unconvincing. "In a sense," said Charles, "we're starting from the wrong end. We are putting down why we suspect someone, whereas we should be thinking, from that person's point of view, why they should want to kill Willy."

"Would that make the list any fuller?"

Charles had to admit that it would not. "What we've got to do is to work out who was involved with Willy—emotionally, artistically, financially. So far it seems the only person from Derby he knew well is a guy called Sam Wasserman, who is currently touring Europe."

"You say he's the only person you can connect Willy with?"

"Except for his wife. But I can't count her because she has nothing to do with the group. Unless she has an ally who's at Derby . . . A lover maybe or . . ." Lack of conviction in what he was saying brought him to a halt. "Nope."

"And she's the only person up here with whom he seems to have had dealings?"

"Yes."

"Oh, Charles, Charles." The Laird shook his head pityingly. "There's someone you've overlooked."

"Is there?"

"Yes. And you have all the information to work out who. I know you do." He watched for reaction and then repeated slowly, "I know you do."

Charles suddenly realized who was meant. "Good Lord, yes. You. The house."

"Exactly. You see, there is a direct financial relationship between me and Willy Mariello. He bought my house. I think I should go down on our list of suspects."

"But that's daft. If you were the murderer, you wouldn't draw any attention to your connection with the victim?"

"Ah, Charles, I may look like the innocent flower, but be the serpent under't. You mustn't rule out any possibility. There, I've put my name down. Declaration of interests, like the Liberals keep asking M.P.'s to make. Now what about you?"

"Me?"

"Your declaration of interest. Had you any motive to murder Willy Mariello?"

Charles laughed. "No."

"Good. Now we know where we stand." James Milne smiled. His reserve was gone and he looked set to enjoy the game of detection. "Now, what about the other forty-odd?"

"What indeed? Presumably I must try to meet them all and find out if any of them knew Willy well. And also what he did over the weekend before he died."

"Yes. And how long have you got to complete this major investigation?"

"My show finishes a week today."

"Hmm. I fear we may find time defeats us."

"Yes. I hope not."

"So do I. But perhaps, Charles, I hope it a little less than you."

"Why?"

"Because I don't yet fully believe that we're on to a case of murder. I'll come along with you for the ride, but I'm not convinced of the existence of a destination."

The Laird was going to dinner with friends, so Charles left him about seven. He was no nearer the solution of the murder, but at least he had an ally. And the cataloguing power of James Milne's mind could be a useful complement to his own haphazard methods.

On the first-floor landing he paused. The revue piano had given up its usual stuck-in-the-groove repetition and was playing a whole tune. A girl was singing. He could not catch the lyrics, just hear the husky purity of her voice. Anna. He felt a strong desire to go into the room on some pretext just to see her. But no. She had said it was better they should keep their relationship a secret and she was right. He did not fancy the gossip and innuendo of forty students.

No. He still had the key to the flat. He'd go back there and wait for her to return and continue his rejuvenation. Later.

On the ground floor the only sign of human occupation was the presence of old socks, creeping like firedamp from the men's dormitory. Charles was about to leave and find a pub for the evening when he heard a slight sound from the basement. He crept down the stairs towards the glow of the sitting-room.

Michael Vanderzee was slumped on the sofa with a glass in one hand and a half-full bottle of Glenmorangie malt whisky in the other. He perceived Charles's approach blearily. "I didn't know there was anyone in the house. Thought they'd all buggered off."

"I've just been having a drink with the Laird."

"Oh, that old poof," said Michael ungraciously.

Charles did not bother to challenge the gratuitous insult, though on reflection he thought it was misplaced. He had not thought before about James Milne's sexual status, but, when he did, neuter seemed the most appropriate definition.

However, Michael was not trying to drive Charles away. On the contrary, he seemed delighted to have a witness of his lonely drinking and an audience for his self-pity.

"Charles Paris, you may work in bullshit commercial theatre, but at least you are a professional." The drink accentuated the Dutchness of his voice as he delivered this back-handed compliment. "Surrounded by bloody amateurs in this place. It's an impossible situation for any creative work. You can't create with amateurs."

Charles grunted sympathetically and sat astride a chair. "Have a drink," said Michael, feeling that perhaps he should offer his audience some reward for its attention. "There's a cup on the table."

The cup was chipped and handleless, but the malt tasted good. When he reckoned that Charles was sitting comfortably, Michael began. "No, I shouldn't have taken this job. Amateurs have no concept of theatre. Look at it. This evening I should have been working, improvising, creating something, and what happens? Half my cast are rehearsing for some bloody revue, half of them are doing some dreary Shakespeare crap, half of them aren't interested . . ."

"And half of them get stabbed . . ."

"Yes." He nodded vigorously. "Though he wasn't a lot more use to me when he was alive."

"What do you mean?"

"Never came to bloody rehearsals. Didn't participate in the concentration exercises or movement classes, any of the workshop stuff. I mean, how can you build an ensemble with people like that? He hadn't any acting talent anyway."

"Then why did you cast him in your show?"

"I didn't cast him. Look, I'm offered this job—"

"You mean you're nothing to do with the university?"

"Good God, no." Michael was severely affronted. "I'm a professional director. They booked me to get some professional feel into their production. And then like bloody amateurs they don't give me enough time to get it together properly. Everyone off for other rehearsals. Do you know how long it takes to build up an ensemble?"

"About four years?"

"Well, four weeks anyway. And four weeks' work. Not four weeks doing bourgeois revues and middle-class Shakespeare."

"No, of course not. You were saying how Willy Mariello came to be in the show . . ."

"Yes. O.K., I take the job. I go to Derby to hold auditions. And already I'm told that Willy is doing the music and, since Rizzio's a guitarist and he has a couple of songs, O.K., he's playing Rizzio too."

"Who told you this?"

"Sam Wasserman, the guy who wrote this crappy play."

"Is it crappy?"

"Yes, but it doesn't matter."

"Why not?"

"My style of direction doesn't need a good play. In fact the play can get in the way. It's only a starting point from which the totality emerges—the iron filing dropped into the acid which produces the perfect crystal." He added the last image with great satisfaction, albeit dubious chemistry. Then he looked at Charles with pitying contempt. "I suppose you still think a play has got to have words."

Charles smiled apologetically. There was no point in alienating such a ready source of information. "Yes, I am a bit of an old fuddy-duddy on that score. I expect Sam Wasserman probably thinks words are quite important too."

"Maybe."

"He sounds an interesting bloke. I'd like to meet him."

Michael gave a snort of laughter that could have meant anything. "You should get a chance quite soon. He's coming up to Edinburgh."

"For the opening in the Third Week?"

"No, before that, I hope. We've been sending telegrams all over Europe for him. He's going to come up and take over the part of Rizzio."

"Oh really." That was very interesting. "He plays guitar too?"

"Yes. He was going to do the music for the show himself until Willy was brought in."

"Ah." That was also interesting. "So everything's back to where it started?"

"I suppose so. More drink?"

"Thank you." Charles held out his cup and the malt was sloshed in like school soup. Trying desperately to sound casual, he asked, "What did you think of Willy Mariello?"

"Useless, unco-operative bastard. Ruining my production. From my point of view, his death was the best thing that could have happened."

It was an uncompromising statement of hatred. So much so that Charles felt inclined to discount it. A murderer would be more guarded . . . Unless it was an elaborate double bluff . . . Oh dear. The further he got into the business of detection, the further certainty seemed to recede. Still, keep on probing. Try to find out some more hard facts. Again he imposed a relaxed tone on his voice. "Were you rehearsing last weekend?"

"Of course. I rehearse whenever I can get my cast together. I am trying to create something, you know."

"Of course. So Willy was rehearsing all weekend?"

"No. That's a good example of what I mean. He rehearses on Saturday with his usual bad grace. Sunday—no sign of him. Monday he is not there and I am so furious I break the rehearsal and I go up to his house to drag him back—by force if necessary."

"Was he there?"

"Oh yes, he's there. Calmly decorating. Plaster dust everywhere, paint brushes, so on and so on."

"Did you get him to rehearsal?"

"Yes, till mid-afternoon. Then he slipped off again when we had a break."

"Hmm. Perhaps he wanted to get back to his decorating."

"Yes. Or to the girl."

"Girl?"

"Yes. When I finally got him out on the Monday morning, he called out 'Good-bye' to someone upstairs."

CHAPTER 6

By Sunday August 18th Edinburgh was beginning to feel the Festival. Over-night the city was full of tourists—tweedy music-lovers on leisurely promenades, earnest Americans decked with rucksacks and guide-books, French and Japanese drawn by the twin attractions of culture and Marks and Spencer pullovers. The residents who had not escaped on holiday wore expressions of resignation, hardened to the idea of their streets clogged with ambling foreigners, their early nights troubled by returning revue audiences and the distant massed pipes and drums of the Military Tattoo.

Because that Sunday was the day when it all started officially. In the words of the Festival brochure, "The twenty-eighth Edinburgh Festival will be opened with a Service of Praise and Thanksgiving in St. Giles' Cathedral on Sunday August 18th at 3 p.m. Later, starting from the Castle Esplanade at 9:45 p.m., relays of torch-bearing runners will light a bonfire on Arthur's Seat."

And in the little halls of Edinburgh on that Sunday morning

would-be cultural torch-bearers blew earnestly at the smoulderings of what was in many cases incombustible material. Experimental and university groups realized that their rehearsal time was running out and put on a spurt to justify the extravagant claims of their publicity. There were dress rehearsals for at least a dozen "funniest revues on the Fringe," some twenty "revolutionary new plays" and three or four "new artistic concepts which would flatten the accepted barriers of culture." If all these ambitions were realized, British theatre would never be the same again.

In the Masonic Hall in Lauriston Street Charles Paris was trying to realize more humble ambitions and finding it hard work. The lighting technician he had been allocated was a fat and contemptuous youth, whose blue denim had faded and dirtied to the color of sludge. He was known as Plug, and Charles found it difficult to call anyone "Plug."

It had been made clear that, considering the exacting demands of creative amateur theatre, there was not going to be much time or effort left for him, a mere professional. "Um . . . Plug?" he said exploratively, "I wonder about the chances of moving the back-projector round. If it stays there, I'm going to be masking the slides."

"That'd mean moving the screen too," Plug grunted accusingly.

"Yes, it will."

"Can't be done. Haven't got the extension leads."

"Can't you get them?"

"Shouldn't think so."

Charles bit back his anger. It was difficult dealing with amateurs. In a professional context, no problem; he could have bawled the guy out, justified because a service that was being paid for was not being provided. But the amateur relies on goodwill and there did not seem to be much of it in evidence.

So he gritted his teeth and played stupid, apparently bowing to Plug's technical expertise and working the youth round till he did what was required as a demonstration of his abilities. It was important, Charles had gone to considerable trouble to have slides made of Hood's woodcuts. They had originally been printed with the poems and the crude humor of the pictures extended the range of the verse. In a one-man show it is important to give the audience as much varied stimulus as possible.

By application of simple child psychology he got the back-projector and screen moved and started a run. It was not easy. With only two stage areas in use, the lighting plot was simple. But Plug refused to rehearse the cues on their own, saying that he would pick them up on a full run. Then, in spite of the carefully marked-up script that Charles had given him, he proceeded to get every single effect wrong.

The one benefit of the run was that it tested Charles' knowledge of his words, because whether he moved to the table or the lectern, there was a guarantee of total darkness on that area. And whenever he turned to the back-projection screen, he was confronted either by a blank or the wrong slide.

It was also a useful concentration exercise. In the darkness beyond the stage people kept wandering in and out. Plug greeted them all loudly and conducted irrelevant conversations at the top of his voice. Charles was ignored like a television in the corner of the room.

The show limped to its close. As he stood at the lectern to read the final *Stanzas,* "Farewell, Life! My senses swim . . . ," he was amazed to find the light was actually where it should be. It had taken the whole show to get one cue right, but at least it offered hope. Encouraged, he put more emotion into the poem. It approached its end with the dying fall he had intended.

> *"O'er the earth there comes a bloom—*
> *Sunny light for sullen gloom.*
> *Warm perfume for vapor cold—"*

Then, before "I smell the Rose above the Mould," the pause held long and dramatic.

Too long. Too dramatic. Plug snapped the lights out before the line was delivered.

Charles's reserves cracked. "Oh, for Christ's sake!"

"What's up?" Plug grunted from the darkness.

"That's not the cue. There's another line."

Plug did not seem unduly concerned. He brought up the house lights. "Never mind."

"And then, after the last line, there's supposed to be a three-second pause and a five-second fade down to black."

"Oh."

"It's clearly marked in the script."

"Yes."

Charles decided there was little point in concealing his feelings. "That was pretty abysmal."

Plug nodded sympathetically, unaware that the comment referred to him. "Hmm. Perhaps you need more rehearsal."

"I think it's you who needs more rehearsal. None of the cues were right."

Plug's silence indicated that this was an unworthy attack on his life work. Charles continued, "So let's have one run-through of just the cues and then do the whole show again."

"There's not much point."

"Why not? The show opens tomorrow."

"Yes, but I won't be doing the lights then. I'm only here for the rehearsal."

Charles tried to find out what would be happening about his lights in the actual show from the Company Manager, and Brian Cassells was confident that everything would be all right. Charles, who found Brian's confidence increasingly unnerving, was not convinced.

"Oh, incidentally, Charles, will you be going down to the Fringe reception?"

"What's that?"

"At five o'clock. Royal Mile Center. It's sort of to launch everything. You know. Press'll be there and all that."

"Then I'll certainly come." Any chance of publicity must be taken. He was not too optimistic of the "D.U.D.S. of the Fringe" poster bringing audiences flocking to see him.

Since the pubs were not open on Sunday, he had cabbage lunch with the rest of the group. The conversation was all of the coming shows. Willy Mariello's death had been almost forgotten. Charles looked round the table. Anna was not there. He suddenly wished she was, or wished that he was with her somewhere keeping the blues at bay.

The loud T-shirted crowd joked and attitudinized. He felt old and envious. Their values were so simple. What they were doing on the Fringe was the most important thing that had ever happened; that was all there was to it. Their shows consumed all their thought and energies.

Except for the thoughts of one person—the murderer. He or she must be feeling regret or anxiety or something. But the lunchtime crowd showed no signs of guilty conscience. They all seemed interchangeably brash and cheerful. Pam Northcliffe was up the far end of the table as nervously bright and giggly as the rest. Communal excitement had replaced the short tempers of earlier in the week.

Martin Warburton was not there. Charles wondered if he would be sharing in the group gaiety if he were. There was still a lot to be found out about Martin Warburton. That afternoon might be a good opportunity to read *Who Now?*—a Disturbing New Play.

It was disturbing. The language was good, there was some sense of structure, but the content was frightening. As the title implied, questions of identity figured large. None of the characters seemed to have a fixed personality; they were chameleons who took on the color of different forms of violence. There was a woolly Leftish political message coming through the monologues that made up the play. Its main tenet seemed to be that, come the Revolution, the bourgeois would be destroyed. But it was the way in which they were going to be destroyed that was disturbing. Images of bombings, secret beatings and firing squads abounded. Continually blood welled, bones cracked, corpses twitched and entrails spilled. So much blood.

Under normal circumstances, Charles would have put it down to over-writing. Some of the extended metaphors even reminded him of his own adolescent literary excesses. But even so, and even given a young person's insensitive ignorance of the real facts of death, there was something obsessive about the play. A morbid preoccupation with violence unbalanced the writer's considerable natural talent.

And became uncomfortably relevant in the light of Willy Mariello's death.

About half past four Martin Warburton suddenly appeared in the men's dormitory. He seemed in a hurry and had dropped in to collect something from his suitcase. Charles was lying on his campbed checking through *So Much Comic* . . .

"Oh, Martin, I've read your play."

"Ah." He seemed embarrassed.

"I'd like to talk about it."

"Ah."

"Now? If you're walking down to this reception, we could chat on the way."

"I'm not going to the reception." Martin hesitated. He was improvising. "I'm going to meet someone down at . . . er . . . Dean Village."

"Oh. O.K. Well, some other time."

"Yes."

Charles started off with some of the *Mary* cast to walk to the Royal Mile Center. Just as they were about to cross Princes Street to go up the Mound, he realized that he had not brought any of his hand-outs. Even a playbill offering one of the DUDS of the Fringe was better than no publicity. Brian Cassells would not have thought to take any. With some annoyance, because it was a warm afternoon, he started back along Princes Street.

He was waiting for the lights to cross Charlotte Street when he saw Martin over the other side striding purposefully along Lothian Road. In the opposite direction from Dean Village.

Charles was not aware of making the decision, but it seemed natural to cross over Princes Street and follow. He was some fifty yards behind his quarry and there were enough meandering tourists about to make the pursuit look casual. He kept his eyes fixed on the blue denim back ahead.

Martin turned left along Castle Terrace which skirts the great Castle rock, then crossed over Spittal Street and climbed up towards Lauriston Place. Maybe going to the Masonic Hall. The scene of the crime. There were no rehearsals that afternoon. Everyone was going down to the reception. Or perhaps Martin was aiming for the Mariellos' house in Meadow Lane. Charles felt a spurt of excitement.

There were less people about in this part of the old town, so he dawdled. He did not want to be noticed if Martin stopped suddenly.

But the boy did not stop. The blue denim back continued its progress. Past the Masonic Hall, no hesitation. Past the Meadow Lane turning. On past the Infirmary, looking neither left nor right. Charles began to feel it was a long walk.

And it continued. On past the University Union with its cloth banner advertising Russell Hunter in *Knox*. On to Nicholson Square and then suddenly right, along the broad pavement of Nicholson Street. Martin still kept up his even, preoccupied pace, with Charles alternately lingering and hurrying along behind.

The whole thing seemed pointless. Charles could not really think what he was doing, playing this elaborate game of cops and robbers when he should be snatching much-needed publicity at the reception. Perhaps Martin was just going out for a walk. Something innocuous. Something—

Martin had disappeared. The fact jerked Charles out of his reverie. One moment the denim back had been moving smoothly along, the next it was gone. In the middle of a parade of shops. No chance of having turned up a side street.

Cautiously Charles moved forward to where he had last seen Martin. All the shops were Sunday shut. Their fronts were separated by doors which served the flats above. Gently Charles pushed the one nearest to where he had last seen Martin.

It was a heavy door, but it gave. The stone hall was dark and suddenly cool. A pram. A bicycle. Stone stairs, a metal rail. And attached to the top of the door a heavy chain that was part of some antiquated system to open it from the flats above.

Just an ordinary hall of an ordinary tenement block. Silence. He could not start barging into private flats at high tea time on an Edinburgh Sunday afternoon. Anyway, what was he looking for? He went out into the street again.

The names on the old-fashioned bell-pushes told him nothing.

McHarg, Stewart, Grant, Wilson. He waited for about five minutes, apparently intrigued by a display of dusty Pyrex in an adjacent shop. Martin did not re-emerge. It was after half past five. Charles set off for the Royal Mile Center.

At the entrance he was asked to identify himself.

"Charles Paris."

"Not your name. Who are you with?"

"Oh, Derby University Dramatic Society."

The result was that he entered the upstairs assembly room with a red card badge bearing the legend "D.U.D.S." It did not seem very positive advertising.

Entering the room was difficult: it was so full that he had to ease one shoulder in as a wedge and wriggle the rest of his body in after it. Some people had glasses of drink. Infallible instinct tracked its source and he slid and sidled over to a long table.

The drink was a pink wine-cup of minimal alcoholic content. Charles looked out across the throng. A swarm of cultural locusts was buzzing loudly and milling round the red badges which bore the names of newspapers, radio or television companies.

Everyone had a badge. *Radio Clyde* bounced on the forceful breasts of a young reporter. *Bradford* clung to chain mail worn to publicize their play *The Quest.* *B.B.C.* flopped on well-cut mohair. *Nottingham* sagged on a dirty T-shirt.

And everyone forced literature on everyone else. Charles had only to stand there to become a litter-bin for hand-outs and programs. He kicked himself for wasting time following Martin and not getting his own publicity.

A glance at the cultural treats the literature offered revealed that there was not much he would want to see, but it was at least varied. There was *Problem 32* by Framework Theatre—"ten young designers creating an hour's theatre in their own terms." The World Première of *Scots Wha Hae,* a new Scots comedy from the group that brought you *The De'il's Awa'* and *Cambusdonald Royal.* Paris Pandemonium Projects offered *Chaos, Un Collage de Comédie.* Under the intriguing title *Charlotte Brontë and her Scotsmen,* Accolade were presenting "psychological deduction of her relations with men in her last years (reduced prices for students and Old Age Pensioners)." Or there was Birkenhead Dada with *We Call for the Decease of Salvador Dali*—"Shocks, poems and perversions; indefensible personal attacks; new levels of tastelessness."

In other words the Fringe was much as usual. But with decreasing conviction. Charles remembered the heady days of the late fifties and early sixties when Edinburgh was the only outlet for experimental drama in Britain. The recent spread of little theatres in London and other major cities had eroded that unique position. And the Edinburgh Fringe seemed less important. Less truly experimental. Too many of the university groups were doing end-of-term productions of classics rather than looking for new ideas.

"Not a lot, is there, Charles?"

He looked up and recognized one of the *Guardian* critics. "Just thinking the same. How long are you up?"

"A week. A week of sifting dirty sand looking for diamonds. Which probably don't exist."

"Sounds fun."

"But what are you doing up here?"

"My one-man show on Thomas Hood. *So Much Comic, So Much Blood.*"

"Oh, I'd like to see that. Did it at York, didn't you?"

"Yes."

"Hmm. I missed it there. Haven't seen much publicity."

"No, it's been a bit thin on the ground. Last-minute booking."

"Ah. Well, give me the details." The critic wrote them down on the back of a Theatre Wagon of Virginia, U.S.A. handout that looked depressingly disposable. "Right, I'll be along."

"And spread the word among your colleagues. Or rivals."

"Will do, Charles." The critic edged off into the throng.

It might be worth something. But he should have brought the hand-outs. His own printed sheet stood more chance of survival than jottings on the back of someone else's.

The crush got worse rather than better. Over on the far side of the room Anna's cropped head was instantly recognizable. She was talking enthusiastically, surrounded by a crowd of journalists. He felt a momentary pang of jealousy, a desire to go over and claim her. But no, she was right. Better to keep it quiet. Later they'd be together. The thought warmed him.

"Hello." Pam Northcliffe wormed her way between a green velvet suit and a coat of dishcloth chain mail. She looked flushed and breathless. There was an empty glass in her hand which Charles filled from a jug on the table. "Oh Lord." She took a sip at it. "A few people, aren't there?"

"Just a few. How are you?"

"Oh. Pissed, I think." She giggled at the audacity of her vocabulary. He was surprised. He felt he could have poured that pink fluid into himself for a year and not registered on the most sensitive breathalyzer. Still, Pam claimed to be pissed and certainly she was much more relaxed and forthcoming on what she thought of her fellow-students. A wicked humor flashed into her observations and at times she even looked attractive.

Charles decided that this confidential mood was too good to waste from the point of view of his investigations. The crowd was beginning to thin out, but he did not want to lose her. "You rehearsing now?"

"No, they're doing the *Dream* at seven thirty—a run as per performance. I'll be doing props for the revue at eleven—if I'm sober enough."

"Come and have another drink. That'll sober you up."

She giggled. "Everywhere's closed on a Sunday."

"No. We can go up to the Traverse."

The Traverse Theatre Club had moved since Charles had last been there doing a strange Dürrenmatt play in 1968. But he found the new premises and managed to re-establish his membership. (The girl on the box-office was distrustful until he explained his credentials as a genuine actor and culture-lover. Too many people tried to join for the club's relaxed drinking hours rather than its theatrical milestones.)

The media contingent from the Royal Mile Center seemed to have been transplanted bodily to the Traverse bar. But the crush was less and Charles and Pam found a round wooden table to sit on. He fought to the counter and brought back two glasses of red wine as trophies. "Cheers, Pam."

"Cheers." She took a long swallow. Then she looked at him. "Thank you?"

"What for?"

"Bringing me here."

"It's nothing."

"No, it's kind of you. I know it's only because you feel sorry for me."

"Well, I . . ." He was embarrassed. He had not done it for that reason, but his real motive was not much more defensible. "What do you mean?"

"You're just being kind. Taking me out of myself. And I appreciate it." She spoke without rancor. "I know I'm not very attractive."

He laughed uneasily. "Oh, come on. What's that got to do with it? I mean, not that you aren't attractive, but I mean . . . Can't I just ask you for a drink because I like your company? Do you take me for a dirty old man? I'm old enough to be your father." (And, incidentally, old enough to be Anna's father.)

He was floundering. Fortunately Pam did not seem to notice; she wanted to talk about her predicament. "I never realized how important being pretty was. When I lived at home, my parents kept saying I was all right and I suppose I believed them. Then, when I went to Derby, all that was taken away. What you looked like was the only thing that mattered and I was ugly." Charles could not think of anything helpful to say. She seemed quite rational, not self-pitying, glad of an audience. She continued, "You had to have a man."

"Or at least fancy one?"

"Yes. A frustrated romance was better than nothing. You had to assert yourself sort of . . . sexually. You know what I mean?"

Charles nodded, "Yes. Have a sexual identity. At best a lover, at worst an idol." He played his bait out gently. "A public figure, maybe . . . A symbol . . . Perhaps just a poster . . ."

Pam flushed suddenly and he knew he had a bite. "I found the poster torn up in the dustbin."

"Ah." She looked down shamefaced.

"Did you love Willy Mariello?"

"No. It was just . . . I don't know. All this pressure, and then Puce came to play at the Union and I met him. And, you know, he was a rock star . . ."

"Potent symbol."

"Yes. And lots of the other girls in the hall of residence thought he was marvellous and bought posters and . . ." She looked up defiantly. "It's terrible emotional immaturity, I know. But I am emotionally immature. Thanks to a middle-class upbringing. It was just a schoolgirl crush."

"Did you know him well?"

"No, that's what makes it so pathetic. I mean, I knew him to say hello to, but nothing more. He didn't notice me."

"You never slept with him?"

Her eyes opened wide. "Oh Lord, no."

"So why the rush to get rid of the poster?"

"I don't know. That was daft. I was just so confused—what with the death, and the police asking all those questions . . . and then you asking questions . . . I don't know. I got paranoid. I thought somehow if my things were searched and they found the poster that I'd be incriminated or . . . I don't know. I wasn't thinking straight."

It rang true. The brief mystery of the poster was explained. But there must be more to be found out from Pam. "What did you feel about Willy when he was dead?"

"Shock. I mean, I hadn't seen a dead body before."

"Nothing else?"

"No, I don't think so."

"No sense of loss?"

"Not really. I mean, it wasn't real love, just something I'd built up in my mind. In a way his death got it out of my system, made me realize that I didn't really feel a thing for him. Anyway, it had been fading ever since we came up here."

"As you saw more of him?"

"Yes." She grinned ruefully. "He became more real. Just an ordinary man. And perhaps not a very nice one. Anyway, I didn't really feel the same about him after that business with Lesley . . ."

Charles picked up the last few words as if they were the ash of a vital document in a murderer's fireplace. "Business with Lesley?"

"Yes, I . . . well, I haven't mentioned it to anyone, but . . . it may be nothing, just the way it seemed . . ."

"What?"

"It was after we'd been up here about a week. Willy suddenly started to take an interest in Lesley—that's Lesley Petter who—"

"I know about her. Go on."

"I think he was probably after her, fancied her, I don't know. Anyway, one evening, after we'd been rehearsing, we were all having coffee back at Coates Gardens and Willy said he was going for a walk up to the Castle and did anyone want to come with him. Well, I said yes sort of straight off, because, you know, I thought he was marvellous and . . . But then I realized that he'd only said that as a sort of pre-arranged signal to Lesley. It was meant to be just the two of them.

"I was awfully embarrassed, but I couldn't say I wouldn't go when I realized. So the three of us set off and I dawdled or went ahead or . . . wishing like anything I wasn't there.

"We went up to the Castle Esplanade and wandered around, and I, feeling more and more of a gooseberry, went on ahead on the way back. I started off down the steps that go down to Johnstone Terrace."

"Castle Wynd South."

"Is that what it's called, yes. Anyway, I was nearly at the bottom, and suddenly I heard this scream. I turned round and saw Lesley, with her arms and legs flailing, falling down the steps."

"And that was how she broke her leg?"

"Yes. I rushed up to where she'd managed to stop herself, and Willy rushed down. She was in terrible pain and I shot off to phone for an ambulance. But just before I went, I heard her say something to Willy, or at least I think I did."

Charles felt the excitement prickling over his shoulders and neck. "What did she say?"

"She said, 'Willy, you pushed me'."

CHAPTER 7

"Be thou my park, and I will be thy dear,"
(So he began at least to speak or quote;)
"Be thou my bark, and I thy gondolier,"
(For passion takes this figurative note;)
"Be thou my light, and I thy chandelier;
Be thou my dove, and I will be thy cote;
My lily be, and I will be thy river;
Be thou my life—and I will be thy liver."

BIANCA'S DREAM

THE SHOW BIZ RAZZMATAZZ of first nights was invented before the development of lunchtime theatre. There is something incongruous about flowers and telegrams for a first lunch. Charles did not get any, anyway. There was no one to send them. Maurice Skellern was the only person outside Edinburgh who knew the show was happening and he was not the sort to spend his client's money on fulsome gestures. Charles deliberately had not told his ex-wife Frances that he was going up to the Festival as another hack at the fraying but resilient umbilical cord that joined him to her.

But the first night excitement was there. He walked from Coates Gardens to the Masonic Hall with a jumpy step, a little gurgling void of anticipation in his stomach. To his relief, the odious Plug had been replaced by an amiable young man called Vernon, who was not only efficient in the rehearsal but was also staying for the show. It made Charles feel more confident. And more scared. With the technical side under control, no excuses were possible, it was his responsibility entirely.

He calmed himself by hard work. One run of the show for Vernon's benefit, to get the cues right, then a quick double-check through all the slides; finally as-per-performance run which was depressingly pedestrian. As it should be. Charles believed in the old theatrical adage about bad dress rehearsals leading to good first nights.

A few more details checked, then down to the pub about twelve-thirty for a quick one. Just one; mustn't risk slurring. Vernon was quiet and reassuring, a good companion for last-minute anxieties. Yes, he would hold the last fade. Yes, he would anticipate the slide of *The Last Man* sitting on the gallows. No, he didn't think there was too much serious stuff in the program. No, he didn't think the dark suit was too anonymous.

Back at the hall Brian Cassells was in charge as Front of House Manager. Apparently he felt that evening dress was obligatory for this rôle, though he looked a little out of place penguined up at lunchtime. He admitted to Charles that advance sales were not that good (three seats), but he had great hopes for casual trade during the next twenty minutes.

Sharp on one fifteen the show started. Charles had felt on the edge of nausea as he waited to enter in the blackout, but as usual actually being onstage gave him a sense of calm and control.

The imperfect masking of the hall's windows meant that the audience was visible, but he did not dare to look until he had received some reaction. The watershed was *Faithless Nellie Gray;* nothing expected on *I Remember, I Remember* and the rest of the preamble. But the first Pathetic Ballad should get something.

> *Ben Battle was a soldier bold,*
> *And used to war's alarms;*
> *But a cannon-ball took off his legs,*
> *So he laid down his arms.*

Yes, a distinct laugh. And the laughs built through the ensuing stanzas. Not a big sound, but warming.

Emboldened, he inspected the audience as he recited. About twenty, which, on the first day of the Festival, with negative publicity, was not bad. On the second glance he realized that a lot of it was paper, members of D.U.D.S. who had not been allowed in free. There was a little knot of revue cast, dark figures grouped around Anna's shining head. James Milne leaned forward in his seat with intense concentration. There were only about eight faces Charles did not recognize. And some of those might be complimentaries for the critics. Maurice Skellern was not going to be over-impressed by ten per cent of fifty per cent of that lot.

But it was an audience. And they were responding. Charles enjoyed himself.

The Laird insisted on taking him out to lunch. They went to an Indian restaurant on Forrest Place and managed to persuade the waiter it was still early enough for them to have a bottle of wine. After a couple of glasses Charles felt better. The immediate reaction after a show was always emptiness, even depression, and the ability to remember only the things that went wrong. Gradually it passed, alcohol always speeded the process.

So did enthusiastic response to the show. And James Milne was very enthusiastic. He had only known the familiar poems of Hood, the ones which have become clichés by repetition, *No-vember, A Retrospective Review, The Song of the Shirt* and the inevitable *I Remember, I Remember*. The broadening of the picture which Charles's show had given obviously excited him. The punning and other verbal tricks appealed to his crossword mind. "I had no idea there was so much variety, Charles. I really must get hold of a *Complete Works.* Is there a good edition?"

"There's an Oxford one, but I don't know if it's in print. You might be able to pick up a second-hand one somewhere. Or there are some fairly good selections. But look, if you want to borrow mine, do. I should know my words by now." He held the copy across the table.

The Laird was touched. By his values, lending a book was the highest form of friendship. "That's very kind. I'll look after it."

"I know you will."

"And I'll make it a priority to find one for myself. Oh, you know I envy that kind of facility with words. Not just the facility—we all happen on puns occasionally—but the ability to create something out of it. It must be wonderful to be a writer."

"I don't know. It was hard graft for Hood. If he hadn't had to work so hard, he might have lived longer."

"Yes, but at least it's congenial graft. I mean, writing, you're on your own, you get on with it, you don't have to keep getting involved with other people. You just write and send your stuff off and that's it. A sort of remote control way of making a living."

Charles laughed out loud. "James, you've got it all wrong. Hood would disagree with you totally. He didn't just sit at a desk toying with his muse and packing the products off in envelopes to editors. All his life was spent scurrying round, selling his own work, sub-editing other people's, setting up magazines. No question of remote control, his Liveli-Hood, as he kept calling it, was very much involved with other people."

"But some writers don't have to do all that, Charles."

"Very few. In my own experience of writing plays, about ten per cent of the time is spent actually writing; ninety percent is traipsing around like a peddler, hawking the results to managements or television companies."

"Oh dear. So what you are saying is that a writer's life is just as sordid and ordinary as everyone else's?"

"If not more so. Hood himself, in his *Copyright and Copywrong,* said of writers, 'We are on a par with quack doctors, street preachers, strollers, ballad-singers, hawkers of last dying speeches, Punch and Judies, conjurers, tumblers and other diverting vagabonds.'"

"How very disappointing. I think I'd rather forget you told me that and keep my illusions of ivory towers and groves of Academe."

They talked further about writing. James Milne admitted that he would have liked to produce something himself, but never got around to it. "Which means perhaps that I haven't really got anything to say."

"Maybe. Though writing doesn't have to say anything. It can just be there to entertain," said Charles, reflecting on his own few plays.

"Hmm. Perhaps, but even then the writer must get a bit involved. Begin to identify with his characters."

"Oh, inevitably that happens."

The Laird paused for a moment, piecing his thoughts together.

"I was wondering if there could be anything of that behind this murder."

"What do you mean? Anything of what?"

"Identification. I mean, if there's anything in the actual situation of the killing, the way it happened."

"I'm still not with you."

"Willy Mariello was playing David Rizzio in a play based on the life of Mary, Queen of Scots. Now there are certain obvious parallels between Willy and Rizzio. There's the Italian name, for a start. I know there are lots of Scots with Italian names, but it's a coincidence. Then they both played the guitar."

"So what you're suggesting," Charles said slowly, "is that someone got obsessed with the whole Mary, Queen of Scots story and identified with Rizzio's murder and . . . Incidentally, who did kill Rizzio?"

"A lot of people, I seem to recall. I think Darnley was the prime mover. Who's playing Darnley in the show?"

"I don't know. I could check. And you think when we've got that name we've got our murderer?" He could not keep a note of skepticism out of his voice.

"It's just another possible line of enquiry. Something that struck me."

"Hmm."

"Well, we're not getting far on any other tack are we?"

Charles hesitated. "No."

"You haven't found out anything else, have you?"

"No," he lied. For some reason he did not want to tell anyone about Pam Northcliffe's story of Willy and Lesley. Not yet.

The Laird was going to browse round some bookshops, but Charles did not feel like it. He was still wound up after the performance, and, since licensing hours did not permit his usual method of unwinding, he decided an aimless stroll round Edinburgh might do the trick.

The stroll soon ceased to be aimless. He had only gone a few hundred yards and was turning off George IV bridge into Chambers Street when he saw Martin Warburton. Striding along on the opposite side of the road with the same expression of blinkered concentration that he had had the day before. And again heading for Nicholson Street.

It is a lot easier following someone when you know where he is going and Charles felt confident of Martin's destination. He was right. The boy again disappeared behind the blue door.

The excitement of seeing the same thing happen two days running quickly gave way to confusion as to what should be done about it. Charles still did not know which flat Martin had gone into and did not feel in the mood for an elaborate masquerade as a reader of gas-meters to gain access. Apart from the risk of illegal impersonation, what would he say if he did find Martin? There was probably some simple explanation for the boy's actions. He had friends living in the flats. Maybe even a girlfriend. Something quite straightforward. Charles was just letting his imagination run riot and suspicion was clouding his judgment.

But he did not want to go. He might be on the verge of some discovery. Better join the bus queue opposite while he worked out a plan of campaign.

As he stood with the laden housewives and noisy schoolchildren he knew it was not really getting him anywhere. No plan of campaign emerged. If he really wanted to find out what Martin was doing, then the only course was to enter the flats. Otherwise he might just as well give up the whole business, leave Willy Mariello to the police and forget any detective fantasies he might be nurturing.

A bus arrived and the queue surged forward, canny housewives wedging themselves into good seats and practiced schoolchildren scampering upstairs to good fooling-about positions. One or two of them gave curious looks to the man at the stop who still queued altruistically without taking his due prize of a seat. The maroon and white bus passed on.

Charles felt exposed and ridiculous on his own at the bus-stop. He turned to go, determined to chuck the whole business and resign himself to just being an actor, when he heard the bang of a door on the other side of the road.

It was the blue one, and a thin figure was walking away from it towards the center of the city. Walking with a determined gait, but not walking like Martin Warburton. It was a slightly unnatural heavier step.

And not looking like Martin Warburton either. A woolen hat gave the impression of short hair. A beard and moustache. Glasses. Dressed in an old donkey jacket and shapeless twill trousers. A khaki knapsack slung across one shoulder. And this strange ponderous walk.

It was the figure whom Charles had seen the previous week on the steps down to the Mound. And it was Martin Warburton in disguise.

By eleven o'clock that evening Martin's identity games did not seem very important. One reason was that afternoon's adventures had not led to anything. Charles had continued tailing his disguised quarry halfway across Edinburgh until Martin had disappeared inside the Scottish National Portrait Gallery in Queen Street. Rather than risk raising suspicions by a confrontation inside the building, the self-questioning sleuth had waited twenty minutes some way down the road. Then he had followed the donkey jacket back to Nicholson Street, missed a few more buses while the young man was reconverted into Martin Warburton and trailed behind that familiar figure back to Coates Gardens. All of which left Charles with sore feet and the feeling that if Martin wanted to do his Edinburgh sightseeing in disguise, that was his own affair. And that Charles Paris needed a drink.

Which accounted for the other reason why Martin's behavior seemed unimportant. Charles was satisfyingly pissed.

After solitary refueling at the pub, he had found Anna with the rest of the revue team at Coates Gardens. He had taken her out for a meal, to celebrate the opening of his show and keep her mind off the opening of hers. They went to the Casa Española in Rose Street and, since Anna was in a high state of nerves, he had to eat most of a large paella and drink all of the wine. A fate which he embraced with fortitude and which contributed to his present well-being.

It had also been encouraging to see Anna nervous. She was as jumpy as a kitten and it was the first time he had seen her lose her cool at all. Which made her seem more human. And even nicer.

Charles thought of her warmly as he sat in the Masonic Hall and fingered her key in his pocket. He had the drunkard's feeling of sexual omnicompetence and longed to be with her in the bed over the Lawnmarket. It would not be long. After the revue. He would go discreetly back to the flat and then, after the company giggles and congratulations, she would join him.

The lights dimmed. Not bad; the house was two-thirds full. He sat back in the right mood to enjoy *Brown Derby*—"Simply the Funniest Late-Night Revue on the Fringe."

If it was, it did not say a lot for the others. *Brown Derby* was a hotch-potch of styles. Decrepit jokes that should have been allowed quiet deaths were resuscitated and paraded as new. Dull irrelevant puns were presented as wit. The ill-digested influence of television comedy made for uncomfortable production. Though there were flashes of humor, the show was heavy going, and never heavier than in its topical material. The comments on the British political scene showed neither insight nor understanding and the piece on the American presidency was frankly embarrassing. Ten days after President Nixon's resignation was not the time for a naïve and tasteless parody of Adolf Hitler in his bunker (including some pretty tired jokes about golf).

And it was not a case of a brilliant new team struggling valiantly against unworthy material. The cast was not good. If acting at its most basic is making oneself heard and not bumping into the furniture, they failed as actors on two counts. They were rarely audible and kept tripping over chairs (especially during the extended blackouts between sketches, with the result that the lights usually came up on some puzzled youth lying full length on the upturned furniture). They had almost no talent.

Except for Anna. She was extraordinarily good and, given the lack of competition, dominated the show completely. Singing, dancing, flashing through a variety of accents and costumes, she was the only person onstage with any concept of pace or comedy. The direness of the material she had to perform only highlighted her skill.

Charles was amazed. Anna was a beautiful girl, but onstage she was animated by an extra charge that intensified her beauty. A real stage presence. He could feel the men in the audience responding to her. When she came on for her last number *A Bunny Girl's Lament* (a reasonable idea, marred by flabby lyrics), dressed in full

Playboy Club kit, showing her long brown legs, the audience broke into spontaneous applause. It was not just that she looked sexy; she managed to incorporate an archness which distanced her from her material and was also extremely funny. Anna Duncan was that rare creature, a woman who can be funny onstage without sacrificing either her dignity or her sex appeal.

It was late when she tapped on the door of the Lawnmarket flat. The first night junketings must have gone on a bit. Perhaps the *Brown Derby* cast had been drowning their sorrows. Or perhaps they were celebrating, thinking that the enthusiastic final applause for Anna was meant for all of them.

She looked him straight in the eye. "Well, what's your cool professional assessment?"

"Can you take it?"

"Yes."

"Well, I'm afraid I thought the show was terrible. The only constructive suggestions that I can make are that your writers should go and sell vacuum cleaners, your male cast should join the Army and your director should become a monk."

"Hmm." The navy blue eyes kept their level gaze fixed on him. She knew there was more to come.

So he let it come. "I would also like to say that you are one of the most talented young actresses I have ever seen."

She smiled and allowed herself a slight relaxation of relief.

"Charles, I asked for your cool professional assessment."

"That was my cool professional assessment."

"Hmm. Sounds biased." But she was obviously delighted.

"Biased nothing! I may also happen to think you are the best screw in the world, but I do genuinely believe that you are exceptionally talented as an actress. Now come and make love."

She grinned suddenly. "You talked me into it."

It was even better. They were completely together. He rolled apart from her and cradled the strong slender body in his arms. Her breasts were slack against his ribs, her breath soft on his shoulder. He recited gently into her hair.

" 'O, happy times! O happy rhymes!
For ever ye're gone by!
Few now—if any—are the lays

Can make me smile or sigh.'
But you're one of them. You can make me smile and sigh."

"I don't think Thomas Hood meant 'lay' that way," she murmured lazily.

"No, I don't think he did."

"Incidentally, I liked your show. I think I was too uptight over dinner to mention it."

"Thank you. Mutual admiration society."

"Hmm." There was a long pause. He wondered if she had gone to sleep. But she spoke again. "Do you really think I'm good?"

"Yes."

"Good enough to make it in the professional theatre?"

"Yes."

"In spite of all you said about needing to be tough and calculating, and needing lots of help?"

"I'll help you, Anna."

Soon she was asleep. Charles lay thinking. He could help her. Get her work, maybe. Even cast her in plays he was directing. He felt useful and wanted to give to her. To give a lot. Was it so ridiculous for a man of nearly forty-eight to go round with a girl in her early twenties? His experience could help her. He felt something for Anna that he had not felt for a long, long time. Possibly even love.

CHAPTER 8

O William Dear! O William Dear!
  My rest eternal ceases;
Alas! my everlasting peace
  Is broken into pieces.

MARY'S GHOST

TUESDAY, AUGUST 20TH was an unsettling day.

It started all right. Charles felt at one with Anna and at one with the world. She left the flat at about half-past nine. (Michael Vanderzee was champing at the bit to get his workshop sessions restarted after the lay-off caused by the revue's opening.) Charles had a leisurely breakfast of floury bacon rolls at the Poppin and then, as a token gesture to detective work, he went back to the Scottish National Portrait Gallery to see if he could work out the reason for Martin's visit.

The Gallery was well laid out and should have been interesting, but he was not in the mood for inspecting the faces of people he had never heard of. The whole business of searching for clues and motives was beginning to bore him.

He was gazing at a wax model of William III when he remembered the newspapers. The day after a first night (or at least a first lunch) and he had not yet checked to see if there were any notices. The rest of the portraits could wait. He hurried out under the disapproving glare of the large-nosed faces of Scotland's heritage.

There was a big newsagents on Princes Street. Rather than behaving logically and starting with just the *Guardian,* he went mad and bought every available daily. Which meant a great deal of waste paper; *So Much Comic* . . . had so far failed to capture the interest of the nationals.

He stood in the street reading and dropped the inadequate newspapers one by one into a litter-bin. Nothing in the *Guardian;* so much for his conversation at the Fringe Reception. Charles realized he was being naïvely optimistic to expect to be noticed on the first day of the Festival, particularly with negative advertising.

Only the *Glasgow Herald* left. He opened it without hope, and on the review page, there it was.

> *So Much Comic, So Much Blood,* Masonic Hall, Lauriston Place. Thomas Hood is now remembered, if at all, for about three poems which recur in anthologies. It was therefore a pleasant surprise to get a broader view of the poet's work from this enchanting lunchtime show. Charles Paris has compiled a skillful program from poems and letters, which maintains a fine balance between humor and pathos without ever slipping into sentimentality. He performs the show with the clarity and understatement which are the hallmark of real talent. Do try to catch this. It's only on for the first week of the Festival and I guarantee more laughs than in most of the late-night revues.

Charles could not control an ebullient smile. What he held in his hands was a good old-fashioned rave.

Thanks to the review and a couple of large Bell's, he arrived at the Masonic Hall at a quarter to one in high spirits and totally devoid of nerves. He felt confident as he waited in the wings for the lights to go down.

From that point on the day deteriorated. For a start, the show did not go well. A second performance is always difficult, because of the feeling of anticlimax. And the size of the audience did not augur well for the circulation figures of the *Glasgow Herald.* There were about twenty, apparently under doctor's orders that laughter was injurious to health. Puns and wisecracks vanished into the spongy void of the hall.

And, to add to that, Frances was in the audience. The woman he had married, to whom he had given the unfortunate name of Frances Paris. He recognized her as soon as the show started from her loyal, and solitary, laughter. When he stopped to consider, it was quite logical that she should be in Edinburgh. She came up most summers to give a couple of her sixth formers a quick cultural immersion. There were two girls sitting with her, one black and one white.

Charles was very fond of Frances, but he wished she was not there. Since he had walked out on her twelve years before, they had remained friendly and he had even gone back to her from time to time. She made no demands on him, but her presence, just when he was feeling secure of his relationship with Anna, was embarrassing.

He tried not to be too off-hand when she came round backstage; he had no desire to hurt her. She looked harassed and was obviously having difficulty controlling her two charges outside the school context. The white girl was dumpy and called Candy; the black girl was splendidly tangible and called Jane; both regarded Edinburgh as an opportunity to be emancipated and *meet men*.

Husband and wife exchanged Edinburgh addresses and parted amicably with vague intentions to meet up again. The encounter brought a little cloud of depression into Charles's sunny outlook.

It was not until about half past six that the cloud started to look stormy. The *Mary* cast had been rehearsing all afternoon, but most of them were released for the evening, because Michael Vanderzee wanted to work on the Mary/Bothwell scenes for an hour until Anna had to go to the revue. After a cabbage supper at Coates Gardens, the actor playing John Knox (nicknamed 'Opportunity Knox' by the rest of the cast) suggested a trip to the pub. Darnley, Ruthven and Cardinal Beaton thought it was a good idea. So did the new David Rizzio, Sam Wasserman. Charles decided that he too would like a drink.

In the Haymarket pub, he discovered that student unrest manifests itself in reluctance to be first to the bar, so he bought the round. Without conscious engineering, he found himself alone at a table with Sam.

The author of *Mary, Queen of Sots* was a young American with fine blond hair, a woffly ginger moustache and black-rimmed round glasses. He wore a thick check lumberjack shirt, the inevitable blue jeans and yellow-laced brown boots. He had arrived in Edinburgh that day, just in time to hear the boom of the one o'clock gun fired from the Castle and become immediately embroiled in one of Michael Vanderzee's workshops.

"That was after two solid days' traveling. I got Mike's telegram from the Poste Restante in Brindisi, and I just dropped everything and came. I mean, my God. I really care about this show . . ."

As soon as Sam started speaking, Charles realized why the tête-à-tête had been so easily arranged. Sam Wasserman was a bore, one of those instantly identifiable bores who has the ability to make the most interesting anecdote tedious, who can destroy by endless detail. But as well as qualifying as one of this international type, Sam also demonstrated that refinement of the quality which is peculiar to earnest young American academics. A glaze crept over Charles' eyes as the monologue continued.

". . . In fact, *Mary, Queen of Sots* derives directly from the presentation techniques I developed in a show based on the Boston Tea Party for my Master's thesis at U.S.C. . . ."

"U.S.C.?" Charles queried weakly.

"University of Southern California. I did my Master's there before coming to Derby. In Drama and Creative Writing. When I say my project was based on the Boston Tea Party, I mean of course loosely based. It concentrated on the ethnico-political problems of the American Indians. Viewed of course from a Socialist standpoint. The central allegorical symbol was the fact that the Boston Tea Party was perpetrated by white men disguised as Indians. White usurping the place of red. Like corpuscles. I used the analogy of leukemia."

Charles concentrated and tried to nudge the conversation in the direction he wanted. "But you come to this show in rather macabre circumstances."

The nudge was insufficient; Sam needed actual derailment. "The macabre is very much an integral part of my writing. And the bizarre. Another image I developed in the U.S.C. show," he steamrollered on, "was the unusual ability of the Navajo Indians to walk along girders at great height as if they were on the ground. It's a different spatial concept. I related that to the myopic nature of the social services . . ."

"Oh." Charles found himself nodding like a toy dog in the back of a car. He made another supreme effort to manhandle Sam off his monologue. "What I meant was that Willy Mariello was killed with a knife and that's why you're here actually taking part in *Mary, Queen of Sots.*"

For a moment it seemed to have worked. Sam looked straight at him and was silent for a long time before his continuation showed that Charles had failed. "Well, of course, *Mary* is an entirely different proposition, in spite of certain similarities of technique. And in fact, from an allegorical point of view, it's very apt that the show should be born in an atmosphere of violence.

"You see, the basic allegory of *Mary, Queen of Sots* is the historical parallel. The original Mary's life was stained with blood. In my version, Mary, Queen of Scots represents Scotland and the natural wealth of her oil resources."

"Oh yes," Charles mouthed, wilting.

"Yes," said Sam, as if it were a surprising affirmation. "Now Mary's two husbands, Lord Darnley and the Earl of Bothwell, I take to represent England and the good old U.S. of A., the two countries who want to control her wealth. Queen Elizabeth, who ordains her execution, is the Arab states, who hold the real power in oil politics. Neat, huh?"

Charles, suffering from mental indigestion at the thought of this labored allegory being expounded in Creative Writing, nodded feebly. But he saw a slight chance. "Where does David Rizzio fit into this scenario?"

"David Rizzio represents the ecological lobby who might argue against the exploitation of oil resources in favor of a more medieval economic structure. For that reason, he gets killed off pretty early." Sam chuckled at his own intellectual audacity.

It might be a tiny lever to shift the conversation and Charles seized it. "But not killed off as early as Willy Mariello was."

"No."

Before Sam had time to relate the death to one of his allegories, Charles pressed on. "You must have been pretty cut up to hear about Willy."

"Shocked certainly. I mean one is always shocked to hear of a young person's death; it's a kind of suspension of continuity. And obviously there was a dramatic element in this particular event."

"But you must have felt this more. To lose a friend . . ."

"I didn't know Mariello that well."

"I thought it was through you that Willy came to be in this show in the first place."

"That's true, but only indirectly. I suppose the suggestion that he should do the music came from me—I put it up to the D.U.D.S. committee—but that was on the recommendation of someone else."

"Who?"

"A girl involved in the society suggested it. I thought it was a good idea, because, you know, he was a professional musician and into rock music and I, well, I've got a kind of basic musical knowledge, but really my talent lies with *words*. And certainly the settings Mariello did for my lyrics were infinitely superior to anything I could have done. He changed the odd word here and there and I had to pull him up on that, but basically it was great. Besides, I believe very strongly in people working together under a kind of creative umbrella unit."

"Why do you think the girl recommended Willy to you?" Charles asked slowly.

"Well, like I say, he was very good. And he'd been hanging round the Derby campus for a bit and apparently, after the group he was with split up, he wanted to try something different . . ."

"And?"

"Well, I kind of got the impression that there might be a kind of thing going on between him and this girl. They both played it pretty close to the chest, but I sort of got this feeling that they wouldn't mind being involved in something together."

"Oh," said Charles, and then asked the question he had been putting off. "Who was this girl?"

"A girl called Anna Duncan. She's now playing Mary in my show. I don't know if you know her."

"Oh yes," said Charles, "I know her."

* * *

That evening he met James Milne back at Coates Gardens and found the Laird eager for another Dr. Watson session. Charles had suddenly become unwilling to pursue the business of detection, but he could not avoid a cozy chat over malt whisky.

Sherlock Holmes was always way ahead of Dr. Watson in his deductions, but he rarely actually withheld information from his sidekick. Charles Paris did. There were things he wanted to be sure of, half-formed ideas that could not be shared until they had hardened into facts.

They talked mostly about Martin Warburton. Charles told of his long tracking expeditions and the discovery of Martin's second identity.

"But surely that makes him our number one suspect?"

"I suppose so." Charles hoped he sounded convinced.

"It's fairly bizarre behavior."

"Yes, I agree. Certainly Martin is in a very strange mental state. He's all mixed up and he has some violent fantasies. I think he's probably suffering from overwork—you know, just taken finals—but that doesn't make him a murderer. His disguise may be for criminal purposes, or it may just be that he needs to escape into another identity."

"Hmm. That sounds like psychological claptrap to me."

"You don't subscribe to a psychological approach to crime?"

"I dare say it's very useful in certain cases, but I think it's often used to fog perfectly straightforward issues. Every action has some sort of motive, and I'm sure that Martin Warburton has a real motive for dressing up as someone else."

"And you don't regard an inadequacy in his personality as a real motive?"

"I regard it as a formula of words. A motive is theft or blackmail, that sort of thing. Revenge even."

"But Martin might take on another identity because there's something in his own that he can't come to terms with."

"I don't really know what you're talking about."

It was so easy for the Laird, insulated from life in his library, just as he had been insulated with his mother at Glenloan House and insulated in the staffroom at Kilbruce School. Because he had never encountered any unpleasant realities, he assumed they did not exist. Or if they did, they were simple things that could be cut up like sheets of paper, not made of material that frayed and tore and could never be properly divided.

"But, James, come off it. When we last spoke you were talking of an obsessional killer, someone for whom the Mary, Queen of Scots story had a macabre significance."

"I didn't quite say that."

"You were moving in that direction. And an obsessional killer hasn't got one of your nice neatly defined motives like theft or blackmail or revenge."

"Yes, he has. The very obsession is the motive. It's not a sane motive, but it's real to the murderer."

"Therefore you've got to understand the psychology of the murderer." Charles felt that it was a mild triumph.

"Yes, but the process is simple. Assume an inverted logic, and the motivation makes sense. You don't have to delve into inadequacies of personality and compensation and all that humbug."

"I don't think we're going to agree on this point." Charles was beginning to lose the little interest he had in their discussion. His mind was elsewhere, and not enjoying the trip. But he felt he should simulate some concern. "So if Martin, say, is an obsessional killer, what do you reckon is the motive for his walking round the city of Edinburgh in disguise?"

"It must be something to do with the planning of his next crime."

"I see." Charles tried not to sound contemptuous. "So what do you think we should do about it?"

"I think we should keep a close eye on him."

"Yes, fine. I must go." He rose with almost rude abruptness. "I've got to . . . um . . . go." He could not think of a polite excuse. He could not think of anything except the ordeal ahead of him. The ordeal of seeing Anna.

When it came, it was not really an ordeal. She arrived, flushed and excited after the revue. There had been a B.B.C. producer in the audience who (according to Brian Cassells, who had buttonholed the poor man departing and forced an opinion out of him) had liked Anna's performance. She was very giggly and charming as she described Brian's earnest relaying of the news and imagined his clumsy handling of the encounter. Charles warmed to her in spite of himself.

But he felt detached because of the tiny infection of suspicion inside him. He kept wanting to ask her about Willy, to know if they had had an affair and, by doing so, cauterize the wound before it spread to dangerous proportions. But he could not do it. Not when she was so lovely. It would spoil everything.

They drank some port that Anna had bought and giggled into bed. And they made love. As good as ever, tender, synchronized, good. Except that Charles felt he was watching the two of them like a picture on the wall. Immediately after, they switched off the light and Anna, who was exhausted by *Mary* rehearsals and the revue, slipped easily into sleep.

Charles did not. He felt better for having seen her; his imagination could not run riot while she was actually there. But the doubt remained. He wanted to excise it, cut it out of his mind. The only way to do that was to ask her pointblank. But he knew he couldn't. Not to her face. He contemplated ringing her up, even ringing her up in a different identity, pretending to be a policeman or . . . No, that was stupid.

He reasoned with himself. All right, so say she had been having an affair with Willy Mariello. So what? Charles had no particular claim on her and, anyway, he never worried about a woman's previous lovers; they didn't concern him. Jealousy over something that was over was pointless. And a lover couldn't be more over than Willy.

That was the worrying bit. Not that Anna had slept with the Scottish lout, but that he had been murdered. Again Charles reasoned with himself and calmed himself with thoughts that there might be no connection between the two facts. Indeed, they weren't both definitive facts yet. And they could be investigated.

Yes, a bit of investigation would put his mind at rest. He plumped up his pillow and turned over. Anna's breathing had a soporific rhythm. But he did not sleep.

CHAPTER 9

There's some have specs to help their sight
Of objects dim and small
But Tim had specks within his eyes,
And could not see at all.

TIM TURPIN

THE FIRST PART OF the investigation to set his mind at rest was another call on Jean Mariello.

She opened the door and leaned against it uninvitingly. "What do you want? There's nothing more I can tell you."

"Please, just a couple of questions. I think I'm on to something."

"Big deal. Listen, Mr. Paris. I'm very busy packing. The only thing that interests me about Willy is how soon I can forget he ever existed. And I don't want to play cops and robbers."

"Please give me five minutes."

"Oh . . ." She hovered between shutting him out and letting him in. Then she drew back. "Five minutes." She looked at her watch.

Charles entered the hall and moved into the front room. Jean Mariello gained some of the satisfaction she would have got from slamming the door in his face by slamming it behind him. "Right. Ask."

Charles looked around. There were suitcases and cardboard boxes brimful of belongings. In the corner household rubbish and decorating rubble was swept into a neat pile. "You're going?"

"Yes, the house is on the market. I'll never come back here."

"You're leaving Edinburgh?"

"Yes. I'm moving in with a man in the folk group. In Newcastle."

"Won't you miss it?"

"Edinburgh, yes. This house I hope I never see again."

"It's a nice enough house."

"Look, I never lived here. Willy only bought the place a few months ago. I've been on tour. The only times I ever saw it, it was covered with paint brushes or plaster dust or other evidence of Willy's latest ideas of home décor. He had the knack of converting every place we lived in into a pigsty. He'd suddenly get sick of his surroundings and want to change it all—smother everything with paint, take down a door . . . and never finish the job. We got turned out of one flat after he decided to take down the partition between the bedroom and sitting-room. Living with Willy was not an experience that gave one a feeling of home. I feel nothing for this place."

"Oh well, it's in reasonable condition. You should get a good price for it."

She snorted contemptuously. "The building society should get a good price for it."

"Ah. Still, Willy . . ."

She shook her head. "Willy had no money. He spent everything he made with Puce, not that there was much left after all the agents and managers had taken their bites. There may be a few royalties to come, but they'll go on the bank loan he got for the deposit on this place and the arrears on the mortgage."

"Arrears?"

"Yes. Willy got the mortgage on the basis of his earnings last year and the assumption that that level of income would continue. Then the band split up and he had virtually nothing. I don't think one single repayment has been made to the building society. Mind you," she added bitterly, "I only discover this when he's dead and I have to go through his mail."

"So you're not exactly a rich widow?"

He got a scornful "Huh" for that. "Mr. Paris, I can't believe that you came here to talk homes and gardens and mortgages. And if you didn't, your five minutes and my patience are running low."

"I'm sorry. But just before I ask what I really came for, tell me why Willy bought this house."

"It fitted the image of what he wanted to be. Saw himself as a great landowner, in his ancestral home in front of his blazing fire. The man of property, Willy, like all social upstarts, couldn't wait to be rich enough to be Conservative. The Socialist pose, the sub-hippy world of rock music—that meant nothing to him really. It was only a stage he had to go through. He wanted to be stinking rich with servants to do everything for him. Trouble was, he was a bloody awful business man and couldn't keep any money for more than five minutes."

There was a pause. Jean Mariello looked at her watch and Charles realized he could not beat about the bush any longer. "I really wanted to ask you about Willy's sex life."

"Oh. Well, of recent years I'm not really an expert on that."

"No. I wanted to know about another woman."

"I didn't take a great deal of interest in his other women either."

Charles ignored the rebuffs and ploughed on. "When he was in Derby—you know, he stayed after the band had played there—do you know if he had a girl then?"

"I assume so. I can't think he stayed for the scenery."

"He never mentioned a girl?"

"No. We didn't discuss our private lives." She glanced at her watch.

"Do you know if he had a girl around recently? You know, in the week before he died?"

She laughed incredulously. "I wasn't here much of the time. You know that. What do you want me to do—say if I found stains on the sheets or hairs on the pillow?"

"Yes, if necessary."

That took her aback. She paused and then said in a softer voice, "All right then, I would say, from the evidence of dirty laundry, that Willy did commit yet another desecration of our marriage bed between the Friday when I left and the Tuesday when he was killed."

"Yes?"

She spoke slowly, as if unwillingly dredging her memory. "Oh yes, he'd had someone. Hairs on the pillow, all the old familiar signs."

"What color hairs?" asked Charles breathlessly.

"Blonde." She looked at her watch. "Five minutes. Goodbye, Mr. Paris. We won't meet again."

The audience for *So Much Comic, So Much Blood* was larger and they saw a competent performance by Charles Paris. There were some laughs, although the show had no more animation than a slot-machine. As Charles' voice wove its way through Hood's tortuous puns, his mind was elsewhere.

After the show, he gathered his possessions together for a quick exit. There was something important that had to be done before three o'clock.

The women's wards in the Royal Infirmary off Lauriston Place are much the same as in other hospitals. The one Charles entered had the usual mixture of patients. An old lady stared ahead with liquid blue eyes, her long white hair radiating over the pillows. A plump bed-ridden blonde chattered to a morose husband. A homely housewife's face still registered surprise at being hospital-ized and half-listened to the sympathy of a lady in a hat. Screens hid one bed and prompted unhealthy thoughts. A thin, thin woman with shiny skin lay as still as her pillow. And, in the cor-ner bed, was a young girl with her plastered left leg raised on a pulley.

Visiting ended in ten minutes; no time to waste. "Hello. Are you Lesley Petter?"

The girl looked up and acknowledged that she was. Brown hair, shrewd brown eyes, well-proportioned but unremarkable features. Hers was the sort of face that needed emotion to animate it; in repose it was ordinary.

Charles' approach had brought some light into her eyes. Any-thing was more interesting than the pile of magazines, thrillers and ragged-edged French novels.

"I'm Charles Paris."

"Oh. You've taken over my lunchtime show."

"Yes. It's an ill wind."

She laughed wryly. "How's it going?"

"O.K."

"It's about Thomas Hood, isn't it?"

"Yes." He did not want to elaborate, though the girl's intelligent eyes indicated sensible opinions on the subject. "I'm really here for a purpose."

"Of course." She was disappointed, but philosophical. "Though I can't think what purpose of yours could involve me."

"No. Maybe it doesn't involve you." He tried to think of a way to phrase his questions. "I . . . there's . . . I don't know, your group . . . D.U.D.S., there's something strange going on there."

"It must seem strange to an outsider coming in."

"No, I expect that, as a middle-aged man with a bunch of whizz-kids. I mean strange in . . . well, there's Willy Mariello's death."

A shutter of caution flicked across her eyes. "Yes. That was terrible."

"And, of course, your accident."

"Yes." She seemed anxious to move the dialogue into a more flippant direction. "Somebody must have whistled in the dressing-room or quoted Macbeth or had real flowers onstage or broken another of the show business taboos."

Charles laughed. He was also relieved at the postponement of his questions. "You know it all. Do you want to go into the theatre?"

"Yes, I did. But . . . I don't know how good I am as an actress. Oh, I'd done bits all right, but the thing I'm really good at is dancing." She looked down the bed at the grotesque suspended limb.

"It'll heal all right."

She patently did not believe his diagnosis, though she said "Oh yes" as if there were no question.

Charles retreated to safer ground. "Anyway, I'm sure you must be a good actress. I mean, you were playing Mary and doing the revue and . . ."

"I got the parts, yes. I don't know how I'd have done them, whether I'd have got good press or . . ."

"Well . . ." He could not think of anything suitable.

"Anna got a very good notice for the revue." It was just a statement, without malice or jealousy.

"Yes, I gather she did." Charles instinctively and defensively made it sound as if he hardly knew who was being referred to.

"And I think she'll be better than I would have been in *Mary*."

"Who knows." He found himself blushing. "As I said, it's an ill wind."

"Yes."

There was a slight pause. A bell sounded, muffled, from an adjacent ward and he blurted out his question. "Lesley, did Willy Mariello push you down those steps?"

She looked at him in amazement and opened her mouth to reply. But she swallowed the instinctive answer and said in a controlled voice, "No. No. Why should he?"

It was controlled. Charles was not convinced. "Are you sure he didn't? I heard a rumor to the contrary."

"People shouldn't spread rumors," she said sharply. There was confusion in her face. "Listen, Willy's dead. My leg's broken, there's nothing can be done about that. Does it matter?"

"Yes, it does."

"Well, I don't know. To be quite honest I don't." She was floundering, an essentially nice girl unable to come to terms with something unpalatable. "I was confused when it happened and I suppose I turned on the nearest person. I . . . I don't know. I mean, would Willy do something like that? What had he possibly got to gain from doing it?"

Charles restricted himself to answering the first question. "Willy was capable of that sort of thing; he was a lout."

She looked shocked at this speaking ill of the dead. A bell was rung loudly in the corridor outside the ward. There was a rustle of parcels and final messages from the other visitors. Lesley looked at Charles pleadingly. "If he did it, I'm sure it was only high spirits, or horseplay or . . ."

"You mean he did do it?"

"I don't know. I . . ."

"Did he push you?"

"Yes, he did."

Charles left her with assurances that he would try to visit again. And he meant to. Poor kid, stuck in hospital in a strange city where all her friends were too busy to remember her.

The brown eyes were troubled when he left. And it was not just loneliness. She had managed to convince herself since the accident that it really had been a mistake, an unfortunate overflow of youthful exuberance. Now she had been forced to destroy that illusion and her kind nature was finding it difficult to believe that anyone could be so evil.

Charles had no difficulty in believing it. To him the human capacity for evil suddenly seemed infinite.

CHAPTER 10

*Thus Pleasure oft eludes our grasp
Just when we think to grip her;
And hunting after Happiness,
We only hunt a slipper.*

THE EPPING HUNT

TWO THINGS WERE CLEAR. One, a confrontation with Anna was now unavoidable. And two, he could not face that confrontation himself. He still treasured a hope that everything would be all right, that there was an innocent explanation for the disturbing chain of events that his logic was joining up. And, if his suspicions proved unfounded, he did not want to let them blight his budding relationship with the girl. There was too much at risk. She was the first woman to touch his emotions for years.

He considered the possibilities of disguise, but rejected them. As an actor, he was capable of convincing physical transformations, and he had used disguise before to gain information. But then he had not been trying to hide his identity from people he knew; here he would be trying to fool a girl he had been sleeping with. No disguise would work at close quarters under those circumstances. Even the varied wardrobe of Edinburgh's many old clothes shops and the wizardry of film make-up with foam rubber padding, latex masks and colored contact lenses would not stand close scrutiny.

He regretted that he could not use the excitement of dressing up to take his mind off the depressing tracks it was moving along. And, like most actors, he found it easier to perform difficult tasks in character than as himself. He visualized appearing to Anna in a total disguise, confirming her innocence by a few well-placed questions, then unmasking and making a joke of it.

But it was just a fantasy. He was being influenced by Martin Warburton and the strong attraction of channeling unpleasant parts of himself into another identity. The fact remained that dressing up would not work.

He contemplated interrogation by telephone. A disembodied voice could be convincingly disguised. But that introduced the problem of an identity. Who would Anna be likely to give information to in a telephone conversation? There were only two answers —someone she knew or a policeman. The first was out and Charles did not feel inclined to risk the second. On a previous occasion he had had it pointed out to him that impersonation of a policeman is a serious offence. And if Anna did have something criminal to hide, the last person she would tell about it was an investigator who had some other justifiable reason for meeting her and who could introduce relevant questions into the conversation with some pretence at casual enquiry.

Which meant an accomplice. It was Wednesday. Gerald Venables should be back from his weekend in Cannes. Charles rang his Grosvenor Street office from a call-box in the Royal Mile.

Gerald was back. "How's the sleuth-work going, Charles?"

"I don't know really. I might be on to something."

"Anything I can do?" There was immediate excitement in the voice. Gerald, who spent his entire life dealing with the peccadilloes of contract-breaking in his show-business legal firm, was fascinated by what he called "real" crime. He had a Boy's Own Paper enthusiasm for anything shady. "Wills to check out, blood samples to analyse, stool pigeons to third degree, hitmen to rub out? You name it, I'll do my best."

Charles wished he could share this detective fiction relish for the case; it all seemed depressingly real to him. "There is something you can do for me. I'm afraid it involves coming up to Edinburgh."

"That's all right. One of my clients is in the Actors' Company *Tartuffe*. There's a film contract on the way for him. I could arrange to have to come up and discuss it."

"Is it urgent?"

"No. But he's not to know that."

"You mean he's going to be footing your bill?" Charles had to remonstrate on behalf of a fellow actor.

"Don't worry. You should see the money they're paying him for the movie. And he can set me against tax. Really I'm doing him a service."

"Hmm." There was never any point in arguing with Gerald on money, it was a subject he had made his own. "Look, how soon do you think you can get up?"

"If Polly can fix me a flight, I'll be up this evening." It was typical of Gerald that he would not insult his client's money by contemplating rail travel.

But it was good from Charles' point of view. "Good. If you can make it, there's a revue I'd like you to see at eleven o'clock. Oh, and could you bring one of your little cassette recorders?"

"Conversation you want to tape?"

"That's it."

"Secretly?"

"Exactly. Do you think you'll be able to make it tonight?"

"Do my best. Can I ring you back?"

"No, I'm in a callbox."

"Ring me again in an hour and I'll tell you what gives."

Charles had decided that he could not face another night with Anna until his suspicions had been exorcised. Then, he kept telling himself, then we can bounce back together again and it'll be even better. Maybe he'd stay in Edinburgh longer than his week. Maybe even away from Edinburgh they could . . .

But not till this was sorted out.

He left the callbox and went down Cockburn Street to the Accommodation Bureau. He picked up his bag from Coates Gardens and by five o'clock was installed with Mrs. Butt in the Aberdour Guest House in Dublin Street, booked for two nights.

He rang Gerald's office from Mrs. Butt's pay-phone. Polly's efficiency had worked wonders and her boss was already in a taxi on *o cab?*

the way to Heathrow. He would reach the Princes Street terminal in a coach from Edinburgh (Turnhouse) Airport at about ten.

The next move involved seeing Anna. After a couple of bracing whiskies in a Rose Street pub, he went back to Coates Gardens, where, as he anticipated, another cabbage dinner was drawing to its blancmangy end. He signaled to Anna, who left the table discreetly and met him in the empty hall.

The lie slipped out easily. "Look, I'm sorry. Can't come tonight. An old friend called Alastair Newton came to see the show at lunchtime. He's invited me to dinner at his place. It's some way outside Edinburgh, so he suggested I stay the night there and he'll give me a lift in the morning. It's a bugger, but I can't really get out of it."

Anna looked disappointed, which did not make the deception any easier. Then she grinned. "I could do with some sleep, anyway."

He grinned too. She was beautiful and the navy blue eyes looked so open and honest, he wished the script of the last few days could be rewritten and all the promptings of suspicion cut out. He felt confident that it would be all right. Probably they would even be able to laugh about it afterwards.

"But tomorrow . . ." he hazarded, "be O.K. if I come round after the revue as per usual?"

"As per usual. Of course." There was a lot of warmth in her voice. But she was still discreet and did not want them to be seen together. "Better get back."

As she turned to go, he took her hand and leaned forward to kiss her. Their lips came together.

A creak on the stairs from the basement made Charles recoil guiltily. Anna as usual kept her cool and glanced towards the person who was staring at them. She looked back at Charles. "See you then, then." With unruffled poise she went back to the dining-room. Martin Warburton stood aside to let her pass, looked at Charles, gave one of his abrupt laughs and hurried out of the front door, slamming it behind him.

It didn't matter. Anna was the one who wanted to keep the affair quiet, and somebody was bound to twig sooner or later.

Charles remembered that he had left his toothbrush in the first-floor bathroom. On the landing he met James Milne hurrying angrily downstairs. "Oh hello, Charles. I've spoken to them before about slamming that door. Not only is it bad for the actual door, it also disturbs the neighbors and I get complaints. Did you see who it was?"

"It was Martin Warburton."

"Ah." The Laird's tone changed from angry to confidential. "Actually I wanted to talk to you about Martin Warburton. Come upstairs and have a drink."

"Have to be quick. I've got to go out to dinner." It was important to maintain the lie.

"Won't take long."

More malt in the leather-bound library. The Laird stood by his marble mantelpiece to give drama to his pronouncement. "Further to our discussion about Martin's disguise, I followed him this morning."

"From here?"

"Yes, all the way to Nicholson Street as you described. I waited and he came out with the beard and what have you, and then I followed him again. Guess where he went this time?"

"Not a clue." Charles found it difficult to get excited about Martin's bizarre doings. He had decided that they were irrelevant to the investigation.

"The Palace of Holyroodhouse," said James Milne dramatically. "Now why should he go to the National Portrait Gallery and Holyrood in disguise?"

"I don't know. Maybe he's embarrassed about being a tourist."

This flippant answer was not well received by the Laird who thought that Martin was definitely the murderer. Charles wished he could share that simple faith; it would be a relief from the forbidding tangle of thoughts that filled his head. But he did not feel inclined to tell his confidant what he knew. It would be better to play along with this Martin theory.

James Milne elaborated. "I think there's some strange tieup in his mind. It's all connected with the Mary, Queen of Scots story, I'm sure. Rizzio was only the first of a sequence of murders of people close to that particular lady."

"I'm a bit hazy about the details of her life. I just remember that she was very tall and when they executed her they lifted the head up and her wig came off."

"What unusual details you pick on, Charles. I'm sure one of your psychologists would have something to say about the selective processes of your mind. But let me tell you, there's quite a lot more significant stuff in the unfortunate queen's story. I know it fairly well—as a schoolboy I spent one long wet holiday at Glenloan reading everything available on the subject. As you probably know, Mary was the daughter of James V of Scotland and Mary of Guise—"

Charles was in no mood for a schoolmaster's lecture. Worry made him less tolerant than usual. "James, I'm sorry. I do have to go."

"Well, let me lend you a book on the subject. I won't give you one of my heavy schoolboy tomes. But there's Antonia Fraser's biography. Popular, but none the worse for that." His mental catalogue took him straight to the right volume on the shelf.

Charles was eager to leave now. He reached out for the book with muttered thanks, but James Milne kept hold of it and said with a twinkle, "If I might quote from the Great Unknown, Sir Walter Scott, 'Please return this book; I find that though many of my friends are poor arithmeticians, they are nearly all good bookkeepers.' Not a bad joke, considering the source."

Charles smiled politely and managed to leave. He was in no mood for swopping literary references. He found a pub in Dundas Street where he was unlikely to meet any of the D.U.D.S. and whiled away the time till Gerald's arrival with the co-operation of Bell's Whisky, Ltd.

The solicitor arrived at the terminal immaculate in a Prince of Wales check three-piece suit. He carried an overnight bag that looked like a giant pigskin wallet and obviously contained the neatly pressed shirt and pajamas of a travel advertisement. "Hello, buddy. Wise me up on the gen."

Charles cringed at the number of thrillers Gerald must have read, and suggested that they talk in a pub.

"Why not in the hotel bar? Then I can check in and dump the bag."

"Which hotel?"

"The North British." It had to be. Typical of Gerald. Polly had managed to fix it, and somehow the client would manage to pay for it.

Posh hotels were not Charles' usual style, but whisky's whisky anywhere. They sat in a dark corner and Gerald leaned towards him conspiratorially. "O.K. Spill the beans," he whispered unsuitably.

"Listen, is your firm engaged in any big film productions at the moment?"

"We always are. Setting up a colossal Hudson movie out in Spain. Starts filming in September if we get the contracts sorted out."

"Have you got a stake in it?"

"The firm has." The answer was discreet. Gerald never admitted his dabbling in film production, though it was common knowledge that he doubled his already considerable income by judicious investment.

"So it wouldn't be too difficult for you to pose as a film producer?"

"It would hardly be a pose," he replied smugly, and then realized that this was tantamount to an admission of financial interest in films. "That is, I'm sure I could manage."

"Right. What I want you to do is to go to a revue called *Brown Derby* at the Masonic Hall in Lauriston Place. It starts at eleven. Now there's a girl in that show called Anna Duncan. She's a good actress, but even if you don't think so, I want you to go round after the performance, introduce yourself as a film producer, say you'd like to talk to her about various ideas and would it be possible to meet for lunch tomorrow." His treachery tasted foul on his tongue, but it was necessary. He had to know.

Gerald's eyes were sparkling with excitement. "And tomorrow?"

"You take her out for lunch. I'll fill you in on what to ask her."

"O.K. And that's the conversation you want recorded?"

Charles nodded. "If it can be done."

"No sweat." The colloquialism again seemed to run counter to the Prince of Wales check. "Do you think I should use a pseudonym?"

"Don't see why you shouldn't use your own name. If you don't mind."

"No, of course not." He was a little crestfallen at losing this dramatic element, but brightened again immediately. "Is this girl Anna Duncan your Number One Suspect?"

Charles could not bring himself to answer that question, even in his own mind. "I wouldn't say that. Just need some information from her, that's all. But it's difficult for me to get it myself."

"Aren't you going to give me all the details of the case so far?"

"Tomorrow. There's no time now. You've got to get to the revue."

They made a rendezvous for the next morning and Charles went back to the Aberdour Guest House. A half-bottle of Bell's did not go far enough and he spent a long miserable night with patches of sleep.

Daylight did not speed time up much, and Gerald's arrival at Dublin Street at half-past ten added another delay to the program. Anna had a tight rehearsal schedule for *Mary* and would not have much of a break for lunch. The assignation had therefore become a dinner date, which extended the agony of waiting by eight hours. Apart from that, all had gone well the previous evening.

Charles then gave Gerald an edited version of the events surrounding Willy Mariello's death and indicated the information he required, with some hints as to what he considered the most effective way of doing it. He hoped that he was judging Anna's character right, and that she would respond in the way he anticipated. But all the time he felt increasingly despicable for the elaborate deception.

At one fifteen he did a performance of *So Much Comic, So Much Blood* without thinking about it. The audience had swelled to nearly eighty and seemed appreciative, but he hardly noticed. He even had a discussion with some dreary Welsh academic about whether

Hood's work contained High Moral Seriousness, but only the reflexes of his mind were working. The rest of it was churning with guilt and anxiety.

In the afternoon he tried to pull himself together and entertain thoughts of the other possibilities of the case. What he should really do was to retrace Martin Warburton's visit to Holyrood and see if it prompted any ideas. But even as he thought of it, he knew he could not be bothered. All his thoughts centered on Anna.

As he meandered through the city, he met Frances sitting on a bench in Princes Street Gardens. She had managed to lose Candy and Jane on a sightseeing coach tour of Edinburgh, and was appreciating the break. Charles knew she could tell he was upset, but he refused to unburden himself to her. He knew she would be understanding and reassuring. That was her most infuriating quality, the way she understood him. It was an option he did not want to take. Guilt about Frances joined the mess of unpalatable thoughts in his head.

He hardly listened to what she said. Most of it was about Candy and Jane, the shows they had seen, how exhausting she was finding it, how she'd need a proper holiday after this, how she even thought of staying up in Scotland for a few days to recuperate after the girls had gone. Charles sat, half-hearing and restless. Suddenly he created an appointment and rose. They made vague plans to meet for dinner in the next couple of days when he was clearer about his movements, and he slouched off, not daring to look back at the pain in her eyes.

It was still a long time till the pubs. He approached a cinema, but when he got there changed his mind and continued his aimless perambulation.

At last five o'clock arrived. The whisky did not work. It was as if he had a heavy cold and was numb to its powers. Half past seven came and he thought painfully of Gerald and Anna meeting in the Cosmo Ristorante in North Castle Street. He felt powerless, as if he was watching an accident from too far away to prevent it.

It was nearly ten o'clock when Mrs. Butt grudgingly admitted Gerald Venables to the Aberdour Guest House. He was flushed with excitement or wine and carrying a briefcase which contained his cassette recorder. "Got a specially long tape. I don't know what the quality will be like. I could only put the case on the table and hope for the best."

Charles was not in the mood for talking. "Let's hear it."

Gerald produced the recorder with all the pride of a schoolboy showing his Cycling Proficiency Certificate. He switched the machine on and wound the tape back. Then, as it started, he fiddled with the dials to get the optimum sound.

The quality was not bad. Gerald's own voice was distant because the microphone had been pointing away from him, but he filled in where his original questions were inaudible. There was a lot of interference from dishes being delivered and cutlery clattering, but most of Anna's answers were perfectly clear. Charles got a strange frisson from hearing her voice. It was not attraction exactly, and it was not guilt, but a mixture of emotions he had never encountered before.

The tape started with an amusing dialogue between Gerald and the waiter, who felt certain that Signor would prefer to put his case on the floor. This was followed by the detailed business of ordering. Gerald did not stint himself, and, encouraged by example, nor did Anna. The client in the Actors' Company was certainly going to pay for advice on his film contract.

After these preliminaries, Gerald started explaining why he was in Edinburgh. As a film producer, he was setting up a new movie, meeting some of the other backers, enjoying the Festival . . . and possibly even doing a bit of casting.

Anna's reaction to this was non-committal and Charles began to feel redoubled guilt. If she were innocent what he and Gerald were doing was unforgivable. No aspiring actress should have her hopes manipulated in such a way.

Gerald's distant voice then started to outline the plot of the film he was setting up, according to their plan. He dropped a few suitably substantial names and spoke airily of the locations in Spain and Finland. In fact, it was not all untrue; it was based closely on the film that he really was setting up. The only bit that was complete fabrication was that one part remained uncast. The part of a young girl, whose lover (a considerable film star was playing the part), a terrible lout, treats her cruelly and is stabbed to death halfway through the film. "Of course," purred the distant voice, "that's going to be really difficult, that's the bit that'll call for real acting. The girl's got to express this complex emotion when he's killed. She knows he's a slob, but . . . tricky. I think they should go for Diana Rigg or someone of that stature, but the director's got this crazy idea about finding an unknown. He must've read too many film magazines."

The first course was delivered. Gerald expertly checked the wine and the sound of Niagara Falls showed that Anna's glass had been adjacent to the microphone. Nothing much happened for a while except for eating and pleasantries. The waiting was purgatory for Charles. Then Gerald's voice resumed its tactics. "I'm sorry. All this talk of people being stabbed. I read in the papers about that terrible accident in your group. I shouldn't talk about it."

"It's all right." Anna's voice came through, very clear and controlled. But was the control genuine, or was there just a fraction too much, a hint of acting?

Gerald continued apologizing. "No, I'm sorry. Shouldn't have mentioned it. It's just that kind of thing's such a shock. You must have all felt that. But think how much more terrible it must be if the person who dies is a lover or someone close. It doesn't bear thinking of."

"No. It's terrible." Charles tried to prise apart the layers of intonation to understand what she meant. Was she rising to the bait? He was torn between the desire to vindicate her and the intellectual satisfaction of having his psychological approach proved right.

Gerald's voice went on, more subdued than ever. "That's the trouble. Every tragedy leaves someone behind. I suppose this . . . Mariello, was that his name? . . . I suppose he had a girl somewhere . . . oh, it's ghastly . . ."

"Yes, he had a girl . . ." There was no question about the way she said the line. She played it subtly, wasting none of her talent for drama. But its meaning was undeniably clear. Charles Paris understood that meaning and understanding hurt like physical pain.

Gerald's recorded reactions were unnecessary, but the tape ploughed relentlessly on. "You mean . . . you?"

"Yes. Willy and I were lovers." The voice was very soft, genuinely moving. There was a long intake of breath and a sob. "Were . . . lovers."

"I'm so sorry. I had no idea. I wouldn't have raised the matter if I'd had an inkling . . ." Gerald's lying protestations continued and Anna's tearful assurances that she had got over it mingled with them. She was playing the scene for all it was worth.

Her unfinished antipasta was taken away and she calmed down sufficiently for the gentle questioning to begin again. "That must have been absolutely terrible for you. To be there and . . . oh, I'm sorry. And it wasn't that you had been lovers? I mean, you still were right at the end?"

There was a long pause which Charles interpreted as Anna being thrown by the question and not knowing which way to jump. Eventually, the voice came back, quiet, but well projected. "Yes, right at the end."

"Good God." The shock sounded genuine. Gerald had played his part well too. "You've been thrown into almost exactly the same situation as the girl in this film. It's amazing." Charles no longer felt guilty about the deceit. Guilt was being forced out of his mind by swelling anger as he listened to Gerald laying the next snare. "Bereavement is an awful thing. It's so difficult to explain to anyone what you really feel, the true nature of your emotions.

"And of course it's even more complex for the girl in this film. Her lover is, as I said, not very loving. A real bastard, in fact, keeps doing crazy things, cruel things, criminal things. I think the character's overdrawn. No woman would stay with a man like that."

"I don't know . . ." Again just a simple remark infused with all the art her considerable talent could muster.

"But surely . . ."

"What, all that not speaking ill of the dead business? Why should I worry? He's dead, and when he was alive, it was not his goodness I loved him for. I knew his faults. He could be cruel, oh yes, and evil." She was warming to her performance. "He'd do crazy things. Wicked things, and he'd say he'd done them for me."

Gerald had only to grunt interest; she needed no prompting. "I mean, take an example. Recently, he nearly killed someone for me.

Yes." She let the drama of it sink in. "There was a girl in our group who would have been in the revue. She had the part I'm playing. And one day I must have said to Willy that I envied her. I don't mean I was jealous; she was a sweet girl, I liked her—but I must have said what a super part she had or something. And do you know what Willy did?"

"No," said Gerald, on cue.

"He pushed her down some stone steps."

"Good God."

"Yes. It was so cruel. No, I'm sorry, you were wrong when you said I didn't know what it was like to love a bastard. I do, to my cost."

Charles rose suddenly and switched off the machine.

"She really was very moving," said Gerald. "Very. And you reckon this is all significant information? *Cherchez la femme,* that's what they always say in detective stories. Frailty, thy name is woman. Is it Raymond Chandler who calls them frails?"

"Is there much more?" Charles snapped.

"A couple of courses. She did perk up a bit after that."

"After she'd finished her audition."

"Yes, I suppose you could say that."

"I'll spool through and see if there's anything relevant."

"No, I'll do it, Charles," said Gerald hastily. "Incredibly pretty girl, I must say. Sort of navy blue eyes. Do you know her well?"

"I thought I did."

"Oh." Understanding dawned. "Oh." Gerald busied himself spooling on and playing snatches of the tape. It was mostly general talk about films and the theatre. At one point Charles's ears pricked up.

". . . had a lot of experience acting?" asked Gerald's voice.

"Yes. Only at university level, of course."

"But you want to go into the professional theatre?"

"Oh yes. I've had one or two offers."

"What sort of thing?"

"Well, I've been asked to play Hedda Gabler at the Haymarket, Leicester . . ."

"The cow!" Charles shouted inadequately. With the unquestionable logic of the last piece of a jigsaw puzzle, his own rôle in the proceedings dropped into place. He was just a prop in the oldest theatrical scene of all—the casting couch.

Gerald spooled on and started playing another extract. "Well, as you know, from last night," said Anna's voice, "the show comes down about twelve fifteen and—" He stopped the tape abruptly.

"What was that?" asked Charles.

"Nothing."

"Switch the damned thing on!" Gerald was powerless against this outburst of fury and sheepishly pressed the button. Anna's voice continued, "We could meet after that if you like."

"I'm at the North British down on Princes Street. If you meet me in the foyer, say twelve thirty . . ." Gerald grinned weakly at the sound of his own voice.

"O.K. See you then." Anna's tone was poisonously familiar.

Charles switched off the recorder and turned to his friend. "Ah," said Gerald, "now don't get the wrong impression. What I thought was, if you were planning a confrontation with her, you'd want to know where she was, and I thought that'd be handy. I mean, for heaven's sake, you didn't think that I'd . . . ? I mean, I'm a married man. Kate and I have a perfect relationship and . . ."

He was still mumbling apologetically as Charles stormed out of the room.

At first he just walked furiously without noticing where he was going, but eventually calmed down enough to think what his next step should be. It was midnight and now a confrontation with Anna was unavoidable. All the delicate feelings which had held him back before had been driven out by anger.

He knew her movements well by now. At twelve fifteen the show came down; he could meet her then at the Masonic Hall. Or he could go back to her flat to wait. But a perverse masochism made him reject both possibilities. At twenty past twelve he took up his position outside the North British Hotel. He leant against the corner of the building, at the top of the steps down to Waverley Station, and prayed she would not come. That at least would spare him the final twist of the knife in his wound. The idea of her deceiving him with Gerald was the most intolerable of all the foul thoughts he was suffering. He would wait till a quarter to one and then go up to the flat.

At twelve thirty she came. He heard the clack of heels and saw the familiar figure walking purposefully along Princes Street towards him. She was wearing the pale yellow shirt with foxtrotting dancers on it and the velvet trousers she had worn when he first took her out to dinner. That made it worse.

As she came close, he shrugged his back off the wall and stepped forward to face her. The pain was too intense for him to find words. He just stood there, rocking on his heels.

Anna did a slight take on seeing him, but when she spoke, her voice was even. "Charles. Hello. I thought we'd arranged to meet up at the flat."

He managed to grunt out, "Yes."

"It's just as well I've seen you actually, because I won't be there till later. I've got to meet someone in the North British."

He almost felt respect for the directness of her explanation until the lie followed. "It's an aunt of mine who's up in Edinburgh very briefly."

"You're visiting your aunt at twelve thirty a.m.?"

"Yes. I've been rehearsing all day, so there hasn't been another opportunity. I'll get back to the flat as soon as I can." She smiled. It was the same smile, the one he had warmed to all week. He realized suddenly that Anna was a perfectly tuned machine. She had all the charm and skills of a human being and knew how to use them like a human being, but inside, controlling everything, was the cold computer of selfishness. Sex, emotions, other people were nothing but programs to be fed in to produce correct results quickly. Charles knew that he could never again believe anything she said. She was not governed by ordinary principles of truth, but by the morality of advantage.

"You're lying," he said sharply. "You're going to the North British to see Gerald Venables. You're going to see him because you think he's a big film producer and can help your career. In the same way that you slept with me because I direct plays, and with Willy Mariello because he was a pop star and might have useful contacts." He wished the accusations carried some dignity rather than sounding clumsy.

A spark of anger came into the navy blue eyes when she started to speak, but it was quickly smothered. Her voice kept its level tone. "I see. You set Gerald Venables up?"

"Yes."

"And he isn't really a film producer? The part he was talking about doesn't exist?"

"He is a sort of occasional film producer. But no, the part doesn't exist."

She flared. He had hit her where it hurt most, in the career. "That was a dirty trick."

For a moment he almost felt a twinge of guilt until he reminded himself of the situation. Anna carried such conviction in her acting. She went on. "I suppose I should have realized that it was unwise to mix with old men. They only get clinging and jealous."

That stung him. "Good God! Do you think I set all this up as some elaborate charade to test your affection for me?" He almost shouted the words. A tweedy middle-aged couple who were passing turned curiously.

"I can't think of any other reason why you should do it."

That sounded genuine, but then everything she said sounded genuine. Charles was not going to be stopped now. It was a time for truths. And accusations.

"I set Gerald up to get certain information from you."

"Like what?"

"Like the fact that you and Willy Mariello were lovers."

"So what? At least he was my age. You see, you are jealous. Jealous of someone who's dead. Anyway, Willy and I were finished. It happened while we were in Derby. We thought it would continue while we were up here, but it didn't."

"You told Gerald it did, right up to Willy's death."

"Oh, you've been spying carefully. That wasn't true. I just said that to sound more like the girl in the film."

That again sounded plausible. The set-up may have been too heavy, and Anna may just have given any information that seemed likely to help her to the part. But Charles was not checked. "Did Willy want the affair to end?"

"No. He got clinging too. Kept trying to win back my affections. But I'd outgrown him."

"How did he try to win back your affections?"

"Silly things."

"Like pushing Lesley Petter down the steps by the Castle?"

That did shake her. There was a long pause before she replied. "Yes. I suppose that was an attempt to get me back."

"Did you suggest it?"

"No, I did not!" she snapped. "I may have mentioned that I was understudying her, that the parts she was playing were good ones, but no . . ."

Charles could imagine her "mentioning" with all the innocence of Lady Macbeth. "Listen, Anna, you're in serious trouble."

"What on earth do you mean?"

"Murder is a serious business."

"What? Are you accusing me of murder?"

"Yes."

"You're off your head. Whom am I supposed to have murdered?"

"Willy."

"Good God." Now she really did look lost, stunned by the accusation. "It never occurred to me that he was murdered. And how in heaven's name am I supposed to have done it? And why, for God's sake?"

"Why first. You incited Willy to nobble Lesley."

"That's not true. It was his idea."

"Quite! He did it, thinking that you'd be grateful and bounce back into his arms. It gave him a hold over you and you were forced to go back to him."

"I didn't."

"But then he became, as you say, clinging. He was a nuisance, he proved to be without influence in show business circles, but he was not easy to shake off because of your shared guilt over Lesley. So you killed him."

She was staring at him in frank amazement. "And how am I supposed to have done the murder?"

He recapitulated all the business of the knives lying unattended at Coates Gardens before the killing. "It was a long chance. The switch was likely to be discovered before the photo-call. But it might work. And it did."

Anna gave a slight smile. "But surely, if, as you say, Willy and I were back together, I would have been sleeping at his place and gone straight to the Hall for rehearsal. I wouldn't have gone to Coates Gardens at all during the relevant period."

That was a blow to Charles' logic. But she had lied so much that she might be lying over that as well. "You could have crept out in the night."

"Oh yes, informed by some psychic source that the knives were lying there?"

"Yes," he asserted, conviction wavering.

"Well, you're wrong. I wasn't sleeping with Willy. But I do have an alibi for the period. I spent that night in the Lawnmarket flat with someone else."

"Who?"

"Its owner. A bloke called Lestor Wanewright. He was the reason I broke with Willy. I met him out in Nice while I was on holiday. He has a villa there. We came back here together and he stayed until he had to return to London on business. That was on the morning of Willy's death. Lestor went straight to Waverley Station and I went straight to the Masonic Hall for rehearsal."

"Why should I believe that?"

"You can check it. Lestor works for his father in London. Wanewright's, the merchant bank."

"But you took up with me only two days later."

She shrugged. "Aren't you flattered?"

"No. You only wanted me for what I could do for you."

"Yes. I quite liked you too."

"Oh yes." There was no danger of his believing anything she said now. Except about Lestor Wanewright. That rang true. If she just wanted an alibi, she had got it with Charles' own assumption that she had been with Willy (a flaw he had overlooked in his argument). The fact that she gave a checkable alibi with Lestor Wanewright meant it was true.

"Good-bye. Charles. I don't think we'll see a lot of each other now."

"No."

She walked off, still brisk and purposeful. Lovely, but not human. Charles leant back against the North British Hotel wall and let the warring emotions inside him fight it out for themselves.

One thing he was sure of. Anna Duncan was a dishonest bitch and a whore. But she was not a murderer.

CHAPTER 11

Even the bright extremes of joy
Bring on conclusions of disgust,
Like the sweet blossoms of the May,
Whose fragrance ends in must.

ODE TO MELANCHOLY

WHEN THE LONG NIGHT ended and light returned, Edinburgh had lost its charm. The bubbling spirits with which Charles had arrived had been ebbing for days and the previous evening's events had finally flushed them away. Unsustained by hope and excitement, he felt tired and miserable. And above all, he felt stupid. He saw himself from the outside—a middle-aged man infatuated with a young girl, thinking she could halt the processes of time. He was a figure of fun from a Restoration comedy, the elderly dupe, no doubt dubbed with some unsubtle name like Sir Paltry Effort. The more he thought about the fantasies he'd had of himself and Anna, the way his mind had raced on, the more depressed he felt. Overnight his new lease of life had been replaced by an eviction order.

At about nine he rang Frances. He convinced himself he rang so early to catch her before she went out to the eleven o'clock concert of Mahler songs at Leith Town Hall; not because in his abject state he needed her understanding.

They fixed to meet for dinner, as if it were a casual arrangement. But she knew something had happened and he rang off curtly to stem the flow of sympathy down the phone. He was not ready for that yet.

Then there was Gerald to sort out. Charles did not want to lose a friend over some bloody woman at his age. He went to the North British and summoned the solicitor from a late breakfast.

Gerald came into the hotel foyer wiping his mouth and blushing vigorously. "Charles, hello," he said with manufactured bonhomie.

"Hello. I came to thank you for last night."

"Oh . . . um. It was . . . er . . . nothing. I hope I got you the information you wanted."

"Yes. It proved I was on the wrong track."

"Oh, I'm sorry."

"Mind you, that was a relief in a way."

"Ah." Gerald looked at him in silence, uncertainly, as if he half-expected to be punched on the nose. "Look, old man, about the . . . er . . . other business . . ."

"Forgotten it already."

"Oh good. But, you know, it's the sort of thing that . . . er . . . well, it was just a joke, but it's the sort of thing . . . I mean, the girl did seem to be virtually offering herself . . ."

"I know."

"Yes. But it's sort of . . . not the sort of thing to make jokes about. I mean, say you were at home . . . with us. Kate's got a . . . you know . . . a rather limited sense of humor in some ways."

"It'll never be mentioned."

"Oh good." Relief flooded into Gerald and he seemed to swell to fill his expensive suit. "Care for a cup of coffee?"

When they were seated with their cups, the solicitor started asking about the case.

"I don't know," Charles replied despondently. "I was working on the theory that Anna had done it."

"Good God. I thought you just wanted information out of her."

"Otherwise you wouldn't have been so anxious to lure her back to your bed?"

"Charles! You said you wouldn't mention it."

"I'm sorry."

"So who's the next suspect? Who are you going to turn the heat on now?"

"God knows. I can't think beyond Anna. All my other lines of inquiry are confused. Anyway, my last performance is tomorrow. Now all I want to do is get the hell out of Edinburgh."

"But what about the case?"

"I don't even know if there is a case. Suppose Willy Mariello died by an accident? That's what everyone else thinks. Why shouldn't they be right."

"But Charles, your instinct—"

"Bugger my instinct. Look, even if it wasn't an accident, who cares? No one's mourned Willy much. One slob less, what does it matter if he was murdered? It's certainly not my business."

"You mustn't take that attitude."

"Why not?" he snapped. "I'm an actor, not a detective. If I were a detective, I'd have been sacked years ago for incompetence. There are some things one can do and some one can't. It's just a question of recognizing that fact before you make a fool of yourself. And I know that I have as much aptitude for detective work as a eunuch has for rape."

"So you don't think you'll pursue the case?"

"No."

"Hmm. I'm getting a plane back shortly."

"Yes. Well, thanks for your help."

"It was nothing."

"See you in London, Gerald."

"And if you change your mind, and do go on investigating, let me know how you get on."

"Sure. Cheerio." Charles slouched out of the hotel.

Apparently he did a reasonable performance of *So Much Comic, So Much Blood* to an audience of one hundred and twenty at lunchtime. He did not really notice it. All he was thinking was how soon he could get out of Edinburgh.

That involved tying up professional loose ends. Which meant a call on Brian Cassells at Coates Gardens. Charles hoped that the

Mary cast were rehearsing at the Masonic Hall; he did not want to meet Anna Duncan. Ever again.

His hope proved justified. The house was unusually quiet. The Company Manager was in his office, as usual pressing Letraset on to sheets of paper. "Thought we might need a bit of puff for *Who Now?* Opens on Monday in your lunchtime slot. Got to keep ahead in the publicity game or no one knows a show's on."

"No, they don't," said Charles pointedly, thinking of the publicity his show had got.

But irony was wasted on Brian. "I've changed 'A Disturbing New Play' to 'A Macabre and Bloody Exposition of Violence by Martin Warburton.' Pity I have to hint; I'd like to add '. . . who stabbed Willy Mariello.' That'd really bring the audience in. Still, the police are probably still investigating, so we may get some more publicity."

Charles searched the Company Manager's face for a trace of humor after this pronouncement, but it was not there. "Stabbed to death rather implies a positive act, like murder, Brian. Doesn't fit in with an accident."

It was a half-hearted attempt to see if the average member of D.U.D.S. harbored any suspicions about Willy's death. Brian obviously did not. "Oh, that's just semantics. You mustn't get too hung up on meaning, you've got to think of the impact of words."

"Hmm. Are you going into advertising?"

"I might think of it if I don't get this Civil Service job I'm up for."

"You'd be very good at it."

"Thank you." Again totally unaware that a remark could be taken two ways.

"Actually I wanted to talk about money." They arranged that Brian would send a check to London when the miserable fifty per cent of the miserable box office was worked out. Charles was not expecting much; in fact he could work out exactly how much by simple arithmetic; but he preferred not to. That always left the possibility of a pleasant surprise.

But he knew the payment would not begin to cover his expenses. It hurt to think how much lavish meals for Anna figured on those expenses. The classic fall-guy, the duped sugar-daddy—he felt a wave of self-distaste.

Have to make some more money somehow. Maybe the B.B.C. P.A.s' strike would soon be over and the telly series would happen. It was the first time he had thought outside Edinburgh since he arrived. A line echoed in his mind. "There is a world elsewhere." Was it Shakespeare? He could not recall. But it was melancholy and calming.

He hoped to leave Coates Gardens without meeting James Milne, but failed. So he was left with the unattractive prospect of Sherlock Holmes telling Dr. Watson that he had given up investigation.

"Anything new?" the Laird hissed eagerly as they met in the hall. He swiveled his white head left and right in an elaborate precaution against eavesdroppers. Charles was getting sick of enthusiastic amateur sleuths—Gerald with his inept slang, James Milne with his melodramatic whispering.

"No, not a lot." He tried unsuccessfully to make it sound as if that exhausted the subject.

"You haven't been following Martin again."

"No, I've . . . er . . . no." He had not mentioned any suspicions of Anna to his confidant and it seemed pointless to start just as the Dr. Watson role was becoming redundant.

"But you must have been following some line of investigation the last couple of days."

"Yes, I have, but I . . . don't really want to talk about it."

"Something personal?"

"Yes, I found it involved someone I knew well and . . ." He hoped that might edge the conversation in another direction. The Laird's old-fashioned values would surely respect a chap's discretion about his private affairs. I mean, dash it all, when there's a lady in the case . . .

But James Milne's curiosity was stronger than his gentlemanly outlook. "And where are those suspicions leading you?" he asked with some excitement.

"Nowhere. Well, I mean they've led anywhere they're going to lead. And produced nothing. I just want to forget about the case now."

The Laird looked at him quizzically. "But you were so keen on it before. I mean, it was your idea that there was anything to investigate. And now you've managed to persuade me there's something in it. You can't just drop it."

"I can. I have."

"But don't you think we ought to do some more investigation of Martin's movements and behavior?"

"Sorry. I've lost interest."

"Oh. And you're leaving tomorrow."

"Yes."

"Ah. Well. I'd better return your Hood." James Milne ignored Charles' remonstrance that it didn't matter, found the volume immediately and handed it over.

"Enjoy it?" Charles saw a way out of the awkwardness into the impersonal area of literary criticism.

"Yes," came the morose reply.

"Amazing feeling for words."

"Yes."

"There's a lot of discussion as to whether it's a purely comic gift. I mean, in some cases a pun does reinforce a serious statement. You know, like that line from *A Friendly Address to Mrs. Fry*. 'But I don't like your *Newgatory* teaching.' "

"Yes." The Laird responded in a predictably brighter tone.

Charles pressed home his advantage. "And some of the wholly serious poems aren't bad. Did you try *The Plea of the Midsummer Fairies*?"

"Yes. Sub-Keats, I thought."

"Right. But *The Song of the Shirt's* O.K. if hackneyed, and *The Bridge of Sighs* is quite moving. And did you read *The Dream of Eugene Aram*?"

"No," said the Laird, "I've never heard of it," and relapsed into gloom. Charles felt churlish for his proposed defection. He needed to soften the blow of his departure. "Look, let's meet for a farewell drink in the morning. At the pub by the Masonic Hall. See you there about eleven. Before my last lunchtime. O.K.?"

The Laird nodded, but he looked downcast and Charles felt that he had let the man down.

* * *

Dinner with Frances was refreshing in that, unlike Gerald Venables and James Milne, she did not encourage him to continue with his detective work. In fact, when he gave her a selective résumé of his investigations, she positively discouraged him. Murder, in her view, was an extremely unpleasant business, and when inadvertently it did occur, it belonged by right to the police and not to untrained amateurs. It could be very dangerous. Although they were separated, Frances retained a maternal protective instinct for her husband. This regularly manifested itself in warm socks and sensible Marks and Spencer shirts for birthdays and Christmas.

They ate in Henderson's Salad Bar, a bit of a comedown from the places where he had squired Anna, but excellent food and better value. Charles began to relax. As he did, the exhaustion that had been stalking him all day caught up. He nearly nodded asleep into his lentil stew. Frances reached out and held his hand. "You're dead."

"Mmm."

"Been overdoing it."

"I suppose so."

"Early night."

"Good idea."

"I'm pretty exhausted too. Those two girls have been leading me such a dance. Still, thank God they get a train back tomorrow. It can't come soon enough. I think I might stay in Scotland for a bit."

"Don't you have to chaperone them home?"

"No. Put the two little horrors on the London train and from that moment they're on their own."

Charles smiled weakly at the incipient relief in her voice. "And then you'll have a few days' holiday?"

"Yes. Bliss. Before term starts." She hesitated. "I don't suppose . . ."

"What?"

"I don't suppose you'd fancy a few days' holiday. If we could book up somewhere . . ."

It was strange to see her blushing. Blushing for propositioning her own husband. He felt the familiar ridge of the kitchen-knife scar across her thumb. His eyelids were heavy with sleep as he replied, "I've heard worse ideas."

There was quite a party at the pub before Charles' performance on the Saturday. A lot of the D.U.D.S. who had never said hello to him decided they had no obligation to say good-bye, and any money that the show might have made was anticipated in large rounds of drinks for people he did not know.

But Charles didn't mind. A night's sleep had done wonders. Alcohol and company meant that he only felt the occasional twinge from thoughts of Anna or Willy's death. Recovery from both obsessions would take time, but it was possible.

Frances was there, celebrating the departure of a King's Cross train from Waverley Station. And, by a stroke of incredible luck, they had arranged a holiday. Stella Galpin-Lord, who was in the party, justified the expense of the vodka and Campari she ordered by fixing them up in a hotel at Clachenmore on Loch Fyne. In fact she had been booked in for a week herself, but had just heard that the acting friend who was meant to join her had got a part in a film and had to cancel. The need for a consoling drink after this disappointment explained her presence in the pub. But her loss was Charles' and Frances' gain. A phone call clinched the change of booking. Charles was so excited about the speed with which it happened that he did not have time to question the wisdom of going on holiday with his ex-wife.

He felt affectionate towards all of the Derby crowd and, now that his departure was imminent, even indulged himself in a slight regret that it was over. Sam Wasserman was talking earnestly (and no doubt allegorically) to Pam Northcliffe. She had her back to Charles, but he could imagine the glaze of boredom slowly covering her eyes. Frances was gamely trying to conduct a conversation with the lighting man Plug (who'd got to do the sodding cue sheets for *Who Now?*, but who'd heard there was a free drink going). Martin Warburton was gesticulating wildly as he expounded one of his theories to Stella Galpin-Lord. They all seemed animated and cheerful except for James Milne who sat slightly apart with a half of "heavy."

Since the Laird was the first person he'd invited to the get-together, Charles felt he should not neglect him and sat down at the same table with his pint.

"Are you really giving the investigation up, Charles?"

He found it difficult to meet the older man's eyes. "Yes."

"I'm sure we ought not to. I mean, if something else happens, we'll feel terrible."

"What else can happen?"

"Another crime."

"Why?"

"I don't know. It's just . . ." The Laird leaned closer and whispered. "I am convinced there's something odd about Martin's behavior. We ought to find out more. We can't just leave it."

This was unsettling. Deep down Charles agreed. But he had managed to push that agreement so far down that it hardly troubled him. He would have to make some concession to his conscience. "What, you mean investigate the flat in Nicholson Street?"

"Something like that, Charles."

"How about Holyrood?" With sudden inspiration. "We'll go this afternoon." The Laird looked relieved that something was being done and Charles felt it was a satisfactory solution. It gave the illusion of interest on his part and was a pleasant way of spending an afternoon. A visit to Edinburgh's famous palace would be a fitting farewell to the city.

"Drink?" The word was spoken sharply close behind Charles. He turned to see Martin Warburton holding a couple of empty glasses. "I'm getting a round."

Charles looked at his watch. "Better not have any more. I'll want a pee in the middle of the show."

James Milne also refused politely, but Martin did not turn away immediately. He stood still for a moment and said, almost to himself, "Holyrood."

"Yes," said Charles. "We're going down there this afternoon." And then, as an explanatory probe, "Have you ever been there?"

"Oh no," Martin replied slowly. "No, I haven't."

* * *

The last performance of *So Much Comic, So Much Blood* went very well; it justified the *Glasgow Herald*'s enthusiasm. It was possibly helped by the alcoholic relaxation of its presenter, and certainly by the vigorous reactions of an alcoholic contingent in the audience. Charles was left with the melancholy emptiness that follows a good show, and an urgent awareness that the pubs closed at two thirty.

A few more drinks and he parted with the D.U.D.S. in a haze of goodwill. Frances went off to scour Edinburgh for gumboots which she assured Charles would be essential for the West Coast of Scotland. James Milne waited for him outside the Masonic Hall while he slipped in to have another pee and pick up his belongings.

The stage crew were already in, setting up the scenery for a lighting rehearsal of *Who Now?* Martin Warburton, as writer, was deep in conference with Plug, the electrician. Charles picked up the holdall that he had left onstage. "Did all the slides go in, Plug?"

"Sure."

"Cheerio then."

" 'Bye." Charles swung the holdall cheerfully on to his shoulder.

"Good-bye, Charles Paris," said Martin Warburton.

The guide at the Palace of Holyroodhouse was a jovial gentleman with a green cap, green jacket and tartan trews. The effort of showing a mixed bag of international tourists round the old building ten times a day (or even more during the Festival) had not blunted his good humor, though it did give a staged quality to some of his jokes.

Charles let it all wash pleasantly over him. He even felt confident that the alcohol would not wear off until the pubs opened again at five. After the stresses of recent days he owed himself a real Saturday night blinder.

Meanwhile information about Scotland's history and art poured out from the guide. Charles II rebuilt the palace . . . George IV wanted to be painted wearing a kilt . . . you can tell the carving's by Grinling Gibbons because of his signature of five peas in a pod . . . the present Queen holds garden parties in the gardens here

. . . the harpsichord by Johann Rucker of Antwerp is still in working order . . . the portraits of fictitious kings of Scotland are by
Jacob de Wet . . . and so on and so on.

Occasionally Charles would be shaken from his reverie by a hiss
from the Laird. "Do you think that might be significant?"

"What?"

"Sixteenth-century tapestry of the Battle of the Centaurs."

"Why?"

"Well, it's violent, isn't it? And Martin's very obsessed with violence."

Charles would feign interest for a moment and then mentally
doze off again. With the confidence of alcohol, he knew that so far
as he was concerned the Mariello case was over. The relief of that
decision gave him the freedom to look at the case objectively. He
saw the long trail of his mistaken suspicions dragging on like a
Whitehall farce, with him as the overacting protagonist, always
opening the wrong door after the crooks had fled, after the pretty
girl had put her clothes back on again, or after the vicar's trousers
had been irrevocably lost.

And, without the pressure of having to think about it, a new logic
crept into the case. First, the greatest likelihood was that Willy
Mariello had died accidentally. And if he had not, then the only
person with whom he was directly connected was James Milne,
through the house sale. Perhaps there had been some motive
there; perhaps even (taking a cue from Michael Vanderzee's insin-
uation) there had been a homosexual liaison between Willy and the
Laird. Perhaps, perhaps. Motivations and suspicions took on the
expendable and detached fascination of a crossword. Perhaps one
day someone would make the effort to find out the facts. Preferably
a policeman. Certainly it would not be Charles Paris. Detective
work, he reflected, was a slow and unrewarding business, like reading Dickens for the dirty bits. Not for him. He followed the guide
through a film of alcohol.

The oldest parts of Holyroodhouse, in the James IV Tower, are
kept till last in the guided tour. These are the apartments of Mary,
Queen of Scots and her second husband, Lord Darnley, and it is
impossible to enter them without a sense of excitement.

Darnley's bedroom is downstairs and there is a little staircase that leads up to the Queen's room. Next door is the supper room where David Rizzio, her Italian secretary, musician and companion, was murdered by Darnley, Patrick Lord Ruthven and other disaffected noblemen. On his body there were found between fifty and sixty dagger-wounds.

"And there," said the guide dramatically, "is the very spot where it happened." Then, with a quick switch into the practiced joke, "There's no use looking for bloodstains. There's only a brass plaque there and it's a different floor. But everything else is just as it was."

"Everything?" Charles queried facetiously. "Is it the same clock?"

"What clock?" asked the guide, confused for the first time on the tour.

"Well, the clock . . ." Charles turned slowly round the room. There was no clock. "Then what's the ticking?"

He looked slowly down at his holdall, lowered it to the floor and, with great care, unzipped it. The other tourists watched with frozen fascination.

There was no question. He had seen enough newspaper pictures from Northern Ireland to recognize the untidy arrangement of a clock face and wires.

So had the rest of the party. In the panic and screams that followed as they all rushed for the narrow spiral staircase, he could hear the Laird's voice, high with fear. "A bomb! He could have killed us all! A bomb!"

CHAPTER 12

The dog leapt up, but gave no yell,
The wire was pulled, but woke no bell,
The ghastly knocker rose and fell,
  But caused no riot;
The ways of death, we all know well,
  Are very quiet.

JACK HALL

BOMBS IN PUBLIC PLACES are police matters, and cannot be well investigated by half-hearted amateurs. Charles found it a great relief when the blue uniforms moved in. He felt he could have gone on snooping in the dark for ever; the police had the advantage that investigation was their business. And they got on with it very efficiently.

An Army bomb disposal expert saved Queen Mary's historic apartments from destruction. As Charles sat waiting to be interviewed at the Edinburgh City Police Headquarters in Fettes Avenue, he wondered what would have happened if the device had gone off. The wholesale destruction of twenty-odd tourists and a guide might have put Rizzio's murder in the shade. And it would have needed a hell of a big brass plaque.

He had assumed that the bomb had not reached its detonation time when it was discovered and received an ugly shock when the findings of the bomb disposal expert were communicated to him. It had been set for twenty minutes earlier. The minute hand on the clock had reached its brass contact screw fixed in the clock face; it was only luck that had prevented it going off. The device's construction was amateur and the motion of Charles' holdall appeared to have broken one of the inadequately soldered joints in the wiring. But for the cavalier, drunken way he had manhandled the bag, the bomb would have worked.

He found its failure small comfort. The intention was no less destructive. The bomb was an unsophisticated weed killer and acid device, which might not have been too devastating in the open, but in an enclosed space like the supper room . . . He didn't like to think about it. Particularly as he had been carrying the thing. Even in the unlikely event of his surviving the blast, he would have been typecast for the rest of his life as Long John Silver or Toulouse-Lautrec.

When he talked to the police, he was amazed at how much they knew. The assumption that they had written off Willy Mariello's death as an accident and were just waiting for this to be officially confirmed in the Procurator-Fiscal's report proved to be naïve. Ever since the stabbing they had been investigating and keeping an eye on the D.U.D.S. They knew about Martin's dual identity and had been following his movements with particular interest.

It all made Charles feel crassly amateur. Not only because his own stumbling investigations seemed so pathetic, but also because it showed he had an outdated image of the police as thick village constables whose only function was to have rings run round them by the brilliant amateur sleuth. That was the way it was in most of the plays he had ever been in, and plays were about his closest contact with the police. What he had taken in this case to be their lethargic inactivity had been discreet investigation, gathering together sufficient evidence for an arrest.

And they reckoned the bomb was probably enough evidence. Certainly enough to justify a search of the flat in Nicholson Road.

There was no question in the police's mind of investigating anyone but Martin. Like the Laird, they reckoned that his behavior was suspicious and, unlike Charles, they were not held up by vague woolly liberal notions that the boy was misunderstood and must have other explanations for his actions. Charles felt as he had in

Oxford when, after an elaborate midnight climb back into college over walls, across roofs, down drainpipes and through dons' bedrooms, he had discovered that the main gate was open.

He also felt rather out of it, though at the center of operations. At least on his own abortive investigations he could maintain the illusion of doing something important in his own right. Here at the police headquarters he was just a source of information, politely asked to wait, filed for reference when necessary. They were interested in what he knew, not what he thought.

So rather than stage-managing dramatic dénouements himself, he found out at second hand what had happened. The search at Nicholson Street had provided plenty of evidence to convict Martin. It was a positive bomb factory, chemicals and components scattered around on tables without any attempt at concealment. There was also an unpleasant collection of knives and other weapons, including a meat cleaver. The boy's fantasies of violence took a disturbingly tangible form.

What the police did not find at the flat was Martin Warburton himself. And, though they found a bottle of spirit gum substitute and a brush, there was no sign of his false beard or glasses. So it was possible that he was somewhere in Edinburgh in his disguise.

They tried the obvious places, which were Coates Gardens and the Masonic Hall, but he was not at either. Apparently he had left the theatre after a disagreement with Plug over some lighting effect. That was shortly before three, and nobody had seen him since.

The case had changed from a whodunnit to a manhunt.

Charles was thanked courteously for his co-operation by the police and asked to keep them informed of where he would be contactable if he left Edinburgh.

It was then about seven o'clock. Frances, he knew, had got a ticket for the Scottish Opera's *Alceste* at the King's Theatre. Denied her calming therapy for his shattered nerves, he saw no reason to change his plans of earlier in the day, and got drunk.

At the Police Headquarters James Milne and Charles had arranged to meet for coffee in the flat the next morning to talk through what had happened. Charles had found the truth of Dr. Johnson's dictum about the proximity of death concentrating a man's mind wonderfully, and regained his flagging interest in the case.

About eleven on the Sunday he arrived at Coates Gardens. "Do you mind if I have something a bit stronger than coffee?"

"Still in a state of shock? So am I."

"Well, mine's only an indirect state of shock, James. I was so shocked yesterday that I had to have a great deal to drink for medical reasons. That's why I need something stronger now. Hair of the dog."

The Laird chuckled and reached for the malt whisky bottle. "Well," he said when they were sitting and the first gulp was irrigating Charles's dehydrated head, "it seems that I was on the right track."

"About Martin?"

"Yes."

"Hmm. Of course, I knew there was something wrong with him right from the start. Now I come to think of it, the first night I was here, I heard someone crying in the bathroom—I'm sure it was him. Obviously in the throes of a nervous breakdown. A schizoid condition, aggravated by overwork for his finals."

"All work and no play . . ."

"Makes Jack a nutter, yes."

" 'Much study had made him very lean . . .' "

" 'And pale and leaden-eyed.' " Charles completed the quotation automatically without thinking. Martin's case seemed more relevant than literary games. "What surprised me was that all his fantasies manifested themselves in a real way. Usually with that type all the action's in their minds."

"Not, it seems, in this case, Charles."

"No." He paused for a moment, ruefully. "Poor kid. He was so mixed up. He seemed so much the obvious suspect that I never really considered him." He laughed. "I must get a less subjective view of criminals."

"What do you mean?"

"Look at me—on this case I miss out the obvious solution just because Martin's someone I like and feel sympathy for. Instead I go off into wild suspicions of more or less everyone else I meet."

The atmosphere between them was friendly enough for a confession. "Do you know, I even suspected you at one point."

"Really? Why?"

"God knows. My mind wasn't working very well. I suspected everybody. Still, even if we didn't know about Martin's bomb factory, I think I'd have to cross you off my list now. The average murderer doesn't deliberately try to get himself blown up."

"No." They laughed.

Then Charles sighed. "I wish I'd got it all a bit more sorted out in my mind. I mean, it's now clear that Martin planted the bomb, and presumably planned Willy's death as well, but I still don't see exactly why."

"He was unbalanced."

"Yes, but . . . I don't know. I suppose I've got a tidy mind, but I'd like to find some sort of method in his madness, some logical sequence."

"What about the Mary, Queen of Scots thing I suggested a few days ago?"

"That would explain the Mariello stabbing, I suppose. Willy was playing Rizzio, so there might be some identification there, but what about the bomb?"

"Darnley was blown up with gunpowder, Charles."

"Was he? Good God."

"Yes, I'm sure he was. At the instigation of Bothwell, as I recall."

"Bothwell? But that's who Martin's playing in *Mary, Queen of Sots*. And . . . yes . . . he talked to me once about how easy it was to identify with people from history."

"There you are then."

"Let's work it out. He's in this show about Mary, Queen of Scots and gets obsessively involved with her life . . ."

"A life surrounded by intrigue and murder."

"Exactly. He identifies with Bothwell and—I say, it's just struck me. I bet there's a portrait of Bothwell in the Scottish National Portrait Gallery."

The Laird nodded excitedly. "There is. It's a miniature. And it's the only extant picture of him."

"Yes." Charles pieced it together slowly. "Right. Martin identifies so completely that, in his confused mind, he becomes Bothwell and Sam Wasserman's awful play becomes reality. And that reality suits his existing obsessions about violence."

"So Rizzio has to be stabbed. Willy Mariello doesn't exist for Martin; he actually is David Rizzio. And Martin must have said something that made Willy afraid of him, which explains what Willy told me in the Truth Game. By a stroke of luck, the stabbing looks like an accident, and so Martin is free to plan his next murder, that of Darnley . . ." His racing thoughts were suddenly brought up short. "But that's strange. If he was living the reality of the play, why did he identify me with Darnley and not the bloke who's actually playing the part?"

"Perhaps he was just getting a bit confused," the Laird offered.

"That's a bit lame. I'm sure if the obsession's as complicated as it seems to be, there must be some logic behind it, some sort of crazy justification for his action."

"You don't think there's anything missing in the historical Mary story?"

"I don't know. What happened to Bothwell in the end?"

"I think he died in prison. Insane."

Charles smiled grimly. "I'm afraid that part of the identification could be horribly apt too. No, there's something we're missing. Why does he turn on me as Darnley?"

"Because he thinks you're on his trail?"

"Doesn't really fit the historical obsession bit. Unless . . ." The solution flashed into his mind. "Good God! Anna!"

"What?"

"Anna Duncan. She's playing Mary. And Willy Mariello had an affair with her. Martin must have seen them together and killed him out of jealousy. And then me. He saw us together downstairs a couple of days ago."

"You and Anna?"

Charles felt himself blushing, but the picture was developing too quickly for him to be discreet. "Yes, we were having an affair, and after he saw us together, he started to identify me with Darnley. So I had to be blown up."

"Leaving Anna to him?"

"I suppose so. But don't you see, James, this may give us a lead on what he's likely to do next."

"Why?"

"Who's the next person to be murdered in the Mary, Queen of Scots saga?"

The Laird pondered with infuriating slowness. "Well, I think actual murders are a bit thin on the ground after Darnley. There are plots and battles, but I don't think any more major figures were actually murdered."

"None at all?"

"No. Well, not until Mary herself had her head cut off. There are a lot of Scots who still regard that as a murder."

Charles sprang to his feet with a feeling of nausea in his throat. "No! I must get to the Lawnmarket." All he could think of was the fact that among other weapons in the Nicholson Street flat the police had found a meat cleaver.

He was so relieved to see Anna open the door of the flat that it took a moment before he realized the situation's inherent awkwardness. She looked at him and the Laird without emotion. "Good morning."

Urgency overcame Charles' embarrassment. "Have you seen Martin?"

"Yes."

"What, here?"

"Yes, he was here."

"When?"

"He left about half an hour ago."

"And how long had he been here?"

A hard look came into the navy blue eyes. "Listen, if you're playing another of your elaborate games—"

"I'm not. This is serious. We've got to find Martin. He's in a dangerous state."

"Certainly in a strange state. He was babbling on about the police being after him or something."

"That's true."

"Why?"

"They want him for the murder of Willy Mariello and the attempted murder of Charles Paris."

Her mouth fell open and an expression of frozen horror came over her face. Charles realized it was the first spontaneous reaction he had ever seen from her.

"Where is he now?"

"I don't know, Charles. He came here last night in an awful state and begged to stay. I thought he was mad, so I didn't argue."

"Just as well. I think you were next on his list."

"What?" She started to cry with shock, and looked human and ugly. But Charles did not have time to notice. "Have you any idea where he was going?"

"No, but he was dressed up."

"Disguised?"

"Yes. I thought he was joking when he suggested it, but he was so fierce and insistent that I let him have the stuff."

"What stuff?"

"A smock and a handbag of mine. And a curly dark wig I've got. And my sunglasses."

"He was wearing all that when he left?"

"Yes."

"Thank you." He turned to rush away.

"Charles?" she whispered.

"Yes."

"Do you think he really might have murdered me?"

"Yes, Anna. I do."

As he ran down the steps from Lady Stair's Close towards Waverley Station, he knew it was a long chance, but he could not think of anywhere else to go. If Martin wanted to get out of Edinburgh, that was the quickest way. Charles had a feeling that there was a London train at two o'clock. In twenty minutes.

The cold sweaty feeling of his hangover mixed with the hot sweaty feeling of running. Ambling tourists turned bewildered faces towards the middle-aged man pelting down the road in the calm of a Sunday afternoon. James Milne was a long way behind him, doing the ungainly penguin run of a man with things in his pockets.

Charles sped down the taxi-ramp into Waverley Station and

halted in the sudden cool shade, gasping to get his breath. Then he moved slowly towards Platform 1-19 where the London train would leave. It had not yet arrived.

He stalked along the railings that ran the length of the platform and peered through at the passengers, who stood waiting with their luggage. They all looked extremely ordinary. He walked on. The women were very womanly.

He stopped and looked at one back view again. The clothes were right. Red smock, blue jeans, curly hair, handbag dangling casually from one hand. It must be.

But he hesitated. There was something so feminine about the stance. And no trace of anxiety.

But it must be. Martin's chameleon-like ability to take on another personality would enable him to stand differently, to think himself so much into the part that he was a woman. Any actor could do it to a degree and a psychopath could do it completely.

Charles moved with organized stealth. He bought a platform ticket and walked through the barrier. Then he advanced slowly towards the "woman." People peered along the line and started to gather up their luggage. The train was coming. He quickened his pace.

He was standing just behind his quarry when the train slid protesting into the station. Even close to, the figure looked womanly. Charles waited a moment; he did not want to risk a suicide under the oncoming wheels. But as the passing windows slowed to a halt, he stepped forward. The curly head was close to his face. "Martin," he said firmly.

The violence of the blow on his chest took him by surprise. He had time to register the skill of the boy's make-up as he fell over backwards.

The shove winded him and it was a moment before he could pick himself up again. By that time Martin had charged the barrier and was rushing through the dazed crowd in the main station. Charles set off in gasping pursuit.

The boy was at least two hundred yards ahead when Charles emerged into the sunlight, and running up the hill which the older man had just descended. Martin was young and fit and moving with the pace of desperation. Charles was hopelessly out of condition on the steep gradient and could feel the gap between them widening.

Then he had what seemed like a stroke of luck. Martin was keeping to the right of the road as if he intended to veer off down the Mound into Princes Street where he would soon be lost in the tourist crowds. But suddenly he stopped. Charles could see the reason. James Milne was standing in his path. Martin seemed frozen for a moment, then sprang sideways, crossed the road and ran on up the steps to the Lawnmarket, retracing Charles' footsteps.

In fact, going straight back to Anna's flat.

Realization of the girl's danger gave Charles a burst of adrenalin, and he surged forward. As he passed the Laird on the steps he heard the older man gasp something about getting the police.

Martin was spreadeagled against the door in Lawnmarket when Charles emerged from Lady Stair's Close. The boy was hammering with his fists, but Anna had not opened the door yet. No doubt she was on her way down the five flights of steps. Charles screamed out Martin's name, turning the heads of a party of Japanese in tam o'shanters.

The youth turned round as if he had been shot and froze again like a rabbit in a car's headlights, unable to make up his mind. Charles moved purposefully forward. It had to be now; he had no energy left for a further chase.

He was almost close enough to touch Martin, he could see the confusion in the young eyes, when suddenly the youth did another sidestep and started running again. Charles lumbered off in pursuit, cursing. If Martin made it down to the Grassmarket, he could easily lose his exhausted hunter in the network of little streets of the Old Town.

But Martin did not do that. He did something much more worrying.

Instead of breaking for the freedom of the Grassmarket, he ran back across the road and up towards the Castle. In other words, he ran straight into a dead end. With a new cold feeling of fear, Charles hurried after him, up between the Tattoo stands on the Esplanade and into the Castle.

The fear proved justified. He found Martin standing on the ramparts at the first level, where great black guns point out over the New Town to the silver flash of the Firth of Forth. A gaping crowd of tourists watched the boy in silence as he pulled off the wig and smock and dropped them into the void.

Charles eased himself up on to the rampart and edged along it, trying not to see the tiny trees and beetle people in Princes Street Gardens below. "Martin."

The look that was turned on him was strangely serene. So was the voice that echoed him. "Martin. Yes, Martin. Martin Warburton. That's who I am." The youth wiped the lipstick from his mouth roughly with the back of his hand. "Martin Warburton I began and Martin Warburton I will end."

"Yes, but not yet. You've got a long time yet. A lot to enjoy. You need help, and there are people who will give you help."

Martin's eyes narrowed. "The police are after me."

"I know, but they only want to help you too." This was greeted by a snort of laughter. "They do. Really. We all want to help. Just talk. You can talk to me."

Martin looked at him suspiciously. Charles felt conscious of the sun, the beautiful view of Edinburgh spread out below them. A peaceful Sunday afternoon in the middle of the Festival. And a young man with thoughts of suicide. "Don't do it, Martin. All the pressures you feel, they're not your fault. You can't help it."

"Original Sin," said the boy, as if it were a great joke. "I am totally evil."

"No."

For a moment there was hesitation in the eyes. Charles pressed his advantage. "Come down from there and talk. It'll all seem better if you talk about it."

"Talk? What about the police?" Martin was wavering.

"Don't worry about the police."

Martin took a step towards him. Their eyes were interlocked. The boy's were calm and dull; then suddenly they disengaged and looked at something over Charles' shoulder. Charles turned to see that two policemen had joined the edge of the growing crowd.

When he looked back, he saw Martin Warburton launch himself forward like a swimmer at the start of a race.

But there was no water and it was a long way down.

And Brian Cassells got another good publicity story.

CHAPTER 13

A plague, say I, on all rods and lines, and on young or old watery
danglers!
And after all that you'll talk of such stuff as no harm in the world about
anglers!
And when all is done, all our worry and fuss, why, we've never had
nothing worth dishing;
So you see, Mr. Walton, no good comes at last of your famous book
about fishing.

A RISE AT THE FATHER OF ANGLING

CHARLES WATCHED THE SUN-GOLD surface of the burn change in seconds to dull brown and then become pockmarked with heavy
drops of rain. He heard a rustle of P.V.C. behind him as Frances
tried to rearrange her position at the foot of the tree to keep the
maximum amount of water off her book. The rain was no less
cheering than the sun.

As he knew from previous experience, if you do not like rain,
there's no point in going to the West Coast of Scotland. The whole
area is wet. Wet underfoot like the surface of a great sponge. Everywhere the ground is intersected with tiny streams and it is never
completely silent; there is always the subtle accompaniment of running water. The wetness is not the depressing damp of soggy socks
and smelly raincoats; it is stimulating like the sharp kiss of mist on
the cheek. And it is very relaxing.

Charles twitched his anorak hood over his head and thought
how unrelaxed he still felt. Suffering from anoraksia nervosa, his

bad!!

528

mind suggested pertly, while he tried to tell it to calm down. But it kept throwing up irrelevant puns, thoughts and ideas. He knew the symptoms. It was always like this after the run of a show. A slow process of unwinding when the brain kept working overtime and took longer than the body to relax.

The body was doing well; it appreciated the holiday. Clachenmore was a beautiful place, though it hardly seemed worth putting on the map, it was so small. Apart from a tiny cottage given the unlikely title of "The Post Office," there was just the hotel, a solid whitewashed square with a pair of antlers over the door. Every window offered gratuitously beautiful views—up to the rich curve of the heathery hills, sideways to the woods that surrounded the burn (free fishing for residents), down over the vivid green fields to the misty gleam of Loch Fyne.

So the situation was relaxing. And being with Frances was relaxing. Arriving at a strange hotel with an ex-wife has got the naughty excitement of a dirty weekend with a non-wife, but with more security. And Frances was being very good, not talking about defining their position and not saying were they actually going to get a divorce because it wasn't easy for her being sort of half-married and half-unmarried and what chance did she have of meeting someone else well no one in particular but one did meet people, and all that. She seemed content to enjoy the current domestic idyll and not think about the future. A line from one of Hood's letters came into his mind. "My domestic habits are very domestic indeed, like Charity I begin at home, and end there; so Faith and Hope must call upon me, if they wish to meet."

But he did not feel relaxed. He did not mind lines of Hood flashing into his head; that was natural; it always happened after a show; but there were other thoughts that came unbidden and were less welcome. He closed his eyes and all he could see were the writhing coils of the fat gray earthworms he had dug for bait that morning. That was not good; it made him think of worms and epitaphs. What would Martin Warburton's epitaph be? He opened his eyes.

The fish seemed to have stopped biting. Earlier in the day he had a good tug on his borrowed tackle and with excitement reeled in a brown trout all of five inches long. Since his most recent experience had been of coarse fishing, he had forgotten how vigorous even tiny trout were. But since then they had stopped biting. Perhaps it was the weather. Or he was fishing in the wrong place.

Even with the rain distorting its surface, the pool where he was did not look deep enough to contain anything very large. But there were supposed to be salmon there. So said Mr. Pilch from Coventry who came up to Clachenmore every summer with the family and who liked to pontificate in the lounge after dinner. "Oh yes, you want to ask Tam the gamekeeper about that. Actually, he's not only the gamekeeper, he's also the local poacher. Only been working on the estate for about five years, but he knows every pool of that burn. Good Lord, I've seen some monster salmon he's caught. They put them in the hotel deep-freeze. Mind you . . ." Here he had paused to attend to his pipe, an aluminum and plastic device that looked like an important but inexplicable electronic component. He had unscrewed something and squeezed a spongeful of nicotine into the coal-bucket. "Mind you, what you mustn't do is ask *how* Tam catches the fish. Oh no, I believe there are rules in fishing circles. But you know, he goes through the water in these waders stalking them, and he can tell the pools they're in—don't know how he does it, mind—and he's got these snares and things, and his ripper. It's a sort of cord with a lot of treble hooks on. Well, he whips them out of the water on to the bank and then gets the Priest out—you know why it's called the Priest? It gives the fish their last rites. Vicious little device it is, short stick with a weighted end. Anyway, down this comes on the fish's head and that's another for the deep-freeze. Highly illegal, but highly delicious, eh?"

However, the salmon were playing hard to get. So were the trout. So, come to that, were any fresh water shrimps that might be around. Obviously the recommended bunch of worms on a large hook ledgered to the bottom was an insufficient inducement. Charles turned to Frances, and put on his schoolboy party-piece voice. "A recitation—*The Angler's Farewell* by Thomas Hood.

> *Not a trout there be in the place,*
> *Not a Grayling or Rud worth the mention,*
> *And although at my hook*

With attention *I look*
I can ne'er see my hook with a Tench on!"

Frances clapped and he bowed smugly. 'IthangyouIthangyou, for my next trick, I was thinking of going for a walk to work off some of Mrs. Parker's enormous breakfast in anticipation of her no doubt enormous lunch. Do you want to come?"

"I'm nearly at the end of this book actually and I'm quite cozy." She looked cozy, tarpaulined in P.V.C. mac and sou'wester, crouched like a garden gnome at the foot of the tree.

O.K. What are you reading?"

"Your *Mary, Queen of Sots.*"

"Oh Lord. That's not my book. I should have given it back. Borrowed it from someone in Edinburgh. Ha, that reminds me of Anatole France."

"Hm?"

"Never lend books, for no one ever returns them; the only books I have in my library are those that other people have lent me. A quote."

"I didn't know you were given to gratuitous quotation."

"The bloke who lent me the book would have appreciated it."

Some Victorian spirit of Nile-source-searching prompted him to go upstream towards the spring that fed the little burn. Any hopes of finding the source before lunch were soon dashed by the stream's unwillingness to get any narrower and the steepness of the gradient down which it came. Centuries of roaring water had driven a deep cleft into the rock. Tumbled boulders enclosed dark brown pools, fed from above by broad creamy torrents or silver threads of water.

The banks were muddy and the rocks he had to climb over shone treacherously. More than once he had to reach out and grasp at tussocks of grass to stop himself from slipping.

At last he came to a part of the burn that seemed quieter than the rest. There was still the rush of water, but it was muffled by trees arcing and joining overhead, which spread a green light on the scene. Here were three symmetrical round pools, neatly stepped like soup plates up a waiter's arm.

He identified the place from Mr. Pilch's descriptions in the lounge after dinner. "Some of the pools up there are incredibly deep, just worn down into the solid rock by constant water pressure. Makes you wonder whether we take sufficient notice of the potential of hydro-jet drilling, eh? Mind you, it takes a few centuries. Still, some of those pools are supposed to be twenty feet deep. Tam claims to have caught salmon up there, though I can't for the life of me imagine how they get that high. Maybe by doing those remarkable leaps you see on the tourist posters, eh?"

But Charles did not want to think about Pilch. The enclosing trees and the muffled rush of water made the place like a fairy cave. It was magical and, in a strange way, calming. Puffed by the climb, he squatted on his heels at the foot of a tree, and started to face the thoughts which regrettably showed no signs of going away.

He knew why he was restless. It was because the explanations he had formed for recent events in Edinburgh were incomplete. Now Martin Warburton was dead, that situation looked permanent. The frustration was like getting within four answers of a completed crossword and knowing from the clues that he had no hope of filling the gaps. He could put down any combination of letters that sounded reasonable, but he would not have the satisfaction of knowing he was right. And with this particular crossword, there would not be a correct solution published in the following morning's paper.

It was partly his own fault for wanting a clear-cut answer rather than the frayed ends of reality. A basic misconception, like his idea that the police were way behind on the case.

But he could not get away from the fact that the tie-up of Martin's motivations which he and the Laird had worked out was unsatisfactory. There were too many loose ends, stray facts that he had found out and still required explanations. Though the main outline was right, there were details of Martin's obsessive behavior that were not clear.

He worked backwards. Martin's suicide demonstrated that, at least in his own mind, the boy was guilty of something. The discovery of the Nicholson Street bomb factory made it reasonable to suppose that one of the causes of his guilt was the device planted in Charles' holdall.

But what evidence was there that he was also responsible for killing Willy? Certainly in retrospect it looked likely. Martin had actually wielded the murder weapon and Rizzio was an obvious first victim in his macabre game of historical reconstruction. But if the murder was carefully planned, the actual execution was a bit random. Assuming Martin had switched the real knife for the treated one, he still had no guarantee that he would be given that one for the photo call. Willy might have been killed by another unsuspecting actor, but would that have given Martin the requisite thrill? Charles felt ignorant of how accurate a psychopath's reconstruction of events has to be for him to commit a murder; it is not a well-documented subject.

But at least he faced the fact that he wanted to tie up the loose ends. Just for his own satisfaction. After lunch he would be organized like James Milne, sit down with a sheet of paper and make a note of all the outstanding questions of the case. Feeling happier for the decision, he set off down the hill to the hotel.

"Three days ago, you know, I wouldn't have believed it possible to eat one of Mrs. Parker's lunches within gastronomic memory of Mrs. Parker's breakfast, and certainly not with the prospect of Mrs. Parker's dinner looming deliciously like an enemy missile on the horizon."

Frances laughed as she watched him put away his plateful of cod and chips without signs of strain. "It's the famous Scottish air. Sharpens the appetite."

He took a long swallow from his second lunchtime pint of Guinness. "Did you finish the book?"

"Yes."

"Good. Then you can tell me. I want some details about the Earl of Bothwell."

"All right." She sat expectant, her schoolmistress mind confident of its recently acquired knowledge.

"Well, we know Bothwell killed Darnley by blowing him up at Holyrood. What I want to—"

"We don't know any such thing. Holyrood's still standing. The house where Darnley was staying, the one that was blown up, was in the Kirk o'Field. And anyway, Darnley wasn't blown up; he was strangled."

"Really." Charles took it in slowly. "Then what about the murder of David Rizzio? Bothwell didn't do it on his own, I know. Who was with him on the—"

"Bothwell wasn't involved in the murder of David Rizzio. Really, Charles, I thought you had a university education."

"A long time ago. And I read English."

"All the same. My fourth formers could do better. Rizzio was savagely murdered by Lord Darnley, Patrick Lord Ruthven (who rose from his sick bed), Andrew Ker of Fawdonside, George Douglas, um . . ." Her new storehouse of information ran out.

"Really?" said Charles, even more slowly. "Really." Martin had read History at Derby. If he were in the grip of psychopathic identification with an historical character, surely he would at least get the facts of his obsession correct. Charles began to regret the glibness with which he had assumed that Willy's death and the bomb were automatically connected.

"Hello. Everything all right?" Mr. Parker, who owned the hotel and was owned by Mrs. Parker, appeared at their table with the glass of whisky that was a permanent extension of his hand.

Charles and Frances smiled. "Yes, thank you," he said, tapping a stomach that surely could not take many more of these enormous meals without becoming gross. "Excellent."

"Good, good."

"Can I top that up for you, Mr. Parker?"

"Well . . . if you're having one."

"Why not? I'll have a malt."

"Mrs. Paris?"

"No, I'll—"

"Go on."

"All right."

It started to rain again heavily. Long clean streaks of water dashed against the window panes. It was cozy over the whisky.

Charles proposed a toast. "To Stella Galpin-Lord, without whom we wouldn't be here."

"Stella Galpin-Lord," said Mr. Parker, and chuckled. "Yes, Stella Galpin-Lord."

"You know her well?"

"She's been here four or five times. Stella the Snatcher we nickname her."

"Snatcher?"

"Oh, I'm sorry. Perhaps she's a friend of . . ."

"No," said Charles in a mischievous way to encourage indiscretion.

"Well, we call her the Snatcher, short for cradlesnatcher. Let's say that when she comes here it tends to be with a young man."

"The same young man?"

"No. That's the amusing thing. Always books as Mr. and Mrs. Galpin-Lord, but, dear oh dear, she must think we're daft or something. I mean, I can't believe they're all called Galpin-Lord."

"It is a fairly unusual name."

Mr. Parker chuckled. "It's not our business to pry. I mean, I don't care about people's morals and that, but I must confess Mrs. Parker and I do have a bit of a giggle about the Mr. and Mrs. Galpin-Lords." He realized that this sounded like a lapse of professional etiquette. "Not of course that we make a habit of laughing at our guests."

"No, of course not," Charles reassured smoothly. "But you say it's always younger men?"

"Yes, actors all of them, I think. Mutton with a taste for lamb, eh? Sorry, I shouldn't have said that."

"Hmm. And thanks to her latest actor getting a job, here we are."

"Yes."

"All the more reason to toast her in gratitude. Stella Galpin-Lord."

Mr. Pilch edged over from the table where Mrs. Pilch and the little Pilches were finishing their apricot crumble. "Oh, er, Mr. Paris. Tam the gamekeeper's going to take me up the burn to see if we can bag a salmon. With the right sort of fly, of course." He winked roguishly at this. "I wondered if you fancied coming . . . ?"

But Charles felt rather full of alcohol for a fishing trip. And besides, he wanted to start writing things down on bits of paper. "No, thanks. I think I'll have a rest this afternoon."

"Perhaps there'll be another chance." Mr. Pilch edged away.

"Sure to be, Mr. Paris," whispered Mr. Parker confidentially. "I'll ask Tam to take you another day. See what you can get. Actually, when our Mrs. Galpin-Lord was here last summer, she went off with Tam and they got a fifteen-pounder. Not bad."

"And did the current Mr. Galpin-Lord go with them?"

"Oh no." Mr. Parker laughed wickedly. "I daresay he was sleeping it off. Eh?"

The rest of the afternoon seemed to lead automatically to making love, which, except for the Clachenmore Hotel's snagging brushed nylon sheets, was very nice. "You know," murmured Frances sleepily, "we do go very well together."

He gave a distracted grunt of agreement.

"Do you think we could ever try again?"

Another grunt, while not completely ruling out the idea, was not quite affirmative.

"Otherwise we really ought to get divorced or something. Our position's so vague." But she did not really sound too worried, just sleepy.

"I'll think about it," he lied. He did not want to think about the circle of going back to Frances again and things being O.K. for a bit and then getting niggly and then him being unfaithful again and her being forgiving again and and and. . . . He must think about it at some stage, but right now there were more important things on his mind.

The lunchtime alcohol had sharpened rather than blunted his perception and he was thinking with extraordinary clarity. The whole edifice of logic he had created had been reduced to rubble and a new structure had to be put up, using the same bricks, and some others which had previously been discarded as unsuitable.

Thinking of the two crimes as separate made a new approach possible. Blurred and apparently irrelevant facts came into sharp focus. Red herrings changed their hue and turned into lively silver fish that had to be caught.

It came back again to what Willy was doing over the few days before he died. The melodrama with Anna and subsequent events had pushed that line of inquiry out of his mind, but now it became all-important and the unexplained details that he had discovered were once more significant pieces in his jigsaw.

He slipped quietly out of the brushed nylon sheets without disturbing the sleeping Frances, then dressed and padded downstairs to the telephone in the hotel lobby.

First he got on to directory inquiries. Then he took a deep breath, picked up the phone again and dialed the operator. London could not be dialed direct, which made his forthcoming imposture more risky, but he could not think of another way. By the time he got through, the Clachenmore operator, the London operator, Wanewright the Merchant's Bankers' receptionist and Lestor Wanewright's secretary had all heard the assumed Glaswegian tones of Detective-Sergeant McWhirter. If it ever came to an inquiry by the real police, there was a surfeit of witnesses to condemn Charles Paris for impersonating a police officer.

Fortunately Lestor Wanewright did not show any sign of suspicion. When the Detective-Sergeant explained that, in the aftermath of the deaths in Edinburgh, he was having to check certain people's alibis as a matter of routine, the young merchant banker readily confirmed Anna's statement. They had been sharing his flat in the Lawnmarket from Sunday, August 4th, when they had arrived back from Nice until Tuesday, August 13th, when he'd had to go back to work again. Yes, they had slept together over that period. Charles Paris felt a slight pang at the thought of Anna, but Detective-Sergeant McWhirter just thanked Mr. Wanewright for his co-operation.

Charles stayed by the phone after the call, thinking. He had two independent witnesses to the fact that Willy Mariello had slept with a woman at his home during the three or four days before his death. Jean Mariello had spoken of blonde hairs on the pillow and she had no reason for making that up. And, according to Michael Vanderzee, Willy had called good-bye to someone upstairs when dragged off to rehearsal on the Monday before he died.

True, Willy's sex life was free-ranging and the woman might have been anyone. But Charles could only think of one candidate with, if not blonde, at least blonded hair, and a taste for younger men.

It was nothing definite, but he still felt guilty about Martin's death. If there was anything that invited investigation, he owed it to the boy's memory to investigate it.

With sudden clarity, Charles remembered the first time he had seen Willy Mariello, on the afternoon of his death. He saw again the tall figure striding ungraciously into the Masonic Hall. Followed a few moments later by Stella Galpin-Lord, who was sniffing. Had she been crying? The memory seemed to be dragged up from years ago, not just a fortnight. But it was very distinct. He remembered the woman's face contorted with fury in the Hate Game.

That decided him. He picked up the phone again and asked for an Edinburgh number.

At first there seemed to be a crossed line, a well-spoken middle-aged woman's voice cutting across James Milne's, but it cleared and the two men could hear each other distinctly. "James, I've been thinking again about some aspects of the case."

"Really. So have I."

"It doesn't all fit, does it?"

"I think most of it does." The Laird's voice sounded reluctant. He and Charles had worked out a solution that was intellectually satisfying and he did not want their results challenged. It was the schoolmaster in him, the academic hearing that his theory has just been superseded by a publication from another university.

"You may be right, James. But for my own peace of mind, there are one or two people I'd just like to check a few details with. So I'm coming back to Edinburgh."

"Ah. And you're asking me to put my Dr. Watson hat back on?"

"If you don't mind."

"Delighted. You'll stay here, of course?"

"Thank you."

"When are you arriving?"

"Don't know exactly. It'll be tomorrow some time. As you know, I'm out here at Clachenmore and getting back involves a taxi to Dunoon, ferry across the Clyde to Gourock, bus to Glasgow and God knows what else. So don't expect me till late afternoon."

"Fine. And you'll tell me all then?"

"Exactly. Cheerio."

Then something odd happened. Charles heard the phone put down the other end twice. There were two separate clicks.

Two separate clicks—what the hell could that mean? He was about to dismiss it as a vagary of the Scottish telephone system when a thought struck him. There were two extensions of the same telephone at Coates Gardens, one in the Laird's flat and one in the hall. Perhaps what he had taken to be a crossed line at the beginning of the call had been someone answering the downstairs telephone. And the first click was that person putting their receiver down. In other words, someone could have heard all of the conversation.

Only one woman likely to be in Coates Gardens had a middle-aged voice.

The journey to Edinburgh developed another complication when he tried to order a taxi. The only firm for miles was in Tighnabruiach and there was a funeral there the following morning which was going to appropriate every car; they could not get one to the Clachenmore Hotel until half past two in the afternoon.

There was nothing to be done about it. It just meant another morning's fishing and another of Mrs. Parker's gargantuan lunches. There were worse fates.

The next morning was very, very wet. Rain fell as if God had upturned a bottomless bucket. Frances decided that she would not venture out; she curled up on the sofa in the Lounge with *Watership Down*.

"What do you think about fishing?" Charles asked, hoping Mr. Parker's reply would excuse him from going out.

"Yes, not bad weather for it."

Damn. Charles started to pull on his anorak. "Actually," Mr. Parker continued, "Tam was asking if I thought you'd like to go after some salmon."

That sounded a lot more attractive than pulling worms out of damp clods in the hope of another five-inch trout. "Really? Is he about?"

"Was earlier. There was a phone call for him. I'll see."

Tam was found and was more than willing to conduct a guided tour of the salmon pools (no doubt in anticipation of a substantial tip). His only reservation, which Mr. Parker interpreted to Charles, was that he did not approve of women being involved in fishing, and did Mrs. Paris want to come? Charles set his mind at rest on that point, and then took stock of his guide.

The gamekeeper was a man of indeterminate age and impenetrable accent. His face was sucked inwards and shriveled like perished rubber. He wore a flat cap and a once-brown overcoat with large pockets on the outside (and no doubt even larger ones on the inside).

Tam's mouth opened and uttered strange Scottish sounds which might have been asking if Charles was ready to go straight away.

"Yes," he hazarded. "Will I need a rod?"

Tam laughed derisively. Legal fishing methods were obviously a myth created for the tourists.

They set off, following the burn up the hill. Conversation was limited. Tam would occasionally comment on things they passed (a dead sheep, for example) and all Charles' acting skill would be required to choose the right "Yes," "Really?" "Too true," "Did they indeed?" or omnipurpose grunt. He did not have the confidence to initiate subjects himself, reacting was safer. Mr. Pilch's words came back to him. "They're a proud lot, the locals. Oh yes, you have to be careful what you say. And they have this great loyalty to their masters. In many ways, it's still an almost feudal society. Very poor though, I'm afraid. Not a lot of jobs available around here. It'll change of course when the oil comes—if it comes, which heaven forbid. You know there are plans to put up platforms just outside Loch Fyne? I hope they don't ruin the West Coast. Eh?"

None of that offered very promising conversational topics. What's it like being proud? Or living in a feudal society? Are you really very poor? What is your feeling about the proposed development of natural oil resources off the West Coast of Scotland? Somehow none of these seemed quite the right question to ask Tam, and fortunately the gamekeeper did not appear to find the silence irksome.

At last he indicated that they had reached their destination. It was the linked series of pools where Charles had been the day before. Again the trees overhead changed the note of the running stream and the heavy dripping of rain was muffled.

"Do the salmon really get up this far?"

Tam managed to communicate that they certainly did. He had got a twenty-pounder out of a good half mile farther up into the hills.

"Whereabouts do they go? Do we just look for them swimming about in the pools?"

Apparently not. In these conditions they lay still just under the bank. The skill was to spot them and whip them out of the water quickly. Tam would demonstrate.

They edged slowly down the slippery rocks to the water's edge. As they drew closer, the noise of the water increased. Swollen by rain, the cataracts pounded down on the rocks below. It was easy to see how the deep cleft had been worn down into the rock over the years.

Silently and efficiently, Tam lay down on the rocks at the water-side and peered into the bubbling green depths.

"Anything?" Charles hissed and was reprimanded by a finger on Tam's lips. The gamekeeper slid crabwise along the rocks, still looking down. Then he froze for a moment and got up.

"Big one," he whispered. Either Charles was getting used to the accent or it was clearer close to.

"Where?"

"Directly under that rock. Have a look. But be quiet and don't move suddenly."

Charles eased himself down to a kneeling position and, with his hands gripping the slimy edge of the pool, moved his head slowly out over the water.

At that moment his left hand slipped. It saved his life. As his body lurched sideways, he saw the flash of the brass head of Tam's Priest as it came down. The blow aimed to the skull landed with agonizing force on Charles' shoulder.

The shock of the attack stunned him even more than its violence. For a moment he lay there, the rocks hard under his back, his hair soaked with spray from the pounding water just below. Then he saw Tam advancing towards him with the Priest again upraised.

The gamekeeper must have thought he had knocked his victim

out; he was unprepared for the kick in the stomach that Charles managed from his prone position. Tam staggered back clutching himself, reeled for a moment at the water's edge, then fell safely on to the rocks.

Charles had one aim, which was to get the hell out of the place. Winding his assailant had given him the opportunity. He scrambled manically over the slimy rocks, grabbing at tussocks and branches to heave himself up the gradient. His right arm screeched with pain like a gear lever in a broken gearbox. But he was getting away.

He turned for a moment. Tam was standing now, but Charles had the start. Then he saw something whip out and uncoil from the gamekeeper's hand. As the treble hooks bit into his leg and he felt the inexorable pull down towards the boiling cauldron below, Charles knew it was the ripper.

CHAPTER 14

IN THE TRAIN FROM Glasgow to Edinburgh Charles said a little prayer of thanks, and reflected how frustrating it must be for God only to be in demand in times of danger, like a brilliant tap-dancer waiting for tap-dancing to come back into fashion. Still, God had saved his life and Charles Paris was suitably grateful.

There was no other explanation than divine intervention. The pain from his shoulder and the long furrows gouged in his left leg made the scene hard to forget. He could see the bank slipping past him as he was dragged painfully down to the water. He could feel the kick in the stomach with which Tam had immobilized him, and see the Priest again raised for a blow that was not going to miss.

And then, as Charles closed his eyes and vainly attempted to put his mental affairs in order, the threat vanished. Almost literally. The blow seemed a long time coming, so he crept one eye open. And Tam had disappeared.

The gamekeeper's foot must have slipped on the rocks and, caught off balance, he had fallen into the water. The force of the stream had swept him over the ledge of one pool and into the next,

543

where he floated round like a giant facecloth with a bubble of air caught in it.

Charles had tried to disengage the ripper from his leg, but the pain was too great, so he used a long stick to guide the body to the water's edge. Then, using both arms (though the right one felt as if it was being severed from his torso with a blowlamp), he had heaved the sodden mass on to the bank.

To his amazement, he found that Tam was still alive, unconscious, but with a strong heartbeat and pulse. Rediscovering a scrap of knowledge that had lain dormant since some aunt had given him a Boy Scout diary in his teens, Charles turned the body over and, after working the shoulders for a few minutes, was rewarded by a flow of water from the injured man's mouth. He then reckoned it was safe to leave Tam there; there was no danger of either death or escape. The body was propped up against a mossy bank and Charles started his painful course back to the hotel.

Mr. Parker took control with instant efficiency. Suddenly Clachenmore did not seem so isolated. A doctor was summoned and a party of local forestry workers who were in the bar went off to fetch Tam.

The doctor did not comment on the story of two men slipping on the bank, Tam falling into the water and Charles getting tangled in the hooks and banging his shoulder on a rock; he just got on with the job. Removing the barbs of the hooks was the worst bit, but he was used to it. He explained that a pair of pliers was an essential part of a doctor's equipment in that area, though most of the hooks he came across tended to be lodged in the cheeks of people walking behind over-enthusiastic fly-fishermen. Treble hooks, he admitted, were trickier, but the principle was the same—push the hook through until its barb stood clear of the flesh, snip if off with the pliers, and then work the remains of the hook out. While this excruciating operation was conducted, Charles made a rash vow that he would give up fishing; he had never thought what it felt like for the fish before.

In spite of the pain they caused, the scrapes on his leg were not deep. The highest one needed a couple of stitches, but the others were just cleaned and dressed. The shoulder presented even less problem. There was nothing broken, just severe bruising. The doctor strapped it into a sort of sling and went to tend the still-uncon-scious Tam, who had just been brought back.

Charles was patched up in time for lunch. Frances sat opposite him, looking anxious, but respecting his promise to explain every-thing in detail when it was over. There was an atmosphere of shock in the dining-room. Even Mr. Pilch was subdued and did not get far pontificating to his children on Stone Age relics in Argyll.

At two thirty the taxi had arrived and, against doctor's orders and Frances' advice, Charles had started the journey to Edinburgh. Which was why he was sitting in the train, thanking God and ask-ing God if He could see fit to spare a little more protection for the confrontation to come.

Stella Galpin-Lord had recommended Clachenmore. She knew Tam. By the attempt on Charles' life, she had nailed her colors to the mast, but it was a mast that only Charles Paris could see, and she thought Charles Paris was dead. His best weapon was going to be surprise.

She did look surprised to see him when he found her at the Ma-sonic Hall. She had just given her nightly peptalk to the cast of *A Midsummer Night's Dream* (which now only had three more revisual-ized performances to run; then in the third week of the Festival *Mary, Queen of Sots* took over). After Clachenmore Charles found it strange to think in terms of dates again. He reminded himself that it was now Thursday, August 29th.

"Stella. I'd like to talk."

"Certainly. I must say, this is a surprise. I thought we'd seen the last of you when you went to Clachenmore."

"Yes," he said grimly.

"Didn't you like it there?"

"There were . . . things I didn't like."

They went to the pub near the Hall where they had last met. She had another of her vodka and Camparis; he had a large Bell's. The pain from his patched-up wounds made concentration difficult, but he did not intend to talk for long.

Stella raised her glass. "Well, this is an unexpected pleasure."

"I want to talk about Willy Mariello."

The brusque statement took her completely off her guard. She blushed under her make-up, and lowered the glass as if she were afraid she might drop it. "Willy Mariello?" she echoed stupidly. "But he's dead."

"Yes. As you well know, he's dead." She mouthed at him, unable to form words. "And, Stella, I think his death may have something to do with what he was doing in the few days before he died."

"It was an accident," she croaked. "It couldn't have been anything to do with—"

"Couldn't it? Let's just suppose for a moment it could. I have become very interested in what Willy was doing over those few days. So far all I can find out is that he did a bit of rehearsing, a bit of decorating in his house . . . and he slept with a woman other than his wife."

The blush spread to the stringy parts of her neck the make-up had missed. "So . . . what are you saying?"

"That you were that woman."

"What if I was? Who do you think you are—the bloody Edinburgh Watch Committee? If two people are attracted to each other and want to sleep together, what bloody business is it of yours?"

"None at all. So when did this little affair start?"

"We met in a pub on the Saturday night. It was obvious he was attracted to me." Charles wondered. He had a more likely vision of Willy, furious at Anna's rejection of him, on the lookout for anything, so long as it was female. "And I went back to his house that night."

"I see."

Stella saw some meaning that Charles had not intended in his remark. "I suppose you're going to say something about our age difference."

"No, I'm not." His own recent behavior would make such comment hypocritical. Anyway, it was irrelevant. "And the affair continued for a few more nights?"

"Yes."

"Until the Tuesday morning when he told you to get lost."

Her eyes flashed under their lash-stretched lids. "He did not! It was my idea. I thought it unsuitable that it should continue. I believe in love on impulse; I don't think one should be tied."

A suitable philosophy if no one's ever tried to tie you and you have to make all the running, Charles thought. But he did not say it. "I see. Well, thank you for telling me that. I'm sure it's something the police don't know."

She gaped and her real age showed. "What do you mean? Surely the police think Willy's death was an accident . . . ? Or, if it wasn't, that that boy Martin—"

"If it wasn't, I feel we should tell them everything we know about the few days before he died."

"I don't think it's relevant."

"You don't. I do. Perhaps there are other things we ought to know about the period. I mean, what *was* Willy doing?"

"Willy—he was, as you said, rehearsing and decorating. The place was full of plaster dust and paint and all kinds of rubbish. Look, Mr. Paris, I'd like to know why the hell you're asking me all these questions."

"Because, Miss Galpin-Lord, I believe that, after a quarrel with Willy Mariello, in which he probably made disparaging remarks about your looks and general appeal, you arranged for him to be killed."

Her face crumbled until it looked of pensionable age. "What? Murder?"

"Yes."

"And what proof do you have of this?"

"The proof comes from the fact that when you realized I was on to you you arranged to have me murdered too. Only unfortunately Tam the gamekeeper failed in his attempt, which is why you see me here now."

"Tam?" Her voice was very weak.

"From Clachenmore. Now, come on, you set me up to go there because you knew Tam was to hand if necessary. Don't pretend you don't know him."

"I know who you mean, but I don't know him well."

"Well enough to know how poor he is and what he'd be prepared to do for money."

"But how am I supposed to have arranged this?"

"Simple. You rang him at the hotel. I know he had a call this morning."

"Don't be ridiculous. I hardly know the man." Now she was almost shouting.

"You've known him ever since he started working at Clachenmore."

"I've only seen him there a couple of times."

"Then maybe you knew him before. In his previous job. It was somewhere in the same area."

"I didn't know him then. Not at all. I've never even been to Glenloan House."

"Where?"

"Glenloan House."

There was only one other person Charles had ever heard use that name, someone who once owned a house in Meadow Lane.

He moved quickly and efficiently, as if the actions he had to make were long premeditated and rehearsed.

A streetlamp outside the house in Meadow Lane showed it to be dark and empty. Fortunately, there was nobody about to see him enter. He moved towards the front door, thinking to break one of the glass panels and reach round to the catch, when a sudden memory stopped him. The window catch Jean Mariello had complained about had been forgotten in the rush of her leaving, and the sash slid up easily.

Inside he was glad of the light from the streetlamp, which gave a pale glow to the white room.

Relevant memories came back. Again he saw Willy sitting opposite him in the Truth Game, long brown hair grayed with plaster dust. He remembered Stella's repetition of the fact that he had been decorating; Jean Mariello's words about her husband—"He'd suddenly get sick of his surroundings and want to change it all"— "Saw himself as the great landowner in his ancestral home in front of his blazing fire. The man of property."

It was on the left. When he looked along the wall, he could see the light catch on the slight prominence of plaster where the fireplace had been filled in. There was a central heating radiator fixed to the wall across it.

The radiator swiveled on its brackets to lie nearly flat on the floor. Behind it the plaster was more uneven, as if done in haste. Even in the pale light available, it was clear that the paint over this area was newer than in the rest of the room.

He was lucky. The pile of rubble which he had noticed when he last saw Jean Mariello was still there. He found a rusty screwdriver and started to chip away at the new plaster.

Willy had made the task easier by the slapdash way in which he had replaced the bricks. As he flaked off plaster and dug into the mortar, Charles tried to visualize the scene. Willy Mariello, the spoilt child, saw things going against him. The group had split up. His new career as an actor was not going to lead to instant stardom. His marriage was in shreds and Anna had rejected him. Bored and frustrated, he suddenly decided he was sick of his house. Where was the fireplace he had dreamed of?—replaced by bloody central heating. It would be a big job to change it. But Willy was impulsive; he did not like to go the boring correct way about things. Smash the fireplace covering first, and then see if he liked it.

But something had made him decide to fill the space in again. Charles prised away one brick, but the light did not reach the void. If only he had a torch. He began to be acutely conscious of the pain in his shoulder as he drove the screwdriver in the recalcitrant mortar. He was sweating.

He had to remove six bricks before he could see anything in the space. But as the sixth was worked out of its socket, the light flowed in and he shared the revulsion that Willy Mariello must have felt at the discovery. In spite of the discoloration of dirt and time and the decay of the fabric of the trousers and sock, what he saw had once been a human leg.

Nausea rising in his throat, he made himself confirm the initial impression. But there was no doubt. He found flesh dried down on to bone. It seemed that there was a complete body in the fireplace.

Again his movements were automatic. As he rose he realized how long he had been kneeling on the floor. The pain burned in his tattered leg. He decided to use the front door.

As he opened it, a large block of stone from the portico crashed down in front of him. It was the slab carved with the date, 1797. If he had not remembered the faulty catch and broken into the house the obvious way, it would have killed him.

CHAPTER 15

At last he shut the ponderous tome,
With a fast and fervent clasp
He strain'd the dusky covers close,
And fixed the brazen hasp:
Oh, God! could I so close my mind,
And clasp it with a clasp!

THE DREAM OF EUGENE ARAM

JAMES MILNE OPENED THE door of his flat. "Ah," he said. It was not an expression of surprise, just an acknowledgment of information received. "Won't you come in?"

"Thank you."

"Malt?"

"Thank you." It was exactly as before, both sitting in their comfortable chairs with their glasses of malt whisky, surrounded by books.

"I heard you had arrived in Edinburgh from one of the Derby students."

"Yes. I know you knew I was here."

The Laird understood. "You've been to Meadow Lane?"

"Yes. As you see, the slab missed me. One of your little plans that didn't work."

"Ah well." The man did not seem emotional, just tired. "After that, I'm surprised you came round here on your own."

"You mean the malt could be poisoned or you could have a gun hidden somewhere?"

"It's possible."

"No. That's not your style. The method must be indirect, done without you present. Then you can just shut your mind to the fact that it ever happened, and go back to your books."

"You seem to understand me very well, Charles."

"I think I do. Various things you said. Something about envying a writer his ability to live by remote control."

"Yes. And you said writing wasn't like that."

"It isn't."

The Laird chuckled, as if their old conviviality had been re-established. Then he was silent for a moment. "Right, how much do you know?"

"Just about everything. As you see from my face and hands, I've been dismantling a wall."

An expression of pain cut across Milne's face. "So you've seen it?"

"Just as Willy Mariello did."

"Yes. He came and told me on the morning before he died."

"And did he say he was going to the police?"

"No, no, that wasn't his idea at all. He suggested that I was a wealthy man and . . ."

"Blackmail. That would fit everything I've heard of Willy. And sort out his mortgage arrears. He could live off you for the rest of his life."

"I don't know. That's what he suggested. Regular payments or . . ."

"He'd go to the police." The Laird nodded. "And that was why you had to kill him."

There was a slight hesitation before a muttered "Yes."

"Who was it, James?"

The man looked flustered and pathetic. "No one. It was . . . just someone I knew . . . a . . . no one . . ."

"Who?"

"A boy. From the school. From Kilbruce. A pupil of mine. He was called . . . Lockhart." The Laird put his words together with difficulty. "He was a good boy. I liked him. He seemed interested in my books and . . . He . . . used to come round for tea or . . . That was all, really. In spite of what they said, that was all.

"Then one evening he came round . . . he wasn't in school uniform . . . and he said he was going to run away to London, and he'd left a note at school and sent one to his parents. I said I thought it was foolish, but I couldn't stop him. And that . . . I'd miss him . . . Just that, nothing more.

"But when I said it, he said something . . . vile . . . a comment on why I'd miss him. He said . . . it was just like all the others . . . that I . . . It wasn't true!" His hands were kneading the arms of his chair rapaciously. "I don't know what happened then. I . . . he was dead. Perhaps I strangled him, I don't know. But suddenly he was dead.

"Then I knew I had to get rid of the body. The men had just finished installing the central heating. I thought of the fireplace. There were no development plans for the area. The house wouldn't be demolished, and no one was going to revert to open fires after central heating had been put in." (No one except an impulsive fool like Willy Mariello, Charles reflected wryly.) "It'd never be found out while I was alive, and there was nobody to mind when I was dead. So that's what I did."

"And everyone assumed the boy had gone to London as he said, and disappeared?"

"Yes. You keep reading of cases of kids doing that."

There was a long pause. "And you managed to live in the house and forget it?"

"Yes. It had been so quick. Sometimes I really thought it hadn't happened, that I'd read about it in a book or . . . I didn't think about it."

"Just as you wouldn't have thought about me if Tam had drowned me or if that piece of masonry had crushed my skull."

"Exactly," he said with engaging honesty. "I've always found it difficult to believe in the reality of other people. You know, I like them, but if I don't see them, it's as if they'd never existed. Except my mother, she was real."

His eyes glazed over and Charles pulled him roughly back on to the subject. "Right. So we know why you had to kill Willy Mariello."

"Yes. The dagger was just a trial run, really. I never thought it would work. But I saw them downstairs at lunchtime on Tuesday and thought that'd do until I found a better way. There was a long chance it might work." A gleam of intellectual satisfaction came into his eye. "And it did. The perfect remote control crime."

"Yes," said Charles wryly. "And then I rather played into your hands by confiding in you as my Dr. Watson."

"You did. At least it made me fairly certain that I wasn't on your list of suspects. That is, until the middle of last week."

"Why? What happened then?"

"You started getting evasive, which seemed odd. I felt you were holding something back. But what really scared me was when you said you were going to give the case up, because it involved some-one you knew well. I thought you were on to me then."

"Good God. That wasn't what I meant at all. I was talking about Anna. You know, I told you I was having an affair with her. Well, at that stage I was suspicious of her."

"Oh." The Laird sounded disappointed. "Then I needn't have planted the bomb."

"It was you!" Charles sat bolt upright in his chair.

"Yes. I'd been building up your suspicions of Martin Warburton to keep the heat off me anyway. But I did follow him and I actually managed to break into the Nicholson Street flat. When I saw all the bomb-making equipment I knew it might be useful. Martin seemed in such a bad state that he wouldn't be able to give a coherent account of his movements. So when I thought you were on to me, I picked up the bomb and waited my chance. Once it was planted, all I had to do was stay with you until it was discovered and you'd cease to be suspicious of me. The fact that it happened at Holyrood just added drama to the situation."

"So the break in the connection was deliberate? You knew the thing wouldn't blow up?"

The Laird nodded smugly, pleased with his own cunning. Charles began to realize just how detached the man's intellectual processes had become from his emotional reactions. For him life was an elaborate mental game, in which passion was an intruder. The Laird expanded on his plot. "And then of course Martin War-burton played into my hands completely. I knew he was in a confused state, but suicide was more than I could have hoped for. It made the whole thing cut and dried, a complete case with a problem and an unquestionable solution. And, from my point of view, a perfect sequence of crimes, which neither I nor anyone else need ever have thought about again.

"And if you hadn't worked it all out at Clachenmore, or even if Tam (who incidentally was my mother's gamekeeper for years and would do anything for me) had made a clean job of dispatching you, it would have worked." Charles was again amazed by the detached way in which the man could talk to someone he had twice tried to murder. The Laird went on in the same level tone. "By the way, what was it made you sure it was me."

"Ah, well . . ." Charles was damned if he was going to admit the circuitous route by which he had reached the solution. And then suddenly his mind joined two incidents whose significance he should have seen long before. *"The Dream of Eugene Aram,"* he pronounced confidently.

"What?"

"Hood's poem. When you returned my book, I asked if you had read it and you said 'No,' quite vehemently. But then later you quoted from the poem . . ."

The Laird supplied the words as if in a trance.

" 'Much study had made him very lean
And pale and leaden-eyed.' "

Charles nodded, confident in his lies. "So that made me wonder why you wanted to divert my attention from *Eugene Aram.* I looked back at the poem and there it was—the story of a schoolmaster who committed a murder and was not found out for many years until the body was discovered. Obviously you didn't want to set my mind on that track."

The Laird agreed tonelessly. "I didn't think you'd noticed."

"Ah," said Charles with what he hoped was subtle intonation. And then he quoted from *The Dream of Eugene Aram.*

" *'Then down I cast me on my face,*
And first began to weep
For I knew my secret then was one
That earth refused to keep:

Or land or sea, though he should be
Ten thousand fathoms deep.

So wills the fierce avenging Sprite,
Till blood for blood atones!
Ay, though he's buried in a cave,
And trodden down with stones,
And years have rotted off his flesh,—
The world shall see his bones!' "

"I see. And that's what made you suspicious?"

Charles had not the hypocrisy to say yes; he let the silence stand. James Milne did not seem to mind. On the contrary, he looked serene, almost pleased at the literary resolution of his case.

There was a long silence, during which he refilled their glasses. Then he sat back in his chair and took a long swallow. "The question now is, Charles, what happens next?"

"Yes."

"I suppose you feel bound to go to the police?" There was a hint of pleading in his tone, but Charles ignored it.

"Yes, James, I'm afraid I do. Not because I hate you or anything like that. As I said to you once, I have a stereotyped view of murderers as wicked people I dislike. You don't fit that. I like you and I'm sorry to have to do this.

"I'm not even particularly shocked by some of your crimes. I don't know about the boy, what the rights and wrongs were, but that sounds like a moment of passion, a sudden burst of insanity that could happen to any of us given the right sort of provocation. I don't even mind that much about Willy Mariello. He was a slob whom nobody seems to have mourned. And, as for your attacks on me, they were a logical consequence of your position and my actions.

"But, James, I can't ever forgive you for the crime you didn't commit—Martin Warburton's suicide. That boy was mixed up beyond belief. But he was very talented and at a difficult time in his life. He needed help. What you did by your elaborate framing of him was to put the boy under pressures that few people completely in control of their senses could manage. I know you didn't think about him as a person; he was just a counter in your game of self-concealment. And it's because you didn't think of him as a person that I regard you as a dangerous man, who should probably be put away."

There was another silence. James Milne did not look shattered, like a man whose life had just been ruined, but piqued, like a debater who had just lost a point. He rose with a sigh. "Perhaps we should go to the police then."

"I think we should."

"I'll take a book." He turned round to the shelves and instinctively found a leather-bound copy of Oscar Wilde's *De Profundis*. "I dare say there'll be a lot of sitting around at the police station."

"Yes," said Charles, "I dare say there will."

CHAPTER 16

My temples throb, my pulses boil,
I'm sick of Song, and Ode, and Ballad—
So, Thyrsis, take the Midnight Oil
And pour it on a lobster salad.

TO MINERVA—FROM THE GREEK

CHARLES SPENT A LOT of time with the police over the next couple of days and did not make it back to Clachenmore. Frances joined him in Edinburgh on the Sunday. They booked into the Aberdour Guest House, where Mrs. Butt patently did not think they were married.

Frances wanted to get back to London to prepare for the new school term, but Charles persuaded her to stay till the Tuesday morning so that they could attend the first night of *Mary, Queen of Sots.* His stay at the Festival would not be complete without that. He also managed to fit in a visit to Lesley Petter, who was cheerful at the prospect of leaving the Infirmary in a couple of days.

On the Monday they arrived at the Masonic Hall at seven, half an hour before the show was due to start, to find Pam Northcliffe and others energetically piling up the chairs from the back of the hall. They were watched by an unamused group of young men in tracksuits.

"Pam, what's going on?"

"Oh Lord, Charles, hello. There's been the most frightful cock-up, I'm afraid. This lot say they're booked in here for badminton on Monday nights. Apparently it was only cancelled for the two weeks and they aren't going to budge."

"Whose fault is it?"

"Brian Cassells booked it."

"Say no more. Where is he? Surely he should be flashing his dinner jacket and sorting it out."

"Oh, he's gone."

"Gone?"

"Yes, he got the Civil Service job he was after, so he's gone to have a holiday in Italy before it starts."

"Tell me, which Ministry is the job in?"

"Social Services, I think. He'll be doing pensions."

That seemed apt. There was some justice after all. Charles could visualize a glowing career for Brian withholding money from old ladies.

"So is the performance off?"

"Oh no. The show must go on. Sam says so," Pam announced with pride.

"Why? Is Sam directing?"

"Yes. As well as playing Rizzio and Bothwell and doing the music."

"Where's Michael Vanderzee?"

"Ah. He had an offer to go and direct Humpe's *Gangrene* at the Almost Blue Theatre."

"And he went?"

"Oh yes. It's a chance in a lifetime."

"Of course."

At that moment Sam Wasserman appeared from behind the curtains, distraught in doublet and hose. "Pam, Pam darling, my tights have laddered."

"Don't worry, darling, I've got a needle and thread in my bag. Oh Lord, I'd better go."

"O.K. Good luck." Pam bustled off, blushing. Charles decided he and Frances had time for a drink. And might need one.

They did. The audience was tiny. Brian Cassells' theory about morbid publicity being good publicity had proved incorrect and the average Edinbourgeois was too affronted by the title alone to consider seeing the show. The atmosphere in the hall was not helped by the full houselights necessary for the badminton and the pounding feet and occasional curses of the players.

But ultimately it was the play that made the evening a disaster. Sam Wasserman's leaden allegories proved no more lively onstage than they had when he described them. They were presented in the metronomic blank verse that can only be produced by a Creative Writing course and were mixed with songs that provided as much contrast as a bread-filled sandwich.

Charles tensed up when Anna came on, looking very beautiful in her Tudor costume. But when she spoke, he relaxed. There was no real pang, just the impression that she was rather theatrical. She was talented, but mannered. Two years at drama school might make her quite good.

At the interval Charles and Frances snuck out to the pub, giggling like schoolchildren. And somehow they omitted to return for the second act.

On the train back to London on the Tuesday morning Charles gave Frances an edited version of the whole case. When he came to the end, she tut-tutted. "Charles, I can't think why you've suddenly developed this very dangerous hobby. Why can't you take up golf or bowls like most middle-aged men?"

"I don't know. It's not deliberate. It's just if I get into a situation I have to find out what happened, find out the truth, I suppose."

"Well, you did in this case."

"Yes. Mind you, I took my time. I think I must have barked up every tree in the park before I found one with anyone in it."

At King's Cross Underground Station, they paused for a moment, slightly embarrassed. Then Charles kissed Frances good-bye. She caught the Northern Line to Highgate and he caught the Circle Line to Bayswater.

Cast, In Order of Disappearance

To Lucy

CONTENTS

1

CINDERELLA ALONE

"CHARLES, CHARLES LOVE, it's your cue."

Charles Paris jerked out of his doze. He looked down for the script on his knees, but *The Times* crossword with two completed clues stared blankly up at him. He dropped the paper, opened his script, and looked hopefully at the little actress next to him for the page number.

"Page 27, Line 4," the producer snapped with all the exasperation of a large mortgage in Pinner and another nineteen years till his BBC pension.

"Sorry . . ." said Charles, trying to remember the producer's name. "Sorry, love," failing to do so.

He read his lines with leaden incomprehension. A twinge of guilt for having done no preparation soon passed when he heard the lines he was reading. Wasn't anyone writing good radio plays any more? As his scene ground to a halt, he looked across at the spindly raffia-haired youth responsible. The Author sat by the producer in a twisted attitude of intense concentration or bad piles. Every now and then he winced as another nuance of his writing was steamrollered.

The play reached its denouement with all the impact of a wet dishcloth, and there was a ripple of dejected laughter. "Well," said the producer, "now the real work starts. But first let's send the lovely Sylvia for some tea."

Charles took the opportunity to go to the Gents and lose lunchtime's excesses of wine. To his annoyance the Author joined him at the adjacent urinal. Charles resolutely pretended he hadn't noticed.

"Um, Charles . . ."

"Yes."

"I hope you don't mind my saying . . ."

"No, of course not."

"Well, I'd seen the Inspector rather Grand Guignol . . ."

"Ah."

"And I thought you read him rather . . ."

"Yes . . . ?"

"Well, Petit Guignol."

"Ah," said Charles Paris. "I'll try to do something about it."

Even Arctic nights end, and so, somehow, did the day in the studio. Charles's performance, however Grand its Guignol, was fixed on tape. It all seemed to matter less as he stood in the BBC Club and the first large Bell's glowed inside him. It was December 3rd and the short walk from Broadcasting House to the Club had been breathtakingly cold after the recycled warmth of the studio.

Sherlock Forster (known to his intimates as Len) was an undemanding companion. A distinguished radio actor and a great pissartist, he had been playing the murderer in the play and was now slumped against the bar, caressing a large Riesling, his toupée'd head deep into the *Evening Standard*. "Hoarding outside said 'Motorist Shot Dead.' Thought it might have pushed the bloody Arabs out of the headlines," he said to no one in particular.

"Did it?" asked Charles.

"No such luck. Main story's still bloody petrol queues. 'Motorist Shot Dead' is way down the column."

"Where'd it happen?"

"Just off the M4 somewhere. Apparently the bloke'd run out of petrol, got out of the car, and some bugger shot him."

"Poor sod."

"Police are treating it as a case of murder."

"Shrewd of them. Anything else in the paper?"

"Well, the Archbishop of Canterbury's being driven round in a Morris Minor to save petrol. And a couple of Cabinet ministers turned up at the House in a Mini."

"Chauffeur-driven, no doubt."

The second large Bell's changed the glow within Charles to a feeling of positive well-being. Forty-seven years old and still attractive to women. The lack of matinée-idol good looks which had kept him from being a star in the Fifties was no longer a disadvantage. He had worn better than a lot of his contemporaries. Hair still grew thick and only lightly silvered at the temples. He looked at Len's theatrical toupée and felt grateful.

Life, Charles reflected, was not too bad. Even financially, for once. He was still flush from a ghastly television series in which he'd minced around some unlikely Tudor monarch in doublet and hose for a couple of months. And when he'd drunk through that money, or when the taxman caught up with him, something else would happen. He cast a professional eye round the bar. A few standard-issue BBC spinsters; one or two attractive younger secretaries, sentried by men; nothing worth chatting up.

"Petrol, bloody petrol," said Len. "There's nothing else in the paper. Look at this—'Attractive 19-year-old model Patti Winchester isn't worried. She's been showing a leg and riding her bicycle for months now.' "

Charles glanced over. "Tatty."

"Hmm. Footballer Bobby Lithgoe has bought a bicycle too."

"Wow."

"And Marius Steen has put the Rolls in the garage."

"Steen? What does it say about him?"

" 'Impresario Marius Steen, the man behind such stage successes as *One Thing After Another, Who's Afraid of the Big Bed Wolf?* and, of course, his current smash-hit at the King's Theatre, *Sex of One and Half a Dozen of the Other,* phoned today at his Berkshire home, said, "We'll leave the Rolls in the garage and use the Datsun." ' "

"He's got a good publicity machine. It's just a straight plug for that bloody *Sex of One . . .*"

"Clocked up a thousand performances last week."

"God. How revolting."

"Big party on-stage at the King's on Saturday."

"It'll probably run forever. There's no justice." Charles picked up Len's empty glass. "Another one of those?"

"Why not?"

Predictably the BBC Club had led to the George, the George to a small pub off Drury Lane, and at about mid-night Charles, having lost Len somewhere along the line, found himself leaning against a banister in the Montrose with a pint in his hand.

The Montrose (a small theatrical drinking club off the Haymarket) was full as usual. A lot of rooms on different levels, shoddy like converted bedsitters, overflowing with actors talking and gesturing loudly.

". . . got a *Z-Cars* coming up. Small part, but nice . . ."

". . . and he said to William, 'You've got as much humor as a crutch!' She was furious . . ."

". . . working towards a modern commedia format . . ."

". . . ultimately it's a matter of identity . . ."

"Hello, Charles." A voice detached itself from the rest and Charles focused on a small blonde girl in front of him. "Jacqui."

Jacqui had a top-floor flat in Archer Street, opposite a casino whose lights usually flashed yellow all night. But now with the power restrictions, they were dark. Only the blue glow of a solitary street-lamp touched their anemic neon tubes. But there were still the noises of the casino—the hum and slam of taxis, the shouts of drunkards and the chatter of Chinese gamblers in the street below.

Charles looked at Jacqui with pleasure. She was an actress-cum-dancer-cum-most-things he'd met in pantomime at Worthing. He'd been Baron Hardup, Cinderella's father; and she had been a Villager, White Mouse and Court Lady (for the Finale). They'd had quite a pleasant time in Worthing. It was good to see her again.

But she looked upset. Charles filled his glass from the bottle of Southern Comfort and slumped back onto the white fur of the bed, shaking a small oil-lamp on the bedside table. "And you can't get in touch with him?"

"No. I've tried both the houses. And the office."

"I wouldn't worry, Jacqui. He'll call you."

"Maybe." She still looked tense and hurt. Strange, how a girl like that, who'd had everyone and done everything, could be so affected by one dirty old man not getting in touch with her. And Marius Steen of all people.

Jacqui stretched out her strong dancer's legs and stared at her toes. "No. He often doesn't call for weeks on end. He's moody. Sometimes he doesn't want me around. I'm his secret vice. Just a tottie. I mean, if he's going to a do with the Queen Mum, he can't take a tart along." Charles grunted uncomfortably. "No, that's what I am. I don't really want to be more than that. He's an old man, he's nice to me, we have a few giggles, that's all. It couldn't possibly last. I know that." She sounded as if she was bravely repeating a formula she didn't believe.

"When did you last see him?"

"Saturday afternoon."

"For God's sake, what is it now? Only Monday. Give him a chance."

"I know, but this time I think it's over."

"Why?"

"When I rang, there was a message. Said I wasn't to contact him again."

"Ah."

Jacqui poured herself a large glass of Southern Comfort and took a savage swallow at it. "Bugger him. I'm not going to get miserable about an old sod like that." She rose and flopped down on the bed beside Charles. "There are other men."

"Still older men, I'm afraid."

"You're not old."

"I'm forty-seven."

"That's cradle-snatching by my standards," she said with a wry laugh. Then she stopped short. "Old sod. It's all because of the knighthood."

"Hmm?"

"His last ambition. Reckoned he might get one this New Year."

"Services to the Theatre?"

"I suppose so. And I suppose I let down the image. Well, I don't care about him." She snuggled up to Charles.

"Jacqui, am I being used merely for revenge? As a sex-object?"

"Yes. Any objections?"

"No."

Charles kissed her gently. He felt protective towards her, as if she might suddenly break down.

Her tongue flickered round the inside of his mouth and they drew apart. "You smell like a distillery," she said.

"I am a distillery," he replied fatuously and hugged her close to him. She had a comforting little body, and the smoky taste of her mouth was familiar. "Hmm. We had a good time in Worthing. We were better than the dirty postcards."

Jacqui smiled closely into his eyes and her hand fumbled for his zip. She couldn't find the little metal pull-tag. An exasperated breath. "You know, Charles, I always think it's simpler to take your own things off. If you're both in agreement."

"I'm in agreement," said Charles. He rolled over to the side of the bed and fumblingly undressed. When he turned round, Jacqui was lying naked on the bed, familiar in the pale street light. "Charles."

"Must take my socks off. Otherwise I feel like an obscene photo."

He lay down beside her and hugged her, warm on the fur. They held each other close, hands gliding over soft flesh.

After a few moments Charles rolled away. "Not very impressive, am I?"

"Don't worry. It doesn't matter."

"No." A pause. "Sorry. I'm not usually like this."

"I know," Jacqui said meaningfully. "And I know what to do about it."

He felt her moving, a soft kiss on his stomach, then the warmth of her breath as it strayed downwards. "Jacqui, don't bother. I'm not in the mood. It's the booze or . . ."

"OK. Poor old Baron Hardup."

"I'm sorry, Jacqui."

"Don't worry. All I really need is a good cuddle."

"Tonight I'm afraid that's all I can offer you." And he hugged her very closely like a teddy bear in his arms. In a moment he had sunk into a heavy, but troubled sleep.

2

THE FAIRY GODMOTHER

As Charles walked past the manicured front gardens of Muswell Hill, he tried to piece together his feelings. It was a long time since he had been so churned up inside. For years life had jogged on from hangover to hangover, with the odd affair between drinks, and nothing had affected him much. But now he felt jumpy and panicky.

Impotence is perhaps not unusual in a man of forty-seven. And anyway it probably wasn't impotence, just the dreaded Distiller's Droop. Nothing to worry about.

But that wasn't the important part of his feelings. There was a change in his attitude to Jacqui. He felt an enormous need to protect the girl, as if, by failing in bed, he had suddenly become responsible for her. She seemed desperately vulnerable, like a child in a pram or an old man in a launderette. Perhaps these were paternal feelings, the sort he had somehow never developed for his daughter.

Together with this new warmth came the knowledge that he had to go and see Frances. "Marriage," Charles reflected wryly as he clicked open her wrought-iron gate, "is the last refuge of the impotent."

She wasn't there. Still at school. Not even six o'clock yet. Charles had a key and let himself in. His hand instinctively found the light-switch.

The house hadn't changed. As ever, a pile of books to be marked on the dining table, concert programs, an old Edinburgh Festival brochure. Earnest paperbacks about psychology and sociology on the bookshelves. Auntie May's old upright piano with the lid up. And on top, that terrible posed photograph of Juliet with pigtails and a grim smile over the brace on her teeth. Next to it, the puzzle jug. Then that windswept snapshot of him, Charles Paris, taken on holiday on Arran. It was a real LP sleeve photograph. Better than any of that expensive rubbish he'd had done for *Spotlight*.

He resisted the temptation to raid the drinks cupboard, switched on the television and slumped into the sofa they'd bought at Harrods when flush from selling the film rights of his one successful play.

He heard the guarded voice of a newscaster, then the picture buzzed and swelled into life. The news was still dominated by petrol and the prospect of rationing. Charles couldn't get very excited about it.

Police had identified the motorist shot off the M4 at Theale. A blurred snapshot was blown up to fill the screen. It had the expression of a man already dead. There had been no petrol in the victim's car; the back right-hand wing was dented; he had been shot through the head and left by the roadside. Police were still trying to find a motive for the killing.

"In the second day of the Sally Nash trial at the Old Bailey, a 17-year-old girl, Miss C., told of sex-parties at London hotels. A lot of show-business people—" Charles switched over to the serious face of Eamonn Andrews talking to someone about petrol rationing. He switched again and got a sizzling snowstorm through which a voice imparted mathematical information.

"Sodding UHF." He got down on his hands and knees in front of the box and started moving the portable aerial about. The snowstorm varied in intensity. Then he remembered the UHF contrast knob and went round the set to turn it.

"Television repair man." He'd been too close to the sound to hear Frances come in.

"Hello." He stood up. "Look. The picture's perfect."

"Are you doing an Open University degree?"

"No. I was just getting it right. It's the UHF contrast."

"Ah." She looked at him. "How are you?"

"Bad."

"I thought so. Do you want something to eat?"

"I don't know."

"That means yes. Did you have lunch?"

"Pie in a pub."

"Ugh." Frances went into the kitchen and started opening cupboards. She continued talking through the serving hatch. It was restfully familiar.

"I went down to see Juliet and Miles at the weekend."

"Ah."

"Nice to get out of town."

"Yes."

"They said they'd love to see you. You should go down, it's a lovely place."

"Yes. I will. At some stage. How's Miles?"

"Oh, he's doing very well."

"Ah." Charles visualized his son-in-law, Miles Taylerson, the rising executive, neat in his executive house on his executive estate in Pangbourne with his executive car and his executive suits and his executive haircut. "Do you like Miles, Frances?"

"Juliet's very happy with him."

"Which I suppose," Charles reflected, "is some sort of answer." Thinking of his daughter made him think of Jacqui again and he felt a flutter of panic in his stomach.

Frances produced the food very quickly. It was a dish with frankfurters and sour cream. Something new. Charles felt jealous at the thought that she was developing, learning new things without him. "Tell you what," he said, "shall I whip down to the off-licence and get a bottle of wine? Make an evening of it."

"Charles, I can't 'make an evening of it.' I've got to be at a PTA meeting at 7:30."

"Parents-Teachers? Oh, but can't you—" He stopped. No, you can't come back to someone you walked out on twelve years ago and expect them to be instantly free. Even if you have kept in touch and had occasional reconciliations. "Have a drink together later, maybe."

"Maybe. If you're still here."

"I will be."

"What is the matter, Charles?"

"I don't know. Male menopause?" It was a phrase he'd read in a color supplement somewhere. Didn't really know if it meant anything.

"You think you've got problems," said Frances.

She was always busy. Two things about Frances—she was always busy and she was never surprised. These, in moments of compatibility, were her great qualities; in moments of annoyance, her most irritating traits.

The next morning she cooked a large breakfast, brought it up to him in bed, and hurried off to school. Charles lay back on the pillows and felt mellow. He saw the familiar gable of the Jenkinses opposite (they'd had the paintwork done blue) and felt sentimentality well up inside him. Each time he came back to Frances, he seemed to feel more sentimental. At first. Then after a few days they'd quarrel or he'd feel claustrophobic and leave again. And go on a blinder.

The impotence panic seemed miles away. It was another person who had felt that nausea of fear in his stomach. Long ago.

They had made love beautifully. Frances's body was like a well-read book, familiar and comforting. Her limbs were thinner, the tendons a bit more prominent and the skin of her stomach loose. But she was still soft and warm. They had made love gently and easily, their bodies remembering each other's rhythms. It's something you never forget, Charles reflected. Like riding a bicycle.

He switched on the radio by the bedside. It was tuned to Capital Radio—pop music and jingles. So that's what Frances listened to. Strange. It was so easy to condemn her as bourgeois and predictable. When you actually came down to it, everything about her was unexpected. What appeared to be passivity was just the great calm that emanated from her.

When he was dressed, he needed human companionship and so rang his agent. "Maurice Skellern Artistes," said a voice.

"Maurice."

"Who wants him?"

"Maurice, I know that's you. It's me, Charles."

"Oh, hello. How'd the radio go?"

"Ghastly. It was the worst script I've ever seen."

"It's work, Charles."

"Yes, just."

"Were you rude to anybody?"

"Not very. Not as rude as I felt like being."

"Who to?"

"The producer."

"Charles, you can't afford it. Already you'll never get another job on *Doctor Who*."

"I wasn't very rude. Anything coming up?"

"Some vacancies on the permanent company at Hornchurch."

"Forget it."

"Chance of a small part in a *Softly, Softly*."

"Put my name up."

"New play at one of these new fringe theatres. About transvestites in a prison. Political overtones. Written by a convict."

"It's not really *me*, is it, Maurice?" in his best theatrical knight voice.

"I don't know what is *you* any more, Charles. I sometimes wonder if you want to work at all."

"Hmm. So do I."

"What are you living on at the moment?"

"My second childhood."

"I don't get ten per cent of that."

"No. What else is new?"

"Nothing."

"Come on. Give us the dirt."

"Isn't any. Well, except for the Sally Nash business . . ."

"Oh yes?"

"Well, you know who the disc jockey was, for a start . . . ?" And Maurice started. He was one of London's recognized authorities on theatrical gossip. Malicious rumor had it that he kept a wall-chart with colored pins on who was sleeping with whom. The Sally Nash case gave him good copy. It was the Lambton affair of the theatre, complete with whips, boots, two-way mirrors and unnamed "show-business personalities." For half an hour Maurice named them all. Eventually, he rang off. That's why he was such a lousy agent. Spent all his time gossiping.

By the Thursday morning Charles's mellowness felt more fragile. When he woke at nine, Frances had already gone to school. He tottered downstairs and made some coffee to counteract the last night's Beaujolais. The coffee tasted foul. Laced with Scotch, it tasted better. He drank it down, poured a glass of neat Scotch and went upstairs to dress.

The inside of his shirt collar had dark wrinkles of dirt, and his socks made their presence felt. Soon he'd have to get Frances to wash something or go back to Hereford Road and pick up some more clothes.

He sloped back downstairs. Frances's *Guardian* was neatly folded on the hall chest. No time to read it at school. Organized read in the evening. It had to be the *Guardian*.

Charles slumped on to the Harrods sofa and started reading an article on recycling waste paper. It failed to hold his attention. He checked the television times and switched on *Play School*. The picture was muzzy. He started fiddling with the UHF contrast knob. The phone rang.

"Hello."

"Charles."

"Jacqui. Where on earth did you get this number?"

"You gave it me ages ago. Said you were contactable there in the last resort."

"Yes. I suppose it is my last resort. What's up?"

"It's about Marius."

"Yes?"

"I tried to contact him again. Went to the house in Bayswater. It was a stupid thing to do, I suppose. Should've left him alone. Should be able to take a bloody hint. I don't know."

"What happened?"

"He wasn't there. But this morning I had a letter."

"From Marius?"

"Yes. It wasn't signed, but it must be. It's horrid. Charles, I'm shit-scared."

"Shall I come round?"

"Can you?"

"Yes." A pause. "Why did you ring me, Jacqui?"

"Couldn't think of anyone else."

After he had put the phone down, Charles switched off *Play School*. He took an old envelope from the table and wrote on it in red felt pen, "THANKS. GOOD-BYE. SEE YOU." Then he left the house and set out for Highgate tube station.

3

WHO WAS AT THE BALL?

CHARLES LOOKED AT the sheet of paper. It was pale blue with a dark bevelled edge and, on it, scrawled in black biro capitals, was an uncompromising message. Basically, it told Jacqui to get lost when she wasn't wanted. And basically was the way it was done. The language was disgusting and the note anonymous. "Charming. Are you sure it's from him?"

"No one else had any reason."

"And is the language in character?"

"Yes, he never was very delicate. Particularly when he was angry. Could be quite frightening."

"Paper familiar?"

"Yes. He had it on his desk at Orme Gardens. Some headed, some plain like this."

"Hmm. Well, there's only one way to treat shit of this sort." Charles screwed the note up into a dark glass ashtray and set it on fire with the table lighter. When the flame had gone, he blew the black ash carefully into the wastepaper basket. "When did it come?"

"It was on the mat when I got up. About eleven. A bit after."

"Come by post?"

"No. Plain envelope. On the table."

Charles leant over and picked it up. Blue, matching the paper. Told him nothing. "And I suppose you didn't . . . ?"

"See anyone? No."

"It's a fairly nasty way of breaking something off, isn't it?"

"Yes." She looked near to tears. "And I thought it was going so well."

"Perhaps he's just a nasty man."

"He could be, I know. But with me he was always kind. When we were in France, he—"

"When was this?"

"We went in August, came back in October. Marius's got a villa down the South. Sainte-Maxime. It's a lovely place. Private beach."

"Very nice."

"Anyway, he took me there to recuperate."

"What from?"

"I'd had an abortion."

"His baby?"

"Yes. He fixed it up, but it didn't quite go right. I was ill. So he took me out to Sainte-Maxime."

"And he was there all the time?"

"Yes. He'd been ill too—had a minor heart-attack. He was meant to be resting, though, of course, being Marius, he was in touch with the office every day."

"It was just the two of you out there?"

"Mostly. Some friends of his dropped in, theatre people. And Nigel for a bit."

"Nigel?"

"His son."

"Oh, yes." Charles remembered someone once mentioning that Steen had a son. "I didn't think they got on."

"That was ages ago. They made it up, more or less. Nigel works in the business."

"And while you were out in France, it was all OK? Between you and Marius?"

"Yes. We had a marvellous time. He was very silly and childish. And kind."

"And now he sends you notes like that. You can't think of any reason for the change in his attitude?"

Jacqui hesitated. "No. Would you like some lunch?"

While she cooked, Charles went down to the off-licence and

bought a bottle of wine. It was obvious from Jacqui's manner that she did have an idea why Steen had changed. And that she was going to tell him. It was only a matter of waiting.

The lunch was unremarkable. Jacqui was a frozen food cook. He remembered it from Worthing. Endless beefburgers and cod steaks with bright peas and diced vegetables. But the wine made it passable. They talked back to Worthing, hedging round the subject of Steen. Eventually, as Charles drained the bottle evenly into their two glasses, he asked, "What do you want me to do, Jacqui?"

"What do you mean?"

"You've brought me round here for a reason."

"I was frightened."

"Yes, but there's something else."

"Yes." She looked very vulnerable. Again he felt the sense of debt that had started when he failed her in bed. The contract was unfulfilled. If he could not serve her in one way, he would serve her in another. It's strange, he thought, is this what chivalry's come to?

"I do want you to do something for me, Charles. It's sort of awkward. You see, I think I know . . . I think I might know why Marius is behaving like this. He might think . . . you see . . ." Charles bided his time. Jacqui looked at him directly and said, "You've heard of all this Sally Nash business?"

"Yes. Is Marius involved in that?"

"Not really. Not with the prostitutes. It's just . . . well, she, Sally Nash, used to be at some parties that we went to."

"Just ordinary parties?"

"Well . . ." Jacqui smiled sheepishly. "No, not ordinary parties really. Things happened."

"I didn't know that was your scene. I thought you only slept with one man at a time and . . ." Charles tailed off, embarrassed.

"No, it's not my sort of thing. But Marius was into all that. Only a bit. Nothing very serious."

"Hmm."

"Don't sound so bloody superior. It's easy for a man. If you're a girl you have to get interested in what your bloke's interested in. If he's mad on football, you watch *Match of the Day*. If it's two-way mirrors, well . . ."

"Was it like that in the South of France?"

"No. It was only a couple of times we ever did it. Last June. There was a party in Holland Park, and one near Marble Arch."

"But they were Sally Nash's parties?"

"She was there."

"And what's the danger? Are you going to be called as a witness?"

"Bloody hell." She looked very affronted. "Look, I may be a tart, but I'm not a whore." Charles tried vaguely to work out the distinction, but fortunately Jacqui clarified. "All these girls they're calling in the trial do it for money."

"I'm sorry. Then what's the . . . ?"

"There are some photographs."

"Of you and Steen at the party?"

"Yes. With some other people."

"Naughty photos?"

"A bit naughty. But I think that's why Marius doesn't want to be seen with me."

"Why? Are the photographs going to come up in court?"

"No, they aren't. But Marius must think they will. It's the only explanation."

"But if you're both in the photos, he could be identified anyway. It doesn't make any difference whether he's seen with you or not."

"No, Charles. The point is, they can't tell it's him. His face is covered."

"Don't tell me—with a black leather mask."

"Yes."

"Really? I was joking."

"Well, it is."

"But you, on the other hand, are not covered?"

"No. Far from it."

"Hmm. How do you know they won't come up in court?"

"Because I've got them. I paid a lot of money for them."

"Did someone blackmail you?"

"No. The Sally Nash trial started on Friday, and I bought them off the bloke who took them on Saturday."

"How much?"

"Thousand quid."

Charles looked at her quizzically and she explained. "Marius had given me some money to buy a car, but it hardly seems worth buying one now, with all this petrol scene."

Charles reflected momentarily on the difference between a tart and a whore and decided he was being a bit harsh. Particularly as Jacqui continued, "I wanted to give them to Marius as a present. Set his mind at rest. And now I can't get to see him. I daren't send them through the post or letter-box, because his secretary'll see them . . ."

Suddenly Charles's role in the proceedings became very clear to him. "And so you want me to deliver them?"

Armed with an innocuous-looking brown envelope, Charles Paris returned to his room in Hereford Road, Bayswater. It was a depressing furnished bedsitter, which he'd moved into when he left Frances. Nothing except his clothes and scripts gave it any identity. The furniture had been painted grey by some earlier occupant, but was mostly obscured by drip-dry shirts on wire hangers. A low upholstered chair with wooden arms sat in front of the gas-fire. There was a small table covered with paper and carbons, a rickety kitchen chair, a single bed shrouded in yellow candlewick, and in one corner, inadequately hidden by plastic curtain, a sink and gas-ring.

Whenever Charles entered the room, fumes of depression threatened to choke him. Every now and then, in a surge of confidence, he would consider moving, but he never got round to it. The room was somewhere to sleep and he did his best to ensure that that was all he did there.

He got back about five and, before the atmosphere of the room had time to immobilize him, opened the cupboard, got out a half-full bottle of Bell's and poured himself a healthy measure. After a substantial swallow, he felt he could look at his surroundings. It was more of a mess than usual. Candlewick in disarray on the unmade bed, coffee cup with a white crust on the table. Cold December air was gushing through the open window. He remembered leaving it to air the place on . . . when was it? Monday? Yes, Monday, December 3rd. The day he'd done that bloody awful radio play.

He slammed the window and put on the gas-fire. It hissed resentfully but came alight (which was more than it sometimes did). He felt strongly in need of a bath, stripped off his grubby clothes and put on a shapeless towelling dressing-gown. Taking a five-pence from his change, he went down to the bathroom on the first landing, checked that the water wasn't running hot, and fed the meter.

Then he remembered soap and towel. Upstairs again to get them. Inevitably, the bathroom door was locked when he returned. The sound of running water came from inside.

Charles hammered on the door and shouted abuse, but the strange sing-song voice that replied over the sound of water told him it was useless. One of the Swedish girls. There seemed to be hundreds of them in the house. And, he thought as he savagely stumped upstairs, all of them old boots. They really shattered the myth of Scandinavian beauty, that lot. Spotty girls with glasses and rugger-players' legs. He slammed the door, picked up the whisky bottle and fell into the chair.

The gas-fire spluttered at him as he sat and thought. There was something odd about the whole business with Jacqui. Her explanation about the photographs seemed unconvincing. In fact, her account of Steen's sudden change of behavior didn't ring true either. A man in his position who wanted to get rid of a girlfriend needn't go to the length of obscene notes.

For a moment the thought crossed Charles's mind that he was being used in some sort of plot. To carry something. What? Drugs? Or just what Jacqui said it was—dirty pictures? But it seemed ridiculous. A much simpler explanation was that she was telling the truth.

The way to find out, of course, was to look in the envelopes. He'd known since he had had the photographs that sooner or later he would. And, he reasoned, Jacqui must have assumed he would. She hadn't asked him not to; the envelope was unsealed. But he still felt slightly guilty as he shuffled them into his hand.

There were six, and they were exactly what Jacqui had said they would be—obscene pictures of her and Marius Steen. Perhaps obscene was the wrong word; they didn't have any erotic effect on Charles; but they intrigued and rather revolted him.

The photographs had the posed quality of amateur dramatics. Steen's body was old, a thin belly and limbs like a chicken's. The tatty little leather mask made him look ridiculous. But, Charles was forced to admit, the old man was rather well endowed.

But it was the sight of Jacqui that affected him. There she was in a series of contrived positions—astride Steen, bending down in front of him, under him on a bed. The sight was a severe shock to Charles; it made him feel almost sick. Not the acts that were going on; he'd seen and done worse, and somehow they seemed very mild and meaningless on these shoddy little snapshots. But it was the fact that it was Jacqui which upset him. He didn't feel jealousy or lust, but pity and again the urgent desire to protect her. It was as if he was seeing the photographs as her father.

A click and silence told him that the gas meter had run out. Blast, he hadn't got a ten p. Brusquely, he shoved the photographs back into the envelope, sealed it and dressed. Then he started his campaign to get to see Marius Steen. It was half past seven. He went to the call box on the landing and rang up Bernard Walton, currently starring in *Virgin on the Ridiculous* at the Dryden Theatre.

4

PRINCE CHARMING

GEORGE, THE STAGE DOORMAN at the Dryden Theatre, looked at him suspiciously. "What's your name?"

"Charles Paris. Mr. Walton is expecting me."

George's face registered total disbelief and he turned to the telephone. Charles wondered vaguely if the old man had recognized him. After all, he'd come in every night for eighteen months during the run of *The Water Nymph* only ten years before. But no, the name Charles Paris meant nothing. So much for the showbiz myth of the cheery old "never forget a face—I seen 'em all" doorman. George was a bloody-minded old sod and always had been.

"Mr. Walton's not back in his dressing-room yet."

"I'll wait." Charles leaned against the wall. The doorman watched his visitor as if he expected him to steal the light fittings.

There was a big poster of the show stuck up just inside the stage door. It had on it an enormous photo of Bernard in hot pursuit of a cartoon of two bikini-clad girls. That's stardom—a real photo; supports only get cartoons.

Charles thought back to when he'd first met Bernard in Cardiff —a gauche, rather insecure young man with a slight stammer. Even then he'd been pushy, determined to make it. Charles had been directing at the time and cast him as Young Marlow in *She Stoops to Conquer*. Not a good actor, but Charles made him play himself and it worked. The stammer fitted Marlow's embarrassment and Bernard got a very good press. A couple of years round the reps playing nervous idiots, then a television series, and now, entering his second year in *Virgin on the Ridiculous,* nauseating the critics and wowing the coach parties.

"Could you try him again?" George acquiesced grudgingly. This time he got through. "Mr. Walton, there's a Mr.—what did you say your name was?"

"Charles Paris."

"A Mr. Charles Paris to see you. Oh. Very well." He put the phone down. "Mr. Walton's expecting you." In tones of undisguised surprise. "Dressing-room One. Down the—"

But Charles knew the geography of the theatre and strode along the corridor. He knocked on the door and it was thrown open by Bernard, oozing bonhomie from a silk dressing-gown. "Charles, dear boy. Lovely to see you."

Dear boy? Charles balked slightly at that and then he realized that Bernard actually thought himself Noël Coward. The whole star bit. "Good to see you, Bernard. How's it going?"

"Oh, *comme ci, comme ça.* Audience love it. Doing fantastic business, in spite of all the crisis, or whatever it's called. So I can't complain. I'm just opening a bottle of champagne if you . . ."

"Do you have any Scotch?"

"Sure. Help yourself. Cupboard over there."

"Bernard. I've come to ask you a favor." May as well leap straight in.

"Certainly. What can I do for you?"

"You know Marius Steen, don't you?"

"Yes, the old sod. He owns half this show. You know, if Marius Steen didn't exist, it would be necessary to invent him."

Aphorisms too, thought Charles. Noël Coward has a lot to answer for. Generations of actors who, without a modicum of the talent, have pounced on the mannerisms.

"The thing is, I want an introduction to him." At that moment, the door burst open and Margaret Leslie sparkled into the room, her tiny frame cotton-wooled in a great sheepskin coat. "Maggie darling!" Bernard enveloped her in his arms. "Darling, do you know Charles Paris? Charles, have you met Maggie?"

"No, I haven't actually, but I've admired your work for a long time." Charles could have kicked himself for the cliché. It was true, though. She was a brilliant actress and deserved her phenomenal success.

"Charles Paris?" she mused huskily. "Didn't you write that awfully clever play *The Rate-payer?*" Charles acknowledged it rather sheepishly. "Oh, I'm enchanted to meet you, Charles. I did it in rep. once. Played Wanda."

"Glenda."

"Yes, that's right."

"Charles was an incredible help to me at the beginning of my career," said Bernard with professional earnestness. "I would have got nowhere without him. But nowhere."

Charles felt diminished by the compliment. He'd have preferred Bernard to say nothing rather than patronise him. It was the gratitude of the star on *This Is Your Life* thanking the village schoolmaster who had first taken him to the theatre.

"Charles was just asking me about Marius."

"Oh God," said Maggie dramatically and laughed.

This put Charles on the spot. He didn't mind asking Bernard a favor on his own, but it was awkward with Maggie there.

"You said you wanted an introduction?" Bernard prompted.

Nothing for it. He'd have to go on. "Yes. I . . . er . . ." he'd got the story prepared but it was difficult with an audience. "I've written a new play. Light comedy. Thought it might be Steen's sort of thing."

"Oh, I see. And you want me to introduce you, so that you can try and sell it to him."

"Yes." Charles felt humiliated. He'd never have sunk to this if he were actually trying to sell one of his plays. But it was the only possible approach to Steen he could think of. "I hope you don't mind my asking . . ."

"No. Of course not. Old pals act. Happy to oblige." And Bernard was. He was the great star and here was an old friend, less successful, wanting to be helped out. Charles winced at the thought of what he was doing. "Is it urgent, dear boy?"

"It is a bit. There's an American agent nibbling."

"Ah." Bernard's tone didn't believe it. "Well, you leave it with me, old chum. Have I got your number?"

Charles wrote it down. Margaret Leslie, who was wandering restlessly round the room, picked up a script from a table. "Is this the new telly, Bernard?"

"Yes, it's awful. Not a laugh in it. I do get a bit sick of the way they keep sending me scripts to make funny. Here's a new show—may not be much good—never mind, book Bernard Walton, he'll get a few laughs out of it. I probably could, but I should get a bit of support from the script-writers. You ought to write something for me, Charles," he added charmingly.

"Not really my style, Bernard."

"Oh, I don't know."

"Bernard," Maggie hinted, "I think we ought to . . ."

"Lord, yes. Is that the time? Charles, we're going out to eat. Why not join us? Going to the Ivy. Miles'll be there, John and Prunella, and Richard, I expect. I'm sure they could make room for another."

Charles refused politely. He couldn't stomach an evening of bright showbiz back-chat. Outside the theatre he gulped great lungfuls of cold night air, but it didn't cleanse him inside. He still felt sullied by what he'd have to do—to crawl to someone like Bernard Walton.

There was only one solution. He hailed a cab and went to the Montrose. If he couldn't lose the feeling, perhaps he could deaden it.

A tremendous hammering at the door. Charles rolled out of bed and groped his way over to open it. One of the Swedish girls was standing there in a flowered nylon dressing-gown. Charles had time to register that she looked like a dinky toilet-roll cover before his head caught up with him. It felt as if it had been split in two by a cold chisel and someone was grinding the two halves together.

"Telephone." The Swedish girl flounced off. Charles tried to make it down the stairs with his eyes closed to allay the pain. He felt for the receiver and held it gingerly to his ear. "Hello?"

"Charles, I've done it!" Bernard's voice sounded insufferably cheerful. Charles grunted uncomprehending. "I've spoken to Marius."

"Ah."

"Well, I haven't actually spoken to him, but I spoke to Joanne—that's his secretary—and I've fixed for you to see him this afternoon at four. That's if he's back. Apparently he's been down at Streatley since the weekend, but Joanne says he should be back today. Got some charity dinner on."

"Look, Bernard, I . . . er . . ." Charles's smashed brain tried to put the words together. "Thanks very . . . I . . . er . . . don't know how—"

"Don't mention it, dear boy." Bernard's voice sounded as if it were opening a fête, big-hearted and patronizing. "Do you know Marius's office?"

"No. I—"

"Charing Cross Road. Milton Buildings. Just beyond the Garrick."

"Ah. Look, I . . ."

"My dear fellow, not a word. I just hope it does you some good. Always glad to oblige. You helped me in the early days. Eh?"

If anything could have made Charles feel sicker, it was Bernard's bonhomie.

By quarter to four the pain in his head had subsided to a dull ache. He found Milton Buildings in Charing Cross Road without too much difficulty, though the entrance was narrow, shuffled between a café and a bookshop.

Inside, however, the buildings were spacious. The board downstairs carried an impressive list of theatrical impresarios, agents and lawyers. "Marius Steen Productions" was on the second floor. Charles traveled up in the old-fashioned cage lift. The envelope in his inside pocket seemed to bulge enormously. He felt as he had in Oxford, the first time he had taken a girl out with a packet of French letters in his wallet. He remembered the sense of an obscene lump under his blazer, revealing his intentions to the entire university. Didn't know why he'd bothered. Virginal Vera, besotted with phonetics. Middle English and nothing else. The time that one wasted. He felt a twinge of embarrassment for the gaucheness of his youth.

"ENQUIRIES" and an arrow in gold leaf on the wall. It pointed to a panelled oak door. Charles knocked. "Come in."

A secretary was sitting behind a solid Victorian desk. This must be Joanne. Unmarried, about forty, but not the standard over-made-up spinster secretary. She looked very positive and rather attractive in a forbidding way. Unmarried by choice, not default. She rose to meet him. "You must be Mr. Paris."

"Yes."

"I thought I recognized you from the television."

"Ah!" There's no answer to that, but it's gratifying.

"Mr. Paris, I'm so sorry. I would have tried to contact you, but I hadn't a phone number. I'm afraid Mr. Steen hasn't come up from the country."

"Oh dear."

"Yes, I'm sorry. I thought he'd be back today. It appears that he's reading some scripts and . . ."

"Oh, that's all right."

"There's no one else who could help? Mr. Cawley deals with a lot of the management side."

"No, I don't think so."

"Or Mr. Nigel Steen should be in town later. He'll certainly be here over the weekend."

"Has he been down at Streatley?"

"He went down yesterday. Perhaps he could . . . ?"

"No, no thanks, I wanted to see Mr. Marius Steen personally."

"Ah. Well, I'm sorry. I explained to Mr. Walton that . . ."

"Yes. Don't worry."

"Perhaps you could let me have your number and then I'll give you a call when Mr. Steen is back in town and we could fix another appointment."

"Yes."

So that was it. Charles left the office with his pocketful of pornography, feeling flat. He wandered along the Charing Cross Road, trying to think what to do next, Galahad on hearing that someone else had found the Holy Grail, Knight Errant without an errand. He rang Jacqui from Leicester Square tube station and reported his lack of progress.

"You say he's in Streatley now?"

"Yes."

"And Nigel's coming up to town?"

"Probably, but, Jacqui, don't try to contact him. Leave it to me. I'll get in touch with him after the weekend."

"Yes . . ." Wistful.

"I'll sort it out, Jacqui."

"Yes . . ." Drab.

Charles wandered aimlessly through Leicester Square to Piccadilly. A cartoon cinema was offering Tom and Jerry and Chaplin shorts. He hovered for a moment, but his mind was too full to be sidetracked. He had to find out more about Marius Steen. So he went down the steps to Piccadilly Underground station and bought a ticket for Tower Hill.

5

SPECIALTY ACT

THE OLD PEOPLE'S HOME was designed for daylight. Plate glass welcomed the sun in to warm the inmates who sat in armchairs, waiting. But now it was dark. The nurse hadn't been round yet to close the curtains and Charles Paris and Harry Chiltern looked out on galvanized frames of blackness. The offices around were empty and dead, street lights in the backwater thought unnecessary in the emergency. The windows seemed more forbidding than walls.

"I saw some program on the television the other day," said Harry after a moment's musing. "All the club comics it was. Just telling gags. Terrible. No technique. Or do I mean all the same technique? I tell you, I've seen more variety in a tin of sardines.

"They don't have variety now. Not even the word. Variety with a big V. Used to mean something. No, I rang a mate in the Variety department at the BBC. Couple of years back, this was. He said, it's not Variety any more, it's Light Entertainment. Light Entertainment—now that's a different thing altogether.

"I mean, when Lennie and I done our act, we worked on it. Worked hard. A few gags, monologue—that was Lennie's bit—a few more gags, I'd do my drunk routine, and finish with a song and a bit of tap. I mean, rehearsed. Not just standing up there telling some joke you heard from a man in a pub. It was an act. People who come to see the Chiltern Brothers knew they'd get a real show. Get their money's worth. No, this television, I don't hold with it. Entertainment in your living room. That's not the place for entertainment—it's for your knitting and your eating and your bit of slap and tickle. You gotta go out—that's part of the entertaining. Make a night of it, eh?"

"Yes. I suppose the television's on all the time here."

"From the moment it starts. Some of the old biddies stuck in front all day long, watching—I don't know—how to speak Pakistani, or what kiddies can do with a cotton-reel. All bleeding day long. I tell you, there's one old cripple, ugly old bird—more chins than a Chinese telephone directory—sits there nodding away at the testcard when it's on, doesn't notice. Mind you, it's a lot more interesting than some of the programs, eh?"

Harry Chiltern cackled with laughter and subsided into silence as the nurse at last arrived to draw the curtains. "Evening, Mr. Chiltern."

"Evening."

"I see we've got a visitor. Hello." The nurse smiled conspiratorially at Charles. Harry contemplated his highly polished shoes until she had left the room. "Silly old cow. Thinks we're all gaga. 'I see we've got a visitor.' Who's we, eh? Apart from Georgie Wood, eh?" He laughed again, then stopped suddenly. "Come on." He eased himself out of the chair.

"What?"

"She's off now, doing the other curtains. We can whip down to the Bricklayers for a pint."

"Should you?"

"Bloody hell, Charles. If I'm going to snuff it, I'd rather snuff it with a pint in my fist than one of their bloody mugs of Ovaltine. Come on."

The Bricklayers' Arms was one of those modern pubs that capture all the atmosphere of an airport lounge. Hanging red lights shone on leatherette couches and framed relief pictures of vintage cars. Pop music pounded from the jukebox.

Still, it was a pub, and a pint. Harry seemed to appreciate it. He took a long swig, put the glass down and wiped his mis-shaven upper lip contentedly. Charles thought it might be the moment. "Harry, I wanted to ask you about Marius Steen."

"Oh yeah. Old Flash Steenie. Why?"

"I'm going to see him about a play I have written." The lie slipped out easily enough. "What's he like?" Harry didn't seem to react. "You knew him round the halls, didn't you?"

"Oh yes. Just thinking about him. Steenie. Tough old bugger."

"Where did he come from?"

"Poland, I think, originally. His parents come over in—I don't know—early twenties, I suppose. When Marius was about fifteen. He done all kinds of things in the business. I mean all kinds. Wrestling promotions, girlie shows, Variety. I think he even been on the boards himself in the early days. Yes, he was. Never saw him, but I heard he was terrible. Even says so himself, I think. He did a whistling act, maybe. Or specialty of some sort. Fire-eating perhaps it was? Hey, d'you hear about the fire-eater who couldn't go anywhere without meeting an old flame? Eh? Made him feel really hot under the collar." Harry chuckled. "Made that one up, y'know. Didn't have any of this script-writer nonsense in my day. You did your own act, and it was yours all the way. Yes." He gazed absently ahead, and raised his glass to his lips with a trembling hand. Charles feared he might have to prompt again. But the old man continued.

"I first met Steenie at . . . where? Chiswick Empire, I think it was. Me and Lennie was some way down the bill and Steenie was managing this tap-dance act, as I recall. Think it was that. I don't know. He'd always got so many acts going."

"All Variety stuff?"

"Oh, yes. Didn't do none of your Oh-my-Gawd theayter till after the war—second big job, you know. No, he was going round the halls, picking up the odd act, putting shows on, making money. Making money. Always knew where every penny was. Tight as a bottle-top. You hear him squeak every time he moves."

"What was he like?"

"I don't know how to answer that. Hard as nails. A real bugger, particularly about money. Made a lot of enemies."

"What sort of people?"

"People who hadn't read the small print of their contracts. Never missed a trick, old Steenie. I remember, one bloke, mind-reader he was—Steenie booked him for some Variety bill, forget where it was now. Anyway, opens first night—this mind-reader comes on—audience really gives him the bird. Lots of audiences were like that. Mind you, Lennie and I could usually get them round. Lennie had this thing, when the act was going bad, he'd . . . ah, Lennie—God rest his soul. Got them wetting themselves up on the clouds, I daresay. . . .

"Anyway, this mind-reader act got the real bum's rush, no question. So Steenie sacks him. Fair enough, that's what you'd expect. But Steenie doesn't pay him nothing. Some let-out he'd got in the contract. Bloke may have been able to read minds, but he couldn't read a bleeding contract. Eh? Mind-reader got quite nasty. Tried to do old Steenie over."

"What happened?"

"Not a lot. Steenie had Frank with him."

"Frank?"

"Don't know what his real name was. Everyone called him Frank after Frankenstein—you know, the old monster. He was Polish and all, I think. Probably had some unpronounceable name. Ex-wrestler."

"A sort of body-guard?"

"That's the idea. Steenie needed one of them, the way he done business."

"Did he ever do anything illegal?"

"Ah, what's illegal? He was no more illegal than most of the fixers in this business. If you mean, could the law have got him, no. He'd never do nothing himself but, you know, things might happen. Frank was a big boy to have lean on you."

"Is he still around?"

"Frank? No, he must be dead. Or shovelled off into the Old Folks like me. One of those big muscle-bound Johnnies. Go to fat when they stop training. Die of heart failure, most of them."

"Do you reckon Steen would have found a replacement?"

"I don't know. He'd got a well-developed sense of self-protection, you know, always carried a gun in the glove-pocket of the car. Probably got another bruiser after Frank. But perhaps you don't need that sort of thing in the old lee-gitimate theayter. Only thing you have to look out for is the nancy-boys, eh?"

They laughed. Harry looked into his glass as if he could see for miles and Charles nudged him back on to the subject. "Do you know Steen's son?"

"Nigel, isn't it?"

"That's right."

"Yeah, I met him. Nasty bit of work. Oh, nothing criminal. Just a bit slimy. Often happens. Old man does well and the kids don't quite make it. I don't suppose you'd remember old Barney Beattie. Vent act. Dummy called Buckingham. Barney and Buckingham. Great they were. Barney, he had these two sons—tried to set up a song and dance act. Nothing. Nothing there. Hooked off every stage in the British Isles, they was. It happens like that." The old man drained his pint reflectively.

"Can I get you another one, Harry?"

"No, it's my throw."

"Oh, but I'll . . ."

"I can still pay my way." And with dignity he took the two glasses over to the bar. He looked small in the crush and it was some time before the order got through. Then he returned, face contorted with concentration as he tried to keep the glasses steady in his blotched hands.

"There." With triumph. "Put hairs on your chest, Charlie."

"Thanks."

"Now, where were we? Yes. Steenie's boy. Ain't got the old man's talent, none of it. Been involved in one or two real disasters. You know, putting on drag shows, that sort of spectacle. But he ain't got the touch. Old Steenie, he'd make money out of a kid's conker match; Nigel'd close *The Mousetrap* within a week."

"Do they get on?"

"Father and son? God knows. Sometimes they do, sometimes they don't. Great arguments, old man used to keep disowning the boy. Then they'd be as thick as thieves again. He likes all the family bit, Steenie. Wife died—oh, years ago, so the boy matters a lot. Jews are like that, aren't they?"

"Yes."

"You want to know a lot about them, don't you?"

"Just interest."

"Yes." A pause. "You know, Charlie my boy, from the way you says that I can tell what you really want is the dirt. All right then—"

he edged closer so that he was whispering rather than shouting over the jukebox "—here's the nastiest rumor I've ever heard about Steenie—really nasty rumor. Dancer he knew—she was on a bill with me and Lennie down the Hackney Empire. Steenie was putting the show on, and he'd got a thing going with this bint Veronica. Always put it about a bit, Steenie. Had a lot of lead in his pencil, that boy"—the image of the photographs flashed across Charles's mind—"Anyway, this girl gets knocked up, and when Steenie finds out about it, he don't want to know. Won't talk to her, doesn't know her, gives her the boot. Out of the show.

"Well, this Veronica won't put up with this—comes round the theatre between shows one night—really drunk—really—I don't like that in a woman—and she's swearing and effing and blinding —big shout-up with Steenie—going to tell his wife, all that. Next morning she's found floating face-down in the Thames.

"All right. Could have fallen in. Could have decided to do away with herself. But nasty rumors at the time said she could have been helped in. Certainly her being off the scene was handy for Steenie. And Frank wasn't round the theatre the night she disappeared. It's a long time ago, though. Just rumors."

"Do you think Steen would be capable of that sort of thing, Harry?"

"If someone was in his way, Charlie, he'd be capable of anything."

"I see, a real bastard."

There was a long pause. "Yes, a real bastard." Harry chuckled. "But you can't help liking him. One of the most likeable lumps of shit I ever come across."

They talked a bit more, but Harry was tiring quickly. He seemed to be having difficulty with the second pint, and had only drunk a third of it when he looked at his watch. "Better be on my way, you know, Charlie. Not as young as I was."

"Will there be trouble when you get back?"

"No. I'll pretend I've had a turn or something. Ah, you know, I don't like that place. Still, not for long."

"Are you moving somewhere else?"

Harry smiled. "Join Lennie. Won't be long now. Still, can't complain."

"A whole lifetime in the business."

"Yes. Did our first show when we was four. And our last one three years ago on some stupid television thing about the music-hall. Seventy-four years in the business, that was, Charlie. Seventy-four."

"And you wouldn't have had it any other way."

"Good God, yes. It was Lennie who wanted all that. I wanted to be a professional footballer."

6

TRANSFORMATION SCENE

CHARLES TRIED TO THINK it all out on the Saturday morning. He'd woken without a hangover and even done a token tidying-up of his room. Then out for a newspaper and some rolls, and he was sitting in front of the gas-fire with a cup of coffee. Glance at the paper; no particular interest in petrol queues or Ireland without Whitelaw, so he settled down to think about Jacqui and Steen.

What he had heard from Harry Chiltern was disturbing. True, the business about the dancer in the Thames sounded a bit too melodramatic—the kind of story that gets embroidered over the years—and probably started out just as an unfortunate coincidence. Charles discounted the facts of it; but it was significant that Marius Steen attracted that sort of accusation. It didn't bode well for Jacqui.

Then there were the photographs and her own story. Something didn't ring true there. He pieced it together. In June, Jacqui and Steen went to a party, which was attended by Sally Nash, now on trial at the Old Bailey on charges of controlling prostitutes. At this party a fairly insipid orgy took place. Some pictures were taken by a nameless photographer. All through this period (according to Jacqui) things were swinging between her and Steen. She even got pregnant by him. He arranged an abortion which went wrong and they went off to the South of France to recuperate. And there, apparently, had an idyllic time.

This idyll had continued up until the previous Saturday, December 1st, when they last met. That was the day after the Sally Nash trial started, and the day that Marius Steen's terrible show, *Sex of One and Half a Dozen of the Other,* celebrated a thousand performances. And from that day on Jacqui had been unable to contact Steen. He had very deliberately told her to get lost, and when she didn't take the hint, he'd sent her an obscene note. And according to Jacqui, the reason for this must be Steen's fear of her being associated with him in the Sally Nash case because it might affect his chances of a knighthood. It was preposterous. Nobody would behave like that.

Charles wasn't sure whether Jacqui believed she was telling the truth or not. She might have her own reasons for obscuring the issue. But, leaving that aside for a moment, he tried to make some sense of Steen's behavior.

The simplest explanation was that he had just got tired of Jacqui. That was quite possible, however well she thought the affair was going. He was a man who had always put it about a bit, as Harry Chiltern said. Jacqui was an attractive enough bit of stuff, but there were hundreds more like her and why should he stick to one? He'd be very unlikely to stay with her or marry her, particularly with a knighthood in the offing. As Jacqui herself admitted, she wasn't the sort of consort for a "do with the Queen Mum."

And, Charles's mind raced on, Steen could have picked up a new tottie at the *Sex for One* . . . party on the Saturday night. That would explain the sudden change in his affections.

But as he thought of it, Charles knew the explanation was inadequate. Even if that had happened, it didn't justify the violence of Steen's attempts to get Jacqui off his back.

No, Steen's behavior certainly suggested that he regarded her as a threat in some way. Perhaps she had tried to blackmail him . . . ? Yes, that made sense. She had actually tried to use the photographs . . . perhaps to blackmail him into marrying her. (That would tie in with the pregnancy in the summer—an earlier attempt to force Steen's hand.) She could have tried the blackmail approach on the Saturday afternoon; then, when Steen cut up rough, she realized she'd overstepped the mark and brought in

Charles as a go-between to patch things up. That would even explain why she took him back to Archer Street from the Montrose. She'd just gone down there to look for any good-natured sucker.

But the new explanation wasn't much more satisfactory than the first. For a start, Charles didn't like to think of Jacqui in that light. And also he doubted whether she had the intelligence to be so devious. The only convincing bit was the thought of Steen as a frightened man. What was it he was afraid of?

Charles marshalled his knowledge of blackmailers' habits. It was limited, all gleaned from detective novels. He got out the brown envelope and spread the photographs on his lap. His reaction to them had numbed. They just seemed slightly unwholesome now, like used tissues. Just photographs. What would Sherlock Holmes, Lord Peter Wimsey, Hercule Poirot and the rest have made of that lot? Charles made a cursory check for blood-stained fingerprints, the thread of a sports jacket made from tweed only available in a small tailor's shop in Aberdeen, the scratch marks of an artificial hand or the faint but unmistakable aroma of orange blossom. The investigation, he concluded without surprise, yielded negative results. They were just photographs.

Just photographs. The phrase caught in his mind. Negative results. Yes, of course. Where were the bloody negatives? Jacqui had paid out a thousand pounds for something that could be reproduced at will. A very rudimentary knowledge of detective fiction tells you that any photographic blackmailer worth his salt keeps producing copies of the incriminating material until he's blue in the face. It would be typical of Jacqui's naïveté to believe that she was dealing with an honest man who had given her the only copies in existence.

If this were so, and the photographer was putting pressure on him, then Steen's reactions were consistent. He had reason to be frightened. But why should he be frightened of Jacqui? Charles shuffled through his pockets for a two p piece and went down to the phone.

"Jacqui?"

"Yes." She sounded very low.

"All right?"

"Not too good."

"Listen, Jacqui, I think I may be on to something about the way Steen's behaving."

"What?" She sounded perkier instantly.

"Jacqui, you've got to tell me the truth. When you bought those photographs . . ."

"Yes?"

"Did you buy the negatives, too?"

"No. I didn't. But he'd destroyed them. He said so."

"I see. And did you mention to Steen that you'd got the photographs at any time?"

"No. I wanted it to be a surprise—a present. He had mentioned them vaguely, said he was a bit worried. So I fixed to get them."

"When were they actually handed over to you?"

"Last Saturday evening."

"And you never mentioned them even when you tried to ring Steen?"

"I started to. On the Sunday evening when I first rang him. I spoke to Nigel. I said it was about the photographs, but even before I'd finished talking, he gave me this message from Marius to . . . you know . . . to get lost."

"Right. Give me the name and address of the bloke you got the photos from."

As Charles limped along Praed Street, he began to regret dressing up for the encounter, but when he reflected on the exceptional violence of blackmailers in all detective fiction, he decided it was as well to conceal his identity. The disguise was good and added ten years to him. He'd grayed his temples and eyebrows with a spray, and parted his hair on the other side. He was wearing the démodé pin-striped suit he'd got from a junk-shop for a production of *Arturo Ui* ("grossly overplayed"—*Glasgow Herald*) and the tie he'd worn as Harry in *Marching Song* ("adequate if uninspiring"—*Oxford Mail*). He walked with the limp he'd used in *Richard III* ("nicely understated"—*Yorkshire Post*). He wasn't sure whether to speak in the accent he'd used in *Look Back in Anger* ("a splendid Blimp"— *Worcester Gazette*) or the one for *When We Are Married* ("made a meal of the part"—*Croydon Advertiser*).

"Imago Studios," the address Jacqui had given him, proved to be in a tatty mews near St. Mary's Hospital in Paddington. The downstairs stable-garage part had apparently been converted into a studio. On the windows of the upper part the curtains were drawn. Charles rang the bell. Nothing. He rang again and heard movement.

The door was opened by a woman in a pale pink nylon house-coat and pink fur slippers. She had prominent teeth and dyed black hair swept back in the style of a souvenir Greek goddess. Her face was heavily made up and eyelashed. Charles couldn't help thinking of a hard pink meringue full of artificial cream.

She looked at him hard. "Yes?"

"Ah, good afternoon." Charles plumped for the *When We Are Married* accent. "I wondered if Bill was in." Jacqui had only given him the Christian name. It was all she knew.

"Who are you? What do you want with him?"

"My name's Holroyd. Bill Holroyd." On the spur of the moment he couldn't think of another Christian name. He grinned weakly. "Both called Bill, eh?"

"What's it about?"

"Some photographs."

"What is it—wedding or portrait? Because my husband—"

"No, no, it's a more . . . personal sort of thing."

"Ah." She knew what he meant. "You better come in."

She led the way up the very steep stairs. The large nylon-clad bottom swished close to Charles's face as he limped up after her. "Can you manage?"

"Yes. It's just my gammy leg."

"How did you do it, Mr. Holroyd?"

"In the war."

"Jumping out of some tart's bedroom window, I suppose. That's where most war wounds came from."

"No. Mine was a genuine piece of shrapnel."

"Huh." She ushered him into a stuffy little room lit by bright spotlights. It was decorated in orange and yellow, with a le-opardette three-piece suite covering most of the carpet. Every available surface was crowded with small brass souvenirs. Lincoln imps, windjammer bells, lighthouses, anchor thermometers, knights in armour, wishing wells, everything. On the dresser two posed and tinted photographs rose from the undergrowth of brass. One was the woman, younger, but still with her Grecian hair and heavy make-up. The other was of a man, plumpish and vaguely familiar.

The woman pointed to an armchair. "Sit down. Rest your shrapnel."

"Thank you."

She slumped back on to the sofa, revealing quite a lot of bare thigh. "Right, Mr. Holroyd, what's it about?"

"I was hoping to see your husband."

"He's . . . er . . . he's not here at the moment, but I know about the business."

"I see. When are you expecting him back?"

"You can deal with me," she said. Hard.

"Right, Mrs. . . . er?"

"Sweet."

"Mrs. Sweet." Charles was tempted to make a quaint Yorkshire pleasantry about the name, but looked at Mrs. Sweet and decided against it. "This is, you understand, a rather delicate matter . . ."

"I understand."

"It's . . . er . . . the fact is . . . Last summer I was down in London on business and . . . er . . . it happened that, by chance . . . through some friends, I ended up at a party given by . . . er . . . well, some people in Holland Park. Near Holland Park, that is . . ."

"Yes." She didn't give anything.

"Yes . . . Yes . . . Well, I believe that . . . er . . . your husband was at this particular party . . ."

"Maybe."

"In fact, I believe he took some photographs at the party."

"Look here, are you from the police? I've had enough of them round this week."

"What?" Charles blustered and looked affronted for a moment while he took this in. Obviously the police had been making enquiries about the Sally Nash case. Marius Steen's anxiety was justified.

"No, of course I'm not from the police. I'm the director of a man-made fibers company," he said, with a flash of inspiration.

"Thank God. I couldn't take any more of that lot."

"No, no. The fact is, Mrs. Sweet, that . . . er . . . I am, you see, a married man. I have two lovely daughters at boarding school and . . . er . . . well, I have become rather anxious about these . . . er . . . photographs."

"Yes." She didn't volunteer anything.

"I have come to the right place, have I? I mean, your husband was at this party in . . . ?"

"Yes. He was there." She paused and looked at him, assessing. "Well, Mr. Holroyd, I think I know which photographs you are referring to. Of course, photography's an expensive business."

"I understand that, Mrs. Sweet. How much do you think your husband would part with the . . . er . . . photographs for?"

"Two thousand pounds."

"That's a lot of money." The price has gone up, thought Charles. "And would that be for the negatives as well?"

"Ah, Mr. Holroyd. How shrewd you are. No, I'm afraid not. The photographs *and* the negatives would cost you five thousand pounds."

So, as he suspected, Jacqui had been done. A thousand pounds for one set of photographs; there might be any number of others about. Bill Holroyd blustered. "Oh, I don't think I could possibly raise that."

"That's the price. Mind you, when things start moving in a certain court case, they might get even more expensive."

"Oh, dear." Charles let a note of panic creep into Bill Holroyd's voice and looked anxiously around the room.

"No point in looking for them, love." It was "love," now she knew she had the whip hand. "You won't find them here."

"How do I know you've got them?"

"I'll show you." She opened a drawer in the dresser, pulled out a folder and handed it to him. "Only copies, love. You'll never find the negatives, so don't try."

"No." Charles opened the folder and looked at all the photographs. There were a lot and they included some identical to the set still bulging in his pocket. His hunch about the morals of blackmailing photographers was right. He handed them back. "You don't think there's any possibility that the price might be—"

"Five thousand pounds."

"Hmm." (A pause, while Charles tried, according to the best Stanislavskian method, to give the impression of a man torn between the two great motives of his life—love of money and fear of scandal.) "Of course, it would take me some time to put my hands on that amount of money. Some days."

"I can wait." She smiled like a Venus fly-trap. "I'm not so sure that you can. Once they start getting deeper into this trial, I'm sure the interest in photographs of this sort will—"

"Yes, yes. I'm sure it won't take too long. It's unfortunate not having my bank in London. It's in Leeds. But . . . er . . . perhaps by Wednesday . . . Would Wednesday . . . ?"

"I'll be here. With the negatives."

"Oh good." Although he was only acting the part, Charles felt Bill Holroyd's relief. And in his own character he'd found out what he wanted to know. If there were other copies of the photographs, there was no doubt that Bill Sweet was blackmailing Steen. Steen had assumed from Jacqui's message to Nigel that she was involved too. Charles was relieved that the information put her in the clear; she had been telling the truth. All he had to do now was what she had asked—get to see Steen, give him the photographs and explain that Jacqui was nothing to do with Bill Sweet. If Sweet himself continued his blackmail, that wasn't Charles's concern.

Mrs. Sweet rose from the sofa. "That's our business concluded. I'm glad we reached agreement in such a reasonable way. Would you like a drink?"

"Oh, thank you very much." Perhaps a little too readily for Bill Holroyd. "That is to say, I don't make a habit of it, but perhaps a small one."

"Gin?" She went to the door.

"That'd be . . . very nice." Charles just stopped himself from saying "Reet nice." Would have been too much.

After a few moments, Mrs. Sweet returned with a bottle, poured two substantial gins, added tonic and proffered a glass. Charles rose to take it. They were close. She didn't move back. "Cheers, Mr. Holroyd."

"Cheers."

She looked at him, hard. "You like all that, do you, Mr. Holroyd?"

"All what?"

"Parties. Like the one in Holland Park."

"Oh . . . well. Not habitually, no. I'm a respectable man, but, you know, one works very hard and . . . er . . . needs to relax, eh?"

"Yes." She sat back on the sofa and motioned him beside her. "Yes, I find I need to relax too, Mr. Holroyd."

"Ah." Charles sat gingerly on the mock leopard. He couldn't quite believe the way things appeared to be going, and couldn't think of anything else to say.

But Mrs. Sweet continued, softly. "Yes, and relaxation becomes increasingly difficult." Her hand rested gently on top of his. The scene was getting distinctly sultry.

Charles decided to play it for light comedy. "I go in for a certain amount of golf, you know. That's good for relaxation."

"Oh, really." Her hand was moving gently over his. Charles stole a sidelong glance. The mouth was parted and thickened lashes low over her eyes. He recognized that she was trying to look seductive, and, while he didn't find her attractive (rather the reverse), he was intrigued by the sudden change in her behavior.

Mrs. Sweet leaned against him, so that he could feel the lacquered crispness of her hair on his ear. Her hand drew his to rest casually on her thigh. "I've never played golf."

"Oh, it's a grand game," said Charles fatuously. In spite of himself, he could feel that he was becoming interested. Her perfume was strong and acrid in his nostrils. "Champion game."

"But I'm sure you play others." Quite suddenly the grip hardened on his hand and he felt it forced into the warm cleft between her legs. Instinctively he clutched at the nylon-clad mound.

But his mind was moving quickly. Mrs. Sweet and her husband were blackmailers. This must be a plot of some sort. "Where's your husband?"

"A long way away."

"But wouldn't he mind if—"

"We lead separate lives. Very separate lives now." Her face was close to his and he kissed her. After all, he reflected, I am one of the few people in the world who isn't worth blackmailing. And Bill Holroyd was already showing himself to be pretty gullible, so it's in character.

Mrs. Sweet reached her free hand down to his flies. No impotence problem this time. Charles began to consider the irony of life —that with Jacqui, whom he found very attractive, there was nothing, and yet with this nymphomaniac, who almost repelled him . . . but it wasn't the moment for philosophy.

Mrs. Sweet stood up and stripped off the housecoat. There was a crackle of static electricity. Her underwear was lacy red and black, brief and garish, the kind of stuff he'd seen in Soho shops and assumed was the monopoly of prostitutes. Perhaps she was a prostitute. The thought of another dose of clap flashed across his mind. But he was by now too aroused to be sidetracked.

He hastily pulled off his clothes and stood facing Mrs. Sweet.

"It doesn't show," she said.

"What?"

"Your war wound. The shrapnel."

"Ah. No. Well, they do wonders with plastic surgery." He advanced and put his arms round her, fumbled with the back of her brassiere. "The front," she murmured. It unclipped.

They sank down on to the leopardette sofa and he slipped off the crisp lacy briefs. Underneath he'd expected her to be hard and dry, but she was very soft and moist. Again he thought of meringues. And as he had her, he emitted grunts which he hoped were in character for the director of a man-made fibers company.

7

CINDERELLA BY THE FIRESIDE

CHARLES FELT DISTINCTLY JADED as he walked along Hereford Road. Mrs. Sweet had kept him at it some time. He ached all over, and felt the revulsion that sex without affection always left like a hangover inside him. It was half-past four and dark. No pubs open yet. He felt in need of a bath to wash away Mrs. Sweet's stale perfume.

As he entered the hall of the house, he heard a door open upstairs. "He is here," said a flat Swedish voice. There was the sound of footsteps running downstairs and Jacqui rushed into his arms. She was quivering like an animal. He held her to him and she started to weep hysterically. A podgy Swedish face peered over the banisters at them. "You are an old dirty man," it said and disappeared.

Charles was too concerned with Jacqui even to yell the usual obscenities at the Swede. He led the trembling girl into his room. She was as cold as ice. He sat her in the armchair and lit the gas-fire, poured a large Scotch and held it out to her. "No. It'd make me sick." And she burst out crying again.

Charles knelt by the chair and put his arm round her shoulders. She was still shivering convulsively. "What's happened, Jacqui?"

The question prompted another great surge of weeping. Charles stayed crouching by her side and drank the Scotch while he tried to think how to calm her.

Eventually the convulsions subsided to some extent and he could hear what she was saying. "My flat—they broke into my flat."

"Who did?"

"I don't know. This morning I came back from doing the weekend shopping and it was—it had all been done over. My oil lamp—and the curtains pulled down and all my glasses smashed and my clothes torn in shreds and—" She broke down again into incoherence.

"Jacqui, who did it?"

"I don't know. It must have been someone who Marius—who Marius—" she sobbed.

"Why should he—"

"I . . . I tried to ring him again."

"Jacqui, I told you not to do that."

"I know, but I . . . I couldn't help it . . . I had to ring him, because of the baby."

"Baby?"

"Yes, I'm pregnant again and . . ."

"Does Steen know?"

"Yes. We knew a month ago, and he said we'd keep this one and he wanted a child and . . ." Again she was shaken by uncontrollable spasms.

"Jacqui, listen. Calm down. Listen, it'll be all right. Steen's only acting this way because he's frightened. There's been a misunderstanding about those photographs." And Charles gave an edited version of his findings at Imago Studios.

By the end of his narrative she was calmer. "So that's all. Marius thinks I'm involved with this Bill Sweet?"

"That's it. Jacqui, you might have known he'd keep the negatives."

"I never thought. I hope you tore him off a strip when—"

"I didn't see him. I saw his wife."

"What was she like?"

"Oh." He shrugged non-committally. "Listen, Jacqui, it'll be all right now. You can stay here. You'll be quite safe. And go ahead as planned. I'll somehow get to see Steen, deliver the photographs and explain the position. Then at least he'll take the heat off you.

And turn it on Sweet, where it belongs." He laughed. "I must say, Jacqui, I don't care for your boyfriend's methods."

Jacqui laughed too, a weak giggle of relief. "Yes, he can be a bastard. You think it'll be all right?"

"Just as soon as I can get to see him. I mean, I don't know about the emotional thing—that's between the two of you—but I'm sure he'll stop the rough stuff."

There was a pause. Jacqui breathed deeply. "Oh, it really hurts. My throat, from all that crying."

"Yes, of course it does. You're exhausted. Tell you what, I'll get you pleasantly drunk, tuck you up in bed, you'll sleep the sleep of the dead. And in the morning nothing'll seem so bad."

"But my flat . . ."

"I'll help you tidy it up, when we've got this sorted out."

"Oh, Charles, you are great. I don't know what I'd do without you, honest."

" 'S'all right." He took her hand and gripped it, embarrassed, like a father with his grown-up daughter. Then suddenly, brisk. "Right, I'm hungry. Have you had anything to eat?"

"No, I . . . I've felt sick. I—"

"Haven't got anything here, but—"

"I couldn't go out."

"Don't you worry. It was for just such occasions that fish and chips were invented."

"Oh, no. I'd be sick."

"Don't you believe it. Nice bit of rock salmon, bag of chips, lots of vinegar, you'll feel on top of the world."

"Ugh."

It's strange how fish and chip newspapers, out of date and greasy, are always much more interesting than current ones. It's like other people's papers in crowded tubes. You can't wait to buy a copy and read some intriguing article you glimpse over a strap-hanging shoulder. It's always disappointing.

In the fish and chip shop Charles noticed that his order was wrapped in a copy of the *Sun*. On the front page was the tantalizing headline, "Virginity Auction—see page 11." The fascination of page 11 grew as he walked home. Who was auctioning whose virginity to whom? And where?

This thought preoccupied him as he entered his room. Jacqui was lying on the bed, fast asleep. Curled up in a ball on the candlewick, she looked about three years old.

He made no attempt to wake her. In her state sleep was more important than food. The Virginity Auction—he settled down in front of the fire to find out all about it. He slipped a hot crumbling piece of fish into his mouth, placed the warm bag of chips on his knees and turned to page 11.

Bugger. He'd only got pages 1 to 8, and the corresponding ones at the back. He'd never know where virginities were knocked down, or how one bidded. A pleasant thought of nubile young girls being displayed at Sotheby's crossed his mind.

There wasn't much else in the paper. It was the last Wednesday's —all bloody petrol crisis. The titty girl on page 3's midriff was stained and transparent with grease from the fish and chips. It looked rather obscene, particularly as the word "Come" showed through backwards from the other side of the page.

Charles turned over and stopped dead. There was a photograph on the page that was ominously familiar. He had last seen it on a dresser, surrounded by brass souvenirs.

Fiercely calm, he read the accompanying article.

M4 MURDER VICTIM IDENTIFIED

The man whose body was found early on Monday morning by the M4 exit road at Theale, Berks, has been identified as 44-year-old William Sweet, a photographer from Paddington, London. Sweet was found shot through the head at the roadside beside his grey Ford Escort, which appeared to have run out of petrol.

Interviewed at his Paddington studios, Sweet's wife, Audrey, could suggest no motive for the killing. Police believe Sweet may have been the victim of a gangland revenge killing, and that he may have been mistaken for someone else.

Charles put down the fish and chips and poured a large Scotch. He could feel his thoughts beginning to stampede and furiously tried to hold them in check.

Certain points were clear. He ordered them with grim concentration. Marius Steen must have killed Sweet: Sweet had put the pressure on about the photographs, Steen had fixed to meet him and shot him. Charles grabbed an old AA book that was lying around. Yes, the Theale turn-off was the one you'd take going to Streatley. Sweet was shot Sunday night or Monday morning. Marius Steen was in London certainly on the Saturday night, because he was at the *Sex of One* . . . party. And in Streatley during the week. He was therefore likely to have been driving through Theale late on Sunday. As Harry Chiltern had said, there was always a gun in the glove compartment. A glance at the map made Charles pretty sure that that gun was now in the Thames.

Other facts followed too. Mrs. Sweet was holding out on the police. It was nonsense for her to say no one had a motive for murdering her husband. As Charles had discovered, she knew about the Sally Nash party photographs. All she had to do was to tell the police about her husband's blackmailing activities and very soon the finger would point at Steen. For reasons of her own, she wasn't doing that. Probably just didn't want to lose a profitable business.

But the most chilling deduction from the fact of Bill Sweet's murder was the immediate danger to Jacqui. If he'd shoot one person who challenged him, Marius Steen would do the same to anyone else he thought represented the same threat. He'd tried to frighten Jacqui off with the telephone messages and vicious note, but if she persisted . . . Charles shivered as he thought what might have happened if Jacqui had been in the flat when her "visitors" called that morning. He looked over to the child-like form on his bed and felt a protective instinct so strong he almost wept.

Confrontation with Marius Steen couldn't wait. Charles must get down to Streatley straight away. If the man was down there . . . Better ring the Bayswater house to check. But he hadn't got the number. It seemed a pity to wake Jacqui. He opened her handbag, but the address book revealed nothing.

No help for it. "Jacqui." He shook her gently. She started like a frightened cat, and looked up at him wide-eyed. "Sorry. Listen, I've been thinking. I want to get this sorted out, like as soon as possible. There's no point in your being in this state of terror. I am going to try and see Steen tonight. Get it over with."

"But if he's in Streatley—"

"That's all right. I don't mind." He tried to sound casual, as if the new urgency was only a whim. "My daughter lives down that way. I wanted to go and visit her anyway."

"I didn't know you'd got a daughter."

"Oh, yes."

"How old?"

"Twenty-one."

"Nearly as old as me."

"Yes."

"Like me?"

"Hardly. Safely married at nineteen to a whizz-kid of the insurance world—if that's not a contradiction in terms. Anyway, the reason I woke you was not just bloody-mindedness. I want to ring Steen's Bayswater place and check he's not there. It's a long way to go if he's just round the corner."

Both the phone numbers Jacqui gave were ex-directory. Charles paused for a moment before dialing the Bayswater one, while he decided what character to take on. It had to be someone anonymous, but somebody who would be allowed to speak to the man if he was there, and someone who might conceivably be ringing on a Saturday night.

The phone was picked up at the other end and Charles pressed his two p into the coinbox. A discreet, educated voice identified the number—nothing more.

"Ah, good evening." He plumped for the Glaswegian accent he'd used in a Thirty-Minute Theatre ("Pointless"—*The Times*). "Is that Mr. Marius Steen's residence?"

"He does live here, yes, but—"

"It's Detective-Sergeant McWhirter from Scotland Yard. I'm sorry to bother you at this time of night. Is it possible to speak to Mr. Steen?"

"I'm afraid not. Mr. Steen is at his home in the country. Can I help at all?"

Charles hadn't planned beyond finding out what he wanted to

know and had to think quickly. "Ah yes, perhaps you can. It's only a small thing. Um." Playing for time. Then a sudden flash of inspiration. "We're just checking on various Rolls-Royce owners. There's a number-plate racket going on at the moment. I wonder if you could give me Mr. Steen's registration."

The discreet voice did so. "Thank you very much. That's all I wanted to know. I'm so sorry to have troubled you. Good-bye."

As Charles put the phone down, he tried to work out what on earth a number-plate racket might be. It was quite meaningless, but at least he'd got the required information.

He tried the Berkshire number. The phone rang for about thirty seconds, then after a click, a voice gave the number and said, "This is Marius Steen speaking on one of these recorded answering contraptions. I am either out at the moment or busy working on some scripts and don't want to talk right now. If your message is business ring the office—" he gave the number "—on Monday, if it's really urgent, you can leave a message on this machine, and if you want money, get lost." A pause. "Hello. Are you still there? Right then, after this whiney noise, tell me what it is." Then the tone, then silence.

The voice was striking. Charles felt he must have heard Steen being interviewed at some stage on radio or television, because it was very familiar. And distinctive. The Polish origins had been almost eroded, but not quite; they had been overlaid with heavy Cockney, which, in turn, had been flattened into a classier accent as Steen climbed the social ladder. As an actor, Charles could feel all the elements in the voice and begin to feel something of the man. He dialed the number again just to hear the voice and find out what else it could tell him.

The message itself was odd. The first reaction to "if you want money, get lost" was that Steen must be referring to potential blackmailers, but then Charles realized how unlikely that was. Any of Steen's friends might ring him, so the message had to have a more general application. Most likely it was just a joke. After all, Steen was notorious for his success with money. And notoriously tight-fisted. Tight as a bottle-top, as Harry Chiltern had said. For him to make that sort of joke on the recording was in keeping with the impression Charles was beginning to form of his character.

And in spite of everything, that impression was good. Somehow Steen's voice seemed to confirm Jacqui's view. It was rich with character and humor. The whole tone of the recording was of a man who was alive in the sense that mattered, the sort of man Charles felt he would like when he met him. And yet this was also the man who had recently shot a blackmailer through the head.

Somehow even that seemed suddenly consistent. A man as big as Steen shouldn't have to be involved with little second-rate crooks like Bill Sweet. Charles felt more hopeful about his mission, certain that when he actually got to Steen, he'd be able to talk to him and clear Jacqui from his suspicions.

He tried Juliet and Miles's phone number in Pangbourne, but there was no reply. No doubt out for the evening talking insurance at some scampi supper. Marius Steen might be out too, but he was bound to return at some stage, and the more Charles thought about the urgency of the situation, the more he was determined to meet the man.

He said good-bye to Jacqui. She refused the cold remains of the fish and chips, so he took the whole package out to the dustbin at the front of the house (no need to worry her about the Sweet murder if she didn't know—and it appeared she didn't). He caught a train from Paddington to Reading, arrived there to find the last train to Goring and Streatley had gone, and, after a considerable wait, got a minicab.

It was only when he was sitting in the back of the car that he actually thought of the risk he was taking. Because of a mild affection for a tart he now seemed unable even to make love to, he was going to confront a man he knew to be a murderer with copies of the photographs for which a man had been killed. Put like that, it did sound rather silly. Fortunately, there had been time to buy a half bottle of Bell's on the way to Paddington. Charles took a long pull. And another one.

The car drew up outside a pair of high white gates. The driver charged an enormous amount of money "on account of the petrol crisis" and swore when he wasn't given a tip to match. As the car's lights disappeared round the corner, it occurred to Charles that he should perhaps have asked the man to wait. If Steen turned nasty, he'd be glad of a quick getaway. But the thought was too late.

It was now very cold, the night air sharp and clear. The moon was nearly full and shed a watery light on the scene. It gleamed dully from a puddle outside the gates, which were high and solid, made of interlocking vertical planks. A fluorescent bell-push shone on the stone post to the right. Charles pressed it for a long time. It was now after midnight. Steen might well be in bed.

He pressed the button at intervals for about five minutes, but there was no reaction. His quarry might not be back yet, or perhaps the bell wasn't working. Charles tried the latch of the gate; he had to push hard but eventually it yielded.

He stood on a gravel path, looking at the house. It was an enormous bungalow, with a central block roofed in green tiles which shone in the moonlight. From this main part smaller wings spread off like the suburbs of a city. To the right there was a ramp down to a double garage on basement level. The whole building was painted the frost white of cake icing and its shine echoed the gleam of the silent Thames behind. No lights showed.

The main door was sheltered by a portico with tall columns, an incongruous touch of Ancient Greece grafted on to the sprawling modern bungalow. The door itself was of dark panelled wood with a brass knocker. Since there was no sign of a bell, Charles raised the enormous ring and let it fall.

The noise shocked him. It boomed as if the whole house was a resonating chamber for the brass instrument on the door. Charles waited, then knocked again. Soon he was hammering on the door, thud after thud, a noise fit to wake the dead. But there was nothing. The rush to Berkshire had been pointless. The photographs still bulged in his inside pocket. Marius Steen was not at home.

8

INSIDE THE GIANT'S CASTLE

"It would have all been easier, Daddy," said Juliet, "if you'd had some sort of regular job. I mean, acting's so unpredictable."

"No, no, darling," said Miles Taylerson, judiciously, "not all acting. I mean there are regular jobs in acting—you know, directors of repertory companies, or in serials like *Coronation Street* or *Crossroads*."

Charles, seated in Miles's karate-style dressing gown, gritted his teeth and buttered, or rather battered, a piece of toast.

"No, but, quite honestly, Daddy, I do worry about you. I mean, you haven't set anything aside for your old age."

"This is my old age, so it's too late now," Charles pronounced with facetious finality.

But unfortunately that was not a conversation-stopper for Miles; it was a cue. "Oh, I wouldn't say that, Pop"—Charles winced—"I mean, there are insurance plans and pension plans for people of any age. In fact, in my company we have rather a good scheme. I know of a fellow of over sixty who took out a policy. Of course, the premiums are high, but it's linked to a unit trust, so it's with profits."

"I thought unit trusts were doing rather badly," Charles tried maliciously, but Miles was unruffled.

"Oh yes, there haven't been the spectacular rises of the first few years, but we could guarantee a growth figure which more than copes with inflation. I know a case of a fellow who—"

Charles couldn't stand the prospect of another textbook example. "Miles, I didn't come down here to talk about insurance."

"Sorry, Pop. It's only because we're concerned about you. Isn't that so, darling?"

"Yes. You see, Daddy, Miles and I do worry. You don't seem to have any sense of direction since you left Mummy. We'd just feel happier if we'd thought you'd made some provisions for the future."

"Exactly, darling. And, Pop, now you've got the advantage of someone in insurance actually in the family, it makes it so much easier."

"What? You mean it's easier than having some creep loaded with policies pestering me at my digs—"

"Yes."

"—to have a creep in the family doing exactly the same thing."

A pause ensued. Miles went very red, muttered something about "things to get on with" and left the room. Charles munched his toast.

"Daddy, there's no need to be rude to Miles."

"I'm sorry, but it is tempting."

"Look, he's been jolly tolerant. You arriving completely unannounced in the middle of the night, using our house as a hotel. We might have had people staying. As it is, he's put off his fishing so as to entertain you—"

"That was entertainment? My God, what's he like when he's not making an effort?"

Juliet ignored him. "And I think you might show a bit of gratitude. Daddy, I do wish you'd just get yourself sorted out."

Oh, sharper than the serpent's tooth it is, to have an ungrateful father. But, Charles reflected, even sharper to have a middle-aged daughter of twenty-one. Where had he gone wrong, as a parent? There must have been a moment when Juliet had shown some spark of individuality which he failed to foster. Some moment when she, as a child, was on the verge of doing something wrong, and he could have fulfilled a father's role and made her do it. But no, his daughter had always been a model of sobriety, good works and even chastity. A virgin when she married at nineteen. In 1973. So much for the permissive society.) It's disappointing for a father.

Miles reappeared, incongruously dressed in brand-new green waders, a brand-new camouflage jacket and brand-new shapeless hat. "Look, Pop, sorry we got heated."

"No one got heated. I was just rather rude to you."

Miles laughed in man-of-the-world style. "Jolly good, Pop. That's what I like. Straight talking. Eh? Look, what I wondered was, would you like to come fishing with me? Got time for a couple of hours, then a quick pint at the local, while Juliet gets the lunch. What do you say?"

"Well, I should be—" Charles remembered his mission.

"We could go into Streatley, there's a nice pub there."

"Oh, all right." It was important to get there and a lift in Miles's odious yellow Cortina was as good a way as any other. He graciously accepted the olive branch.

Charles persuaded a rather grudging Miles that he had time for a quick bath before they left. It was still only half-past nine. Apparently it was Miles's fishing that got them up so early. Charles wondered. To him, getting up early on a Sunday seemed sacrilegious, particularly if you had a woman around. Some of the best times of his life had been Sunday mornings. Toast, newspapers, and a warm body. Not for the first time, he tried to visualize his daughter's sex-life. It defied imagination. Perhaps a regular weekly deposit with a family protective policy and a bonus of an extra screw at age twenty-five.

As he lay in the marine blue bath (matching the marine blue wash-basin and separate lavatory), laced with Juliet's bubble bath, Charles thought about the Steen situation. It seemed a long way away and he focused his mind with an effort. Assuming he could see Steen and hand over the photographs, it would soon be over. Now Bill Sweet was dead, there was no one else to put on the pressure. Charles conveniently put the circumstances of Sweet's death to the back of his mind. He didn't feel any obligation to see justice done in that matter. If Steen was a murderer, that wasn't his business. Let the police deal with it. If they really wanted to find a motive for the murder, they should grill Mrs. Sweet. She could supply them with a few answers.

But did Mrs. Sweet know about Steen? Had she realized who was responsible for her husband's death? In fact, did she know all the details of his blackmailing activities or was she just cashing in as much as possible? If Mrs. Sweet was in the picture, she might continue the pressure on Steen, and that could have unpleasant repercussions for Jacqui. It suddenly became rather urgent to find out how much Mrs. Sweet knew.

The trouble with modern architect-designed houses on estates (what's the alternative to an architect-designed house—a milkman-designed house? a footballer-designed house?) is that there's no privacy. The telephone in the Taylersons' executive home was situated in the middle of the open-plan living area, which had unimpeded access to the kitchen area, the sitting area and the upstairs area. In other words, Juliet and Miles were bound to hear every word of any telephone conversation. But there was no alternative.

The ringing tone stopped. "Hello."

"Ah, Mrs. Sweet. It's . . . er . . . Bill Holroyd." The old *When We Are Married* voice.

"Ah, Mr. Holroyd." Interest.

"Yes . . . er, the reason I'm ringing is . . . er . . . I've just heard about your husband . . ."

"Yes." No emotion.

"I wondered if . . . er . . . this changed the situation?"

"No. You deal with me."

"Yes. Er . . . nasty business." No reaction. "This doesn't mean that the . . . er . . . police . . . would . . . er . . ."

"Don't worry. I haven't told them a thing."

"Oh, good."

"Yes. You just give me what you owe and you'll never hear about that particular business again."

"Fine. There was . . . er . . . something else. One or two of my friends were also at the party . . ."

"Yes."

"A Mr. Phillips, a Mr. Cuthbertson, a Mr.—" he tried desperately to think of a name "—Taylerson. They . . . er . . . wondered if they featured in the photographs."

"Yes, I rather think they did. You'd better put them in touch with me."

"Yes." Charles was getting the information he wanted. Obviously Mrs. Sweet hadn't a clue who any of the people in the photographs were. But best to be sure. "Mr. Taylerson in particular was anxious. He seemed to think he might feature in some pictures with a blonde girl. And a mask." The Steen and Jacqui photographs were the only ones that fitted the description.

"That's Mr. Taylerson, ah." She didn't know. "Perhaps I'd better get in touch with him. Do you know his address?"

Charles resisted the temptation to give Miles's address, funny though the image of his son-in-law being blackmailed with dirty photographs was. "No, I think I'd better put him in touch with you."

"Yes, do that. And I'll see you Wednesday."

"Yes."

"With the money."

"Yes."

"And . . ." the voice continued with studied casualness, "perhaps you'd better double the money . . ."

"What?"

"Mr. Holroyd, you remember yesterday afternoon?"

"Yes."

"Well, would you believe it, Mr. Holroyd, there's a camera trained on that sofa."

"Oh."

"I'm sure you wouldn't want your wife and two lovely daughters to—"

"No."

"Ten thousand then, Mr. Holroyd, and you'll have the whole album."

"But I—" The line went dead. Charles felt enormous relief that he wasn't Bill Holroyd. Bill Holroyd was a man with problems. Still, it explained Mrs. Sweet's sudden change of behavior. Oh dear, and he'd thought it was his own animal magnetism.

Charles turned to see Miles and Juliet standing open-mouthed in the kitchen doorway. "Sorry about that. Talking to an actress friend. Always fool about like that. Putting on voices."

"Yes," said Miles in a very old-fashioned voice. "I suppose a lot of that sort of thing goes on with actors and . . . you know. Perhaps we can go fishing now."

"Just one more call. Will be quick, I promise. What's the code for Streatley from here?"

Again it was a recorded answer. Steen's voice gave the number. "Marius Steen speaking. Not available at the moment. Ring later, or leave a message after this noise."

Miles had the complete kit. Not only the shining new camouflage clothes, but various shining new containers of tackle. A waterproof khaki bag to hang from one shoulder, a long black leather rod-case to hang from the other, and an assortment of neatly dangling nets, stools and bait-boxes. As he laid out his instruments on squares of cloth like a surgeon, he said, "You know, Pop, fishing's a very good relaxant. Relaxation is important to anyone in an executive position."

They were sitting on the bank opposite Steen's house, Miles on a new folding chair of shining chromium tubes, Charles on a relegated wooden stool. He had chosen the location deliberately, assuring Miles that it was a very promising swim, that the swirlings of the current denoted barbel pits and that the overhanging trees were a good lie for large pike. It was all nonsense, but it was in the right language and Miles was impressed.

So Charles had a good view. The bungalow didn't look so large from the back, just discreetly expensive, a low white outline from which the lawn sloped gently down to a neat concreted waterside. To the left there was a small boat-house whose locked doors gave on to the river.

The bungalow showed no sign of life, and there had not been any when they had driven past on the road. Charles had persuaded Miles to stop and tried ringing the bell on the gate. No reply.

But somebody had been there overnight. Not only was there the evidence of the changed recording on the telephone. The puddles outside the bungalow gates showed fresh tire-marks. Steen was certainly around somewhere; it was just a question of waiting; and, in the meantime, fishing.

"I think the thing for these sort of conditions," said Miles, "is a swimfeeder."

"Ah."

"Yes. Quite definitely. Filled with a gentle and bread-paste mixture, with a couple of gentles on a number twelve hook, I think it'd be a cert for bream."

"Maybe."

"Yes. Or roach."

"Hm."

"Well, that's what it recommended in this angling magazine I was reading. I reckon these are the sort of conditions it described. More or less."

"Yes." Charles flipped his line out into the water. He'd been lent an old relegated rod with two mottled bamboo sections and a greenheart tip, a plastic center-pin reel and a yellowed quill float. He'd put a couple of maggots on a small hook. He sat and watched the quill being borne along by the current and then leaning over as it tugged at the end of the swim.

"Have you plumbed?" asked Miles.

"I beg your pardon?"

"Plumbed the depth of the swim. You'll never catch anything if you don't do that. You see, what the angler has to do with his bait is to make it imitate as nearly as possible the conditions of nature. In nature things don't dangle awkwardly in the water. They flow, carried along by the current, a few inches above the bottom. Depending on the season, of course."

"Of course."

"Would you like a plummet? I've got one."

"No thanks. I'm trying to give them up."

Miles was silent, preoccupied with opening his latest piece of equipment. Proudly he stripped off the packaging and screwed a limp length of fiberglass to the end of his sleek fiberglass rod. Charles looked on with an expression of distaste which Miles took for admiration. "Swingtip."

"Ah."

"Best sort of bite-detector for bottom-fishing."

"Ah." Charles reflected how Miles always talked out of books. His son-in-law was the least spontaneous person he'd ever met.

Nothing came naturally; it all had to be worked at. Whatever interest he took up, he would begin by a painstaking study of the language and then buy all the correct equipment, before he actually did anything practical. Fishing was the latest accomplishment which Miles thought the young executive should not be without.

Again Charles found himself wondering about Miles and Juliet's sex-life. Had that been approached in the same meticulous way? "Well, here we are on our honeymoon, Juliet darling. What I will do, when we are in bed and an atmosphere of mutual trust and relaxation has been established, is to practice a certain amount of foreplay. This is likely to begin with a kneading or massaging of the breasts in an accelerating stroking motion. This will be followed by manual clitoral stimulation . . ." The idea was intriguing. Charles wondered if he was becoming a dirty old man. But it *was* intriguing. Guiltily, he disguised his interest in a standard father-in-law question. "Miles, have you and Juliet thought of having a family?"

Miles sat up with irritation. He'd just been trying to squeeze a split-shot on to his line and it had popped out of his fingers. "Yes, Pop, we have. We reckon in about four and a half years I should have gone up at least a grade, so, allowing for the usual increments, and assuming that the mortgage rate doesn't rise above the present eleven per cent, I should think we could afford to let Juliet stop work then."

There was no answer to that, so Charles sat and looked out over the water to Steen's bungalow. Nothing. It was very cold. The air stung his face and he felt the ground's iciness creep into his feet through the soles of Miles's relegated gum-boots. His body was stiff and uncomfortable. Always got like that when he sat still for a long time. He felt his years. A sure sign he needed a drink.

Miles had now completed the cat's cradle at the end of his line, and had loaded the perspex tube of his swim-feeder with a porridgy mash of bread and maggots. Two favored maggots squirmed on the end of his size twelve hook (hooked, no doubt, as the books recommend, through the small vent in the thick end). Miles rose to his feet and fiddled with the knobs of his gleaming fixed-spool reel. "The important thing," he quoted almost to himself, "is to remember it's not brute force with a fixed-spool reel; just a controlled flick."

He made a controlled flick. The line jerked and maypoled itself around the rod. The contents of the swim-feeder sprayed from their case like shotgun pellets and landed with a scattering plop in the middle of the river. Charles didn't say anything, but controlled his lips and looked at his float. As he did so, it submerged. He struck, and reeled in rather a good perch.

Four hasty pints before the pub closed at two saw Charles through lunch, and there was a bit of wine too. "Le Piat Beaujolais Primeur," said Miles "—young, robust and slightly petillant, ideal with meat dishes." (Obviously he had read a book on wine too.) The combination of alcohols anaesthetized Charles so that he could even watch the holiday slides of Tenerife without excessive pain.

They were not very varied—"Juliet in front of a shop . . . and here's Juliet in this bar place . . . and this one's of Juliet sitting on a rock . . . and here's Juliet in a boat—that was the day we went for a boat trip. . . ." Obviously, Miles did not trust her with his camera or there might have been a matching sequence of "Miles in front of a shop . . . Miles in this bar place . . ." etc. References in the commentary to shutter speeds, and exposures and lenses demonstrated that Miles had read a book on photography too. Charles let it all flow over him. Time was suspended, and he was too fuddled for darker thoughts.

The peaceful mood lasted until he stood alone on Goring Bridge. Miles and Juliet had offered him a lift to Pangbourne Station, but they'd got some people coming and were very relieved when he said he'd get a minicab to Reading. Miles had been dropping heavy hints about how difficult it was to get petrol and how he intended to use the Cortina "for emergency uses only." (By moving up from the level of salesman in his insurance company, he'd sacrificed a firm's car and was rather careful about using his own.)

When the cab came, Charles left in a surge of family effusiveness, and then, feeling like the hero of some of the terrible thriller films he'd been in during the fifties, he told the driver to go to Steen's home instead. As they approached Streatley, he lost his nerve and asked to be dropped by the bridge. The driver, with the predictability of all motorists over the last few weeks, commented on the petrol crisis, overcharged grossly, and drove off into the night.

The bridge at Goring is long and narrow; there are two spans to an island in the middle; one side is Streatley, the other Goring. Charles stood on the narrow pavement, leaning on the wooden parapet, and looked down into the water, which seemed infinitely deep in the darkness. Somewhere the church bells rang in the distance, calling the faithful to evensong. Their old-fashioned domesticity seemed incongruous as his thoughts darkened.

The pressure which had been building up all weekend was nearing some sort of explosion. The Steen business had to be sorted out that evening. Charles felt an uncomfortable sense of urgency. It was now nearly a week since Bill Sweet's death on Sunday December 2nd, and Jacqui was still in great danger. Charles had known the full implications of the situation for only twenty-four hours, but he had a sick feeling that time was running out. A sense of gloom blanketed his thought as he looked down to the dark water and heard the hiss of it rushing over the invisible weir ahead of him. Somewhere down in the depths, he felt certain, lay Marius Steen's gun, thrown away after the murder was committed.

He'd wasted the day. The fishing, the slides of Tenerife were all irrelevant; he should have been dealing with Steen. It was one of the most important responsibilities of his life. And this was one he couldn't shirk. It must be done straight away. He looked at his watch. Nearly seven. The pubs would soon be open. Just a quick drink for a bracer and then it must be done.

It was twenty past nine when he left the cozy fireside of the Bull. He was braced to the point of recklessness. Two hours of sipping Bell's and listening to the quacks of the local Scampi and Mateus Rosé crowd made the whole issue seem much simpler. If Steen was there, Charles had only to tell him the truth; if he wasn't, then he could leave the photographs with an anonymous note explaining Jacqui's innocence. He couldn't think why it hadn't occurred to him earlier, as he marched briskly (after a bit of trouble with the door latch) out of the pub.

The moon was fuller than the night before, but its light was diffused by cloud. He could see quite clearly as he climbed the hill out of the village. It didn't feel as cold as it had earlier in the day. He stopped to relieve himself into the roadside bushes and almost lost his balance as a car screeched round the corner in a clatter of gravel. He zipped himself up and strode onwards. A strange sense of purpose filled him, even a sense of honor. Sir Galahad nearing the end of his quest. Marius Steen, the giant who seemed to have been looming over his life now for a week was about to be confronted. A fragment repeated itself inappropriately like a *mantra* in Charles's mind. "My strength is as the strength of ten, because my heart is pure."

He was almost disappointed when he reached the gates. He'd expected a great brazen trumpet hanging, with a legend in outlandish characters—"Who dares to brave the giant's wrath, let him sound this trump." And in the trees, clattering sadly, the armor of those who had dared, and failed in the combat. He turned to look at the trees, but they were bare. And the only sound was the wind breathing on their branches.

Charles leaned unsteadily against the gate-post and pressed the fluorescent button. He didn't wait for any response, but pushed open the heavy white gates with a scrunch of gravel. The bungalow again seemed to have grown in the moonlight, and was now a Moorish temple, where the infidel foe lurked. A light shone through a chink in the curtains of a window above the garage door.

No one appeared as Charles approached the front door, but he felt as if he was being watched. Suddenly the night had become very silent. He beat a tattoo with the doorknocker, and again its reverberations filled the whole world. But no one came. The quarry was lying low.

Charles pushed the door but it was very solid. He backed away and looked along the front of the house. The windows appeared to be shut firm. Garage? He walked heavily down the ramp and grasped the handle that should lift the door up and over. Locked.

But he had reached a pitch where he couldn't give up. He stumbled round the side of the house, through the flower beds, feeling the windows. All were tightly locked.

Round the back of the bungalow he was suddenly aware of the

slow wash of water at the end of the lawn. There was no other sound and no light was visible on this elevation. But he knew Marius Steen was inside.

There was a small door which corresponded with the back of the garage. He walked up a crazy-paving path and tried the handle. Braced for a shove he nearly overbalanced when the door gave inwards.

It was very dark. He blinked, trying to accustom his eyes to the change, but still couldn't see much. There were no windows and only a trickle of light came in through the door behind him. From what he could see, it illuminated a pile of boxes. Perhaps he was in some sort of storeroom rather than the garage. He moved slowly forward, groping ahead with a breast-stroke motion.

But discretion was difficult in his alcoholic state. There was something in the way of his foot, then an object with a sharp edge fell agonizingly onto his ankle. Whatever it was precipitated an avalanche of other objects which thundered down around him as Charles fell sprawling to the ground.

He lay frozen, waiting for some reaction, but there was nothing. It was only his tense state that made the crash sound so loud. Gingerly, he reached forward, found a wall and levered himself up against it. Then he felt along to a door frame and followed its outline until he found a light-switch.

The sudden glare was blinding, but when he unscrewed his eyes, he could see he was in a kind of windowless utility room. There was a washing machine, a spin dryer, a washing-up machine, a deep-freeze and rows of neatly hanging brooms and mops. Above these was a cluster of meters, fuse-boxes and power-switches. Deep shelves on the opposite wall contained boxes of tinned food and crates of spirits. There was a spreading honeycomb of a wine-rack, full and expensive-looking.

And on the floor Charles could see what had caused his fall. A pile of boxes lay scattered like a demolished chimney. He knelt down and re-piled them. They were heavy, as he knew from the numbing pain in his shin. He looked at the writing on the boxes. "Salmon," "Trout," "Strawberries." "Do not refreeze." Marius Steen certainly knew how to live.

When he had finished piling the boxes up, Charles looked once more round the room and his eyes lighted on the very thing he needed at that moment—a torch. It was a long, black, rubber-encased one, hanging from a hook by the back door. He took it down, switched on, turned off the light and opened the door into the rest of the house.

He was in the garage. It was large, but dominated by the huge form of a dark blue Rolls-Royce. Remembering a detail with sudden clarity, Charles knelt down and looked at the left-hand side of the front bumper. There was a little dent, which he'd lay any money corresponded to the dent in the back right-hand wing of Bill Sweet's Ford Escort. The door of the Rolls was not locked. Key in the ignition, nothing in the glove compartment and the petrol gauge read empty.

Charles moved round the great car, looking for any other clues it might give. He felt his foot slip under him and sat down with a jarring shock, landing uncomfortably on a spanner and a piece of plastic tubing. Fate seemed determined to translate his dramatic mission into slapstick.

He found the door which led to the body of the house, along a corridor and into the large hall. All the walls were hung with hunting prints which were anonymously expensive, bought on advice by a man without natural taste. Two enormous china Dalmatians stood guarding the front door. They seemed to reflect more of their owner's personality. They were Steen the showman; the prints were Steen the man who wanted to gatecrash high society, the man who wanted a knighthood.

There were no lights in evidence, except for a slight glow from the top of a short flight of steps, which must lead to a room above the garage. The room whose light Charles had seen from the front.

He moved purposefully up the stairs and began to feel faint. The drink was telling; he felt his energy wane. He had to get the interview over quickly.

The first room he came to was a kind of study, equipped with telephones, typewriters, and copying machines. The walls were covered with framed photographs of stars from Marius Steen's shows, scribbled with effusive messages. It was a sentimental showbiz touch that again didn't fit the man's character. What he felt was wanted, rather than what he wanted. Bernard Walton's face grinned patronizingly down from the wall.

The study was empty; the light came from the adjacent room. Charles switched off his torch with a dull click and moved towards the half-open door. Through its crack he could see a plush bedroom, dominated by a large four-poster bed. Curtains obscured his view, but the shape of the covers told him that the bed was occupied.

As he entered the room, exhaustion threatened to swamp him, but still he moved forward. Now, in the light of a bedside lamp, he could see Marius Steen lying back on the pillows asleep. The great beak of a nose, familiar from countless press photographs, rose out of the sheets like the dorsal fin of a shark. One large hand lay, palm upward, on the cover.

"Wake him, tell him and go." Charles formulated his thoughts very simply with desperate concentration. He staggered forward to the bedside and stood there, swaying. As he reached for Steen's hand, he heard a car drawing up outside the gates. He clutched at the hand in panic, and felt the coldness of death.

9

INTERVAL

CHARLES WOKE AS IF his body was being dragged out of a deep pit, and memory returned slowly to his pounding head. He didn't like it when it came. He could see Steen's face in its pained repose, and felt certain that he was up against a case of murder.

He was lying in bed in Miles and Juliet's spare room. Vague memories of getting there. The rush from Steen's bedroom out through the garage and utility room, as he heard a car stopping on the gravel and footsteps approaching the garage door. Then he remembered skulking breathless behind the bungalow until the car was safely garaged, a rush through the gates, staggering along the road till a police car stopped, warnings—"Had a few too many, haven't you, sir? Still, won't charge you this time. But watch it"— and ignominious delivery on Miles and Juliet's doorstep.

He heaved himself out of bed and limped downstairs. The bruise on his ankle was cripplingly painful and he felt his forty-seven years. Too old to be involved in this escalating round of violence.

Juliet stood staring at him as he made it to the kitchen chair. She appeared not to have inherited Frances's forgiving nature. "Really, Daddy, what a state to come home in."

"I'm sorry, love."

"Miles was furious."

"Oh well." There were more important things than Miles's sensibilities.

"I mean, the police coming here. What will other people on the estate think?"

"You can tell them the police weren't coming for you or Miles."

"They wouldn't think that!"

"Miles can tell them it's just his drunken father-in-law."

"I don't think they'd find that very amusing." She turned away to make coffee. "Honestly, Daddy, I don't think you have any concept of human dignity."

That hurt. "Listen, Juliet *darling*. I think I probably have more knowledge of the really important things that give a person dignity than . . ." But it wasn't worth explaining; she wouldn't understand. "Oh, forget it. Shouldn't you be at work?"

"I'm not going in till after lunch. There's not much to do and . . . well, I was worried about you."

It was the first softening Charles could ever remember hearing from Juliet. It warmed him. "Thank you."

"Honestly, Daddy, I don't know what you're up to half the time. That peculiar phone-call yesterday morning, and now all this. What on earth were you doing in Streatley anyway? I thought you had taken the cab to Reading."

"Yes, I know. The thing is, I had to change my plans. It's all rather involved, but . . ." He paused, and all the boiling thoughts inside him strained for an outlet. He had to tell someone. Why not Juliet? "Marius Steen is dead."

"Yes, I know." Her answer was cool and unconcerned.

"How do you know?"

"It was on the radio this morning. On the *Today* program."

"What? How did it say he died?"

"Heart attack, I think it was. Here's your coffee." As she placed the cup in front of him, Charles looked at his daughter, wondering if she could be involved in this grotesque business. But in her face, as easily read as her mother's, there was nothing devious; she was telling the truth. "Anyway, Daddy, why do you tell me that? Was it Steen you went to see last night?"

"No."

"I didn't know you knew him."

"I didn't." He sipped the coffee. It wasn't what he needed. His body felt dangerously unstable and bilious. "Juliet, could you get me a drop of whisky?"

"At this time in the morning? Daddy"—with all the awe of a television documentary—"are you an alcoholic?"

"I don't know. I've never thought about it. Where does liking a drink stop and being an alcoholic start?"

"I should think it starts when you need a *hair of the dog* the next morning." Juliet italicized the unfamiliar phrase.

"Well, I do need one now."

"I don't know whether I should—"

"Oh, get it!" he snapped impatiently. As Juliet scurried shocked to the cocktail cabinet, Charles asked himself whether he was in fact an alcoholic. On balance, he decided he probably wasn't. He could do without drink. But he wouldn't like to have to. It was an old joke —a teetotaller knows every morning when he wakes up that that's the best he's going to feel all day. Drink at least offers some prospect of things improving.

He felt Juliet's shocked eyes on him as he poured whisky into his coffee and drank it gratefully. It made him feel more stable, but desperately tired. Waves of relief washed over him. Steen had died of a heart attack. Thoughts of murder had been prompted only by the events of the previous week and the melodramatic circumstances of the discovery of the body. All the contradictory details evaporated. Charles believed what he wanted to believe. The pressure was off. "Juliet love, what's the time?"

"Twenty past ten."

"Look, I think I'll go back to bed for a bit."

"But you must have something to eat." Frances's eternal cry.

"When have you got to go to work?"

"Have to leave quarter to two."

"Wake me at half-past twelve. Then I'll have something to eat. I promise."

It wasn't until after lunch and Juliet's departure that Charles remembered about Jacqui, still lying low at Hereford Road. The public announcement of Steen's death had sapped the urgency out of him and yesterday's imperatives no longer mattered. Jacqui was just the frayed end of an otherwise completed pattern and it was with reluctance that he dialed his own number.

Jacqui answered. All of the Swedish girls must be out at their various Swedish employments. Her voice was guarded, but not panic-stricken. "Charles? I wondered when you were going to ring. I was just about to leave."

"Jacqui, I've got some bad news . . ."

"It's all right. I heard. On *Open House*."

"What?"

"The radio."

"Ah. Well, I'm sorry."

"Thank you." There was a pause, and Charles could feel how fiercely she was controlling her emotions.

"Jacqui, I'm afraid I never got the photos to him."

"That hardly matters now, does it? Nothing much matters now."

"Jacqui . . ."

"I'll be all right."

"Yes. I suppose that's the end of it, isn't it?"

"I wouldn't count on that."

"What do you mean?" Charles had an unpleasant feeling he was about to sacrifice his recently-won calm.

"Do you think he died of a heart attack, Charles?"

"Yes."

There was a grunt from the other end of the line, a sound between exasperation and despair. "Charles, I can't talk about it now. I'm too . . . I'll talk when—"

"Tomorrow?"

"Yes, if I feel O.K. Come round when you . . . Evening. Eight or . . ."

"O.K. I'll be there. Archer Street. You'll be all right now?"

"Like hell." The phone went dead.

Before Charles left the house in Pangbourne, he took the envelope of photographs out of his inside pocket and looked at them. With Steen's death they had changed. Already they had the air of curios or souvenirs—oddities from another age. The erotic quality had drained from them and they seemed like sepia prints in an album of someone else's relations. Mildly interesting, but ultimately irrelevant.

He looked around for somewhere to destroy them. The trouble with architect-designed houses on estates is that they have nothing like an open fire. The central heating was fired by oil. (Miles had already spoken gloomily of the inevitable price rises which the Middle East situation must precipitate. As he said portentously, "You know, Pop, the days of cheap fuel are over.") The cooker was electric. There was no convenient stove to consume the evidence.

Charles took a giant box of matches from the kitchen and went out into the garden. The forty-foot-long area was neatly organized. A potting shed of conspicuous new timber, a patio area protected by a screen of lattice-work bricks, a path of very sane crazy-paving winding diagonally across the lawn, a meticulous row of cloches. Only the winter shagginess of the grass gave any hint of rampant nature or humanity.

It had started to rain. Big heavy drops that were cold as they fell, penetrating, on his head and shoulders. In the far corner of the garden Charles saw what he was looking for. Neatly screened by another low wall of lattice-work bricks were a compost heap, bound in by wooden slats, and an empty metal incinerator. He lit the photographs one by one and let the flimsy black rectangles of ash drop into the bin. Finally he burnt the envelope, then stirred the dampening fragments into a black unrecognizable mash.

10

SECOND ACT BEGINNERS

THE OBITUARY APPEARED in *The Times* the next day, Tuesday December 11th.

MR. MARIUS STEEN
Impresario and Showman

Mr. Marius Steen, CBE, the impresario, died on Sunday. He was 68. Born in Warsaw in 1905, his full name was Marius Ladislas Steniatowski, but he shortened it for convenience when his parents came to England in 1921. His father was a tailor and for some years the young Steen helped him in his business. But already the attraction of entertainment was strong; Steen spent most of his limited pocket-money on tickets for the music hall and in 1923 launched himself as Mario, the Melodic Whistler. In spite of changes in name and act, he was never a success as a performer, but became increasingly interested in the business of promotion and management. The first act he managed was Herbert and his Horrible Dogs in 1924.

Soon he was progressing from individual acts to the presentation of complete shows. Though he started with wrestling and all-girl revues, by 1930 he was presenting variety bills at music halls all over the country. Through the Thirties he centralized his activities on London and, in 1935, had his first major success with the spectacular revue *Go with the Girls.*None of these early productions had a great deal to recommend them artistically, but Steen always maintained that success must be measured by public reaction alone. And by that criterion his shows were highly successful.

Steen continued presenting revues, with an increasing reliance on scripted comedy rather than just dancing girls, until the outbreak of war. Then he moved into the cinema and, with his customary unflagging energy, set up a series of films in keeping with the jingoistic spirit of the times. Of these the most memorable was *Brothers in Battledress*, directed by William Hankin.

After the war Marius Steen continued to put on shows and gradually he forsook revue for musicals and light comedies. *What's in the Box?* was one of the greatest successes of 1953, and in 1960 Steen's purchase of the King's Theatre off Shaftesbury Avenue heralded a string of commercial triumphs, including *One Thing After Another*, which ran for three years, and, currently, *Sex of One and Half a Dozen of the Other*.

Steen maintained his interest in the cinema and put money into many ventures including the highly successful Steenway Productions, which makes horror films. He was also a major shareholder in three commercial television companies, and was at the time of his death interesting himself in the production of programs for network on the new commercial radio station.

Marius Steen was often criticized for his healthy disrespect for "Art" and there are many stories of this supposed philistinism which he loved to tell against himself. (On first hearing of Michelangelo, he is reputed to have asked "Michael who?" His alleged description of opera as "fat gits singing" is probably apocryphal.) He was a forthright man who made enemies, but was loved and respected by his friends. He had no hobbies, maintaining that if a person needed hobbies, then there was something wrong with his work. He divided his time between his houses in London and Streatley and a villa in the South of France. In 1969 he was awarded the CBE for services to the theatre.

Marius Steen married Rose Whittle in 1934. She died in 1949 and he never remarried. He leaves a son.

Charles was impressed. It was quite an achievement for anyone in the theatre to command that many column inches in *The Times*. The obituary seemed like a washing of the body. It cleaned Steen up. The existence of the photographs, all the sordid aspects of the man's life were rinsed away by the formalized prose. The Western ritual of death was observed—the obligation to remember the most dignified image of the deceased. Like those ghastly American mausoleums where the embalmed corpse is presented at its best, dressed and smiling, prior to burial. But Charles had a nagging feeling that, however Marius Steen was tarted up in death, his corpse would not lie down.

Charles arrived at the Archer Street flat with a two-liter bottle of Valpolicella from Oddbins and a determination to be very slow on the uptake in any discussion of Steen's death. Jacqui looked ghastly when she opened the door. Her face was pale and her eyes were puffy red slits.

"Are you all right?"

"I will be, Charles. I'll just sit down for a moment."

"Can I get you a drink?"

"No. It'd make me sick. But help yourself."

The events of the last few days had made Charles forget about Jacqui's flat being done over, but inside it the evidence was all too clear. She had obviously made some attempt to tidy up. There were two cardboard boxes in the middle of the room full of bits of glass and torn clothes. But the curtains were still hanging shredded from their rails, and the bed smelt of oil from the smashed lamp. The little room looked sad and crippled.

He didn't make any comment, but found an unbroken glass and filled it with Valpolicella. "Do you want to go out to eat, Jacqui?"

"No, I couldn't."

"Hmm." The silence was obtrusive. Feebly he repeated himself. "Do you feel all right?"

"Charles, the bloke I loved and whose kid I've got has just been murdered."

"I'm sorry." He stolidly avoided reacting to the word "murdered." Jacqui softened. "I'll get you some food later. When I can face it."

"Don't worry about that. Not particularly hungry."

"No." Again they were conscious of the silence. Then Jacqui burst out. "He always was a little sod."

Charles was genuinely amazed. "Who?"

"Nigel."

"Nigel Steen?"

"Well, who else?"

"Why do you suddenly bring him in?"

"Because he killed Marius, that's why."

This new direction of thought was too sudden for Charles to take in. Deliberately, he slowed down. "What on earth do you mean? You haven't got any reason for saying that."

"Of course I have. Who else stood to get anything out of Marius's death?"

"I don't know. I would have thought Nigel was doing all right anyway. He didn't need to murder anyone. Presumably he'd have got everything when his father went. He only had to wait."

"He's greedy. Anyway, things may have changed. Maybe he had to move fast."

"What do you mean?" Charles asked patiently, determined to humor her through this crazy new idea.

"Marius was thinking of changing his will in favor of me and the baby."

"Oh yes." Charles tried to sound believing, but failed.

"Yes, he bloody was. He was even talking about us getting married."

"When was this?"

"First in the South of France. Then when I told him about the baby he was more definite. He said he'd felt awful about the abortion last time, and he wanted to keep this one and marry me and start again."

"And cut Nigel out of the will?"

"I suppose so."

It didn't sound very plausible. Even if Steen had ever had such intentions, the events of the last week made it clear that he had changed his mind. And the whole idea of remarriage and disowning Nigel was the sort of novelette situation that would appeal to Jacqui. Still, he couldn't be completely brutal with her. "Why didn't you mention this before?"

"It was a secret. Between Marius and me. It was all going to be secret. Even when we married it was going to be a secret for a bit. But now he's dead . . ." She broke down.

Charles calmed her and forced her to drink a little wine. But when she was composed again, he felt he had to be cruel. If Steen had been murdered (and he had no cause to believe that that was the case), then it was something to do with the Sweets and the blackmailing business. It was dangerous for Jacqui to go around blaming his son. She was quite capable of going to the police and making accusations which, since she hadn't a shred of evidence, could only lead to trouble. This nonsense had to be stopped.

"If what you say is true, how do you explain Steen's behavior during the past week? Hardly the actions of a devoted husband-to-be."

He could see from her face that that really hurt, and also that it was something she hadn't been able to work out satisfactorily for herself. "Well, Nigel kept him from me. Marius went off to Berkshire—where he didn't want to be disturbed. He'd often do that," she added defensively, "go off with a great pile of scripts, looking for his next show. And then Nigel left all those messages for me."

"And he sent the note?"

"Yes."

"Pity I burnt it. We could have got the handwriting analysed," he said skeptically.

"That note's just the sort of thing the little sod would do."

"Jacqui, why, if Nigel had decided to kill his father anyway, did he bother to give the impression you were out of favor?"

"So that, when he'd done it, nobody would believe me when I said about us getting married. They'd think we'd had a quarrel."

It was ingenious, but Charles didn't feel very inclined to accept the reasoning. "All right then, when did Nigel do the murder?"

"Sunday evening. When he says he found the body."

"How do you know he found the body? It wasn't in the papers."

"I rang Morrison. He told me."

"Who's Morrison?"

"Sort of odd-job man at Orme Gardens. He was meant to be the chauffeur, but Marius liked driving himself. I rang Morrison and he told me Nigel had driven down to Streatley and found the body dead in bed at about quarter past eleven on Sunday night. Well, Marius never went to bed before one, so I don't believe that for a start."

"I think you may have to believe it." Charles told her about his movements on the Sunday night, concluding, ". . . so it must have been the arrival of Nigel's car that made me run out of the place."

"And you are sure Marius was dead?"

"Quite sure. He was cold. He had been dead some time."

"Perhaps Nigel had come earlier and killed him and then arranged to come back and find the body."

"I hate to sound like a detective, but there was a puddle outside the front gate and only one new set of tire-marks between the Saturday night and the Sunday night. They must have been Steen coming back on the Saturday. I know he did come back because of the new tape on the Ansaphone."

"Perhaps Nigel killed him on the Saturday night." Jacqui was desperate to hang on to her theory, but she could feel it slipping away. Charles shook his head. "I'm sorry, Jacqui, but you must face the facts. Marius had a history of heart trouble—you say he'd had a minor attack before you went to France in the summer. He was a man of 68—worked hard all his life—never made any concessions to age. Is it surprising that he should die a natural death from a heart attack? Apart from anything else, if there were suspicious circumstances, the doctor wouldn't have signed a certificate. So far as we know there's been no suspicion of foul play."

"The doctor must have been in league with Nigel," Jacqui insisted truculently.

"If there was any mark on the body, the undertaker would notice."

"There are poisons which don't leave any trace."

"Jacqui, my love"—he deliberately sounded patronising. Having chosen the role of the infinitely reasonable older man, he was determined to stick to it—"you have read too many detective stories."

That finally silenced her. She sat still for a full five minutes, then stood up brusquely. "I'll get you some food."

* * *

It was another of Jacqui's frozen meals. This time fish steaks with still-frozen centers and bright slivers of French beans. Charles consumed most of the Valpolicella and tried to steer the conversation away from anything to do with Marius Steen. It was difficult. Small talk kept erupting into some new accusation or burst of crying from Jacqui. Charles found it a strain and was relieved when the meal was over and he felt he could decently leave. "You get to bed, Jacqui. You look absolutely knackered. I'd better be off."

"Yes. Charles."

"Yes."

"Do you mind staying?"

"No. O.K." He lied. She obviously needed him, and so the awkwardness must be prolonged.

"I don't mean . . . you know . . ." she said feebly, and the waif-like expression on her strained face made it difficult to grasp immediately what she did mean. Then he realized she was referring to sex. It seemed incongruous in relation to the events of the last week.

"Of course not. No, I'll stay. As long as you need someone around."

"Just for the night. I didn't sleep at all last night. It was awful. I kept hearing things and imagining. Just tonight. I'll be all right tomorrow. Got to be. Sort out what I'm going to do about the baby. I'll have to get rid of it."

"Jacqui, you must keep the baby." Charles had long since ceased to delude himself that he had any immovable principles on anything, but he felt something approaching that on the subject of abortion. Without having a particular reason, like Catholicism, he found it unjustifiable. He tried to argue in his mind against this conviction, because he was frightened by feelings of such strength. Granted, he'd say to himself, I've never been in a situation where an abortion has been necessary. Natural caution has prevented me from getting anyone into trouble. If it happened, no doubt that principle would crumble like any other. But the instinct remained strong.

And as Jacqui's suffering face looked up at him, he knew he had said the right thing. There was relief and determination there, in spite of her words. "But I can't look after a baby on my own. I can hardly look after myself."

She sounded so plaintive that Charles laughed and Jacqui even managed a brief grin. "Don't worry"—at his most avuncular—"something'll happen."

"What? Nothing can, now Marius is dead."

"Something will happen," he repeated with a confidence whose basis he didn't like to investigate. "Now, where am I going to sleep?"

"Oh, with me. It's daft for you to get a stiff neck on the sofa when there's room in my bed."

So they settled down, Charles in shirt and underpants, Jacqui in silk pajamas, cradled in his arms. It was eight days since they had last lain on the bed together, and sex seemed as far away now as then. But this time Charles's feelings were mellower. It seemed all right that this sad and trembling body should lie in his arms. There was a lot to be said for cuddling. Now he seemed to find it even more attractive than screwing. Perhaps it was the approach of old age, sliding into impotent fumblings. As he fell asleep, Byron's lines floated through his fuddled mind.

> *We'll go no more a-screwing*
> *So late into the night,*
> *Though the heart is still as loving*
> *And the moon is still as bright.*

When he woke, he was alone in the bed. He could hear Jacqui being sick in the bathroom. It was a nostalgic sound, taking him back to the flat in Notting Hill where he and Frances had started their married life; and started Juliet; and, in a way, started living apart. Nappies boiling on the gas-stove, the sweet smell of breast milk—it all came back. "I am degenerating into a sentimental old fool," he thought as he rolled out of bed.

Jacqui came in as he was pulling on his trousers, and sat down, looking drained. "O.K.?" he asked.

"I will be. I hope I will. It's ghastly. Look." She closed her eyes grimly and pointed at the table. There was a letter which had been opened and shoved back into the envelope.

"Can I read it?" Jacqui nodded. Charles pulled the papers out. There was a short letter and a smaller envelope, which had also been opened. The letter was on paper headed "Cohn, Jarvis, Cohn and Stickley—Solicitors and Commissioners for Oaths."

Dear Miss Mitchell,
On the instructions of my client, Mr. Marius Steen, I am sending you the enclosed letter. I have no knowledge of its contents, but was instructed to send it to you as soon as I heard news of Mr. Steen's death.
Yours sincerely,
Harold Cohn

"Can I read the other one?"
"Go ahead."
He opened the envelope. The letter was written in a sprawling hand, writing that had once undergone the discipline of copperplate, but long ago broken loose from its restrictions and now spread, thick and unguarded, over the page.

2nd November
Dear Titty . . .

Jacqui was studying Charles's face and anticipating his reaction. "Marius always called me that." Charles continued reading.

If you get this letter, I am dead. So I'm sorry. The old heart or some other bit of my body has given out and fouled the system and I've gone. So that's a pity. Not because I haven't had a good run, just that I'd like the run to continue. I'm a winner and I want to go on winning. And when you came on the scene, I started enjoying my winning even more.
As you know, I wanted to marry you. Depending on when you get this letter, I may already have married you. If not, believe me, it's all I want to do. I only care about you and the little bastard in your belly. I'm sure he'll turn out better than the other one.
And the main purpose of this letter is to tell you and your beauti-

ful body not to worry. If Marius is dead, Marius will still look after you. There'll be money for you and the baby. Call him Marius.

Love,
Marius

Charles looked up at Jacqui. In her face was discomfort and sadness, but also an unmistakable gleam of triumph.

11

ENTER THE FUNNY POLICEMAN

HE THOUGHT HE MUST be going soft in the head. To have tried to help Jacqui in the matter of the photographs was illogical, but at least generous, getting her out of an awkward situation. But assisting her investigations into a perfectly natural death as if it were murder was little short of lunacy.

She had read so much into Steen's letter. Channeling all the pain of her loss into arguments to support her theory, she leapt on to the promise of provision for her and the baby, and to the sentence, "I'm sure he'll turn out better than the other one." To her mind, these proved conclusively that Marius had decided to change his will in her favor, and that Nigel had got wind of this and forestalled his father's plans by killing him. Charles put up all the arguments skepticism could muster, but somehow ended up agreeing with Jacqui that it was at least worth further investigation.

Which was why, on Thursday December 13th, he was taking Gerald Venables out to lunch. Gerald had been a contemporary at Oxford, who had read Law and acted a little. He had been elected Treasurer of the Oxford University Dramatic Society and, as such, demonstrated the prime motive of his life—an unashamed love of money. This motive led him after university away from the Theatre and into the Law. He joined a firm of solicitors specializing in show-business contract work, became a partner within five years and thereafter just made more and more money. The subject fascinated him; he always talked about money; but did it with such an

650

ingenuous enthusiasm that the effect was not alienating. At worst he was boring, in the same way that a golfer or a photographer or a dinghy-sailor or any other person obsessed by a hobby is boring.

When the Stilton was produced, Gerald undid another button of his exquisitely cut tweed waistcoat and patted his paunch beneficently. "What is it, Charles? Are you putting some work my way? I'd better warn you, my rates, which were always pretty high, are now almost beyond belief."

"I anticipated as much. It's not exactly work. I don't know how you'd define it. . . ."

"Ah, if it isn't readily defined, it's automatically at double the rate."

"Yes. It's a matter of investigation—or do I mean snooping?"

"That's what solicitors are for."

"Exactly. The point is, I know solicitors individually are totally immoral"—Gerald nodded assent as if accepting a compliment—"and I suppose, as with any other bunch of thieves, there is honor among you." Again Gerald graciously inclined his head. "So no doubt you scratch each other's backs." The third nod was very positive. "What I want you to do is to find out some information from another solicitor."

"Officially?"

"Unofficially."

"Ah. Comes more expensive."

"I thought it might."

"What do you want to know, Charles?"

"You've heard of Marius Steen, bloke who's just died?"

"Of course. Been involved in a lot of contracts with him. He was a real shark, totally immoral." Gerald's voice carried a hint of respect as he made this tribute.

"So you know his solicitor?"

"Harold Cohn. Of course. He's the hardest bargainer in the business." A diffident smile. "Present company, of course, excepted."

"Of course."

"And you want to know about the old man's will?"

"How the hell did you know that?"

"Because there's nothing else anyone could possibly want to

know about a man three days dead. There has been quite a lot of speculation on the matter in professional circles."

"Any conclusions?"

"Rumors, but nothing definite."

"Do you think you could find out?"

Gerald smiled blandly. "I wouldn't have thought it was beyond the realms of possibility." A waiter was hovering at his shoulder. "We'll have coffee, won't we, Charles? And a Cognac, perhaps. Yes, two Cognacs." He looked thoughtfully over the table. "Now I wonder why you would be interested in Steen's will, Charles. You're hardly expecting to be a beneficiary, are you?"

"No. Hardly."

Gerald looked at him, puzzled. He didn't like being in a position of ignorance on any subject, and started probing. "Whoever it goes to, there's a lot."

"Yes."

"Steen did all right. Even with estate duty, it'll be worth having."

Charles nodded, determined not to give anything away. Gerald tried another tack. "You want to find this out for yourself?"

"Yes."

"It'll be public knowledge soon. If you can only wait a few—"

"I want to know as soon as possible."

"Well, Charles, you are a dark horse." Gerald sat back in his chair and sipped his Cognac. It was amusing for Charles to see him in this state, his usual poise unbalanced by childlike curiosity. "Charles, is it a crime?"

"What do you mean?"

"Are there any suspicions about the will? Surprise heirs in Australia, forgery, skulduggery with birth certificates, secret codicils?" Gerald threw out the ideas like baits, hoping to catch some reaction. Charles smiled in a way that he knew was infuriating.

Gerald was suitably infuriated. "Oh, for God's sake, Charles. You can tell me. Look, if I know the circumstances, it'll make my enquiries much easier." Charles continued to smile. Gerald was reduced to infantile tactics. "Listen, if you don't tell me why you want to know, then I won't find out for you."

"Oh dear. Then I'll have to ask someone else."

Gerald looked rattled, but controlled himself, smiled and said,

"Charles, if there's anything suspicious, I want to know. Look, I'm a sucker for that sort of thing. Always reading detective stories. I don't know, it's a fascination. It's my hobby, if you like."

"I thought your hobby was money."

"That's my main one, but I can't resist suspicious circumstances. It's been a life-long ambition of mine to be involved in something mysterious, a crime. I don't mean the sort of official crime I deal with as a solicitor. I mean real cloak-and-dagger investigation stuff." Charles remained silent. "Listen, if you are involved in crime, from whatever side of the law, you need a solicitor. Oh, Charles, do tell me!" he burst out petulantly, but still got no reaction. "Listen, if you are investigating a crime—"

"And what on earth makes you think I am?"

"I don't know. Something about the way you're behaving. Listen, if you are, I won't charge you anything."

"You what?"

"I will undertake any investigations free . . ."

"Gerald, are you feeling all right?"

". . . so long as you let me in on all the details."

"Hmm." Charles was circumspect. It was a very good offer, an amazing offer, considering who it came from. But he himself felt so far from convinced there was any crime to investigate, that he had no desire to spread ill-founded suspicions. "Gerald," he began slowly, "if there were something fishy, and I were to tell you, could I trust your discretion?"

"Of course." Gerald was affronted. "I am a solicitor."

"That's what I mean. All right, I accept your offer."

"So there is a crime?"

"Maybe."

"All right, give me the dirt." Gerald made no pretence of maturity now. He was an eager child. Charles remembered that Gerald had always been like that. It was the same quality that made his fascination with money so inoffensive. Not for the first time Charles reflected that growing-up is a myth; getting older is just an intenser form of childhood. "I'll give you the dirt," he said, denying the child his treat, "when you tell me about the will."

"You bugger," said Gerald. But he agreed to the deal.

When the bill was brought to Charles, it was enormous. It was a long time since he'd eaten out in this style and he was shocked by the escalation of prices and VAT. "Think yourself lucky," said Gerald, as Charles counted out the notes. "If we hadn't come to an agreement, you'd be paying for my time as well."

Charles didn't tell Jacqui about their new ally in investigation when they met up that evening to report progress. He just said he'd met his solicitor friend who reckoned he could find out the details of the will.

Jacqui was in quite a state. She'd been down to Goring for Marius's funeral (having found out the time by ringing Morrison at Orme Gardens). At the church she'd ended up in the cliché situation of being frozen out by Marius's relatives. It was the stereotyped picture beloved of cartoonists—the family (Nigel and a few cousins), trim in their black on one side of the grave, and the floozy (Jacqui), in an unsuitable black cocktail dress and purple fur-collared coat, weeping on the other. The burial had been a small affair. Marius was against cremation; he wanted to lie in an English grave with a marble headstone. A memorial service in St. George's, Hanover Square, was to follow, for Steen's theatrical and business acquaintants. No one spoke to Jacqui or even acknowledged her, except for Morrison. By the end of the ceremony she was so upset that she hadn't the nerve to go to the house with the small party of mourners, and caught a train straight back to London.

However, she had managed to have a few brief words with Morrison and questioned him about Nigel's movements over the weekend of his father's death. (She assured Charles she had been subtle in her questioning, but he dreaded to think what she meant by subtlety. If there were any alarms to start, he had no doubt she'd set them jangling.) From Morrison she had found out a significant fact, which would have deterred anyone less prejudiced in their conviction of Nigel Steen's guilt. The young man's car, a Jensen Interceptor, was out of action at the relevant time. It had had brake trouble and Morrison, who was an expert mechanic, had offered to mend it over the weekend. He'd attended to the brakes on the Saturday, but then, feeling unhappy with the alignment of the wheels, had started work on them. He was a perfectionist, and the job took a long time. When he left the vehicle on the Saturday evening, all four wheels were off, and they were in that state when he returned to the job on the Sunday morning. He didn't finish work until the evening, and it was then that Nigel drove off down to Berkshire, and found his father dead. In reply to the question as to whether Nigel could have used the Datsun, Morrison couldn't say. Miss Menzies had filled it with petrol on the Friday afternoon and used it on the Monday morning. No doubt she would have noticed if it had been used in the interim.

"Who's Miss Menzies?" asked Charles.

"Joanne. Marius's secretary."

"Oh yes. I've met her. Hmm. And you actually managed to get all that information without Morrison getting at all suspicious?"

"Yes. Anyway, what if he did get suspicious? He doesn't like Nigel any more than anyone else."

It seemed to be a feature of the case that no one had a good word to say for Nigel Steen. Not having met the man, and basing his conclusions on other people's prejudices, Charles decided that young Steen's main offence was that he was not his father. From all accounts he didn't sound as if he had the spunk to be a murderer.

"Where does Nigel live?"

"I think he's got a flat near Knightsbridge, but he's never there. Spends all his time in Orme Gardens or at Streatley."

"Father's boy?"

"I wouldn't say that."

"How did they get on, Jacqui?"

"I don't know. I hardly ever saw them together, and Marius never talked about Nigel. But you've seen the letter."

"Yes. And did Joanne like him?"

"Did she like who? She liked Marius." Was there a hint of jealousy there?

"No. Nigel."

"I don't think she liked him."

"Hmm. Then I think perhaps she's due for a visitation."

Charles was making-up next morning in Hereford Road when the phone rang.

"Hello. Oh, Maurice, I was just making-up."

"What for? You working and not telling me?"

"No, just for fun. Practice."

"Well, I think it's about time you did some work. You seem to have taken the three-day week to heart too quickly."

"Three-day week?"

"Don't you read the papers?"

"I haven't yet this morning."

"Heath's going to put the whole country on a three-day week. Save power. And stop television at half-past ten in the evening."

"Really."

"Yes. Think of all the ten per cents of all those series I won't be getting. Johnny Wilson had a repeat scheduled for late evening. That'll be off."

"I'm afraid I'm not very in touch."

"I'll say. Look, you know that *Softly Softly* I said might be coming up?"

"Yes."

"Well, it hasn't."

"Oh. Thanks."

"But there is something. Had a call from the casting director of a new horror film yesterday. They're looking for someone to play this sort of deformed hunchback, part werewolf, part vampire. I told them you were made for the part."

"Thank you very much."

Silence punctuated with gasps from the other end of the line showed that Maurice was roaring with laughter at his own witticism. He always laughed noiselessly, his jaw snapping up and down as he took in great gulps of air. Charles waited until he'd recovered sufficiently to continue.

"Sorry, just a little joke. But really, it is that sort of part. They seemed quite keen when I mentioned you. Said 'Yes, we like using the old fifties stars everyone's forgotten.' "

"Thank you again. What would it involve?"

"Two weeks' filming early January—if this three-day week nonsense doesn't interfere. At some stately home. Forget where exactly, but within reach of London."

"Hmm. What's the film called?"

"The Zombie Walks!"

"Oh God. Who's directing?"

"Never heard of him. Some name like Rissole. It's being set up by Steenway Productions."

"Oh really. I'll take it. Check the dates."

"Your diary's not exactly crowded, is it?"

"Money good?"

"Goodish. I'll ask for double."

"Good lad. Thanks for that."

"My pleasure. If I don't do things for you, you're clearly not going to do anything for yourself."

"Cheerio, Maurice. Keep smiling."

"What, with my worries? Cheerio."

Work, too. And dressing-up. Charles was beginning to feel unaccountably cheerful. He rather relished the idea of secret investigations. With a jaunty step he went upstairs to his room to continue making-up.

Disguise is a matter of presenting oneself to the person deceived in an unexpected context. Then come tricks of stance and movement. Actual changing of coloring and features are less important. And Charles was quite pleased with his disguise. Certainly Joanne Menzies appeared not to recognize him, although he'd rather regretted choosing the character of Detective-Sergeant McWhirter of Scotland Yard when she revealed that she'd been brought up near the Kyles of Bute. But she seemed to accept the Glaswegian accent and his story of having left Scotland for London in his teens.

He had phoned her at Milton Buildings, saying that he had a routine enquiry to make about the Datsun, would have asked for Mr. Marius Steen but, owing to the recent regrettable happening, wondered if she could help. She was efficiently affable, and invited him to come round straight away. So there he was, on the Friday morning, sitting opposite her, in the same chair that, only a week before, Charles Paris had occupied.

Detective-Sergeant McWhirter wore a nondescript brown and green suit, a Marks and Spencer pale yellow shirt and brown knitted tie. His shoes were stout brown brogues, suitable for the tramping from place to place which takes up most of a detective's time. When he entered the room he had hung up a pale mackintosh and a trilby hat. His hair was dark brown and slicked back with Brylcreem. He had thick horn-rimmed glasses, a heavy shadow and rather bad teeth. On his wedding finger was a worn gold band. He was the sort of man nobody would look at twice. No doubt a conscientious worker; no doubt a good husband and father; but totally unremarkable.

Miss Menzies couldn't be very helpful about the Datsun, though she answered all his questions very readily. Detective-Sergeant McWhirter explained that he was investigating a robbery in Pangbourne on Saturday night. An eye-witness claimed to have seen a yellow Datsun in the area at the relevant time, and McWhirter was painstakingly investigating all of the local Datsun-owners. The local police had told him that Mr. Steen possessed such a vehicle, and he was just making a routine check on the whereabouts of the car at that time.

Miss Menzies felt certain it was in the garage at Mr. Steen's Orme Gardens house all over the weekend. When Mr. Steen rang on Friday afternoon to say he wasn't certain whether or not he was returning to London at the weekend, she had checked the petrol in the car in case he might want it.

"This was Mr. Marius Steen who rang?"

"No. This was his son Nigel. He rang to say that he was coming up to town that evening . . ."

"The Friday?"

"Yes. But that his father was still deep in his scripts, and wasn't sure of his movements. So I thought I'd better get some petrol in case Mr. Marius Steen did come up to town over the weekend. You know what it's like getting petrol at the moment."

Detective-Sergeant McWhirter nodded sagely, imagining his eleven-year-old Morris Traveller and the increasing difficulties of driving the wife and kids around. The foam rubber pads in Charles Paris's cheeks were beginning to feel acutely uncomfortable.

"I was lucky," Miss Menzies continued. "I managed to get a full tank. It's the garage I always go to."

"And the tank still registered full on the Monday?"

"Yes."

"And it wouldn't have done that if it had been driven down to Streatley and back?"

"Good heavens, no." Miss Menzies looked at him as if he was mad.

"I'm sorry," said Detective-Sergeant McWhirter stolidly. "I do have to check all the details. Some cars have a petrol gauge that stays on full for a long time. If it's not properly adjusted."

"Yes, of course. I'm sorry. The Datsun's does actually. It stays on "full" for quite a while and then drops rather fast."

"But it wouldn't stay on full all the way to Streatley and back?"

"No. It's pretty good on petrol, but not that good. Might just about make it one way without registering, but certainly not both. Anyway, nobody could have got into the garage at Orme Gardens. It's always locked."

"Of course. Sorry about all this. We have to check. I'm afraid a detective's life is mostly spent chasing up blind alleys and wasting people's time."

"That's quite all right."

"Good." Detective-Sergeant McWhirter rose to leave and then paused. "That was very good of you, to look after the petrol. Part of your normal secretarial duties?"

"I am more of a personal assistant to Mr. Steen than a secretary. I mean, I was."

There was just a slight chink in her armor and he pressed a little further. "Yes. A sad loss."

"Yes." He noticed how strained she was looking, much older than a week before. Though she was still immaculately groomed, there seemed somehow less poise about her, as if appearances remained, but the will had gone.

"So I suppose it's all up to the son now."

"I suppose so." She couldn't disguise the contempt she felt.

"Always sad for the family, this sort of thing. Is his wife still . . . er . . . ?"

"She died years ago."

"Ah. And he never thought of remarrying?"

"No, he didn't." She pronounced the words with sudden emphasis, and Charles saw clearly the situation which Jacqui's words —"She liked Marius"—had hinted at. Joanne Menzies had loved

Marius Steen. Whether the love had ever been reciprocated or consummated he didn't know—though Steen's reputation made it likely—but the new fact opened interesting avenues of thought. She loved Steen, and she was passionately against his remarriage. The controlled force of her emotion when speaking of it had been frightening. A woman with feelings of that intensity might be capable of any action if she thought the man she loved was seriously in love with someone else. It added a new dimension to the picture.

12

THE UGLY SISTERS

WHEN CHARLES GOT BACK to Hereford Road, there was a Swedish scrawl on the note pad—JERRY VENERAL RING. After a few moments' deciphering he rang Gerald Venables's number.

"Charles, look, we can't talk on the phone." Gerald was obviously taking all the detective bit to heart, and entering into it with the spirit of a child's game of Cops and Robbers. "Listen, I've found out about the 'you-know-what.' We must meet somewhere and talk."

"O.K. Where and when?"

"Two o'clock. The back bar of the Red Lion in Waverton Street."

"Why? Is it quiet there?"

"No, but you can be overheard in quiet places. The Red Lion's so noisy, nobody'll hear a word," said Gerald with complete seriousness.

"All right, Peewit."

"What do you mean—Peewit?"

"Code-name. I'll be wearing a carnation. What's the password?" Charles put the phone down, imagining the expression on Gerald's face.

He was out of costume and looked like Charles Paris when he arrived in the back bar of the Red Lion. Squeezing past the milling lunchtime crowds he found himself pressed closely between Gerald and a rather busty Australian. "Who's she?" he hissed.

"No idea. Where's your carnation?"

"That was a joke."

"Oh." Gerald sounded genuinely disappointed.

"Well, you recognize me, don't you?" Gerald was forced to admit he did. "So, what gives?" Charles shouted above the din.

"Ssh."

"What gives?" Softer.

"I beg your pardon."

"Oh, for God's sake."

Eventually, as the lunchtime crowds subsided officewards and the pub was left to a few loud tourists, they found a quiet corner and sat down with their drinks. Charles had a pint and Gerald a dry martini (Charles almost expected him to ask for it "shaken not stirred"). The solicitor looked round with conspicuous caution.

"The will is very interesting," he hissed. "Well, not so much the will as the whole situation. Basically, Nigel gets everything, but he's got a lot of it already.

"Marius Steen made over his three houses and about 75 per cent of his other assets to his son some years ago. You know, the old gift *inter vivos* dodge, to avoid estate duty."

"I'm sorry. I don't know the old gift *inter vivos* dodge. I'm very stupid about the law."

"So's everyone. That's what lawyers thrive on. What it basically means is that if someone makes a gift during his lifetime and doesn't die for a given period, that gift is free of estate duty, or partly free. There's a sliding scale. If the donor dies more than seven years after the gift, there's no duty at all payable. If he dies in the seventh year the whole duty is reduced by 60 per cent, if in the sixth by 30 per cent, and in the fifth 15 per cent." Gerald was talking very fast and fluently, as he always did on the subject of money, but Charles reckoned he had got the gist. "When was the gift made, Gerald?"

"Nearly six years ago."

"So Nigel had absolutely no motive to kill his father. In fact, it was in his interests that the old man stayed alive."

"Ah. That's it, is it?" Gerald's eyes narrowed in the manner of a thousand television thrillers. "I think you'd better tell me the whole story, Charles."

So he got the whole story, and when it was spelled out, the catalogue of suspicions and circumstantial evidence did sound pretty feeble. Gerald was clearly disappointed. "That all hinges on Nigel Steen having a financial motive to kill his father, and, as you just observed, he very positively didn't have such a motive."

"And it wouldn't have made any difference even if Marius Steen remarried?"

"It would have made a difference in the disposition of that part of the estate which hadn't been given away. But the gift of the rest couldn't be revoked. He had given away all rights in the property. You know, the freeholds were made over by deeds of gift by way of conveyance, and the—"

"Please talk English."

"All right. Basically, all of the property is Nigel's—exclusively. Marius could not have any beneficial interest in any part of it. In other words, he couldn't benefit from the property or the dividends on the shares, or any part of the gift."

"So what did he live on?"

"Interest from the remaining shares. Still quite a substantial amount, but only a tiny part of the whole."

"And how could he still live in the houses?"

"He actually paid rent."

"So if Nigel had wanted to, he could have turfed his father out of his own houses."

"Yes. Because they weren't his own houses. They were Nigel's."

"And what about the business? He still seemed in charge there."

"Only in an advisory capacity. He made no profit from any of it."

"Good God. So there again Nigel could have ousted him."

"Could have done, but wasn't daft. He knew the business depended completely on his father's skill and instinct. No, Steen had organized it all very meticulously to avoid death duties. Nigel has been an incredibly wealthy young man for years."

"How wealthy?"

"Certainly worth more than a million."

"Shit." Charles was impressed. "And if none of this had been done what sort of death duties would have been charged?"

"80 per cent."

"Blimey. The Government gets its pound of flesh, doesn't it. But Steen didn't go the full seven years."

"No, he died just before the six came up. So estate duty is only going to be reduced by 30 per cent. Makes a nasty hole in Nigel's assumed possessions."

"And certainly rules out any motive for murder."

"Yes. The only motive for killing Marius Steen could be sheer bloody-mindedness on somebody's part—a desire to make things really difficult for Nigel. Is there anyone around who hates him that much?"

Though everyone seemed to despise Nigel, Charles hadn't met anyone whose feeling seemed strong enough to amount to hatred. It was Marius Steen who inspired violent emotions, not his son. "And there's no mention of any legacy to Jacqui in the will?"

"None at all."

"Hmm. I wonder what Marius Steen's letter meant."

Charles felt depressed as he walked through Soho to Archer Street that evening. For a start there was the gloomy news he had to pass on to Jacqui. And then London itself was depressing. It was cold and dark. Display lighting was out, as Edward Heath began his schoolmasterish campaign of mass deprivation, keeping the whole country in until the miners owned up that they were in the wrong. Time would show that the campaign had misjudged the reactions of the British public. Shops were dark, cold and uninviting. Familiar landmarks, like the neons of theatres and cinemas, disappeared. It was like the blackout, which Charles could suddenly remember with great clarity. A fifteen-year-old in gray flannel wandering around London in school holidays with an adolescent's apocalyptic vision, praying that he would lose his virginity before the bombs came and blasted him to oblivion.

He took a couple of wrong turnings in the gloom and was angry when he reached Jacqui's flat. He prepared an account of the will situation to break to her brutally. There was no point in kid gloves; she had to know sooner or later.

But he didn't get the chance to drop his thunderbolt. Jacqui opened the door in a state of high excitement, more color and animation in her face than he had seen since the Steen affair started. "Charles, come in. Bartlemas and O'Rourke are here!"

William Bartlemas and Kevin O'Rourke were a legend in the world of British Theatre. They were a middle-aged couple, whose main activity was the collection of memorabilia of the two great actors, Edmund Kean and William Macready. Bartlemas had an enormous private income, and the pair of them lived in a tall Victorian house in Islington, which was filled to the brim with playbills, prints, prompt copies, figurines and other souvenirs of their two heroes. They identified with them totally. Bartlemas was Kean, and O'Rourke Macready. In theory they were writing a book on the actors, but long since the fascination of collection for its own sake had taken over and work on the collation of evidence ceased. They spent all their time travelling round the British Isles, visiting auctions and antique shops, following hints and rumors, searching for more and more relics of their idols. But they always rushed back to London for the first night of every West End show. It was a point of honor that, if they were in the country, they'd be there, sitting in the middle of the fifth row of the stalls, both resplendent in Victorian evening dress, clutching shiny top hats and silver-topped canes. Quite what their role in British theatre was, was hard to define, but they knew everyone, everyone knew them and managements even came to regard their presence on a first night as an essential good luck charm. In the camper and more superstitious regions of the theatre world you'd often hear the sentence, "My dear, Bartlemas and O'Rourke weren't there. The notices'll be up within the week."

In appearance they fell rather short of their ideals. William Bartlemas was not tall, probably only about five foot seven, but his angular body gave the illusion of height and his knobbly limbs moved with adolescent awkwardness. His head was crowned with an astonished crest of dyed hair. It had that brittle crinkly texture born of much hairdressing, and was ginger, of a brightness to which nature has always been too shy to aspire. Kevin O'Rourke was tiny, with the pugnacious stance of a jockey and all the aggression of a butterfly. He was balding, and had countered the problem by combing what remained forward in a Royal Shakespeare Company Roman Plays style. The dyed black hair was as tight as skin over his head, except at the front where there was a curly fringe like the edge of a piecrust. The two always dressed identically—a grotesque pair of Beverley sisters. Today they were in oyster grey velvet. Meeting Bartlemas and O'Rourke was an unforgettable experience, and a fairly exhausting one. They talked non-stop in an elaborate relay race, one picking up the thread as soon as the other paused for breath.

They were delighted to see Charles. He had only met them once briefly at a party, but they remembered him effusively. "Charles Paris," said Bartlemas, "lovely to see you. Haven't talked since that marvellous Bassanio you did at the Vic"—that had been fifteen years before—"lovely performance."

"Yes," said O'Rourke, "you always were such a clever actor . . ."

"Sensational," said Bartlemas. "What are you up to now? My dear, we've just been on the most shattering binge in North Africa."

"For months and months and months . . ."

"In Morocco, of course. O'Rourke disgraced himself continually. So much to drink, my dear, it wasn't true . . ."

"And Bartlemas almost got arrested more than once . . ."

"Oh, I didn't. Not really . . ."

"You did, dear, you did. I saw it all. This Moroccan policeman was watching you with a distinctly beady eye. And I don't think it was your perfection of form that intrigued him . . ."

"Well, be that as it may. We go off, we leave the collection and everything, miss all those divine first nights, just simply to have a holiday, to get away from everything . . ."

"But everything . . ."

"And we come back to hear this shattering news about Marius. Oh, it's too sad."

"Too sad. We were just telling Jacqui here, we are absolutely desolated . . ."

"I mean he was so strong. And such a chum too . . ."

"I don't know how we'll survive without him, I really don't."

"It's terrifying. If someone like Marius who was so robust . . ."

"So full of living . . ."

"If he can just pop off like that . . ."

"Then what chance is there for the rest of us?"

They both sat back, momentarily exhausted. Charles opened his mouth to speak, but missed the chance. "So of course," said Bartlemas, "as soon as we heard the ghastly news about Marius, we just had to rush round here . . ."

"Immediately," said O'Rourke. "Because of *our secret.*"

They paused dramatically and gave Jacqui time to say, "Charles, they've got a new will. Marius made another will."

Charles looked round at Bartlemas and O'Rourke. They were glowing with importance. "Yes," said Bartlemas, "we witnessed the will and he gave it to us to look after it . . ."

"Which is a pity," said O'Rourke, "because that means we can't inherit anything . . ."

"Not that he had anything we'd really like to inherit. I mean, nothing to do with Edmund and William . . ."

"No, but it would have been nice to have a little memento, wouldn't it, Bartlemas?"

"Oh yes. Yes, it would. You see, what happened was, we were in the South of France in the summer, when Jacqui and Marius were out there . . ."

"At Sainte-Maxime . . ."

"Yes. Marius's villa. Lovely spot . . ."

"Oh, lovely . . ."

"And suddenly, one night, after Jacqui had gone to bed, Marius suddenly said he was going to make a new will, and there was someone on holiday down there who was a solicitor—"

"Not his usual one?" Charles managed to slip in.

"Oh no, not dear Harold," said Bartlemas.

"No, not Harold," echoed O'Rourke. "This was a rather sweet young man Marius found in a casino . . ."

"And anyway, Marius said this boy was coming over and he was going to draw up a new will, and would we witness it? . . ."

"So of course we said yes . . ."

"Well, we were so *intrigued*. It was so *exciting* . . ."

"And we've got it with us, and we were just about to show it to Jacqui when you arrived."

"Look," said Bartlemas, and, with a flourish, produced a sealed envelope from his inside pocket. At this gesture both he and

O'Rourke burst out into riotous giggles. "I'm sorry," said O'Rourke when they had calmed down, "it's just that that was the gesture Edmund Kean is supposed to have used on the 'Is this a dagger?' speech in *Macbeth* at the New Theatre Royal, Drury Lane, in 1823."

"Oh," said Charles, as Bartlemas and O'Rourke went into new paroxysms of laughter. Again it took a little while for them to calm down and when they had, Bartlemas, with mock solemnity, handed the envelope to Jacqui. "Of course," he said conspiratorially, "we know what's in it, don't we, O'Rourke?"

"Oh yes, Bartlemas." They both sat back with smug smiles on their faces and looked at Jacqui, like favorite uncles watching a child unwrap their Christmas present.

Jacqui opened the envelope, pulled out a document and looked at the sheet for some long time. Then she looked up, perplexed. "It's all in funny English."

"That's because it's a legal document," said Charles. "They are always incomprehensible. It's a point of honor among lawyers never to be understood."

"You read it, and tell me what it means." Jacqui handed the document over.

"We could tell you what's in it," said Bartlemas.

"Yes, but we won't," said O'Rourke coyly.

Charles read the will.

I, MARIUS LADISLAS STENIATOWSKI, commonly known as MARIUS STEEN, and hereinafter referred to as such, of 173, Orme Gardens, London, W2 and "Rivalon," Streatley-on-Thames in the County of Berkshire, Theatrical Impresario, HEREBY RE-VOKE all wills and testamentary documents heretofore made by me AND DECLARE this to be my LAST WILL.

1. I APPOINT WILLIAM DOUGLAS D'ABERNON BAR-TLEMAS and KEVIN CORNELIUS O'ROURKE to be jointly the Executors of this my WILL.

2. In the event of my dying before remarriage, I DEVISE and BEQUEATH all of my real and personal estate whatsoever and wheresoever not already disposed of as to my freeholds in fee simple and as to my personal estate absolutely to the issue of my union with JACQUELINE MYRTLE MITCHELL, the property to be

held in trust for the said issue, the trust allowing a monthly sum of not less than FIVE HUNDRED POUNDS to the said JACQUE-LINE MYRTLE MITCHELL to pay for the upbringing of the said issue, this arrangement to cease on his or her attaining the age of twenty-one years, whereupon a quarter of the remaining estate— whether in freehold property, stocks, shares or chattels shall be granted in perpetuity to the said JACQUELINE MYRTLE MITCHELL, and the remainder to be granted to the said issue. In the event of the said JACQUELINE MYRTLE MITCHELL dying before the child attains twenty-one years, all of the estate shall devolve upon the said child and be held for him or her in trust, as my executors and their appointees shall advise.

IN WITNESS whereof I the said MARIUS STEEN the Testator have to this my LAST WILL set my hand this fifteenth day of October One Thousand Nine Hundred and Seventy-Three.

SIGNED AND ACKNOWLEDGED by the abovenamed MARIUS STEEN the Testator as and for his LAST WILL in the presence of us both present at the same time who at his request in his presence and in the presence of each other have hereunto subscribed our names as witnesses:

William Bartlemas

17, Ideal Road,
Islington

Keanophile
Kevin O'Rourke

17, Ideal Road
Islington

Macreadophile

Jacqui was looking at him eagerly. Obviously she had understood the gist of the will and just wanted confirmation. Charles grinned. "Basically you'll be all right. You can afford to have that baby."

"What, and the baby'll get everything?"

"Not exactly, no." And Charles explained briefly about the gift *inter vivos* to Nigel. "So what we're talking about is only 25 per cent of Marius Steen's assets other than the houses. Mind you, it's still more money than you've ever seen in your life."

Bartlemas and O'Rourke had been silent too long and burst again into stereo action.

"Ooh," said Bartlemas, "fancy all that going to little Arse-hole . . ."

"Who?"

"Nigel," said O'Rourke patronizingly. "Everyone calls him little Arsehole. Why on earth would Marius make all that over to him?"

"It's the family thing, isn't it," said Bartlemas. "Marius always wanted to found a dynasty."

"But I thought he and Nigel didn't get on." Charles was still rather puzzled by the whole gift business.

"Well, it varied, didn't it, O'Rourke?"

"Oh yes, up and down all the time . . ."

"I remember, there was a time when Nigel ran off to America . . ."

"With some woman, ghastly actress . . ."

"But ghastly. Marius was awfully upset. Nigel stayed away for two, three years . . ."

"All of that, Bartlemas, all of that. Then he came crawling back . . ."

"Tail between his legs. Woman had left him . . ."

"Who could blame her? Marius really did the prodigal son bit . . ."

"Oh yes, you couldn't move in Orme Gardens for fatted calf. All the great reconciliation, my son, my son . . ."

"It's the Jewish character, you know. Love of the family. Terribly important to them . . ."

"You're right, O'Rourke. That's what it is." This was pronounced with finality and followed by a breath pause. Charles, who was beginning to understand the technique of conversation with Bartlemas and O'Rourke, leapt in. "When was it this reconciliation took place?"

"About five or six years ago," said Bartlemas.

"Ah, that figures. It must have been then, in a final flush of family feeling, that he made everything over to Nigel."

"Yes."

"And, so far as one can tell, he regretted it ever after."

"Yes," said O'Rourke. There was a pause. "Jacqui," said Charles. "I didn't know your middle name was Myrtle."

"It was after an aunt," said Jacqui.

13

WHO DOES THE SLIPPER FIT?

THE NEW WILL was passed over to Gerald Venables, who got in touch with Harold Cohn of Cohn, Jarvis, Cohn and Stickley, and the law began the grindingly slow processes on which it thrives. Charles thought that the whole affair was now out of his hands, and, though it was unsatisfactory that so many questions remained unanswered, at least some kind of justice had been done. Nigel got most of the estate, but would be more than a little embarrassed by estate duty; and provision for Jacqui and her baby would be sorted out in time. If the police persevered, they were bound to crack Audrey Sweet's defense and find out about the family blackmailing business. Then they had only to check through the photographs and the Sally Nash guest lists (which, as the case at the Old Bailey trickled on inexorably, were becoming public property anyway) to find their murderer. Charles even felt a twinge of pity for Mrs. Sweet. She was a desperate woman, her incompetent attempts at blackmail motivated only by a desire to get as much money as possible in her new widowhood. It was now three days since Bill Holroyd had promised to bring her ten thousand pounds and by now she must realize the likelihood of his appearance was decreasing.

It was Saturday December 15th. Christmas was coming, but without much conviction in a darkened Britain. The cold shops with their sad gas-lamps were full of Christmas shoppers feeling sorry for themselves, and shoplifters having a field day. The ever-present possibility of bombs made buying presents even jollier.

Charles rose late and managed to beat one of the Swedes into the bathroom. He returned to his room wrapped cosily in his towelling dressing-gown and sat in front of the gas-fire with a cup of coffee. Now that the excitements of the last fortnight were over, he would have to think again about getting some work. True, he'd got *The Zombie Walks* coming up, but that wasn't going to make him a millionaire, and the old overdraft was getting rather overblown. Perhaps the answer was to write another television play. But, even if he could write the thing quickly, all the subsequent processes took such a bloody long time. Getting the thing accepted, rewritten, rewritten, rewritten, rehearsed, recorded, edited, scheduled, rescheduled, rescheduled, rescheduled ad infinitum. Not much likelihood of getting a commission either. Charles Paris wasn't a big enough name these days. And no doubt, with the prospects of a three-day week and early closedown, none of the television companies would commit themselves to anything.

But as he tried to think of his work (Charles had long since ceased to grace it with the name of "his career"), his thoughts kept returning to the Steen situation. There was something fishy about the whole set-up. He tried to think himself into a detective frame of mind. What would Sherlock Holmes do in the circumstances? He would sit puffing on his pipe, Dr. Watson goggle-eyed with admiration at his side, and suddenly, by a simple process of deduction, arrive at the complete solution. Somehow Charles Paris, sitting on his own in a towelling dressing-gown, hadn't quite the same charisma. Or the same powers of deduction.

Reflecting sadly on his inadequacy, Charles rose to get dressed. He opened the dull gray wardrobe and pulled a pair of trousers off a hanger. As he did so, he noticed that there was a dark smudge on the seat. It smelled of petrol. He was about to put his trousers back and take out another pair, when a sudden thought stopped him in his tracks.

The trousers he was holding were the ones he'd been wearing at Streatley the previous weekend. And he must have got the mark on them when he slipped over in Steen's garage. The scene came back to him with immediate clarity of detail. The enormous bulk of the blue Rolls illuminated by his torch, then suddenly his feet going from under him, slipping in a pool of petrol, landing on a spanner and a piece of tubing.

A piece of tubing. And the Rolls petrol gauge registered empty. Joanne Menzies' words about the Datsun came back to him—"It's pretty good on petrol, but not that good. Might just about make it one way without registering, but certainly not both." But what was simpler than to drive the car to Streatley, siphon petrol out of the Rolls into it (possibly even siphon some into a can as well, to top it up near London) and then drive back? Charles decided that a visit should be paid to Mr. Nigel Steen.

Joanne Menzies still looked drawn and strained when she ushered Detective-Sergeant McWhirter into Mr. Steen's office on the Monday afternoon. The policeman thanked her and stood deferentially until he was invited to sit down.

The man who made the invitation was very like his father, but without the vitality that had distinguished Marius Steen. Nigel had the same beak of a nose, but, without the dark eyes, its effect was comic rather than forceful. His eyes were blue, a legacy from the English rose whom Marius had married; and his hair was light brown rather than the black which his father had kept, only peppered with gray, until his death. The general effect was of a diluted Marius Steen, ineffectual and slightly afraid.

Nigel was ostentatiously smoking a big cigar to give an illusion of poise. He flashed Charles what was meant to be a frank smile. "Well, what can I do to help?"

"I'm very sorry to bother you," said Detective-Inspector Mc-Whirter slowly, "and I do very much appreciate your putting yourself out to see me. Particularly at what must be a very distressing time for you."

"That's quite all right. What is it?" With a hint of irritation, or was it anxiety?

"I have already spoken to your secretary on the matter and she proved most helpful." Charles reiterated his lies about the theft in Pangbourne on the Saturday night.

"But you see, since I spoke to her, we have had another witness's account of having seen a yellow Datsun in the Goring area. And they identified your number plate. I mean, you can never trust members of the public; they are extraordinarily inaccurate in what they claim to remember, but I can't discount anything. All I'm trying to do is to establish where your father's Datsun was on that night, and then stop wasting your time."

"Yes." Nigel drew on the cigar and coughed slightly. He was clearly rattled. Not a man with a strong nerve, and certainly on the surface not one who could carry out a cold-blooded murder. He capitulated very quickly. "As a matter of fact, I was in Streatley in the Datsun on that Saturday night."

Charles felt a great surge of excitement, but Detective-Sergeant McWhirter only said, "Ah."

"Yes. I'd phoned my father in the evening, and he didn't sound too well, so I drove down to see how he was."

"And how was he?"

"Fine, fine. We had a few drinks together, chatted. He seemed in very good form. Then I drove back to London."

"Still on the Saturday night?"

"Yes. It's not far."

"No, no, of course not." Charles was about to ask about the subterfuge of the full petrol tank, but decided that Detective-Sergeant McWhirter might not be in possession of all the relevant facts for that deduction. As it happened, Nigel continued defensively without needing further questions.

"You're probably wondering why I didn't mention this fact before. Well, to tell you the truth, your boys asked me when had I last seen my father alive and I said Friday instinctively, and then by the time I'd realized my mistake, it was all written down, and, you know, I thought if I changed it, that'd only create trouble."

It sounded pretty implausible to Charles, but Detective-Sergeant McWhirter gave a reassuring nod. "Yes, of course, sir. And you're quite sure that while the car was down in Streatley, the thieves who I'm after wouldn't have had a chance to take it and use it for their break-in?"

"No, that would be quite impossible. I put the car in the garage and I'm sure I'd have heard it being driven off. Anyway, I wasn't down there very long."

"No. Oh well, fine, Mr. Steen. Thank you very much." Detective-Sergeant McWhirter rose to leave. "I think I'd better start looking for another yellow Datsun."

"Yes. And . . . er . . . Detective-Sergeant . . ."

"Yes?"

"Will you have to mention the discrepancy in my story—you know, my confusion about when I last saw my father—?"

"Good Lord, no. That's quite an understandable mistake in a moment of emotion, sir. So long as an account's written down somewhere, no one's going to fuss about the details. After all, there wasn't anything unusual about your father's death. If there had been any grounds for suspicion, it'd be a different case." And Detective-Sergeant McWhirter laughed.

Nigel Steen laughed too, Charles thought a bit too heartily. But perhaps he was being hypersensitive and letting his suspicions race like Jacqui's.

"Anyway," the Detective-Sergeant continued, "I don't have anything to do with your father's death. Different department, you know."

"Yes, of course."

"Well, good-bye, Mr. Steen. And thank you again for your help. If only more members of the public were as cooperative as you have been, our life would be a lot easier."

They shook hands. Nigel's felt like a damp facecloth. Detective-Sergeant McWhirter went through into Miss Menzies's anteroom. "All sorted out now?" she asked brightly.

"Yes, thank you, Miss Menzies."

"Hmm. We've seen quite a lot of you lately."

"Yes," said the Detective-Sergeant casually, unprepared for what happened next.

Miss Menzies suddenly stood up, looked him straight in the eyes and said, "Do you know it's a very serious offence to impersonate a police officer?"

"Yes," said Detective-Sergeant McWhirter slowly, waiting to see what came next.

"I rang up Scotland Yard to tell you something this morning, and they'd never heard of you."

"Ah."

"And from the start I thought your accent was a bit phoney. I know a lot of people who come from Glasgow."

"Yes." There was a pause. Then Charles continued, still in his discredited Glaswegian. "Well, what was it you rang up the Yard to tell me?"

Joanne Menzies looked at him coolly. "You've got a nerve. But I think you're probably doing something I'd sympathize with, so I'll tell you. I checked with Morrison, the chauffeur at Orme Gardens, and he was suspicious that the Datsun may have been used on the Saturday night."

"Yes, I know. I've just got that from Mr. Nigel Steen."

"Ah." She sounded disappointed that her information was redundant. "You're suspicious of him too, aren't you?"

"Maybe."

"No maybe," she said, "you are. Incidentally, 'Detective-Sergeant,' what's your real name?"

"Charles Paris."

"Ah." Her eyes widened and she nodded slowly. "Very good." It was a warming compliment, from someone who knew about the theatre. "Well, Charles, if there's anything else I can tell you, or I can find out for you, let me know."

"Thanks." As he was leaving, he turned and looked at her. "You hate Nigel Steen, don't you?"

"Yes," she said simply.

Christmas intervened and the business of investigation was suspended. Charles told Jacqui the new information he'd gleaned, but met with little luck in following it up. When he rang Joanne to check Nigel's movements in the week before Steen's death, a strange female voice answered and informed him that Miss Menzies had already gone up to Scotland for her Christmas holidays. Gerald Venables was getting a very slow response from Cohn, Jarvis, Cohn and Stickley on the matter of the new will, and also seemed preoccupied with family arrangements and Christmas drink parties. His enthusiasm for the cloak-and-dagger business of detection seemed to have waned.

Charles felt his own sense of urgency ebbing too. Though he got excited at each new development in his investigations, he soon became disillusioned again. And Joanne's seeing through his disguise made him a bit wary. He had no particular desire to break the law. Detection was a serious business, and perhaps he should leave it alone. The days of the gifted amateur investigator were over. It was better to leave everything to the police, who with superior training and equipment must stand a greater chance of uncovering crime.

And each time Charles looked at his progress it seemed more negative. Though he had enjoyed his little investigations and masquerades, his only real discovery was that Nigel Steen had tried to disguise the fact of driving down to Streatley on the night of Saturday December 8th. And though the visit could have given him an opportunity to kill his father, and then drive down the next day to discover the body, that was the one crime which every logical motive screamed against. By killing Marius then, Nigel would have been sacrificing a great deal of money. Duties at 80 per cent on an estate of a million, only reduced by 30 per cent, because of the donor's death before the end of the sixth year (to borrow Gerald Venables's terminology) would mean that Nigel would be paying more than half a million in estate duty. Whereas if he only waited till the seven years were up, all the given property would be his without any tax. It's a rare character who commits murder in order to lose a million pounds.

And the only other fact, hanging around in the background, was Bill Sweet's death, which, by some fairly dubious reasoning and some circumstantial evidence, could be laid at Marius Steen's door. But Marius Steen was dead. Why bother him now?

The Montrose was open over Christmas and so, along with a lot of other divorced and debauched actors, Charles Paris spent a week sublimely pissed.

He was feeling distinctly drink-sodden when the phone rang on the morning of January the 3rd, 1974. He wanted to be picked up and wrung out like a floor cloth to get the stuff out of his system.

He lay in bed, hoping the phone would go away or someone would answer it. But the Swedish girls were still in Sweden for the holidays and he was alone in the house. The phone went on ringing.

He stumped savagely downstairs and picked up the receiver. "Hello." His voice came out as a croak.

"It's Jacqui." Her voice was excited again, bubbling. "Charles, I've been to the police."

"What?"

"About Nigel. I went to Scotland Yard this morning and saw an Inspector and told him all about our suspicions, and about how we knew Nigel had been down at Streatley that Saturday—"

"I hope you didn't tell him how we found out."

"No, I didn't. I didn't mention you at all."

"Thank God for that."

"Anyway, the Inspector said it all sounded very suspicious and he's going to authorize an aupopsy—"

"Autopsy."

"Yes. Anyway, he's getting an order to have Marius exhumed and check the cause of death. He took everything I said very seriously." The last sentence was pronounced with pride. There was a pause; she was waiting for him to react. "Well, what do you think, Charles?"

"I don't know. In a way, I think it's asking for trouble . . ."

"Oh, Charles, we've got to know whether or not Marius was murdered."

"Have we? It's all sorted out. The baby's being looked after . . ."

"Charles, do you mean that?"

"No."

"We've got to know."

"Yes. When's the exhumation to be?"

"Quite soon. Probably next Monday."

"And when will the results be known?"

"End of next week. There should be an inquest on Friday."

"You realize that, by doing this, you have virtually made a public accusation of murder against Nigel?"

"Yes. And that is exactly what I meant to do."

* * *

Ten days passed. In America, with the tide of Watergate rising around him, President Nixon celebrated his sixty-first birthday. In England wild storms swept the country, and commuters were infuriated and inconvenienced by the ASLEF dispute. Housewives started panic buying of toilet rolls. And in a churchyard in Goring, the body of Marius Steen was moved from its grave after a stay of only four short weeks. Then it was opened up and samples of its organs were taken and analysed.

All of these events, international and domestic, seemed unreal to Charles. Since sobering up after Christmas he had degenerated into a deep depression. Inactivity and introspection left him lethargic and uninterested in anything. His usual solutions to the problem—drink and sex—were ineffectual. He drank heavily, but it gave him no elation, merely intensified his mood. And his self-despite was so strong that he knew reviving an old flame or chasing some young actress would only aggravate it. He tried to write, but couldn't concentrate. Instead he sat in his room, his mind detached, looking down on his body and despising what it saw. Forty-seven years old, creatively and emotionally sterile. He thought of going to see Frances, but didn't feel worthy of her warmth and eternal forgiveness. She had sent him four stout dependable Marks and Spencer shirts for Christmas, nursing him like a mother who respects her child's independence. He'd sent her Iris Murdoch's latest novel. In hardback, which he knew she'd think an unnecessary extravagance.

His only comfort was that the following Monday he was to start filming *The Zombie Walks*. Though he didn't view the prospect with any sort of enthusiasm (he'd been sent a script, but hadn't bothered to read it) he knew that activity of some sort, something he had to do, was always better than nothing. Eventually, if enough kept happening, the mood would lift without his noticing its departure and he would hardly remember the self-destructive self that went with it.

But as he walked through the dim streets of London to Archer Street on the Friday evening, the mood was still with him. He felt remote, viewing himself as a third person. And he had a sense of gloom about the findings of the inquest.

When Jacqui opened the door of her flat, he knew from her face that his forebodings had been justified. She was silent until he'd sat down. Then she handed him a glass of Southern Comfort and said, "Well, that's that."

"What?"

"According to the coroner, Marius died of natural causes."

"A heart attack?"

"They had some fancy medical term for it, but yes, that's what they said."

"Well." Charles sighed. He couldn't think of anything else to say. Jacqui looked on the verge of tears, and, as usual, converted her emotion into a violent outburst. "Little Arsehole's been clever, the sod. He must have given Marius an electric shock, or injected air into his veins, or—"

"Jacqui, you've been watching too much television. That sort of thing just doesn't happen. I'm afraid we have to accept the fact that Marius did die from natural causes, and that all our suspicions of Nigel have been slander, just based on dislike and nothing else."

"No, I don't believe it."

"Jacqui, you've got to believe it. There's nothing else you can do."

"Well, why did he go down to Streatley on the Saturday night, and make such a bloody secret of it?"

"I don't know. Perhaps for the reasons he said. He was worried about his father, so he went down, they had a few drinks, then he came back to London."

"Oh, for Christ's sake, that won't wash."

"Why not?"

"He and Marius didn't get on at the time. We know that from the new will and the letter to me and—"

"Perhaps they had another reconciliation."

"Piss off, Charles. There's something fishy and Nigel's behind it. Marius was murdered."

"Jacqui, the most sophisticated forensic tests have proved that he wasn't."

"Well, they're wrong. They're all bloody wrong. Nigel paid them off. He bribed them."

"Now you're getting childish."

"I am not getting bloody childish!" Jacqui stood up and looked as if she was about to hit him. Charles didn't respond and after a frozen pause, she collapsed into a chair and burst out crying. When he had calmed her, she announced very coolly. "I'm not going to stop, Charles. I'll get him. From now on there's a war between Nigel and me."

"Well, you certainly nailed your colors to the mast by setting up the post-mortem."

"Yes. And I'm going to win." Thereafter she didn't mention anything about either of the Steens for the rest of the evening. She cooked another of her frozen meals (country rissoles) and Charles drank moderately (a rather vinegary Spanish Rioja). Then they watched the television. She had just bought (in anticipation of her legacy) a new Sony portable ("I'll be sitting about a lot when I get very big"). There wasn't much on the box, but that night it was preferable to conversation. At ten-thirty, by Government orders, came the closedown. Charles rose and after a few mumbled words about thanks, and keeping in touch, and being cheerful, and seeing himself out, he left.

Jacqui's flat was on the top floor and the bulb in the light on her landing had long since gone and not been replaced. As Charles moved forward to the familiar step, he felt his ankle caught, and his body, overbalancing, hurtled forward down the flight of stairs.

The noise brought Jacqui to the door and light spilled out over the scene. "Charles, are you all right? Are you drunk, or what?"

He slowly picked himself up. The flight was only about ten steps down to the next landing, and though he felt bruised all over, and shocked, nothing seemed to be broken. "No, I'm not drunk. Look."

And he pointed up to the top step. Muzzily outlined in the light was a wire, tied tightly between the banisters on either side. It was about four inches above the step. Jacqui turned pale, and let out a little gasp of horror. "Good God. Were they trying to kill me?"

"No!" said Charles, as he leaned, aching, against the wall at the foot of the flight. Suddenly he realized the flaw in the will Marius Steen had so hastily improvised in the South of France. "I don't think it was you they wanted to kill. Just your baby."

14

SLAPSTICK SCENE

THE ZOMBIE WALKS was one of the worst film scripts ever conceived. The Zombie (played by a well-known Horror Film Specialist) had walked for a thousand years in a subterranean cavern which was broken open by an earthquake in Lisbon. By means not specified, from Portugal he arrived in Victorian England, where he got the idea that Lady Laetitia Winthrop (played by a "discovery" from the world of modeling, whose acting talent was 36-23-36) was his long-lost love from a world before the subterranean cavern. He therefore determined to seize her from Winthrop Grange where she lived with her father Lord Archibald Winthrop (played by a well-known character actor who did commercials for tea bags). After the Zombie's travels through Victorian London (where, incidentally, he committed the crimes attributed to Jack the Ripper) he arrived at the Grange and enlisted the help of Tick, a deformed coachman of evil character (played by Charles Paris). As the Zombie progressed, he committed murder after murder, and his victims, rather than dying and lying down, became zombies too, until at the end Winthrop Grange was besieged by a whole army of the walking dead. Had it not been for the activities of Lady Laetitia's lover, bold Sir Rupert Cartland (played by an odious young actor who'd risen to prominence by playing a tough naval lieutenant in a television series) making with the garlic and the wooden stakes (a bit of vampire lore crept into the script), Lady Laetitia and her father would have been turned into zombies and carried back to the subterranean cave, where they would never be heard of again. Which, to Charles's mind, wouldn't have been a bad thing.

They were filming at Bloomwater, a stately home in Berkshire which had been built by Sir Henry Manceville, an eccentric noble-man, in 1780. Manceville had designed it himself as a great Gothic palace and even incorporated the specially-built ruins of an abbey into one wing. It was a monumental folly, which could have been made for horror films. In fact, had the cinema been invented at the time, it probably would have been. Sir Henry Manceville had been obsessed with ghosts and, in later life, when his eccentricity slid into madness, he used to terrify his servants by walking the Long Gal-lery, dressed in a sheet, dragging a length of chain and wailing piteously.

Bloomwater's present owner was a more prosaic figure, Sir Lio-nel Newman, the paper magnate. He was a man who, like Marius Steen, had risen from humble origins to immense wealth and had surrounded himself with all the symbols of the established aristoc-racy. His association with Marius Steen had been the reason why Bloomwater was being used for the filming.

Charles found that, as ever, making a film involved much more hanging around than actual work. The director, a little Cockney who glorified in the name of Jean-Luc Roussel, generated an im-pression of enormous activity as he buzzed around checking cam-era angles, getting the lighting changed, demonstrating the special effects and bawling out the continuity girl. But very little actually seemed to get done.

Charles didn't find many sympathetic characters among the cast. The Horror Film Specialist was surrounded by an admiring coterie of lesser horror film specialists and most of their conversation re-ferred back to previous triumphs. ("Do you remember that *Dracula* when your fang got stuck in the girl's bra?"; or "I'll never forget that girl who had hysterics during that human sacrifice"; or "Do you remember that take as the Werewolf when you forgot your line and said 'Bow-Wow'?") They all sat around, reminding each other of things they all remembered, each waiting his cue for the next reminiscence to be slotted in.

So Charles went off on his own most of the time. He sat in the Library (later to be the scene of the appallingly-written quarrel between Lord Archibald and Sir Rupert) and did the crossword or played patience.

On the Wednesday morning of the first week of the schedule he was sitting with the cards spread before him and feeling fairly secure. The film world still has an outdated generosity in its dealings with actors. The big-spending Hollywood myth retains its influence and the Zombie cast were well looked after by Steenway Productions, with cars organized to get them to and from the set. The early starts were a disadvantage, but Charles had minimized that by staying with Miles and Juliet and having the car pick him up at six. Then he could sleep through the drive and the laborious business of make-up. Quite cozy. And the money was good.

He also felt as secure as he could about Jacqui. The shock of the trip-wire incident had worn off and she was fairly well hidden. He'd wanted to send her off to some relative in the country, but she didn't seem to have any family. In fact, when they went into it, it was amazing how few people Jacqui had to call on. No family, or at least none she kept in touch with, no girlfriends. The center of her life had always been men, either one at a time or many. A lot of girls end up promiscuous, when all they're looking for is friendship. Jacqui's lack of other resources explained both her desolation when Steen seemed to have dropped her and her reliance on Charles. (Even her leaping into bed with him again. She needed to keep up her continuity of male companionship, and humbly thought she had nothing to offer but sex.)

Charles had considered parking her on Frances in Muswell Hill, but the incongruity of the thought of the two women together was too great. So in the end he had given her his keys to the room in Hereford Road. He felt fairly confident that Nigel Steen, or whoever was mounting the campaign against her, did not know of any tie-up with Charles Paris. Hereford Road was dangerously near Orme Gardens, but it was only a short-term solution while the film lasted. Jacqui was likely to stay in most of the time with her portable television; her pregnancy made her quite content to do so. Obviously she'd have to go out to the shops from time to time, but she'd had her hair dyed black on the Saturday, bought a new winter coat and a large pair of dark glasses. That should keep her safe. Charles could imagine Jacqui quite happy in her enforced confinement.

Hers was not a demanding character, and so long as she felt some evidence of a man's care (which living in Charles's room would give her) she would not need more. When the Zombie had finished his walk, a more permanent method of protecting her for the next four months would have to be found.

They'd considered going to the police, but agreed that, after the embarrassing *débâcle* of the inquest, further accusations from Jacqui against Nigel Steen would sound more like the ramblings of a paranoid than anything else. It was safer for her simply to go underground. Charles rang daily to check everything was all right.

So he felt secure as he sat looking over the rolling lawns of Bloomwater. To add to his pleasure, the patience came out. He was just laying the cards down for another game, when he heard the door open behind him. He turned and the girl who had just come in let out a little scream.

For a moment he couldn't think what was worrying her, until he remembered his make-up. His own hair was hidden under a latex cap from which a few gray wisps straggled crazily. His eyes were red-rimmed and sagging, his nose a mass of pustules, and his teeth had been blacked out with enamel. The whole face had the unearthly green tinge of dead flesh, which Jean-Luc Roussel was convinced was the mark of a zombie.

"I'm sorry," said Charles. "I'm afraid I do look rather a fright."

"Oh, that's all right. I just wasn't expecting it." The girl looked about sixteen and recently aware of her considerable attractions. Her black hair was swept back in the careless style that only the most expensive hair-dressing can give. She was wearing check trousers and a red polo-necked sweater that accentuated the perfect roundness of her bra-less small breasts. For the first time in over a month Charles felt certain that he hadn't lost interest in sex.

"I take it you're in the film," said the girl.

"No, I always look like this. You're making fun of my natural affliction."

The girl was checked for a moment, then laughed. "That's not fair. Who are you?"

"I am Tick, the deformed coachman," he said in his First Witch voice ("Macabre in the extreme"—*Plays and Players*).

She laughed again. Obviously she was still at an age to be

amused by funny voices. Charles felt distinctly inclined to show off. "No, who are you really?" she asked.

"Charles Paris."

"Oh, I think I've heard of you," she said, polite but uncertain. "Ooh, just a minute. Were you ever at the Royal Shakespeare Company at Stratford?"

"Yes, a long time ago."

"About seven years?"

"Yes."

"Did you play Cassius in *Julius Caesar?*"

"Yes."

"Ooh. I thought you were marvellous. We went in a school trip. We all got quite silly about you."

"Oh," said Charles, in what stage directions describe as a self-deprecating manner. This was all rather playing into his hands. Seeds sown unknowingly long ago. Cast your bread upon the waters, and it will come back buttered. "Who are you then?"

"I'm Felicity Newman. I live here. Daddy owns this place." (The "Daddy" caught the slight quack of an English girls' public school. It was a sound Charles had always found exciting.) "I'm fascinated by all this filming. Somebody's going to show me round, a friend of Daddy's. I want to work in films."

"With your looks I should think you'd stand a very good chance."

"No, silly." She was still sufficiently girlish to blush at the formula compliment. "Not that side of films. The production side. I'm doing a secretarial course and want to get in that way. Daddy knows quite a lot of people in the cinema."

Yes. Charles felt sure that Daddy could pull the odd string on his daughter's behalf. Sir Lionel Newman put a great deal of money into film production. Charles even had a feeling that he was a major shareholder in Steenway Productions. "And how come you're not doing your secretarial course today?" he asked in the Morningside accent which he had drummed into the cast of his production of *The Prime of Miss Jean Brodie* ("Slow-moving"—*Evening Argus*).

She giggled. "Oh, I just took the day off. How do you do that Scottish accent?"

She was easily impressed, but Charles felt like indulging himself in a little *tour de force*. He went through his entire gamut of the accents of Scotland, from his Hebridean fisherman through to the harsh tones of Glasgow. Indeed, he was in full flood in his Detective-Sergeant McWhirter voice, to an accompaniment of giggles from Felicity, when he heard a voice behind him. "Ah, there you are."

He stopped in mid-flow and turned to see Nigel Steen standing in the doorway. Steen looked annoyed, but it was difficult to tell whether or not he had recognized the voice. "Felicity. I'm sorry to have kept you. Shall we start our tour?"

"Yes. Certainly, Nigel." She was suddenly downcast, obviously sharing the world's lack of enthusiasm for Marius Steen's son. "Do you know Charles Paris?" she asked.

"No, I don't think we've met," said Nigel Steen, and he looked at Charles intently.

The scenes to be shot were rescheduled and Charles didn't in fact do anything that day. When this truth, which had been apparent from early morning, was finally recognized by Jean-Luc Roussel and Charles was released, it was about five o'clock. In a state of some exasperation, he was about to organize his car back to Pangbourne, when Felicity appeared round the corner of one of the make-up caravans. "Hello," she said brightly, "do you fancy a drink?"

It was exactly what Charles did fancy (or at least part of what he fancied), so he said so. "Come on," said Felicity, and led him round the back of the house and through a herb-garden into a large modern kitchen. "This is the part of the house we actually use. The rest's just for show." She led him upstairs to a homely-looking sitting-room, and opened the drinks cupboard. "What?"

"Scotch, please."

She took out a bottle of Glenfiddich and poured a wine-glassful. "Hey. Stop."

"Why?"

"It's an expensive malt whisky."

"I know," she said superciliously, and passed him the glass. He took a long sip. It was very welcome. Felicity still looked rather piqued at his assumption of her ignorance of drink lore. He tried to open out the conversation. "Still keen on films after seeing them in action for a day?"

"Yes," she said shortly, and then, to show her sophistication in the matter of alcohol, "I think I'll have a gin and tonic."

"So it was a good day?" Charles knew he sounded horribly patronizing.

"All right. The company could have been better."

"Nigel Steen, the great impresario."

"Shit," she said unexpectedly. "He's a creep, always has been. I've known him for years. Daddy knew Marius. I think they had plans for matchmaking. Yeugh."

"Not your type?"

"God, no. I don't know what my type is really, but it's not that. Ergh. He made a pass at me once. It was horrible, like being groped by liver. Actually, he invited me out tonight, probably with an ulterior motive. I told him I was otherwise engaged."

"Are you?"

"No. Not unless you'd like me to cook you a meal."

"Oh well . . . I'm sure that you don't want—"

"It's no sweat. I'm doing this Cordon Bleu course as well as the secretarial thing, and I need the practice."

So they both agreed to show off for the evening. She demonstrated her culinary skills with a splendid Chicken Kiev and Dauphinoise potatoes, and he kept her entertained with a variety of accents and theatrical reminiscences. Felicity raided her father's cellar for a couple of bottles of an excellent Château Margaux. "He'll never notice. Doesn't know a thing about wine. Just takes advice all the time."

"Where are your parents?"

"Oh, they've gone to Jamaica. As soon as all these lighting restrictions came in, Daddy said he wasn't going to stay in England and they pissed off." Felicity's lapses into strong language, which were meant to make her sound cool, only made her sound immature. But appealing.

Charles found it very difficult. This girl was plainly throwing herself at him, and he knew that if he took advantage of something so easy, he would really feel shabby. And she looked sixteen. Possibly even under age. There is a point where going around with younger women stops and cradle-snatching begins. And Charles prided himself that he had never knowingly taken advantage of anyone (anyone, that is, who didn't deserve it).

It would have been easier if he hadn't found her attractive. Usually the sort of woman who makes such blatant advances is eminently resistible. But in Felicity's case, she was not impelled by the plain girl's need to take the initiative, but by youthful enthusiasm and social immaturity. Charles was determined to resist her.

But as the alcohol warmed and relaxed him, he could feel lust beginning to take the upper hand. When he had finished her excellent chocolate mousse, he made an immense effort of will, and rose to his feet. "I think I'd better be off now. I'm doing my big scene tomorrow. Perhaps I can ring for a minicab."

She didn't move. "What's your big scene?"

"My death. The death of Tick, the deformed coachman shot down by Sir Rupert Cartland, as he rushed along the gallery to capture the abysmal Lady Laetitia Winthrop."

"You needn't go."

"I must." Well done, Charles. The Festival of Light would be proud of you.

Felicity rose very deliberately from the table, walked towards him, and pressing her body close to his, kissed his lips. Charles stood like a carved idol receiving the homage of the faithful. He gave nothing. "I think I had better go."

"Why?" She used that word disconcertingly often.

"Well, I . . . um . . . you know . . ." It was difficult to think of a good reason at a moment like this.

"If you don't find me attractive, you can say so. I'll survive."

"It's not that. You gotta believe me, it's not that." He dropped into American to hide his confusion.

"Are you worried about my age?"

"Yes. Amongst other things."

"Listen, Charles. I am eighteen, which is not only two years above the age of consent, but is also now the age of majority. And I'm on the Pill, so you needn't worry about that."

Her frankness was very confusing. Charles felt himself blushing. "Um . . . you mean, you're not a virgin?"

Her short derisive laugh made him feel suitably patronised. "Charles, I lost my virginity when I was twelve, and since then quite a few other things have happened." The weakness of the ending of her sentence again revealed her youth.

Charles could feel his resolve slackening, but made one last effort. "I'm too old for you, Felicity."

"You're not as old as the man who had me first."

"Oh. Who was he?"

"Marius Steen."

The next day Charles was feeling elated. He had parted from Felicity on good terms after breakfast; she had returned to continue her courses. He'd rung Jacqui, and she was fine. To crown the day, he was going to film the death of Tick, the deformed coachman, and he enjoyed a bit of ham as much as any other actor.

They rehearsed the scene in the morning. Tick crept in through the window of the dining room and surprised Lady Laetitia Winthrop playing at her virginals (a likely story). He carried a rope with which to bind her. When she saw him, she let out a little cry (that bit took ages to rehearse: every bit that required Lady Laetitia to do more than flash her tits took ages), then turned and ran to the end of the room. Tick cried out, "Not so fast, my proud beauty!" (really), and pursued her. She ran up the stairs to the minstrels' gallery with Tick in breathy pursuit. (That was filmed in long-shot from the other end of the room.) Then a quick close-up of Lady Laetitia cowering panic-stricken against the wall. (That took a long time too. "For Christ's sake," said Jean-Luc Roussel, "panic-stricken, not bleeding constipated! Imagine he's going to cut yer tits off!") Then a long-shot from behind Sir Rupert Cartland's shoulder as he forced open the dining-room door, saw the scene of Tick advancing menacingly on his beloved (or "that silly bitch," as he always called her off the set), raised his pistol, cried, "No, you monster" and shot the deformed coachman. Tick stopped and staggered. Cut to close-up of blood trickling from his face as he fell against the rail. Cut to shot of stuntman falling backwards over rail to the floor.

When the rehearsal was finally over, they adjourned for lunch in the billiard room, where the covers on the tables had a splendid buffet laid on them. Charles piled up his plate and sat on his own in the corner. To his surprise, two men came over and joined him. They were called Jem and Eric; he recognized them; they'd been around since the filming started. Jem was one of those burly figures who proliferate on film-sets. His role was ill-defined except to himself and other members of his union, but he spent most of his time carting scenery around and moving heavy props into position. Eric was a smaller, colorless man who worked in some clerical capacity in the production office. They never said much on the set except to each other. Nobody took much notice of them or expected them to start up any form of conversation, so Charles was surprised when Eric addressed him by name.

"Yes?"

"There's a bit of a query on your contract," said Eric in his flat London voice. "Been a typing error on some of them. Maybe on yours. Anyway, we want to send a duplicate just in case. It doesn't change anything."

"O.K. Fine."

"Don't seem to have your address. Where should we send it to?"

Charles gave him the address of Maurice Skellern Artistes.

"Oh, we want it signed quickly. Wouldn't it be better if we sent it to your home?"

"No. My agent deals with all that kind of stuff."

"Oh. Oh well, fine. We'll send it there then." And Jem and Eric wandered off.

It gave Charles an uncomfortable feeling. True, it might be a genuine enquiry, but it could be Nigel Steen relating him to Jacqui for the first time. If so, a new hiding-place must be found quickly. Yes, it was fishy. If a new contract had to be signed urgently, why hadn't Eric brought it to him there and then, rather than posting it? Still, there was a bit of breathing space. Maurice would never give away the Hereford Road address and very few people knew it. Even friends. Charles hated the place so much he always arranged meetings in pubs, and never took anyone there. But the incident was disquieting.

He soon forgot it as the filming restarted. It was painfully slow. Lady Laetitia had forgotten all she'd been taught in the morning and everything had to be rehearsed again. Charles felt he would scream at another repetition of "Not so fast, my proud beauty!" But progress was made and, shot by shot, Jean-Luc Roussel was satisfied. ("Not bleeding marvellous, but it'll have to do if we're going to get it all in before the bleeding electricians have their bleeding break.")

Eventually Lady Laetitia and Tick made it to the minstrels' gallery. Then there was a long break as the cameras were set up for the dramatic shot over Sir Rupert Cartland's shoulder. Make-up girls fluttered in and out with powder puffs. Electricians looked at their watches and slowly pushed their arc lights about. Jem handed Sir Rupert his props. Sir Rupert complained that one of the buckles on his shoes was loose (the shot was only going to reveal his right ear and shoulder). Eventually all was ready. *"The Zombie Walks: Scene 143, Take One"*—the clapper-board clapped shut. Tick advanced on his prey cowering constipated against the wall. The doors of the dining room burst open. Sir Rupert Cartland cried, "No, you monster," and a shot rang out.

Charles Paris felt a searing pain as a bullet ripped into his flesh. He crumpled up in agony.

15

POOR OLD BARON!

CHARLES REALLY THOUGHT he was dying when he woke up the next morning. Cold tremors of fear kept shaking his whole body. It wasn't the wound that worried him, though his arm still ached as though a steam-hammer had landed on it. Head and body felt disconnected and the foul taste in his mouth seemed to his waking mind a symptom of some terrible decay creeping over him from within.

For once it wasn't alcohol, or at least not just alcohol. The Battle Hospital in Reading had given him a sedative to take if necessary when he was discharged. The wound was clean and dressed; there was no point in keeping him inside with such a shortage of hospital beds. So the film company organized a car to take him from Reading to Pangbourne. Jean-Luc Roussel himself had come to the hospital and fretted and fluttered about like a true Cockney sparrow. Steenway Productions was very anxious about the injury; it is the sort of thing all film companies dread, because it inevitably leads to enormous claims for compensation.

They had tried to find out how the accident had happened. The gun was a genuine late-Victorian revolver (another anachronism in a film so full of them that its period could be any time between 1700 and 1900). How live bullets had got into it no one could imagine. The props people said they hadn't touched it; it had come like that from the place of hiring. The hiring firm were very affronted when rung up, and assured the film company that they only ever supplied blanks. No doubt a further investigation would follow.

The thought of substantial compensation didn't comfort Charles much. It was the taste of death in his mouth that preoccupied him. He staggered out of bed and cleaned his teeth, but the taste was still there. He put his hands on the marine blue wash-basin and his body sagged forward. The face in the mirror of the marine blue bathroom cabinet looked terrified and ill. Partly he knew it was last night's sedative, coupled with a large slug of Miles's Chivas Regal. Coming after the sleepless night spent with Felicity, it was bound to affect him pretty badly. But more than that it was the shock, a feeling that left his body as cold as ice, and sent these involuntary convulsions through him.

He started to dress, but almost passed out with the pain from his arm. To steady himself he sank down on the side of the bed. At that moment, Juliet came into the bedroom. "Daddy, are you all right? I heard you moving and—"

Charles nodded weakly.

"You look ghastly," she said.

"I feel it. Here, would you help me get dressed? This bloody arm . . . I can't do anything."

Very gently his daughter started to help him into his clothes. As she bent to pick up his trousers, she looked just like Frances. "Daughter and wife whom I'll leave when I die"—the phrase came into his maudlin thoughts and he started crying convulsively.

"Daddy, Daddy."

"It's just the shock," he managed to get out between sobs.

"Daddy, calm down." But his body had taken control and he couldn't calm down.

"Daddy, get back to bed. I'll call the doctor."

"NO . . . I can't go back to bed, because I've got to get to London. I've got to get . . . to London. I've got to get to London." Suddenly the repetition seemed very funny and his sobs changed to ripples of high-pitched giggles. The situation became funnier and funnier and he lay back on the bed shaken by deep gasps of laughter.

Juliet talked calmingly to no avail. Suddenly her hand lashed out and slapped his face. Hard. It had the desired effect. The convulsions stopped and Charles lay back exhausted. He still felt ill, but the hysterics seemed to have relaxed him a bit. Juliet helped him back under the bedclothes. "I'm going to get the doctor," she said, and left the room.

Charles dropped immediately into a deep sleep where lumbering Thurber cartoon figures with guns in their hands chased him through a landscape of pastel green, dotted with red flowers. There was no menace in their attack. He was running hand in hand with a girl who was Juliet or Felicity, but wearing Frances's old white duffel coat. They stopped at a launderette. The girl, whose face was now Jacqui's, clasped his arm and said, "It's a pity the *Battleship Potemkin* is booked for Easter." She kept hold of his arm and shook it till it became elastic and extended out of its socket like a conjuror's string of handkerchiefs.

"Mr. Paris." Charles opened his eyes warily, disgruntled at being dragged out of his dream. "Mr. Paris. I am Doctor Lefeuvre."

"Hello," said Charles sleepily.

"It's rather difficult you not being one of my regular patients, but since your daughter is, I'm stretching a point. She's told me about your accident yesterday, but I gather that's not what's troubling you?" The voice had a slight Australian twang. Charles looked at Doctor Lefeuvre. A man in his mid-thirties with dull auburn hair and a freckled face behind rectangular metal-rimmed glasses. He had very long hands, which were also covered in freckles and sported three gold rings.

"I don't know, Doctor. I just feel very weak and ill."

"The arm's all right?"

"It feels bruised, but that's all."

"Only to be expected. Let's just have a look at the dressing." He cast his eye expertly over the bandage on Charles's arm. "It's been very well done. When are you due to go back to the hospital?"

"They'll change the dressing next Monday."

"That seems fine. I won't meddle with it then. But otherwise you're feeling run down and ill. It's probably just shock."

"Yes."

"I'd better have a look at you." And the doctor began the time-honored ritual of taking temperature and pulses. In fact, Charles felt better now. His body had regained some warmth and the sleep had relaxed him. He just felt as if he'd run full tilt into a brick wall.

Doctor Lefeuvre looked at the temperature. "Hmm. That's strange."

"What?"

"You seem to have a slight temperature. Just over a hundred. That's not really consistent with shock. Let's take your shirt off. There. Not hurting the arm?"

"No."

"Hmm." The doctor started probing and tapping. "Let's have a look at your throat. Open. There. Tongue down. No, down. Yes. Is your throat at all sore?"

"A bit. Sort of foul taste in my mouth."

"Yes. Hm. That's strange. You haven't been in contact with German measles recently?"

"Not to my knowledge, no."

"No. Hmmm. Because, on a cursory examination, I would say that is what you've got. There's a slight rash on your chest, hardly visible. The temperature and the sore throat are consistent."

"Oh. Well, what should I do about it?"

"Nothing much. It's not very serious. If you're feeling bad, stay in bed. It'll clear up in a couple of days. You don't have to rush back to work, do you?"

"No, they've reorganized the shooting schedule."

"Oh." Doctor Lefeuvre obviously didn't understand what that meant, but equally obviously it didn't interest him much either. "Look, I'll prescribe some penicillin." He scribbled on his pad. "You'd better check with Battle Hospital, tell them you're going to take it. Just in case they want to put you on something else."

"Fine."

"Good. Oh. I'd better just have your address and National Health Number for the records." Charles gave them, digging the number out of a 1972 diary which was so full of useful information he'd never managed to get rid of it.

"Right." Doctor Lefeuvre gathered his things together and prepared to leave.

"So there's nothing special I should do? Just rest?"

"Yes. You'll feel better in a couple of days. The rest won't do the arm any harm either."

"O.K."

"Oh, there is one thing of course with German measles."

"Yes."

"You mustn't be in contact with anyone who's expecting a baby. If a woman gets German measles while she's pregnant, it can have very bad effects on the unborn child."

Charles dressed with Juliet's help (he didn't like staying in bed alone) and rang Jacqui as soon as the doctor had left. He didn't mention the "accident" at Bloomwater because it would only upset her. In fact, she sounded particularly cheerful; it was the first morning she had woken up with no trace of sickness, and was cheered at the thought of entering the "blooming" phase of pregnancy. No, nothing disturbing had happened. Nobody had rung. She was quite happy in her little prison.

Charles felt fairly confident of her safety for the time being. Though the shooting on the film set, if it wasn't accidental, implied that Nigel Steen knew of his involvement, he still might not have realized the direct connection with Jacqui, and certainly was no nearer getting the Hereford Road address. But she would have to be moved soon. Charles determined to ring Frances and ask her to take the girl in. It would be a strange coupling, but Frances wouldn't refuse. He explained to Jacqui about the German measles.

"Oh no, for God's sake keep away from me," she said. "The child is born blind or something terrible."

"Don't worry. I'll stay away."

"How long are you infectious?"

"I should be better in two or three days. But I don't know how long the quarantine period is. It's probably just as well I haven't been near you for the last week. Don't worry though. I won't come back till I'm quite clear of it. I'll ring Doctor Lefeuvre and check."

"Who?"

"Doctor Lefeuvre."

"Australian?"

"Yes."

"Good God."

"Why. Do you know him?"

"Yes. He was the one who did my abortion in the summer."

"What? But it wasn't a legal one, was it?"

"No. Marius got Nigel to fix it up?"

"Was Lefeuvre the family doctor?"

"I suppose so. Marius didn't talk about doctors. He kept saying he was never ill."

"So it was probably Lefeuvre who was called in when Marius died."

"Yes, it was. He was at the inquest."

"He was? Jacqui, for Christ's sake. Why didn't you tell me this before?"

"I didn't think it was important. Is it?"

"Jesus!" But there was no time to explain. And no point in worrying her. "Jacqui, just sit tight. Don't worry about anything." He slammed the phone down. "Juliet, can I have your car keys? I've got to go up to London immediately."

Juliet emerged dazed from the kitchen area. "But you can't take the Cortina. Miles'll be furious."

"I haven't got time to worry about Miles. Give me the keys."

Juliet was amazed by the sudden force of his personality and held out the keys, as if hypnotized. "But, Daddy, you can't drive with that arm."

"I bloody can."

16

BACK AT THE FIRESIDE

BEING BACK IN LONDON was a disappointment. The mad drive up the M4 with pain like barbed hooks turning in his arm had all been for nothing. He had screeched to a halt in the residents' parking bay in an unimpressed Hereford Road, let himself in, banged on his own door and, keeping his distance, ordered Jacqui to go off to the pictures for the afternoon. Then he'd driven round to the surgery of Drs. Singh and Gupta, with whom he was registered, only to find that both were out on their rounds. He rushed to St. Mary's Hospital, Paddington, and, after the hours of waiting that are statutory in hospitals, finally persuaded a callow houseman to examine him and pronounce him clear of German measles. It was evident from the young man's circumspect excitement that he thought he'd got his first genuine schizophrenic hypochondriac. Charles ended up with a clean bill of health and a parking ticket.

As he sat in his drab room in Hereford Road, it all seemed a bit futile. The dark fears of the morning had subsided into childish fantasies. He felt he should be watching the road from behind the curtains, waiting for the badmen to arrive at High Noon, while in the background a voice intoned "Do not forsake me, O my darling." But since his windows faced the back of the house, it was impossible. And in the familiar banality of his room thoughts of approaching badmen seemed ridiculous. He just felt tired and ill again. The excitements of the day had put him back considerably. Pain throbbed in his arm with agonizing regularity. He felt himself drifting asleep.

Suddenly the phone rang. Swedish feet in wooden sandals clumped down the stairs past his door, then up again, paused, knocked, said "Telephone" and continued back to their room.

He went down and picked up the dangling receiver. "Hello."

"Hello. It's Joanne Menzies."

"Oh. Hi."

"Charles, can we meet and talk? About Marius's death."

"Yes, sure. Have you got anything new?"

"Not really. But I'm just convinced there was something fishy going on."

"Yes. There are a lot of things that don't fit. When do you want to meet? After work?"

"I'm not at work."

"Oh."

"I came back after Christmas to the news that my services were no longer required by Mr. Nigel Steen. A year's salary in lieu of notice."

"That's a substantial pay-off."

"Yes. Hush-money, no doubt. Where shall we meet?"

"Do you mind coming round here? I'm not very well."

"Fine. What's the address?" Charles gave it. "I'll be round straight away." He put the phone down and had a moment's doubt. Was he wise to give Joanne Menzies his address? She seemed straight enough, but her motives weren't absolutely clear. Oh well, if she told Nigel Steen, fair enough. Charles's suspicions of Dr. Lefeuvre made him think his address was already common knowledge. At least he was here now, and could supervise moving Jacqui to another hideaway. He rang Frances's number to make his strange request, but there was no reply. It was only five o'clock. No doubt she was supervising the school debating society or another of her public-spirited activities.

Joanne Menzies arrived quickly and they started talking over a glass of whisky. Charles gave the shortest possible explanation of his sling—"an accident on the film set." He didn't want to voice any suspicions until he felt a bit surer of Joanne's allegiances. "So. What do you think is fishy?"

"No one big thing, Charles. Just a lot of dubious details."

"Like . . . ?"

"Like the way Nigel lied over that Saturday night, all the subterfuge over the petrol in the Datsun. Like the way he's been behaving since his father's death—and the week before, come to that—"

"How's he been behaving?"

"Very twitchy. Jumps whenever the phone rings. As if there's something he's frightened of."

"What else?"

"The way I've been dismissed. All right, I was Marius's personal assistant and there's no reason to assume that Nigel would want to take me over in the same role. But it was rather sudden. And a year's salary is excessive—out of character too for someone as mean as Nigel."

"Hmm. So you think that Nigel murdered Marius?"

"That's the obvious thing to think."

"Except for the findings of the inquest."

"Yes." Joanne spoke with the same contempt Jacqui had shown for the high achievements of forensic science.

"And the fact that Nigel had no motive. It was in his interests that his father should live at least until the seven years were up." Joanne's face revealed that she didn't know about the gift, so Charles gave a brief résumé of the legal position. He finished up, "You know, we are not the only people who are suspicious of Nigel and would attribute any crime to him. But the fact remains that, in the matter of Marius Steen's death, we have not a solitary shred of evidence to go on. Just prejudice and dislike."

"Yes. I'm sure he's done something, though." Her conviction was reminiscent of Jacqui's, overriding little details like facts.

"All right, Joanne, let's talk through it all again. Actually, one thing you said interested me. You said Nigel was twitchy the week before the murder—I mean, the death."

"Yes."

"I thought he was in Streatley that week."

"Only part of it. He went down on the Thursday to go through some business things with Marius, then came back on the Friday late afternoon—just after you came round about your play. Was that another blind, by the way?"

" 'Fraid so."

"Why?"

"Too complicated to explain." He didn't want to bring in the Sweets and the implied charge of murder against the dead man. "So look, let's trace through the movements of the two of them. Where were they on the Sunday, that'd be what . . . ?"

"The 2nd of December."

"Right."

"I think they were both in Orme Gardens. Then Marius drove to Streatley that night to read the scripts on his own?"

"Was that unexpected?"

"No, he'd been talking about it. He'd noticed a slight waning in the receipts on *Sex of One* . . . though I think it was just the power crisis and the railways. Anyway, he felt he had to make a decision on the next show for the Kings."

"And when he did one of these script-reading sessions, he used to cut himself off completely?"

"Yes. Just switch on the Ansaphone."

"I see. So when did you last speak to him?"

"Small hours of Sunday morning. At the *Sex of One* . . . party."

"Oh yes. A thousand performances. Ugh. Let's continue their movements. Marius is in Streatley. Where's Nigel, say on the Monday morning? Milton Buildings?"

"No, he came in after lunch."

"Was that unusual?"

"No. Particularly considering the late night we'd all had on the Saturday."

"Right. Incidentally, how was Marius at the party?"

"In marvellous form—leaping around like a boy of twenty. Dancing with all the girls." The pride was evident in her voice.

"Including you."

"Yes."

"You loved him, didn't you?"

"Yes."

"Did you know he was contemplating remarriage?"

"I knew."

"Did you mind?"

"Yes, but if it made him happy . . . If Marius wanted something there was no point in trying to stop his getting it."

"No." Her answers sounded perfectly honest. "Let's continue

our tracing movements. Which car did Nigel go down in on the Thursday?"

"His own. The Interceptor. It was after that that he complained about the brakes to Morrison."

"Right. And then he goes down again in secret on the Saturday in the Datsun. The Datsun, the Datsun. You know there's something at the back of my mind about that Datsun and I can't think what it is." He looked round the room for inspiration. It was an untidy mess. Jacqui's occupation hadn't improved it; she wasn't the sort of girl who immediately revolutionized a place and gave it a woman's touch; she just spread her belongings over the widest possible area. A flouncy negligée and a pair of tights lay over one chair; the tiny television was perched on another; a soggy packet of frozen spinach lay beside the gas-ring; on the crumpled candlewick of the bed an *Evening Standard* was open at the entertainments' page so she could decide which film to go and see.

A thought suddenly illuminated Charles's brain like a flash of lightning. "That's it. The *Evening Standard*."

"What?" Joanne was left floundering as his mind raced on. Very clearly he saw himself standing in the BBC Club with Sherlock Forster and hearing the name of Marius Steen, the name that had come to dominate his life. When was that? It was a Monday. Yes, Monday the 3rd of December. After that terrible play. And what had the paper said? Something about Marius not using the Rolls, but sticking to the Datsun. Oh, if only he could remember the details.

There was one person who could help. Johnny Smart, who'd been at Oxford with him and edited one of the university magazines, landed what seemed then an amazing job on the *Evening Standard*. In the years since he'd sunk into alcoholic indifference in the same job, which at his present age was less amazing. With a murmured excuse to Joanne, Charles rushed to the telephone and rang the paper. Fortunately Johnny was still there—a stroke of luck considering that the pubs were open. In rather breathless fashion, Charles explained that he wanted to find out who researched and wrote an article about the petrol crisis in a late edition on Monday 3rd of December.

Johnny thought he could probably find out. It was bound to be one of the young reporters. Why didn't Charles come down and join them at Mother Bunch's? A lot would be down there at this time of night. He'd be there himself except that the newsroom was on sodding tenterhooks waiting to see if Heath would call a sodding snap election and they'd have to bring out a sodding slip edition. He'd be down in half an hour though.

Just as Charles put the phone down, Jacqui returned. She had been to see *Enter the Dragon* and started to tell him all about the code of *kung fu* as he hurried her upstairs. Joanne recognized Jacqui the moment the dark glasses came off and Charles felt the room temperature drop as the two women faced each other. Still, he hadn't time to worry about that. Leaving strict instructions to Joanne to stay there at all costs and to both of them under no account to let anyone in, he hurried to the Cortina and set off for Fleet Street.

Reporters are proverbially heavy drinkers, and it took a few bottles of *bonhomie* with Johnny Smart before Charles could actually get down to the business for which he had come. He sat in the broad circle of young journalists in Mother Bunch's Wine House and, with the rest of them, sank glass after glass of red wine. Eventually Johnny drew him to one side with a shock-haired young reporter who sported horn-rimmed glasses and a velvet bow tie. His name was Keith Battrick-Jones. Charles explained his mission.

"Bloody hell," said Keith Battrick-Jones. "Done a lot of stories since then. I don't know if I can remember that far back. When was it?"

"Monday December 3rd. Six, seven weeks ago. It was a sort of round-up of people's reactions to the petrol crisis. Pictures and comments. There was Steen . . ." The boy looked blank. ". . . and some footballer . . ." Still blank. ". . . and a leggy girl on a bike—"

"Oh shit. I remember. Yes. Crappy idea, wasn't it? Somebody thought of it at an editorial conference, and Muggins here had to ring round all these celebrities to get comments. As usual, the interesting people told me to piss off, and I ended up with the same old circle of publicity seekers."

"Can you remember phoning Marius Steen?"

"No, I don't think I can. If it was Monday morning, I must have had a skinful the night before. No, I . . . oh, just a minute though. I remember. I rang through and I got some old berk being facetious on an Ansaphone. So I told the machine what it was about, and moved on to a golfer and one of the Black and White minstrels."

"But Steen did phone back?"

"Yes. Made some fatuous comment about using the smaller car. Well, we'd got a library picture of him, so we put it in."

"And you are sure it was Marius Steen himself who spoke to you?"

"I don't know. I've never met the bloke."

"Was it the same voice as the one on the Ansaphone?"

"Oh no. It was much more cultured. And younger."

17

THE BROKER'S MEN

CHARLES HAD A LOT of wine inside him as he drove along the Strand on his way back, but he was thinking with extraordinary clarity. Suddenly Nigel had two secret trips to Streatley to explain, not one. If he had been at the *Sex of One . . .* party, he must have driven down some time between the small hours of the Sunday morning and when he rang Keith Battrick-Jones on the Monday morning. That was, of course, assuming that he had gone down on his own. It was possible that he had been in the Rolls with his father on the Sunday night.

If that were the case, and Charles's other conjecture was correct, he must have witnessed Marius shooting Bill Sweet on the roadside at Theale. That might well explain the twitchiness which Joanne had noticed during the ensuing week. Possibly Nigel had shot Bill Sweet himself? But no, that was nonsense. He had nothing to do with the Sally Nash affair, and the Sweets represented no threat to him. If anyone had committed murder on the lonely turn-off from the M4, it must have been Marius.

At Hyde Park Corner, a taxi traveling from Knightsbridge suddenly cut across the front of the Cortina and Charles had to slam on all his brakes. The shock jarred every bone in his body and he felt as if he was about to pass out. There was nothing else coming. He swung the car across the yellow line and stopped by the marble colonnade at the roadside. His body was in agony. Slowly the total blinding pain broke down into individual centers of hurt. First there was his arm, with its bone bruised by the bullet. That pain seemed to swell and swamp the others. Then there were the bruises on his knees and elbows that he'd received from the fall over the trip-wire at Jacqui's. And then, lower down the league of pain, there was the dull ache of an old bruise on his ankle.

Suddenly, he saw in his mind the utility room at Streatley and a scattered pile of boxes. Some words of Gerald Venables reverberated in his head. Dr. Lefeuvre's role came clearly defined into focus, and Charles Paris knew what Nigel Steen's crime was.

As he walked up the stairs at Hereford Road, he was glowing with the intellectual perfection of it. Not the intellectual perfection of the crime—that was a shabby affair—but the intellectual perfection of his conclusion. Suddenly, given one fact, all the others clicked neatly into position. As he drove back, he had tried each element individually, and none of them broke the pattern. He was looking forward to spelling it all out to Jacqui and Joanne. Actual evidence was still a bit short on the ground (burning the vicious letter to Jacqui and the Sweet photographs had shown a regrettable lack of detective instinct). But he felt sure facts would come, now the basic riddle was solved.

The door of his room was open, the lock plate hanging loose. A cold feeling trickled into his stomach as he went inside. It was dark. He switched on the light. A body lay tied, gagged and struggling on the floor by the bed. Joanne. There was no sign of Jacqui.

He fumbled with the knots of Jacqui's tights which had been tied cruelly round Joanne's mouth. She gave a little gasp of pain as he tightened to release them, and then she was free to talk. "Two men . . . someone must have let them in the front door . . . they took Jacqui . . ."

"Did you see them?"

"They had stockings over their heads. One was big and burly, the other was smaller . . ."

"Yes. I know who they are." He cut her other bonds free with a kitchen knife. "Come on. We must follow them."

"Where to? How do we know where they've gone?"

"I think it's Streatley. And I pray to God I'm right. For the sake of Jacqui's baby."

18

KING RAT

THEY ROARED DOWN the M4, fifty miles an hour limits contemptuously ignored. They swung off the motorway at Theale, past the
scene of Bill Sweet's death, and on, through the dark roads, past
Tidmarsh, Pangbourne, Lower Basildon, towards Streatley. About
a mile outside the town, the Cortina suddenly lost power and pop-
popped to a stop at the roadside. "Sod it. Bloody petrol. The whole
case hinges on it, and I forget to fill up."

"He might have a spare can," said Joanne. But there was nothing in the boot. Miles's odious efficiency was absent when actually
needed. "I'll have to walk the rest." Charles started off into the
gloom.

"What shall I do?" Joanne's voice floated after him.

"Get the police." He stumbled on, occasionally trying a little
jogging run. His body ached all over and the wounded arm felt as if
it were dropping off. The strain of the last few days was beginning
to tell, and he knew he hadn't got much energy left. If it came to
violence, he wasn't going to do too well. He didn't relish facing Jem
and Eric (he felt sure it was they who'd carried Jacqui off).

Sweat trickled down his sides in spite of the cold. His clothes
were heavy and awkward. Still the road seemed to stretch onwards
endlessly, darkness replacing darkness, as he staggered forward.
Occasionally a car would pass, fix him like a moth in its headlights,
and then vanish.

Eventually he was at the top of the slope that led down to the little towns of Streatley and Goring, separated, like their respective counties of Berkshire and Oxfordshire, by the River Thames. Revived by the proximity of his goal, Charles hurried painfully onwards along the road to the familiar white gates. It occurred to him that being on foot was probably an advantage; a car drawing up on the gravel would be heard from the house. And in his position he needed advantages.

He opened one gate slowly, trying not to let it scrape on the gravel. Then he moved round on to the flowerbed at the side of the path, to muffle his footsteps. The house looked quiet and the same, except for a strange car parked by the front door. Again, as on the previous occasion, there was a chink of light from Marius Steen's bedroom. Was it possible that Charles's previous luck could be repeated and he'd find the door to the utility room open? Keeping to the lawn, he crept silently to the back of the garage, moved in close to the door and felt for the handle.

He closed his eyes, uttered a silent prayer and turned the knob. For a moment the door seemed firm, but then, blissfully, it gave.

He sidled into the utility room, treading with remembered caution, and reached for the light switch. The room had been tidied since his last visit. All the tins and boxes were neatly on their shelves, and, thank God, the torch was still in its place. He took it and started to put into action a plan that had half-formed in his mind during the run from the stranded Cortina.

He locked the door by which he had entered and put the key in his pocket. Then he turned his attention to the door that opened into the garage. There was no lock on that one. For a moment he stood, defeated, but then, memory working overtime, he moved into the garage, opened the door of the Rolls, and shone his torch over the dashboard. With a small grim smile of satisfaction, he went back to the utility room and looked at the power switches. He closed his eyes and memorized their positions. Then one by one, with a series of quick movements, he switched them all off. He scurried into the safety of the great car.

There was a murmur of voices from the room above, then the slow sound of people feeling their way downstairs and towards the garage. The faint glow of a match shone through the door from the house. Charles shrank into the deep upholstery of the Rolls's front seat.

There were two voices, a deep slow one, and a higher London whine. Jem and Eric, as he'd thought. They went into the utility room. Charles heard the scrape of a match, then a muttered curse. With another prayer, he turned the key in the ignition of the Rolls. It started immediately. He found first gear and eased the great machine slowly forward until it hit the utility room door, closed it, and pinned it fast. Then he pulled on the hand-brake and leapt out.

The hammering of Jem and Eric followed him, as he rushed upstairs with the torch to Marius Steen's bedroom. As he entered it, one of the prisoners found the switches, and the lights came on again.

The scene which they revealed was an ugly one. On the bed, Jacqui lay unconscious. She was on a sheet, naked with her legs spread apart. Another sheet was crumpled over her thighs. On either side of her, blinking in the sudden light, were Nigel Steen and Dr. Lefeuvre. Laid out on a cloth on a stool were a row of bright instruments. A scalpel gleamed in the doctor's long freckled hand.

Nigel was the first to speak. "Charles Paris . . . You are taking a very great risk."

"Nothing to some of the risks you've taken, Steen."

There was a silence. Nobody moved. Then came the sound of renewed battering from downstairs. Dr. Lefeuvre dropped his scalpel with the other instruments, gathered them up in the cloth and put them in his bag. "I'm leaving, Steen."

Panic flashed into Nigel's face. "You can't do that. I need your help."

"No, Steen. Get out of this one on your own."

"You've got to help me."

"No."

"You did the other things for me."

"Not for you. For money."

"I'll tell the police what you've done."

"I think that unlikely. It might involve too much explanation of your own activities. Anyway, I will have left the country by then. I'd planned to go back to Australia when I'd made enough. And, thanks to you"—he tapped the case—"that time's come."

"But—"

"Good-bye, Steen." Dr. Lefeuvre left the room. Neither Charles nor Nigel spoke as they heard his footsteps on the stairs, the slam of the front door, the gates being opened, and his car departing in a scurry of gravel.

"What do you want, Paris? Money?" said Nigel Steen suddenly.

"No."

"I could give you a lot. I'll pay for silence."

"And then set your thugs on me the first time my back's turned. No, thank you."

"Then what do you want?"

"Just to talk. See if what I think is correct—until the police come."

"I see. Come through here."

Nigel Steen led Charles, with what was meant to be a lordly gesture, into the study next door. He sat behind the desk and offered the older man a plush leather seat. "Well now," in deliberately even tones, "what is all this about the police? Shouldn't I be calling them to get you, as a common house-breaker?"

"You could try, but I think they'd find your case more interesting."

"Do you? Why? What are you accusing me of? The inquest has already proved I didn't murder my father."

"I know. That's not what I am accusing you of."

Nigel's face went pale. "What are you accusing me of then?"

"I'll tell you. Stop me if I'm wrong. This is the story as I see it. On Saturday December 1st, your father Marius Steen went to the party on stage at the King's Theatre to celebrate the one thousandth performance of *Sex of One and Half a Dozen of the Other*. He enjoyed the party, danced, drank and generally had a whale of a time.

"The following day, Sunday December 2nd, your father, because of his exertions, suffered a second heart attack, and died. You, with a shrewd sense of your own advantage, realized that you were now liable to pay one hell of a lot of estate duty on your father's gift to you because of his inconvenient death; but that if he had died a fortnight later it would be six and not five years since the property was made over to you. If you could maintain the illusion that your father was still alive for another fortnight you would be saving—say the property was worth one million—about £240,000. A quarter of a million pounds has been the motive for far worse crimes than the one you contemplated.

"Obviously, you needed help. And it was to hand. Dear Dr. Lefeuvre, who had already arranged at least one abortion for you, was always susceptible to bribery, or, if not that, to blackmail. All he had to do was to come round when you called and sign the death certificate with all particulars correct. Except the date.

"Now there was a problem, of course. The police might want to see the body; the undertaker certainly would. How to preserve it? Why not the good old deep-freeze? Keep the old man in there, get him out in good time to defrost, maybe even put him in a hot bath to remove any traces of his preservation. And there you are.

"So, late on the Sunday night, with your father's body propped up in the Rolls, you drive to Streatley, move a few boxes out of the deep-freeze and put your father in. On the Monday, after making one mistake by phoning the *Evening Standard*—and I can sympathize with your reasons for that mistake; after all, it was a heaven-sent opportunity to assert your father's continued existence—anyway, after that you get a train back to London . . . I'm guessing there, but it's not important.

"So it was all set up, and your father's known habit of shutting himself up with his scripts made the deception all the easier. The only fly in the ointment was Jacqui. If she kept on trying to contact your father, it could be awkward. Still, she was on her own, and not very brave. A little intimidation should keep her quiet. An anonymous letter, and, when that didn't work, Jem and Eric doing her flat over. Easy.

"On the Thursday you return to Streatley, to maintain the myth of your father's continuing business interests; and perhaps to check a few details with Dr. Lefeuvre. Or even to put the pressure on him, maybe?

"Then on the Saturday, something rattles you. You lose your nerve, drive down to Streatley in secret, change the tape in your father's Ansaphone, prepare the body and move your whole schedule forward a week. That, I must confess, is the bit I don't understand. By doing that you made the whole crime worthless. You were losing money. No doubt you had your reasons.

"But when the new will came to light, you were liable to lose even more money. So, seeing the flaw in its hastily drawn up provisions, you started your vendetta against Jacqui's child, a vendetta that Dr. Lefeuvre was about to complete when I arrived. No doubt, before that you used the cruder talents of Jem and Eric. Certainly, when you realized my connection with the case at Bloomwater, they were the bully-boys you turned on to me.

"Well, I think that sums up most of my conclusions. How am I doing?"

He looked up at Nigel Steen. The man's face was white and mean and he was pointing an automatic pistol at Charles's chest. But he still tried to maintain some shreds of panache. "Very good," he said slowly. "How did you know about the boxes in the freezer?"

"Ah, I must confess I have been in this house before. Just before your dramatic discovery of your father's corpse, I . . . er . . . fell over the boxes. They were heavy and had the words 'Do not refreeze' written on them, but I didn't immediately realize the significance of that. Sorry. I was a bit slow on the uptake."

"I see. Well, since I am going to kill you anyway—an intruder in my house, I met you, drew my gun; you attacked me and in the ensuing fight the gun went off, unfortunately killing you—I—"

"If that's as successful as your other crimes, I think I'm fairly safe."

"Quiet!" Nigel waved the gun. "Let me fill in the details. One thing you were wrong about is the extent of my crime. The things you describe could be classed as fraud and harassment maybe, but in fact there is a murder involved."

"Yes, I know." Steen looked at him open-mouthed, robbed of the drama of his pronouncement, as Charles continued, "Bill Sweet's murder."

"Whose?"

"Bill Sweet, the man who was found shot dead at Theale."

"Oh, was that his name? I didn't know."

"You mean you didn't know his connection with your father?"

"No. Was there one?"

"What happened, Steen?"

"We came off the M4 and suddenly there was this maniac in the middle of the road, flagging us down. I swerved to avoid him and hit his silly little car. I tried to drive on, but he came at me with some story of having run out of petrol. Then he looked in the car, saw my father crumpled up and started to speak. I panicked and shot him. I went through his pockets—for some reason they were full of dirty pictures. I took them and his wallet and threw the lot, with the gun, into the river."

"Why his wallet?"

"To disguise his identity. I don't know. I panicked. I wanted to forget all about him—pretend it hadn't happened."

"And that's why you haven't moved the Rolls since that night. You even left your father's keys in it. You seem to do rather a lot of panicking, don't you? Not a very impressive criminal."

"If my plan had worked, it would have been a masterstroke. To save a quarter of a million—that's the sort of thing my father used to do." The envy in his voice was almost pathetic.

"But you could never do what your father did, could you, Nigel? Business, women, even crime. You just never made it." Nigel Steen's knuckles whitened around the gun and Charles uttered another silent prayer. He seemed to be getting very religious all of a sudden. "Because you never had the guts to carry anything through," he continued. "Why didn't you carry this one through?"

"Because of you, you little sod." Nigel spat the words out.

"Me?"

"Yes, you and your bloody Detective-Sergeant McWhirter business. When you rang up that Saturday and checked the registration of the Rolls, I thought the police were on to the Theale murder."

"Good Lord." Charles had completely forgotten about the first entrance of McWhirter. It came back to him vaguely. And that had actually ruined Nigel's crime. Charles could have chosen any excuse for the phone call and it was pure chance that he had lighted on the meaningless "number-plate racket!" "So that's what made you drive down in the Datsun, and move the plan forward, and lose a quarter of a million pounds?"

"Yes."

"Good Lord." Charles was absolutely flabbergasted, but he hadn't really got time to analyse his reactions. Nigel was still pointing a rather businesslike gun at him. "Nigel, I'd put that thing away. The police are coming. You stand a chance as things stand at the minute. They need never find out about Sweet's murder. Just get you on the other charges."

"I don't believe you, Paris. You're bluffing. There aren't any police coming."

"There are." Charles prayed that he was speaking the truth. "Joanne Menzies is getting them."

"So, she was involved with you. The bitch."

"I think you'd better hand that gun over, Nigel." Charles rose to his feet.

"Don't move! I'll shoot you!" Nigel held the gun away from him, as if he was afraid of the bang it would make. Charles felt himself sweating.

He tried desperately to control his voice. "No, Nigel, you won't shoot me. This is cold blood, Nigel. Something you've got to think about. Not like shooting Sweet in a moment of blind panic. Not like doing it by remote control, having Jem set up a trip-wire. This is you committing a crime, Nigel."

The two men faced each other. Their eyes were interlocked and the gun pointed directly at Charles's heart. The pause seemed endless.

Suddenly the doorbell rang. Nigel tensed as if to fire, and Charles closed his eyes. Then he heard the clatter of the gun falling on to the desk. He looked at Nigel Steen and saw the glint of tears in his eyes as the young man rushed out of the door.

Charles collapsed like a glove puppet with the hand withdrawn, and stood for a long moment, sagging. The doorbell was still ringing. But before he went downstairs, he crept into Marius Steen's bedroom.

Jacqui was still unconscious, breathing heavily under the anaesthetic. Gingerly, Charles raised the sheet that lay over her thighs. There was no blood, no sign that she had been touched. As he looked down at the body he used to love, he thanked God for letting him arrive in time.

When he opened the door downstairs, he heard the roar of a motorboat leaving from the boathouse at the back. On the doorstep in front of him stood Joanne Menzies, alone. She was breathless. "I couldn't get the police. Didn't see a phone. I've just walked from the car."

So it had been a bluff. Charles started laughing, clear ripples of relief shaking his body. He clasped Joanne in his arms, not for love or lust, just sheer joy at being alive.

The speedboat was found splintered against Goring Bridge. It had missed the lock and been driven full-tilt down the hard steps of the weir. Nigel Steen's body was found in some weeds nearly a mile downstream. Whether the death was suicide, or a result of his natural aptitude for failure, was never established.

19

FINALE AND CURTAIN CALL

BARTLEMAS AND O'ROURKE's tall Victorian house in Ideal Road, Islington, was like a chaotic museum. Every available wall surface was covered with memories of Kean and Macready; even in the lavatory the twin deities looked down beneficently on lesser mortals.

A battered life-size carving of Kean as Shylock greeted Charles as he entered the front door. The beak of a nose seemed strangely reminiscent of Marius Steen. O'Rourke took his coat. "You know, people keep saying we ought to hang coats on Shylock's arm . . ."

"But we're sure Edmund wouldn't like it," said Bartlemas, appearing from nowhere in a shiny apron with an advertisement for "Camp Coffee" on it.

"No, he wouldn't. The party was really Bartlemas's idea . . ."

"Oh, I wouldn't say that, O'Rourke. Let's say we arrived at the idea mutually . . ."

"Yes, let's. Nearly everyone's here. Do go through. Bartlemas, do you want a little succor with your vinaigrette?"

"Wouldn't say no, O'Rourke. Excuse us. Titivating the goodies. Do go through . . ."

"Just toddle through . . ." They vanished in a shimmer of saxe-blue silk shirts.

The sitting-room had two walls devoted to prints of Edmund in all his greatest roles, and the other two to William. Between them, sitting with drinks, were Joanne Menzies and Gerald Venables.

Gerald rose to greet Charles in typical style. "Hello, old boy. What's the budget going to do to your savings then?"

"I haven't got any."

"Wise feller." Charles greeted Joanne and helped himself to a large Scotch. Gerald continued. "Do you realize, Charles, that if these Labor Johnnies go and slap on this gift tax they're talking about, crimes like young Nigel Steen's won't be worth committing."

"His wasn't worth committing anyway, as it turned out."

"No. Fascinating, though, from the legal point of view. Do let me in on any more of your detective work, won't you, Charles?"

"There won't be any more, Sherlock Holmes."

"Oh, I'm sure there will. How's the arm?"

"Healed up long ago. A nice scar though."

"And a good story to go with it."

The conversation drifted. Joanne talked about her new job in a concert agency. Bartlemas and O'Rourke came in and talked about the first night of Gielgud's Prospero ("Doing it again, dear") at the National. Charles felt detached and rather sad. A little parcel had arrived through the post that morning from the old people's home at Tower Hamlets. Harry Chiltern had died, and asked that all his possessions be sent to Charles. It was depressing to think that he was the closest friend that the old man had, and it stirred all the usual guilt feelings—should have gone to see him more often, and so on. The package contained a watch, a silver cigarette case, a Ronson lighter and *Stanley Matthew's Book of Football*.

It suited Charles's melancholy mood well. Nothing much seemed to be happening. He had finished shooting the rescheduled scenes of *The Zombie Walks* without meeting Felicity again. (However, the episode was not without profit, since the film company had paid very substantial compensation for his "accident.") He was now involved in a dreary radio serial, which was driving him slowly mad with boredom. Life went on, at its usual alcoholic level.

A ring at the doorbell announced the late arrival of Jacqui, blonde again and resplendently pregnant in a long red and white flowered dress. It was so far from her usual style that Charles thought she must have undergone some violent change of personality. She greeted him slightly gushingly, and that again struck a false note.

The reason for the change soon became apparent. Given Jacqui's simple character, it could only be a man. Her escort followed her into the sitting-room. It was Bernard Walton.

"Hello, Charles. Dear boy. Joanne, darling. Hello, all you lovely people. Haven't met you, have I, sir, but I'm sure we'll get on. Tell you what, Jacqui and I were thinking of tootling on to the midnight matinée at the Parthenon after this lot. It's a charity thing—something to do with April Fools' Day. Perhaps that means it's raising money for a looney bin. Whole thing will probably be a ghastly no-no, but everyone will be there. What do you all say to the idea?"

Bartlemas and O'Rourke were terribly enthusiastic, and the others mumbled politely. Charles didn't even mumble. He knew what wasn't his scene.

The dinner was very good, though the conversation tended to be dominated by Bernard's stories of his new television series and the director who was disastrous, but disastrous. At one point, however, they did get around to Marius Steen and the circumstances of his death.

"What I never could understand," said Gerald, "was why Steen, who was so good with money, made such a cock-up of that final will. I mean, just leaving it to the baby, or making it dependent on the baby's survival. It's insane."

"But you see, dear," said Bartlemas, "he only got that one together in a hurry . . ."

"Yes," said O'Rourke, "he was going to sort it all out properly when he got back to England. I mean, the so-called solicitor he found out at Saint Maxime was a boy, hardly even qualified. Just got his articles—I always think that sounds rude." A snigger. "So the will was only a stop-gap. But when Marius felt better, he forgot about it . . ."

"Yes. He was intending to get married, you see."

Gerald nodded. "Of course. Remarriage would revoke all previous wills."

But Charles was intrigued by something O'Rourke had said. "When Marius felt better? What did you mean by that?"

"Oh no! Didn't we tell you?" O'Rourke's eyes opened wide.

"I don't think we did, O'Rourke . . ."

"Oh well, you see, Marius had this heart attack while we were out there. Not a bad one, but it frightened him. That's why he was in such a rush about the will . . ."

"That's right. And that's why he made us witnesses and executors . . ."

"Doesn't that sound grand . . ."

"Yes, because we were the only people there . . ."

"And then he gave us the will and the other papers and he said to us, just before we toddled off to Morocco—"

"Just a minute, O'Rourke," Charles interposed. "What other papers?"

O'Rourke looked at Bartlemas and both of them opened their eyes wide and put their hands over their mouths in mock horror. "Oh no, Bartlemas, we haven't . . . !"

"We have, O'Rourke . . ."

"Forgotten all about them . . ."

"Oh no!"

"Where did we have them last?"

"Well, we certainly had them when you were cleaning that playbill of William as Lear at the Theatre Royal, Covent Garden . . ."

"And then we . . ."

"Ooh. Do you know, I think I left them in my dinki-doodi-den . . ."

"Oh, no, Bartlemas!"

"I'll scurry up and get them straight away."

There was a brief pause. Nobody quite liked to ask what Bartlemas's dinki-doodi-den was. Fortunately he scurried back before the silence became awkward.

"Here it is, acres of bills and things."

Gerald assumed control and looked through the papers while the others watched. Then he chuckled. "The old sod."

"Who?" asked Jacqui.

"Marius Steen. He'd really got it in for Nigel. He must have regretted that gift business."

"Why? What did he do?" asked Charles.

"Marius wrote a letter to his son last November—this is a copy of it—complaining in humble terms about how he'd left himself short by the gift and not taken inflation into account, and would Nigel let him have a small income from various shares and properties? And here's the agreement duly signed by Nigel."

"And what does it mean?"

"It means that Marius was retaining a beneficial interest in the gift."

"What?" asked Jacqui blankly, which saved the embarrassment of someone else's asking.

"It means that the whole gift thing was invalid. Nigel would have had to pay duty on the whole estate without reduction."

"Good God," said Charles. "You can't help admiring the old bugger. Making his own son sign away his fortune."

"Yes. He was an amazing character. He understood money," said Gerald with respect, "and, having made one mistake, determined that most of it would die with him."

"Will it affect my inheritance?" Jacqui asked anxiously.

"Ah, who knows?" Gerald smiled. "That all has to be sorted out by solicitors and accountants."

Charles gave a mock yawn. "I know. Endless meetings, confabulations, discussions and mumblings about the law. Where does all that get you?"

"Rich," said Gerald smugly.

At half past eleven, they all left the house to go to the April Fools' Midnight Matinée at the Parthenon. Bartlemas and O'Rourke had dressed in their Victorian first-night gear specially. They looked like a pair of Dickensian undertakers.

The bright young theatrical crowd (including Gerald, who had decided he would go after all) piled into Bernard Walton's Bentley, leaving Charles and Joanne on the pavement outside the house. "See you," yelled Jacqui out of the window as the great car roared off.

"How've you been?" Charles asked Joanne.

"All right."

"You still miss Marius?"

"Yes, but the new job's very busy, so it's not too bad."

"Good. Do you fancy a drink somewhere?"

"Thanks very much, but no, I don't think so. I've got to be up early in the morning."

Charles found a cruising taxi to take Joanne Menzies home. Then he hailed another for himself and gave the driver the address of the Montrose.

ABOUT THE AUTHOR

SIMON BRETT is the author of more than twenty novels, including fourteen Charles Paris mysteries, four Mrs. Pargeter mysteries, and two novels of psychological suspense, *Dead Romantic* and *A Shock to the System*, which was made into a film starring Michael Caine. He has also published a collection of short stories, *Tickled to Death*. Known as an anthologist and a television and radio dramatist, Brett is a former president of the British Crime Writers' Association. He and his family live in England.